CONTR

GEORGIA I. HESSE, for 19 [...] *Francisco Examiner and Chronicle,* is the author of guidebooks on France and Paris and has contributed articles on travel to almost all major North American magazines and newspapers. She was a Fulbright scholar at the University of Strasbourg.

BRUCE ALDERMAN, the Paris bureau chief for *Variety,* is working toward his doctorate in French history. He has been a correspondent associated with Reuters in southern France and has worked for *Time* and *Newsweek* magazines in Paris.

CHARLA CARTER is a free-lance fashion editor and journalist in Paris. She has contributed articles on fashion and cultural affairs to the American, British, and Australian *Vogue* magazines, to the American *Elle,* and to *Vanity Fair, European Travel & Life,* and *Passion, The Magazine of Paris.*

FRED HALLIDAY divides his time between Paris and Connecticut. He is a frequent contributor to *Food and Wine, Connoisseur,* and *Travel & Leisure* magazines.

EDWARD HERNSTADT is a free-lance writer who has lived in Paris for four years. He was until recently the managing editor of *Paris Passion* magazine.

STEPHEN O'SHEA is a Canadian writer and journalist who also translates French fiction and screenplays into English. He has lived in Paris since 1981.

JONATHAN WEBER is a Senior Editor of *World Link* magazine in Geneva. A former correspondent for Fairchild Publications, his articles have also appeared in the *International Herald Tribune, Paris Passion* magazine, and other publications.

THE PENGUIN TRAVEL GUIDES

AUSTRALIA

CANADA

THE CARIBBEAN

ENGLAND & WALES

FRANCE

IRELAND

ITALY

NEW YORK CITY

THE PENGUIN GUIDE TO FRANCE 1989

ALAN TUCKER

General Editor

PENGUIN BOOKS

PENGUIN BOOKS

Published by the Penguin Group
Viking Penguin Inc., 40 West 23rd Street,
New York, New York 10010, U.S.A.
Penguin Books Ltd, 27 Wright's Lane,
London W8 5TZ, England
Penguin Books Australia Ltd, Ringwood,
Victoria, Australia
Penguin Books Canada Ltd, 2801 John Street,
Markham, Ontario, Canada L3R 1B4
Penguin Books (N.Z.) Ltd, 182-190 Wairau Road,
Auckland 10, New Zealand

Penguin Books Ltd, Registered Offices:
Harmondsworth, Middlesex, England

First published in Penguin Books 1989
Published simultaneously in Canada

1 3 5 7 9 10 8 6 4 2

ISBN 0 14 019.902 0
ISSN 0897-683X

Printed in the United States of America by
R. R. Donnelley & Sons Company,
Harrisonburg, Virginia

Set in ITC Garamond Light
Designed by Beth Tondreau Design
Maps by Vantage Art, Inc.
Illustrations by Bill Russell
Editorial services by Stephen Brewer Associates

THIS GUIDEBOOK

The Penguin Travel Guides are designed for people who are experienced travellers in search of exceptional information that will help them sharpen and deepen their enjoyment of the trips they take.

Where, for example, are the interesting, isolated, fun, charming, or romantic places within your budget to stay? The hotels described by our writers (each of whom is an experienced travel writer who either lives in or regularly tours the city or region of France he or she covers) are some of the special places, in all price ranges except for the lowest—not the run-of-the-mill, heavily marketed places on every travel agent's CRT display and in advertised airline and travel-agency packages. We indicate the approximate price level of each accommodation in our descriptions of it (no indication means it is moderate), and at the end of every chapter we supply contact information so that you can get precise, up-to-the-minute rates and make reservations.

The Penguin Guide to France 1989 highlights the more rewarding parts of the country so that you can quickly and efficiently home in on a good itinerary.

Of course, the guides do far more than just help you choose a hotel and plan your trip. *The Penguin Guide to France 1989* is designed for use *in* France. Our Penguin France writers tell you what you really need to know, what you can't find out so easily on your own. They identify and describe the truly out-of-the-ordinary restaurants, shops, activities, and sights, and tell you the best way to "do" your destination.

Our writers are highly selective. They bring out the significance of the places they cover, capturing the personality and the underlying cultural and historical resonances of a city or region—making clear its special appeal. For exhaustive detailed coverage of cultural attractions, we suggest that you also use a supplementary reference-type guidebook, such as a Michelin Green Guide, along with the Penguin Guide.

The Penguin Guide to France 1989 is full of reliable and timely information that is revised each year. We would like to know if you think we've left out some very special place.

ALAN TUCKER
General Editor
Penguin Travel Guides

40 West 23rd Street
New York, New York 10010
or
27 Wright's Lane
London W8 5TZ

CONTENTS

MAPS

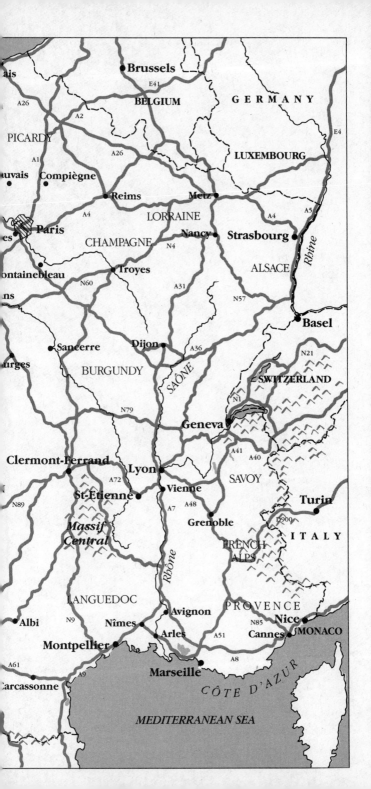

OVERVIEW
FRANCE: A LAND FOR ALL REASONS

By Georgia I. Hesse

Georgia I. Hesse, for 19 years the Travel Editor of the San Francisco Sunday Examiner & Chronicle, *now contributes articles on travel and related subjects to many magazines and newspapers, including* Travel/Holiday, Condé Nast's Traveler, *the Toronto* Star, *the* Chicago Tribune, *and the* Atlanta Journal/Constitution. *She is the author of a number of travel guidebooks, including one on France. She was a Fulbright Scholar at the University of Strasbourg, and has been awarded the Order of Merit by the French government.*

"**A**sk the travelled inhabitant of any nation, In what country on earth would you rather live?—Certainly in my own, where are all my friends, my relations, and the earliest and sweetest affections and recollections of my life. Which would be your second choice? France."
—Thomas Jefferson, *Autobiography,* 1821

There are as many reasons to visit France as France has cheeses (265, according to Charles de Gaulle), such as:

- to live *la vie en rose* in Paris, or
- to potter through little villages lost in the snooze of yesteryear, or
- to appreciate art in all its various forms, including that of living, or
- to transport yourself with haute cuisine (*mousseline de brochet, ragout de homard et morilles à*

5

la crème de Sauternes) or with everyday cooking (*choucroute garnie*), or

- to sit in a shady square in Senlis, north of Paris, and think that "modern" France began there a thousand years ago.

Looking at the map of France is looking at the head of a dog, a boxer, perhaps: The scruff of his neck is the Pas-de-Calais on the Belgian border, his head joins the body of Europe along the Alps and the Black Forest. The two ears are lower Normandy and Brittany, and his muzzle bites down on Andorra and Spain. It's a very square and handsome head, with Tours as an eyeball.

Ancient as it is in essence, France brought all its parts together only as recently as 1860, when Savoy became the final region to join that whole of which Hugues Capet was crowned king in 987. Of the regions known by their traditional names, such as Alsace or Burgundy, there are today 22, while a Revolutionary "reform" in 1790 established 96 *départements*. (Enthusiasts of France and of trivia will enjoy knowing that the number of each *département* is used for the last two figures of car registration numbers and first two of postal codes.)

Fortunately, travel patterns have changed since the famous days of "If it's Tuesday, it must be Belgium." It's no longer smart to take in the well-known high points of all France (much less all Europe) at one sitting. The informed wanderer now considers the country region by region as suited to his or her own inclinations, choosing to see what he or she can at fairly low speed and planning to return another time.

But few travellers call upon France without stopping to pay their respects to **Paris**, which, in the last several years, has sprinted forward like a runner in the Bois, leading even Parisians to wonder where all the energy (not to mention the money) is coming from. Jane Kramer (the worthy successor to the *New Yorker*'s Genêt) pinpoints de Gaulle as the last long-distance runner, who, she says "planned to leave himself to the French, and in a sense he did." Presidents since, however (Georges Pompidou, Valéry Giscard d'Estaing, François Mitterrand), have appeared to share Mitterrand's view that France cannot have a *grande politique* without a *grande architecture*.

In the race, Parisians, their visitors, and *la culture* are the clear winners. (Culture is to the French as football to Americans; Kramer wrote a couple of years ago that "One of the first duties of the French press is to distract the French from a fatal suspicion that France and civilization may not be entirely synonymous as concepts.")

No one knows today's Paris who does not know the Musée National d'Art Moderne (sometimes dubbed Chez Pompidou); the Forum des Halles (almost ten years old now but still overlooked by many foreigners; not without reason, some might say); Musée Picasso in the reborn Marais; la Géode (with the world's largest projection screen) at the Cité des Sciences et de l'Industrie (in Parc de la Villette); the controversial and astonishingly successful Musée d'Orsay; the violently debated new pyramidal glass entrance to the Louvre by I. M. Pei; the Musée des Arts Décoratifs in the new Louvre; the Grande Arche de la Défense, or the Tête Défense (also known irreverently as Mitterrand's square bagel).

The latest *chantier* (construction site) is in Bercy, up-river from Notre-Dame, where rises the new headquarters of the Finance Ministry, which will be the largest government building in Europe.

If Mitterrand's dreams come true, the new Opéra de la Bastille (his "people's opera") will open on July 14, 1989, at the place de la Bastille.

Paris so dominates its immediate region, the **Ile-de-France**, that many of the Ile's riches go unexploited by travellers. After all, the Ile-de-France once *was* France; its lures are as many and as diverse as the autumn leaves in the valley of the Chevreuse: Versailles, Fontainebleau, Chartres, Giverny, etc.

But France is not completely Paris.

France generally is conceived of as a garden, a rich, fat land where good things grow, an earth carefully tended and trimmed throughout generations and centuries, nature made to order. Indeed it is.

France is also rugged, untamed, wild, mean as a sudden *mistral.* The hexagonal garden is walled in by hills, *massifs,* and mountains on several sides: the Vosges and Jura ranges on the northeast; the Alps (Mont Blanc in France is Europe's highest peak, at almost 16,000 feet) and Alpes-Maritimes on the east; the Pyrénées on the south; and the Massif Armoricain in the northwest—windblown Brittany. The spine of the Massif Central has helped keep the Auvergne among the least trammeled regions of the country.

Following Paris, **Provence** and the Côte d'Azur (the Riviera) lure more extra-European visitors than any other part of France, though surely no North American or Australian would go to France for the beaches alone, having more than a sufficiency of better ones at home. No; it's the essence of the region as a whole—the sun falling on old cultures and old stones, the air scented with roses and orange blossoms and basil and thyme and garlic, the welcoming inns with shaded gardens, the hillside picnics of salade Niçoise and a chilled rosé (perhaps Tavel) and a regional cheese (Pélardon or Bleu des Causses?), the countrysides that look like Impressionist paintings—and vice versa.

The **Côte d'Azur** is where the fashionable action is, and has been since the mid-19th century, when Cannes was discovered and made chic by Baron Henry Peter Brougham and the Brits who followed him there. (Provence proper, on the other hand, is where most action isn't, and where almost no one wants it.)

Burgundy and the **valley of the Rhône** fit neatly into a Provence-Côte d'Azur itinerary, whether you travel by *autoroute,* by back roads that twist like intestines, or by train. Burgundy is as rich in lures as the wines that bear its name; a distinctive cuisine for one, more Romanesque churches than you can shake a sculpture at, Gallo-Roman art and archaeology, tiny towns and pine forests, and two major cities, Dijon and Lyon.

Another complete trip could (and should) be confined to the northeast alone, to **Champagne** and **Lorraine and Alsace**, with sidesteps into Picardie and Franche-Comté. These are the lands of the fatted calf and the stuffed goose, of storybook villages and refreshingly rural pastures and lanes, of a cocktail of cultures ("Let them speak German," Napoléon said of the Alsatians, "as long as they think in French"), the whole seen through a (wine) glass, lightly.

Along the **Loire River** (". . . mirroring from sea to source a hundred cities and five hundred towers," wrote Oscar Wilde), travellers wander in an oval path from Paris to Brittany, to Normandy, and back again. When the sun is out, they will move in a lazy, erratic pattern, one hopes, rather like a butterfly in search of sweets on every side.

The **Loire**, with its Renaissance châteaux and its white wines, is serene and civilized, the very essence of the notion of France. Like Alsace, **Brittany** is a land of its own, fiercely independent, unbendingly individual, a land of fishermen, saints, and puzzling standing stones. **Normandy**, on the other hand, is a dream of green, of soft and creamy cheeses (Camembert!), a tapestry of good things growing, torn on the west by the beaches of World War II.

Culinary as well as cultural adventures begin in **Bordeaux** in southwest France, leading devotees into the valleys of the **Dordogne**, the Isère, and the Lot; down into the Guienne and Gascony; to modish resorts and Medieval villages; to caves sheltering prehistoric art; to Basque towns climbing the foothills of the **Pyrénées**.

In some respects, southwest France (with names on the land such as Landes, Gers, Tarn, Languedoc-Roussillon) is the largest and most complex of the regions, with an inheritance of linguistic confusions, religious upheavals, and economic and agricultural dislocations. It is also one of the most rewarding.

The queen city of the central south, **Toulouse** is France's fourth largest and one of the oldest; some scholars say it was founded before Rome. Its climate, its several architecturally remarkable structures, emphasis on the arts, and university-inspired liveliness make it a rewarding destination, while it also serves as jumping-off point for such smart, smaller cities as Auch and Albi to the west and east.

South of Toulouse, major routes and little roads as provocative as afterthoughts run through country unfamiliar to most foreigners where still walk the ghosts of prehistoric man, of insurgents and heretics, of pilgrims and hermits and troubadours.

Savoy and **Dauphiné** in winter are empires of ice and snow, of toney resorts such as Chamonix and Megève and Flaine. The Winter Olympics will be staged around Albertville in 1992. In summer, these places constitute the promised land of mountaineers and lovers of lakes (including Le Bourget, France's largest) and Alpine scenery. Pretty spa cities such as Aix-les-Bains and Evian attract those who arrive "to take the waters"; beautifully sited old Grenoble is an attention-getter in its own right.

Cooking in the French Alps tends to be just that— cooking rather than cuisine. The specialties are hearty and filling; *gratin,* for instance, a family of crusty potato-cheese dishes. Wines are light, dry, refreshing as the mountain air.

Clearly, France—with 55.6 million inhabitants, who occupy a space smaller than Texas—is inexhaustible. So it is that, in one volume, we have not attempted to exhaust, not even to completely cover, France. We are not encyclopedic; we have made choices.

Largely skipped, *hélas,* is Franche-Comté (Free Country), which extends south from Alsace-Lorraine to the Rhône-Alpes region, backing up against the Jura mountains and Switzerland. The big city is Besançon, where Victor Hugo was born and watches have been manufactured since the 17th century. It has an excellent Musée des Beaux-Arts. Mountains and high plateaux make driving very pleasant in Franche-Comté; the most remarkable architectural achievement there is Le Corbusier's Chapel of Notre-Dame at Ronchamp, 20 km (13 miles) northwest of Belfort.

We have not explored the multiple personalities of Languedoc-Roussillon, although we discuss **Carcassonne.** From Montpellier to Béziers to Narbonne to Perpignan, the frequent traveller to France will find new excitements: especially inland from Collioure to Céret or in the Massif Canigou over to Prades (the setting for the annual Pablo Casals festival), to the sensational abbey of St-Michel-de-Cuxa (from the cloister of which came the stones now at the Metropolitan Museum of Art's Cloisters in New York), to St-Martin-du-Canigou (a walk or Jeep ride from Casteil).

Some roads remain undriven in these pages: the corkscrew of 906 from Alès north of Nîmes to Le Puy. Some city streets also remain to be ambled through: those of Périgueux and Limoges, of La Rochelle and Lille.

We leave those trips for another time.

USEFUL FACTS

When to Go
France, like other major European destinations, swarms with tourists in June, July, and August. The best weather and fewer crowds make September and October the finest months for general sightseeing, followed by late April to mid-June (although early springs can be rainy). Christmas-New Year's holidays bring throngs to the ski slopes; plan a ski vacation for mid-January to early May (depending on resort altitudes), but *not* on school holidays.

Entry Documents
In addition to a valid passport, *visas are required* for citizens of the United States, Australia, Canada, and all other countries except members of the European Economic Community, Andorra, Monaco, and Switzerland.

(The regulation also applies to French possessions in the Caribbean, South Pacific, and elsewhere.) To obtain a visa, check *well in advance* of a trip with the nearest French Consulate.

Arrival at Major Gateways by Air

From North America and elsewhere outside Europe, most travellers to France arrive at Paris's international airports, **Roissy-Charles-de-Gaulle** (21 km/14 miles north via A 1 or RN 2), and **Orly** (15 km/9 miles south via A 6 or RN 7).

Note: There are two *aérogares* at De Gaulle, Aérogare 1 and Aérogare 2, and Aérogare 2 has two terminal buildings, A and B. Before arrival and, especially, before departure, it's wise to check where, precisely, your plane will land or take off. That's particularly important when you are picking up a rental car at the airport or when instructing the taxi driver in Paris where to deliver you.

The third international airport, old Le Bourget, is served by business aviation.

Paris has two major in-town terminals: **Invalides** at 2, rue Esnault-Pelterie, on the Left Bank near the Pont (Bridge) Alexandre III, and **Porte Maillot/Palais de Congrès**, northwest of the Arc de Triomphe at the end of avenue de la Grande Armée. Invalides occupies a fairly small former railroad station, whereas Maillot sits within a skyscraping complex that's a veritable town in itself, with shops, cinéma, cafés, a parking lot, disco, Métro station, etc. There are also two giant hotels: the 1,012-room Méridien at Porte Maillot itself and, across the boulevard at Palais de Congrès, the 940-room Concorde Lafayette.

Airports are linked to the two terminals with frequent departures of buses marked **Cars Air France**. These coaches leave from the sidewalks in front of baggage pick-up areas at Orly, from Porte (Gate) 36 at De Gaulle's Aérogare 1; and Porte A5, Terminal A, and Porte B6 at Terminal B, both Aérogare 2. Directional signs are well placed.

The trip from Charles-de-Gaulle to Maillot takes about 30 minutes and costs just more than $6 at this writing. From Orly to Gare Montparnasse (a scheduled stop) or Invalides, it's about 26 minutes at $5.50. Connections between the two airports take 75 minutes at approximately $11. (Between the airport and Invalides, stops will be made upon request at Porte d'Orléans and Duroc.)

Buses bound from De Gaulle to Porte Maillot also make outdoor stops at **place Charles-de-Gaulle/Etoile** on the avenue Carnot side.

For travellers with considerable luggage, Cars Air France are preferable to the RATP buses discussed below. Both downtown air terminals are more handily located for travellers staying around the Champs-Elysées or place de la Concorde areas than for those going to the heart of the Left Bank or Ile-de-la-Cité.

RATP (city) buses connect Charles-de-Gaulle to the train stations Gare de l'Est and Gare du Nord ($6), Charles-de-Gaulle to place Nation ($6), and Orly-Ouest/Orly-Sud to place Denfert-Rochereau ($3.50).

Roissy-Rail links Charles-de-Gaulle by train to the Gare du Nord and such stops as Châtelet, Luxembourg, Port Royal, Denfert-Rochereau, and Cité Universitaire. Orly-Rail runs between Orly-Ouest/Orly-Sud and Gare d'Austerlitz with intermediate stops; the two airports are also connected by coaches. Both rail systems are integrated with city-wide Métro services.

Taxi fares between the airports and Paris range from about $16 to $50, depending upon the airport (De Gaulle is slightly farther out), destination within the city, traffic conditions at the time, luggage surcharges, etc. A 10 percent tip is standard. The hotel concierge will estimate the charge rather accurately.

Arrival by Train

Paris maintains six railroad stations, served by trains from some 6,000 communities in France as well as from all European countries. They are Gare d'Austerlitz (on the southwest of town), Gare de l'Est (east), Gare de Lyon (southeast), Gare Montparnasse (west), Gare du Nord (north), and Gare St-Lazare (northwest). Passengers entering the country will have their passports and visas checked on the train before border crossings.

Cities served from the stations are as follows: from **Austerlitz**: Tours, Bordeaux, Toulouse, Madrid, etc.; from **Est**: Reims, Strasbourg, Frankfurt, Zurich, etc.; from **Lyon**: Lyon, Dijon, Provence, Nice, Barcelona, etc.; from **Montparnasse**: Brittany, La Rochelle, etc.; from **Nord**: Lille, Brussels, Amsterdam, Hamburg, and also for boat-trains to Boulogne, Calais, Dunkirk; from **St-Lazare**: Normandy, boat-trains to Le Havre, Cherbourg, etc.

Arrival by Sea from Britain

At least nine companies maintain ferry, hydrofoil, and Hovercraft services across the English Channel (*La Manche,* The Sleeve, in French). Check out Brittany Ferries (Tel: 0752-21-321 or 0705-27-701, Plymouth); Commodore Shipping Services (Tel: 0534-71-263, Jersey); Condor (Tel: 0481-26-121, Guernsey); Emeraude Ferries (Tel: 0534-74-458, Jersey); Hoverspeed (Tel: 0304-21-62-05, Dover); Irish Continental Line (Tel: 001-77-43-31, Dublin); Sally Line (Tel: 01-409-05-36, London); Sealink (Tel: 01-834-23-45, London); and Townsend Thoresen (Tel: 01-734-44-31 or 01-437-78-00, London).

As examples of available services, Brittany Ferries sails between Plymouth and Roscoff, Poole-Cherbourg, Portsmouth-Caen-St-Malo, Cork-Roscoff; Hoverspeed (Hovercraft) between Dover and Boulogne-Calais; Sealink (major car ferries) from Dover to such French connections as Calais, Dunkirk, and from Weymouth and Portsmouth to Cherbourg; Townsend Thoresen out of Dover to Calais and Boulogne, and Portsmouth to Cherbourg and Le Havre.

Both day and overnight services are available. Most ferries carry automobiles and all Hovercraft will board them. Condor's hydrofoils serve foot-passengers only. Across the narrowest span and via hydrofoil or Hovercraft, the trip can be as short as 35–40 minutes; all ferries take several hours, particularly on wide, rough runs. Overnight accommodations should be booked well in advance of the trip unless you don't mind sleeping in the lounge.

Around France by Train

French Railways S.N.C.F. (*Société Nationale des Chemins de Fer Français*) operates the most advanced rail transportation system in the world with the fastest scheduled service (more than 150 m.p.h.) on high-speed **TGV trains** (*Trains à Grande Vitesse*).

At this writing, the following schedules are maintained: Paris-Lyon-St-Etienne (two hours to Lyon); Paris-Avignon-Marseille-Toulon-Nice (even with a train change and multiple stops, Nice may be reached in eight hours); Paris-Dijon (one hour, 20 minutes or so); Paris-Nîmes-Montpellier; Paris-Macon-Geneva (around four hours); Paris-Lausanne-Berne; Paris-Besançon-Beaune-Chalon-sur-Saône; Paris-

Aix-les-Bains-Chambéry-Annecy (with connections to ski resorts); Paris-Lyon-Grenoble; Rouen-Lyon; Lille-Douai-Arras-Lyon.

The system will be extended to Brussels and London, to Bordeaux, Brittany, and Strasbourg, to Basel and Zurich in Switzerland, and to central Germany.

Air-conditioned TGV trains consist of eight cars with 111 coach-type seats in first class, 275 coach seats in second class, and a bar car. Several first-class cars provide dining service at the seat, airline-style, during meal hours (hot meals). Second-class passengers receive a cold meal. Snacks, sandwiches, drinks, cigarettes, and newspapers are sold for both classes in the bar car.

In addition to TGVs, S.N.C.F. offers services by Eurocity, Corail, and Turbo trains, as well as special "touristic" trains in summer with entertainers aboard.

For information outside Paris, check French National Railroads (S.N.C.F.) offices in London, New York, San Francisco, Beverly Hills, Chicago, Miami, Montreal, and Vancouver.

Special fare discount programs are available: Eurailpass, Eurail Youthpass, Eurail Saverpass, 9-Day Eurail Flexipass, France-Vacances Pass, and the new, extremely flexible France Rail'n Drive Pass, combining train travel and car rental.

Eurailpasses are sold at offices of the French National Railroads in New York, San Francisco, Beverly Hills, Miami, and Chicago in the United States (Chicago address, 11 East Adams St., 60603, (312) 427-8691); in London (179 Piccadilly, W1 OBA, (01) 499-21-53); in Montreal and Vancouver in Canada (Montreal address, 1500 Stanley St., Suite 436, (514) 288-8255). In addition, on certain lines, Motorail *trains-autos-couchettes* make possible overnight, in-berth travel while cars are carried on the same train.

Renting a Car and Driving

A valid driver's license from the country of residence is required; minimum age is 23 years, or 21 for credit card holders. All vehicles must be insured; if you are renting a car licensed in France, the rental company will take care of the paperwork. The major rental car companies in France are Avis, Budget-Milleville, Citer, Europcar, Hertz, Interrent, and Mattei. International car rental credit cards are accepted for payment, with no deposit required. Other cards accepted are American Express, Carte

Blanche, Carte Bleue Visa, Air France, Air Inter, Diner's Club, and Eurocard.

The most economical plan for rental periods of one month or more is Renault's Financed Purchase-Repurchase lease plan, by which the driver purchases a new Renault, paying basic charges in advance and signing a promissory note for the balance of the cost. The note is discharged by return of the car in good condition to Renault at an agreed time. The cost includes unlimited mileage, government taxes, factory guarantee, registration, and insurance.

For information on Renault Purchase-Repurchase, inquire of: Auto Europe, Camden, Maine; Avis, Garden City, NY; Peugeot, New York City; Europe by Car, New York City; France Auto Vacances, New York City; Kemwell Group, Harrison, NY; Renault Overseas, New York City; A.M.C. Renault, Brampton (near Toronto), Canada; Inter-Car, Montreal; Renault U.K. Ltd., London; Renault Australia, Saint Leonards, NSW.

Local Time

Paris is one hour east of Greenwich Mean Time, which means by the clock it's one hour ahead of the U.K., six hours ahead of New York and the non-Maritime east coast of Canada, and nine hours ahead of California and western Canada. Sydney, Australia, is ten hours ahead of Paris. For short periods during Daylight Savings Time there will be an hour's variance because the countries go on and off Daylight Savings Time at different times.

Currency

The basic unit is the *franc,* which is divided into 100 centimes; there are banknotes for 10, 50, and 500 francs and coins of 5, 10, and 20 centimes and ½, 1, 5, and 10 francs. When travelling in France, check listings at major banks or in the *International Herald Tribune* and other newspapers for current exchange rates.

Telephoning

The telephone area code for Paris is 01; for all other places in France, the area code is incorporated in the first two digits of the phone number. The international country code for France is 33.

Electric Current

Current in France is 220 V, 50 cycles AC. North American-made appliances require adapters.

Business Hours and Holidays

Banks in France are open from 9:00 A.M. to 4:30 P.M., except on Saturdays, Sundays, and holidays. Banks usually close at noon the day before a holiday. When banks are closed, currency exchanges are open at Charles-de-Gaulle and Orly airports in Paris; from early morning until at least 9:00 P.M. at railway stations Austerlitz, Est, Lyon, St-Lazare, and Nord; Crédit Commercial de France at 103, avenue des Champs-Elysées is open daily except Sundays from 8:30 A.M. to 8:00 P.M., and Union de Banques à Paris at 154, avenue des Champs-Elysées is open on Sundays and holidays from 10:30 A.M. to 6:00 P.M.

Most department stores are open Mondays through Saturdays from 9:30 A.M. to 6:30 P.M., though some are closed on Monday mornings. They are usually open until 9:00 or 10:00 P.M. one or two evenings a week. Smaller shops close between noon and 2:00 P.M.

Fashion boutiques, perfume stores and the like are open Tuesday through Saturday from 10:00 A.M. to noon and 2:00 P.M. until 6:30 or 7:00 P.M.

Hairdressers close Mondays and are usually open on Saturdays from 9:00 A.M. to 6:00 or 7:00 P.M. Food shops are open Tuesdays through Sundays from 7:00 A.M. until 1:30 P.M. and from 4:30 to 8:00 P.M. (except bakers, open from 2:00 to 8:00 P.M.). Food shops may close at noon on Sunday.

The French in general celebrate ten national holidays: New Year's Day, Easter Monday, Labor Day (May 1), Ascension Day, Whit Monday, Bastille Day (July 14), Assumption Day (August 15), All Saints Day (November 1), Armistice Day 1918 (November 11), and Christmas Day. The Alsace also celebrates Good Friday and December 26.

In addition, some businesses in rural areas may close for one of the hundreds of local celebrations.

Credit Cards

Visa, paired with the French *Carte Bleue,* and MasterCard, affiliated with Eurocard, are the most widely accepted international cards in France in establishments small as well as large, rural as well as urban. American Express and Diner's Club are widely accepted in major shops, restaurants, and hotels. Gasoline credit cards are not accepted.

For Further Information

In 1987 the French Government Tourist Offices (F.G.T.Os.) around the world consolidated various activities under the umbrella of Maison de la France. Offices are maintained in New York, Chicago, Dallas, Los Angeles, San Francisco, Montreal, Toronto, Sydney, and London. The addresses of the major offices are: 610 Fifth Avenue, New York, NY 10020-2452, Tel: (212) 757-1125; 1981 McGill College, Suite 490, Montreal, Quebec H3A 2W9, Tel: (514) 288-4264; 178 Piccadilly, London W1V OAL, Tel: (01) 493-6594; 33 Bligh Street, Sydney N.S.W. 200, Tel: (612) 231-5244.

BIBLIOGRAPHY

MICHAEL BAIGENT, RICHARD LEIGH, and HENRY LINCOLN, *Holy Blood, Holy Grail.* This book has been called revolutionary, astonishing, bizarre, speculative, controversial. Whatever you've thought before about the Cathars, the Knights Templar—or Jesus—this will make your eyes and mind swivel.

SAMUEL CHAMBERLAIN, *Bouquet de France.* Whether he's supping in Strasbourg or climbing about Carcassonne, the epicurean is always entertaining.

MARSHALL DILL, JR., *Paris in Time.* From the birth of Paris on the Ile de la Cité to its scrubbing at the hands of André Malraux, here is the great city and how it came to be.

DAVID HUGH FARMER, *The Oxford Dictionary of Saints.* Here are the stories of some of history's strangest people (many of them French) by an English historian, once a monk.

NOEL RILEY FITCH, *Sylvia Beach and the Lost Generation.* Literary Paris of the 1920s–'30s gathered at the book club of Shakespeare and Company. Here's what they did and said and thought: James Joyce, F. Scott Fitzgerald, et al.

JANET FLANNER (GENET), *Paris Journal 1944–1971.* Two volumes. No single writer has ever brought Paris's politics, art, daily life, and enchantment to reality as does Genêt, in her columns from *The New Yorker,* excerpted here.

JANET FLANNER (GENET), *Paris Was Yesterday*. Selected from the journalist's *Letter From Paris* articles in *The New Yorker,* these well-chosen pieces bring to life the people and passions of Paris, from 1925 and the adored Josephine Baker to the *gaieté Parisienne* that preceded World War II.

FORD MADOX FORD, *Provence*. This is less a story of Provence than an evocation of it, a love letter to it; it is a literary *bouillabaisse*.

HUGH FORD, *Published in Paris*. The Lost Generation of American and British writers, printers, and publishers paints the glory years in Paris from 1920 to 1939.

HELEN GARDNER, *Art Through the Ages*. Published first in 1926, this is the amateur's best introduction to the arts, from cave paintings to Picasso.

FRANCES GIES, *Joan of Arc*. You thought you knew Joan of Arc; have you met Joan of Arc? Here, in a most unusually structured history, Mrs. Gies makes the real Joan stand up.

FRANCES GIES, *The Knight in History*. For six centuries the Medieval knight dominated the battlefields and stirred the imagination of the western world. Here are the Crusaders, the Knights Templar, and individual heroes such as the Breton Bertrand du Guesclin, who changed the world that came after him.

FRANCES and JOSEPH GIES, *Marriage and the Family in the Middle Ages*. A rewarding turn away from heroes and kings to daily life: What was the family, how did it bring us to today?

ANTHONY GLYN, *The Seine*. Glyn is the best companion you could want on an amble: easygoing, anecdotal, curious, and thoughtful.

PHILIP and MARY HYMAN, and ROSEMARY GEORGE, *Webster's Wine Tours France*. Georges Bertrand is one of the talented new winemakers of Corbières and Aloxe-Corton may be visited daily: This book is as helpful as a *tire-bouchon*.

ERNEST HEMINGWAY, *A Moveable Feast*. Here is the Paris for which the world is nostalgic, the days of wine and cafés.

JAMES A. HUSTON, *Across the Face of France*. The liberation and recovery of post-World War II France as seen by an American who served there.

MICHAEL JACOBS and PAUL STIRTON, *The Knopf Traveler's Guides to Art*. The volume on France is an essential handbook for the traveller who doesn't want to miss a Gérôme in Vesoul or the tomb of a duke in Dreux.

JOHN JAMES, *The Traveler's Key to Medieval France*. This guide and introduction to sacred architecture will be invaluable to anyone who knows once you've seen one church you haven't seen 'em all.

AMY KELLY, *Eleanor of Aquitaine and the Four Kings*. Beautifully written, endlessly fascinating, this book is more difficult to put down than any murder mystery. The family that created half of 20th-century France still lives.

EMMANUEL LE ROY LADURIE, *Montaillou, the Promised Land of Error*. Peasants who lived more than 600 years ago live once again in the days of the Albigensian heresies; ethnography at its best.

ALEXIS LICHINE, *New Encyclopedia of Wines and Spirits*. This is the classic compendium for the discerning drinker.

BRIAN N. MORTON, *Americans in Paris*. Where did Henry Adams live and write, where did Isadora Duncan dance in the gardens, where did Elsa Maxwell entertain? See Paris in the company of dozens of Americans from Louis Armstrong to Carnegie.

FRANCES MOSSIKER, *Madame de Sévigné*. No letter-writer ever has surpassed Madame de Sévigné's style or substance. Mossiker catches her in full literary flight.

JAMES POPE-HENNESSY, *Aspects of Provence*. A wanderer in the great tradition, educated and urbane, takes us by the hand from Lady Blessington's Nîmes to Merimée's St-Maximin.

JOHN REWALD, *The History of Impressionism*. Specialists will admire and amateurs enjoy this source-book on almost everybody's favorite painters.

WAVERLEY ROOT, *The Food of France*. The late, great writer-gourmet is here at his hungry best.

MORT ROSENBLUM, *Mission to Civilize*. The French, they are a funny race; a senior foreign correspondent watches them ticking and tells us how they do it.

JOHN RUSSELL, *Paris*. The erudite art critic for *The New York Times* chooses Dufy, Cartier-Bresson, et al., to help him create the most beautiful and provocative coffee table book on the world's handsomest city.

GILES ST. AUBYN, *The Year of Three Kings, 1483*. During the dramatic year of 1483, three kings ruled over England— Edward IV, Edward V, and Richard III. Here is the intriguing gang battle of the War of the Roses, seen from across the Channel.

KATHERINE SCHERMAN, *The Birth of France*. Beautifully written, learned, and humorous at once, this book belongs in the library of everyone who cares about France.

DESMOND SEWARD, *The Hundred Years War*. The endless, spaghetti-like tangles and twists of the French-English inheritance struggles from 1337 to 1453 are described in all their fascinating and intricate detail by a precise historian and excellent writer.

DESMOND SEWARD, *Prince of the Renaissance*. No one who meets François I in these pages will ever look at the Loire's great châteaux in the same way again. Here in finest moments and with flaws lives the man who had more effect on France than any leader since Charlemagne.

ANDRE L. SIMON, editor, *Wines of the World*. As readable as it is authoritative, this volume belongs on every imbiber's bookshelf.

BARBARA TUCHMAN, *A Distant Mirror*. Here is the 14th century in all its glittering accomplishments and dreadful agonies; indispensible to an understanding of how modern France came to be.

PATRICIA WELLS, *The Food Lover's Guide to France*. Where to buy olive oil in a working mill, where to bite a *baguette* in Aix: It's all here.

THEODORE ZELDIN, *The French*. A witty writer spies on everyone from Montand to Mitterrand and tells how to deal with them.

We don't want to burden you with yet another essay on the greatness of French letters and philosophy. But to be fairly knowledgeable about the country and people of France—and, not coincidentally, to get more out of any visit to the country—there are some writers you should read or reread. We suggest them to you here as a reminder, a mouth-watering checklist presented in no particular order:

Colette, Marcel Aymé, Marcel Proust, Jean Anouilh, Jules Romains, Jean-Paul Sartre, Simone de Beauvoir, André Maurois, Paul Claudel, Françoise Sagan, Alexandre de Saint-Exupéry, Henry de Montherlant, Jean Giraudoux, Jean Giono, Romain Gary, Jacques Duhamel, François Rabelais, Joachim du Bellay, René Descartes, Pierre Corneille, Blaise Pascal, Françis–duc de La Rochefoucauld, Jean-Baptiste Poquelin (Molière), Jean de la Fontaine, Jean Racine, Jacques-Bénigne Bossuët, Jean de la Bruyère, Charles-Louis de Secondat (Baron de Montesquieu), Pierre Carlet de Chamblain de Marivaux, François-Marie Arouet (Voltaire), Denis Diderot, Jean-Jacques Rousseau, Pierre-Augustin Caron de Beaumarchais, François-René (Vicomte de Châteaubriand), Alphonse-Marie-Louis de Lamartine, Alfred-Victor (Comte de Vigny), Honoré de Balzac, Victor-Marie Hugo, Louis-Charles-Alfred de Musset, Pierre-Jules-Théophile Gautier, Charles-Marie-René Leconte de Lisle, Gustave Flaubert, Charles-Pierre Baudelaire, Paul-Marie Verlaine, Emile-Edouard-Charles-Antoine Zola, Alphonse Daudet, Henri-René-Albert-Guy de Maupassant, Stephane Mallarmé, Jean-Nicolas-Arthur Rimbaud, Jacques-Anatole-François Thibault (Anatole France), Stendhal (Marie-Henri Bayle).

PARIS

By Stephen O'Shea

Stephen O'Shea, a writer and journalist who has lived in Paris since 1981, has written for British, American, Canadian, and French magazines on many aspects of Parisian and French life.

Paris has captivated the Western imagination for so long that even people who have never visited the city sometimes feel nostalgia for it. The mere mention of its river, the Seine, summons up thoughts of beauty, youthful heartbreak, and the creative dissipation that has lured foreigners to the city since Medieval times. With its superb restaurants, its districts devoted to high fashion, and its relentlessly romantic vistas, Paris is known throughout the world as Europe's pleasure dome. It is also a city marked by a turbulent past, its rich intellectual, artistic, and religious heritage surviving in museums, galleries, landmarks, churches, and the way Parisians speak and act in everyday life.

The modern metropolis has kept alive one Parisian tradition above all others—the city and its inhabitants remain fascinated by novelty. Anyone travelling to France, whether for the first or fifteenth time, must have an exceptional excuse not to want to go to its capital.

MAJOR INTEREST

Museums
The Big Three: Louvre, Orsay, Pompidou
Noteworthy: Cluny, Picasso, Rodin

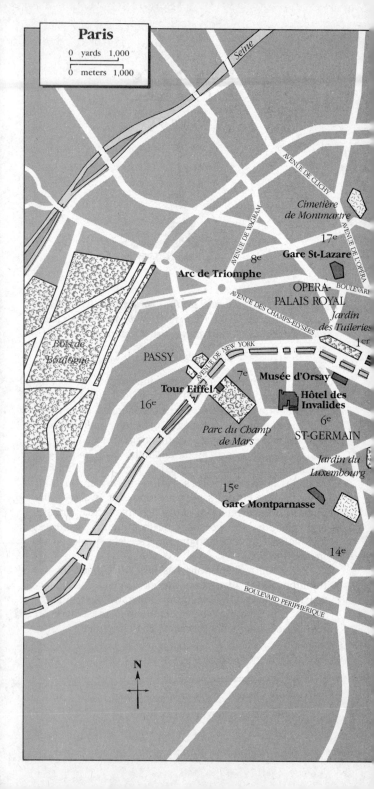

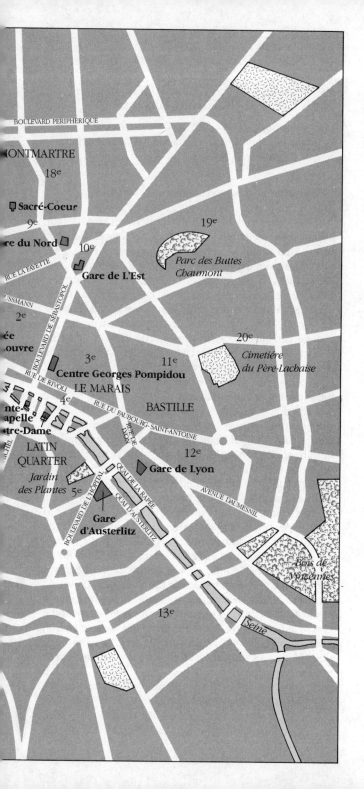

Sights
Notre-Dame, Sainte Chapelle, Champs-Elysées,
   Eiffel Tower, Trocadéro, Invalides

Neighborhoods
Bastille, Latin Quarter/St-Germain, Marais, Opéra–
   Palais Royal

Parks
Bois de Boulogne, Luxembourg, Tuileries

It is best to consider Paris as a performance. Certain districts of the city hold center stage for a time, then step back to let other neighborhoods reappear in the spotlight. The changing nature of this show is a source of both pride and distress to lovers of Paris, fuelling countless café counter arguments and public controversies. A familiar Parisian boast is that one lives or works in a *quartier qui monte,* that is, an area where positive, usually trendy, change is taking place. In present-day Paris, the Bastille district is undergoing such change. Those opposed to the trend point to dubious developments (the underground Les Halles complex, for example) as an indication that their contemporaries have absolutely no idea of what they are doing.

Over the centuries a literary cottage industry has sprung up, with distinguished authors bemoaning the imminent destruction of the city's soul. Victor Hugo, in *Les Misérables,* went into loving detail about the warren of Medieval alleyways eliminated by the cutting of the boulevards in the middle of the 19th century. However, much of Paris's later fame, and much of its charm, is associated with these broad thoroughfares. In the same way, the Eiffel Tower was almost universally loathed by the literary upon its opening a hundred years ago. Guy de Maupassant said he enjoyed the view from the top of the tower because it was the only place in the city where he wasn't forced to look at the damn thing. Still, successive generations of artists came to use it as a symbol of the city, and it is now almost impossible to imagine Paris without its iron mast. At any given period of its history, Paris has been described as a shadow of its former self or as a disfigured beauty, yet the show still goes on, changing for each generation and, as befits its quarrelsome audience, provoking heated disagreements.

One of the principal reasons Parisians harbor such strong emotions about their city is the accessible, human scale on which it is built. Unlike greater London, which sprawls across miles of the Thames Valley, or even Manhattan, stretching out in a seemingly endless procession of linear neighborhoods, Paris is compact and easy to understand. The Seine, too, is not so much a physical barrier, like the Thames or the East River, as it is a beautiful boulevard for barge traffic. The metropolitan area, with its population of ten million, may be gigantic, but central Paris, its 20 *arrondissements* (districts) spiralling out from the Louvre district, can easily be crossed on foot in an afternoon.

Even more coherent is the city's growth. From an island settlement of Gauls huddled together in the midst of a watery plain to a 19th-century capital incorporating the hills that hem in the lowlands created by the Seine, Paris has grown outwards in ever-widening rings. Roman Lutetia spilled over onto the Left Bank; the 12th-century battlements of King Philip II Augustus encompassed a bustling town extending from the drained marshes of the Right Bank to the monastery vineyards of the Left; and Louis XVI's Farmers-General Wall, a source of pre-Revolutionary irritation, formed a circuit of customshouses concentric to the present-day perimeter. The city's pie-shape would have a geometric elegance pleasing to all Cartesians, except that the crescent formed by the Seine bisects the circle so unequally that the true focal point of the city lies a little off center, like the human heart. After all, this is Paris.

THE ISLANDS
The Ile de la Cité

The birthplace of the city and the symbolic center of the nation, this small island in the Seine was first settled by the Parisii Gauls in the third century B.C. Long a miniature of French society, with the three Estates of clergy, nobility, and commoners crowded together, the Cité is now inhabited more by presences than by people. It is a place where the legendary and fictional have as great a right to exist—in French, *droit de cité*—as do the historical and factual. In the mind of the modern visitor, Quasimodo and Esmeralda loom larger than Abélard and Héloïse (who lived and loved at 9, quai aux Fleurs) as characters of Medieval Paris, and even Inspector Maigret, calmly puffing a pipe in his office at 24, quai des Orfèvres, seems far more believable than the fantastic relics once housed in the Sainte Chapelle. Romans, Norsemen, Knights Templar, and Jacobin revolutionaries have all passed this way, remembered not so much in stone as in the imaginative works they have inspired.

There are, however, two other forces that have left a lasting mark on the island. Church and State, wary partners throughout French history, have had dramatic clashes here. On the present-day Cité the standoff between the two is far more benign than it has been in the past, but it remains striking nonetheless. Notre-Dame Cathedral squares off opposite the sprawling central police station, and the Sainte Chapelle is dwarfed by a 19th-century courthouse. The Conciergerie, a vestige of the residence of Medieval kings, is less a symbol of State power than of its destructiveness: It was used as a prison during the Reign of Terror.

The colorful history of Church-State jostling on the island stretches as far back as Roman times. For more than four centuries the Ile de la Cité was the administrative and spiritual center of the bustling Roman provincial town of Lutetia. Foundations of houses from this period and the street plan of an ancient neighborhood are on view in an artfully designed archaeological crypt beneath the square in front of Notre-Dame. Fittingly, the Roman governor most closely associated with his "dear Lutetia" was Julian the Apostate, a troublemaker in both spiritual and temporal domains. As Emperor from 361 to 363, Julian overthrew the Christian orthodoxy imposed on the Empire by his uncle, Constantine the Great. When, from his balcony at the Prefect of Gaul's residence on the island, the 29-year-old devotee of the old gods first heard his legions acclaim him sole Augustus of the Roman world, the Cité's long tradition of rivalry between the sacred and the profane was born.

Certain events springing from this rivalry are the stuff of legend. On the western tip of the island, the **Square du Vert-Galant**, now a favorite spot for lovers, King Philip the Fair brutally put an end to the crusading confraternity of Knights Templar on March 11, 1314, by first torturing, then burning its leaders at the stake. Legend has it that Grand Master Jacques de Molay, before being consumed by the flames, invoked God to visit a curse on the malevolent King's family. Within a generation, the monarch and all his legitimate issue had met violent ends as France and England plunged into the Hundred Years War.

Above this park, on the **Pont Neuf**, stands an equestrian

statue of Henry IV, the king whose wedding celebrations were marred by the massacre of his fellow Huguenots and whose reign was marked by an uneasy truce between prelates and certain factions within the nobility. When Henry for dynastic reasons consented to convert to Catholicism (thereby ensuring the continuation of the royal Bourbon line he began), the famous impiety, "Paris is worth a Mass," became the catchphrase to describe the depth of his religious conviction. The king was later murdered by Ravaillac, an ardent Catholic who did not share his cavalier attitude toward the faith. It is fitting that Henry's statue stands on the western, "secular" part of the island.

In 1804, an even more celebrated instance of clerical nose-tweaking occurred on the island, this time at the making of a modern emperor. In the midst of his solemn coronation ceremony at Notre-Dame, Napoléon I snatched the crown out of the hands of an astounded Pope Pius VII and placed it on his own modest head. So that none of the assembled notables in the devastated church would miss the point about where true legitimacy and power lay, he then crowned Josephine de Beauharnais his empress. Jacques-Louis David's vivid rendering of the event now hangs in the Louvre.

Still, the two great works of religious architecture adorning the Cité attest to periods when Church and State coexisted peacefully. During the long reign of the pious King Louis IX (Saint Louis) in the 13th century, a nascent style of architecture, only later stigmatized as "Gothic"— thus, barbarian—by its Renaissance detractors, came to maturity in the Ile-de-France under the supervision of such master builders as Pierre de Montreuil. In 1246, Louis called on Montreuil to build a reliquary worthy of the objects he had obtained from the Holy Lands. A partial inventory: the Crown of Thorns, a piece of the True Cross, a vial of the Virgin's milk, and Jesus Christ's swaddling clothes. Montreuil's construction, the **Sainte Chapelle**, erected in 33 months of frantic activity, more than matched the extravagance of the monarch's faith. Even at a remove of seven centuries, the chapel inspires awe, with its upper sanctuary seeming to be built entirely of brilliant stained glass. In the late afternoon, when the sun strikes the building, visitors studying the biblical scenes depicted in the 13th-century windows of this sanctuary will get the distinct impression that they are standing inside a large jewel. The light suffusing the upper chapel at this time of

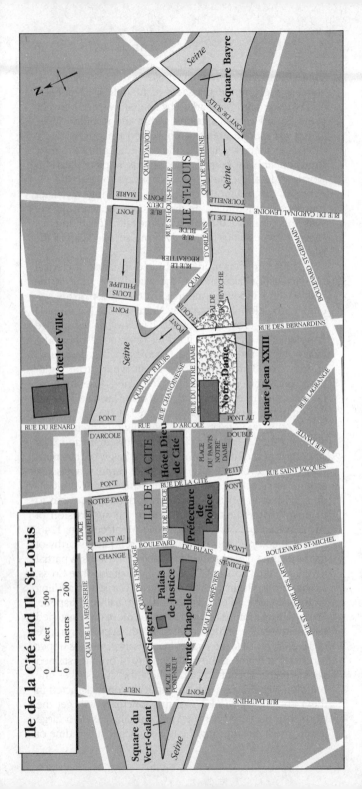

Ile de la Cité and Ile St-Louis

feet 500
meters 200

N

Square Bayre

Seine

QUAI D'ANJOU

QUAI DE BÉTHUNE

PONT MARIE

RUE DES DEUX PONTS

RUE ST-LOUIS-EN-L'ILE

ILE ST-LOUIS

RUE BUDE

RUE D'ORLÉANS

RUE LE REGRATTIER

PONT LOUIS PHILIPPE

QUAI ST-LOUIS

QUAI DE LA TOURNELLE

PONT DE LA TOURNELLE

Seine

PONT DE SULLY

RUE DU CARDINAL LEMOINE

BOULEVARD ST-GERMAIN

Hôtel de Ville

Seine

QUAI AUX FLEURS

QUAI DE L'ARCHEVÊCHE

RUE DE L'ARCHEVÊCHE

RUE DES BERNARDINS

QUAI DE LA CHANOINESSE

RUE DU NOTRE DAME

Notre-Dame

Square Jean XXIII

RUE LAGRANGE

RUE DU RENARD

PONT

RUE D'ARCOLE

PONT D'ARCOLE

ILE DE LA CITÉ

Hôtel Dieu de Cité

RUE DE LA CITÉ

PLACE DU PARVIS NOTRE-DAME

PONT AU DOUBLE

PONT AU PETIT

RUE SAINT JACQUES

RUE DANTE

PLACE DU CHÂTELET

PONT AU CHANGE

PONT NOTRE-DAME

RUE DE LUTECE

Préfecture de Police

BOULEVARD DU PALAIS

PONT ST-MICHEL

BOULEVARD ST-MICHEL

QUAI DE LA MÉGISSERIE

QUAI DE L'HORLOGE

Conciergerie

Palais de Justice

Sainte-Chapelle

QUAI DES ORFÈVRES

RUE ST ANDRÉ DES ARTS

PONT NEUF

PLACE DE PONTNEUF

PONT

RUE DAUPHINE

Square du Vert-Galant

Seine

day has not grown any dimmer since the distant age of belief it first illuminated.

A more comprehensive example of the spirit of the age is **Notre-Dame**. Begun in 1163 and not completed until 170 years later, the cathedral is the collective work of generations of architects and craftsmen. At the time of its construction, the symbols of the power and the glory of the Church were being transferred from isolated monasteries in the countryside to the burgeoning cities and towns. Slowly, Romanesque architecture—with its massive pillars, rounded arches, and thick, almost windowless, walls that suggested a fortress Church standing alone against a hostile world—gave way to the graceful lancets of the so-called Gothic, with innovative flying buttresses strengthening walls that could now be pierced by huge stained-glass tableaux. As naves soared higher, and such embellishments as statuary and rose windows became ever more accomplished, the great cathedrals came to serve as spectacular illustrations of the teachings and ultimate message of the Medieval Church. The populace was both edified and awed by these sanctuaries, learning the lives of the saints and martyrs from the portals and windows as their eyes were inexorably drawn heavenward by the lines of the building. The large square cleared in front of Notre-Dame during the 19th century betrays an anachronism: The cathedral's façade was designed to be viewed at close quarters, its balanced composition sweeping the eye up the bell towers and beyond.

However solemn and instructive its purpose, Notre-Dame was never a museum. The church served as a refuge from civil authority in Medieval times, sheltering criminals and vagrants from the law. Markets were set up inside it and messy everyday life went on beneath the towering vault. Hence, the Notre-Dame of today, constantly filled with hundreds of people raising dust as they walk and talk their way around the ambulatory, is not so much a victim of mass tourism as its beneficiary, marked by the very human informality that reigned within it during the Middle Ages. The Sunday evening organ recital, jammed with listeners, chatterers, and worshippers, is a particularly good time to visit the church. So too is the *heure bleue,* when the morning sun strikes the north rose window and fills the transept with an otherworldly blue.

A commanding view of Paris is the reward for those hardy enough to climb the 387 steps up the north tower of Notre-Dame. The famous gargoyles perched over the void (some of them 19th-century confections of Viollet-le-Duc, the architect who restored the church) look as if they can, indeed, frighten away demons. Viollet's renovation project was made possible after Victor Hugo's *The Hunchback of Notre-Dame* had raised public awareness of the cathedral's perilous state of dilapidation. The Revolution had taken its toll: Most of the statuary was destroyed, including the façade's 28 Kings of Judah, mistakenly thought to be the Kings of France; much of the glasswork was smashed; the old bells, excluding the 17th-century Emmanuelle, which still sounds today, were melted down; and the Goddess of Reason cult, which put a pretty ballerina atop a pile of dirt in the transept, caused extensive structural damage. In fact, it was only the cathedral's transformation into a wine warehouse for military hospitals during the last phase of the Revolution that prevented it from being demolished altogether.

The spirit of Revolutionary excess is far more palpable at the **Conciergerie**. Although the building dates back to the 14th century (as does its remarkable outdoor clock), Parisians usually associate it with the early 1790s, when it held nobles and revolutionaries who had fallen from favor. Visitors can see the cells of Marie Antoinette, Danton, and Robespierre, as well as the courtyard where women and men prisoners were momentarily reunited before being led away to their deaths. A raised corridor at one end of the great Gothic room is known as the "rue de Paris," a reference to Monsieur de Paris, the name given to the city's executioner. From this vantage point the beauty of the large hall can be best appreciated—even if its historical associations are somewhat sinister. The Medieval kitchens, with their colossal hearths for roasting animals on spits, recall the earlier, more festive days of the Conciergerie.

Toward the western end of the Cité lies its most picturesque residential district, the **Place Dauphine**. A triangular oasis of greenery, the spot is known throughout the city for its quiet charm. The houses lining two of the triangle's sides are a study in differing styles of architecture. Surrealist André Breton extravagantly proclaimed the square the "sex of Paris," which may be why Henry IV, the monarch famous for his dalliances, seems to be riding toward Place Dauphine from his place of glory atop the Pont Neuf.

Ile St-Louis

After the surfeit of history on the neighboring island, it is a relief to visit Ile St-Louis, a fairly recent creation in a city as old as Paris. Developed by land speculators and parvenus of the 17th century, the island is characterized by houses that have what is called *du ventre,* the bellylike sag of old constructions. A provincial calm reigns on this small island, which is best viewed at dawn, when the different shades of gray (bridges, houses, and river) make it particularly beautiful. A walk around the island on the quais alongside the Seine is a romantic experience—and useful, if you are planning to sleep under a bridge. Of the six bridges leading from the Ile St-Louis, the most remarkable is the **Pont Marie**, with its elegant stone arches all of a different size.

Now a playground for weekenders in search of mellow but modern restaurants and shops, Ile St-Louis has always been outside of the mainstream of Paris life. As its rich occupants left for more-spacious accommodations elsewhere in the city, the island became a haven for artists. Its most famous resident was Charles Baudelaire, who used to frequent the Hôtel de Lauzun, where members of the Club des Haschischins ingested hashish in suitably exotic surroundings. Today, things are considerably tamer, the consumption of Berthillon sherbet being the islanders' principal sensual indulgence. The resident creative community is consequently less lean than it was during the island's bohemian heyday, with such patrons of the arts as the Rothschilds and the widow of President Pompidou now living in the quaint neighborhood. The best reminder of the island's good old days of poetic self-destructiveness lies across the Pont de Sully on the Right Bank. At the first intersection there is a statue of Arthur Rimbaud in what can only be called a hallucinatory pose. His head and shoulders are dreamily separated from the rest of his body.

THE LEFT BANK
The Latin Quarter

For a long time simply called the Université (the other two districts of Paris were Cité, being the island, and Ville, being the Right Bank), the Latin Quarter embraces the area from the place Maubert on the east to the Odéon on the west, with the Montagne Ste-Geneviève as its southern boundary. Immediately opposite the south flank of Notre-Dame is the **Maubert quarter**, a maze of old streets dotted with restaurants and exotic food shops. Once famed for the rats that infested the tanneries lining the Medieval confluence of the Seine and Bièvre (today an underground stream), the area is now the last word in left-wing genteel, housing successful academics, psychoanalysts, and politicians. The uniformed policemen on the narrow rue de Bièvre guard the house of the most successful of them all, François Mitterrand.

Farther downstream, across the old Roman road to Orléans, now called the rue St-Jacques, is another late-Medieval quarter that survived the great boulevard building of the 19th century. Unlike its neighbor, the **St-Séverin quarter** has nothing genteel about it. It is the area of Paris that counts the most bouzouki players per square foot, and its tiny streets are crammed with Greek restaurants and takeout counters. Before deploring the current commercial state of the neighborhood, detractors should consult historian Robert Darnton's *Great Cat Massacre,* a study of the mock trial and execution of the area's cats that took place on the rue St-Séverin in the 1730s. It gives a fair idea of the grotesque entertainments enjoyed by the scribes, printers, and clerics who used to live and work in these streets. Fittingly, this peculiar neighborhood houses the minuscule theater (Théâtre de la Huchette) where nightly performances are given of Paris's longest-running show, two very absurd plays by Eugene Ionesco: *La Cantratrice Chauve* and *La Leçon.*

Despite the recent commercialization of the area, the St-Séverin quarter and the slightly more pleasant **St-André district** on the other side of the busy place St-Michel are still associated with eight centuries of student life. Even now, two decades after Paris universities were dispersed throughout the city, this part of the Latin Quarter remains the symbolic home of student pranks— the hapless stroller or motorist who ventures into the area on Mardi Gras will get pelted with eggs and flour. This offense, however annoying, pales in comparison with the duels, cuckolding, and bawdy singing that once passed as normal behavior in the district. As early as the 12th century, students from the numerous religious colleges on the Cité found respite from their taskmasters in

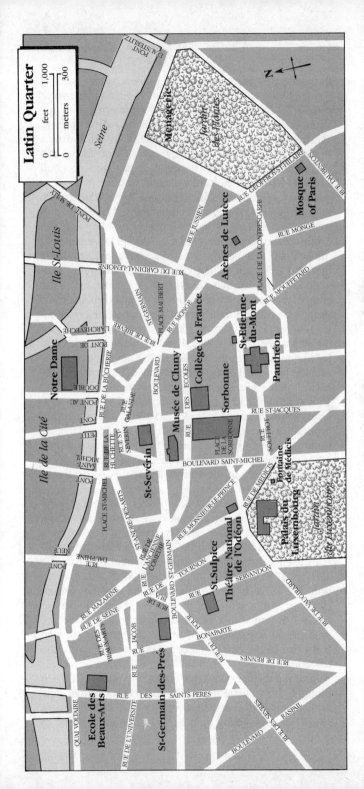

Latin Quarter

feet 1,000
meters 300
0

Seine

Ile St-Louis

Ile de la Cité

PONT D'AUSTERLITZ

Ménagerie

Jardin des Plantes

RUE GEOFFROY ST-HILAIRE

Mosque of Paris

RUE JUSSIEN

Arènes de Lutèce

RUE MONGE

PLACE DE LA CONTRESCARPE

RUE MOUFFETARD

RUE DU CARDINAL-LEMOINE

PONT DE SULLY

RUE ST-GERMAIN

PLACE MAUBERT

RUE MONGE

Collège de France

St-Etienne-du-Mont

Panthéon

RUE DE L'ARCHEVÊCHE

PONT DE BIÈVRE

Notre Dame

PONT AU DOUBLE

RUE DE LA BÛCHERIE

RUE GALANDE

BOULEVARD ST-GERMAIN

Musée de Cluny

RUE DES ECOLES

Sorbonne

RUE ST-JACQUES

PONT AU

PETIT PONT

RUE DE LA HUCHETTE

RUE ST-SEVERIN

St-Sévérin

RUE DE LA SORBONNE

PLACE DE LA SORBONNE

RUE SOUFFLOT

PONT ST-MICHEL

QUAI SAINT-MICHEL

PLACE ST-MICHEL

BOULEVARD SAINT-MICHEL

RUE DE MÉDICIS

Fontaine de Médicis

PONT NEUF

QUAI DES GRANDS-AUGUSTINS

PLACE ST-ANDRE-DES-ARTS

RUE MONSIEUR-LE-PRINCE

Palais du Luxembourg

Jardin du Luxembourg

RUE DE VAUGIRARD

RUE DAUPHINE

RUE DE L'ANCIENNE COMÉDIE

BOULEVARD ST-GERMAIN

RUE DE TOURNON

Théâtre National de l'Odéon

SERVANDONI

RUE MAZARINE

RUE DE SEINE

RUE DE BUCI

RUE DE

RUE DU FOUR

BONAPARTE

St.Sulpice

RUE DE RENNES

QUAI VOLTAIRE

RUE DES BEAUX-ARTS

RUE JACOB

RUE DE

RUE DE

Ecole des Beaux-Arts

RUE DE L'UNIVERSITÉ

RUE DES SAINTS PÈRES

St-Germain-des-Prés

BOULEVARD

RUE DE SÈVRES

RASPAIL

N

the alehouses of the area. Irreverence was the order of the day, with the inspirational choral singing known as the Ecole Notre-Dame finding its counterpoint in the licentious parodies belted out in Latin Quarter taverns. The best-known of these is the collection called "Carmina Burana." As Latin was the language of instruction and discourse in this quarter (hence its name), students of all nations were in on the earthy pleasantries.

Often tradition was flouted because it impeded knowledge. In Ian Littlewood's anecdotal *Paris: A Literary Companion,* a Medieval observer reports stumbling across a group of body snatchers at the St-Séverin cemetery— medical students, one hopes—intent on circumventing the Church's ban on the dissection of cadavers. Such applied skepticism has always been the hallmark of the area, ever since its earliest days when gifted rhetoricians drew crowds with their formal disputations. Pierre Abélard, in particular, was an idol of the neighborhood for his sheer genius in debate, handling contradictions and heckling with elegance and advancing novel ideas on the relation between Reason and Revelation, the central problem of Medieval thought. His successors in the 13th and 14th centuries had a far more organized system of colleges at their disposal, and scholasticism found fertile ground for development in the scores of religious institutions then housed in the Latin Quarter. Thomas Aquinas, Albertus Magnus, and many other great thinkers spent stimulating years in the Université, as this collection of schools was called.

The only substantial physical relic of this period is the **Musée de Cluny**, a rich repository of art from the Middle Ages housed in a 15th-century mansion. The tapestry series on display in Room XI, "The Lady and the Unicorn," is in itself worth a visit. Illustrated by animals from the allegorical bestiary that inhabited the Medieval imagination, the subjects of the tapestries are the five senses. However, the meaning of the sixth and final tapestry in the series remains a beautiful mystery. Alongside the museum lie the extensive ruins of the splendid Roman baths that in the days of Lutetia occupied this part of the Left Bank.

South of the Cluny are two competing giants of French thought, the Collège de France and the Sorbonne. Now undistinguished in appearance, they have been eminent rivals ever since King Francis I founded the Collège in

1530 as an intellectual counterweight to the dominant Sorbonne. Even today, the **Collège de France** prides itself on its anti-institutional slant, admitting anyone wishing to attend its public lectures. In recent years, Michel Foucault, Claude Lévi-Strauss, and Raymond Aron have given lecture series to halls packed with the studious, the curious, and just plain groupies. All one needs to attend is an ability to decipher the arcane timetables posted outside the building.

Although most of its buildings date from the last century, the **Sorbonne** is one of the oldest universities in the world. Founded in 1253 by Robert de Sorbon, the confessor of Saint Louis, it quickly rose to preeminence among French universities, specializing in the study of theology and the defense of orthodoxy. A latter-day alumnus, Cardinal Richelieu, poured funds into restoring its facilities, and it is his impressive mausoleum, a 17th-century chapel, that overlooks the place de la Sorbonne. Paradoxically, this square, though it bears the name of an academy notorious for its ponderous resistance to change, has come to symbolize youthful revolt in France. The television footage beamed live around the world every generation or so, showing French students squaring off against the police, sent in with their Plexiglas hoplites to restore order in the Latin Quarter, often originates from the place de la Sorbonne.

The most spectacular and far-reaching in effect of these outbursts occurred in May 1968, when a carnival spirit reigned in the quarter, and the joyful anarchy and explosion of radical political thought almost toppled the central government. Chafing at the outdated formalism of university life and impatient with an older generation affected by its wartime experience, the *soixante-huitards* (68ers) helped loosen the conservative bonds inhibiting French society. The revolt's climactic moment, both scorned and admired for its utter uselessness, was the occupation of the neighboring Odéon, the theater of an august state company that in the 1960s had been a showcase for contemporary drama under the direction of Jean-Louis Barrault. Although Barrault later lost his job for making clear where his sympathies lay, his Odéon will always be remembered for the spread of the movement's most dangerous idea: *L'imagination au pouvoir!* (power to the imagination!). The legacy of this slogan and the revolt it inspired are still hotly debated in France today. For many Parisians now in early middle age, the acrid smell of tear gas that drifts over the capital from time to time is not so much a nuisance as it is a fragrant reminder of youth.

The Montagne Ste-Geneviève and the Contrescarpe

Two peculiar landmarks stand atop the Montagne Ste-Geneviève, a glorified hill named after the fifth-century saint who convinced fleeing Parisians that Attila the Hun would bypass their town (which he did). The **Panthéon**, originally a pious project of Louis XV and Louis XVI, had the singular destiny of reaching completion just as the Revolution broke out. It passed the first century of its existence as an imposing question mark on the landscape, with successive regimes giving it to, then taking it from, the Church. Its definitive role as national mausoleum and temple of the Republic was established with the political stability of the late 19th century, when the body of Victor Hugo was installed with great pomp in its huge crypt. Other illustrious Frenchmen who now lie here are Voltaire, Rousseau (who poetically face each other for eternity), Emile Zola, Jean Jaurès, and Jean Moulin, the Resistance leader murdered by Klaus Barbie's men. The interior of the sanctuary is stridently nationalistic, and the enormous tableaux and other turn-of-the-century celebrations of the spirit of France unsuited to modern tastes. At the same time as a reactionary Church was elevating its basilica of Sacré Coeur (yet another case of dubious esthetics) on Montmartre, the progressive Third Republic was dressing up the Panthéon in the trappings of secular mysticism. The two domes still compete for attention.

The other striking monument on the hill is, indeed, a church, but it suffers from an earlier clash, relating almost entirely to taste. The interior of **St-Etienne-du-Mont** is Gothic—it is the only church in Paris to have kept its rood screen—yet the façade is a mishmash of Renaissance elements. Despite its confusing exterior, the church is of a rare beauty and provides a peaceful setting for a regular series of concerts (frequently featuring works by Vivaldi). Blaise Pascal, hedging his bet on salvation, is buried here—not across the way in the Panthéon with the two giants of the Enlightenment.

Many of the streets winding down from the hilltop have considerable charm, particularly the **rue Mouffe-**

tard, which follows the old Roman road from Paris to Lyon. Nothing from that distant Roman period exists here nowadays, although *la Mouffe* has kept the 20th century at bay much longer than most Paris neighborhoods have. Its upper stretch near the place de la Contrescarpe, despite a bewildering number of restaurants, is prized by sentimental Parisians fond of the local characters who are an enduring part of the human landscape of this quarter. On warm afternoons, an elderly birdlover known in the neighborhood as Madame Pigeon can usually be seen tending her flocks, always ready to share her encyclopedic knowledge of *la Mouffe* with passersby. Farther down the street toward its southern end the scene becomes unbearably picturesque, especially when the Mouffetard market opens for daily business. From behind the mounds of fruit and vegetables voluble merchants harangue shoppers in the flat accents of the native Parisian; in the cafés the clocks have stopped at the year 1900. The façade of the building at 134, rue Mouffetard is easily Paris's most elaborately decorated storefront.

The other attractions of this *arrondissement* (the fifth) are notable for their diversity. Near the Seine, the **Jardin des Plantes** is a quiet haven of Enlightenment natural sciences, encompassing a small zoo (where the sans culottes gaped in astonishment at the exotic animals that had been freed from royal menageries), rows of flower beds and herb gardens, mineralogical displays, musty old pavilions, and a cedar-of-Lebanon that was planted in 1734. As is so often the case in this city, history has made strange bedfellows: The immediate neighbor of this Enlightenment garden is an enclave of non-Western values. The spiritual center of the hundreds of thousands of Muslims who have settled in France since the period of decolonization and subsequent North African immigration, the **Mosquée de Paris** is striking not only for its Hispano-Moorish beauty, but also for its symbolic importance. As a new multiconfessional, multiracial France takes shape for the future (not without some bitter resistance from antediluvian nationalists), the cultures and customs of North Africa are more and more entering the French mainstream with the maturing of each successive generation. Although admittance to the mosque itself is reserved exclusively for the faithful, the adjoining gardens, tearoom, study center, and *hammam* (steambaths) have become a meeting place for France and Islam, with

Parisians of all backgrounds frequenting the facility. After a sybaritic evening spent in a Paris restaurant, many head to the mosque's soothing *hammam* for relief. Be sure to pick your night of excess carefully: The bath is open to women on Mondays, Tuesdays, Wednesdays, Thursdays, and Saturdays, and to men on Fridays and Sundays. Movie fans will be interested in knowing that Rita Hayworth married the son of the Aga Khan in this mosque.

Just a javelin's throw from the mosque and the Jardin des Plantes lies the Roman amphitheater. Much restored, the **Arènes de Lutèce** is an oasis of antiquity in the midst of a busy neighborhood, a perfect place to relax on a warm summer's day and watch the men play *boules* or the boys torture their younger brothers. For those with a taste for more organized carnage, the last week of June is particularly satisfying, for it is then that a professional stuntmen's association stages mock gladiator battles and other edifying spectacles in the arena.

St-Germain-des-Prés and the Jardin du Luxembourg

The **Pont des Arts**, an aptly named footbridge linking the galleries of the Louvre to the Left Bank, draws visitor and Parisian alike to its unobstructed view of the Ile de la Cité to the east and the often brilliant sunsets over the Seine to the west. The baroque edifice closing off the perspective to the south—the Institut de France—is notable for its dome, which, like Richelieu's Chapel of the Sorbonne, serves as a monument to a 17th-century cardinal with a flair for statecraft and intrigue. In this case the ostentatious prelate was Cardinal Mazarin, the gray eminence who ensured the transition from Louis XIII to Louis XIV.

The domed building is also home to the **Académie Française**, which is charged with removing, or at least recording, impurities that have crept into the French language. Admission to the Academy marks the official consecration of a French intellectual during his lifetime, although many intellectuals are quick to point out that truly great artists and thinkers have often been passed over in favor of inoffensive mediocrities. This may be a sour-grapes argument, or, more probably, the usual Parisian attitude of deference and derision toward the *académiciens*. The Academy's closest neighbors most clearly express these mixed feelings. Opposite the refined read-

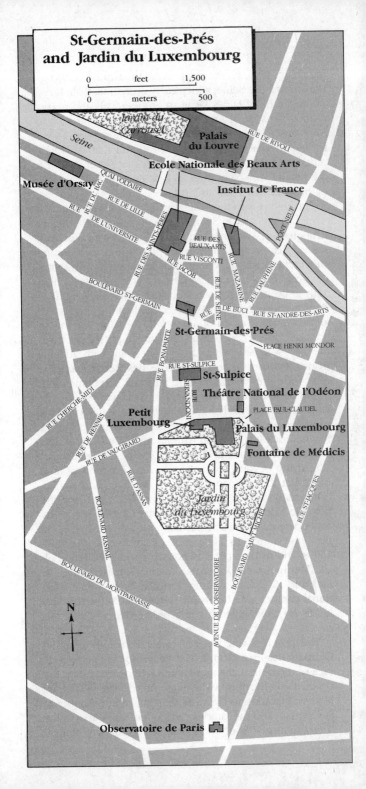

St-Germain-des-Prés and Jardin du Luxembourg

0   feet   1,500
0   meters   500

Jardin du Carrousel

Seine

RUE DE RIVOLI

Palais du Louvre

Ecole Nationale des Beaux Arts

Musée d'Orsay

QUAI VOLTAIRE

Institut de France

RUE DE LILLE

RUE DE BAC

RUE DE L'UNIVERSITE

RUE DES SAINTS-PERES

PONT NEUF

RUE DES BEAUX-ARTS

RUE VISCONTI

RUE JACOB

RUE MAZARINE

RUE DAUPHINE

BOULEVARD ST-GERMAIN

RUE DE SEINE

RUE DE BUCI

RUE ST-ANDRE-DES-ARTS

St-Germain-des-Prés

RUE

PLACE HENRI MONDOR

RUE BONAPARTE

RUE ST-SULPICE

St-Sulpice

Théâtre National de l'Odéon

RUE FERNANDONI

PLACE PAUL-CLAUDEL

Petit Luxembourg

Palais du Luxembourg

Fontaine de Médicis

RUE CHERCHE-MIDI

RUE DE RENNES

RUE DE VAUGIRARD

RUE D'ASSAS

Jardin du Luxembourg

RUE ST-JACQUES

BOULEVARD RASPAIL

BOULEVARD DU MONTPARNASSE

AVENUE DE L'OBSERVATOIRE

BOULEVARD SAINT-MICHEL

N

Observatoire de Paris

ing rooms beneath the dome stand the windswept book-stalls lining the Seine, which carry everything from faded photographs of James Dean to erotic novels and quirky monographs (as in a recent find, *Women Who Said No to Napoléon*). The *bouquinistes* (booksellers) are Paris's tribute to chaotic erudition, a tradition that is slightly older than the Academy itself: They first set up shop on the nearby Pont Neuf three decades before the founding of the Académie Française in 1635.

Through a short passageway in the Academy's west wing lies the rue de Seine, the main street of the **Beaux Arts quarter**. Two small squares at its lower end contain statues that seem to have been placed here as a parting shot at the Academy: Voltaire, a true immortal, snickers at the *académiciens,* and Carolina, a naked girl, stares defi-antly at the temple of official culture. The young nude is doubly appropriate, for she also stands at the entrance to an area given over almost entirely to the study and sale of art. Galleries, art bookstores, and art-supply shops crowd the narrow streets, which are often teeming with students from the nearby **Ecole Nationale des Beaux-Arts**. The cafés here are welcoming and informal, sometimes sub-jected to impromptu concerts by what may rank as the world's worst brass band, *le fanfare des Beaux-Arts.* This mix of art and frivolity has long made the neighborhood a magnet for esthetes of all nations. An ailing Oscar Wilde, who said of the rates at his hotel at 13, rue des Beaux Arts, "I'm dying beyond my means," is also reported to have looked at the wallpaper from his deathbed and sighed, "One of us will have to go." Parallel to Wilde's street is the tiny rue Visconti, one of the quarter's oldest. Formerly called rue des Marais-St-Germain, it was nicknamed "Lit-tle Geneva" for its Huguenot inhabitants in the mid-1500s, and in later periods housed Racine, Molière, Bal-zac, Merimée, and Delacroix. Stendhal's masterpiece, *The Red and the Black,* was first printed here. A recent fic-tional creation, the loathsome Grenouille of Patrick Süs-kind's *Perfume,* killed his first red-headed virgin in this street.

The most renowned spot of the Left Bank is the **place St-Germain-des-Prés**, from which the visitor can get a good idea of the radical changes Paris has undergone over the centuries. To the north is the Beaux Arts district with its late Medieval façades; to the west, the 18th-century Faubourg St-Germain and the famous cafés of postwar Paris; to the south, the broad avenues of the 19th century and the tall

Tour Montparnasse (a high-rise office tower) of the 20th; and to the east, the abbey church of St-Germain itself, a remnant of a time when this area was meadowland (*les prés*) cultivated by Benedictine monks. The Romanesque lines of the distinctive bell tower hint at the sanctuary's considerable age—Pope Alexander III consecrated the enlarged choir of this church only a few days before laying the cornerstone of Notre-Dame. Founded in the times of the Merovingian kings, the monastery recovered from the ravages of Viking raids in the ninth century and became prosperous around the year 1000, when the Cluniac reform of the Benedictines infused the order with renewed faith and vigor. Since then St-Germain has always figured prominently in the Parisian landscape, for many centuries as a rich country estate just beyond the city walls.

To the modern mind, St-Germain-des-Prés is associated with the Paris of the 1940s and 1950s, when prominent artists and intellectuals frequented the **Deux Magots** and **Flore** cafés. Simone Signoret, in her autobiography, *Nostalgia Isn't What It Used to Be,* gives a vivid description of the wartime Flore and its cast of artists, writers, and charlatans living a precarious existence in Nazi-occupied Paris. Just a few blocks away on the boulevard Raspail, the Hôtel Lutetia served as Gestapo headquarters. After the war—perhaps because of it—existentialism and its message of hopelessness as a spur to action became the vogue in these literary cafés and in the nearby **Brasserie Lipp**, with Jean-Paul Sartre and Simone de Beauvoir reigning as the undisputed sovereigns of daytime St-Germain. Night was the province of Boris Vian, a gifted writer and trumpeter who celebrated the cult of jazz in the many cellar clubs of the district. As France became embroiled in the Indo-Chinese War and memories of right-wing Vichy collaborators remained fresh, many of the intellectuals of St-Germain turned to Moscow for political inspiration—just as, at the same time, they were turning to New Orleans for enjoyment.

The contradictions are different now, as is the intellectual tenor of café life, but St-Germain has kept faith with some of its traditions. The center of France's publishing industry and, as such, the quarter of Paris with the greatest profusion of bookstores, it is also a popular area for nightlife. The **boulevard St-Germain** is lively well into the small hours of the morning, the crowds growing younger as one advances eastward to the Latin Quarter. The two districts converge at the place Henri Mondor, a cinema-lined square dominated by a statue of Georges-Jacques Danton, a former resident of the area. Down the rue de l'Ancienne Comédie is the **Procope**, the café (now a restaurant) where revolutions—intellectual and political—had been hatched since the late 17th century. Behind the Procope runs an inconspicuous alleyway called the cour du Commerce-St-André, built alongside the Medieval ramparts erected by King Philip II Augustus (a vestige of a tower can be seen inside number 4). Nearby, at number 9, a certain Dr. Guillotin tested a machine that was to inspire terror in royalist and revolutionary alike. Danton, whose statue now stands proudly a few feet away in the square, was one of its many victims.

Slightly off the beaten track and, mercifully, much quieter than the boulevard, is the lovely square and fountain in front of the **church of St-Sulpice**. Slightly bombastic in appearance for a simple parish church built for the lay community that had grown up around the St-Germain monastery, St-Sulpice is best viewed at sunset, when the fading light softens the harsh stone and unforgiving classicism of its façade. Among the devotional works inside the church are three striking tableaux by Eugène Delacroix (whose studio on the nearby place Fürstemberg can be visited). The emptiness of the square outside of St-Sulpice is relieved only in June at successive antiques and poetry fairs that take place around the central fountain. As befits a literary neighborhood, the given name of this fountain, les Quatre Points Cardinaux (the Four Cardinal Points), is an elaborate pun: Depicting four churchmen facing the cardinal compass points, the fountain honors prelates whose defense of the Gallican church against Vatican interference guaranteed that they would not rise far in the Roman hierarchy—hence, they were *point* (which also means "not at all") cardinals.

By far the best way to escape the bustle of both the Latin Quarter and St-Germain-des-Prés is to enter the **Jardin du Luxembourg**, a large expanse of greenery to the south of these districts. It is arguably the city's most entertaining park. In its western reaches, near the Orangerie, old men play interminable games of chess, young couples afflicted with romantic melancholia stroll through the *jardins à l'anglaise*, which are dotted with statues of literary greats, and, at the *Grand Guignol*, the French equivalent of Punch and Judy, the real stars of the show are the enthusiastic young spectators. A formal French garden, flanked by terraces adorned with statues of great French women of the past, makes up the central part of the park. A long prospect to the south opens onto the tree-lined avenue de l'Observatoire, so called for the domed observatory visible in the distance. Yet another institution inspired by the Enlightenment, the observatory fought to make its meridian the division between Eastern and Western hemispheres, but lost this honor to Greenwich. As a result, the linear arbor leading from the Luxembourg is a rather prosaic 2° 20′ 14″ E.

The eastern edge of the Luxembourg encloses one of the most beautiful spots in the city, a rectangular pond surmounted by a three-tiered fountain on which the lovers Galatea and Acis are watched over by the giant Polyphemus. Overhanging plane trees cover the water with an uneven carpet of leaves, beneath which golden carp swim about languidly. Although the statuary dates from the Second Empire, the Italianate pond, called the **Medici fountain**, has remained unchanged since the early 17th century, when the widowed queen of Henry IV ordered the construction of the neighboring **Palais du Luxembourg**. Marie de Mèdicis, who felt no compunction about raiding her late husband's treasury at the Bastille for funds, wanted to reproduce here the Pitti Palace of her beloved Florence. Though thwarted in this grand design, she managed to complete the palace and gardens even while plotting and counterplotting intrigues during the regency of her young son, Louis XIII. Rubens's 21 tableaux depicting her life, now hanging in the Louvre, do not represent Marie's final fate: death in exile, ultimately outfoxed by Richelieu. Her sumptuous palace is now occupied by the French Senate, a respected but powerless group of legislators. For readers of Dumas *père,* uninterested in such contemporary niceties, the place to continue musing about Richelieu's perfidy is in the quiet neighborhood between the Luxembourg and St-Sulpice: At 12, rue Servandoni lived the thorn in the Cardinal's side, the musketeer D'Artagnan.

In the 1920s the Jardin du Luxembourg served as the inexpensive alternative to the nearby cafés of **Montparnasse**. Although still a thriving boulevard dotted with restaurants, cafés, and movie houses, Montparnasse retains little of the flavor of its wild days when John Glassco, in his hilarious *Memoirs of Montparnasse,* could write about partying with Kiki (Man Ray's model), cajoling Emma Goldman out of a post-Bolshevik funk, and drinking heavily with French surrealists and American writers. Café society, especially at the **Coupole** and the **Select**, can still be slightly subversive, even if the spread of offices following the erection of the Tour Montparnasse has made the area more business-minded. Aside from its Lost Generation lore, which is still powerful enough to make you self-conscious about writing so much as a postcard in these cafés, the area has two further attractions: a Breton enclave near the rue Edgar Quinet, with crêperies and cider-fuelled merriment, and a small theater district on the rue de la Gaîté. But Zelda and her friends have long gone.

From Orsay to the Eiffel Tower

The Faubourg St-Germain, stretching from the rue des Saints-Pères to the Invalides, has remained frustratingly impenetrable to the commoner, its aristocratic 18th-century homes and gardens hiding behind massive stone gates. Developed when the nobility left the cramped streets of the old Marais district for the then wide-open spaces of the Grenelle Plain west of the St-Germain abbey, the Faubourg lost its ancien régime exclusiveness with the coming of the Revolution and the Bonapartes. The early-19th-century salons of the lovely Madame Récamier and brilliant Madame de Staël restored some of the quarter's lost cachet, and even today a few fading dynasties match wits and offspring in the Proustian calm of their Faubourg drawing rooms. Still, most of these fine old homes are now occupied by government grandees, and the prospect of an elegant ministry here undoubtedly fuels the ambitions of provincial politicians. The Hôtel de Matignon, its property encompassing Paris's largest private park, is reserved for the Prime Minister, the public figure who is expected to thrive best in the miasma of French party politics. Fittingly, Matignon's fashionable rue de Varenne address was on the calling card of French history's most formidable political survivor, Charles-Maurice de Talleyrand.

If the houses of the Faubourg remain closed to the curious, at least some elements of their decor are on view—and on sale—to the public in the **Carré Rive Gauche**, a grid of streets bordered on the north by the quai Voltaire. Its concentration of antique and furniture shops makes window shopping here a rewarding pastime, particularly in May, when the Carré's Days of the Extraordinary Object give pride of place to some truly weird creations foisted on old and new money alike. An entertaining appraisal of the Carré appears in "Old Paris,"

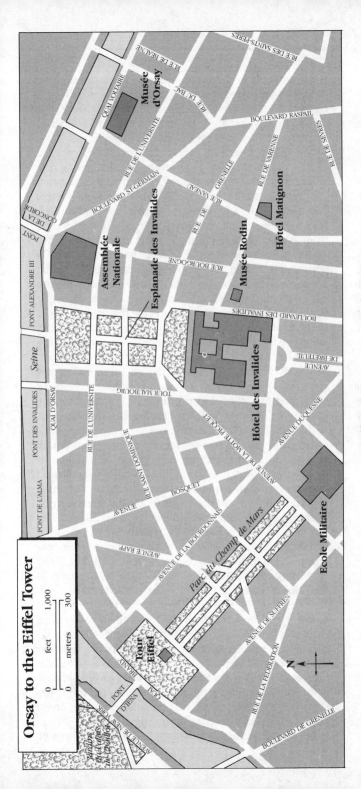

Orsay to the Eiffel Tower

feet 1,000
meters 300

Musée d'Orsay
QUAI VOLTAIRE
RUE DE BEAUNE
RUE DES SAINTS-PÈRES
RUE DU BAC
BOULEVARD RASPAIL
RUE DE L'UNIVERSITÉ
BOULEVARD ST-GERMAIN
RUE DE GRENELLE
RUE DE VARENNE
RUE DE SÈVRES
Assemblée Nationale
RUE VANEAU
RUE DE
Esplanade des Invalides
RUE BOURGOGNE
Hôtel Matignon
PONT DE LA CONCORDE
Musée Rodin
PONT ALEXANDRE III
BOULEVARD DES INVALIDES
Seine
Hôtel des Invalides
PONT DES INVALIDES
TOUR MALBOURG
AVENUE DE BRETEUIL
QUAI D'ORSAY
RUE DE L'UNIVERSITÉ
PONT DE L'ALMA
RUE SAINT-DOMINIQUE
AVENUE DE LA MOTTE PICQUET
AVENUE DU QUESNE
AVENUE BOSQUET
AVENUE RAPP
AVENUE DE LA BOURDONNAIS
Parc du Champ de Mars
Ecole Militaire
AVENUE DE SUFFREN
Tour Eiffel
QUAI BRANLY
PONT D'IÉNA
AVENUE DE LA FÉDÉRATION
AVENUE DE NEW YORK
Jardins du Palais de Chaillot
BOULEVARD DE GRENELLE

N

a sardonic essay by Saul Bellow: "Who would have thought that Europe contained so much old junk? Or that, the servant class having disappeared, hearts nostalgic for the bourgeois epoch would hunt so eagerly for Empire breakfronts, Récamier sofas, and curule chairs?"

Nostalgia for the 19th century runs even deeper at the nearby **Musée d'Orsay**, a refurbished Belle Epoque railway terminal that houses the city's rich artistic legacy from the period 1848–1914. The creation of this mammoth new way station in the art lover's tour of Paris brought about the removal here of the collection of French Impressionists from its quaint isolation in the Jeu de Paume pavilion of the Tuileries. In many ways, its transfer to a train station is appropriate, given the Impressionists' conviction that scenes from everyday life, whether in the country or in the city (indeed, the Gare St-Lazare served Claude Monet as inspiration), were worthy subjects for the painter. Some critics have faulted the Orsay for being indiscriminate in its all-embracing sweep of the 19th century and for giving *pompier* excesses as much exposure as recognized masterpieces. Whatever its contradictions in presentation and contents, Orsay stands as a striking testament to France's continued expertise in converting old buildings to new uses. Whether the result is philistine is a question that visitors must answer for themselves.

The Hôtel Biron, an older example of a successfully converted building and the only 18th-century home in the area that is open to the public, stands at the opposite corner of the Faubourg St-Germain. In 1910 the French government reserved this property for the use of artists, among them Isadora Duncan, Henri Matisse, Rainer Maria Rilke, and Auguste Rodin. Rodin later signed an agreement bequeathing his work to the State in exchange for freedom to work and live in the Hôtel Biron at public expense. The result of this ideal arrangement is the **Musée Rodin**, a quiet, sensual place where such sculptures as *The Kiss, The Thinker,* and *The Burghers of Calais* blend in surprisingly well with their neoclassical surroundings. Recently, the work of the gifted Camille Claudel, the mistress of the sculptor—her high-strung genius brought her to a tragic end in an asylum for the insane—has belatedly emerged from her lover's shadow and received public recognition in its own right. Her life story is often cited by French feminists as a cautionary tale of great talent frustrated by misogynist times.

The Rodin museum's low-key celebration of the arts of

love is in contrast to the full-blown cult of martial glory displayed by the neighboring **Invalides**. An imposing Parisian landmark since its completion in 1706, the Invalides is Louis XIV's legacy to the capital he shunned for Versailles. The king's numerous wars of conquest, although successful in expanding the borders of France and ensuring his reputation as Europe's most powerful monarch, brought about great human misery, some of which this veterans' hospital tried to alleviate. The humanitarian impulse was gradually supplanted by the desire to make the building a showplace for French arms: Indeed, the Revolution, hardly sympathetic with past royal initiatives, made the place a Temple of Mars, and the Invalides became a museum honoring French soldiery. Thus it is appropriate, if anachronistic, that Jules Hardouin-Mansart's superb domed church is principally known as the mausoleum of Napoléon Bonaparte, the greatest soldier France has ever produced. In the eyes of French nationalists, the stature of the two historical figures connected with the Invalides, the Emperor and the Sun King, augments its prestige, making the place a symbol of the grandeur of their country. For those of other political persuasions, the evocation of grandeur is a defense of absolutism and should, like the Invalides itself, be avoided.

These two strong opposing viewpoints, the desire for a strong central authority and the egalitarian impulse, have been at war in the French mind since 1789, and the struggle is still evident in the contemporary Fifth Republic, in which a multitude of elective offices are dwarfed by the tremendous power of the President. The bridge linking the Esplanade des Invalides to the Right Bank is a more striking illustration of this long-standing ambiguity. Built for the World's Fair of 1900, when many politicians of the Third Republic were fighting the antidemocratic forces of Church and Army (on such issues as public education and the Dreyfus Affair, respectively), the **Pont Alexandre III** honors the most absolutist regime of its time, the Russia of the Tsars. True, anti-Prussian motives had made France and Tsar Nicholas II unlikely allies, yet the mere fact that Paris, the reputedly godless, regicidal capital of a progressive republic, could build such an exuberant monument to an autocrat is still something of a wonder today. It is also our good fortune: The bridge's ornamentation and statuary (the central groups depict the Seine and Neva rivers) make it an overdone Belle Epoque gem and, as such, very photogenic.

Farther downstream, the river is spanned by the **Pont de l'Alma**, famous for the Zouave (French-Algerian soldier) standing at its base as the city's unofficial marker of high and low waters. It may come as a relief to know that the bridge's neighboring attractions have nothing to do with art or politics. On the Left Bank is the public entrance to the sewers of Paris, a 19th-century engineering achievement that can be visited—whenever the Seine is well below the Zouave's feet—on Mondays and Wednesdays and the last Saturday of every month. Across the river on the Right Bank lies the main embarkation point for the **bateaux-mouches**, the monstrously large glass tour boats that ply the Seine year round. Contrary to the prejudices of seasoned travellers, these boats are not tourist traps. A quick tour of Paris's riverfront is beautiful day or night, providing you can put up with a tiresome recorded spiel in every major European language (it's best to sit outside). The dinner boat, however, takes too long to make the circuit but not long enough to allow for a leisurely Parisian feast; far better to take the regular cruise and dine at a good restaurant on shore.

The westernmost part of this large swath of the Left Bank is taken up by the **Champs de Mars**, the elegant park that once served as a parade ground for the Ecole Militaire. When Napoléon was graduated from this academy in 1785, his instructor's prescient evaluation of Bonaparte read, "Will go far, if circumstances permit." Aside from its military past and its rare status as a Parisian park where you are allowed to sit on the grass (a little beyond the midway point to the river, off the side alleys), the Champs de Mars is most famous for its riverside monument, the **Eiffel Tower**. Built for the World's Fair of 1889, the tower was intended to be the iron icon of France's industrial and engineering might—and to be a temporary structure. Civic pride over having the world's tallest structure at that time forestalled demolition, and the invention of the wireless gave Gustav Eiffel's implausible creation a new lease on life as a radio mast. Its ironwork seems surprisingly light and delicate to 20th-century eyes, particularly when viewed from directly beneath the structure, and recent renovations have been hailed by all Parisians as a success. The new nighttime illumination creates the illusion that the tower is covered in cheap gold-colored paint, making it the world's largest souvenir of itself. Long a symbol of the industrial age, the Eiffel

Tower is now entering its second century as Paris's most unexpected tribute to postmodernism.

THE RIGHT BANK
The 16th *Arrondissement* and the Bois de Boulogne

There are few places where the performance aspect of Paris is more in evidence than on the Right Bank across the Seine from the Eiffel Tower. The hilltop **Palais de Chaillot**, built for the 1937 World's Fair at the place du Trocadéro, forms a large Art Deco backdrop to the play of fountains in the gardens sloping down toward the Seine. Monumental statues adorn these fountains, which send their powerful jets of water spraying out over a long reflecting pool. This area and the terrace above, a striking lookout over the Left Bank, are the playgrounds of roller skaters, skateboarders, break dancers, and members of other strenuous urban subcultures who suspend their year-round cavorting at Chaillot only for such special occasions as Bastille Day, when the place is brilliantly illuminated by fireworks.

The two wings of the palace make up an impressive cultural complex containing a major national theater and three large museums: the Musée de la Marine (begun by Louis XIV's minister, Jean-Baptiste Colbert), the Musée de l'Homme (the showcase of French anthropology), and the Musée des Monuments Français (featuring reproductions of the finest works of art to be found in the French provinces). Down the avenue Président-Wilson are three other museums of note. The **Musée Guimet** houses a world-famous collection of art from the Orient, while two neighboring palaces, **Galliéra** and **Tokyo**, respectively exhibit clothing fashion since the 18th century and the municipality's modern art holdings. The Tokyo Palace was built for the 1937 World's Fair and, like its larger contemporary atop the Chaillot hill, serves several purposes. The gallery's photographic exhibits are extremely popular with Parisians, especially during the biennial Mois de la Photo, a citywide celebration of the camera held in November. It also houses France's cinémathèque, which contains the celluloid archives of the nation and has several screening rooms open to the public.

On the southern slope of the Chaillot hill stretches the

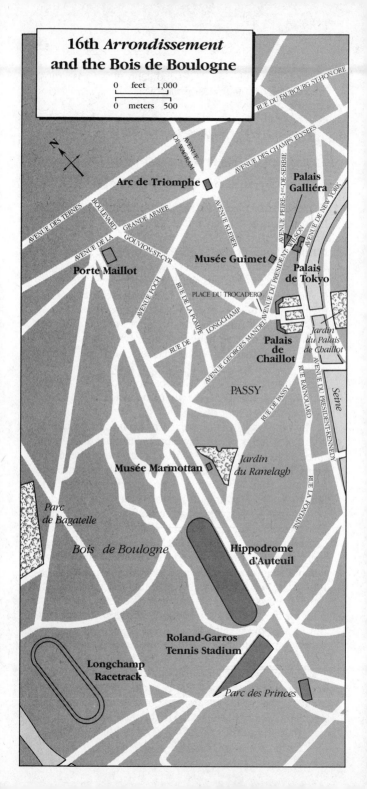

16th *Arrondissement* and the Bois de Boulogne

0   feet   1,000

0   meters   500

RUE DU FAUBOURG ST-HONORÉ

AVENUE DE WAGRAM

AVENUE DES CHAMPS ELYSÉES

Arc de Triomphe

AVENUE PIERRE-1er-DE-SERBIE

Palais Galliéra

AVENUE DES TERNES

BOULEVARD

GRANDE ARMÉE

AVENUE KLÉBER

AVENUE DE NEW YORK

AVENUE DE LA

GOUVION-ST-CYR

Musée Guimet

Palais de Tokyo

Porte Maillot

AVENUE FOCH

RUE DE LA POMPE

PLACE DU TROCADERO

AVENUE DU PRÉSIDENT-WILSON

Jardin du Palais de Chaillot

RUE DE

LONGCHAMP

AVENUE GEORGES MANDEL

Palais de Chaillot

RUE DE PASSY

PASSY

RUE RAYNOUARD

Seine

AVENUE DU PRÉSIDENT-KENNEDY

RUE LA FONTAINE

Musée Marmottan

Jardin du Ranelagh

Parc de Bagatelle

Bois de Boulogne

Hippodrome d'Auteuil

Roland-Garros Tennis Stadium

Longchamp Racetrack

Parc des Princes

quiet neighborhood of **Passy**. Literary pilgrims can visit the house at 47, rue Raynouard, where Balzac lived from 1840 to 1847. Constantly beset by creditors, the author of the *Comédie Humaine* became one of its most colorful characters by residing in this suburban hideout expressly to evade bill collectors (an exit at a lower level made it easy for him to disappear at the sound of a door knocker). Balzac's coffeepot, in which he brewed the stuff that kept him awake and writing through the long nights, now sits idly on display.

Passy and its environs have since been swallowed up by the 16th *arrondissement,* the district of Paris known for its splendid isolation. Long a bucolic retreat for aristocrats, artists, and diplomats (Benjamin Franklin spent many years in Passy), the area developed into a fashionable residential quarter at the close of the last century, when most of its stately apartments were built. Today, the 16th is home to the Parisians satirically known as the BCBG (*Bon Chic, Bon Genre*), the well-scrubbed, well-off, well-dressed conservatives who can be seen, their dogs at their feet, sipping drinks in the fashionable cafés of the place du Trocadéro and place Victor Hugo. At night this residential district is dead, especially in the summer months when its inhabitants answer the call of the civilized and move out to their country homes. Passy's Jardin du Ranelagh serves as a nursery for their impeccably turned-out toddlers and as an elegant antechamber for visiting lovers of Monet—nearby is the **Musée Marmottan**, where many of the painter's greatest works are on exhibit.

Although the 16th is deserted at night, the same cannot be said of the neighboring **Bois de Boulogne**, which as soon as the sun sets becomes the hunting ground of peculiar human fauna. In the daytime, however, the 2,200-plus-acre park is populated with more innocent pleasure seekers who stroll, jog, cycle (bikes can be rented near the Jardin d'Acclimatation), or ride horses through its maze of forest pathways. On the urging of Napoléon III (in perhaps the only of his many town-planning initiatives to be universally applauded by Parisians), the designers of the Bois set about creating a Hyde Park for Paris, their Anglophilia driving them so far as to plant a Shakespeare Garden at its heart. This enclosure features all of the flora the Bard ever mentioned in his works. Of the park's many attractions (restaurants, artificial lakes, country clubs, children's playgrounds), the oldest is Bagatelle, a country pavilion that the Count of Artois constructed in the record time of seven weeks to win a bet with his sister-in-law, Marie Antoinette. However charming this *folie* may be, it is Bagatelle's floral gardens that more truly merit a visit. The azaleas (April) and roses (June and July) draw crowds of admirers who the resident peacocks assume to be well-wishers. The combination of colorful flower beds and proud peacocks can be quite spectacular.

Peacocks of the human variety are on display at the Bois de Boulogne's most famous attraction, the **Longchamp racetrack**. On the first Sunday in October, the plumage becomes extravagant at the main event of the season, the Prix de l'Arc de Triomphe, Europe's richest horse race. The Longchamp tradition stretches back to Second Empire days of ostentatious social jockeying, and still retains a certain cachet. Auteuil, the other track of the Bois, is definitely the poor cousin, although its immediate neighbor, the Roland-Garros tennis stadium, has lately risen in social standing, and tickets to the French Open in May are now very difficult to obtain. South of the Bois is another sports venue, the Parc des Princes, where French soccer and rugby matches are played.

From the Arc de Triomphe to the Tuileries

From atop the **Arc de Triomphe**, Napoléon's monument to his military invincibility (completed 21 years after Waterloo), the visitor has a good view of imperial Paris and the 12 avenues radiating from the Etoile, the star. Far to the west are the towers of La Défense, a suburban business district where striking skyscrapers and wind-tunnel esplanades successfully suggest the might of corporate France. A massive new arch, glorifying communications and media, is being built at La Défense as the final monument in the prospect that runs from the Louvre's place du Carrousel, up the Champs-Elysées, and out of the city. All told, this triumphal way counts three arches (Napoléon is celebrated by another Arc de Triomphe, smaller and more graceful, at the eastern end of the Tuileries), an Egyptian obelisk (in the place de la Concorde), and an equestrian statue by Bernini (in the place du Carrousel).

It should hardly come as a surprise that Bernini's horseman is Louis XIV, Napoléon's ancien régime counterpart in the grandeur stakes.

In fact, the whole failed point of the Champs-Elysées is grandeur. From its beginnings, when Louis XIV's landscaping genius, André Le Nôtre, first laid it out as a tree-lined prospect stretching from the Jardin des Tuileries to a distant, elevated horizon, the avenue was intended to represent the sublime and the permanent. Instead, it has been the theater of the temporary, largely because its development took place during France's stormy 19th century. When the avenue was saddled with a name evocative of the gods walking the Elysian Fields, its fate as colossal irony was sealed. From the Palais de l'Elysée, Louis-Napoléon (the Emperor's nephew) engineered the overthrow of the Second Republic in order to set himself up as a mid-century Augustus, leading Karl Marx to remark of this Bonapartist replay on the avenue, "History occurs first as tragedy, then repeats itself as farce." As Emperor Napoléon III, Louis lived in absolutist style in the 16th-century Tuileries palace, only to be run out of the country in 1870 after being utterly humiliated in the war against Bismarck's Prussians. A year later, embittered Parisians put the palace to the torch during the Communard uprising, thereby giving notice that they had had enough of imperial pretensions from their rulers. The avenue's opulent mansions, built by 19th-century capitalists who were as ostentatious as Faubourg-St-Germain aristocrats were discreet, gradually fell under the wrecker's ball, to be replaced by office buildings and apartments. (A remarkable survivor stands at number 25.)

Today the Champs-Elysées serves as a stage for Republican spectacles. The French president resides in the Palais de l'Elysée, receiving dignitaries in a style that the building's best-known tenant, Madame de Pompadour, would find congenial. On July 14, Bastille Day, the avenue becomes a parade ground for the army, the latest in French weaponry passing in review of the president and thousands of patriotic Parisians. As on other anniversaries of martial significance, a giant tricolor hangs from the Arc de Triomphe, giving rise in many hearts to what is sardonically called *"cocorico"* ("cock-a-doodle-do," or chauvinistic nationalism). Whatever misfortunes have befallen the French army in the past one hundred years, the grandiose—and to many Frenchmen, moving—sight of the flag billowing above the tomb of the unknown soldier is a reminder of past sacrifices and victories.

Fortunately, the avenue's aspirations to grandeur are overshadowed by its pursuit of the frivolous. Despite its historical significance, the **Etoile,** for many Parisians, is simply the most exhilarating place in the city to drive, especially at night at a fast clip. (Do not even consider walking across the Etoile to get to the Arc; take the lifesaving underground passageway instead.) The best way to visit the **Champs-Elysées,** luckily, is on foot, with occasional stops to watch everybody watching everybody else. Here is where the urban myth of the extortionate price of coffee in Paris actually has some grounding in fact, so be prepared to nurse a demitasse of espresso for as long as you care to sit and stare. The walker should also cross the street at least once, pausing in the middle of the roadway to get the full effect of the monumental symmetry and the blinking lights of the long lines of traffic. The speed at which this traffic whizzes past accounts for the absence of cyclists: The only time they appear in any number is at the end of July, when the month-long Tour de France bicycle race concludes here in a blaze of publicity.

For all its bright lights, the modern-day showiness of the Champs-Elysées is fairly empty and need only be taken in once. Cinemas, airline offices, car dealerships, and chain restaurants line the street, with a few shopping arcades scattered about for the benefit of luxury souvenir hounds. At number 127, the Paris tourist office provides a mine of information about festivals, concerts, and special events taking place in the city. On the nearby avenue George-V is one of the city's most popular permanent shows, the daring girlie revue of the **Crazy Horse Saloon,** a perennial favorite of visiting Middle Eastern potentates. The area stretching to the east of George-V contains a large number of restaurants and fashionable boutiques, especially in the quarter around the elegant **avenue Montaigne,** which is vying with the rue du Faubourg St-Honoré (to the north and parallel to the Champs-Elysées) for the title of the city's most exclusive thoroughfare. **Faubourg St-Honoré** is longer, older, and more established, but the scents wafting from passersby are just as expensive as those on Montaigne, and the avenue itself is broad, tree-lined, and uncongested. The street can also lay claim to the new fine-art auctioneering facility of Paris, Drouot-Montaigne; the theater (Théâtre des Champs-

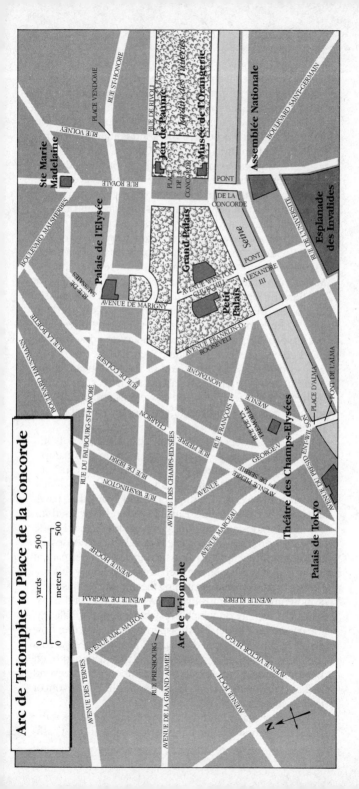

Arc de Triomphe to Place de la Concorde

Ste Marie Madeleine

Palais de l'Elysée

Jeu de Paume

Musée de l'Orangerie

Musée de l'Orangerie

Assemblée Nationale

Esplanade des Invalides

Grand Palais

Petit Palais

Théâtre des Champs-Elysées

Palais de Tokyo

Arc de Triomphe

PLACE VENDOME

RUE ST-HONORE

RUE DE RIVOLI

PLACE DE LA CONCORDE

RUE ROYALE

RUE VOLNEY

BOULEVARD MALESHERBES

RUE DE PENTHIEVRE

RUE DE LA BOETIE

AVENUE DE MARIGNY

RUE DE LA CONCORDE

Seine

PONT DE LA CONCORDE

PONT ALEXANDRE III

BOULEVARD SAINT-GERMAIN

RUE DE L'UNIVERSITE

AVENUE WINSTON CHURCHILL

AVENUE FRANKLIN-D.-ROOSEVELT

BOULEVARD HAUSSMANN

RUE DU FAUBOURG-ST-HONORE

RUE DE COLISEE

CHARRON

RUE DE BERRI

RUE DE PONTHIEU

AVENUE DES CHAMPS-ELYSEES

RUE WASHINGTON

RUE PIERRE 1er DE SERBIE

RUE FRANÇOIS 1er

AVENUE MONTAIGNE

AVENUE MATIGNON

AVENUE PIERRE 1er DE SERBIE

AVENUE GEORGE V

AVENUE MARCEAU

PLACE D'ALMA

PONT DE L'ALMA

AVENUE DU PRESID.-ENT-WILSON

AVENUE HOCHE

AVENUE MAC MAHON

AVENUE DES TERNES

AVENUE FOCH

AVENUE DE LA GRAND ARMEE

RUE PRESBOURG

AVENUE DE WAGRAM

AVENUE KLEBER

AVENUE VICTOR HUGO

N

0   yards   500

0   meters   500

Elysées) in which Nijinsky was booed at the premiere of Stravinsky's *Rite of Spring;* and a fashionable mix of diplomats, TV people, and haute couturiers.

The avenue Montaigne meets the triumphal way at the fountains and flowerbeds of the Rond-Point des Champs-Elysées. At this midway mark of the Champs, shaded pedestrian alleyways take over from the lively business district. The northern side of the avenue, near the avenue de Marigny, holds a stamp, coin, and old postcard market on Thursdays, Saturdays, and Sundays, a charming outdoor affair that draws a good number of the city's eccentrics. This green belt, now sedate and often deserted, is forever linked with the most extravagant of Parisian vogues, the *Incroyables* and the *Merveilleux* (the Incredible and the Marvelous) of the post-Revolutionary period. Fashion for strollers through this area at that time dictated outlandish, immodest dress, and a relaxing of morals encouraged the type of libertine behavior that previously had been the preserve of the nobility. Revolutionary fervor even demanded new diction: The rolling French of the aristocracy was so detested and the accent of the Caribbean so admired that the letter "r" was abolished from speech altogether. Couples tempted to be incwedible and mawvelous in the area's secluded shrubbery should remember that times have changed.

The sole intersection breaking up the greenery is impressive for its double vista: the long view up the Champs-Elysées to the west and the broad avenue Winston Churchill leading south to the distant dome of the Invalides. Flanking this avenue are the Grand and Petit Palais, pavilions built for the World's Fair of 1900 and now used for the more important temporary art exhibitions and trade shows to come to the city. (The Petit Palais also houses the museum of the city of Paris, which includes a permanent collection.) A pleasant, inexpensive way to enjoy this imposing urbanism entails catching the **number 83 bus** at the Rond-Point des Champs-Elysées. As this is one of the two routes in the city on which every bus has a rear balcony, the passenger can stand in the open air and watch the show go by. At sunset this ride down the Champs-Elysées, across the Alexandre III bridge, briefly along the quays of the Left Bank, then on to the Jardin du Luxembourg and beyond makes even the most blasé Parisians take their noses out of their newspapers.

The other major landmark of the Champs-Elysées is the **place de la Concorde**, an impressive combination of rushing traffic, beautiful streetlamps, imposing statues of women representing the major cities of France, allegorical fountains, and, of course, the obelisk. The view from the Concorde is special as well. The two buildings on the northern side of the square, occupied by the Hôtel Crillon and the ministry of the Navy, are colonnaded palaces designed by Jacques-Ange Gabriel for Louis XVI. The rue Royale, separating the two buildings, gives onto the Corinthian excess of the **church of the Madeleine** (Mary Magdalene). Impossible as it may seem, even more pillars are evident to the south, where the Napoleonic façade of the Assemblée Nationale, France's fractious parliament, stands facing the square from the Left Bank. On the east and west sides equestrian groups by Coustou (the *Horses of Marly*) and Coysevox (the *Winged Horses*) guard the entrances to the Champs-Elysées and Tuileries, respectively.

Like the Champs-Elysées, the Concorde does not live up to its name for the simple reason that the square has traditionally been associated with discord. During the 1770 wedding celebrations of Louis XVI and Marie Antoinette, 133 people died in a stampede caused by panic over exploding stores of fireworks. In 1793–4, the square was the Revolution's most prestigious execution site, and 1,119 prisoners rode the tumbrils the length of the rue St-Honoré to their final appointment here. Among those whose heads rolled were Danton, Charlotte Corday (Marat's assassin), Robespierre, Marie Antoinette, and Louis XVI. Two decades later the Bourbons came back into power and decided to adorn the square with a distinctly apolitical obelisk that Mohammed Ali, Viceroy of Egypt, offered to them. However, by the time the 3,000-year-old gift arrived in Paris, the Bourbons had once again been shown the door and the Orléanist usurper of their throne, King Louis-Philippe, had the pleasure of welcoming the exotic monument to Paris. In later Republican days, the Concorde became the theater of the white-hot *revanchard* sentiment over the loss of Alsace and Lorraine to the Prussians in 1873. The statue of Strasbourg was smothered in flowers for more than 50 years, and the timorous few to oppose the cult of the lost provinces were soon punished. A fashionable ice-cream merchant on the rue Royale had his shop destroyed for daring to put a German flag in his window (his property was quickly snapped up by an enterprising waiter named Maxim Gaillard, and thus Maxim's was born). In 1934 the most violent riot of modern times in France took place at the Concorde, with members of extreme-right groups rushing the Assemblée Nationale to throw parliamentarians into the river. Fifteen died and 300 were wounded, many of them on the **Pont de la Concorde**, the one Paris bridge to have been constructed with building material freed in another memorable riot. Much of its stone comes from the Bastille, demolished in 1789.

By contrast, the **Jardin des Tuileries**, although it too was the scene of memorable incidents in the Revolution, is almost always associated with the gentler pastime of doing absolutely nothing. A formal French garden designed by Le Nôtre, the Tuileries has been a favorite Parisian promenade since the 17th century, its pools, terraces, and statuary unerringly lined up by landscape geometers. The sole exception is modern: a series of sensual female nudes sculpted by Maillol and scattered about the park's eastern extremity. For those uneasy about idling away too much time on a vacation, however lovely the surroundings, the arcades of the commercial rue de Rivoli that run the length of the Tuileries' northern edge are always ready for shoppers.

A more edifying antidote to lazing about the Tuileries can be found at the two galleries near the place de la Concorde. The **Jeu de Paume**, now bereft of Impressionist glory, holds temporary exhibits, while the **Orangerie**, containing the superb Manet, Cézanne, Renoir, and Douanier Rousseau canvases of the Walter-Guillaume collection, remains one of the city's most surprising—and least visited—small galleries.

The Louvre and Châtelet

When King Philip Augustus decided to construct the **Louvre** in order to protect Paris while he was off gallivanting with Richard the Lion-Hearted on the Third Crusade, he unwittingly created the architectural hobbyhorse of the French nation. Few buildings in the country have been so assiduously rebuilt, extended, and modified. The result is a glorious monster, glaringly imperfect yet miraculously possessing three fine expressions of the builder's art: the Cour Carrée (a courtyard built over the course of several reigns that shows the shift from Renaissance to Baroque to Neoclassical in French architecture); the Galerie du Bord de l'Eau, the center section of the riverside wing built for Henri IV; and the Colonnade de Perrault, the imposing easternmost façade constructed for Louis XIV.

The latest expression of the 700-year-old tradition of tinkering with the Louvre—an underground concourse of shops, conference rooms, and restaurants designed by I. M. Pei—was inaugurated in 1988.

The newcomer departs from its underground discretion only once, in a tall, pyramid-shaped skylight that rises from the middle of the Cour Napoléon. However one feels about this daring addition to the Louvre, there can be no doubt that the modern facility meets several needs. It provides a glimpse of the formerly inaccessible Medieval palace (visitors can now walk underground through the moats), cleans up the confusion that once reigned in the Cour Napoléon, and, in rationalizing the Louvre's entranceway, gives some order to a museum that has long been notorious among art lovers for playing hide-and-seek with its cultural treasures. The reorganization of the Louvre's collections, some of which are gathering dust out of view, is expected to continue until the year 2000— that is, if obstacles such as the one encountered in the mid-1980s, when a French finance minister pettishly refused to move his offices from the building's northern wing, can be successfully circumvented. A compromise allowing the minister in question to hang on to his fancy address was eventually struck, but not before Parisians had enjoyed an unseemly fight between private vanity and public interest.

Once inside the Louvre it is easy to forget these recent squabbles and to thank the Revolution for finally opening the building to the public, in 1793. Louis XVI had considered, but never adopted, the idea. The first sight for many visitors, the monumental Daru staircase, crowned by the *Winged Victory* of Samothrace, is a foretaste of the masterpieces to follow and of the enjoyment to be derived from them, provided, of course, the temptation to sprint through the entire building at one go can be resisted. As many of the paintings come from the private collections of Bourbon and Valois monarchs, it is hardly surprising that the Louvre is particularly rich in art from Italy, the country long synonymous with civilization for France's rulers. As is only natural, French painting is also well represented, particularly in the giant tableaux from the early 19th century. Other famous collections include a priceless selection of Flemish and Dutch masters and, for classicists, extensive Greek and Roman holdings. France's enduring fascination with the pharaohs, spurred by Napoléon's adventures on the

Nile, is evident in the museum's large Egyptology department. In the northwestern wing of the building, along the rue de Rivoli, is a newly refurbished Musée des Arts Décoratifs. Given over to the traditional arts from Medieval times to the present (with an annex devoted to haute couture), this museum forms a practical counterpart to the more famous collection of art for art's sake to be found elsewhere in the palace.

Associated in the modern mind with two women, the *Venus de Milo* and the *Mona Lisa,* the Louvre must often have seemed to its royal occupants more aptly represented by another artwork now in the museum, Hieronymus Bosch's *Ship of Fools.* The history of the Louvre, for seven centuries home to the French Court, is rich in incident and intrigue. In the **Petite Galerie** visitors can still see the apartments of the Renaissance Valois monarchs. Their turbulent reign during France's religious wars made the Louvre a nest of plotting noblemen, minions, mistresses, and royal bastards. The 16th-century Louvre was a place of vicious rumor (about sexual and religious practices), suspect foreign connections (the Protestants with England, the Catholics with Spain), and frequent poisonings. Paris, a Catholic fief—it is often forgotten that Loyola founded the Society of Jesus on Montmartre—showed little tolerance for the winds of reform reaching France from Geneva, while the Huguenots, disciples of John Calvin, viewed the capital as a sink of corruption under the baleful Italian influence of Catherine de Médicis, the Queen Mother. As the number of Huguenots steadily grew among nobles and commoners alike, many powerful French Catholic clans, led by the Guise family of Lorraine, saw a threat to the secular and ecclesiastical connections that were the sources of their great wealth and power. In 1572, at the wedding of Catherine's daughter, Margaret of Valois, to a Huguenot prince, Henry of Navarre (later Henry IV), the Catholic faction hit upon an expedient solution to the problem posed by French Protestants: Kill them all.

Accordingly, early in the morning of August 23, the eve of the feast of Saint Bartholomew, bells in the rear belfry of St-Germain l'Auxerrois, the church opposite the Louvre's eastern façade, chimed the signal for the slaughter to begin. Daggers and swords drawn, the king's men raced through the Louvre killing Huguenot wedding guests in their beds, while armed bands of thugs were dispatched to roam the city and murder at will. News of this bloodbath sent both Catholic and Protestant Europe reeling in shock and disgust, no group more so than the Huguenots themselves, whose aristocratic spokesmen had suddenly disappeared. Today, a statue of the leader of the movement, Gaspard de Coligny, the Admiral of France murdered by his king on St. Bartholomew's Day, looks reproachfully at the Louvre's northern façade, his monument discreetly—perhaps a bit too discreetly—placed behind the grillwork separating the rue de Rivoli from a Protestant oratory. The Huguenots gained a respite from persecution two decades later when the bridegroom of that memorable wedding party became King Henry IV, converted to Catholicism, and promptly decreed religious toleration in the Edict of Nantes. Unfortunately, his grandson, Louis XIV, set the clock—and France's development—back by revoking the edict and driving the Huguenots into exile.

The neighborhood east of the Louvre has lost all trace of its colorful past, commerce and theater being its principal modern occupations. The quai de la Mégisserie is the capital's shop for pets and edible animals, with ducks, rabbits, geese, hamsters, kittens, and white mice competing for attention. The relative scarcity of dogs at this market is puzzling, for the incautious pedestrian in Paris quickly realizes that the city's canine population is large and uninhibited. At the corner of the quai and the Pont Neuf stands the Samaritaine department store, much like its competitors in all respects but one: Its circular rooftop observation deck offers, for free, a superb view of Paris and the Seine.

Performing Arts

The next major intersection to the east is **Châtelet**, formerly the dungeon, torture chamber, and slaughterhouse of the city. Since the 19th century the square has been given over to the performing arts: music at the Théâtre Musical de Paris; dance and drama at the Théâtre de la Ville. The latter, the stage on which Sarah Bernhardt reigned as queen of Paris theater, is the municipality's *riposte* to the national companies scattered throughout the city: Odéon, Comédie Française, and Chaillot. Other such state-subsidized theaters as the Bouffes du Nord (home to Peter Brook productions) and Ariane Mnouchkine's Cartoucherie, where her imaginative troupe works out of an old ammunition factory in the eastern Bois de Vincennes, have received interna-

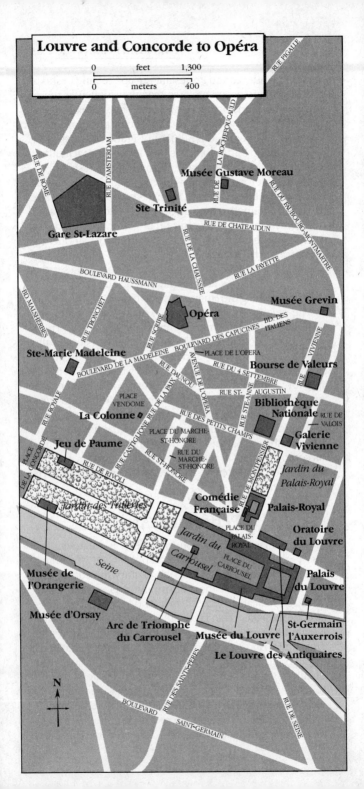

Louvre and Concorde to Opéra

0 — feet — 1,300
0 — meters — 400

RUE PIGALLE

RUE DE ROME

RUE D'AMSTERDAM

RUE DE LA ROCHEFOUCAULD

Musée Gustave Moreau

RUE DE

RUE DU FAUBOURG-MONTMARTRE

Ste Trinité

Gare St-Lazare

RUE DE CHATEAUDUN

RUE DE LA CHAUSSEE

RUE LA FAYETTE

BOULEVARD HAUSSMANN

Musée Grevin

ED. MALESHERBES

RUE TRONCHET

RUE SCRIBE

Opéra

BD. DES ITALIENS

RUE VIVIENNE

Ste-Marie Madeleine

BOULEVARD DES CAPUCINES

PLACE DE L'OPERA

BOULEVARD DE LA MADELEINE

RUE DAUNOU

AVENUE DE L'OPERA

RUE DU 4 SETTEMBRE

Bourse de Valeurs

RUE ROYALE

RUE DE LA PAIX

RUE DE LA PAIX

RUE ST-ANNE

RUE ST-AUGUSTIN

Bibliothèque Nationale

RUE DE VALOIS

PLACE VENDOME

La Colonne

RUE DES PETITS CHAMPS

Galerie Vivienne

RUE CASTIGLIONE

PLACE DU MARCHE-ST-HONORE

Jeu de Paume

RUE DE RIVOLI

RUE DU MARCHE-ST-HONORE

RUE ST-HONORE

RUE DE MONTPENSIER

Jardin du Palais-Royal

DE LA PLACE DE LA CONCORDE

Jardin des Tuileries

Comédie Française

Palais-Royal

PLACE DU PALAIS-ROYAL

Oratoire du Louvre

Jardin du Carrousel

PLACE DU CARROUSEL

Seine

Musée de l'Orangerie

Palais du Louvre

Musée d'Orsay

Arc de Triomphe du Carrousel

Musée du Louvre

St-Germain l'Auxerrois

Le Louvre des Antiquaires

N

RUE DES SAINTS-PERES

BOULEVARD SAINT-GERMAIN

RUE DE SEINE

tional acclaim for their treatments of exotic epics and Shakespeare (the Bard is ever popular in France), while the enduring *cocu* (cuckold) plot device is alive and well in the farces staged in the district of the Grands Boulevards. Paris has scores of theaters, café-theaters (cabarets where gatling-gun French punning is the rule), and performing-art venues. To make sense of it all, the visitor should pick up an inexpensive weekly entertainment guide (*Pariscope* or *Officiel des Spectacles*) at a newsstand; to save money, make a trip to the agency beside the church of the Madeleine in the 8th *arrondissement,* where you can buy a half-price ticket for same-day performances.

Palais-Royal, Place Vendôme, and Opéra

These neighborhoods constitute the "Right Bank" that is meant when the expression is used to suggest Parisian elegance, luxury, and liveliness. This is the Paris of fashion magnates and advertisers, of models with slinky legs sliding out of limousines, tripping into stylish shops along the rue du Faubourg St-Honoré, and strolling down glittering boulevards with a suitably perfect man in tow. Glamour long ago replaced grandeur as Paris's trademark, which is why the triangle formed by the place Vendôme, Palais-Royal, and Opéra districts is now far more emblematic of the city than the Champs-Elysées. First developed when the Parisian bourgeoisie was shaking free of feudal bonds to King and Bishop, this area has significantly few ministries and churches—the presence of two major financial institutions, the Bank of France and the Stock Exchange, indicating its role as the cradle of French capitalism.

North of the Louvre on the rue de Rivoli is the Right Bank's equivalent of the Carré Rive Gauche, the **Louvre des Antiquaires,** today a rich man's flea market, with dozens of shops selling *objets d'art* and antique curios to collectors. To people of more modest means, the building is perfect for wistful window shopping, especially on those rare muggy days when the facility's most un-Parisian feature, air-conditioning, makes it particularly attractive. There is a far quieter place to loiter across the street at the **Palais-Royal,** where a garden enclosed on three sides by graceful if neglected apartments has been open to the public since 1784. The present peacefulness of the spot belies its noisy past, for the musty arcades now lined with booksellers and military-memorabilia shops once housed the Continent's most raucous cafés. The site first served as Cardinal Richelieu's town house, then as a second home to the monarchs (hence its name), before falling, in 1780, into the hands of Louis-Philippe d'Orléans, a high-living, hard-up nobleman who rebuilt the place and opened it to private businesses. His cousin at Versailles, Louis XVI, is reported to have sniffed, "Now that you're a shopkeeper, we'll no doubt see you only on Sundays."

The Palais-Royal was an overnight success, instantly becoming the city's intellectual center, amusement park, and fleshpot. This last unsavory facet of the place lives on in a skipping rhyme still sung, in all innocence, by French schoolgirls, *"Le Palais-Royal est un beau quartier/Toutes les jeunes filles sont à marier"* ("The Palais-Royal is a fine neighborhood/All the girls there are ready to wed"). As for the other attractions, the garden's mountebanks, cardsharps, palm readers, and freak shows competed with the strange cafés of the Palais, each of which had its own peculiar novelty. Outside the Café des Mille Colonnes (formerly at 36, Galerie de Valois) Madame Rollain, the "most beautiful woman in the world," sat on a raised platform to beguile customers, while at the Café Mécanique (formerly at 121, Galerie de Valois) a clever system of dumbwaiters in the center of every table served and took away drinks without the need for human intervention. The cafés of the Palais-Royal also provided a political forum for encyclopedists, democrats, republicans, and rabble-rousers to discuss the ideas and problems of their day with great freedom.

In the summer of 1789, the air rife with rumors about imminent measures to be taken against the city of Paris and the Estates-General, Camille Desmoulins stood up in the Café de Foy at 46, Galerie de Montpensier and incited his listeners to arm themselves against the government. That evening, July 13, they raided the Invalides for guns and later the next day stormed the Bastille, a symbol, if not a true representative (as it then held only seven prisoners) of absolutist repression. Few people thronging the Palais-Royal that evening realized that their revolt would turn into a revolution of unprecedented proportions, bringing down not only a dynasty, but also the entire monarchical principle. It is hard to think of the present-day Palais-Royal as a crucible of modern Europe or a place of great social ferment (tellingly, the French Ministry of Culture now snoozes above the Galerie de Valois), yet this is where the ancien régime collapsed, the educated yet unenfranchised classes who came here having had enough of the web of privilege woven by aristocracy and clergy. Louis-Philippe d'Orléans, who unwittingly lit the fuse by making his palace a safe-house for sedition, was not spared the guillotine, despite the caution he showed by rechristening himself Philippe-Egalité.

He might find the spot more to his tastes today, for, curiously enough, France's ultraconservative streak is nowhere more in evidence than it is here. The 300-year-old Comédie Française performs at the Palais-Royal—and is excoriated by its public whenever it experiments. The installation in 1986 of *Les Trois Plateaux,* a photogenic artwork consisting of truncated black-and-white columns placed in what had been used as the Palais's parking lot, earned its creator, Daniel Buren, a frightening amount of mail marked by pure hatred. Still, the neighborhood has always been a place of controversy: In the Régence Café that once stood across from the Comédie Française, Marx and Engels first decided to form a working partnership. It should be noted that both men were initially drawn to the area by the presence of the **Bibliothèque Nationale**. Located just north of the Palais Royal on the rue de Richelieu, France's national library was first placed here in 1724 by a prescient Louis XV. A complex of 18th-century mansions and Second Empire reading rooms, the "BN"—as it is known to its thousands of scholarly regulars—often puts on temporary exhibits of its most precious holdings.

The **place Vendôme** has never had the questionable connections of the Palais Royal; its serenity has been troubled only by the toppling, re-erecting, melting down, and statue-switching effected on the Napoleonic replica of Trajan's column that stands in its center. Playing musical chairs with monuments, however, was something of a national sport in France during the 19th century, so the fate of the Vendôme column was not exceptional. The fame of the square lies more in its ordered Louis XIV elegance (another example is the place des Victoires, north of the Palais-Royal) and in its prestige. The Ritz, recently refurbished by an Egyptian businessman who also picked up Harrod's on a London shopping spree, gives onto the square, as do several of the world's most exclusive jewelers. At sundown, when the streetlamps blink on and the display windows sparkle, place Vendôme can be captivating, a sensation appropriate to a spot that once housed Dr. Mesmer, an 18th-century physician who treated patients simply by staring at them. Many people, however, are spellbound by the square's suggestion of limitless wealth. As every player of the French version of Monopoly knows, the adjoining rue de la Paix is the city's most valuable piece of property.

The rue de la Paix runs north into the **place de l'Opéra**, the centerpiece of Napoléon III's scheme to make Paris the "most beautiful capital in the universe." His town planner, Baron Haussmann, cut swaths through the historic fabric of Paris by driving wide boulevards into the heart of old neighborhoods, much to the dismay of residents. The police were delighted, for the new layout allowed them to isolate disturbances by deploying on the boulevards, putting an end to the age-old insurgent tradition of erecting barricades and scampering to further adventure through the citywide labyrinth of tiny streets and alleyways. The outbreaks of 1830 (portrayed in *Les Misérables*) and 1848 (which ignited the rest of Europe) haunted the emerging ruling classes of capitalist France, who, although at first sympathetic to the risings, did not want to see things get out of hand. The "arsonist-turned-fireman" syndrome, by which each generation of Parisian bourgeois would begin adulthood as constitutional hotheads and finish it as crotchety reactionaries, was commonplace in 19th-century France, as the newly ascendant elites faced a sustained salvo from a wide range of antagonists. Aside from suffering the indignity of Honoré Daumier's withering caricatures, the bourgeoisie of post-Napoleonic times was shaken in its Gallic complacency by the Anglophilia of the French Romantics, and, on another front, attacked in its religious faiths by the writings of such Positivist visionaries as Claude de Saint-Simon and Auguste Comte. The more the business of France became the making of money, the fiercer became the critique of commerce as a sign of moral depravity—a notion that lurks in the back of the French mind even today. Fuelling the bourgeois-bashing impulse was class hatred born of economic injustice. The misery of the urban working class, the subject of much of Emile Zola's work, stood in stark contrast to the opulent homes on the Champs-Elysées and to the upper classes' most grandiose riposte to their critics, the **Paris Opéra**.

Completed in 1875 after 13 years of construction (and five years after its sponsor, Napoléon III, had been deposed), Charles Garnier's Opéra remains Europe's largest theater and still impresses by its sheer excess. Its colorful monumental staircase, tailor-made for gawking at gowns and tiaras, is a riot of marble and statuary. The same holds true for the reception rooms and the great hall itself, dominated by a six-ton chandelier—which has come crashing down on opera goers only once, in 1896—and a ceiling decorated by Marc Chagall in 1964. Tickets to the Opéra are difficult both to obtain and to afford, although guides rattling off impressive figures about kilometers of upholstery and square meters of stage surface conduct tours daily. It is always a challenge to catch a glimpse of the real phantom of this Opéra: good taste.

The Opéra district was the setting for the 19th-century naughtiness associated with the notion of "gay Paree." To the east stretches the long strip known as the Grands Boulevards (ironically, one of the few broad thoroughfares not created by Baron Haussmann), where the bourgeois, boulevardiers, and soubrettes once came together in a mix worthy of an Offenbach operetta or Feydeau farce. Today, the district is lively but progressively shabbier as you head east, its only real links to the past in its numerous theaters and its **Musée Grévin** (10, boulevard Montmartre), a typical 19th-century entertainment consisting of wax figures, trompe l'oeil devices, and sound and light shows. To the west of the Opéra, the boulevard des Capucines leads prosperously down to the Madeleine, traces of its later Belle Epoque heyday evident in its Edwardian shops and services. To the north, the successors to the Second Empire boulevards and the turn-of-the-century Belle Epoque restaurants now pull in the crowds: The *grands magasins* (big department stores), the triumph of the 20th-century mass market, line up on the **boulevard Haussmann**. It is difficult to say whether the Baron would be flattered or appalled.

Just beyond this bustling commercial neighborhood, hidden in the rue La Rochefoucauld, one of the oddest expressions of France's 19th-century artistic development can be visited. The three floors of the **Musée Gustave Moreau** house most of the prodigious output of this Symbolist painter, whose work inspired the art-and-artifice worshippers associated with fin-de-siècle decadence. A quiet, peculiar place, where every inch of wall space is covered in darkly sensual paintings, the museum seems out of time, awash in a sensibility that could not have had any bearing on the real-life struggles of Moreau's contemporaries. The warmest praise for the painter's works appeared in J.K. Huysmans's Moreau *A Rebours* (Against the Grain), a grotesque tale hailed as "the breviary of decadence." It was this book, infused with the esoteric esthetics of Huysmans and Moreau that was supposed to have corrupted the youthful Dorian Gray. Thus, the pictures in the museum deserve careful study.

Les Halles, Beaubourg, and Le Marais

What Zola called the "belly of Paris" is now its hole. The **Halles** district, for eight centuries the central food market of the city, is an undistinguished pedestrian zone with an underground shopping mall. It also marks the point where the trendy part of the city begins, the blues and greens of the western Parisian wardrobe giving way to the blacks and grays of the east. In ten years—the time it took the government to decide what to do with the yawning crater left by the demolition of the 19th-century market buildings—the area changed from a charming anachronism in the heart of a traffic nightmare to a shining example of gimcrack urbanism. This is in keeping with a long tradition, for Les Halles has never been a genteel or refined neighborhood.

The peep-show area around the rue St-Denis was once the center of cutthroat Paris, the names of such alleyways as Petite and Grande Truanderie (Little and Big Thuggery) giving a fair idea of the locals' profession. However, the former seaminess of the Grande Truanderie's *Cour des Miracles,* where mutilated beggars by day became whole and hearty by night (simply by taking off their contrived handicaps), pales in comparison to the past squalor of the place des Innocents. Currently known for the never-ending parade of urban fauna filing past its central Renaissance fountain (built by Pierre Lescot, architect for much of the Valois Louvre), the square long had the dubious honor of being the city's largest cemetery and charnel house, and the source of horrific anecdotes. An example: One evening in 1780 the southern retaining wall of the overcrowded Innocents cemetery gave way under the weight of the bodies piled high against it. Tenants sleep-

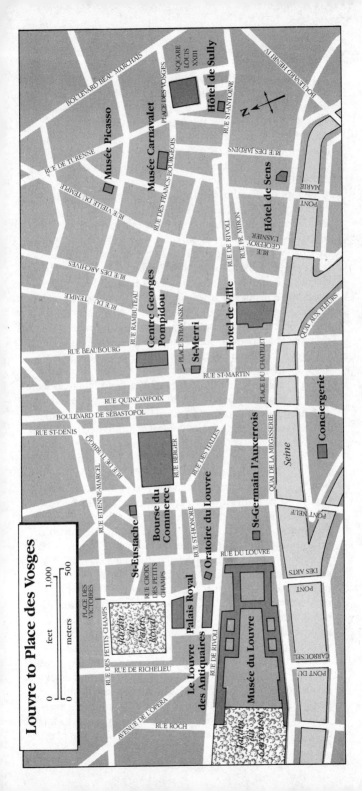

Louvre to Place des Vosges

feet
0   1,000
0   500
meters

Place des Victoires

Jardin du Palais Royal

Le Louvre des Antiquaires

Palais Royal

Jardin du Carrousel

Musée du Louvre

St-Eustache

Bourse du Commerce

Oratoire du Louvre

St-Germain l'Auxerrois

RUE DES PETITS CHAMPS
RUE CROIX DES PETITS CHAMPS
RUE DE RICHELIEU
AVENUE DE L'OPÉRA
RUE ROCH
RUE DE RIVOLI
RUE ST-HONORÉ
RUE DU LOUVRE
RUE BERGER
RUE DES HALLES
RUE ÉTIENNE-MARCEL
RUE ST-DENIS
RUE TURBIGO
BOULEVARD DE SÉBASTOPOL
RUE QUINCAMPOIX
RUE ST-MARTIN
RUE DU TEMPLE
RUE DES ARCHIVES
RUE BEAUBOURG
RUE RAMBUTEAU
RUE VIEILLE DU TEMPLE
RUE DE TURENNE
BOULEVARD BEAUMARCHAIS
RUE DES FRANCS-BOURGEOIS
PLACE DES VOSGES
RUE ST-ANTOINE
RUE DE RIVOLI
RUE FR. MIRON
RUE GEOFFROY L'ASNIER
RUE DES JARDINS
BOULEVARD HENRI QUATRE

Centre Georges Pompidou
PLACE STRAVINSKY
St-Merri
Hôtel de Ville
PLACE DU CHÂTELET
Conciergerie
Seine
QUAI DE LA MÉGISSERIE
QUAI AUX FLEURS

Musée Picasso
Musée Carnavalet
SQUARE LOUIS XIII
Hôtel de Sully
Hôtel de Sens

MARIE
PONT
PONT NEUF
PONT DES ARTS
PONT DU CARROUSEL

N

ing peacefully on the lower floors of the adjacent building (the long, 17th-century construction that still borders the square's south side) were rudely awakened—and almost smothered—by the horde of uninvited and very dead guests crashing into the bedrooms of the living. This disaster spurred efforts to remove the remains from city cemeteries to the catacombs of Denfert-Rochereau—now a ghoulish tourist attraction.

This public-health nightmare, an undisciplined graveyard alongside the city's central food market, has now totally vanished, together with most everything else. The place des Innocents gives out onto an artlessly landscaped expanse whose saving grace lies in the unobstructed view it provides of the **church of St-Eustache**. A 16th-century Gothic behemoth on the outside, St-Eustache impresses even more inside. Its towering nave often resounds with choral singing, and one of its radiating chapels is touchingly dedicated to the butchers, fishwives, and other food merchants who once made up the sanctuary's colorful congregation. Where their stalls once stood, on the sanctuary's southern flank, is a small hemicycle, dominated by Henri DeMiller's 50-ton sculpture of a head lying on its side, staring off into space. Little imagination is needed to see that the eyes are turned toward the solitary pillar at the Halles's western end, an astrological column used by Catherine de Médicis' court seer, Nostradamus.

Across the boulevard Sebastopol lies the **Beaubourg quarter**, yet another pedestrian zone. Whereas the neighboring Halles is entirely given over to commerce, Beaubourg's vocation is modern art. Galleries line its narrow rue Quincampoix, and its ever-popular **Centre Georges Pompidou** has become Paris's biggest tourist attraction, outdrawing the Eiffel Tower and Louvre combined. Opened in 1977 to groans from Parisians dismayed at seeing a mammoth, multicolored, glass-and-steel structure erected in a picturesque old quarter, the facility is now a familiar landmark, its permanent collections recently rearranged, its libraries and vidéothèques chaotic victims of their own success, and its temporary exhibits well, sometimes too well, attended. The large plaza that has been cleared in front of the museum serves as a stage for street musicians, fire-eaters, contortionists, and crackpots who compete for the attention of the crowds with the neighboring mechanical show, Jacques Monestier's ingenious "Defender of Time" clock (affixed to a wall in the adjacent Quartier de l'Horloge). Overlooking the plaza stands yet another clock, the Nemo design group's Genitron, a digital scoreboard that since its installation in 1987, has been neurotically counting down the seconds left in our millenium.

Immediately south of the Pompidou center is the Beaubourg quarter's photogenic showstopper, the **Stravinsky fountain**. The fountain's silly reflecting pool, containing Jean Tinguely's idiosyncratic machines and Nikki de St-Phalle's mobile sculptures, forms an irreverent roof to the underground IRCAM complex, noted for its research into experimental music. The unlikely backdrop to the place Stravinsky is the 16th-century **church of St-Merri**. Some critics think its grace is disfigured by the proximity of such an odd neighbor, but the charge betrays ignorance of the history of the church. Its long association with bizarre practices and secretive sects is indicated by the little figure atop the central portal: Baphomet, a grinning hermaphroditic devil. Nearby, the Tour St-Jacques, the lone vestige of a church that was once the starting point of the pilgrimage to Santiago de Compostela, was a favorite haunt of the mysterious Nicolas Flamel, the alchemist who inspired both fear and respect in 14th-century Parisians. The weird Stravinsky fountain is obviously in good company.

From Beaubourg to the Bastille stretches an area known as **Le Marais** (The Swamp), a reference to its once-marshy soil. A district totally distinct from the rest of Paris, it has retained a late-Medieval flavor, escaping the great changes of the 19th century and narrowly avoiding large-scale demolition in the 20th, thanks to the efforts of culture minister André Malraux in the 1960s. The Marais is studded with magnificent *hôtels particuliers,* aristocratic mansions built when the area was the most elegant urban quarter of France. This was particularly true of the late 17th century, a time of great intellectual ferment in the Marais, the aristocratic *précieuses* holding their salons for the great men of the day: Molière, La Fontaine, Boileau, and La Rochefoucauld. The greatest woman of her time, Madame de Sévigné, lived, wrote, and received in the Hôtel Carnavalet, bequeathing a lively depiction of that glittering milieu in her letters.

The physical evidence of the past is everywhere present in the Marais. Along the rue des Jardins stands a 225-foot-long stretch of the 12th-century city rampart, its original crenellation intact. Bordering a playground, the wall is taken for granted in a neighborhood where stunning courtyards and mansions are commonplace. (If you see an open gate in the Marais, take advantage of the situation to go in and snoop around.) Three great *hôtels* permanently open for public inspection are grouped around the rues des Francs-Bourgeois and Archives: **Lamoignon** (the historical library of Paris); **Carnavalet** (the history museum of Paris); and **Soubise** (the national archives, with a permanent exhibition of important French documents from Merovingian times to the present). On the rue St-Antoine, the **Hôtel de Sully** (named for Henry IV's shrewd finance minister) holds temporary exhibits about other French monuments, although its real interest is intrinsic. Like the interior of the other *hôtels,* the decor of Sully gives the visitor a taste of Baroque splendor. Slightly older than Sully and converted to use as an extraordinary public library is the riverside **Hôtel de Sens**, a half-Medieval, half-Renaissance mansion that once served the fanatical Guise family as a Parisian pied-à-terre for hatching their murderous plots. At nightfall especially, this building looks the part.

A popular *hôtel* among modern visitors is Salé, since 1986 home of the **Musée Picasso**. Created from duties imposed by the French government on the artist's heirs, the collection includes more than 200 paintings and sculptures, handsomely displayed in the 17th-century mansion. The aristocratic neighborhood—the tranquil Parc Royal is just around the corner—seems to suit the master. The only other artist thus honored in the Marais is Victor Hugo, whose former residence at the **place des Vosges** has been converted into a quirky museum concentrating on the great man's private life. His fame, however, is secondary to that of the square, a graceful 17th-century fund-raising project that Henry IV and Sully dreamed up. In the place of the rustic horse-trading market that occupied this spot, a regal square was envisioned, its identical pavilions to be sold off to the highest bidders. The promise of occasional royal occupancy (the Queen's apartment in the center of the north side, the King's in the south) was dangled as prestigious bait, which nobles and rich merchants were quick to snap at. The enterprise was a resounding success, proof that business and beauty can coexist. Even the square's name is tied up with cold hard cash: In 1800, the Vosges was the first region to pay its taxes.

Aside from its relative antiquity in the Parisian landscape, the contemporary Marais is also known for the variety of its human geography. Affluent professionals clever enough to have picked up apartments when the prices were right (in the 1970s) displaced many of the area's artisans, although quaint businesses still exist alongside dance studios and graphic arts wonderlands. The rues Ste-Croix de la Bretonnerie and Vieille du Temple form the meeting place of the old and new Marais populaces, with crewcut gays, trendy designers, and old-time residents strolling past kosher food stores, café-theaters, and antique shops. Nearby, the Square du Marché Ste-Catherine, a restaurant-dotted expanse in the maze of narrow streets, fills pleasantly on summer evenings, while the Bastille Day Bal des Sapeurs-Pompiers (Fireman's Ball) in the firehall on the rue de Sévigné is by far the most entertaining in the city, with its mix of the comfortably fashion-conscious and the casually fashion-oblivious.

Completing this mosaic is the age-old **Jewish quarter** centered on the rue des Rosiers. French Jewry has long maintained a welcoming place for immigrants in the area, once known as the *pletzl* (square) to its Yiddish-speaking newcomers. Today the accents heard here are more likely to be North African, as many Sephardic Jews have moved to France in the wake of decolonization. The rue des Rosiers, although an anachronistic representative of the French Jewish community, is nonetheless a powerful symbol in a country where anti-Semitism ran very strong. Long denied civil rights and subject to sporadic persecutions, the community met its greatest trials in the past hundred years. The turn-of-the-century Dreyfus Affair, which shocked the visiting Viennese journalist Theodor Herzl and strengthened his belief in the need for a Jewish homeland, sullied the French Republic's reputation for tolerance and added further ugliness to the rabid nationalism espoused by such figures as Maurice Barrès. French Jews suffered terribly during World War II, thousands being sent to their death by the Nazi occupiers or their French underlings. A monument to the Unknown Jewish Martyr stands on the rue Geoffroi l'Asnier, and an underground memorial to victims of the Holocaust can be visited at the easternmost tip of Ile de la Cité. However, the rue des Rosiers, its three blocks teeming with life in an otherwise quiet Medieval quarter, remains the most vivid reminder of a hard-won victory over bigotry.

Eastern Paris and Montmartre

The cutting edge of Paris these days is the **Bastille district**, a neighborhood no longer living paradoxically in the shadow of a demolished building. The Bastille was torn down in the heady days of 1789, and for many years thereafter the area, called the Faubourg St-Antoine, was known for furniture manufacture and working-class militancy. Those days are over too, the oldtime *musette* (the Auvergnat accordion music associated with romantic Paris) halls giving way to—or alternating nights with—New Age trend setters, and the district's warehouses are being converted into lofts, studios, and galleries. Gentrification here, however, is in a far less advanced phase than in the neighboring Marais, and the "hot" street of the Bastille, the rue de Lappe, is still a bit daunting to faint-hearted explorers of the night. The Bastille's new **Opéra** (to be opened in 1989), a facility that architect Carlos Ott has designed to make that art form more accessible to a larger public, points to the future of the area as the cultural laboratory of Paris. For the moment, the Bastille is Paris's *quartier qui monte,* possessing a mix of the shabby and the genteel that many young Parisians find compelling.

The improvements in the Bastille area go along with a general redevelopment scheme for the whole of eastern Paris. Long considered the poor cousin of the more historic neighborhoods of central Paris and the wealthy *beaux quartiers* of the west, this large, densely populated section of the city is now experiencing a boom. Slum clearance and renovation here are high on city hall's list of priorities. The canal linking the Bastille to the Seine has been transformed into the Arsenal Marina for pleasure boats, and the rough area behind the Gare de Lyon, Bercy, was chosen as the site for the Palais Omnisports, an all-purpose indoor stadium. The **Canal St-Martin**, stretching from the Arsenal at the Seine, continues underground for a mile or so north of the Bastille, and reemerges as a picturesque waterway threading through a series of locks and pedestrian bridges; it is now lined with artists' studios and new housing projects. A long, lazy barge tour of the canal leaves daily in the summertime from the Arsenal Marina, allowing visitors to take an unorthodox trip that ends close to the most peculiar of Paris's new attractions, the science center at La Villette. A textbook example of centralized planning gone awry (the Villette was built as a giant slaugh-

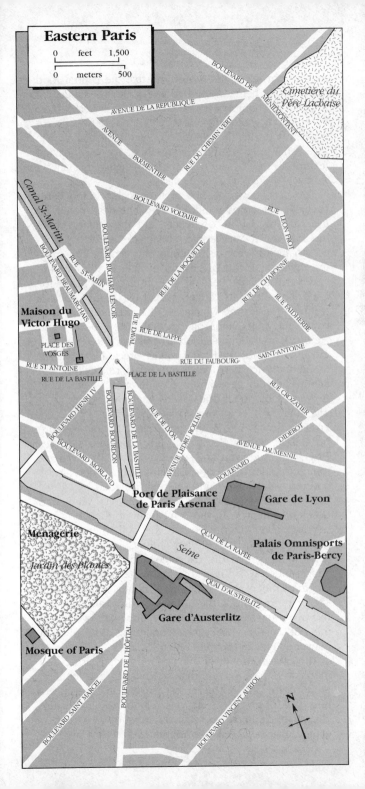

Eastern Paris

| 0 | feet | 1,500 |
| 0 | meters | 500 |

Cimetière du Père Lachaise

Canal St-Martin

AVENUE DE LA REPUBLIQUE

AVENUE PARMENTIER

RUE DU CHEMIN VERT

BOULEVARD DE MÉNILMONTANT

BOULEVARD VOLTAIRE

RUE LÉON FROT

BOULEVARD BEAUMARCHAIS

RUE ST-SABIN

BOULEVARD RICHARD LENOIR

RUE DE LA ROQUETTE

RUE DE CHARONNE

RUE FAIDHERBE

Maison du Victor Hugo

PLACE DES VOSGES

RUE DAVAL

RUE DE LAPPE

RUE DU FAUBOURG- SAINT-ANTOINE

RUE ST ANTOINE

RUE DE LA BASTILLE

PLACE DE LA BASTILLE

RUE CROZATIER

BOULEVARD HENRI IV

BOULEVARD BOURDON

BOULEVARD DE LA BASTILLE

RUE DE LYON

AVENUE LEDRU ROLLIN

DIDEROT

AVENUE DAUMESNIL

BOULEVARD MORLAND

BOULEVARD

Port de Plaisance de Paris Arsenal

Gare de Lyon

Menagerie

Jardin des Plantes

Seine

QUAI DE LA RAPÉE

Palais Omnisports de Paris-Bercy

QUAI D'AUSTERLITZ

Gare d'Austerlitz

BOULEVARD DE L'HÔPITAL

Mosque of Paris

BOULEVARD SAINT MARCEL

BOULEVARD VINCENT AURIOL

N

terhouse at about the same time that the central food market was being moved to the southern suburb of Rungis), the complex ended its career as the city's most conspicuous white elephant when billions of francs were poured in during the 1980s to convert it into a showcase for French and European technology. Its most striking feature is the Géode, a spherical cinema that shows stomach-wrenching documentaries.

The best-known of eastern Paris sights is the **Père-Lachaise cemetery**, a hilltop city of the dead noted for the celebrity of its occupants and the fantasy of its funerary art. A Napoleonic scheme designed to put an end to such horrors as the Innocents cemetery by moving the capital's burial ground outside of the city, the graveyard quickly became the fashionable place for interment—once its caretakers had hit on the publicity stunt of transferring whichever illustrious remains they could get their hands on (e.g., Molière, Abélard, and Héloïse) to the then-suburban hillside. Its reputation grew as wealthy Parisian families erected extravagant monuments to their dead and as its roll call of the famous grew longer with the passing of each generation. It is advisable to tip the gatekeeper in exchange for a map that will help you locate the graves of Marcel Proust, Oscar Wilde, Edith Piaf, Frédéric Chopin, Honoré de Balzac, Sarah Bernhardt, Jim Morrison, Georges Bizet, Gertrude Stein, and scores of others. The strangest tomb of the lot is that of spiritualist Allan Kardec, always covered with flowers and often surrounded by séance holders intent on finding a way of communicating with deceased relatives. In the cemetery's northeastern corner is another pilgrimage site: the wall where, on the night of May 27, 1871, the last of the Communard insurgents were summarily executed after an eerie battle amidst the graves. The Paris Commune, a revolutionary city government that lasted three months and ended in savage repression by the army and wholesale arson by the Communards, was the most spectacular uprising of the 19th century, its legacy a continuing bitter division between Right and Left in French society.

The other redoubt of the Communards is associated more with life and art than with death and politics. **Montmartre**, the northernmost of the city's perimeter hills, was originally a religious refuge, its 12th-century **church of St-Pierre** showing its antiquity in a vaulted ceiling that looks ready to topple over at any moment.

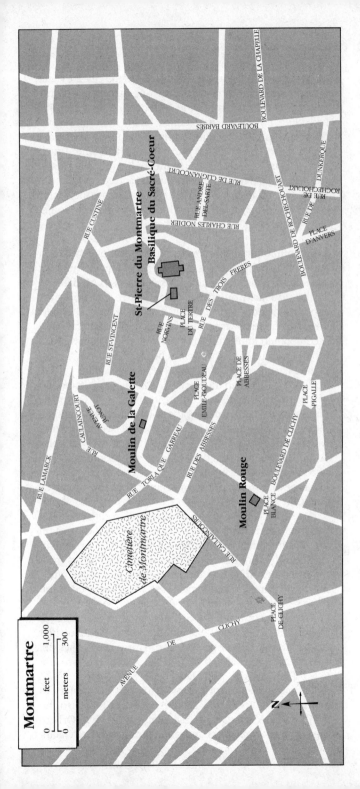

Montmartre

feet 1,000
0

meters 300
0

BOULEVARD DE LA CHAPELLE
BOULEVARD BARBÈS
RUE DE DUNKERQUE
RUE DE ROCHECHOUART
PLACE D'ANVERS
RUE DE CLIGNANCOURT
RUE ANDRÉ DEL SARTE
RUE CHARLES NODIER
BOULEVARD DE ROCHECHOUART
RUE CUSTINE
St-Pierre du Montmartre
Basilique du Sacré-Coeur
RUE DES TROIS FRÈRES
RUE STVINCENT
RUE NORVINS
PLACE DU TERTRE
PLACE EMILE-GOUDEAU
PLACE DE ABBESSES
PLACE PIGALLE
AVENUE JUNOT
Moulin de la Galette
RUE TORLAQUE GARREAU
RUE DES ABBESSES
BOULEVARD DE CLICHY
RUE CAULAINCOURT
RUE LAMARCK
Moulin Rouge
PLACE BLANCHE
Cimetière de Montmartre
RUE CAULAINCOURT
DE CLICHY
PLACE DE CLICHY
AVENUE

N

Monasteries were gradually displaced as the city grew out to meet and engulf this village of wine makers and stone-cutters. By the last half of the 19th century, its windmills had been converted into dance halls (the 20th would change some of them into condominiums), where absinthe fueled much of the merrymaking and where such painters as Renoir (who frequented and painted the Moulin de la Galette) and Toulouse-Lautrec (the Moulin Rouge) found inspiration. Montmartre became the center of cabarets and bohemia, which thanks to the new boulevards more staid Parisians could easily visit for an evening out.

The hill might have stayed a purely local phenomenon had not artists of genius worked a revolution here. At such studios as the Bateau-Lavoir, Picasso, Modigliani, Utrillo, and many others used Montmartre as a subject for experimentation with figurative art, their radical departures defended by writer Guillaume Apollinaire and often accompanied, musically, by Erik Satie. The **Lapin Agile**, a cabaret where the avant-garde mixed with the criminal element, still exists, though it is now peopled by the nostalgic rather than the creative. The same might be said of Montmartre itself, a victim of its own fame. The **place du Tertre** in the warm months is crammed with people looking at the airport art for sale, and the **basilica of Sacré Coeur**, a blemish inflicted on the hillside by a vengeful French episcopacy in the wake of the Commune, has become an obligatory stop for every oversized tour bus in Europe. It's best to visit Montmartre in the winter or not at all.

If you do go to Montmartre, by all means visit the narrow strip on the southern slope, between the crush on the summit and the unrelieved sleaze of Pigalle and Clichy at the foot of the hill. The streets leading up from the **place des Abbesses** are picturesque and quiet, offering lovely, unexpected views over Paris. Here even the most seasoned travellers feel tempted to become maudlin over this extraordinary city, so don't worry if your eyes start misting over. In the springtime bring a handkerchief or, better still, someone you love. This is Paris, after all.

GETTING AROUND
As Paris is a major world capital, there is no mystery to getting there. Charles-de-Gaulle airport in Roissy to the north handles regular international flights, while Orly to the south takes charters and domestic flights. Both facili-

ties are served by **Air France buses** that go to the central city terminals at Invalides, Etoile, and Porte Maillot (the latter being a modern hotel and convention center complex to the east of the city). In addition, **Orlybus**, a regular city transit line, provides an efficient service to Denfert-Rochereau. From Roissy, take the **RER** suburban railway line (look for the sign *Paris par le train*) that follows the B route directly and quickly to the Gare du Nord, Châtelet-Les Halles, St. Michel-Notre Dame, Luxembourg, and Denfert-Rochereau. The cost for all the above is in the 30 to 40 francs range, whereas taxi fare from either airport to the center of Paris runs from 150 francs to 200 francs.

Paris is well serviced by France's efficient SNCF railway system. The city's six major train stations (St-Lazare, Nord, Est, Lyon, Austerlitz, and Montparnasse) are all served by the Métro, city buses, and taxis. Driving into Paris on the major expressways should present no problem except on Sunday nights or the last evening of holiday weekends, when long traffic jams are a certainty. The ring road (called the boulevard Périphérique) can sometimes involve drivers in a challenging game of chicken, especially when merging cars exercise their right of way, unique to this expressway, to zip into the right-hand lane without a moment's hesitation or notice.

When in Paris, walk; it is the best way to see and enjoy the city. Pedestrians usually ignore traffic signals. Avoid the busier streets between 5:00 and 7:00 in the evening—the pollution can be overwhelming. If you like cycling, this is not the city for you.

The public transit system is excellent. The **Métro** (subway) is open from 5:30 A.M. to 1:00 A.M. every day. The different lines are indicated by their termini; thus, you should know the direction in which you are going—*the name of the terminus*—rather than the number or color of the line. A Métro station is usually exited by way of glass doors (a natural mistake is to push the metal frame of these doors—which will not open them—instead of the green glass marked *Poussez*). A book of ten Métro tickets (a *carnet*) costs about 30 francs. Each ticket is good for one ride regardless of the number of transfers made. There are first-class cars in the middle of each train, although this curious class system is only in effect from 9:00 A.M. to 5:00 P.M. If confronted by a ticket inspector—a rare occurrence, except at the Louvre stop in the summer—you must have a valid ticket—or a 100-

franc banknote—to pay the fine. If you are staying in Paris for an extended period, weekly and monthly passes are available.

The **RER** system provides even faster transit within the city, the four lines (A, B, C, D) having far fewer stops in Paris than the Métro. Thus, to go from the easternmost Bois de Vincennes to the central Châtelet-Les Halles transfer station on RER entails only two stops. If you stay within Paris on the RER system, regular Métro tickets can be used, the only novelty being the need to insert them in turnstiles on leaving RER stations. (Never throw away your ticket in the Paris underground.) Leaving Paris on the system (on a day trip to Versailles, Malmaison, or St-Germain-en-Laye, for example) requires purchasing a ticket whose price varies according to the length of your journey. As with the Métro, you must know the terminus of the line you wish to take in order to find the correct platform. Once there, make sure to check the electric signboard: Although RER trains do not skip stops within Paris, once out in the suburbs they may become super-expresses.

The **buses** use the same yellow tickets as the Métro, although there are no transfers between the two systems or even between different bus routes. According to the length of your bus trip, you have to punch one, two, or three tickets in the little box located directly behind the driver. This number is determined by the number of zones you will pass through, as shown on the route map affixed to your bus stop. Information about times, frequency, and last bus runs should also be there. You can always ask fellow bus passengers: They tend to be more civil than the Métro riders (although Britons should not expect to see an orderly queue at a bus stop).

Contrary to Francophobe legend, Paris **taxi** drivers are not swindlers. It is true, however, that they drive like maniacs and that they sometimes have to be persuaded to take a customer who is not going their way. At cab stands the driver cannot refuse you—even if you're just going around the corner.

If you insist on driving in Paris, forget your manners and behave like a spoiled child. For all their admirable qualities, Parisians tend to become arrogant and impatient behind a steering wheel. Avoid driving on weekend evenings, and in central Paris be prepared to spend a good deal of time looking for a parking space. Cars are parked illegally everywhere, but at the high risk of being towed away. A very pleasant experience is to drive around Paris after eleven or so on a week night, past all the floodlit monuments. Cruising down the boulevards and around the Concorde and Etoile is pure, unadulterated fun.

ACCOMMODATIONS

Like any world capital, Paris brims with hotels that range from the exquisite to the execrable. The top end offers incomparable luxury and impeccable service; the bottom end is not worth talking about. Unfortunately, prices fit the same pattern. The hotels listed below are divided into two groups: the palace hotels, as they are called, where willing patrons pay at least 1,500 francs per night for a room and far more for a suite; and the rest, which cost between 100 and 1,500 francs per night. The hotels also fall into three geographic regions: the area around the Arc de Triomphe; the center, stretching from the Opéra to the Marais; and the Left Bank from the place Maubert to the Invalides.

The telephone country code for France is 33; the city code for Paris is 1.

The Palaces
The Ritz. The Ritz is so classy that its name has come to mean sophistication. Bought recently by an Egyptian businessman, the hotel has lost none of the charm, elegance, and snob appeal that made it famous—its neighbors on the exclusive place Vendôme include several of the world's most exclusive jewelers. In fact, the new owner created the Ritz-Hemingway literary award (winners so far include Marguerite Duras and Peter Taylor), a real-life paean to the man who claimed to have "liberated" the Ritz bar in 1944 and then decimated its cellars. The first hotel with a bathroom in the room, it now offers such comforts as window awnings that can be worked while still in bed, Jacuzzi bathtubs, and all business necessities. An excellent restaurant, too.

15, place Vendôme, 75001. Tel: 42-60-38-30; in U.S., (212) 838-3110 or (800) 223-6800.

Meurice. Whenever he came to Paris, Salvador Dalí would swagger through the Meurice lobby, a cape swirling from his shoulders, and brandishing a silver-headed cane, which says a lot about both the hotel's service—to keep such a demanding patron—and its personality—to attract such a commanding one. A block from the Ritz, the Meurice has a long and distinguished tradition; in the 19th century Edmund Rostand and Talleyrand favored it, and today such people as Liza Minnelli and Shirley Temple like to visit. Recent renovations include air-conditioning and remarkably elegant and modern bathrooms. The personal service inspires great loyalty in the customers.

228, rue de Rivoli, 75001. Tel: 42-60-38-50; in U.S., (212) 935-9540, or (800) 221-2340, (800) 448-8355, or (800) 223-9868.

Inter-Continental. Designed by Garnier of Paris Opéra fame, this is the largest of the palace hotels, though that takes away nothing from its level of comfort. Seven courtyards break up the massive building (one of them is a delightful garden café), and the industrious staff negotiates miles of corridors to ensure that everything is just so. The very advanced business center—with FAX, computer, and secretarial facilities—and a central location bordering the Tuileries Gardens makes it popular with the international business set, and VCRs are available for those unwilling to leave the luxury of their rooms.

3, rue Castiglione, 75001. Tel: 42-60-37-80; in U.S., (212) 687-1144 or (800) 327-0200.

Crillon. The Taittinger Champagne family runs the Crillon, and the hotel is suffused with a vivaciousness that recalls the days when men refused to step out-of-doors without a top hat and women felt naked without a triple strand of pearls. The stunning setting—bounded on one side by the place de la Concorde, with views of the Assemblée Nationale and the Eiffel Tower across the river—is matched by a sumptuous decor: Glowing 18th-century wood paneling and marble bathrooms are standard. The intimate service draws such patrons as Edward Kennedy and Richard Nixon from diplomatic and political ranks.

10, place de la Concorde, 75008. Tel: 42-65-24-24; in U.S., (212) 696-1323.

Bristol. The softly lit white façade a block from the Champs-Elysées seems to promise exactly the sort of transcendent service this hotel in fact supplies. From the sixth-floor swimming pool to bathrooms brightened by Lalique windows and shower doors to the bright bouquets of flowers everywhere, this hotel is particularly strong at what the Bristol management considers the basics—for almost anyone else the height of comfort. There are several fine dining rooms and a very pretty garden behind, which contributes to the calm, assured atmosphere. The Bristol is popular with the idle rich and well-heeled businessmen. Lovely Art Deco decor.

112, rue du Faubourg St-Honoré, 75008. Tel: 42-66-91-45; in U.S., (212) 593-2988 or (800) 223-5652.

George V. Like the Ritz, the George V has become synonymous with luxury. The building, situated between the Champs-Elysées and the Seine, was constructed when Art Deco was at its most popular, and its architecture is majestic and completely un–Art Deco: Antiques fill the rooms, and an art gallery is necessary to supply paintings grand enough for the dining room. Recent management changes have restored the hotel to the top rank; today the front entrance is always lined with expensive foreign cars, and a mink-farm worth of coats swings through the main revolving door every night. Large extended suites can be created on certain floors, so this hotel is a favorite for big parties or for people with retinues, and the basement conference rooms draw major meetings and fancy balls.

31, avenue George-V, 75008. Tel: 47-23-54-00; in U.S., (212) 541-4400 or (800) 223-5672.

Plaza-Athénée. The discreet entrance a few doors from the place d'Alma cloaks what is probably the most beautiful of the palace hotels. In the spring, red geraniums blanket the building's façade, and the public rooms on the inside are alive with extravagant floral arrangements. The rooms are large and perfectly appointed, and not a whisper of traffic from the street below is allowed to reach them. During the fall and spring Paris fashion shows, the Plaza Athenée is packed with the most haute of the haute couture crowd (the hotel is reserved for two years in advance), and the Art Deco grillroom supplies top designers from the *quartier* with their daily nourishment. Sour notes and missed cues are illegal at the Plaza Athénée, which has satisfied such guests as Mata Hari and Katharine Hepburn and just about everyone else who has stayed there.

25, avenue Montaigne, 75008. Tel: 47-23-78-33; in U.S., (212) 541-4400 or (800) 223-5672.

Royal Monceau. The strange attraction the Royal Monceau holds for the military must be due to its discreet understatement rather than its elegance: Generals ranging from Ho Chi Minh to Alexander Haig to Dwight Eisenhower (on the night he entered Paris after the Liberation) have enjoyed its privacy and attentive service.

The Monceau appeals to those who take their comfort seriously, offering clients a health club complete with sauna and Jacuzzi as well as a fully outfitted business center. All the pleasures of a palace, but in a less glamorous, more retiring atmosphere.

37, avenue Hoche, 75008. Tel: 45-61-98-00; in U.S., (212) 935-9540 or (800) 221-2340.

Arc de Triomphe and Trocadéro

Named after a great 15th-century general, Louis II de la Trémoille, **La Trémoille** is anything but warlike. Situated in a lovely, late 19th-century building, this lavishly and tastefully decorated hotel provides clients with a private and elegant retreat from the city (Orson Welles once stayed several months and almost never left his room), complete with balconies alive with flower boxes. An intimate, wood-paneled bar leads to an even more intimate dining room, complete with a crackling fire.

14, rue de la Trémoille, 75008. Tel: 47-23-34-20; in U.S., (212) 838-3110 or (800) 223-6800.

The **Raphaël** is like a slightly smaller, slightly clubbier version of the Trémoille. The wood paneling is dark rather than light, the plaster moldings are a bit more elaborate, and thick Oriental rugs cover the marble floors. The very large rooms are favored by high-flying businessmen and those needing personalized service. A very pretty, very distinguished hotel.

17, avenue Kléber, 75016. Tel: 45-02-16-00; in U.S., (212) 477-1600 or (800) 223-1510.

The **Lancaster** is another smaller but no less luxurious option to the palace hotels. Just off the Champs-Elysées, in a gracefully designed building with stained-glass ceilings and a tranquil garden courtyard complete with fountains and statues, the Lancaster offers affluent travellers a graceful home away from home, if you happen to live as Santiago Drake del Castillo did when he built the house in 1899. Run by the Savoy group.

7, rue de Berri, 75008. Tel: 43-59-90-43; in U.S., (212) 535-9530 or (800) 223-5581.

Up the block from the Elysée palace, home to the French president, the **Hôtel d'Elysée** is a very reasonably priced possibility in an expensive neighborhood. The rooms are lovely; some have terrific balcony views, and the ones on the top floor have cozy dormer walls and wood beams. Restoration decor with lots of trompe l'oeil murals.

12, rue des Saussaies, 75008. Tel: 42-65-29-25.

The **Washington** is probably the least expensive hotel in the Champs-Elysées area. Small, simple, and modest, it is quite comfortable and features enormous bathrooms. The wood-paneled lobby is unaffected, and the reception is warm. The Washington is for those who long to roam the rich walks of the eighth *arrondissement* without breaking the bank.

43, rue Washington, 75008. Tel: 45-61-10-76.

The Center

Wedged between the Louvre and the Comédie Française, facing the famed shopping street rue du Faubourg du St-Honoré, and peering up the avenue de l'Opéra, the **Louvre-Concorde** could hardly be more central. A grand, two-story lobby shimmers under the huge crystal chandelier, and, beyond, a formal staircase leads up to the high-ceilinged, comfortable, and fairly expensive rooms. The mirrored dining room can be confusing, but a good outdoor café looks out onto the busy square and Palais-Royal.

Place André-Malraux, 75001. Tel: 42-61-56-01; in U.S., (201) 235-1990 or (800) THE OMNI.

Smack in the heart of the Les Halles area, the **Prince Hôtel Forum** provides character and service at moderate cost in a lively neighborhood. Rooms are sound-proofed to allow proximity to the action without being forced to listen to it all night. With pleasant, recently remodeled rooms in a very old building, the hotel has a full range of services.

83, rue Rambuteau, 75001. Tel: 42-36-15-90.

The **Henri IV** is a tiny, ancient hotel on a similar square, the place Dauphine on the Ile de la Cité. The management is very nice and the rooms are clean, if not particularly tasteful. Be sure to ask for one on the *place,* though, since the airshaft rooms are rather bleak. It's cheap, central, fun, and always packed. Write for a reservation.

25, place Dauphine, 75001. Tel: 43-54-44-53. No credit cards.

Maybe it isn't as opulent as its MGM namesake, but **Le Grand Hôtel Inter-Continental** on the place de l'Opéra is pretty grand indeed. The recently renovated rooms are nicely done up and on the whole tasteful (especially the suites), and the columned and gilded dining room and garden restaurant are spectacular examples of Second Empire taste. The Grand is very large, on the expensive side, and at times a little impersonal, but the service is generally quite good.

2, rue Scribe, 75009. Tel: 42-68-12-13; in U.S., (212) 687-1144 or (800) 327-0200.

A former 18th-century convent named after its most famous resident, the **Baudelaire** is a much more reasonably priced option in the Opéra area than the Grand. The rooms are plain, with an occasional touch of grandeur. The sparkling lobby is dominated by a somewhat Roman fresco, a theme that is halfheartedly repeated throughout the hotel. Conveniently located between the Opéra and the Palais-Royal.

61, rue Ste-Anne, 75002. Tel: 42-97-50-62.

The hotel **Bretonnerie** in the heart of the Marais is the perfect headquarters for people who love wandering the *quartier*'s ancient, charming streets. The moderately priced rooms are neat, though decorated with less than effective attention to matching colors and patterns, and each has a comfortable bathroom. The rooms on the airshaft are a bit dim, so it's best to avoid them. Redolent of a somewhat dated Paris bourgeois life. The management is quite cheerful.

22, rue Ste-Croix-de-la-Bretonnerie, 75004. Tel: 48-87-77-63.

The historic place des Vosges houses only one hotel, an honor reserved by the **Pavillon de la Reine**. This quiet, attractive, and luxurious hotel with a garden courtyard and interestingly decorated rooms (some of the decor is fairly heavy, though) is a favorite of those looking for high style and privacy. There is a nice fireplace in the wood-paneled lounge, but no restaurant.

28, place des Vosges, 75003. Tel: 42-77-96-40; in U.S., (212) 477-1600 or (800) 223-1510.

Just behind the St-Merri church, which bounds the Stravinsky fountain next to the Centre Pompidou (yes, it is central), the small, cozy **Saint Merry** hotel offers an eccentric decor that seems to draw a very attractive clientele. Everything—bedspreads, wallpaper, curtains, even the wastebaskets—bears the same pattern. Several of the church's flying buttresses launch themselves through rooms, which poses a danger for sleepwalkers or sudden wakers. Fun and very reasonably priced.

78, rue de la Verrerie, 75004. Tel: 42-78-14-15. No credit cards.

A pair of neighboring hotels provide accommodation on the very charming Ile-St-Louis. The 17th-century hotel **Deux-Iles** features a very welcoming lobby with flowered couches and white-painted beams. The **Saint Louis** specializes in long stays and is charmingly and tastefully decorated. The former has an old-fashioned quaintness; the latter is clean, simple, and comfortable.

Deux-Iles: 59, rue St-Louis-en-l'Ile, 75004. Tel: 43-26-13-35. Saint Louis: 75, rue St-Louis-en-l'Ile, 75004. Tel: 46-34-04-80; in U.S. for both, (212) 477-1600 or (800) 223-1510. No credit cards at either hotel.

Montmartre offers the modern **Timhôtel**, an extremely well-located member of a medium-priced chain. Bordering the picturesque and quiet place Emile-Goudeau, the hotel has tasteful rooms, some with extraordinary views of Paris. On Saturday mornings, a talented accordion player cranks out old French love songs. Picasso's and Braque's one-time studio, the Bateau-Lavoir, is next door (not open).

11, place Emile-Goudeau, 75018. Tel: 42-55-74-79.

The 18th-*arrondissement* charm almost entirely absent from Sacré Coeur and the place de Tertes blossoms in full on the pretty place des Abbesses and the little market streets bordering it. **Regyn's Montmartre**, overlooking the place, benefits from both its location and the lovely garden courtyard within the hotel (request rooms on the courtyard away from the incessantly ringing church bells). The rooms are pleasantly priced and nicely done up, and the breakfast room is as bright and cheerful as the staff.

18, place Abbesses, 75018. Tel: 42-54-45-21.

Two things particularly recommend the **Hôtel Le Laumière**: its propinquity to both France's Communist Party headquarters—an odd building designed along Stalinist lines—and to what is perhaps the most touching of Paris parks, the Parc aux Buttes Chaumont; and its very low prices. One of the few hotels in the isolated 19th *arrondissement,* Le Laumière is nonetheless a well-run little outpost in a too little explored neighborhood.

4, rue Petit, 75019. Tel: 42-06-10-77. No credit cards.

The Left Bank

Left Bank hotels tend to be smaller and more intimate than those across the Seine and, other than a trio of high-class options, are usually moderately priced.

L'Hôtel is the grandest accommodation on the Left Bank, a sliver of a building on a street crammed with art galleries and character near the place de l'Odéon. Each of the luxuriously appointed rooms has a different decor, and the superb service is as straightforward as the name. There is an excellent piano bar in the hotel. It was here that Oscar Wilde spent his last days dying beyond his means.

13, rue des Beaux-Arts, 75006. Tel: 43-25-27-22; in U.S., (212) 477-1600 or (800) 223-1510.

The **Relais Christine**, opposite a repertory movie house a block from the Seine, is only a half-step behind l'Hôtel in terms of luxury. An abbey in the 16th century, the building features a handsome courtyard and a lovely garden. Breakfast is served in an ancient vaulted cave, and cocktail hour takes place in a clubby, wood-paneled lounge. Medieval artifacts—including beams that still bear the trace of their original paint job, tapestries, and suits of armor—set the tone.

3, rue Christine, 75006. Tel: 43-26-71-80; in U.S., (212) 477-1600 or (800) 223-1510.

The **Lutétia Concorde** was refurbished and rejuvenated a few years ago, and thus recaptured much of the Art Deco glory that made it famous (especially the stunning paneling in the excellent dining room). Some of the rooms are very large (a luxury for which you will pay) and have pretty views of the tree-filled place Boulicaut at Sèvres-Babylone across the street. There are imposing yet comfortable sitting rooms off the lobby.

45, boulevard Raspail, 75006. Tel: 45-44-38-10; in U.S., (212) 593-2988 or (800) 223-5652.

Esmeralda, named after Quasimodo's bohemian flame, has the slightly eccentric, slightly funky character one might expect from such an inspiration. A block from both Shakespeare and Co. and the Seine, the structure was built in 1640; the tiny lobby, with its stone walls and huge wood beams, leads to a handful of uniquely decorated rooms—and a sauna. Such actors as Julie Christie and Jane Birkin, who obviously appreciate a good bargain, have come here for the pleasantly odd atmosphere.

4, rue St-Julien-le-Pauvre, 75005. Tel: 43-54-19-20; in U.S., (212) 477-1600 or (800) 223-1510. No credit cards.

The **Hôtel de Nesle** is one of the most colorful places to stay in Paris. The large, very friendly proprietress takes a personal interest in the young, decidedly anglophone crowd that populates this small hotel on a short side street near the Seine. The office is more like a lounge, or library, with a very Oriental feel. The rooms are adequate and quite cheap, but any inadequacies would be overcome by the Nesle's vivacious personality.

7, rue de Nesle, 75006. Tel: 43-54-62-41. No credit cards.

A true writer's hotel should be slightly seedy and on a bustling egalitarian street, and it should charge egalitarian prices. **Louisiane** qualifies. It housed Sartre and Jacques Prévert in the old days, and it is home to a few real-life writers today. Ask for the round rooms; they embody the absence of sharp edges one finds here.

60, rue de Seine, 75006. Tel: 43-29-59-30.

In the heart of the Latin Quarter, the hotel **St-André-des-Arts** offers rooms ranging from the tiny and cheap on the top floor to the spacious and inexpensive on lower floors. The inner rooms are somewhat shielded from the rollicking street outside, and the clientele runs to artists, dancers, and models.

66, rue St-André-des-Arts, 75006. Tel: 43-26-96-16.

One of Louis XIV's architects designed the **Hôtel des Saints-Pères** in 1658, and the structure reflects the period's fondness for rich decor—including some terrific frescoes and painted panels, and a very pretty little garden courtyard. In warm months, breakfast and tea are served outside. Friendly in a faintly formal way and relatively inexpensive.

65, rue des Saints-Pères, 75006. Tel: 45-44-50-00; in U.S., (212) 477-1600 or (800) 223-1510.

Between the graceful church of St-Germain-des-Prés and the massive St-Sulpice church, the medium-priced **Hôtel de l'Odéon** features a wood-beamed lobby, a warm reception, and some outstanding four-poster beds. Even the smaller rooms have an old-fashioned charm. The location is excellent.

13, rue St-Sulpice, 75006. Tel: 43-25-70-11.

Nestled between the Ecole des Beaux-Arts and the Faculté de Médecine, the rue Jacob boasts the **Marronniers** ("the chestnut trees"), a lovely little hotel complete with a garden patio for breakfast. Ask for a room on the top floor, amid the mansards and cornices, for a view of the bell tower of the church of St-Germain-des-Prés, or for a room just above the garden. Quiet, reasonably priced, personable, and charming, Les Marronniers is just right for a few romantic days in the Latin Quarter.

21, rue Jacob, 75006. Tel: 43-25-30-60. No credit cards.

The **Récamier** is a simple hotel with a dated French decor (flowered wallpaper, pseudo-antique furniture) right on the place St-Sulpice and a three-minute walk from the Luxembourg gardens. Nothing special, except that it is solid, dependable, moderately priced, and superbly located.

3 bis, place St-Sulpice, 75006. Tel: 43-26-04-89.

Also near the Luxembourg gardens, the **Bonaparte**, like Napoléon's parceling out of Europe, is a family affair (the same family has kept patrons happy for several generations). Pleasant rooms and a homey salon have exposed beams and a dash of oddness to give them character. The Bonaparte is a good, less-expensive option.

61, rue Bonaparte, 75006. Tel: 43-26-97-37.

The **Ferrandi** offers 19th-century charm in a period house, which means that some of the rooms tread a delicate balance between pretty and kitschy. Others, though, are truly beautiful, and all are moderately priced. Well-kept and well-run in a quiet neighborhood in the southwest corner of the 6th *arrondissement.*

92, rue Cherche-Midi, 75006. Tel: 42-22-97-40.

The **Quai Voltaire** hotel is nestled on the quay from which it takes its name, square between the Bibliothèque Mazarin and the Musée d'Orsay. Most rooms have superb views of the Seine and unfortunately good acoustics: The traffic from the street below can get loud. The building is old and not all the rooms are in tiptop shape, but it still has the charm—and the rates—that drew composers Wagner and Sibelius.

19, quai Voltaire, 75007. Tel: 42-61-50-91.

Faux marbre walls in the corridors and trompe l'oeil murals in the breakfast room may give one the impression that the **Duc de St-Simon** is not for real. It is, being a very tasteful hotel in a late 17th-century *maison particulier.* The moderately priced rooms are quite pretty, and the suites are very comfortable. There is a garden on the first floor, and the street is particularly picturesque.

14, rue St-Simon, 75007. Tel: 45-48-35-66.

Sixty years ago the **Lenox** was a *pension* favored by such folks as James Joyce and Ezra Pound. Later the Lost Generation prowled its halls. Today the small, welcoming lobby is still welcoming, and the rooms are very nice (especially 22, 32, and 42) and nicely priced. The cozy Art Deco bar is a quiet place for a late drink.

9, rue de l'Université, 75007. Tel: 42-96-10-95; in U.S., (201) 235-1990.

—Edward Hernstadt

DINING

Paris has long had a reputation for its superb cuisine that is justly earned. But in a city of some 20,000 restaurants and cafés, eating well is a surprisingly difficult challenge. Guides are a must: The seemingly similar cafés and small brasseries that line almost every street are too often similar in their mediocrity as well, and too many visitors leave Paris sadly dissatisfied. With a little care, though, you can dine as beautifully as the city's fame promises.

Paris *haute cuisine,* though more expensive than ever, still sets the world standard for sublime and inventive meals served with an emphasis on extreme comfort, and this continuing strength in terms of talented chefs means that there is a reasonably broad range of restaurants that are distinctly less costly (250 to 400 francs per person, rather than 500 francs and up), yet offer innovative and tasty dishes. Bistros and brasseries still form the solid middle level of Paris restaurants, in terms of price (100 to 250 francs), originality, and tastiness of the food. If you want to eat after the witching hour (for most restaurants and cafés, 10:30), these old-time eateries are the best and often only bet. Wine bars take two forms: the modern, which offers *nouvelle* dishes along with a selection of wines, and the traditional, where it is customary to munch on cheese or sausages and Poilane bread. In both, a satisfying repast for less than 100 francs is standard. Cafés and tea rooms fall more or less into the same price range as wine bars: The former feature such traditional snacks as *croques monsieur* and baguette sandwiches, while the latter emphasize tarts (both sweet and with vegetables) and quiches.

HAUTE CUISINE

Gloriously refined meals in sumptuously appointed rooms; attentive waiters hovering discreetly just out of sight; magnificent wines glowing in balloon glasses as one astoundingly subtle and elegant dish succeeds another: the stuff of dreams, perhaps, but in Paris not an impossibility. In fact, the *haute gamme* food business is raging on vigorously, ignoring the death of *nouvelle cuisine* (which some critics have announced), the strengthened franc, and visa restrictions that have so annoyed some Americans and Scandinavians that they have decided to travel elsewhere.

Today the world of fine dining is ruled by chefs rather

than by restaurant owners or the great "names," the Maxims, of yore. Some chefs, like Joël Robuchon, are very low-key, content to remain sequestered in the kitchen, rarely even showing themselves at the end of a service. Others, like Alain Senderens, have cultivated a reputation away from the cutting board (Senderens enjoys his role of "philosopher/chef," making weighty declarations on the state of cooking, and frequently sports ties and eyeglasses of a matching color). But the best chefs, in any guise, are worth the 400- to 900-franc bill that is standard at their restaurants, as well as the straining waistline and general aura of peace on earth and good will toward men that suffuses your amble home. For all of these, reserve at least five days in advance, if not earlier.

Right Bank
Joël Robuchon, at 32, rue de Longchamp in the 16th *arrondissement,* is unquestionably the best mix of the mysterious ingredients that signal greatness in a restaurant. The small main room is intimate and elegant. Huge bouquets of flowers and folding screens of some ancient origin isolate the tables, Roman busts, dated engravings, and tasteful red-velvet banquettes set a refined and harmonious tone. The food is truly sublime: roast duck with spices for two, cooked in an enormous copper casserole with a ring of pastry baked around the rim to seal in every molecule of flavor; *purée de pommes de terre* (the world's best mashed potatoes); rack of lamb baked in a salt and thyme crust; *langoustines,* either in ravioli or with cabbage. The wine list is extensive and excellent, and everyone, from the wine steward to the maître d'hôtel, is remarkably courteous and down-to-earth. The bad news? Reserve at least a month in advance. Tel: 47-27-12-27.

Henri Faugeron is probably the second-best chef in the restaurant-happy 16th *arrondissement*. **Faugeron**'s strange, dark decor—which has touches from nearly every historical period, with Byzantine the leading style—is actually quite pleasant, and the food is consistently notable. His creations are less gaudy and thus less outstanding than those of some of his compatriots, but dishes like the house-smoked salmon, shrimp and cabbage salad, and *ris de veau* with lentil-stuffed ravioli are delectable. The solid cooking (though in these circles, that means eye-opening) and an atmosphere so absurdly formal as to be comfortable make Faugeron a popular spot. The service, as is usual for any of these restaurants, is dedicated.

Faugeron and three other chefs, Les Toques Gourmands, banded together to buy wine in bulk and rented a huge underground warehouse to store their now vast communal cellar, which means that the wine list is quite good, though better on the more recent vintages. 52, rue de Longchamp. Tel: 47-07-24-53.

On the other side of the Arc de Triomphe, at 18, rue Troyon in the 17th *arrondissement,* **Guy Savoy** continues to minister to the hungry in what was once Le Bernardin (now in New York). This is wonderful, because his former headquarters in the rue Duret was just too cramped to contain the faithful who flocked to experience the monk-like Savoy's marvelous mixture of country, traditional, and completely inventive cooking. This young chef is constantly experimenting and growing in the kitchen. The best and most adventurous move: Order *Le menu dégustation* and try Savoy's latest original and beautifully presented dishes. He has a sure touch with *langoustine* and lobster, and his variations on duck are winners. The cheeses are particularly good, and for dessert have his *mille-feuilles* (what in the United States and often in the United Kingdom is served in a heavy-handed and limited version as "Napoleon"); they are always works of art. Tel: 43-80-40-61.

Michel Rostang has side-by-side restaurants in the 17th *arrondissement* (see Bistro d'à Côté, below) and comes to the trade by blood: His father and younger brother run the wonderful La Bonne Auberge in Antibes. Rostang's first-string restaurant, with its formal, fancy, though basically tasteful decor, is a mighty work indeed. The cuisine is varied and moves from the classic bourgeois—his ambrosial ravioli stuffed with goat's cheese in a chicken broth—to the otherworldly—quails' eggs poached inside sea urchins. The delicate rosy lamb, redolent with herbs, is exactly what you dream lamb should be. One possible drawback to the quiet, intimate dinners this restaurant is designed for is the quantity of Anglophones; you suspect that the charming Madame Rostang groups them together. But that is a very minor complaint. Order the Pantagruelian menu if only a seven-course feast will suffice. The cheeses and desserts are delicious, the wine list ample, and the refined atmosphere conducive to those who take their pleasure at the table. 20, rue Rennequin. Tel: 47-63-40-77.

Rounding out the sedate 17th, **Apicius**, at 122, avenue de Villiers, is one of the most recent additions to the pantheon of exquisite restaurants. It is also one of the most casual. The cool, rather small room, the young and attractive Madame Vigato, and the lively atmosphere make Apicius a place for you and friends to eat extremely well and make some noise doing it. Jean-Pierre Vigato is another one of those young and creative chefs who has moved well past the strictures of *nouvelle cuisine* and simply cooks what he thinks is tasty. Grilled pig's trotters and exquisite sautéed foie gras sit side by side on the menu. Other winners include the frog's legs and a lovely, meaty rabbit that is so good you will forever after think of "bunny" as a consumable dish. Desserts are fine though unspectacular, and the varied wine list includes some fairly reasonably priced bottles. Tel: 43-80-19-66.

Champs-Elysées

There is probably a greater concentration of immodestly expensive restaurants in the 8th *arrondissement* than anywhere else in Paris, though unfortunately that does not mean an equal concentration of culinary wonders. Still, four stops in particular are worth the weighty bills: Taillevent, Les Ambassadeurs, the Elysée Lenôtre, and Lucas-Carton.

If style, class, and a dignified atmosphere are as important as cooking, **Taillevent** is the best restaurant in Paris. Set in a well-preserved Second Empire *hôtel particulier* at 15, rue Lamennais in the 8th, Taillevent defines more the art of dining out than that of eating well. The tasteful wood-paneled walls and crystal chandeliers in the main room, or the ornate yet unimposing grandeur of the smaller room; the perfect, understated service (you barely see a waiter until, alerted by some imperceptible gesture or stray thought, one sweeps up to the table an instant before being signaled); the gracious welcome of Jean-Claude Vrinat, the restaurateur who should be a template for all restaurant owners (Vrinat is so gracious, and confident, that he insists the food at Robuchon is the best in Paris); the vast, varied, and surprisingly affordable wine list—all make up the Taillevent dining experience.

Unfortunately, magical, inventive cuisine was left off the list. The food, by Claude Deligne, is awfully good but cannot live up to the experience of eating it. The ingredients are always fresh, the dishes of a modified classicism, and the menu changes frequently (upon request, the house will give diners an outdated one). Order according to what rings true or ask M. Vrinat for his recommendations—everything is tasty, especially the desserts. The bill will be appropriately serious, and be prepared: They don't accept any credit cards. Reserve at least two months in advance for dinner, less for lunch. Tel: 45-63-91-00.

A different kind of style typifies **Les Ambassadeurs**, the majestic dining room of the Hôtel Crillon at 10, place de la Concorde in the 8th *arrondissement,* a stone's throw from both the U.S. and British embassies. The hotel itself was built in 1758 by the architect Jacques-Ange Gabriel and was used as a residence until 1920. Entrance to the restaurant is through the hotel's opulent front hall, past the piano bar and courtyard—which in the summer is itself a delightful spot to lunch—and into a room that looks exactly like what it once was: the imposing grand salon of a fabulous *hôtel particulier.* Red, beige, and white Sienese marble walls and floors greet the eye, and the vast 30-foot windows look out onto the place de la Concorde and the illuminated Egyptian obelisk at the square's center that sits placidly on the same spot where during the revolution of 1793–94 thousands died, their heads sliced from their bodies as neatly as Les Ambassadeurs's chef André Signoret now dices zucchini.

The atmosphere is formal (famed food critic Henri Gault advises that "if you don't wear a tie you will be shot, with a look, anyway, and someone will bring you one") but not at all oppressive. It's as if the staff assumes that if one dines at Les Ambassadeurs, one is a member of an elite club and due all privileges granted thereby, which is a far cry from the haughtiness of the staffs of some top Parisian restaurants. The food is excellent, though not mind-boggling, featuring delicate *langoustine* and sea scallop dishes, a delicious (and exceedingly rich) puff pastry with wild mushrooms, and the very interesting curried oysters (with endives and lime). Go to the Crillon for a romantic or anachronistic meal; the surroundings give you a sense of the extreme luxury that defined the ancien régime. Tel: 42-65-24-24.

In the late 19th century, the Pavillon Elysée was *de rigueur:* The beautiful people of the Belle Epoque, from Edward VII to Toulouse-Lautrec, dined at the Louis XVI-style restaurant. Today the Pavillon, now called the **Elysée-Lenôtre,** tucked away in the 8th *arrondissement*'s Tuileries gardens, designed by André Le Nôtre (no relation to chef Patrick Lenôtre), is one of the most popular and pleasant restaurants in town. Go for dinner to experience the true creativity of this young chef: At lunch the menu (and wine list) is plainer and fractionally less expensive. In the evening richer fare like foie gras, *langoustine,* and sea urchins are the norm.

Schizophrenia, though, is the trope of this elegant eatery, because the Pavillon actually houses two restaurants at 10, avenue des Champs-Elysées: the airy, more consciously pretty **Jardins Lenôtre** on the ground floor, with its terrace overlooking gorgeous flower beds; and the more somber, serious Pavillon itself above. The food is the same in both rooms, so your choice will depend on decor and activity. Upstairs are leather, wood, and private loggias; downstairs has a decidedly more interesting decor: huge "classical" murals with women in togas, birds, fountains, Romanesque columns, an intricate plaster ceiling, and other slightly kitsch elements. The price tag on a meal in either room is stiff, but reservations can be made a day before. Tel: 42-65-85-10.

Lucas-Carton in the 8th *arrondissement* is perhaps the most controversial great restaurant in Paris; master chef Alain Senderens does his best to ensure that. The reservation list is long (at least a month for dinner), the portions are minute, the dishes can miss the mark, and the prices are monumental (a group of eight Americans are alleged to have spent 55,000 francs on a meal—most of it on rare wines). Nonetheless, Senderens prepares some of the best food in the world; order well and a successful meal at Lucas-Carton is as memorable as a feast hosted by Tolstoy's Count Ilya Rostov.

The magnificent Belle Epoque decor announces that something special is at hand: rich, burnished, wood-paneled walls by Louis Majorelle; comfortable, dark-brown banquettes separated into individual dining spaces by carved wood and glass dividers; tall, beveled mirrors; and huge floral arrangements. Senderens, who perhaps considers himself the best-dressed chef in Paris, has outfitted his many waiters, stewards, and captains in sober tuxedos, the pastel shade of the requisite bow tie alone distinguishing each staff member's station.

Senderens is no stranger to the long-renowned restaurant at 9, place de la Madeleine: He worked in the kitchen there more than 30 years ago. In a sense, his return to his beginnings mirrors his philosophy at the stove, where he constantly revives and updates ancient recipes (like the famous honey-and-spice-covered *canard Apicius*). Today Senderens continues to innovate—he was perhaps the first to impose Oriental combinations and ideas on French cuisine—and his masterpieces are extraordinary indeed. Anything with *langoustine,* foie gras, lobster (like the miraculous lobster in vanilla sauce), or game is bound to be impeccable and original. The service has gotten better (that is, less pretentious and pressured), and the wine list is extensive. Senderens's latest obsession is the "marriage of food and wine," so it behooves you to try a *menu dégustation* with selected wines included, or the cheese dish consisting of five cheeses and five (usually unexpected) wines. And be prepared to cash in your Christmas Club fund before you go. Tel: 42-65-22-90.

Center

Alain Dutournier is in a quandary. Au Trou Gascon, his bustling first restaurant, which showcased the constantly evolving imagination of this brilliant young chef, was an unqualified success. But in 1986 Dutournier took a chance and moved from his pleasant but unexceptional former bistro in the 12th *arrondissement* to the **Carré des Feuillants**, an opulent yet charming restaurant at 14, rue de Castiglione, just off the elite place Vendôme. The new restaurant cost a fortune to build, with its odd, half-majestic, half-absurd stone entrance hall—featuring an ice-filled sarcophagus that is used to cool Champagne, and plastic bunches of grapes housing light fixtures—striking blond wood walls, and sober, surreal paintings of monstrous fruits and vegetables being carried to market. This expense has put a heavy financial burden on Dutournier, which sometimes shows itself in hurried service or dishes that don't live up to the very high expectations his cooking has earned.

On the whole, though, Dutournier's new home is a marvel, and it is perhaps the only great restaurant in Paris that exhibits its owner's sense of humor in addition to his commitment to the highest cooking standards. The cuisine is a fascinating mix of southwest traditional and innovation. All the duck dishes are wonderful, as are the foie gras creations (especially the sublime *risotto au foie gras*). Dutournier is especially good at using rustic foods in a sophisticated way, perhaps evidenced most remarkably by his appetizer of cold lentils mixed with fresh raw oysters under a layer of wafer-thin slices of raw sea scallop. The extremely pleasant sommelier, Jean-Guy Loustau, sports one of the most distinguished mustaches in Paris and makes a point of recommending lesser known (and less expensive) wines. Despite its growing pains, the Carré des Feuillants is an extremely enjoyable place to dine. Tel: 42-86-82-82.

When Bernard Pacaud moved l'Ambroisie from its cramped home down the block from the Tour d'Argent, he locked the door and threw away the key. And why not? The old Ambroisie, with only 12 tables, was intimate. It had to be. Because the kitchen was so tiny, it also featured a limited menu. Perhaps now in his refined and sumptuous new restaurant at number 9 on the venerable place des Vosges, in the 4th *arrondissement,* Pacaud will get the recognition his wonderful and quintessentially tasteful (one can detect the full flavor of any ingredient Pacaud chooses to use) cooking deserves.

The restaurant itself is particularly inviting: The high ceilings, massive chandelier, stone walls, and floral displays transform its two rooms into a sanctuary of fine dining. But the fare is the feature here. Pacaud, like the most successful young chefs mentioned above, revels in renovating and adapting traditional recipes and ingredients in dynamic ways. For years his red-pepper mousse dominated discussion of his cooking. Pacaud uses the now-trademark dish as an *amuse-bouche* (literally "amuse your mouth"—an appetizer before the appetizer to get the salivary glands flowing), but try the huge, succulent sea scallops, or meaty, complex wild duck and foie gras "cake." The wine list is costly but good. Reserve at least a week in advance. Tel: 42-78-51-45.

Left Bank

Strangely, there are only two truly fine restaurants on the Left Bank: Olympe and L'Arpège. Michelin still gives the Tour d'Argent its mythic three-star rating, but that must be on the basis of price rather than quality. Certainly the view—of Notre-Dame's spotlit flying buttresses—is unparalleled. And the history is undeniable: Relics include the preserved, glass-domed table where three emperors—Alexander II, the Czar of Russia; his son, Alexander III; and Wilhelm I of Prussia—and Chancellor Bismarck of Prussia once dined; and the signatures of famous customers, including Richard Nixon, that paper the foyer and elevator. But the uninspired food and unbelievable prices make the Tour d'Argent a rip-off. Perhaps after an enormously costly meal the unwary diner won't, as did Jean-Baptiste Grenouille's first master in *Perfume,* fall into the Seine and drown, but he will feel his bank account did.

Dominique Nahmias is the only woman ever discussed under the rubric "great chef," a result not only of the scarcity of "great chefs" but also of the fiercely male bias that dominates the top end of French cuisine. Whatever the case, Nahmias, or **Olympe**, as she and her restaurant are called, is an extremely talented chef. Of the top restaurants, Olympe is the youngest at heart and its clientele the most chic. Accordingly, the decor—a 1930s look dominated by maroon, with genuine carved panels from the Orient Express, and many mirrors—and the hours (dinner is served until midnight) are funky. The cuisine, and, unfortunately, service, can be spotty, but on the whole the former, at least, is magnificent. Game dishes, ravioli (stuffed with lobster!), foie gras, and kidneys (especially the *rognon* suffused with lemon) are the best bets, though Nahmias shows the same sure touch with fish and her ambrosial lamb with rosemary. Desserts are also great (her *mille-feuille* is one of the few in Paris that can rate with that of Guy Savoy), and the wine list is good if expensive. 8, rue Nicolas Charlet, 75015. Tel: 47-34-86-08.

Former Alain Senderens student Alain Passard has mimicked his teacher in two ways only: in his inventiveness and in setting up a restaurant in the former quarters of his old master at 84, rue de Varenne. **L'Arpège** and Passard's own particular and innovative style of cooking now reign in what was once Senderens's Archestrate. The room is no larger, and certainly no quieter, but the tone and prices are different. While it is true that L'Arpège is the best restaurant for the price in Paris, bar none, it would be worth visiting at twice the price. The menu is full of wonderful-sounding and delicious-tasting dishes, including a remarkable rosemary lobster in leek leaves, a sauté of mixed shellfish, and a duck cooked "according to my mother's recipe." Also delectable are the hare and the pigeon. High chairbacks break the tiny space into clearly defined areas, and the service, while a bit slow, is quite friendly. The wine list is somewhat limited, but who cares. Tel: 45-51-47-33.

EXPENSIVE AND MODERATE

Unfortunately, *les crèmes de la crème* are often completely booked up or just too expensive. But there is a second tier of restaurants in Paris that are almost as good as the finest, definitely more accessible, and often far less costly (200–500 francs). Some, like the Jules Verne in the Eiffel Tower, are exceptional for their location or view;

while others, like Le Divellec, feature cuisine of a very high standard.

Right Bank

The management has recently changed at **Pierre Traiteur**, 10, rue de Richelieu, a two-minute walk from the Comédie Française. The quality and general bonhomie, however, has not. Although this 1st-*arrondissement* restaurant could technically be classed a bistro, the atmosphere is so chummy and honest—and predominantly French, with scattered tourists wandering in from the Palais Royal—that it deserves special notice. The foie gras is lovely, as are the house specialties of mackerel in cider and *boudin* (blood pudding, which when properly prepared is delicious) sautéed with onions. The prices are stiffer than at most bistros, but the food is worth it. Tel: 42-96-09-17.

Pile ou Face takes its name—"heads or tails"—from its proximity to the Paris stock exchange, the Bourse. But a meal here is no gamble: The fresh ingredients and careful, frequently original preparation guarantee a toothsome repast. It is also one of the pleasantest restaurants in Paris, situated at 52 bis, rue Notre-Dame des Victoires, in the 2nd *arrondissement,* on two tiny floors in three tinier rooms—none of which has more than five tables. Lunchtime crowds are dominated by huddled stockbrokers plotting their afternoon trades, but at dinner Pile ou Face's true charm comes into play. The lighting is muted, and soft classical music wafts gently through the charming rooms. The comfortable 1930s decor adds to the romantic atmosphere. The service is attentive enough, and the rabbit with rosemary is especially tasty. Tel: 42-33-64-33.

The sign outside **Pharamond** promises a "true" tripe from Normandy, and a genuine *tripe à la mode de Caen* you get—one of the best in Paris. But even if you don't favor that particular specialty, this little restaurant in the heart of the changing Les Halles neighborhood in the 1st *arrondissement* is still worth a visit. The turn-of-the-century decor (mirrored windows, bright ceramic tiles portraying our favorite fruits and flowers, a delicate restored steel staircase leading up to the second floor) and the immaculate table settings and formal service are a joy. So too is the food, with delicious duck and many typical Normandy dishes. The apple cider, also from Normandy, is outstanding. 24, rue de la Grande-Truanderie. Tel: 42-33-06-72.

The **Ambassade d'Auvergne** in the 3rd *arrondisse-*

ment also specializes in a regional cuisine—so success-fully that it could actually be the Auvergnat Embassy in Paris. The comfortable restaurant at 22, rue du Grenier St-Lazare, spread over two floors under low, wood-beamed ceilings, features such specialties as a silky *aligot* (potatoes and Cantal cheese), delicious stuffed cabbage, and lentil cassoulet (usually this hearty mix of sausage, duck or goose, and meats is served with white beans). Two appetizers are also noteworthy: the lentil salad and the chopped cabbage, bacon, and vinegar salad. Everything is good here, though, and there are daily specials to accommodate regular patrons. The res-taurant has recently been renovated, with no loss of either atmosphere or food quality. Tel: 42-77-31-22.

A new and very successful restaurant in a colorful part of town (at 2, place d'Anvers, 75009, a block from Pigalle, one of Paris's more notorious red-light districts), **La Table d'Anvers** features inventive cooking in a funky, slightly tacky room dominated by lacquered oranges and grays. The cook and staff are young and tend to be slow, but they are full of charm and have a will to please. The food is very pleasing indeed, with a delectable oyster salad, plump roast fish, and a very tasty roast shoulder of lamb. The prices are reasonably low, so it's a good place to go with friends to eat in style without paying a fortune. Tel: 48-78-35-21.

Though the food at **Le Dômarais** is very good, its remarkable decor, unique in Paris, is also a compelling reason to try this small restaurant near the National Ar-chives in the Marais district. Passing through a rather nondescript courtyard, you enter what was once the first auction hall in Paris, built during the reign of Louis XVI. The small room is dominated from above by a magnifi-cent glass dome, and intimacy results more from the vertical spaciousness than from the distance between tables. A circular staircase on one side leads up to a catwalk overlooking the opulent salon where jewels and precious objets d'art were once displayed. The cuisine is a fine, slightly *nouvelle* rendering of such standard dishes as veal with foie gras, roast duck with fruit or peppers, and an excellent puff pastry with wild mushrooms. The classical music completes the sensation of dining in a long-gone splendor. 53 bis, rue des Francs-Bourgeois, 75004. Tel: 42-74-54-17.

Deep in the heart of the 11th *arrondissement,* a vast and, for most tourists, untravelled region, lies **A Souscey-**

rac, a restaurant redolent of an old-time dedication to solid, grand bourgeois cooking and a neighborly atmosphere. The bright interior, divided neatly into smaller areas by the ancient oak wainscoting, is as welcoming as the chef, Gabriel Asfaux, who regularly wanders out from the kitchen to gossip with the regulars and make sure newcomers are happy. The food is traditional and leans heavily to game—especially the restaurant's renowned, and today hard-to-find, *lièvre à la royale*. The menu also features such dishes as a particularly rich cassoulet, sausage, foie gras, and a handful of newer creations. To dine in this honest and pleasant restaurant at 35, rue Faidherbe, 75011, is to enjoy the special character of an idyllic French eating experience. Tel: 43-71-65-30.

Despite Alain Dutournier's defection to posher quarters near the place Vendôme (see *Haute Cuisine*), **Au Trou Gascon**, with his wife, Nicole, at the helm, is still a wonderful place to eat. The bustling bistro, with now-decorative brass coatracks behind the banquettes, and lovely plaster half-columns, is as lively as ever, and the food is almost as good as when the Gascon master himself patrolled the kitchen. It is difficult to imagine a more exquisite duck breast: rich, succulent, graced with a fatal half-inch of crackling skin and fat so precisely cooked that it's like a single heavy wafer of manna. The same care and quality mark all the other dishes, from the delectable salmon to the exquisite foie gras and truffle ravioli in a consommé to the escargot and cèpe pancake. The cheeses, both of them, are perfectly ripe, and the wine list is excellent. The collection of Armagnacs is one of the best in Paris. 40, rue Taine, 75012. Tel: 43-44-34-26.

Left Bank

The delightfully rustic **Chez Tante Madée**, 11, rue Dupin, only steps away from the Au Bon Marché department store, seems a little out of place in the sleek 6th *arrondissement*. The small room, with wood-beamed ceilings, stone walls, and a large, welcoming fireplace, conveys a feeling of country comfort, but unfortunately the prices are citified. It's worth it, though, as much for the delicious food as for the pleasant atmosphere (one example of the effort that goes into putting diners at their ease: A kir is brought to the table when you sit down). The shellfish fricasee with fresh pasta and the *ris de veau* are particularly good here, as is the rack of lamb. The service is familiar and perhaps a little slow, but you wouldn't hurry your aunt, so just relax and enjoy. Tel: 42-22-64-56.

Stephane Pruvot is definitely going places. When he took over **Chez Albert** in 1986, the food was almost as stuffy as the longtime clientele. Today the young chef's sharp imagination makes this slightly out-of-the-way, slightly too expensive, but decidedly charming restaurant a grand place to visit. There's plenty of innovation in Pruvot's *nouvelle* dishes, and his classics—like the mouth-watering roast lamb and mashed potatoes that make you wonder why they are not on more menus— demonstrate his authority in the kitchen. The prix-fixe menu is a very good deal. 122, avenue du Maine, 75014. Tel: 43-20-05-19.

Le Divellec is far more expensive than most of the places mentioned here—but rightfully so, since it almost matches the ethereal standards of the "greats." The bright blue-and-white decor promises the sea, which chef Jacques Le Divellec delivers as he knows best: in the form of interesting and stunningly fresh fish dishes—sautéed, poached, steamed, or raw. The oysters with seaweed are particularly good, and Le Divellec never destroys the flavor of a fish with too heavy a sauce. Rather formal service and a lengthy wine list complete the experience. 107, rue de l'Université, 75007. Tel: 45-41-91-96.

La Cagouille, 10, place Brancusi in the 14th *arrondissement,* is another, though far less formal, haven for fish-lovers. Chef Gérard Allemandou does the shopping himself at the fish markets near Orly airport south of Paris, and this care shows in the impeccable freshness of his creations. Simple, straightforward, untainted by anything that disguises the fish, Allemandou's dishes consist of healthy servings of what is seasonal and affordable. The somewhat iconoclastic restaurant has a good, if limited, selection of wines and old-fashioned desserts. No credit cards. Tel: 43-22-09-01.

Jules Verne is for the romantic who doesn't let the possibility that he is doing something "touristy" get in the way of having a good time (the kind of soul who allows himself kitschy but great *bateaux-mouches* rides on the Seine). On the second "floor" of the Eiffel Tower, this elegant, dark restaurant features all the touches such a hybrid—half monument, half deluxe eatery—ought to. What's missing is outstanding cuisine. The food is actually better than might be expected, but it doesn't live up to the impossible standards set by the truly remarkable views (especially at night, when the shimmering plain of Paris is broken only by dozens of spotlit church towers). How could it? But the comfortable black leather chairs and banquettes, somehow more appropriate to a first-class section of an airplane than to a restaurant; the odd paper orchids and designer lamps that grace each table; and the pianist in the bar all add up to a seductive atmosphere. Jules Verne is first and foremost a spot from which to drink in the heady wine of Paris from a deeply romantic perspective. Tel: 45-55-61-44.

If the food at the **Maison Blanche** weren't so good, this completely out-of-the-way restaurant (82, boulevard Lefèbvre in the 15th *arrondissement*) would have vanished in a few weeks. Instead, chef José Lampréia's consistently excellent creations have attracted one of the most chic crowds in Paris to a lovely, rather American room on the outskirts of town. Polished parquet floors, muted off-white walls, vast urns of flowers, and the most confusing bathroom in town—all mirrors, even, it seems, the fixtures—set the tone for such intelligent Lampréia dishes as the tuna with beef marrow or the sweet-and-sour duck. The service can be lackadaisical, but it's fun to people-watch, and the quality of the food and relatively low prices (especially the bargain lunch menu) make a meal in the "white house" worthwhile. Tel: 48-28-38-83.

FOREIGN DINING

Like any city with a large population of immigrants and refugees, Paris enjoys an abundance of foreign restaurants. Some are the fruit of France's traditional ties, either colonial—Vietnam, North Africa, and West Africa—or cultural. Others are the inevitable beachheads established by immigrant communities digging in far from home. A good rule of thumb when considering a foreign restaurant: The more exotic, or chic, the better (good Italian food, for example, just doesn't exist in Paris). The better ventures, though, can be both cultural and culinary adventures.

When in 1954 a guerrilla war for independence erupted in Algeria, a French colonial possession since 1830, France was thrown into sometimes violent confusion. It took Charles de Gaulle, the only statesman whose clout was as strong in the public sector as in the military, to end the political turmoil, suppress a revolt by a handful of renegade generals, and give Gallic blessings to an independent Algeria. In the aftermath of the war, a wave of pro-French Algerians emigrated to France, many of them settling in Paris. Moroccans, too, have moved in by the thousands (Morocco was a French protectorate from 1912 to 1956), as have Lebanese, leaving a troubled land for the city many already considered their spiritual home. Paris's profusion of North African and Middle Eastern restaurants reflects these demographics, and there are now some particularly worthwhile dining stops.

The **Timgad** is Paris Central for authentic North African dishes in a classy and romantic North African setting. Rough stones, a fountain, and carefully dimmed lighting provide the background for excellent couscous, *tagine,* and *pastilla.* 21, rue Brunel, in the 17th. **Le Baalbeck,** an authentic Lebanese restaurant at 10, rue de Mazagran, tucked away in the heart of Paris's small Turkish quarter in the 10th *arrondissement,* is a must for fans of true exotica. There is standard Middle Eastern fare like shish kebabs and *houmous* and also a spectacular show with the meal: Belly dancers writhe around the room, vendors come to the tables with jasmine, and everyone laughs loudly and cavorts to his heart's content.

Vietnamese settlers came to Paris in two waves: after the French humiliation at Dienbienphu and subsequent withdrawal from Indochina in 1954; and then in the 1970s after the American defeat there. As a result, there are many Vietnamese restaurants in Paris, including some with Cambodian or Thai accents.

Le Palanquin is all Vietnamese. Delicate Oriental screens and a gracious welcome set the atmosphere, and the food is well-presented and delicious. The Tran sisters run the comfortable wood-beamed room, at 12, rue Princesse in the 6th *arrondissement,* with quiet charm and complete efficiency. Pleasure awaits, in the form of crab claws in lemon sauce or the other specialties of the house. **Tan Dinh,** at 60, rue de Verneuil in the neighboring 7th *arrondissement,* features high-quality products imported directly from Vietnam. The dishes that result from these links to the homeland are among the most honest and successful in Paris. The soothing red-and-black lacquered decor is both traditional Eastern and obliquely French. No credit cards.

France's former colonial ties with West Africa (Ivory Coast, Benin, Ghana, etc.) and the Antilles (Martinique and Guadeloupe) account for most of Paris's black population. And though the cultures and histories of these two areas are completely different—the Antilles have been very French for centuries—in restaurants and nightclubs they are often hyphenated: Afriques-Antilles.

Unquestionably, the *boîtes de nuit* (nightclubs) are the most exciting representatives of African culture in Paris. The restaurant **Babylone**, however, is an exception to the rule. The walls and ceiling are covered with leopard and other animal skins, and an enormous wood carving completely fills one wall. Plants add to the veld atmosphere, as does the hot young crowd. Babylone is open until 8:00 A.M. for those who prefer to dine late. 34, rue Tiquetonne, 75002.

Though there are many "American" joints in Paris, all serving the requisite burgers and barbecued ribs and chicken, most are either mediocre or simply uninteresting to Anglophone travellers. Two, though, could titillate the sociologically inclined.

The **Spirit of St. Louis** and the Rival Coffee Shop are reverse images of each other. The former is a tiny, beautifully restored restaurant with a completely French decor on the historic Ile St-Louis at 12, rue Jean du Bellay. It was opened by a longtime American expatriate and proffers accurate versions of all-American favorites, including tasty BLTs and a Hawaiian ham, pineapple and all, that any roadside café would be proud of. The **Rival Coffee Shop**, at 59, rue de la Roquette in the 11th *arrondissement* is an even more bizarre combination: Two Frenchmen imported an entire diner from New Jersey (plastic squeeze mustard containers, swivel stools, "juice-o-mat," and all). It's almost a 1950s Americana museum exhibit from French chefs who serve up recognizable renditions of U.S. standbys: breakfast specials with salad instead of potatoes, roast beef sandwiches with an avocado puree, and the like. A study in opposites, these two restaurants make a fascinating pair.

Though the Chinese community in the 13th *arrondissement* includes several fine restaurants, and is quite fascinating to explore, **Chez Vong** in Les Halles takes the prize. The deluxe comfort of the small private rooms, Oriental pottery, lacquer finishes, and subtle lighting is matched by sophisticated, carefully prepared Chinese cuisine. The dim sum is especially good. 10, rue de la Grande-Truanderie, 75001.

For centuries before World War II, the Marais area was home to the majority of Parisian Jews. Nazi raids (aided by the collaborationist government and French police) nearly decimated the community, which has slowly regained some of its former vigor through the influx of Sephardic Jews from North Africa and the Middle East. The rue des Rosiers in the 4th *arrondissement* is the gastronomic center of this community; it features a row of kosher restaurants, butchers, fish-sellers, and a pizzeria.

Jo Goldenberg at number 7 is probably the best-known restaurateur in the Marais. The plate-glass window, bulging with pastramis and smoked fish, incongruously also bears scars from a 1980 machine-gun and grenade attack that killed six. The food is tasty and honest—though not really of New York caliber—the matzoh ball soup is nurturing, and Goldenberg's has the best deli department in the neighborhood. **Chez Marianne** has more of a Middle Eastern menu: *tarama falafel,* stuffed grape leaves. There's also a barrel of pungent, homemade pickles that the sensitive of nose should try to sit far from. Service is very warm. For takeaway as well. 2, rue des Hospitalières-St-Gervais, 75004.

Indian food really came to France via England. Nonetheless, today it is one of the more chic exotic cuisines. The number of Indian eateries is fairly limited, though still proportionally pretty high considering Paris's small Indian community. Two choices in particular stand out. **Vishnou** offers an award-winning mix of traditional dishes and modern innovations in a classic, very intricate, and comfortable decor. The service is also commendable. 11 bis, rue Volney in the 2nd *arrondissement.* The **Ile de Kashmir** has one of the most unusual settings in all Paris: a large, old barge parked at a quai opposite the Eiffel Tower. The boat has been completely redone in luxurious style, with several beautiful dining rooms and an intimate, softly lit bar at the back. All the cuisines of India are offered, and the curry and tandoori dishes are especially tasty. 32, avenue de New York, quai Debilly, 75016.

Isse is widely considered the best culinary representative of a culture whose mounting popularity matches its homeland's increasing presence in Paris: Japan. While the Japanese business profile has been steadily on the rise for years, the proliferation of clothing designers from the East has had at least as important an impact, with the latter adding more than the former to fashion-conscious France's estimation of the Japanese. Two factors serve notice that Isse is the top sushi and sashimi outlet in Paris: the lines outside of 56, rue Ste-Anne in the 1st *arrondissement,* and the predominantly Japanese crowd. The decor is pleasant, though nothing special, and the fish is fresh and of very high quality. No credit cards.

Eastern Europe has probably the most romantic history of involvement with Paris. Artists such as Frédéric Chopin and Franz Liszt left Warsaw and Budapest for the French capital; Czarist Russia (Napoléon's invasion notwithstanding) had strong ties with France; and such writers as Ivan Turgenev, Eugène Ionesco, and Milan Kundera have made their homes here. Little wonder, then, that a host of restaurants representing the region's several cuisines sprinkle the streets of Paris.

Of the many Russian choices, which range from inexpensive restaurants serving blinis, tarama, and brochettes to very elegant caviar emporiums, one of the nicest is **Le Coin du Caviar**. Just off the place de la Bastille at 2, rue de la Bastille, this refined and tastefully decorated restaurant features hot and cold Russian specialties, including delicious blinis, smoked-fish plates, and relatively affordable portions of caviar. The atmosphere is quiet and pre-revolutionary, and vodka is served in carafes frozen in a block of ice.

The **Mazurka** is quite a different enterprise. Two charming little rooms in a slightly seedy part of town in the 18th *arrondissement,* this Polish restaurant (found on a street named after an Italian Renaissance painter) serves healthy portions of hearty country dishes, including great stews and stuffed cabbage. Everyone, from the waiters to the cooks (who look like stereotypes of heavy Polish housewives waiting in line outside a shoe store) to the musicians who sing at the tables, is either a Pole or a near neighbor, so there's an unrestrained Eastern European air to the place. No credit cards. 3, rue André-del-Sarte.

FASHIONABLE RESTAURANTS
In a city as committed to eating as Paris, and as populated with restaurants, it is inevitable that every year a generation of slick new restaurants springs up in the dining-out marketplace. But it is important to note that in Paris high-tech, chic restaurants make up only a fraction of the new

additions. As opposed to New York, say, where the city's frenetic, revolving-door culture compels new ventures to be as up-to-date and as instantly popular as possible, new Paris restaurateurs have long gastronomic traditions to guide them. Thus hundreds of restaurants imitating existing genres open their doors yearly, leaving the culinary avant-garde open to a brave few.

It should be no surprise, then, that having no working model of their own, fast-track entrepreneurs have co-opted ideas found in New York or elsewhere, transplanting them more or less Frenchified, more or less successfully to Paris. Nor should it be a surprise that the majority of these ventures have a decidedly American edge—either overtly, as in popular "American" restaurants like Joe Allen's or Marshal's—or stylistically. This second type of eatery, and other more original attempts, are most worth visiting.

Right Bank

Two years ago **Orève** was one of the most exclusive florists in the rarefied 16th *arrondissement;* this year it is one of Paris's hottest restaurants. Maurice Marty, who proved his mettle with earlier successes in the Halles area (both since sold and rather passé), renovated the huge, gorgeous store, proving that he knows what Parisians will like. The brasserie food is fine, especially considering how many dinners come out of the kitchen each night, and the service is as good as the waiters' prerequisite chic petulance will allow. The restaurant is broken up into seven spaces, so despite the general noise intimacy is possible, and the steel beams that form the hothouse sections are particularly lovely. 25, rue de la Pompe.

The **African Queen** is a restaurant one might find in New York. It is set on three floors (at 34–36, rue Montorgueil in the 1st *arrondissement*) and designed down to the last spoon: The china, chair backs, and door all bear the restaurant's symbol, and everything else, from the muted beige and brown decor to the Christian Duc furniture, has been carefully integrated into a soothing, harmonious whole. The food will be a pleasant surprise for those used to an inverse relationship between the quality of the decor and cuisine. The inventive mix of West African and French *nouvelle* is prepared with care, using fresh and exotic ingredients (such as manioc, coconut, and kiwi). Owner Mai Ollivier is half-tribal North African (Peul), worked for years in West Africa, and brings both a solid restaurant background and her very warm and open personality to the venture.

Were it not for setting, **Cargo** could easily be the latest rage in New York's SoHo instead of in Paris. But the Canal St-Martin, a favored background for *policiers* (detective stories in the James Cain mold), where Cargo occupies the ground floor of an 1850s warehouse perched above a worn but still working lock, is all French. The converted warehouse, with its high ceilings, thick white-painted support beams, and stellar view of the placid yet somehow menacing canal, makes for an airy and pleasant space. Owner Patrice Taravella has filled it with Mallet-Stevens reeditions—very fancy designer furniture indeed. But the bar is great, and the food, a very New Yorkish quasi-*nouvelle,* is light and tasty. 41 bis, quai de la Loire, 75019.

The creator of **The Studio** is very French, but his perfect southern accent carries over to the impeccable Tex-Mex decor and country & western music. The Studio exemplifies the restaurant *à l'Américain* in Paris; it was opened by a Frenchman homesick for the U.S. who intuited that transplanted Americana would be a magnet for young Parisians. He was right, and this actually quite good Mexican restaurant, tucked away in an ancient courtyard at 41, rue du Temple in one of Paris's most ancient neighborhoods, in the 4th *arrondissement,* is packed nightly with a predominantly French—and chic—crowd. One of the city's great summer courtyards, and a fun place to watch people or, when feeling nostalgic, to sup on tacos and nachos while listening to the Flying Burrito Brothers.

The Bastille area is the center of gentrification in Paris. No street shows this more than the 11th *arrondissement*'s rue de Lappe, and no dining spot exemplifies it better than **Tapas Nocturne** at number 17. A sliver of a restaurant just down the block from the very chic dance spot **Balajo**, it specializes in the dainty and tasty appetizers called *tapas.* It can be quite entertaining, but go early, because after 9:00 P.M. even the chic wait in line. No credit cards.

Left Bank
Puzzle, which joined the ranks of the ultra high-tech late in 1987, is just that—a puzzle. It was designed by Philippe Starck, the golden boy of contemporary Paris design, and

opened by neighbor Jean Castel of the still-popular **Castel disco**. But Starck's jittery green-black-and-white-dominated interior and the confused menu bespeak an internationalism gone mad: marble and glass less *pur et dur* ("pure and hard") than kitsch; and a mix of shepherd's pie, pasta in cream sauce, and hamburger with an egg. Plenty of beautiful people, though, decent enough food, and a very interesting decor make Puzzle worth at least a look. 13, rue Princesse, 75006.

Nana, on the other hand, proffers a comfortable, slightly weird eclecticism. Opened at 11, rue de Bernard-Palissy in the 6th *arrondissement* by American Rae Ann Dienstag and her French partner, the place features more or less Russian fare (smoked fish, caviar, vodka, plus some French specialties). Decorated by Peter Bolton—who produced interiors for the Palladium and Area nightclubs in New York—and looking in parts like a faded brothel, in others like a Persian smoking lounge, Nana is a fascinating and fun place to eat and hang out. The welcome is warm and gracious, the crowd beautiful, and the style—slightly ragged luxury—unique in Paris.

The **Café Pacífico** is to Amsterdam, Paris, and London what the Hard Rock Café is to London, New York, and wherever, only better. Created by Tom Estes, a former high-school teacher and wrestling coach and one of the nicest guys ever to pull on a clean white tee-shirt, the Paris branch serves the best Mexican food in town and more brands of tequila and mezcal than you can shake a stick at (17, at last count). Though the happy hour and atmosphere are American, the crowd (and that word is not used lightly here) is mostly French, young, good-looking, and excited. Rowdy and rambunctious, Café Pacífico is not for the fainthearted. 50, boulevard du Montparnasse, 75014.

BISTROS AND BRASSERIES
Bistros and brasseries are perhaps the most typical French restaurants, offering the most traditional dishes and liveliest atmosphere. With some few exceptions (Hemingway eating potato salad and drinking beer at the Brasserie Lipp, or Jean-Paul Sartre dining at his customary table at La Coupole), there is no great literary tradition associated with these styles of restaurant—they were too crowded with well-fed bourgeoisie and more expensive than the lower-rent cafés favored by the ink-stained for several

centuries. Today meals will cost between 100 and 250 francs, depending on the quality of the food or grandeur of the decor.

Contemporary bistro and brasserie menus share many of the same dishes. Generally, bistros serve the rustic dishes Mom and Dad used to cook up, with a devoted emphasis on stews (*pot-au-feu,* cassoulet, *daube*), duck (*confit de canard, magret de canard,* foie gras), internal organs, all the varied and wondrous parts of pigs (including knuckles, feet, ears, sausages, hams—cooked, smoked, or aged—and kidneys), lamb (including the rack, shoulder, saddle, feet, and head), and veal (the standard cuts, liver, kidney, pancreas, feet, and head; one critic, in fact, warns readers away from a restaurant because the owner "insists on buying the head ready-rolled, so you miss out on the brains and tongue"). This hearty and sometimes heavy fare goes down best in fall and winter months, though of course poultry, rabbit, fish, and many of the lighter meats are delicious year-round, especially when washed down with plenty of good wine.

Brasseries take their name from the word for "brewery" and are predominantly Alsatian, or advertise themselves as such, so beer and Riesling wine are plentiful. They tend to stay open later than bistros and often feature fresh seafood and shellfish, *choucroute* (sauerkraut and sausage), chicory salad with bacon and a poached egg, and the like.

Understandably, the area surrounding the old Les Halles food market, until 1968 Zola's "belly of Paris," features a number of excellent bistros and brasseries. Some are still open all night, as they were when hungry farmers and butchers refreshed their weary bodies with liters of beer and wine and huge plates of rich country cooking at 5:00 A.M. Unfortunate victims of the market's move to Rungis, near Orly airport, include the row of colorful brasseries on the rue Coquillière, such as the Pied de Cochon, once a magnet for top-hatted society seeking a plebeian meal after a night's revels, all now renovated, refurbished, and reduced beyond all recognition. Most of the other good spots are spread around the Right Bank, from the Porte Maillot to Nation, with only a cluster of restaurants representing the Left Bank.

Les Halles
Chez Denise (or A la Tour de Montlhéry, to the uninitiated) is a good example of a bistro. The woman behind

the cash register is as formidable as her longtime partner's extensive mustache, but the food is great and the
portions enormous. The salt pork with lentils could feed
a nuclear family or a starving merrymaker wandering in
for a dawn feast. The (three) wines offered are fine, and
the decor—hams swinging from the rafters, signed posters, and sketches of the mustachioed man out front—is
eclectic and warm. 5, rue des Prouvaires, 75001.

On the other side of the rue du Louvre, at 25, rue Jean-
Jacques Rousseau, is the **Epi d'Or**, one of the most typical
bistros in Paris. From the mimeographed menu to the
checked tablecloth to the knickknacks placed around the
room to the gracious hosts, everything bespeaks the
warmth and care that is at the heart of bistros. Portions
are particularly healthy, and everything is hot and hearty.
Desserts are worthwhile, and little touches like the peach
wine evidence the restaurant's conscious effort to keep
up with new developments while maintaining its traditional form.

Five minutes away, the **Fermette du Sud-Ouest** would
be cloyingly rustic if the dishes pork-butcher-turned-chef
Christian Naulet turned out weren't so authentic and
soul-warming. The very high quality of this bistro makes
it without question one of the finest in town. Set on two
floors at 31, rue Coquillière, with enough wooden beams
and rough stone to build a real farm, the Fermette has, as
one might expect, exceptionally good sausages of all
types, including *boudin* and *andouillette* (a rough tripe
sausage that is exquisite when made well and inedible
when not). Naulet also sports a fine mustache. It's best to
reserve; Tel: 42-36-73-55.

At 1, rue de Mail, near the fashionable place des
Victoires (home to several high-toned clothing shops) in
the 2nd *arrondissement,* **Chez Georges** continues a tradition as well: that of the utterly dependable neighborhood
bistro. The long, somewhat stark, mirrored room with its
white tile floor and bright lights is made welcoming by
the sweet, middle-aged waitresses in black dresses and
white aprons. The menu is standard and the food quite
tasty—in season, the garlicky sautéed cepes are delicious.
During the day patrons are a mixed crowd of stockbrokers, bankers from the nearby Banque de France, and
fashion people. The homier evening crowd is made up
mostly of locals. Chez Georges serves an impressive collection of Bordeaux wines. No credit cards.

Chez Pauline, a block from the Palais Royal, onetime

home to Cardinal Richelieu, D'Artagnan's bane, is understandably pretty swank. The charm of the classic decor, complete with stern, avuncular waiters and plenty of flowers, balances somewhat the fact that it's a bit overpriced, as do the excellent boeuf bourguignon and rice pudding. More modern dishes, anathema to many bistro chefs, are also available. Chez Pauline is popular with just about everyone. It's best to reserve. 5, rue Villedo, 75001; Tel: 42-96-20-70.

Bordering Les Halles to the north, **Aux Crus de Bourgogne** is one bistro that has never seen the need to inflate its prices; what the French lovingly call the *rapport qualité-prix* (quality-cost ratio) is very high here. Just off the rue Montorgueil, one of Paris's finest market streets, at 3, rue Bachaumont in the 2nd *arrondissement,* this lovely old room with long communal tables and private booths brightened by red-checked tablecloths and boisterous waiters would cheer even Lear, with good stews, dishes with luscious wild mushrooms (cepes and morels), and, in season, wild game (from duck to boar). Very reasonable wines are served. No credit cards.

If middle-aged restaurateurs prone to flirtation amuse you, **Chez Pierrot,** 18 rue Etienne-Marcel, in the second *arrondissement,* is the place. Monsieur Losson's ministerings are meant to add to the lighthearted atmosphere of this bright, bustling bistro, not offend. And he ministers to the stomach as well, with vast portions of everything: an entire plate of sausages to cut from at will; a vat of chocolate mousse from which to scoop spoonfuls to one's heart's content. The crowd is unified only in its good humor, with businessmen and fashion mavens such as Jean-Paul Gaultier rubbing elbows over their leeks in vinaigrette sauce, *daubes,* and chicken fricassees. No credit cards. Tel: 45-08-00-48.

Benoit is an extremely elegant version of the bistro, and prices are constructed accordingly. From the shrubs outside that protect diners from inquiring eyes to the fresh, white foyer and gracious welcome, to the impeccable decor (unchanged since the restaurant opened in 1912), to the heaping portions of perfectly prepared dishes like the *salade de boeuf,* braised-beef stew, and roast red mullet, everything is of the highest quality. Benoit is so pretty and the food so good that it's quite popular despite the prices. Reservations are a necessity. No credit cards. 20, rue St-Martin, 75004. Tel: 42-72-25-76.

Right Bank

Like the remnant of a richer past, **Chez Georges**—this one at 273, boulevard Péreire in the 17th *arrondissement*—maintains its 60-year-old bistro traditions in the face of the poured-concrete modernity of the Palais de Congrès hotel/shopping-mall/theater center that has transfigured the Porte Maillot across the street. The dining room, created and redone by Art Deco design king Slavik, is run with care by Roger Mazarguil, who has carried on the appetite-enhancing policy of carving succulent slabs of roast beef and leg of lamb right at the table. It's easy to enjoy the high quality, careful preparation, and atmosphere that suggest successful people congregating, though the prices are a little steep.

If Michel Rostang has taken a gorgeous old *épicerie fine* (gourmet grocery store for Proust's crowd) and transformed it into one of the best bistros in town, it is because his talent wouldn't let him do otherwise. At 10, rue Gustave-Flaubert in the 17th *arrondissement,* a few doors down from his eponymous temple of haute cuisine, **Le Bistro d'à Côté**, is a small tile-and-wood room filled with old-fashioned candy jars, ceramic plates, dated tables and chairs that are not uniform, and a variety of other antiques (most are for sale). This attention to detail is mirrored in the service and the food, which is rigorously of the bistro genre—in itself an act of imagination for such an inventive chef. There's a pleasant terrace, and an excellent repast is guaranteed. Best to reserve; Tel: 42-67-05-81.

Nestled in a *quartier* primarily occupied by insurance companies, and thus nearly dead at night, the **Petit Riche** creates its own liveliness. The well-preserved 1882 decor of overstuffed banquettes, brass coatracks, clouded and etched windows, and intricate ceilings fills several small and vivacious rooms, none with more than five tables. The menu is standard and the food competent if unexceptional, but for fans of period restaurants who are looking for a pretty bistro in which to eat, drink, and be merry, the Petit Riche is worth a visit. 25, rue Le Peletier, 75009.

Jean-Paul Bucher has succeeded in creating a chain of restaurants that share almost identical menus, wine lists, and style of service without making them dreary and repetitious. How? By taking old brasseries, each with its own history and decor, carefully renovating them, and limiting the cuisine to the foie gras, Riesling, fresh shellfish, and good grilled meats God intended brasseries to serve. In late 1987 Bucher modified this approach when he bought a restaurant that needed no renovation—La Coupole—thus adding the Paris landmark to a chain that already comprised several of the city's most chic dining-out spots. Bucher's "chain" is most like the Palm restaurants in the U.S. in concept, but the restaurants are not carbon copies of one another.

One warning: Make reservations, and better early or late (all the chain's restaurants are open until 2:00 A.M.), since even patrons with reservations join the hordes waiting for tables at the bars of each of these restaurants.

The **Flo**, two long, low rooms with dark, polished wood walls, stained-glass beer-hall windows, and a pretty zinc bar, was the first to open. Overtly Alsatian, it's the most traditionally brasserie-esque of the five and emphasizes its sometimes mediocre *choucroute*. There is often a Rolls-Royce parked out front, watched over by the trays of fresh oysters, clams, crabs, and other shellfish. 7, cour des Petites-Ecuries, 75010.

Julien, whose fabulous 1889 Belle Epoque decor was created only three years after the more somber rooms of the Flo, is a loud, bright restaurant looking out of place amid its surrounding markets and exotic fast-food shops. The two rooms are separated by a marble bar; the smaller front space is all crisp white linens and crushed velvet banquettes, whereas the main dining area is capped by a magnificent stained-glass dome and made larger by the vast mirrors. 16, rue du Faubourg-St-Denis, 75010. Tel: 47-70-12-06.

Across the street from the Gare du Nord, the penultimate stop for battalions of young men on their way to the trenches of the Somme, one of World War I's most horrible slaughteryards, the **Terminus Nord**'s lovely design only reflects Art Deco's calm postwar precision. Large, airy, sprawling rooms with numerous bouquets of flowers and a huge bar in the center play host to the featured seafood platters, light fish dishes in butter sauces, and other standards. 23, rue de Dunkerque, 75010. Tel: 42-85-05-15.

Probably the most civilized of Bucher's eateries, the **Vaudeville** does not suffer from its nearness (20 yards) to the business of the Bourse. The very pretty 1925 marble-and-mirror walls reflect the chatter of a rather chic crowd, all tucking into trays of fresh oysters (and their shellfish brethren) and thick steaks. In the summer the terrace, which looks out onto the stock exchange's imposing columned façade, is especially fun. 29, rue Vivienne, 75002. Tel: 42-33-39-31.

The **Boeuf sur la Toit**, an Art Deco masterpiece, is the most historic of the bunch. In its heyday, artists, writers, and musicians (such as Jean Cocteau and Pablo Picasso) were drawn to the gorgeous burnished-wood restaurant, with its innumerable mirrors, symmetrical staircases, and little hidden nooks. Because of its beauty and location (not far from the Champs-Elysées), it is probably the most popular as well. 34, rue du Colisée, 75008.

Several big questions come to mind now that the mythic Antoine Magnin no longer minds the stove in the cramped kitchen at **l'Ami Louis**. (As old as the century, he died with his toque on in late 1987.) Will they finally renovate the splendidly decrepit decor, which looks as if paintbrushes were banned from the premises before the war? Will the slabs of foie gras remain as monstrous? Will the French fries crackle as wondrously as they are rushed to the tables? Decidedly overpriced, l'Ami Louis has nonetheless been packed for years with devotees drawn to the almost dreary restaurant by Magnin's magic. The service is haphazard—after they hurl your overcoat onto the 4-inch-wide rail above the table with casual precision, waiters are hard to come by—and the renowned game dishes (pheasant, wild duck) are sometimes disappointing. But the snails and foie gras are terrific, and the sometimes surreal atmosphere is addicting. Make reservations. 32, rue de Vertbois, 75003. Tel: 48-87-77-48.

Better just to call it **Chez Philippe**, like everyone else: Auberge Pyrénées-Cevennes might be too difficult to remember, and this very fine bistro is not one to forget. Stone walls the color of spicy mustard and red-tiled floors make a comfortable setting for the locals and well-to-do businessmen who depend on Philippe Serbource to provide them with regular doses of his excellent foie gras and cassoulet. It is easy to make a pig of yourself over the delicious *cochonnailles* (sausages)—customers are free to serve themselves—but it's best to save room for the tasty stews and southwest specialties. No credit cards. 106, rue de la Folie-Mericourt, 75011.

In the 3rd *arrondissement,* five minutes from Chez Philippe and bordering the place de la République at 39, boulevard du Temple, **Chez Jenny** offers a different kind of fare but with a similar honesty and enthusiasm. A monument to Alsatian traditional garb and cuisine, Jenny features one of Paris's most authentic *choucroutes*—

succulent sausage and sharp sauerkraut—rather than the tasteless, stringy affair many brasseries pawn off on unwary diners. The huge, wood-paneled dining area is well-staffed with buxom, costumed waitresses eager to plunk a liter of Alsatian beer on the table. There's also fresh shellfish, a little out of place amid the cabbage, and a fine roast lamb. While the atmosphere may be a little too fairy-tale, the very reasonable prices are not.

Most demonstrations in Paris gather at the place de la République and march to the place de la Bastille, the Saint Peter's Square of French revolutionary spirit since 1789, when enraged sansculottes destroyed the ominous Bastille prison, a symbol of monarchal arbitrariness, and joyously marched the handful of mostly insane prisoners through the streets of Paris. Today an occasional unfortunate tourist asks directions to the long-gone prison; they would do better to ask the way to **Bofinger**, a block from the Place, at 3–7, rue de la Bastille in the 4th *arrondissement*. Most of Paris regularly visits the restaurant's two delightfully restored rooms, the larger graced by a stunning glass dome put up in 1919, paying homage to the long zinc bar where in 1864 Paris's first draft beer was served.

The decor of the **Train Bleu** at the Gare de Lyon train station epitomizes the grandeur of the high Belle Epoque: comfortable banquettes with plenty of space between them for luggage; seriously romantic blue-dominated murals on all the walls; molded plaster on the ceiling that encloses even more intricate murals; and sometimes infrequent, avuncular waiters (a special, 45-minute menu is available if you have a train to catch). The food and wine list are pretty good as well, but it is really the eye-boggling decor that makes this grand restaurant worth visiting. Gare de Lyon, 20, boulevard Diderot, 75012.

Left Bank

Twenty years ago Allard reigned as one of the great bistros in Paris. Since then M. Allard has died and Fernande, his wife and longtime chef, has retired. But the spirit and high-quality food that had made this deluxe bistro a watchword among gastronomes since 1903 remain; **Allard** is still a culinary force to be reckoned with. The two dining rooms are separated by the kitchen and shimmering zinc bar, and are much brighter when looking past a floral arrangement out the lovely etched windows than when gazing in through the dreary cast-iron bars that protect the windows from high-spirited pass-ersby. People come here to feast on the generous por-tions of the very well prepared stews (such as the deli-cious *navarin d'agneau* or *coq au vin*), escargots, or specials (like the dozen grilled pig kidneys a table of serious diners has been known to consume). It's on the expensive side, but it's a pretty place with high standards. 41, rue St-André-des Arts, 75006.

A few blocks away from Allard, the **Petit Zinc**, also in the 6th, serves up a tasty mix of standard bistro dishes, fresh shellfish, and hearty country specials in a truly republican atmosphere: The waiters treat everyone with the same familiarity, as if each diner were a friend of a friend. The two cramped rooms could use a fresher look, perhaps, though downstairs bustles more than above, and the terrace tables are one of summer dining's most popu-lar stops. The grand old zinc bar that gives the restaurant its name is barely used, but it looks special. 25, rue de Buci.

Perhaps it's not as cheap as it used to be, but the **Restau-rant des Beaux-Arts** is still one of the best deals in town: respectable, sometimes excellent cuisine at bargain prices and an atmosphere that immediately recalls the student days you might imagine after reading too much Baudelaire at the nearby Beaux-Arts school, when hungry artists would throw down the brushes and quit the turpentined haven of the studio for a big boeuf bourguignon and many bottles of rough red wine, arguing endlessly whether that Delacroix fellow was a genius or a charlatan. The good old days are gone, but the mood still remains, fueled by an energetic young crowd and a warm decor (enormous canvases covering the walls). At 11, rue Bonaparte, in the 6th *arrondissement,* this bistro is a good time. No credit cards.

If devotees of the **Brasserie Lipp** worry that the 1987 death of longtime owner and commander-in-chief Roger Cazes will change everything, well they ought. It was Caze's dictatorial personality that ran the famous boule-vard St-Germain landmark, at number 151 on the boule-vard in the 6th *arrondissement* (so well known, in fact, that Lipp once sued a 16th-*arrondissement* café for "imitat-ing" his façade), meting out tables in the rarefied ground-floor room to fellows like François Mitterrand and Yves Saint Laurent, while banishing the unknown or unsuccess-ful to a circle of hell Dante forgot: the upstairs. The quality of the food has declined since Hemingway favored Lipp, and it can at times be quite listless (and overpriced). But the beer is good, and the food far from hopeless, and Caze's nonrepublican attitudes made Lipp a place to be seen being seen. Fun to check out. No credit cards.

Since its opulent 1927 opening party, when 3,000 people consumed over 1,200 bottles of Champagne, **La Coupole** has been a special place. Loud, bright, relentlessly popular—with artists, writers, movie stars, and directors, the young, the rich, the old—and bizarre (it's said that young gigolos proposition older patrons by offering them a dish of ice cream), this brasserie is first and foremost a social experience. The food is usually fine, but it can be cold, raw, or overdone. The bar, discreet and chic, is great fun. Very proper waiters politely serve kirs and ensure that every table has its little dish of tiny shrimps. The vast Art Deco dining room is partially broken up by thick pillars and by the monumental chipped-ice-and-shellfish display in the center of the restaurant. Troupes of waiters and captains dance gracefully around the tables, and one another, while beautiful persons and retirees alike soak in the habit-forming atmosphere of one of Paris's essential experiences. 102, boulevard du Montparnasse, 75014.

WINE BARS AND WINE BISTROS

For all the hoopla in France about wine, wine *bars* are a fairly recent innovation. Wine *bistros*—and there is a difference—have been a Paris institution since a Russian soldier allegedly shouted *"bistro!"* ("hurry!") in an attempt to speed up a laggard barman (circa the Napoleonic wars). These honest *bistrots à vin* are usually grimier and more personable than what the high-tech 1980s has termed a wine bar. Modern, cloned mini-chains can be worth visiting—like the six l'Ecluses, which serve only Bordeaux; the three le Pain et le Vins, created by four chefs who joined together to buy wine (including Henri Faugeron and Alain Dutournier, both mentioned above), which feature some interesting wines and understandably excellent snacks; and Les Domaines, where the Philippe Starck design is so modern it hurts. But these new drinking spots simply lack the character and comfort of Paris's true wine bars.

The **Taverne Henri IV** is a good place to sample an old-style *bistrot à vin*. On the western end of the Ile de la Cité facing the large equestrian statue of Henri IV, the well-liked king whose 1610 assassination probably caused many mourners to visit wine bars, the Taverne specializes in crisp whites from the Loire valley, a selection of fine Beaujolais, and the rare Jura region wines. Add to this farm-fresh cheeses, hams, and sausages, mix in a boisterous owner and a clientele devoted to all of the above, and the result is a terrific place to lunch or taste wines on an afternoon. 13, place du Pont-Neuf, 75001.

People flock to **Jacques Mélac** for four reasons: the moderately priced wines, the lively crowds, Mélac's luxuriant mustache, and the annual harvest of the house grapevine, for many locals a festive occasion inspiring the consumption of vast quantities of wine. Luckily, they are in the right place. The bar is tucked away in the 11th *arrondissement* on rue Léon-Frot, but it is worth the trip: There are fine Côtes-du-Rhône and tempting platters of *charcuterie* and cheese. Hearty lunch specials and dinner are available on Tuesdays and Thursdays, and many of the wines can be bought to take away.

La Tartine would be hard-pressed to have a more interesting history; it kept the leaders of the Russian Revolution fed and oiled. Trotsky lived right around the corner, and Lenin and Tito were also frequent hangers-out. But La Tartine today is the same modest café/*bar à vin* it was then, and its past speaks for itself. Such contemporary luminaries as Gérard Depardieu and Nathalie Baye frequent the bar now, as well as fans of the large wine list (drawn from the nearly 30,000 bottles in the cellar below) and the peasant-bread sandwiches. The atmosphere is warm yet anonymous, made up in equal parts of locals, workers, businessmen, and foreign students. The common ground they share—wine—is a good enough reason to be friendly. 24, rue de Rivoli, 75004.

Two upstart establishments have earned the label "true wine bar" by dint of hard work, a deep knowledge of the Côtes-du-Rhône, and sharp, dry English wit. **Willi's Wine Bar**, named not after acerbic English owner Mark Williamson but after one of Colette's husbands, broke new ground in the Paris wine world. Williamson has created a bar/restaurant with great charm, excellent food, and a weekly choice of often little-known wines by the glass. The rough, stone walls and wood beams play host to an international crowd, fans of both the very large selection of fine wines (especially from the Côtes-du-Rhône) and the atmosphere. 13, rue de Petits-Champs, 75001.

Then, in 1987, Williamson, with partner Tim Johnston,

opened **Juvenile's** (named, oddly enough, after another of
Colette's husbands) just around the corner from Willi's, at
47, rue de Richelieu. The wines are less rarefied, though
no less carefully selected, with an eclectic mix of French,
Spanish, Italian, Californian, and even Australian. The bar's
faintly Spanish air (quite Anglicized) is evident in the
tapas—a variety of inexpensive, delectable appetizers—
and the variety of sherries, which is one of the best in town.
Juvenile's is basically a lower-key, lower-priced alternative
to Willi's. (Despite having English owners, neither bar is an
expatriate haven.)

The **Duc de Richelieu** may share the same street as
Juvenile's (at number 110), but in terms of wine bars it's a
world away. Owner Paul George serves only Beaujolais
(even bottling his own in the basement) and features
some of the best vintage wine in Paris from that abused
region. With extraordinarily civilized hours (it's closed
only between 5:00 A.M. and 7:00 A.M.), good, reasonably
priced food all night, and a rambunctious crowd, the Duc
might not be the classiest wine bar around, but it's one of
the most fun.

Despite its neighborhood—the chic Marché-St-Hon-
oré—**Le Rubis** is as honest and old-fashioned as wine
bars get. From the emptied half-barrels that serve as
tables outside the always crowded bar, to the broad
choice of affordable Côtes-du-Rhône, to the very high
quality cheeses and *charcuterie,* to the wise and wise-
cracking waitresses, Le Rubis is like a movie set of some
imagined 1950s *bistrot à vin.* As one might expect, it is
easy to have a good time there. 10, rue du Marché-St-
Honoré, 75001.

SALONS DE THÉ

Tearooms are the romantic, warm, and welcoming hideaways of all those looking for a light lunch or a cozy spot
to dawdle. Calmer than restaurants, quieter than cafés,
usually graced with classical music and a relaxing atmosphere, tearooms are for foul weather—or for any day
when only a spot of comfort will cure what ails.

Right Bank

There are tearooms and there are tearooms. The **Plaza
Athénée** falls in the latter category. Which is to say that tea
is taken quite seriously at the Plaza, thank you, either in
the Relais, a quiet room washed with gentle harp music,
or in the hall, where the famous and the wealthy come to

refresh themselves after a long day of being famous and wealthy. 25, avenue Montaigne, 75008.

While tea was probably served at **W. H. Smith** during the war, it was with Kuchen rather than scones: Nazi occupying forces transformed the very English bookstore into a *Buchhandler.* Today, though, things are back to normal: Downstairs is one of Paris's leading English-language bookstores; upstairs, what Henry James considered the day's most civilized hour—high tea—is still treated as just that. Great muffins and scones and a variety of teas are served in a pleasant setting. 248, rue de Rivoli, 75001.

A. J. Liebling remembers growing up at **Angelina** when it was called Rumplemeyer's (until 1948). Thousands of French haute-preppies (*bon chic, bon genre;* i.e., the right people with the right stuff) spend their lives here at number 226, down the street from W. H. Smith, as does a broad segment of "beautiful" Paris. History and habitués apart, the famous old room with its green marble tables and mirrored walls is quite pretty, and the hot chocolate should be picketed by the heart-disease center.

The Ritz offers the classiest and most classic tea in town; it is served in a lovely, high-ceilinged room just off the main lobby, complete with formal waiters and table settings, soft music wafting up from a grand piano, and a fireplace. And, ah, the scones and cakes, the tiny smoked salmon or cucumber sandwiches. Dress for the part, both for the hotel, which takes ties as seriously as teas, and for yourself. 15, place Vendôme, 75001.

On a lighter note, **Tea Follies**, on a tree-filled square in the not-too-chic 9th *arrondissement,* typifies the kind of tearoom that is visited for many reasons. Go for lunch and the tasty *tartes salées* or chicken pie, or for Sunday brunch and raisin and bran scones and spinach, or on any afternoon to read the stack of papers that builds up over the course of the day and to look over the month's art show, with works accepted only from customers. A welcoming place, at 6, place Gustave-Toudouze.

A Priori Thé is the best place in town to sit outside on a rainy summer day. It's in Paris's most beautifully restored covered passageway, the Galerie Vivienne, off the rue des Petits-Champs in the 2nd *arrondissement* (sharing space with the likes of fashion designer Jean-Paul Gaultier), so all you suffer is the relaxing sound of rain pattering on the gallery's glass roof. There are comfortable white wicker chairs and rough wood tables, daily lunch specials, and an inviting, equally comfortable atmosphere.

At the unfashionable end of the rue St-Honoré (number 91), **Rose-Thé** is hidden in a courtyard complex of antique shops. The one small room looks like an antique shop itself: None of the tables or chairs matches; they range from deep, overstuffed armchairs to spindly Louis-XVI imitations. Because tables are given out on a first-come-first-served basis, some amusing seating arrangements have ensued, with over-stuffed patrons perched precariously on thin-legged chairs. Rose-Thé has terrific tarts (especially the meat), salads, and desserts. Very pleasant.

Down the block from the Centre Pompidou, but on a street so tiny and aged it appears a world away, **Quincambosse** features some of the best and most intricate salads and tarts in town. The raw stone walls have character, though occasional art exhibits take away from their natural beauty. Great for lunch, less great for sitting around. 13, rue Quincampoix, 75004.

The **Loir dans la Théière** (Lewis Carroll's dormouse in a teapot), on the other hand, is a great place for hanging around in the 4th *arrondissement*. At one end of the rue de Rosiers—number 3—a few doors down from a public steam bath for men and women, this rumpled, comfortable tearoom looks like the common room of some ideal social club. Mismatched tables and chairs, including huge, gratifyingly form-fitting ones near the door, set the tone, and a fairly young crowd that seems to have time on its hands makes for a pleasantly lackadaisical air. Good lunches and cakes.

The plate-glass windows at the **Flore-en-l'Ile** afford a magnificent view of Notre-Dame's flying buttresses, summertime sunbathers, and the organ grinders, storytellers, and mimes who inhabit the pedestrian bridge leading from the Ile St-Louis to the Ile de la Cité. The food is pretty good, and the Flore stocks the famed Berthillon ice cream, which is handy, since lines at the store stretch for blocks during the summer. 42, quai d'Orléans, 75004.

The place Dauphine is a bit odd anyway: a pretty little park dwarfed on one side by the Palais de Justice and guarded on the other by the large statue of a mounted Henri IV. It's no wonder that **Fanny Tea**, at 20, place Dauphine, is odd too. It looks like the library that time forgot, with books and candles all over the place, tea instruments someone's great-aunt left behind back in 1907, and an intense owner. But it does give new meaning to the word *interesting*, and the cakes and pies are awfully good. P.S.: Yves Montand is a neighbor.

Left Bank

The **Village Voice** is first a bookstore and then a tearoom, and it's best to remember this, since books give the store all its character. But this is a lovely, crowded shop that carries an eclectic selection of books as well as good, chewy brownies and rich hot chocolate. Village Voice is a terrific place to come when it's raining, to browse and have a cup of tea while poring over last week's *New York Review of Books* or Henry Miller's *Tropic of Cancer.* 6, rue Princesse, 75006.

Hidden away, at 59–61, rue St-André-des-Arts in the 6th *arrondissement,* not far from the place de l'Odéon, **La Cour de Rohan** is a pretty little tearoom in greens and whites with good furniture. Soothing classical music and fine tarts and pastries make it a nice spot for those rendezvous you hope will linger on. Quite English and yet romantic.

The first mosque built in Paris (Mosquée de Paris) contains a restaurant, a steam bath, and, of course, a tearoom. And what a tearoom! If it weren't so crowded with students from the nearby university, it would be easy to dally all day, sipping small glasses of sweet, fresh mint tea, staring at tiled floors and romantic Eastern architecture. 1, rue Daubenton and 39, rue Geoffroy-St-Hilaire, 75005.

CAFES

Cafés are the traditional Paris spots for a quick lunch, a rendezvous, or just to while away a few hours with a book or a diary. And rightly so. The city is rich with these half-bar, half-restaurants: They come in a variety of guises, offering a wide range of settings, atmospheres, and pleasures. The best are graced with a fascinating history and aspects of the character that originally made them historical.

Right Bank

Fouquets (pronounced, in the English fashion so popular during the Belle Epoque, foo-KETS) is technically a café, though of the rarefied sort. Snacks do not come cheap here, but Fouquets is one of the last remnants, and certainly the classiest one, of the glory that was once the Champs-Elysées before fast-food emporiums, automobile showrooms, and movie theaters overran the avenue. James Joyce was a regular back when dinner was affordable, and today artists of a different sort (journalists and actors) still pack the lively terrace and dining room. The coffee is pretty good, and it is an excellent vantage point for people-watching, as well as a fun place. 99, avenue des Champs-Elysées, 75008.

Another relic, though with less of its former grandeur, the **Café de la Paix** still dominates the large square in front of L'Opéra. It's now a national monument, so it is likely neither to disappear nor to improve. But most of the civilized world at one point or another passes by, so a good afternoon's examination of what Parisians look like this year can be had.

The **Bonne Pecheur** was the first café brave enough to open after the unfortunately ugly Les Halles shopping mall debuted in the late 1970s. Today it is one of the pleasantest in the *quartier* at 14, rue Pierre-Lescot: small, cool (the waiters sport Hawaiian shirts and sunglasses that are at least as chic as the customers'), and person-able. The *bouffe* ("chow") is good as far as café fare goes, and the location is ideal for a sunny afternoon's reading of the paper. A mime who is somewhat less annoying than the norm often provides entertainment, following and imitating innocent passersby.

When the **Café Costes** opened its doors in the 1st *arrondissement* in early 1985, it set off a city-wide design revolution. Philippe Starck's hard-edged neo–Art Deco interior was an instant success, and suddenly everyone opening a bar or restaurant either wanted Starck to de-sign it, or mimicked his approach (Costes's tables and chairs, logo, coffee cups, and more were created by Starck). Today the design still stands up—a little cold, perhaps, but coherent and attractive. As you might expect, Costes is one of the most chic cafés in Paris (and charges accordingly). In warmer months the well-dressed crowd packing the terrace tables present the facing place des Innocents (a centuries-old cemetery) with a sea of de-signer sunglasses and men with ponytails. All the same, Costes can be fun to hang out at.

A few hundred yards away, at 100, rue St-Martin, on the place Beaubourg, another Costes has set up shop in another very trendy café. The **Café Beaubourg**, opened by Gilbert Costes and his brother Jean-Louis in early 1987, takes up where the Café Costes leaves off. Total design is, again, the emphasis, but here comfort seems to have been taken into account. There are different areas with different chair designs to suit the needs of a range of customers. Upstairs, private nooks shield the romantic from inquiring eyes; opposite the bar downstairs, a pile of the week's papers in several languages (French, German, Italian, and English) awaits those settling into the most comfortable chairs for a long stay. The food is particularly good here, especially the breakfast egg dishes and the *café crème*. The crowd here is not as chic as at Costes; some bloods are put off, perhaps, by the portly gents breathing fire, eating glass, and lying on beds of nails across the way.

Of the many cafés in the Marais, two stand out: **Ma Bourgogne** and the Fer à Cheval. The former is nestled under the red-brick arches that make up the arcade of the perimeter of the place des Vosges, once the home of Henri IV. The old-time rattan chairs afford a view of a beautiful little park, where the very fashionable neighborhood's young mothers bring their children to play and where other locals, young and old, come to sunbathe and read in the summer. Inspector Maigret would wander over here from his Ile de la Cité office to drink coffee and ponder his surprisingly light caseload. The **Fer à Cheval**, which was a wine shop in the 1800s and for nearly a century one of the most popular cafés in the *quartier,* takes its name from the lovely horseshoe-shaped marble bar that dominates the small room. A center for troublemakers during the May 1968 student uprising, it's still an excellent hangout. 30, rue Vieille-du-Temple.

One of Paris's odder cafés, the **Clown Bar** is a fairly seedy spot next to the Cirque d'Hiver (Winter Circus), and the bar's name, decor, and patrons take their cue from this location. Photos of circus stars share wall space with decrepit murals of clowns and bareback riders. Although the food and coffee aren't great here, it is worth visiting for the warm, run-down atmosphere. 114, rue Amelot, 75011.

Left Bank

A grand old café with dark-wood walls and a classic long zinc bar, **La Palette** is still a favorite with art and other students. And well it should be. Good, cheap sandwiches; an open, bustling atmosphere; and plenty of history ("what famous painter, then as unknown as myself, could have sat right here?")—all make for a café that seems to define the genre. 43, rue de Seine, 75006.

The Café Deux Magots and Café de Flore are the kings of St-Germain-des-Prés café life. They've been homes away from home to more artists, writers, and thinkers than the Académie Française, and today remain beacons for the intellectually prominent.

The **Deux Magots**, because of its advantageous location opposite the Church of St-Germain-des-Prés, is the more boisterous, and touristy, of the two. (It was behind the church monastery that D'Artagnan was to duel Athos, Porthos, and Artemis and joined the Musketeers against the cardinal's men who suddenly appeared.) A favorite hangout of Cubists and other arty types, Deux Magots became after World War II the second office of Jean-Paul Sartre. Today the prices keep starving artists away, but many glitterati still frequent its hallowed red banquettes. Many street musicians serenade the café during summer months.

The nearby **Flore** (the two cafés are always thought of together) has a more literary tradition, though, in his turn, Picasso moved here after the war. Sartre, Camus, and de Beauvoir made the café the headquarters of existentialism, though today few of the literary set go there to ponder questions of being and nothingness, unless it's to ponder their status as cultural icons. A fine place for a coffee or beer, a breakfast of soft-boiled eggs, or the best Welsh rarebit in town.

The **Select** is the only member of the Montparnasse pantheon of cheap cafés still living and breathing as it once did. The Dome has been renovated so hideously it should be closed to preserve its former greatness; and the Coupole, though open for coffee, is predominantly a restaurant. But the Select (with the two other cafés just mentioned, the 6th *arrondissement* epicenter of all that life had to offer for the Lost Generation) has retained some of its former glory. The grand terrace, at number 99, lets onto the ravaged boulevard Montparnasse, now housing a procession of movie theaters and overshadowed by the drab Montparnasse tower, and is filled with a young crowd reading books and soaking up the sun.

—*Edward Hernstadt*

BARS

In France, drinking is considered an integral part of the process of eating and talking. Thus, the French bounty of alcohol is usually consumed in a restaurant or a café, although neither institution truly does justice to the drinker's art. Fortunately, cosmopolitan influences on

Paris have tempered the Gallic prejudice against going out to any place where chewing and digesting are not the principal activities, as is evident in the foreign origin of many of the city's best watering holes. Because drinking for the sake of drinking is an exotic proposition for many Parisians, prices in pubs and bars can be quite steep. Be prepared to pay 30F and up for a cocktail or a humble glass of beer. So much for the bad news. The good news is that tipping is not required, or even expected, to keep drinks flowing to your table.

The best example of an outpost of the bar culture is **Harry's New York Bar**, an American fixture of the Opéra district since 1911. Its wood-paneled walls are hung with pennants from every notable U.S. college, which contrast with the more discreet Oxbridge coats of arms also on view. A favorite of expatriates and French people who enjoy feeling like expatriates, Harry's famed straw poll of Americans on the eve of presidential elections has been wrong only once (1976, when barflies picked Ford over Carter). The bar is the birthplace of the Bloody Mary (1927) and of the city's most corny Franglais joke: Harry's prints its address as "Sank roo doe noo" (5, rue Daunou).

At the nearby place Vendôme, Americans have yet another home away from home. The bars at the Ritz are still proud of their Lost Generation connections, none more so than the **Bar Hemingway**, a shrinelike affair dominated by a bust of Papa. He is supposed to have liberated this bar in 1944, when, presumably, the dress code was not as strict. Men must now wear a tie. Around the corner from the Ritz, on the rue des Capucines, is a Dublin newcomer to the district, **Kitty O'Shea's**. Named for the woman whose adulterous affair with Parnell caused such a fuss in the late 19th century, the bar is the headquarters for Irish Eurocrats and well-heeled Bretons desperately seeking Celtic camaraderie. And yes, the Guinness is good.

The area near the Etoile is noted for two elaborately ersatz British pubs, the **Lady Hamilton** at 82, avenue Marceau, and the **Winston Churchill**, 5, rue Presbourg. The latter is grander and possesses a greater variety of Scotch whiskey. It also has two cellar bars, one done up in the French conception of a London local, the other in dark Neolithic modern.

The Champs-Elysées district has discos and piano bars by the dozen, many of them far too distracting for serious drinkers. Exceptions are the **Bar des Anglais** (what else?) in the Plaza-Athénée Hotel (25, avenue Montaigne) and the bar at **Le Doyen** restaurant. The latter is the neglected gem of the entire district, set amid the greenery behind the Petit Palais. Summer calls for long, cool drinks on the terrace; winter, for grogs and "medicinal" coffees in the unpretentious elegance of the barroom. Le Doyen is, surprisingly, medium-priced, uncrowded, and 100-percent French.

For haute-couture barflies, the best place to wet one's whistle after a hard day's splurge is in the bar of the **Bristol Hôtel,** at 112, rue du Faubourg-St-Honoré. Gobelins tapestries and huge bouquets of flowers make up the decor.

The Halles district, for all its devotion to play, is not well endowed with decent drinking spots that are not cafés. Its development in the late 1970s, which coincided with a great gush of Americanophilia, has left a legacy of New World barrooms. The best of these is **Conway's** (73, rue St-Denis), a crowded restaurant anteroom cluttered with boxing photos and American sports exotica. Its location, where Les Halles turns sleazy, makes it a point of departure for adventures in respectability or vice, depending on whether you head south or north, respectively. Southward, at Châtelet, the ground-floor room above the **Petit Opportun** cellar jazz club (15, rue Lavandières-Ste-Opportune) exudes mellow, early middle-aged funkiness until four or five in the morning. Northward, on the tiny rue Tiquetonne, **Le Baragouin** gives an idea of what it is to be young, rowdy, and broke in Paris.

The Marais is more of a restaurant than a bar district, except for the city's gay population. Two gay bars in particular should be noted: **Le Piano Zinc,** 49, rue des Blancs Manteaux, which has a cabaret in its cellar, and **Le Swing,** 42, rue Vieille-du-Temple, a relaxed 1950s study in gray. Around the corner, the deliberately shabby **Au Rendez-Vous des Amis,** 10, rue Ste-Croix-de-la-Bretonnerie, is precisely that: a place for friends—of all persuasions—to get together for a drink in the early evening. At the point where the Marais meets the Bastille lies one of the city's handsomest bars. **La Mousson,** 9, rue de la Bastille, prides itself on its imperial connections: not, as one might expect, with Paris's ubiquitous Napoléon, but with the days of the Raj. Mock-rattan furniture, lazy overhead fans, and a few posters of posh ocean liners evoke the world of Kipling and Maugham for well-dressed clients in their twenties and thirties. French is the lingua franca of this corner of the empire.

The Bastille district is, according to *The New York Times,* "thug chic." The area near the rue de Lappe, now the nesting ground of the city's night owls, looks mildly threatening and thus is of great interest for barroom adventurers. Of the many drinking spots, the **Cactus Bleu** (on the rue de Lappe) is the most impressive, overdesigned in accordance with the current tenets of Parisian taste. Where rue de Lappe runs into rue de Charonne, the **Entre Pots** celebrates old advertising campaigns and displays halogen lights for a quietly trendy crowd. If you are uncomfortable with comfort, less genteel places are very easy to find around here.

In the great stretches of the Right Bank off the beaten track, several bars are worth visiting. In the 11th *arrondissement,* the area that promises one day to supplant the Bastille as an up-and-coming neighborhood (Paris is an ever-changing city), the **H₂O** at the place Léon Blum (rue Godefroy Cavaignac) is building a reputation for creative cocktail-mixing, one of the few refinements neglected by French civilization. Farther into the central business district, near the Folies Bergère, **Au Général La Fayette** stands as proof of the constant surprises Paris has to offer. Located on the otherwise unremarkable rue La Fayette, this lively bar is one of the most agreeable spots to quaff ale in the city.

At Montmartre, pseudo-cafés serving a full range of expensive drinks (including pastis, which, after all, is pseudo-absinthe) are the norm. For good downmarket fun, a cramped crêperie-café-piano bar called **Le Tire Bouchon** (on the tiny rue Norvins) should be tried.

The Left Bank is usually associated with café life, and for good reason: Decent bars are hard to come by. One very worthwhile exception is the **Caveau de la Bolée**, a charming hole in the wall hidden away in the rue de l'Hirondelle, a deserted alleyway close to the crowded place St-Michel. Named for the bowls (*bolées*) of cider that poor Sorbonne students favored in Medieval times, this quiet all-night spot is now the haunt of chess fiends, who are sent to the back of the cave to indulge in their sleepless passion. The good old days—or rather, nights—of jazz on the Left Bank are kept alive at such places as **La Paillote**, 45, rue Monsieur Le Prince, a place done up to look like an African hut, and **Birdland**, at the corner of the rues Princesse and Guisarde, a minuscule bar in the heart of St-Germain-des-Prés. Both bars have admirable collections of jazz records.

At Montparnasse, once famous for the cafés and bars

where French surrealists rubbed shoulders and lifted elbows with the young and talented from all over the world, chain restaurants and high rents—fallout from the giant office complex built here in the 1970s—have moved in. The sole bar of the area that is worth a visit nowadays is the **Rosebud** (11 bis, rue Delambre), a tranquil spot where young professionals and failed artists converge over cocktails, chile con carne, and recorded jazz. A friendly place.

—*Stephen O'Shea*

NIGHTLIFE AND ENTERTAINMENT

For the Victorians, Paris was where one came for "culture" and to sow one's oats, which together usually meant the opera, fancy-dress balls, carriage rides in the Tuileries, and perhaps a mistress. For North Americans, Paris symbolized the cynical worldliness that gathered itself under the rubric "Europe" and tempted young men to stray from the straight and narrow. Henry James recognized the compelling character of Paris quite well: Even Lambert Strether in *The Ambassadors,* old and wise enough to know better, was seduced by the city's subtle beauty. Today the world has shrunk, and so too have many of the illusions that served to enliven it. Paris, however, is a city in which illusions are still respected and nostalgia revered. It is also a city that loves the night, and considers it to be as much a territory of the imagination as of the senses.

Today's Parisian "night" can be broken into four categories: *music, spectacle* (revues), *dancing,* and *classical culture* (concerts, opera, dance, and theater). Events change regularly, of course, and visitors are advised to buy the journals *Pariscope* or the *Officiel des Spectacles,* on sale at any kiosk, to see what's playing at the theaters or clubs. Movies are also listed in these publications; *v.o.* means that the film is shown in its original form with subtitles in French; *v.f.* means that it is dubbed.

MUSIC

The French have long been mad about jazz, and Paris has long been a haven for American jazz musicians unable to find an audience, or work, in the United States. A cult sprang up around Josephine Baker in the 1920s, and in the 1940s and 1950s as much good jazz could be heard in Paris as anywhere else in the world. Bernard Tavernier's

1986 film *'Round Midnight* is a touching tribute to the reverence many French people have had for jazzmen and clubs. Today there is a wealth of clubs and piano bars that still feature top American musicians, as well as the leading homegrown practitioners. Venues for contemporary non-jazz genres are far rarer, as are quality French bands for them, but Paris is an important stop on the international circuit and there are always a few rock concerts in town.

Piano Bars

The **Ascot** and the **Ritz** are probably the most elegant piano bars in Paris. The former offers reasonable prices and the subdued horsey interior you imagine exists only in English men's clubs, while the latter offers luxury and refinement in a relaxed, slightly snobby atmosphere. Ascot: 66, rue Pierre-Charron, 75008, until 4:00 A.M. Ritz: 15, place Vendôme, 75001, until 1:00 A.M.

The hotel-auditorium-mall complex at the Porte Maillot has two piano bars: the **Lafayette**, in the hotel of the same name, and the **Lionel Hampton**, in the Hôtel Méridien. They share a common element: Despite the built-in disadvantage of being hotel bars, they are both surprisingly nice. Both have "modern" decor and frequent guest performers. Lafayette: Hôtel Concorde-Lafayette, 3, place de la Porte-des-Ternes, 75017, until 2:00 A.M. Lionel Hampton: Hôtel Méridien, 81, boulevard Gouvion-St-Cyr, 75017, until 10:00 P.M.

Joe Turner, one of the transplanted kings of jazz, has stayed in Paris, he says, "Because I haven't been out of work for 30 years." He parks himself behind a piano and a cigar every night from midnight till dawn at the intimate **Calavados**, pounding out classics in his warm and inimitable style. 40, avenue Pierre-1er-de-Serbie, 75008.

Les Trois Maillets occupies an ancient building in the heart of the Latin Quarter, and offers jazz on two floors. The homey, crowded piano bar above is one of the most pleasant in Paris, drawing fun-loving, knowledgeable crowds. Downstairs in the cramped *cave* groups and combos ranging from jazz to the blues to gospel play every night. 56, rue Galande, 75005.

Clubs

Club action doesn't start until after dinner—10:00 at the earliest—and generally continues until the wee hours.

The better clubs impose a cover charge. Expect fairly costly cocktails in all of these.

Four *boîtes* dominate Les Halles, offering a variety of musical options.

The **Baiser Salé** presents an international mix of styles, from blues to Brazilian, in a comfortable though somewhat expensive club. 58, rue des Lombards, 75001.

The **Slow Club** has one of the best neon signs in Paris and quality swing jazz in a lively setting. 130, rue de Rivoli, 75001.

The **Petit Opportun**, a stone's throw away, is a more traditional club: The bartender in the cramped upstairs room plays rare recordings, while top musicians reign in the charming old *cave* below. 15, rue des Lavandières-Ste-Opportune, 75001.

Distrito, a restaurant cum jazz and rock club, is a new addition to the district. The best local bands play here from midnight till the wee hours. 49, rue Berger, 75001.

Five other Right Bank clubs feature an eclectic choice of genres:

The **Cambridge**, a few blocks from the Arc de Triomphe, is one of the only places in town to hear Dixieland jazz. 17, avenue Wagram, 75017.

The **New Morning** attracts the best foreign artists who come to Paris, and they play everything from jazz to blues to rock. It's a cavernous club in what was once a newspaper printing plant. 5–7, rue des Petites-Ecuries, 75010.

Le Gibus is the only real rock-and-roll club in Paris doing well today, after an unhealthy punk period in the earlier 1980s. It features some very raw, exciting bands. 18, rue du Faubourg-du-Temple, 75011.

The **Cigale**, a former 1890s music hall, has been redesigned by the ubiquitous Philippe Starck and is, as would be expected, exceedingly cool. Plays, special screenings, and music production take place here, as do rock concerts. 120, boulevard de Rochechouart, 75018.

La Chapelle des Lombards, in the hot Bastille area, features salsa and samba music. 19, rue de Lappe, 75011.

Four dependable Latin Quarter clubs present topnotch jazz every night.

Caveau de la Huchette, a center for swing and big-band music. 5, rue de la Huchette, 75005.

Le Petit Journal St-Michel, on three cramped floors,

presenting the leading acts. 71, boulevard St-Michel, 75005.

Le Furstemberg, a lively bar below a busy brasserie. 28, rue de Buci, 75006.

Montana, a tiny bar where Champagne is the house drink and combos squeeze onto the stage. 28, rue St-Benoît, 75006.

Three clubs dominate the music scene in the Montparnasse area.

Le Petit Journal Montparnasse, which is as good as its mate in the Latin Quarter. 13, rue du Commandant-R. Mouchotte, 75014.

Utopia-Jazz Club, an odd bar that is headquarters for blues, bluegrass, and country *à la Française* (just think about it). 79, rue de l'Ouest, 75014.

Dunois, which specializes in the cutting edge of jazz. 28, rue Dunois, 75013.

SPECTACLES

The Las Vegas "girlie revue" took its inspiration from Paris's *grands spectacles*. But, built on schlock as Vegas is, the Nevada versions cannot compare with the sheer exuberance and grandeur of the originals. While there are dozens of supper clubs and small revues in Paris, the rule of thumb is simple: The most famous are, quite simply, the best. Shows typically feature troupes of women dancing gamely without the benefit of tops and balancing enormous gaudy headpieces or dragging long glittering capes; men, usually in supporting roles, traipsing onto the stage in a variety of outlandish outfits; archetypical nightclub singers crooning; and a slew of vaudeville acts performing outside the curtain while teams change the vast and complicated sets.

One more common feature: song and dance numbers that cannot be described without an army of exclamation marks. The world's most beautiful women! Spectacular story lines! Lavish scenery! Unbelievable special effects! Drama! Excitement! These shows are probably the world's finest Grade-B entertainment, and that elevates them to a form of art. They are also terrific fun.

The **Lido** is the most Las Vegas-like of the shows, and probably the most spectacular. An intricate hydraulic system means that finales often include swimming pools or ice-skating rinks and that a real pit is available for the disposal of "virgins" being sacrificed to the gods. 116, Champs-Elysées, 75008. Tel: 45-63-11-61. Dinner at 8:00, shows at 10:15 and 12:15. 495 francs.

The **Folies Bergère** is undoubtedly the best-known show in Paris; it turned 100 in 1987. Charlie Chaplin, Colette, Maurice Chevalier, and Josephine Baker are just some of the entertainers who have graced the boards here, and Manet painted a waitress behind the bar. The opulent sets still include many designed by Erté. The Folies always features a truly talented singer, who shares the spotlight with the dance numbers, something the other shows can't claim. 32, rue Richer, 75009. Tel: 42-46-77-11. Show at 9:00. 78–341 francs.

The **Moulin Rouge** puts on the most stereotypically French spectacle, in keeping with its history. The place is nothing like the dance hall Toulouse-Lautrec created posters for, but still the Moulin has retained its musette character, with plush red banquettes and lights on lamp posts. The shows still feature the can-can, a number that over the years has lost none of its stunning athleticism and drama. Place Blanche, 75018. Tel: 46-06-00-19. Dinner at 8:00, shows at 10:00 and 12:00. 340–495 francs.

The **Paradis Latin**, on the other hand, is a more genuinely French show. Set in a comfortable theater with three long rows of closely packed tables, the spectacle includes old-time singers and lively vaudeville acts, and encourages audience participation. The Paradis has a homier, more intimate feeling than the giants do. 28, rue du Cardinal-Lemoine, 75005. Dinner at 8:30, show at 10:00. 330–485 francs.

The **Crazy Horse Saloon** stages the most exotic show in town, featuring nude dancers sporting bits of ribbon and lace and names like Polly Underground, Tiny Semaphore, and Funny Cumulus. Favorites with businessmen from Japan, the dances are actually a pretty amazing sight: The Western-theme bar is small, so the performers loom enormously on the tiny stage, and the choreographer occasionally manages to be interesting. An experience. 12, avenue George-V, 75008. Tel: 47-23-32-32. Shows at 9:30 and 11:30; weekends at 8:15, 10:35, and 12:50. 465 francs.

DANCING

Three types of dancing spots exist in Paris: old-fashioned tango palaces, where serious practitioners of the art congregate; rich, glitzy discos around the Arc de Triomphe;

and high-fashion clubs favored by the young, artistic, and cool. Discos tend to be extremely expensive and to be geared to middle-aged jet setters, Greek shipping czars, and starlets who haven't quite made it. (If interested, check out Atmosphère, 5th Avenue, Régine's, Olivia Valère, or Castel's at your own risk.) Clubs are generally open until at least 5:00 A.M., and the most popular often have ugly-tempered bouncers and long lines outside. Drinks start at 50 francs, entrance 70 francs and up.

La Coupole is more than a historic restaurant—it is also one of the best dance clubs in town. Downstairs from the famous brasserie, conservatively dressed middle-aged men and women gather to tango the evenings away. Not for those unfamiliar with the precise, erotic dance. 102, boulevard Montparnasse.

Chez Gégène opened just after World War I broke out, and features both tango and musette (typically French accordion songs). A wonderfully folksy and traditional place to dance close, the way men and women were meant to do. 126 bis, quai de Polangis, Joinville-le-Pont.

The **Balajo** has a split personality. Weekday afternoons it is a great dance hall packed with couples swinging around the floor. Monday evenings it is also packed, but with trendy young Parisians twisting to thumping disco and rock songs. Quite fun. 9, rue de Lappe, 75011.

Keur-Samba is the one 8th-*arrondissement* club that everyone loves. Terribly private (one of the hardest to get into) and done up in what Abercrombie and Fitch might consider correct disco decor, the Keur features African music and is popular with the rich and famous. 79, rue de la Boétie. From 11:00.

Le Palace is the old standby of the younger-spirited clubs. The huge space was done over in 1987, and that has helped keep it popular. It tends to have fairly good music, playing less disco and more "dance" tracks (long versions with heavy bass lines) of popular songs. 8, rue du Faubourg-Montmartre, 75009. From 11:00.

The **Locomotive** is one of the newer clubs, but is already very popular. When not used for rock concerts, its three levels—including a large dance floor and the basement, which winds through the boilers of the next-door neighbor, Moulin Rouge—are full of trendy young people. 90, boulevard Clichy, 75018. From 11:00.

Les Bains dominated the club scene in recent years, though that may mean nothing tomorrow. The highly stylized decor and many, many dressed-to-kill artsy types remain, though. The place gets unbelievably crowded on weekends. 7, rue Bourg-l'Abbé, 75003. From 11:30.

The Tango is an intimate, friendly club where young Africans, South Americans, and Parisians squeeze together to dance to the latest hits from two continents. This was an early rap center, too. 14, rue au Maire, 75003. From 11:00.

Over the past few years, the Paris night scene has seen the emergence of the one-night stands, clubs open for one night of the week only. The **Balajo**, on Mondays at 9, rue de Lappe, was the first. Others include the **Bataclan**, 50, boulevard Voltaire, 75011, on Sunday afternoons and the **Royal Lieu**, 2, rue des Italiens, 75009, on Tuesdays.

CLASSICAL MUSIC, DANCE, AND THEATER

Of course, the joys of Paris nights are not limited to jazz and the jitterbug. As a world capital and traditional center of the arts, Paris has long been home to a wealth of talented and innovative musicians, conductors, dancers, directors, and playwrights.

Though Paris today is not the preeminent music center it once was, and the Orchestre de Paris has been called second tier, its concert halls still draw many of the world's greatest artists.

Ballet was invented in France during the reign of Louis XIV, with the Sun King himself often performing in the first dances. Today Paris is home to several world-caliber companies (including the Paris Opera Ballet, directed by Rudolf Nureyev), and every year the world's finest companies, such as the Kirov, the Bolshoi, Maurice Béjart's Ballet of the 20th Century, and the New York City Ballet, grace Paris stages.

The French theater tradition is old, glorious, and alive, as attested to by ongoing productions of Molière and Racine, both of whose plays still crackle with wit and verve. Avant-garde theater was in part developed in Paris, and two of Ionesco's plays, *La Leçon* and *La Cantatrice Chauve,* are still running (though in seriously fatigued stagings) after more than 30 years. Though a 1987 "culture crisis" deprived French theaters and theater companies of a portion of their supporting funds, there are always dozens of reasonably priced plays to be seen, and they run the gamut from Sam Shephard (in bilingual versions) to archaic avant-garde. For most cultural events in Paris, you should reserve tickets well in advance of performances.

The most notable concert halls and theaters in Paris are:

- Les Bouffes du Nord. 37 bis, boulevard de la Chapelle. Tel: 42-39-34-50. Major center for modern theater.
- Centre Pompidou. Place Beaubourg. Tel: 42-74-42-19. Avant-garde music.
- La Comédie Française. 2, rue de Richelieu. Tel: 40-15-00-15. The classic French repertory in a beautiful theater.
- Opéra Comique (Salle Favart). 5, rue Favart. Tel: 42-96-06-11. Opera, dance, and shows.
- Paris Opéra. Place de l'Opéra. Tel: 47-42-53-71. Opera and dance in opulent surroundings. Chagall painted the ceiling.
- Salle Cortot. 78, rue Cardinet. Tel: 43-96-48-48. Concerts.
- Salle Gaveau. 45, rue de la Boétie. Tel: 45-63-20-30. Concerts.
- Salle Pleyel. 252, rue du Faubourg St-Honoré. Tel: 45-63-88-73. Concerts.
- Théâtre de la Bastille. 76, rue de la Roquette. Tel: 43-57-42-14. A leading forum for avant-garde theater, dance, and music.
- Théâtre de la Ville. 2, place du Châtelet. Tel: 42-61-18-83. Concerts and dance.
- Théâtre des Champs-Elysées. 15, avenue Montaigne. Tel: 47-20-36-37. Plays and touring shows (such as Marcel Marceau).
- Théâtre Musical de Paris. Place du Châtelet. Tel: 261-19-83. Concerts, dance, and touring shows.
- Théâtre National de Chaillot. Place du Trocadéro. Tel: 47-278-11-15. Plays and dance.
- Théâtre National de l'Odéon, place Paul-Claudel. Tel: 47-27-81-15. Bold and innovative theater productions.

Many churches feature organ recitals and choral pieces—among them, a regular Sunday concert at Notre-Dame.

Many sporting events are held at the Palais des Sports,

porte des Versailles (Tel: 48-28-40-90), and the main convention center is the Palais des Congrès, 2, place de la Porte Maillot (Tel: 47-58-22-22).

—*Edward Hernstadt*

SHOPS AND SHOPPING

In Paris shopping transcends self-indulgence, for here shopping is not so much an exercise in consumerism as an education in style and taste. For the French, choosing the perfect Brie from an open-air market stall is imbued with the same sense of ritual as selecting a Louis XV commode from a quai Voltaire *antiquaire;* and wrapping a box of candied fruits becomes an art. The French traditions of quality, craftsmanship, and attention to detail can be appreciated painlessly—and with a minimum of pedagogy—by the shopper alerted to Paris's mercantile possibilities and their nuances.

This is a city of serendipitous discovery. Although Paris's well-defined *quartiers* do attract certain habitués—and boutiques and restaurants are often geared toward them—wonderful shops sometimes appear where you would least expect to find them. Explore on foot and, given Paris's cobblestone streets and unpredictable weather, wear good, sturdy shoes. Shopping hours tend to be somewhat *fantaisiste.* Department stores reliably open at 10:00 A.M. and close at 7:00 P.M.; but Paris's smaller boutiques sometimes don't open before 10:30 A.M., close at lunchtime and, if they deign to open for business on Saturday, sometimes close on Monday to compensate. Visa and MasterCard are the most universally accepted credit cards in Parisian stores. Traveller's checks often cause confusion due to fluctuating exchange rates; French francs are consistently welcome.

The city's shopping terrain can be roughly divided into three geographic areas. The Right Bank—traditionally Paris's chic side of the river Seine—now reveals a split personality. Southwest of the Opéra, on the place Vendôme, the rue Royale, the rue du Faubourg St-Honoré, and the avenue Montaigne, luxury reigns. Eastward, at the Palais Royal, the place des Victoires, the recently renovated Les Halles, and the newly rediscovered Marais and Bastille areas, trendy takes over. The Left Bank's St-Germain-des-Prés area remains a bastion of "typically Parisian" fashion as well as an art and antique lover's mecca.

Place de la Concorde

Where to start? First decide on your priorities, or determine the target area you'd like to explore. For a crash course in French *art de vivre,* a good jumping-off point is the grandiose place de la Concorde, which many Parisians consider the hub of the city. Certain Parisian luxury shops demand token homage, and many of these legendary institutions are found on or around the streets radiating from here: **Lalique** crystal, a few doors down from Maxim's restaurant at 11, rue Royale; **Christofle** silver, which supplies much of the world's remaining royalty with its flatware, at number 12; and the city's most glorious—and costly—florist, Lachaume, next door. Farther up the rue Royale are a number of chic fashion boutiques: **Façonnable** and **Cerruti 1881** for classically inclined men (with a small Cerruti women's boutique in between), **Gucci** and **Mario Valentino** for flashy Italian shoes and leather goods, and the American new kid on the block, **Ralph Lauren**, at 2, place de la Madeleine. Tucked off the rue Royale in the cité Berryer (a passageway lifted straight from the pages of Zola) is **The Blue Fox bar**, which offers quiche, salad, and a glass of Bordeaux to an attractive lunchtime crowd of well-dressed shoppers, fashion press attachés, and stockbrokers from the nearby place Vendôme.

The prestigious saddlers-turned-leather-goods house of **Hermès** is a two-minute walk away, at 24, rue du Faubourg St-Honoré. Hardened indeed is the heart that doesn't leap at the sight of a brown-ribboned, orange box from Hermès containing one of the house staples: a silk scarf, a "Kelly" handbag (made famous by its most celebrated advocate, Princess Grace), or the ultimate status accessory, Hermès's pigskin Métro ticket holder.

Sitting smugly in the midst of all this *luxe* is the magnificent Hôtel de Crillon, at 10, place de la Concorde. Its **Obélisque Bar**, reached by the hotel's rue Boissy-d'Anglas side entrance, used to be a watering hole for journalists in the prewar Paris of Janet Flanner and is still an irresistibly romantic rendezvous spot.

Just beside it is the kind of shop that collectors of the rare, the wonderful, and even the slightly kitschy come to Paris for: **Au Bain Marie**, at 12, rue Boissy-d'Anglas. Specializing in *l'art de la table,* Au Bain Marie's huge interior is chockablock with antique and reedited items for the kitchen and dining room: turn-of-the-century silverware purchased from defunct hotels, antique Daum and St.

Louis crystal glasses, Memphis dishes and Thirties Bakelite tableware, and exquisite vintage and modern table and bed linens.

Food

In a country where food has been elevated to the status of religion, it seems only fitting that Paris's highest concentration of luxury food shops be found in the shadow of one of its most illustrious temples, La Madeleine. Here, clustered around the place de la Madeleine, are some of the world's most dazzling names in gastronomy. Merely the windows of **Fauchon**, at 26, place de la Madeleine, are an ode to gluttony. Inside, myriad culinary delights await: fresh foie gras and Beluga caviar, scented oils and out-of-season tropical fruits, as well as a stock of more humble imported goods catering to homesick Americans. Across the street at Fauchon's stand-up lunchroom you can wash down a frothy *pâtisserie* with a cup of some of the best coffee in Paris. On the other side of the *place,* at number 21, is **Hédiard**, *épicier par excellence,* specializing in exotic fruits and vegetables, its own selection of teas, honeys, and spice blends, and fresh-fruit jellied candies known to every Parisian hostess as *les pâtes de fruits de chez Hédiard.* **Caviar Kaspia**, at 17, place de la Madeleine, offers caviar, smoked salmon, and blinis to go (an upstairs restaurant serves the same thing), and next door's **La Maison de la Truffe** supplies fresh truffles from November to March (out of season, they are available dried or preserved for less rarefied palates).

The adjacent rue Vignon boasts the quintessential *fromagerie,* **La Ferme St-Hubert**, at number 21, which in addition to its vast selection of cheeses also serves cheese dishes at its tiny adjoining restaurant; and **La Maison du Miel**, a turn-of-the-century honey shop selling a fragrant array of house honeys and those culled from distant hives throughout the world. While on the rue Vignon, don't miss **Pulcinella**, a small shop with a persimmon awning at 10, rue Vignon that sells wonderful antique jewelry and other collectibles, and at number 11, **Jean Lafont**, one of Paris's oldest and most renowned optometrists, specializing in Clark Kent-style, mock-tortoiseshell spectacles. On the corner of the rue Vignon and the rue de Sèze is the French equivalent of the old corner drugstore, **Pharmacie Leclerc**, whose Belle Epoque-style packaged fine face powders, alcohol-free tonic lotions, and grandmother's-recipe face creams are favorites with Paris-based models and other fashion fauna.

Rue Tronchet and the Grands Magasins

The rue Tronchet is a bustling commercial artery leading north from the place de la Madeleine to the Parisian *grands magasins,* Au Printemps and Galeries Lafayette. On the second floor of number 13, celebrated hatmaker **Jean Barthet** concocts fanciful headgear for Paris couturiers as well as provincial mothers-of-the-bride. At the intersection of the rue Tronchet and the boulevard Haussmann is another throwback to a more genteel era, **Aux Tortues** (at 55, boulevard Haussmann), whose caramel-colored marble façade decorated with bronze elephants has stood since 1864. Although its once-standard stock of tortoise-shell-backed, boar-bristle brushes, ivory pocket combs, and eyelash brushes is dwindling (there is, apparently, no longer a clientele for tortoiseshell hand mirrors at 8,500 francs), Aux Tortues still has the best selection of polished Baltic amber necklaces and ivory and coral chokers in town.

Paris's two major department stores, **Au Printemps** and **Galeries Lafayette**, at numbers 64 and 40, boulevard Haussmann, are wonders of Belle Epoque architecture: Galeries Lafayette's stained-glass dome bathes the entire store in pastel light, and Printemps's top-floor terrace restaurant is known for its elaborate 19th-century decor. They are Paris's answer to New York's Bloomingdale's and London's Harrod's. Both *magasins* have been recently renovated, and a shopper short on time can find at them Paris's best names in beauty, fashion, and interior design.

A distinct advantage for foreigners shopping at one of Paris's department stores is the ease in garnering the *détaxe*—the refund of French excise tax to which visitors from abroad are entitled on purchases of up to 2,200 francs or more if they live within the European Economic Community, or on purchases of up to 1,200 francs if they live outside the EEC. Shoppers from outside the EEC must fill out a special *détaxe* form—with receipts of purchases made within a period of six months—which they surrender to customs for stamped approval when they leave France. Paris's *grands magasins* all have special *détaxe* departments that help to demystify this all-too-often bewildering process.

Check out the labels on a Parisian dandy and chances are that at least one thing he's wearing comes from **Charvet**, *the* Paris men's haberdashery, located a few minutes' walk from *les grands magasins,* down the rue de la Paix at 28, place Vendôme. A seven-floor sanctuary on the majestic, 17th-century place Vendôme, Charvet has offered everything for the impeccable man since 1838—and for such women enamored of masculine classics as the novelist George Sand, who used to have her shirts made here.

Place Vendôme

Clustered around the place Vendôme are France's most prestigious names in *haute joaillerie,* the centuries-old family jewelers Chaumet, Boucheron, Mauboussin, Van Cleef et Arpels—and Cartier, just up the street on the rue de la Paix. With the graceful, curved awnings of the Hôtel Ritz rimming one side, the glittering storefronts of these distinguished jewelers the other, the place Vendôme on a spring afternoon is the closest approximation of Proust's Paris that the city can offer today.

A visitor can prolong the remembrance of Paris past at two neighboring boutiques: **Annick Goutal**'s glorious, gilded scent shop at 14, rue de Castiglione, and **Casse-grain**, 422, rue St-Honoré, stationers and engravers to Paris since Proust's times. Those nostalgic for the more genteel days of steamship and rail travel should stop by **Morabito**, at 1, place Vendôme, whose windows are perennially, defiantly piled high with gleaming black crocodile luggage (which some countries prohibit under customs laws).

Place du Marché St-Honoré

A *place* no less charming, but of an entirely different nature, is the place du Marché St-Honoré, which you can reach by making a left onto the rue St-Honoré from the place Vendôme's southern end and turning left again on the narrow rue du Marché St-Honoré. A fire station occupies the place of honor here, and around it are a jumble of colorful restaurants and boutiques. **Jean-Charles Castel-bajac**, at 31, place du Marché St-Honoré, is a designer-clothing store where fashion often blends couture and cartoon; and wacky accessory designer **Philippe Model**, at number 33, supplies rose-trimmed toques, tasseled suede gloves, and fuchsia silk pumps to Parisiennes with the wit—and the self-assurance—to wear them. A note of austerity recently added to the *place* is the **Comme des Garçons** furniture boutique, at 23, place du Marché St-Honoré, whose minimalist steel creations are the interior-design equivalent of Japanese fashion label Comme des Garçons' purist fashion.

Rue de Rivoli

Do an about-face on the rue du Marché St-Honoré and it becomes—in yet another one of Paris's inexplicable street-name changes—the rue du 29 Juillet, which leads onto the colonnaded rue de Rivoli. If you're looking for gilt Eiffel Towers, Mona Lisa sweatshirts, and Paris-monument printed acetate scarves to take home, any one of the closet-sized souvenir shops on the rue de Rivoli will be able to provide them.

Exceptions to the general tourist-trap ambience of the rue de Rivoli are the English bookshops **W. H. Smith** (which has a cozy English tearoom upstairs) at number 248 and **Galignani**, said to be the oldest bookshop in Europe, at number 224. Visitors hoping to take home with them more than just a memory of Paris streets should check out **Galerie d'Architecture Miniature**'s tiny, hand-made faience reproductions of Paris buildings (206, rue de Rivoli). And **Angelina's**, at number 226, Paris's tearoom *par excellence,* is the gilt-and-mirrored meeting place for chic Parisians, a must for anyone seeking to understand French *belles manières.* Sipping a cup of Angelina's sinfully rich hot chocolate—poured in dollops from tiny porcelain pitchers—over an equally rich chestnut-and-cream Mont Blanc *pâtisserie* is many a Parisian's way of whiling away a long winter afternoon.

If big-game antiques are your bag, **Le Louvre des Antiquaires**, left off the rue de Rivoli, at 2, place du Palais-Royal, is a well-stocked hunting ground. In this highly civilized, three-story gallery are 250 shops devoted to fine French furniture, rich leather-bound books, and heavy bronzes. Unlike the tiny *brocanteurs* you find along the Left Bank's rue du Bac or rue Jacob, whose wares are reminiscent of Grandma's attic treasures, Le Louvre des Antiquaires's offerings are of a decidedly grander sort—and carry price tags to match.

Men for whom the traditional pleasures of smoking and hunting remain as compelling as they were in earlier centuries will find two boutiques here to their liking: **A La Civette**, 157, rue St-Honoré, a *tabac* that has been providing smokers with the tools of their vice—fine Havana cigars, aromatic tobaccos, handmade pipes—since the 17th century, and **Faure le Page**, 8, rue de Richelieu, which sells arms and munitions and other hunting and shooting accessories. This shop, located on the same corner as the Comédie Française since 1716, holds no charm for those who don't share its passion, but it carries a noteworthy distinction: It is here, in 1789, that the Paris mob stole the gunpowder with which they blew up the Bastille.

Palais Royal

Off the place du Palais-Royal are the tree-lined gardens of the Palais Royal, whose graceful stone arcades have stood since 1780, when Louis-Philippe of Orléans built this ground-level shopping mall in Paris's first recorded get-rich-quick building scheme. Colette lived and died in one of the sumptuous apartments overlooking the gardens; the **Grand Véfour** restaurant, which began life here as a café in 1760, boasts a menu with a Jean Cocteau sketch on the cover and a small brass plaque indicating Victor Hugo's habitual dining place. Old mosaic floor tiles outside still proclaim long-gone shopowners' names, their places now occupied by a mixed bag of unusual boutiques.

Here are cloistered shops selling old stamps, antique jewels, beribboned medals and orders. **Didier Ludot**, 24, rue de Montpensier, sells one-of-a-kind antique leather accessories: Hermès bags and belts, crocodile wallets, and shoes. **Costea**, 63–64, galerie Montpensier, offers geometrically shaped *objets d'art* for home and office in stark ebony wood and ivory, tortoiseshell, and shiny nickeled bronze. **Galerie Gerald Lesigne**, 37, galerie Montpensier, is a showcase for naturalistic wrought-iron furniture from the "New Barbarians," the group of young designers who are currently redefining avant-garde Paris interiors.

On the northern end of the gardens is a delightful boutique, **Anna Joliet**, at 9, rue de Beaujolais, which sells music boxes both old and new. Just behind are the turn-of-the-century, glass-roofed shopping **Galeries Colbert** and **Vivienne**. The Galerie Vivienne, in addition to an assortment of tearooms, clothing boutiques, interior-design shops, and the oldest bookstore in Paris—the **Librairie Petit Siroux**—counts **Jean-Paul Gaultier's** post-high-tech Baroque boutique among its tenants. Childhood nostalgics shouldn't miss **Si Tu Veux**, at 62, galerie

Vivienne, which sells charming traditional toys and games—wooden alphabet blocks, farm animal cardboard cutouts, and "real" teddy bears for parents and children weary of computerized fun. The newly renovated Galerie Colbert's **Bibliothèque Nationale Gift Shop**—France's national library is right next door—offers distinctive souvenirs, all adapted from the library's archives.

Place des Victoires

Where the rue des Petits-Champs meets the rue Etienne-Marcel sits the place des Victoires, an elegant 17th-century *place* with an equestrian statue of Louix XIV in its center. Circling it are some of Paris's best fashion storefronts: Kenzo, Thierry Mugler, Stéphane Kélian, Enrico Coveri, Charles Chevignon, Victoire. Its overflow has spilled onto the high-tech rue Etienne-Marcel, which has become the Paris address for the Japanese designers **Comme des Garçons** and **Yohji Yamamoto**, active-wear designers **Marithé and François Girbaud**, the British knitwear house **Joseph Tricot**, and the French ready-to-wear house **Cacharel**. The small streets radiating from the place des Victoires—the rue Croix-des-Petits-Champs, the rue du Mail, the rue Hérold, and the nearby rue de la Coquillière—are full of interesting, affordable fashion boutiques for both men and women.

Les Halles

Next stop on the Right Bank shopping tour is the Les Halles area, which has been the subject of much controversy in the past decade. Out of the rubble of what Zola once called the "belly of Paris" and in the place of the sprawling market that for more than 800 years supplied the housewives, restaurateurs, and market stalls of Paris with fresh produce has risen an ultra-modern shopping complex, Le Forum des Halles. Though totally lacking in charm, this chrome-and-glass monument to modern consumerism does have something for everybody: bookshops, sporting-goods stores, fashionable clothing boutiques, cinemas—if you can find your way around the elaborate labyrinth of escalators.

The surrounding *quartier* is an eclectic mix of chic boutiques and sex shops, trendy bars, and fast-food establishments that draws a particular species of Parisian whose characteristic dress often includes black leather, combat boots, and tin can lid-sized hoop earrings. Les Halles's other shopping options are only a stone's throw from the Pompidou Center, whose entrance, with its motley congregation of fire-swallowers, African drum bands, and mimes, resembles a Medieval fairground. The place Ste-Opportune and the rue de la Ferronnerie are pedestrian areas bustling with enterprising boutiques; the rue du Cygne and the rue Pierre-Lescot are the streets to comb for Fifties and Sixties *fripes,* or secondhand clothes. The **Papeterie Moderne**, at 12, rue de la Ferronnerie, is the place to find life-sized copies of Paris's green-trimmed, blue-metal street signs as well as the bona fide plastic *pâté de campagne* and *terrine de lièvre* signs of French *charcuteries.* Next door, **Opox Rapax**, also at 12, rue de la Ferronnerie, is *the* Paris address for big, bulky, hand-knit sweaters.

La rue du Jour, in the shadow of the imposing St-Eustache church, where Louis XIV celebrated his first communion and Molière was baptized, is the bastion of Paris's wildly successful ready-to-wear designer **Agnès B**. The designer makes simple, relatively inexpensive clothes for men, women, and children, and each category has its own boutique here. Also worth checking out on the rue du Jour: **La Droguerie**, at number 9, a treasure trove of yarns, ribbons, buttons, and beads, where teenage Parisians come to find parts for their first pair of funky earrings; **Pom d'Api**, at number 13, for amusing sneakers and other original shoe styles for tots (the "grown-up" store, **Free Lance**, is nearby, at 22, rue Mondétour); **Claudie Pierlot** and **Oblique**, at numbers 4 and 19, for reasonably priced fashion separates. For those tin can-lid hoop earrings, check out **Scooter**, at 10, rue de Turbigo, which also sells ethnic-inspired, funky sportswear for men and women.

Gourmet Equipment

A five-minute walk away are two establishments for aspiring Cordon Bleu chefs: **A. Simon**, 36, rue Etienne-Marcel, and **E. Dehillerin**, 18–20, rue Coquillière, both vestiges of the days when Les Halles was the city's wholesale market. A. Simon is a family-run business that has been providing restaurateurs and hoteliers with kitchen and dining equipment since 1884. A vast selection of traditional French table items can be purchased here at almost wholesale prices, from the utilitarian stainless steel-and-glass salt, pepper, and mustard-pot sets found on any Paris bistro table to a select choice of Baccarat crystal at a 10 percent saving; also available are Villeroy and Boch porcelain dinner services at 25 to 30 percent less than in Paris department stores. Across the street, at 48, rue Mont-martre, is A. Simon's kitchenware annex, where a stock of Sabatier and Tour Eiffel knives and Cousances and Le Creuset enameled cast-iron cookware await the would-be kitchen wizard. Pots and pans are E. Dehillerin's specialty: shallow cast-iron crêpe pans, weighty steel frying pans, and the shiny copper pots of French country kitchens.

Le Marais

East of Les Halles, tucked in among the jumble of crooked streets, kosher delicatessens, and splendid, half-hidden 17th-century town houses that make up Paris's historic Marais quarter, are a number of unusual boutiques that reflect the *quartier*'s unique character. Stroll along the rue Vieille-du-Temple, a street that has retained much of its old flavor. At number 26 is a delightful shop, **A La Bonne Renommée**, which sells spools of embroidered ribbons, reams of calico, and everything that could be concocted from a combination of the two. At number 47, the smell of fresh-ground coffee wafts from **La Maison des Colonies**, a gleaming emporium of imported coffees and exotic teas. At number 58, **Jean Lapierre** offers 18th-century carved-stone mantelpieces and blackened 17th-century iron coats of arms ferreted out from demolished buildings. **Casta Diva**, next door, is an opera and ballet lover's nirvana: a red-carpeted, red-walled boutique specializing in records, books, magazines, and photographs on opera and dance.

On the adjoining rue des Francs-Bourgeois (which got its name, "the men who pay no tax," in 1332 from the almshouses built there for the poor) is **Janine Kaganski**, at number 41, a mother-and-daughter shop selling 18th-and 19th-century polychrome wood furniture from Bavaria and Alsace painted in gay patterns of flowers and fruit. At number 45, **A l'Image du Grenier sur l'Eau** has over a million vintage postcards for sale—from kitsch to classic Fifties film stills—lovingly amassed by the shop's owner over ten years. **S.M.A.R.T.**, at 22, rue des Francs-Bourgeois, offers artisan-made, hand-painted ceramic tiles for bathrooms, kitchens, or floors—including *tommettes,* the clay-colored floor tiles so popular in Provençal homes. S.M.A.R.T. will also produce tiles of your own design and ship them. At number 17, the idiosyncratic **Jean-Pierre de Castro** sells silver-plated cutlery by the kilo, as well as unusual jewelry fashioned from old knives, forks, and spoons. On **l'Harlequin**'s dusty, floor-to-ceiling shelves at number 13 is a dazzling display of beautiful antique glassware. **Carnavalette**, at number 2, is the place to find the ideal Marais souvenir: an old bound copy of Madame de Sévigné's *Lettres,* which chronicles the day-to-day events of aristocratic 17th-century Paris, or an 18th-century *gravure* of the nearby place des Vosges.

This square, the oldest in Paris, awaits you at the end of the rue des Francs-Bourgeois. Once the scene of elegant courtly parades, raucous festivities, and duels at dawn, the place des Vosges—known in the days of Henri IV as the place Royale—is today a quiet park where children play and old men reminisce on sun-warmed benches. Rows of antique shops, restaurants, and boutiques have sprung up under its stone arcades; don't miss Franco-Italian fashion designer **Popy Moreni**'s clean, geometric, three-floor shopping space at number 13; **Jardin de Flore**'s limited reeditions of antique illuminated manuscripts, and exquisite copies of 17th-century Venetian globes at number 24; and **Librairie Sylvie**'s jumble of books and handmade marionettes at number 26, place des Vosges. Music lovers and those who admire fine workmanship no matter what the craft should stop by **André Bissonet**, just off the north end of the place des Vosges, at 6, rue du Pas-de-la-Mule. Here, in an erstwhile butcher's shop (decor intact), the erstwhile butcher himself, André Bissonet, restores and sells an intriguing array of antique musical instruments: an 18th-century viola, a 17th-century harp, even carnival hurdy-gurdies that have seen better days. (For players of string instruments, **François Perrin's Lutherie**, at 4, rue Elzévir, also in the Marais near the Picasso Museum, buys, restores, and sells violins, violas, harps, and other old string instruments.)

In the past few years the Marais area has become the domain of many of Paris's young, trendy designers. **Azzedine Alaïa's** body-hugging fashions can be found behind a discreet, dark-green lacquered door at 17, rue du Parc-Royal; **Patrick Kelly**'s humorous, sexy clothes at 6, rue du Parc-Royal; **Lolita Lempicka,** who dresses many fashionable Parisians in witty, feminine dresses and suits at 15, rue Pavée; and **Alain Mikli**'s avant-garde eyewear at 1, rue des Rosiers.

La Bastille

A ten-minute walk eastward from the Marais is La Bastille, an area that has emerged in recent years as the latest candidate for the title of "the insider's Paris." The controversial Bastille Opera House opens here in 1989 for the Bicentennial of the French Revolution, and the *quartier*— once a humble working-man's neighborhood—has been sprucing itself up for the expected onslaught of attention. La Bastille now offers a lively selection of offbeat restaurants and gutsy P.M. fare for those in search of alternative forms of entertainment. It's no wonder, then, that **Pom Pin Disques**, a record shop specializing in hard-to-find collector's records from reggae to funk, New Wave to Edith Piaf, at 17, rue de Lappe, stays open sometimes until 2:00 A.M. By day this area, rife with artists' ateliers and galleries, welcomes art amateurs and collectors in search of Eighties alternatives to Picasso and Gauguin. **Galerie Bastille**, at 28, rue de Lappe, which opened in 1979 when La Bastille was still primarily a furniture wholesalers' district, now includes John Cage, Ruffin Cooper, and Michel Faublée among its stable of artists. **Franka Berndt Bastille** devotes its high-ceilinged, cool white-and-gray gallery to constructivist works at 11, rue St-Sabin; and **Lavigne Bastille**, 27, rue de Charonne, to new painters and sculptors.

A space the size of a walk-in closet, **Duelle** (21, rue Daval) displays another kind of art, avant-garde jewelry: papier-mâché bangles in paintbox colors, resin earrings translucent as uncut stones. "I'm on the lookout for pieces with humor," says the lavender-locked owner, Claude Deilhes. Farther down, where the rue Daval becomes the rue de Lappe at number 26, is a shop devoted to the gentleman's game of billiards, **Le Maître Billiardier**, supplying the well-equipped game room with everything from cushioned bistro stools and antique mechanical pianos to the ubiquitous billiard table—from a run-of-the-mill 45,000 franc model to a 450,000 franc claw-footed Charles X antique.

Rue du Pont Louis-Philippe

Double back from the place des Vosges (south on rue de Birague off the *place,* then a right turn) on the rue St-Antoine and trace the rue François-Miron to where the rue du Pont Louis-Philippe leads to the Seine. Number 68, rue François-Miron, is the 17th-century mansion built for Anne of Austria's first woman of the bedchamber in return for her having initiated the 16-year-old Louis XIV in the delights of love. Although fallen into disrepair, the Hôtel de Beauvais is still majestic; its curving, carved-stone staircase is magnificent.

Facing each other on the rue du Pont Louis-Philippe are two boutiques for lovers of beautiful stationery: **Papier +**, at 9, rue du Pont Louis-Philippe, sells heavy handmade papers, fabric-covered notebooks, and photo albums; and **Mélodies Graphiques**, which carries Florence's famous "Il Papiro" stationery items made from marbleized endpapers, at 10, rue du Pont Louis-Philippe.

The Left Bank

Just across the bridge lies the Latin Quarter. Although this Medieval *quartier* retains its status as the intellectual heart of Paris—the Sorbonne, the Beaux-Arts, and the *grandes écoles* are all located here—Sartre's table at Aux Deux Magots is likely to have been usurped by a weary shopper, so dense is the concentration of boutiques in this area. The maze of streets nearest the river—the rues des St-Pères, de Lille, du Bac, de Verneuil, Bonaparte, and Jacob—are a paradise for the antique and art gallery aficionado.

On the river itself, not far from the Ecole des Beaux-Arts, at 3, quai Voltaire, is **Sennelier**, an art-supply shop smelling of chalk and linseed oil that Paris painters have known and loved since 1887. Just behind it, **Robert Montagut** (15, rue de Lille) is a perfectly reconstructed antique Provençal *pharmacie,* whose gleaming niches hold antique apothecary jars of all shapes and sizes on sale for 1,500 to 150,000 francs! Lovers of ballet will find their spiritual home at 14, rue de Beaune, where **La Danse** offers books, magazines, prints, and watercolors on dance, even Degas-esque bronze statuettes of graceful ballerinas. **La Rose des Vents**, at 25, rue de Beaune, sells old ship's wheels, antique brass compasses, and other ancient nautical treasures. **Le Temps Libre**, down the adjacent rue de Verneuil at number 9, offers children's playthings rescued from attic trunks: odd bits and pieces of porcelain dolls and their houses, long-forgotten board games, and other juvenile oddities. Next door is **Parsua**, at number 7, where Parisian housewives bring their heirloom carpets to be restored, and where you can pick up a length of 18th-century Lyonnaise silk for an appropriately princely sum.

The rue Bonaparte leads to the place St-Germain-des-Prés and its surrounding cluster of bookshops. At 31, rue Bonaparte, the **Librairie Bonaparte**'s window is lined with books in many languages on *le spectacle*—ballet, theater, modern dance. The imposing **Librairie F. De Nobele**, next door at number 35, specializes in old tomes and literature related to *les beaux-arts:* fashion, art, design. On the corner of the rue de l'Abbaye and the rue Bonaparte is **Le Divan**, whose name (the kind of tongue-in-cheek reference French wags delight in) means "the couch," indicating this bookseller's bent for psychology and philosophy titles. And sandwiched between the celebrated Parisian cafés Aux Deux Magots and Café de Flore is the no less celebrated **La Hune** bookstore, at 170, boulevard St-Germain, with its wealth of "humanist" books—on poetry, photography, architecture, literature, music, theater, cinema, and fashion. **Elve**, the best place in Paris for old prints, is up the boulevard at 213 *bis.* And those on the trail of Hemingway's Paris shouldn't miss **Shakespeare and Company**, near St-Germain's place Maubert at 37, rue de la Bûcherie. Although today's bookshop is not the Sylvia Beach original, American expatriate owner George Whitman has faithfully reproduced its namesake's bohemian literary atmosphere, offering poetry readings, upstairs beds for itinerant writers, and a mixed bag of English, American, German, and other European-language books.

On the other side of the boulevard St-Germain are hundreds of boutiques. The rues Bonaparte, du Four, St-Sulpice, de Rennes, du Cherche-Midi, and de Sèvres are all showcases for the latest Paris fashions and accessories. A determined shopper short on time can start at the rue du Four and, following the rue de Grenelle westward, encounter an inexhaustible lineup of clothing and shoe shops: Sonia Rykiel, Prada, Boutique D'Emilia, Charles Kammer, Chacok, Christian Aujard, Stéphane Kélian, Miss Maud, Odile Lancon, Claude Montana, Tokio Kumagai, Cerruti 1881, Kenzo, and more. Another St-Germain street attracting a concentration of interesting, affordable fashions is the tiny rue du Pré-aux-Clercs, which begins life just off the boulevard St-Germain as the rue St-Guillaume. Boutiques that sell inexpensive ready-to-wear clothes are Philippe Ben, Irié, Michel Klein, Corinne Sarrut (an ex-Cacharel designer), and Peggy Roche.

Other unique boutiques in the area are **Soleiado**, at 78, rue de Seine, which carries reams of colorful Provençal-print cotton fabrics and a selection of household and fashion accessories made from them; and **Beauté Divine**, 40, rue St-Sulpice, a reconstructed 19th-century store specializing in beauty and bathroom items from bygone eras: Baccarat crystal perfume flacons, ivory nail buffers, antique porcelain pitchers. Another plush turn-of-the-century replica, **Diners en Ville**, at 89, rue du Bac, focuses once again on that popular French preoccupation—dining—but with an emphasis on originality and color. Here are the amusing trompe l'oeil plates the French call *barbotines,* vintage glass and crystal carafes, and refurbished antique paisley tablecloths. Candles to decorate a dining table can be found at **Point à la Ligne** (177, boulevard St-Germain), which sells imaginative fantasy candles: silvery oysters to pile up, as the French do with the real thing, on holiday tables; wax raspberry tarts and watermelon slices. For the kind of lingerie trousseaux are made of, visit **Sabbia Rosa**, 71–73, rue des St-Pères, where sumptuous, lace-trimmed satin nightgowns, camisoles, and sexy tap pants hang in languid pastel rows against lacquered gray walls. For sheer delight, visit **Madeleine Gély**, 218, boulevard St-Germain, a doll-sized boutique—crammed full of umbrellas, parasols, and canes both old and new—that has been in existence since 1834. Gély will still custom-make umbrellas for too-short or too-tall clients in their choice of fabric, and with wood, ivory, or horn handles. For a crash course in traditional Parisian pint-sized elegance, there's **Bon Point** (67, rue de l'Université; furniture at 7, rue de Solférino), which sells the same navy blue coats, gray flannel shorts, and smocked dresses French children have been wearing for decades.

Avenue Montaigne

Coming full circle, you will return to the Right Bank by the Pont d'Alma near the Eiffel Tower and, via the avenue Montaigne, enter a world of unbridled luxury. If your stay in Paris has still not converted you to the gilded life, a stroll down the tree-lined avenue Montaigne will. This is home of much of the haute couture—Dior, Emanuel Ungaro, Guy Laroche, Hanae Mori, with Yves St-Laurent and Givenchy nearby. The crimson-awninged, geranium-banked Hôtel Plaza Athénée presides over the avenue like a serene princess. Its Relais Plaza grill room, with a Thirties ocean-liner decor, is the lunchtime spot for Paris's *beau monde,* and postprandial shoppers need only turn left outside the door to check out Italian jeweler **Bulgari**'s latest creations (27, avenue Montaigne). **Valentino** is just next door, at 17–19, avenue Montaigne; **Chanel**, at 42, avenue Montaigne. **Louis Vuitton**'s newest boutique is at number 54. At number 16 is an extraordinary accessory shop, **Isabel Canovas**, a cobalt-blue, mirrored Ali Baba's cave filled with artisan-made jewel-studded cuffs and earrings, brilliant silk-velour shawls, and embroidered bags. **D. Porthault**, at 18, avenue Montaigne, is where house-proud Parisians buy their bed, bath, and table linens; the store's fresh, floral-print cotton percale bedsheets are world-famous. **Parfums Caron**, at 34, avenue Montaigne, dispenses Caron perfume classics from gold-etched Baccarat crystal urns. **Puiforcat**, next door to **Fouquet**'s 65-year-old sweet shop at 22, rue François-Ier, sells re-edited versions of the streamlined sterling silver table settings and tea and coffee services that made them so popular in Paris in the 1930s. Behind the Plaza Athénée, on the narrow rue de la Renaissance (number 3), is **Hobbs**, a shop specializing in quality Scottish cashmere sweaters in a rainbow of 50 colors and a variety of amusing patterns. And for the best classic man's fedora, there is the 1887-vintage **Motsch Fils**, a five-minute walk away at 42, avenue George-V, a hat shop that also sells Panamas, Homburgs, and hunting caps and boasts one of the most beautiful wood-paneled storefronts in town.

Although the nearby avenue des Champs-Elysées still inspires awe, the recent profusion of pinball halls, flashy cinemas, and fast-food establishments has robbed it of its past standing as Paris's ultimate chic shopping avenue. The fragrance house **Guerlain**, at 68, avenue des Champs-Elysées, is a staunch exception: Its marble walls and atmosphere of hallowed *luxe* make it an obligatory stop for those on the trail of typically Parisian, Old World luxury.

Flea Markets

No shopping devotee could leave Paris without a pilgrimage to one of Paris's *marchés aux puces,* or flea markets: the **Porte de Montreuil** for antique clothing and odd bits of furniture; the **Porte de Vanves** for bric-a-brac; and especially the **Porte de Clignancourt** for more than 3,000 stands selling everything from used clothing to gilded Regency furniture. For serious antique hunters, the Porte de Clignancourt's 200-stand Marché Biron sells what is generally considered to be the *crème de la crème* of the *puces:* old silver- and bronze-framed mirrors, Limoges porcelain, and other treasures. The Marché St-Paul is a scavenger's dream, offering a mixed bag of chipped crockery, old dentist's mirrors, brass candlesticks; and for fabulous vintage Louis Vuitton steamer trunks (complete with old hotel stickers) don't miss Stand 232, Allée 6, of the

Port de Clignancourt's Marché Paul-Bert. Be warned: Although most flea market shopkeepers will arrange shipping of these sometimes unwieldly souvenirs back home, depending on weight and choice of air mail or slow boat, transport could almost double the price of your Paris "bargain."

—Charla Carter

DAY TRIPS FROM PARIS
ILE DE FRANCE

By Edward Hernstadt

Based in Paris since 1984, Edward Hernstadt writes on culture and business. He is the former Managing Editor of the English-language Paris city magazine Passion.

Paris is a city of marvels: old and new, secular and religious, vulgar and exquisite. It is also a modern city and can be as congested and wearying as any other urban center. However, Paris need not be limited by the bounds of the Périphérique: Its 23 centuries of continuous occupation has left a mark on the surrounding countryside. Today the Ile-de-France, as the region is called, encompasses Paris as well as the towns and castles around it: the Medieval villages that traded with or provided a refuge from the city; the religious centers that spread the word of God among peasants; the hunting lodges and country houses of France's kings; and the grand châteaux of the French nobility.

A day in the country can provide both an enriching perspective on the history of Paris as well as the opportunity to spend some time in beautiful valleys and forests. Many destinations are accessible by train; others are best reached by car. Most are on the tourist-bus circuit, but this option could prove constricting, as organized tours are often crowded and don't allow time for dawdling. Finally, all these destinations are within 90 minutes of the capital, and any one will provide a pleasant day's outing.

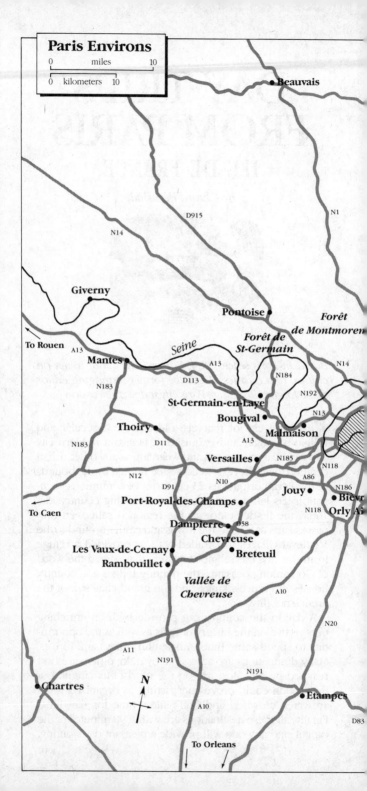

Paris Environs

0   miles   10

0   kilometers   10

• Beauvais

D915

N14

N1

• Giverny

Pontoise •

Forêt de Montmoren

To Rouen ←

Seine

A13

Mantes •

Forêt de St-Germain

A13

N184

N14

N183

D113

N192

St-Germain-en-Laye

N13

Thoiry •

D11

Bougival •

A13

Malmaison •

N183

A13

N185

N118

Versailles •

A86

N12

N10

Jouy •

N186

D91

• Bièvr

To Caen ←

Port-Royal-des-Champs •

Orly Ai

N118

Dampierre •

D58

Chevreuse •

Les Vaux-de-Cernay •

• Breteuil

Rambouillet •

Vallée de Chevreuse

A10

N20

A11

N191

N191

• Chartres

N

A10

• Etampes

To Orleans ↓

D83

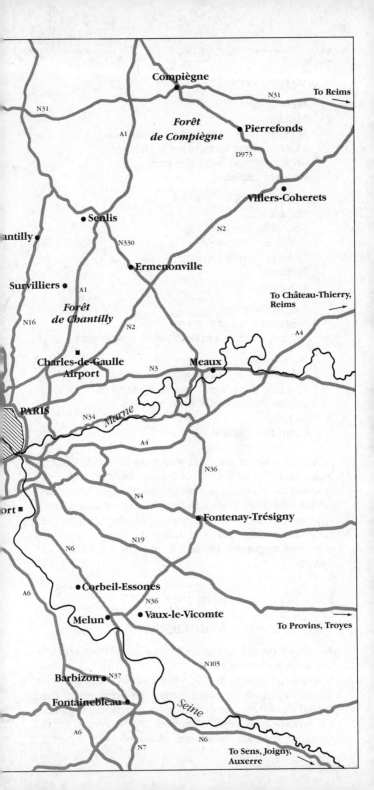

MAJOR INTEREST

West of Paris
Malmaison
St-Germain-en-Laye castle and gardens
Monet's home and garden at Giverny
Thoiry château and game-park
Chartres cathedral

South of Paris
Versailles
Fondation Cartier
Vallée de Chevreuse
Château Vaux-le-Vicomte
Barbizon
Fontainebleau

East of Paris
Medieval town of Provins
Château-Thierry and Bois Belleau battle sites

North of Paris
Pierrefonds and Compiègne Châteaux
Fôret de Compiègne Armistice site
Roman and Medieval town of Senlis
Chantilly
Beauvais cathedral

A brief note on the chief players in the Ile-de-France: François I, the Ramses II of France, built or added to many of the châteaux mentioned, as did Louis XIV. Louis Le Vau and Jules Hardouin-Mansart were the predominant architects of the 17th century; Charles Le Brun, the preeminent decorator; and André Le Nôtre is arguably the most important landscape artist in the history of France.

WEST
Malmaison

For Napoléon and Joséphine, Malmaison was first a house and then a place of refuge. Joséphine bought the pretty brownstone château in 1799 when Napoléon was still first consul, and in it he could escape the pressures of the capital and unwind in the frivolous, completely unpolitical atmosphere Joséphine created. The house and large, beautiful grounds, which are threaded with peaceful paths and rose gardens, remained Joséphine's favorite retreat after Napoléon proclaimed himself emperor in 1804. After their divorce in 1809 she retired to a life of relative calm at Malmaison, living out her days where she had been most content.

Napoléon, too, returned to Malmaison: first in triumph after his escape from Elba in 1814, and then during the darkness that followed his defeat at Waterloo and final exile on Saint Helena island. Napoléon III also owned the château, and it was his wife, the Empress Eugénie, who conceived the idea of the museum, devoted to Napoléon and Joséphine, that eventually opened here in 1906.

The château itself, built in a lovely, symmetrical style, is fairly modest as châteaux go. Because it is small, a satisfying tour can be completed in 45 minutes, allowing ample time to wander through the now-reduced, but still appealing, park and gardens. The most interesting rooms are the council chamber, which is dressed up to look like a campaign tent and is where Napoléon plotted some of his early victories; the library, a heavy, serious room packed with tomes on the art of war; and Joséphine's bedroom, an over-decorated boudoir that reveals both her vanity—it's full of mirrors, toiletries, and jewels—and her extravagance—receipts for some of her luxurious gowns are on display. Occasionally, international horse shows are held on the grounds.

Cafés are well hidden in the town of Malmaison, but a fine lunch can be had at the **Pavillon Joséphine**, a onetime hunting lodge that has recently been converted into a pretty, elegant, and rather expensive restaurant. (191, avenue Napoléon-Bonaparte.) If you drive from Malmaison to St-Germain-en-Laye, there is a fine restaurant in Bougival that is well worth a stop. **Le Camélia**, home of Jean Delaveyne, a founding father of contemporary French cooking, is a rustic spot with wood beams, lace curtains, and a satisfying, subtle cuisine. (7, quai Georges-Clemenceau.) You can reach Malmaison in about 20 minutes on the RER line A; go in the direction of St-Germain-en-Laye and get off at Reuil-Malmaison. By car, leave Paris on the N 13.

Saint-Germain-en-Laye

St-Germain-en-Laye's long and involved history is reflected in the château itself. Originally constructed in the

12th century by Louis VI, who thought the commanding hillside site would be ideal for repelling unwelcome guests, the castle was destroyed, rebuilt, and added to for the next five centuries. The Black Prince, Edward, eradicated the original structure (except for the chapel erected by pious Saint Louis in 1230) during the Hundred Years War, and Charles V rebuilt it in 1368. François I redesigned the castle in 1539, retaining only Charles's dungeon and the chapel. In addition to the kings of France, inhabitants have included Mary Queen of Scots, before her brief marriage to François II, and James II, after England's 1688 Glorious Revolution. Louis XIII died here, and Henri II, Charles IX, and Louis XIV were born here.

In its current (and probably final) form, the castle is shaped like an unbalanced pentagon. None of the rooms is open to the public; most are storerooms and offices for the château's **Musée des Antiquités Nationales**, created by Napoléon III to house prehistoric, Celtic, and Gallo-Roman artifacts. Saint Louis's chapel, almost certainly built for the king by Pierre of Montreuil, who later constructed the Sainte Chapelle in Paris, is open to the public; the bare stone church offers only the beauty of its solemn architecture. The castle's plain stone façade is enlivened by red brick windows and chimneys, and massive stone urns punctuate the balustrade that runs along the roof.

The gardens are the main reason to visit St-Germain. Enter through the gate to the left of the château's main door. A large graveled space opens to lawns, flower beds, and what was once a fountain. To the right, carefully laid-out paths wind through chestnut trees to the more dramatic English garden, where curving paths swing through well-tended lawns (lawns that you actually can sit on, something of a rarity in France) and more flowers. Le Nôtre's masterful Grande Terrasse (about a mile and a half long) borders the ridge. It is one of the most famous promenades in the Paris area and overlooks a steep hill and the Seine. In 1547 a duel was fought on the parterre that splits the two gardens and leads to the terrasse, one of the last of these contests appealing to God's judgment. The formidable La Chataigneraie, one of Europe's great swordsmen, fell to a certain Monsieur Jarnac, who employed a devious Italian ruse and switched his sword to his left hand to administer the killing blow. La Chataigneraie might have survived, but he was so infuriated by defeat that he refused all help and perished on the spot.

The town of St-Germain-en-Laye is quite pretty and merits a stroll. The square facing the château (where the RER exits, and over a convenient underground parking lot) shows signs of the 1980s with its videocassette outlet, a "western" shop, and an American restaurant. Some of the town's other restaurants, however, offer a more sophisticated cuisine. The **Pavillon Henri IV**, at 21, rue Thiers, is the most historic of these: Louis XIV was anointed here, and Alexandre Dumas wrote both *The Three Musketeers* and *The Count of Monte Cristo* while he was a guest. Unfortunately, because of the terrace's fantastic view, it is overpriced. Instead, you might want to try the classic **Cazaudehore**, with its pretty garden (1, avenue du Président-Kennedy) or the more modern **Le 7 Rue des Coches**, on the street of the same name.

To the north lies the vast and beautiful **Forêt de St-Germain**, which is a superb setting for afternoon hikes and picnics. Several interesting buildings are in the forest, including a former hunting lodge rebuilt by Jules Hardouin-Mansart that now serves as a retreat for members of the Legion of Honor. You can reach St-Germain-en-Laye in half an hour via the RER, line A; by car, take N 13 from Paris.

Giverny

Everybody comes here. In the last weeks of autumn, just before the house and gardens close for the winter and after most of the flowers have died, the parking lot at Giverny is still full of tour buses. Even if you shy away from tourists and prefer to discover sites in relative solitude, Giverny is worth visiting.

Claude Monet made Giverny his home from 1883 until his death in 1926. Monet's son left the house to the Académie des Beaux-Arts, which opened the restored property in 1980 as a museum. An enormous amount of work went into replanting the gardens to re-create the palette of colors Monet himself created and then depicted in hundreds of paintings.

His studio—called the Nymphéas—and house have also been renovated; the former is filled with reproductions of his most famous works as well as period photographs that show him in the studio during the teens, when the originals of those same works hung on the walls. The house is a more typical museum. The artist's collection of Japanese prints and more reproductions of his works are hung as the originals were when he lived here, and the rooms look as if Monet had just stepped out to go to the bakery. This exactitude is almost spooky, but the house is actually quite lovely and the kitchen looks, today, like something out of a "do-your-own-rustic-look" catalog.

The raison d'être of the place, though, is the garden: a glorious, floral candy shop in shades of blue, pink, yellow, red, white, and purple. Monet moved through it like a bearded Druid, addressing the flowers by name and coaxing even more brilliant colors from them. Across the road is the water garden, complete with the Japanese footbridge, weeping willows, and the water lilies that inspired so many canvases (including the huge works in New York's Museum of Modern Art and Paris's Orangerie).

Because of the number of tourists, picnics are not allowed, although plenty of suitable spots can be found in the Vernon woods behind Giverny. A tearoom and flower shop share the museum's parking lot, and there are several cafés in Vernon; none, however, is really special. You can reach Giverny in about 90 minutes via SNCF from Paris St-Lazare to Vernon; from the station it's a brisk walk of about 4 km (2.5 miles) along the Seine to the house. Taxis or buses are available. By car, take A 13 from Paris. The museum is open from April 1 through October 31.

Thoiry

The Vicomtesse de la Panouse (information director for the Château Thoiry and wife of the Comte de la Panouse, whose family has owned and lived in the house since 1564), is quick to call Thoiry a marvel, and she is right. The Château Thoiry is an astounding mixture of history, kitsch, aggressive marketing, physical beauty, and unrestrained imagination.

Where to start? In the African game park, where camels, zebras, bears, lions, and other creatures cavort on the château's ancestral grounds? Or perhaps in the museum of gastronomy, where those whose eyes are bigger than their stomachs can view replicas of extraordinary desserts? Or maybe in the reptile house, where snakes and alligators slither in the dark cellars beneath the parterre designed by Le Nôtre. The park also has a pond filled with swans and flamingos, a "city of apes," a children's zoo, and assorted tigers, wolves, and hyenas.

There are tours of the house and its treasures, which include a Sèvres pitcher and basin once used by Marie Antoinette and a small, fascinating archives museum, filled with four centuries of correspondence between the Comtes de la Panouse and various prominent international figures. The whole place is actually quite amazing, and the spectacle of the visitors, many of whom are children, is as interesting as the château. The stables have been converted into a restaurant, tearoom, and conference facility. Classical concerts (with dinner) are offered year-round, most frequently during the summer. The game park is open from April through October. You can reach Château Thoiry from Paris in an hour by car, via A 13, then D 11.

Chartres

Today's visitors to Chartres see the same awesome vista that has greeted pilgrims for centuries: a towering cathedral rising from rough fields, emerging slowly as you near the town and gradually dominating the horizon and countryside. The area has remained as proportionally rural as it was when Edward III laid siege to the town during the Hundred Years War, or when the Prince of Condé attacked it as a center of Catholicism. It is something of a mystery why so magnificent a cathedral, one that set the standard for Gothic cathedrals all over Europe, sprang up so far from any major commercial center.

Chartres has always been a place of worship and a place of pilgrimage. Churches have stood on the same spot as the cathedral for more than two millennia. Before the birth of Christ, Chartres was a center of Druid rites. When the Romans conquered the Gauls, they built a temple to the Earth Mother here. With the rise of Christianity, the icon of this goddess was interpreted as a prefigure of the Virgin Mary, renamed Notre-Dame-sous-Terre, and consigned to a special chapel. Today, the ninth-century **chapel of Notre-Dame-sous-Terre** is still devoted to this pagan idol. Worship of her successor, the Virgin, has long been strong at Chartres: Charles the Bald saw fit to give the church the sacred Tunic of the Virgin in 876.

The first Christian church dates from the fourth century, and successive buildings have been erected and subsequently destroyed by raiders. The present **cathedral of Chartres** was initiated by the bishop of Chartres, Saint Fulbert, after a fire destroyed an earlier structure in 1020. The upper church, crypt, and ambulatory were completed by 1134, when another fire damaged the façade and bell tower. Work then began on the north tower, the impressively Gothic one on the left. It is known as the "new bell tower," although it is actually older than the Romanesque south tower, because its spire wasn't erected until 1506. In 1194 yet another fire destroyed the entire church except for the façade, towers, and crypt. This tragedy rocked the international Christian community, because by then the pilgrimage to the Virgin of Chartres was one of Europe's most popular pastimes.

An appeal was made, and local church authorities pledged their tithes for three years, while the area's burghers responded in kind. A spirit approaching frenzy fueled the reconstruction of the cathedral, and most work was finished by 1220 in a record 26 years; the outside towers were completed 40 years after that. The relative speed with which it was built gives the church a rare coherence of style: It was rebuilt from a single set of plans, and construction was directed by a single, unknown master builder.

If you regard the cathedral from the place Jean Moulin (named after the World War II French Resistance leader who was murdered by Klaus Barbie), the striking main towers will draw your eye first. The towers were begun and completed within ten years of each other (north: 1134–1150; south: 1144–1160), yet the architectural styles are startlingly dissimilar. The north tower is a superb example of Early Gothic techniques; it is built in two stories and has an intricately carved tower. The south tower is unique; its pious severity and balanced proportions contrast dramatically with the sweeping lines of its mate. It is considered one of the world's great examples of the Romanesque style.

The cathedral is famous for its sensitively carved figures. The main, or "royal," portal dates from the mid-12th century, and it is another masterpiece of Romanesque art. Originally designed as the narthex of an 11th-century structure, it later became the main entrance to the cathedral. In hundreds of naïve sculpted figures, the three doors depict Christ's birth, ascension, and Second Coming. To the right is the story of Mary, culminating in the birth of Christ; to the left is the story of his betrayal and ascension; the central door is devoted to the Day of Judgment. The figures are carved with an unusual intensity of expression and a wealth of charm.

The south portal, on the right side of the cathedral, is a fascinating mix of sobriety and gore. At the center of the central bay, a peaceful Christ oversees acts of charity, with the 12 Apostles ranged behind him, each bearing the instrument of his martyrdom (or, in the case of Saint Peter, his symbol). The left bay depicts a host of martyrs in the act of being slaughtered; note particularly John the Baptist being beheaded and Saint Blasius being flayed alive. In the right bay saints performing acts of charity and miracles are depicted.

Inside the cathedral two features are particularly outstanding: the beautiful choir screen, consisting of sculptures depicting the lives of Mary and Christ; and the sublime stained-glass windows. These windows, built in the 12th and 13th centuries (with some later additions), are among the finest in France. Their astounding "Chartres blue" is an intense, luminous shade that has never been reproduced.

While the town surrounding the cathedral has grown greatly over the centuries, it is still quite charming. The **stained-glass museum** (just behind the cathedral) is worth visiting, as are several of the smaller churches in town. A stroll through the *quartier*'s streets is also very pleasant. A number of cafés and tearooms surround the cathedral. You can reach Chartres by car via A 11 and then N 10, or by train from the Gare Montparnasse, in a little more than an hour. You'll be able to see the cathedral from the train station.

SOUTH
Versailles

Versailles is as much a conviction as a château—the conviction that "bigger *is* better" and that "moral ostentatiousness *is* more tasteful." The château is enormous, imposing, imperial, and rock solid, still conveying Louis XIV's message of French omnipotence and his own glory. This is not an unpopular message with the French, who have long struggled to reconcile their longings for monarchal pomp with their pride in the egalitarianism that led to the Revolution. Not surprisingly, the Revolution struck especially hard at Versailles, symbol of the crown's arrogance, and the château has not been a royal residence since Louis XVI was beheaded in 1793.

Versailles is one of the few châteaux in France without a long history of renovations; it was built in two phases, which together turned a sleepy farm town into the apogee of 17th-century luxury. Louis XIII enjoyed hunting and built a small lodge here in 1624. Seven years later he bought the entire town and had the architect Le Roy construct a small château. When his son Louis XIV assumed power in 1661, his first step was to outdo mere mortals like Nicolas Fouquet, whose château at Vaux-le-Vicomte he envied. Louis instructed the architect Louis Le Vau, the decorator and painter Charles Le Brun, and the landscape artist André Le Nôtre to build the grandest, most opulent, most expensive château in France. Louis had another motive: He sought to distance himself and his courtiers from the dangerous political intrigues of Paris.

Work began slowly. Le Vau extended the existing château while Le Brun commanded an army of artisans and Le Nôtre planned and laid out the gardens. In 1678 the architect Jules Hardouin-Mansart took over the design of the château, which occupied him for the next 30 years; during this time he added the two monumental wings and the Galerie des Glaces (Hall of Mirrors). The artists faced enormous logistical problems: The palace and grounds had to be large enough for the entire court—which then comprised some 6,000 people—yet everything had to be decorated and landscaped down to the last cornice and begonia. The numbers that resulted from these requirements are almost too vast to have parallels in everyday life: 36,000 workers were involved; some 3,000 trees were moved in and out of hothouses every season; 1,400 fountains were constructed; and a vast reservoir was built to store water diverted from the river Seine. Although work continued until the end of Louis XIV's reign, the château was in use by 1663.

A heavy cast-iron gate opens onto a large courtyard flanked by two buildings that once housed government ministers. A monumental statue of Louis XIV stands in the Cour Royale (Royal Courtyard), and behind it the Cour de Marbre (Marble Courtyard), constructed from squares of white and black marble, is surrounded by the original château, whose façade is by Hardouin-Mansart. The ministerial wings break up the building's nearly half-mile-long façade. From behind, however, the perspective is striking, with the center of the château set forward to add relief. Statues and vases break the line of the balustrade, and statues of Apollo and Diana cap the central, royal, section.

The apartments are relentlessly luxurious. Marble, gilt, moldings, and frescoes are everywhere. It is difficult to understand how any business requiring concentration could have been accomplished in the palace—the sheer mass and ostentation of the decor is distracting. It is also superbly crafted: Le Brun's team of talented artisans executed his designs with precision and grace. The château may be pretentious, but its decor is the most completely realized of the period.

The chapel, a sumptuous study in white and gold with intricately carved pillars, is one of Hardouin-Mansart's masterpieces. On the second floor, the Grands Appartements, where Louis XIV and his court ate, played pool, and listened to concerts, consists of a series of thematic rooms: of Mars, Venus, Mercury, and Diana; the throne room belongs to Apollo. The staggering **Galerie des Glaces** was in its heyday a ballroom. The mirrored walls reflect Le Brun's ceiling frescoes, which describe Louis XIV's early years, and were designed to show off the wildly expensive costumes of the ladies and courtiers of the court.

Two events that determined the contours of Europe also took place in the Galerie des Glaces. In 1871, after soundly defeating France in a war engineered by Otto von Bismarck to unify the various states of Germany under the leadership of Prussia, Germany announced the German Empire to the world from Versailles. This new Germany also seized the disputed territories of Alsace-Lorraine at the war's end, thus heightening to the tensions that resulted in World War I. And it was here in 1919 that the defeated Germany signed the Treaty of Versailles, the unbalanced document that led indirectly to World War II.

After the heavy luxury of the apartments, which were designed primarily to celebrate the importance and majesty of Louis XIV, the planned beauty of the gardens is a delight. Directly behind the château, steps lead down to two large basins. To the right a parterre wends through flower beds to the Neptune fountain, the largest at Versailles. To the left more gardens lead to the Orangerie, where hundreds of orange and palm trees bloom every summer. Paths lined with statues thread through the garden, which is divided into areas where different geometric patterns dominate. A long central path, the Tapis Vert (green carpet), runs from the center of the château perpendicular to the Grand Canal. It, too, is bounded with statues, and the view of the château façade over gardens and fountains is stunning. The Grand Canal extends to the horizon from the perspective of the château and, as it is laid out on an east/west axis, the setting sun is reflected in it. The gardens behind the Trianons are more rustic; designed in the country style favored in the 18th century, the winding paths are almost emblematically pastoral and lovely to walk along.

Other buildings occupy the grounds, notably the Grand Trianon, the Petit Trianon, and the Hameau. Louis XIV first constructed the Trianon de Porcelain, where he escaped the court with his first mistress, Madame de Montespan. By the time he replaced her with Madame de Maintenon (whom he secretly married after the death of his wife), the porcelain had decayed. So Louis built the **Trianon de Marbre**. It was used principally for receptions by succeeding kings, and in 1962 Charles de Gaulle restored it as a residence for visiting dignitaries. Among those who have enjoyed the royal lodgings are Queen Elizabeth II of England and Leonid Brezhnev. Today it is furnished in the 19th-century style of the Restoration kings. Highlights include the malachite room, which takes its name from the malachite vases and candelabra Czar Alexander gave Napoléon at Tilsit, and the *galerie,* filled with crystal and paintings of the gardens as they looked in the 17th century.

Louis XV commissioned the **Petit Trianon,** and it was a favorite retreat of Louis XVI and Marie-Antoinette. This frivolous queen also built the **Hameau,** a charming, idealized reproduction of what the wealthy imagined farms to be, and she loved to pretend to herd sheep there. Ironically, she was near the Hameau when a messenger brought word that rebellious Parisians were marching on Versailles. Marie-Antoinette fled and never saw the château again. Napoléon III's empress, Eugénie, who sympathized with her, collected many of the late queen's possessions in a little museum there.

Other important sites are spread through Versailles, including the Menus-Plaisirs at 22, avenue de Paris, and the **Salle du Jeu de Paume,** just off the rue Satory (not open for visits). When the Estates-General (the three estates of the clergy, the nobility, and the bourgeoisie) convened in 1789, they met in a makeshift structure erected in the courtyard of the building housing the King's entertainers, the *menus-plaisirs*. Many of the dramatic events that led to the first stage of the French Revolution took place here, including the drafting of the constitution and the Declaration of the Rights of Man. And the Estates-General took the famous "Tennis Court Oath," vowing not to disband until a constitution was accepted by the crown, during the three days they met at the Salle du Jeu de Paume.

Versailles is home to the **Trois Marches**, one of the Ile-de-France's most respected restaurants; a luxurious meal in this very refined house may be a perfect conclusion to a day spent drinking in the opulence of the château. (3, rue Colbert; Tel: 39-50-13-24.) Many other cafés and small restaurants in Versailles offer fine meals. Or you might bring a picnic; it would be hard to find a more inviting picnic spot than the gardens at Versailles. You can reach Versailles, less than an hour from Paris, by car via A 13, N 186, or N 10, or by RER (the château is visible from the station).

Fondation Cartier

In the mid-18th century Baron C. P. Oberkampf opened a cloth factory that eventually employed 1,200 Indian workers and manufactured an instantly popular fabric that put both the Baron and Jouy-en-Josas on the map. Louis XVI gave him a title; Napoléon approved of his methods; and all of France clamored for his *toile de Jouy*. Today the Fondation Cartier, opened in 1984, has taken over Oberkampf's estate and shows works of very contemporary art in an imaginative way on grounds that the Baron's wife landscaped in the English fashion.

You can circumnavigate the park in less than an hour, and this gives you time to gawk at such permanent works as Arman's monumental *Long Term Parking,* a gigantic upright rectangle at least 200 feet tall of wrecked cars and poured concrete. On summer days the wide lawns are perfect for lolling and tanning or reading a book. There's a bookstore, a library, and a very high-tech café, furnished by Pascal Mourgue, that's open on weekends for lunch. The Fondation is 6 km (3.5 miles) from Versailles. You can reach it from Paris via train from the Gare d'Austerlitz to Jouy-en-Josas; on the RER, take direction Sceaux to Massy-Palaiseau; change there for direction Versailles-Chantiers and go to Jouy, where signs point toward the park. By car follow N 118 to Bièvres, then drive west to Jouy.

Vallée de Chevreuse

The Vallée de Chevreuse is actually a series of valleys in 25,000 acres of forest, with the quaint town of Chevreuse at its center, all of it less than an hour from Paris. The only way to see the valley properly is by car or bicycle (and those who favor the latter should be warned that the terrain is extremely hilly). The region is justly famous for its great beauty: narrow roads lined with cypress trees winding through lush forests, streams, and small farms; solemn ruins of Medieval castles and abbeys; and several very lovely châteaux.

By car follow D 91 from Versailles to **Port-Royal-des-Champs**, where you can wander through the ruins of the once famous abbey. Port-Royal reached its peak under the leadership of Mother Angelica, an austere nun who became mother superior in 1602 at the age of 11 and subsequently reformed the practices of the abbey. Later that century the abbey became the center of Jansenism in France and as such was notorious in Catholic circles. Blaise Pascal's sister Jacqueline entered the convent there in 1651; Pascal himself was a defender of Jansenism. Louis XIV decided to close the troublesome abbey in the late 17th century, and a crew of king's musketeers evicted the remaining nuns (who were denounced by the sisters at the Paris Port-Royal Abbey) in a final expulsion some 30 years later.

From Port-Royal follow D 195 east to D 95, and turn off onto N 306 east to Chevreuse. After a walk around Chevreuse and a visit to the beautiful little Hôtel de Ville, continue on D 58 to Dampierre.

The château at **Dampierre** is one of the most charming in the region. Designed by Hardouin-Mansart in 1683 for the Duc de Luynes, it is smaller than most châteaux and set at the lowest point of a gentle valley so that the wooded hills behind dominate and frame the house. The Luynes family still lives here and has opened one of the two wings to tourists. The 45-minute tour (with no chance of escape) provides some insight into how the nobility actually lived. The rooms still exhibit the exquisite workmanship (especially of the wood panels and parquet floors) and classic design of the era. Part of the house was redecorated in the desperately overdone Third Empire style—all trompe l'oeil murals and gilt.

Le Nôtre designed the gardens and park, which are lovely to walk in; stroll through the formal parterre, feed the ducks and swans in the pond or the carp in the moat, and then hike in the woods behind the opulent château, so comfortably placed in this tranquil setting. The stables have been transformed into a fine restaurant (oddly decorated with hundreds of mounted animal trophies, many from Africa). The tiny village offers a few unexceptional restaurants, all within a five-minute walk. The house is open from April to mid-October.

One kilometer (about half a mile) to the south is the **Parc Floral**. Its extensive gardens were created to feature the seasonal brilliance of hundreds of flowers, especially summer roses—there are 150 varieties, including some very old strains.

From Dampierre continue south on D 91 to the **Vaux de Cernay**, a beautiful valley in which you can walk beneath ancient oaks along the Vau stream, past a small waterfall, and perhaps have a picnic beside the Cernay pond. From here, N 306 north leads to **Breteuil**, another very pretty château.

The Breteuil family is one of the oldest in France and has occupied the château since its construction in 1550. An early Norman ancestor, Raoul, possessed a voice so powerful that he once set the entire French army to flight with it. His son William was a compatriot of William the Conqueror, who gave the family its title after the Battle of Hastings. The château was constructed in the simple, but imposing, architectural style of Henri IV. Set on a small promontory in the middle of a park, it presents a formal grandeur to motorists driving up the tree-lined avenue. The building of tan stone and red brick houses an excellent collection of period furniture and china, as well as the family's own wax museum, which depicts famous visitors and momentous events in the life of the Breteuils.

From the Vaux de Cernay continue straight up D 24 to N 10, or take any one of the tiny, badly marked roads and explore the countryside more thoroughly. This beautiful drive makes for a pleasant day's outing.

Vaux-le-Vicomte

Vaux-le-Vicomte is arguably the most perfectly realized château in France. Nicolas Fouquet, minister of finance under Louis XIV, built the first completely planned château and gardens in the country as a monument to his exalted position in France. When Cardinal Jules Mazarin, then first minister, appointed Fouquet finance minister in 1653, the royal treasury had just declared bankruptcy and defaulted on its enormous debts. Fouquet was given the daunting task of reestablishing the crown as a viable credit risk. He proved himself to be one of the most brilliant, able, and loyal ministers ever to work for the crown, yet ambition (his own and that of others), naïveté, and carelessness led him to disaster.

Fouquet's fall came in 1661 after years of conspicuous spending, and a period of courting a woman Louis XIV wanted for himself. He held a ball for the King that gave the word ostentation new meaning: His guests ate off 6,000 silver plates, served themselves from 432 large silver platters, and wiped their mouths with 1,440 linen napkins. Louis was so enraged and envious—he'd just been forced to sell his own silver to pay for one of his many wars—that he wanted to arrest Fouquet on the spot. Remembering his obligations as a guest, though, he graciously refrained and 19 days later sent a musketeer to haul the unfortunate minister off to jail. Before his fall, though, Fouquet gave Le Vau, Le Brun, and Le Nôtre—the architect, decorator, and landscaper responsible for the château at Versailles—the opportunity to design a landscape from scratch, a very rare opportunity indeed, by buying a 1,500-acre expanse on which he changed the course of one river and razed three small towns to make the land "virgin" again. The three artists, the greatest of the era, responded by fashioning a house of matchless grace, an interior that is exquisitely Baroque yet not disturbingly flamboyant, and a park that is the first, and finest, example of the "French" garden.

Le Vau's design is ornate yet harmonious. The Grand Salon, which was unfinished at the time of Fouquet's arrest and remains so today, gives the clearest evidence of his plan's clarity and coherence. Le Brun's paintings, frescoes, trompe l'oeil murals, and cameos are better than anything he did at Versailles. They fill the house's magnificent rooms, as do period furnishings, tapestries, and rush mats (which were widely used in the 17th century, when carpets were still rare). The château is so impeccably preserved it warrants the one- to two-hour tour, and you can easily spend an entire day in the incomparable gardens. That the estate still exists is due to some quick thinking by the Comtesse during the Revolution—she convinced the arts commission to declare it a national monument. In 1875 Alfred Sommier, a sugar magnate and patron of the arts, purchased Vaux after it had been abandoned and restored it.

You can reach the château, an hour from Paris, via A 6 to Melun, then D 215 east. At the sign, turn down a long, elegant, tree-lined avenue and prepare yourself for the sight of this stunning château on the right. There is a café in the refurbished stables. Candlelight tours are available Saturday evenings at 8:30, June through September, and elaborate fountain shows are held on the second and last Saturdays of each month.

For devotees of sublime cooking, **A la Côte St-Jacques**, a luxurious and expensive hotel and restaurant in Joigny about 50 km (30 miles) south on A 6, has one of the finest, most innovative kitchens in France.

Barbizon

Barbizon is a small, quaint town between Vaux-le-Vicomte and Fontainebleau that is best known as the home of most of France's great mid-18th-century artists. Painters like Théodore Rousseau, Jean-François Millet, and Jean-Baptiste-Camille Corot would pack palettes and canvases and head into the idyllic countryside around the town to paint. Charles Baudelaire attacked the Barbizon School, as this group of painters was called, for merely reproducing landscapes; he wrote, "In this silly cult of nature unpurified, unexplained by imagination, I see the evident signs of a general decline."

The surrounding country is still quiet and very lovely, as is the Fontainebleau forest, which bounds one side of the town and offers marvelous walks. On Barbizon's single main street, the rue Grande, are the former studios, now museums, of Millet and Rousseau; both artists are buried in the local cemetery. The Auberge de Ganne, where the artists used to congregate to eat, drink coffee, and chat with neighbors George Sand and the Goncourt brothers, is also a museum. If you want to stay the night, the **Bas-Bréau** is a beautifully restored farmhouse right in town, with rustic, comfortable, well-appointed, and expensive rooms and an excellent restaurant. Leaders of the Seven Nations Economic Group stayed at the inn during their 1984 summit. There are also several other pleasant restaurants in the town. You can reach Barbizon via A 6 or by train from the Gare de Lyon to Melun and then by taxi.

Fontainebleau

Fontainebleau has been a royal residence since the 12th century. It was originally a hunting lodge. Louis VI and Saint Louis came here to hunt stag and boar in the magnificent forests, and Philippe le Bel died here after a fall from his horse. While the town center is a bit run-down in places, there are many beautiful houses, and France's most prestigious business school, INSEAD, is located here. The main post office and town hall are quite pretty, and there are some noteworthy buildings along the rue Grande, as well as a variety of bakers and *traiteurs* (gussied-up delis, basically).

The main entrance to Fontainebleau proper is from the place de Charles de Gaulle, where a gilded cast-iron gate leads to the Cour de Cheval Blanc, or the Cour des Adieux, so named because it was from this courtyard that Napoléon left for exile on Elba. The courtyard is divided into four squares of perfectly manicured lawn bounded by sculpted pine trees. The minister's wing on the left is one of a pair constructed by Gilles Le Breton, whom François I commissioned to rebuild the palace after he pulled down most of an earlier Medieval castle. Its mate was destroyed by Louis XV, who had Jacques-Ange Gabriel build the existing wing. The opposing styles make for a good comparison between 16th- and 18th-century architecture.

The central building, which was expanded by every king from François I to Louis XV, is dominated by the handsome Fer-à-Cheval staircase (a Louis XIII production); it was from this majestic podium that Napoléon, the general who decimated two generations of French youth, bade farewell to his beloved guards, asking them always to look after France: "Her happiness," he said, "is my only thought." While emperor, Napoléon lived at Fontainebleau and not Versailles, where the ghost of the Sun King challenged his position in the pantheon of great Frenchmen. The Louis XV wing (on the left) now houses the Napoléon Museum, which displays uniforms and mementos from the reigns of both Napoléons (closed Tuesdays).

The palace itself is a remarkable monument to the incredible luxury with which the kings of France surrounded themselves. The sheer richness of the decor, which covers every imaginable surface in three centuries' worth of decorative styles, stirs even the most jaded. It is less coherent than Versailles because it is the work of master artists from several centuries, but its variety gives a sense of the wastefulness of French rulers who destroyed superbly crafted rooms and buildings not because they were in need of repair (though this was sometimes the case) but merely because they were unfashionable.

Highlights of the *grands appartements,* which you can visit without a guide, include the fantastically decorated **Chapelle de la Ste-Trinité**, every surface of which is covered with gilt, paint, or carved wood, and the gorgeous **Galerie de François I**. This long hall is made entirely of carved wood, stucco, and painted panels—a style that was created by the Italian decorator Francesco Primaticcio (known in France as Le Primatice), who belonged to the Fontainebleau School. The enormous **Salle de Bal**, with its 40-foot ceiling and wood panels and its exquisite view of the Cour de la Fontaine, and pond and park behind, is undoubtedly the most spectacular room in the palace. Built by François I and completed by Henri II, the room is bathed in light and inspires visions of gowned women swinging on the arms of bewigged men with a cavalry of servants attending to their needs, in a space awash with music, splendor, and an indomitable belief in the future. The less fascinating *petits appartements* and those of Pope Pius VII are open only to guided tours.

The large, pretty park and English garden are well tended and perfect for an afternoon's stroll. Together, they offer a choice of atmospheres: wild (the garden, with its sweeping paths and inviting lawns) or ordered (the carefully geometric park). The Etang des Carpes is filled with large carp; feeding them and watching them splash for the food is a favorite Fontainebleau sport. Pony rides around the parterre are popular among younger visitors to the palace. The place de Charles de Gaulle is ringed with generally reliable cafés and restaurants.

You can reach Fontainebleau in an hour by train from the Gare d'Austerlitz. By car, go via A 6. If you drive do not, at any cost, miss a ride through the magnificent woods. There is also horseback riding along paths once reserved for kings, as well as mushroom picking (in season) and beautiful walks. Picnic spots abound. The forest is also home to the world's premier "boulder garden"—groups of rocks that climbers use to train or improve their technique.

EAST

Provins

The Medieval city of Provins, southeast of Paris, rises from the surrounding fields like a quiet acknowledgment of the earth's long memory. The first records of the village date from the ninth century. In 1120 it provided refuge for Pierre Abélard, one of history's best-known and most unfortunate lovers. His audacious philosophical positions were unpopular with the authorities, and he was forced to flee Paris, leaving the heartbroken Héloïse behind. By the end of the 12th century, Henri le Libéral had solidified the commercial importance of the town, and for 200 years the annual fair of Provins was a major marketplace for merchants from Italy, Germany, Holland, Marseille, and Spain. In the mid-13th century, Edmund of Lancaster, whose coat of arms included the then-rare red rose, was sovereign of Provins, and today the town is famous for the radiant rose gardens below the old ramparts.

Enter the Ville Haute, the Medieval town, through the Porte St-Jean, a 12th-century gate in the 30-foot-thick ramparts. The reinforcements, archers' slits, and walkways along the top of the wall are visible from the gate. Follow the road to the central square, the place du Châtel, where an ancient well is covered by an iron gate. The **Tour de César**, a 12th-century dungeon, still dominates Provins; climb the stairs for a terrific view of the entire region. The **church of St-Quiriace**, behind the tower, dates from 1140, but it wasn't completed until the 17th century. It is in use today, and the sound of hymns on a Sunday does much to emphasize the tangible Medieval quality of this town. Beautiful restored houses, barely visible over their protective walls, share the rest of the hill. The French filmmaker Louis Malle thought the town so unspoiled he used it for the setting of his award-winning 1987 film *Au Revoir les Enfants*.

Several cafés bound the place du Châtel, the best of which is **Au Vieux Grandpère**. You can reach Provins in a little over an hour by car on N 19 from Paris; exit at the Porte de Bercy.

Château-Thierry and Bois Belleau

The château that gave the small town of Château-Thierry its name once commanded the plain of the river Marne from the hill that rises steeply behind the town. The original castle was built in the early eighth century and gradually fell into ruin. Château-Thierry is most interesting for its involvement in the Napoléonic Wars and both world wars. One major battle was fought below its walls, and the town was invaded and liberated three times.

The English came first, conquering the city during the Hundred Years War. Joan of Arc then liberated it in 1429. In 1814 Napoléon fought off the Russo-Prussian army commanded by Marshal Gebhard von Blücher. Then, in 1914, the German army held Château-Thierry for a week before they were forced to retreat. During the last great offensive of the war, the Germans took it once again, and this time held it for almost two months. American troops helped push back the "pocket" of German forces that had penetrated deep into the Marne valley. Both times the attacking army sacked the town.

Château-Thierry has another, more pacific, claim to fame: Jean de la Fontaine, the poet and writer of fairy tales and fables, was born here in 1621. His house is open to the public, and some mementos are on display.

A few kilometers to the north, three monuments commemorate the battles that raged during World War I in the expanse of the **Bois Belleau**. The Aisne-Marne memorial rests on a knoll overlooking the river Marne. A small road winds through placid fields to the massive structure, a symbol of "friendship and cooperation between French and American armies." Families now picnic on the lawns that sweep down from the memorial to the hill's edge, and men play *boules* on the gravel paths. French youths play Frisbee or, more appropriately, baseball instead of their fathers' traditional game. The only impediment to the view of the valley are the chemical plants along the river.

The American cemetery is about a thousand feet away, at the end of a tree-lined avenue. Impeccably tended lawns and rosebushes guard the footpath to the memorial chapel, on whose walls are inscribed the names of every American who fell in the vicious battle for the wooded hill behind the cemetery. The neat rows of crosses and stars extend far into the distance, marking the graves of the 2,288 men who died here. The graveyard's beautiful situation, flush against a hill and under towering trees, is tranquil and a powerful reminder of the war that was supposed to end all wars, the war that so many Americans have forgotten.

Within eyesight a second, almost unmarked cemetery honors the dead of the army that lost. The 8,625 Germans who fell in the battle are buried in a tiny graveyard. Only a small plaque on one of the two stone buildings that front it marks their presence. The ironies of World War I, which abounded during the conflict, are clearly still with us.

You can reach Château-Thierry, a little over an hour from Paris, by car via A 4, and south on D 1. The drives throughout the Marne valley area are often very pretty.

NORTH
Pierrefonds and Compiègne

Set on a commanding hilltop on the southeastern edge of the vast and beautiful Forêt de Compiègne, Pierrefonds is one of the most striking châteaux in France. If you drive here from the north or west you'll wind through small valleys and, quite suddenly, see the majestic towers and battlements of this restored Medieval fortress rise before you. The château was first erected in the 12th century, then was rebuilt by Louis d'Orléans, brother of King Charles VI and regent of France during the Hundred Years War until his assassination by Jean the Fearless in 1407. Eventually the château became the property of François d'Estrées. When he imprudently and unsuccessfully rebelled against the crown, Pierrefonds was partially pulled down and fell into a state of such disrepair that Napoléon was able to buy it in 1813 for only 3,000 francs.

In 1857 Napoléon III, taken with the feudal magnificence of the setting, decided to rebuild the house at great expense, a move that was criticized by those who felt the fortress's *ancien-régime* roots should remain buried. Eugène-Emmanuel Viollet-le-Duc, who directed the restoration, based his design on the walls that remained, and re-created the massive Medieval structure.

And an overwhelming edifice it is. Huge, compelling, secure, and self-contained, the castle controls the entire valley by virtue of its strategic location and its imposing appearance. In design, it is true to 14th-century principles: Only a handful of windows open to the outside, and the eight towers and many archers' slits determine the fortress's interaction with the world. The towers are crowned by (and named after) massive sculptures of King Arthur, Charlemagne, Alexander the Great, and Caesar, among others. The castle entrance crosses a drawbridge and passes through 15-foot-thick walls into a central courtyard. The chapel and the Escalier d'Honneur in the courtyard are both Second Empire; the rest of the buildings and interior, however, are reasonably accurate reproductions of the original castle. The tour is well worthwhile.

The town itself is rather small; a pretty lake with rowboats for rent is at its center. A pleasant café offers lakeside lunches. You can reach Pierrefonds by car in a little over a hour via N 973 from Compiègne, or from Paris by SNCF to Compiègne and then by taxi or bus.

Compiègne has been a favorite residence of French kings since Charles the Bald established a palace here in 873. By the 13th century a bustling town had grown around the castle, and in 1374 Charles V built a château on the site of the current palace. It was at Compiègne, in 1430, that Joan of Arc's inspired military career came to an end when a risky sortie across the river to scout English positions resulted in her capture. Louis XIV, dissatisfied with the accommodations at Compiègne, made additions to the château, claiming that, "At Versailles I live like a king, at Fontainebleau like a prince, and at Compiègne like a peasant." His great-grandson, Louis XV (Louis XIV reigned for 72 years, outliving both his son and grandson), completely rebuilt and enlarged the palace so that his entire court could live here in comfort. Jacques-Ange Gabriel, who built the *hôtels particuliers* facing the place de la Concorde in Paris, oversaw the work and is responsible for the château's classical lines. Wars and revolutions repeatedly interrupted construction—Louis XVI made only one visit to the partially renovated château before the exigencies of the incipient revolution called him back to Paris—and it wasn't until Napoléon I chose it as his imperial residence that the building was finally finished.

Today, Gabriel's imposing façade, which resembles, not coincidentally, many government offices in Paris, faces the pretty place du Palais. The north wing has been given over to an automobile museum, and the rooms at the end of the courtyard, including the Salle des Gardes and the striking Escalier d'Honneur, now house changing art exhibits. Entrance to the château's most beautiful apartments, those of Napoléon and Marie-Antoinette, is just to the right. Guided tours only are offered, but the history of the château is so convoluted that this is a welcome requirement. As you might expect, the rooms are luxuriously decorated in a grand mix of royal styles. The Salon des Cartes contains a fascinating collection of maps of the forest, which Louis XV used to consult for his hunts. The apartments have a stellar view of the well-tended, flower-filled gardens and the park, which extends to the forest.

The church of St-Jacques, where Joan of Arc took communion on the day of her capture, dates from the 13th century and has a very pretty bell tower. The Hôtel de Ville, a good example of Gothic architecture, boasts one of the country's oldest clocks. The town itself is lovely, and a brief stroll through its older sections, with their Tudor buildings and ancient walls, is in order. Many small restaurants and cafés, as well as expensive shops, dot the streets; a good omelette *paysan* is available at the charming **Café des Lombards**, on the street of the same name.

The **Forêt de Compiègne** is another example of the wild beauty of the terrain around Paris. Nobles once hunted game in the forest, and today it's a beautiful area through which to drive or bicycle: Ruins of abbeys, stands of ancient oak trees, and hills offering spectacular views of the forest abound. One particularly fascinating stop is the **Clairière de l'Armistice**, a clearing where on November 10, 1918, Marshal Foch and representatives of the Allied armies and Germany met in the marshal's train car to sign the armistice ending World War I. The site of the rolling battle headquarters has been preserved as a monument to the French military, and a giant statue of Foch, the savior of France, stands here. The display makes no mention of a second armistice signed on this spot: In 1940 Adolf Hitler ordered that occupied France capitulate here in the original train car in which Germany surrendered at the end of World War I. The train car was destroyed in 1945 near Berlin, perhaps to prevent yet another surrender in the Compiègne forest; the car on display now is a reproduction.

You can reach Compiègne by car via A 1 from the Porte de la Villette in Paris, or by SNCF from the Gare du Nord. From the station, cross the bridge into town, turn left at the church of St-Jacques, and continue to the château. A tourist office is located in the Hôtel de Ville.

Senlis

Senlis was a major town in Gallo-Roman times—a first-century amphitheater and the old walls still mark the Roman presence—and, for centuries, was the religious center of France, a bishop's seat until 1901. Today it is a well-preserved little hilltop village with cobblestone streets that echo with history. It was at a gathering of feudal lords in Senlis castle in 987 that the Archbishop of Rheims proposed Hugh Capet as the first king of France.

What makes Senlis special and worth visiting is the palpable sense of antiquity and continuity the town exudes. It's very small, and often crowded, so a few hours are enough to explore the entire village. Wandering through the ancient streets, under Roman gates and past Tudor houses, you might share the sharp and certain feeling that four centuries ago people traversed the same stone paths past the same buildings.

The cathedral of Notre-Dame here was begun ten years before Paris's Notre-Dame and is an excellent example of both early Gothic architecture and the evolution of the style through succeeding centuries. The cathedral is built on a smaller scale than its more famous namesake. Another church in Senlis, the St-Pierre, exhibits both Roman and Gothic design. The town's château is rather modest (perhaps that explains why kings preferred the comforts of Compiègne; Henri IV was the last to stay here), as is the park behind it. The grounds also include a hunting museum.

Jean-Jacques Rousseau lived at Ermenonville, 13 km (8 miles) southeast. You can take beautiful walks through the woods the philosopher loved (once the grounds of the château in which he died) and across the odd Mer de Sable—a vast expanse of sand.

You can reach Senlis by car, a hour from Paris, via A 1, or by SNCF from the Gare du Nord. From the station, walk up the hill to the old town. Ermenonville can be reached by car via N 330 from Senlis.

Chantilly

Chantilly has one of the prettiest settings of any château in France: It rises almost ethereally from the tranquil lagoon that encircles it. Built and rebuilt in fits and starts over seven centuries, the château has seen more than its share of sieges and sacks, and the history of its occupying families is particularly interesting. In the 14th century, Pierre d'Orgemont, then chancellor of France, purchased the property and erected a fortified castle on the ruins of a 10th-century château that had been destroyed in the Jacquerie (the peasant uprising of 1358).

The Montmorency family bought the estate in 1450, and Anne (a man) demolished the fortress and built what is now called the Petit Château—then separated from the main structure by a moat. As high constable of France, Anne was a man of tremendous wealth, energy, and influence—he was a friend and adviser to every king from Louis XII to Charles IX. At home, he was responsible for enlarging the grounds of the estate, as well as building the elegant square that fronts the château. He died at 70 in a battle with Protestants at St-Denis, and it took five stab wounds, two slashes to the head, and a bullet to the spine to kill him.

Henri II was the last Montmorency to rule at Chantilly; he was beheaded at Toulouse for leading a revolt against Cardinal Richelieu. In the tradition of his ancestor, it took 18 wounds, including five bullets, to convince Henri to surrender. In his will, Henri left the cardinal the two Michelangelo *Slaves* that now stand in the Louvre. Henri II de Bourbon-Condé, who married Montmorency's daughter, inherited the estate, and the era of the Condés, the longest-lasting and best-known residents of Chantilly, began. The Grand Condé, Louis II, hired André Le Nôtre to design the renowned gardens and began yet another renovation of the château according to plans by Hardouin-Mansart. The vain Sun King, Louis XIV, was said to be envious of Henri's fountains, which were deemed the most beautiful in France. Henri made Chantilly a center of the arts in France by attracting writers like Jean-Baptiste Molière, Jean de la Fontaine, and Jean Racine. Henri's chef, Vatel, also elevated cooking to the highest levels, at least in terms of artistic temperament: Distraught that a batch of fish hadn't arrived in time to feed Louis XIV and the 5,000 courtiers who accompanied him everywhere, Vatel fell on his sword. Later it was discovered that the fish had, in fact, come. The Château d'Enghien, the last main addition to the house, was built in 1767 for the presumptive heir, the Duc d'Enghien.

The estate was pillaged during the Revolution; the family fled and later died off. Today the castle owes its excellent condition to the Duc d'Aumale, fourth son of King Louis-Philippe. A Bourbon like the Condé family, he devoted himself to completing the restoration begun by his predecessor and repairing the ravages of both time and revolution. Aumale died without an heir and left both the castle and his collections to the Institut de France.

The château, now the **Musée Condé**, houses little of the art that belonged to the family; the bulk of the collection was scattered during the Revolution. The interior is extraordinarily rich, with marble staircases, glowing parquet floors, and ornate tapestries. The museum's collections include a gorgeous 15th-century illuminated manuscript (the Limbourg brothers' famous *Très Riches Heures du Duc de Berry*) and works by Botticelli and Raphael. In the Petit Château a long gallery is lined with canvases depicting the military victories of Grand Condé. The grounds are also outstanding; their manicured lawns and immaculate paths invite leisurely strolls through the relaxed English garden, the wooded park, or along the great canal.

The monumental Grandes Ecuries (stables) across the road from the château constitute one of the best examples of 18th-century architecture in the country and is also open to visitors. The stables are still in use and house a horse museum, complete with dressage demonstrations and Shetland ponies. Race horses that train on the track are also stabled here. The stables and tracks have made Chantilly one of France's equestrian centers, and every June the **Prix de Diane**, the most important race in the world for three-year-old fillies, attracts the most beautiful of beautiful people to the track, their antique Rolls-Royces, colorful summer suits, and formal top hats filling the infield.

The attractive old château village, which is entered through a large gate connected to the stables, has many restaurants and cafés; one of the best is the **Relais Condé** opposite the racetrack at 42, avenue du Maréchal-Joffre. The Captainerie du Château in the castle's courtyard is a pleasant tearoom. You can reach Chantilly by car in less than an hour from Paris via A 1 to Survilliers, and then D 924A, or by SNCF from the Gare du Nord. From the station, you can take a bus or walk up the avenue du Maréchal-Joffre, turn right on the rue du Connétable, and continue on to the château. The walk takes about 30 minutes.

Beauvais

Much of Beauvais was destroyed by savage bombing during World War II, but the mammoth cathedral—the world's tallest—survived. Actually the town has an appealingly stormy history. The Romans dismantled it first after defeating the army of Gaul. In 1429 the Bishop of

Beauvais was run out of town by honest burghers for supporting England in the Hundred Years War; one year later he condemned Joan of Arc to the stake. In 1472 Beauvais got its own heroine, when Joan of the Hatchet rallied the town to repulse an invasion by the Duke of Burgundy. While her townspeople ran along the city walls, panicked by the huge army facing them, Joan took a hatchet to an enemy soldier carrying a banner and hacked him off the wall. The townspeople, inspired by her courage, regrouped and resisted the attack.

The **cathedral of St-Pierre**, which dominates the town (and is in fact the only real reason to visit Beauvais, now a modern provincial outpost laden with neon and roadwork), is a marvel. Some call it a miracle that defies the law of gravity; others call it an act of extreme hubris. The plans were so grandiose and costly that when construction was abandoned four centuries after work began in 1225, the building still had no towers. As it turned out, the structure could not support the weight of the stonework, and by 1284 the cathedral had begun to collapse. Only constant patchwork and jerry-rigging kept it—and keeps it—standing.

Inside, however, the audaciousness of the design seems justified. Majestic, sweeping columns support a ceiling that seems to be miles away, reaching perhaps to heaven. The stained-glass windows are sublime, especially the southern rose window, depicting the creation, and the windows along the north transept, showing ten Sybils, who face ten prophets on the south wall.

From Paris you can reach Beauvais, about 90 minutes away, by car via N 1 from the Porte de la Villette, or by SNCF from the Gare du Nord. From the station, take a bus or taxi. Or, make the long walk up the avenue de la République, then right onto the rue Malherbe; the cathedral will become visible on your left.

ACCOMMODATIONS REFERENCE

▶ **A la Côte St-Jacques.** 14, faubourg de Paris, 89300 **Joigny**. Tel: 86-62-09-70; Telex: 801458; in U.S., (212) 696-1323.

▶ **Bas-Bréau.** 22, rue Grande, 77630 **Barbizon**. Tel: 60-66-40-05; Telex: 690953; in U.S., (212) 696-1323.

CHAMPAGNE

By Georgia I. Hesse

Champagne, which is known to bubble with the world's finest sparkling wines, is just as rich in historical and artistic interest. The region extends from Reims, in the north, to Troyes, the ancient capital, in the south. West to east, it stretches from about Condé-en-Brie (site of a 16th-century château built for Louis de Bourbon-Vendôme) to the valley of the Marne and Alsace-Lorraine (the subject of the next chapter).

Many of Champagne's superb churches and cathedrals are covered in this chapter. To them enthusiasts of architecture can add Laon (Notre-Dame) and Soissons (abbey of St-Jean-des-Vignes and the cathedral of St-Gervais et St-Protais, of which only the transept and choir survived the battles of 1914–1918). Both towns are west of Champagne proper. You will also want to visit **Clairvaux**, near Bar-sur-Aube east of Troyes, with its 12th-century abbey of St-Bernard, one of the most important sites in the history of Christianity. The remains now serve as the local prison. Champagne well remembers World Wars I and II—especially the battlefields along the Marne, although other major battlefields and memorials are westward in Picardie and along the Somme.

Men of letters born in the region (they usually left for Paris as soon as possible) include Chrétien de Troyes, the author of several classic *chansons de geste;* the historian Jean de Joinville; and the fabulist Jean de la Fontaine. Jean Baptiste Colbert, born in Reims, toted about Louis XIV's account sheets in a small black bag called a *bougette*—thus giving a grateful world the word budget.

MAJOR INTEREST

Reims
Cathedral of Notre-Dame
Basilica of St-Remi
The Champagne *caves*
Musée St-Denis
Musée et Hôtel Le Vergeur
Palais de Tau

Epernay
The Champagne *caves*
Abbey of Hautvillers

Troyes
Cathedral of St-Pierre et St-Paul
Musée d'Art Moderne
The ancient *Quartier St-Jean*

Elsewhere in Champagne
Cathedral of St-Etienne in Châlons-sur-Marne
Basilica of Notre-Dame in L'Epine
Colombey-les-Deux-Eglises

Reims

Reims is a light and lively city, seat of a busy university, full of bustling sidewalk cafés and smart shops. Most outdoor action swirls along rue de Vesles and the elongated place Drouet-d'Erlon. Geographically, the cathedral of Notre-Dame is the heart of the city; from it most notable attractions are within walking distance, with the exception of the Basilique St-Remi to the south and the Champagne *caves* to the north and the southeast.

The most important contemporary attraction is the Salle de Guerre, in a technical college near the railroad station. This is where General Dwight D. Eisenhower headquartered during World War II and where, on May 7, 1945, he accepted the German surrender.

Surrounded by cafés and stores ranging from chic to utilitarian, the **Hôtel Paix** is the best headquarters for in-town meandering. A classic, old structure that has been renovated, it offers pleasant and comfortable rooms, a locally respected restaurant, and a bar that is a meeting place for local businessmen as well as visitors.

Reims was capital of Gallic Belgium when Paris was a mere village, and its wines were so renowned that in A.D.

92 the Roman Emperor Dimitian ordered that the vines be destroyed because they were unfair competition to those of Italy. Reims owes its name to a Gallic tribe, the Rèmes, but its Roman conquerors dubbed it Durocortorum and made it capital of Lower Belgium. From the third to the eighth century Reims served as a veritable cradle of saints, producing at least 13, including Remi (properly, Remigius; A.D. 440–533). On Christmas Day of 496, Remi (of the propitious Champagne name) baptized Clovis, the Merovingian king of the Franks, on the site where the cathedral of Notre-Dame stands today. Later kings wished to be consecrated in the same place and with the same oil as was Clovis, and according to history 37 of them were, down to Charles X in 1825. The coronation that has received the most press was that of Charles VII in 1329—thanks largely to Joan of Arc.

Notre-Dame, smack in the center of Reims and reached via rue Libergier if you are coming from the direction of Paris, is justly renowned for its 13th-century stained-glass windows and its superbly sculpted façade, which is best seen and photographed just before twilight, when a dying sun enlivens its tympanum, gables, pinnacles, and statue-filled portals. First admire the entry portals; then take a turn to the left to view the colossal angel sculptures. The harmony of the cathedral's interior is striking; it is highlighted by the previously mentioned 13th-century stained glass, which was restored after World War I.

Just to the right as you face the cathedral is the **Palais du Tau**, originally a residence of the king and later the archbishopric. Within are admirable statues from the Champagne school, among them a fine *Coronation of the Virgin* and a *Goliath*. Among the many worthwhile tapestries, that honoring the life and times of Great King Clovis stands out. The two rooms that constitute the treasury of the Palais du Tau are rich in holy ornaments, talismans, chalices, reliquaries, and objects used in the ceremony of Holy Communion.

Across the *place* and east of Notre-Dame, the **Musée St-Denis** houses in several huge rooms statues, tapestries, grisaille paintings, and French canvases from the 17th to the 20th centuries, including several notable Impressionist works.

Amble up rue de Vesle, turn left at place Royale (a harmonious Louis XVI square), then right at place du Forum and you will reach the **Musée et Hôtel le Vergeur**, home of artworks, furniture, engravings, and the like dating from the days of Old Reims. One room is devoted to some splendid Dürer engravings.

On the southern edge of town, in a quarter called Fléchambault, stands the **basilica of St-Remi**, built in the 11th and 12th centuries atop the saint's tomb. It has endured several reconstructions necessitated by war and remains the repository of many early archbishops and kings of France; the tomb of Remi is behind the altar, which was reworked in 1847.

One of the 19 restaurants in all France rating three stars in the hallowed pages of the *Michelin Rouge* is the elegant **Boyer "les Crayères,"** in a parklike setting near the basilica of St-Remi on boulevard Vasnier. In an impressive, refined mansion, Boyer also offers 15 very expensive bedrooms and one suite suited to diners who may wish to collapse in style after their Cognac. Filet of duck is a specialty.

Many travellers quite naturally gravitate to Reims to pay their respects to—and, perhaps more honestly, to consume—one of civilization's great creations, Champagne. The Gauls were cultivating vines on these hillsides when the Romans arrived, and the early Church encouraged the viticulture that brought cash into monastery coffers. In the 16th century two kings otherwise opposed to each other (François I and Henry VIII) granted their royal favors to the production of this remarkable beverage. Until the time of the little monk Dom Pérignon (1638–1715), Champagne was a still wine, although a naturally perky one. Under the careful tutelege of Pérignon, Champagne began to bubble as it does today (*see* the abbey of Hautvillers, below). Wars and revolutions have come and gone; Champagne remains one of the great French traditions—and foreign-currency producers.

The **Champagne** *caves* of the Champs de Mars quarter (north of the city's center) and the slopes of St-Niçaise hill (to the southeast of town) began as chalk quarries from which the Romans extracted hewn blocks used for building the town and its fortifications. Standing in these *caves* today, 150 feet or so below ground, you look straight up at a small hole of natural light just large enough for one block to fit through at a time (so designed to prevent moisture from entering the quarry). In ancient times, workers hacked downward inside, cutting in triangular fashion, so that at the bottom you stand within a hollowed-out pyramid. (Although many *caves* were formed in this fashion, the best example is that of the house of Ruinart.)

Many of the *caves* (used for storage and such periodic practices as *riddling,* or turning the bottles) and the above-ground offices and sales rooms are open to the public and offer tastings, although because of the short life of an open bottle, such top-of-the-line wonders as Taittinger's Comtes de Champagne are rarely poured.

For maps, informative brochures, and up-to-date information on which houses are open when, inquire at the Office de Tourisme near the Musée St-Denis in Reims. Here visitors usually are welcomed at G.H. Mumm, Piper-Heidsieck, Pommery, Taittinger, and Veuve-Cliquot-Ponsardin.

Epernay

Even today, the people of little Epernay call themselves the *Sparnaciens,* a reference to the Roman name of the town. Vying with Reims as a wine *entrepôt,* the town was owned by the archbishops of Reims from the fifth to the tenth century, when the area was given to the counts of Champagne. A center for trips into the Marne valley, Epernay is more laid-back than Reims. (As British writer Patrick Forbes explained in his book on the region, "By 10 P.M. Epernay is as dead as mutton.")

As a result of being sacked, burned, bombed, and otherwise disturbed during its long history, Epernay today displays few antique monuments that are noteworthy. Instead, airy and green, it is a town suggestive of lazy autumn afternoons, especially if you stroll from the centrally located place de la République east along the **avenue de Champagne**, which is lined with large 19th-century houses in a comfortable mix of Renaissance and Classical styles.

The **Musée des Beaux-Arts** in Château Perrier (19th-century, Louis XIII style) on avenue de Champagne is really three museums; those of wine (with a great collection of labels) and regional archaeology (pottery, glassware, arms, and finds from tombs) are the most interesting.

Here, as in Reims, the *Office de Tourisme* (near Notre-Dame) will advise visitors of the Champagne *caves* that may be visited: **de Castellane** on the rue de Verdun, **Mercier**, and **Moët et Chandon** on the avenue de Champagne are usually open to tourists. Both Mercier and

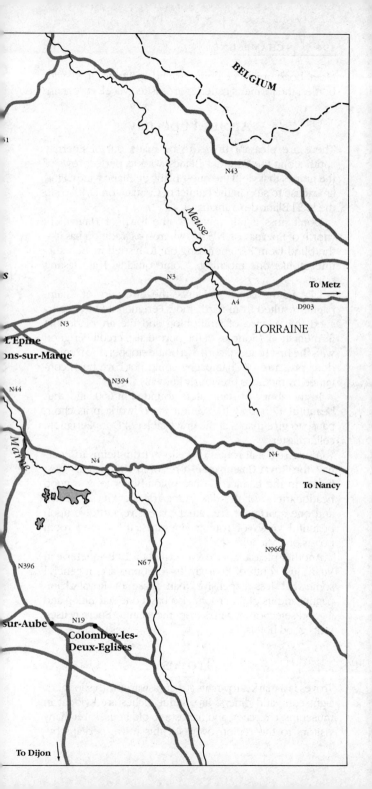

Moët boast miles of underground galleries lined with bottles; the former's galleries are visited via electric train.

Around Epernay

There are pleasant drives to be made out of Epernay south along the Côte des Blancs, with its perfect rows of the grapes that yield the finest Blanc de Blanc wines. Find an excuse to stop in the hamlet of Cramant on D 10 to sip the local Blanc de Cramant.

Don't miss a pilgrimage to the town of Hautvillers (north of Epernay on N 386), where—as tradition has it—the blind Dom Pérignon sang out to his fellow Benedictine monks one morning, "Come quickly; I am tasting stars!"

Like many happy accidents, the discovery of Champagne resulted from hard study: Pérignon had long pursued the science of vinification and the art of double fermentation. (Sources of the period also credit Pérignon with the first usage of cork as a bottle stopper; the tremendous pressure of Champagne could not have been contained by methods previously known.)

In the **abbey of Hautvillers**, founded in 660, and with beautiful 17th- and 18th-century woodwork in its choir, pause to give thanks at the grave tablet of Dom Pérignon, cellarmaster.

Along regional route 51 (yellow) from Reims to Epernay, the **Royal-Champagne**, a restored 18th-century post house in the hamlet of Champillon-Bellevue, is a good headquarters for the discerning traveller. Its 23 rooms and one apartment are rather expensive and give upon beautiful views of rolling vineyards; the dining room boasts one Michelin star.

Another pleasant place to overnight is **La Briqueterie** in Vinay, just south of Epernay. Its 42 rooms are in general somewhat less expensive than those of Royal-Champagne, and its dining room also has a one-star rating and a good selection of wines from the vicinity. Epernay itself lacks good hotels.

Troyes

Troyes is a market town, its streets aswarm with shoppers, sightseers, and diners. Its antique riches are evident in museums, churches, and handsome old houses. Yet many visitors to the region overlook this town, perhaps because it sits beside the Seine just off the direct Sens-to-Burgundy route.

In the 12th and 13th centuries, things were different. Along with Lagny-sur-Marne, Provins (both now considered within the greater environs of Paris), and Bar-sur-Aube (Clairvaux), about 32 miles to the east, Troyes staged an annual Fair of Champagne that attracted merchants from all civilized Europe and established standards for Continent-wide commerce. (Troyes gave its name to our system of troy-weight measurements.)

An original Troyes foodstuff is the *andouillette* (tripe sausage), which was extremely popular in the 16th century. Royalist troops who were supposed to be attacking the city sat down to gorge in the *andouillette* quarter (St-Denis) and were set upon and massacred by Troyes's defenders. Even Louis the Stammerer dined on this delicacy when he was crowned in 878; it may have been responsible for his epithet.

Until recently, the cathedral was Troyes's top attraction. Today, the **Musée d'Art Moderne** (Musée Levy) has taken its place. In 1976 Pierre and Denise Levy presented a part of their enormous art collection to Troyes, their hometown. After arduous restoration, the museum opened in the renovated bishops' palace near the cathedral. Of most significance at the museum are the paintings of the late 19th and 20th centuries, representing almost every major French artist of the period. Also on display are prints, drawings, bronze and African sculptures, ceramics, and glassware.

The façade of the **cathedral of St-Pierre et St-Paul** (in the northeast quarter of town, off the place St-Pierre) was ornately sculpted by Martin Chambiges, who also worked on the cathedrals of Beauvais and Sens. The beautiful Flamboyant rose window remains (Flamboyant style features window tracery with a flamelike rhythm), while the statues of the portals were destroyed during the Revolution. Joan of Arc visited the cathedral in 1429 on her way to the crowning of Charles VII.

Among the fine stained glass from the 13th to 16th centuries, a curious window portrays Christ stretched out across the planks of a wine press as the blood pours out of the wound in his side into a handy chalice. Meanwhile, a vine stalk grows out of his chest, and the 12 Apostles sit on its branches.

Of the other half-dozen major churches in town, visit **St-Pantaléon** for its Renaissance altar screens and statues (in the southwest quarter, off rue Emile Zola) and the **basilica of St-Urbain** (in the center of town, off the place de la Libération) for its superb Gothic choir. The oldest church, **Ste-Madeleine** (on rue du Général-de-Gaulle not far from the railway station), owns a remarkable 16th-century rood screen in Flamboyant style, and a statue of Sainte Marthe dressed as a common woman, the best example of the Champagne school of that century.

Very near the cathedral, the **Musée St-Loup**, in a former abbey (named for the fifth-century bishop whose virtues persuaded Attila the Hun not to sack the town), devotes itself mainly to natural history and regional archaeology. The Musée Historique de Troyes et de la Champagne, in the superb Renaissance Hôtel de Vauluisant, near St-Pantaléon, illustrates the city's history and possesses the only hosiery museum in France. (Stockings, gloves, and hats were even more important to Medieval Troyes than were *andouillettes.*)

Remarkable preservation work is ongoing in the **St-Jean quarter**, where the Medieval fairs were staged. It's the 16th century revisited, from the smartly turned turrets atop the Maison de l'Orfèvre to the recobbled, archaic-looking ruelle des Chats.

Troyes's best restaurant is generally conceded to be **Le Bourgogne** on rue du Général-de-Gaulle near the church of St-Remy. Le Bourgogne's duck liver is a recommended dish; it also has a good cellar of regional wines. A pleasant choice, and more modest, is **Le Valentino** on cour de la Rencontre near the Hôtel de Ville.

As is often the case in provincial French towns, a good hotel is right near the railway station, the **Grand** on avenue Maréchal-Joffre, which is quite reasonably priced and boasts three restaurants, each good in its category: **Le Champagne**, the formal dining room; a grill called **Jardin de la Louisiane**; and the **Pizzéria Grill Aquarius**.

Travellers in search of really off-the-beaten-track towns and villages for overnight stops might take N 19 55 km (33 miles) east toward Bar-sur-Aube and stop just 8 km (5 miles) out at the hamlet of Dolancourt and the unpretentious but comfortable, modestly priced, 16-room **Moulin du Landion,** with its own small park, mill-wheel, and cozy dining room.

Châlons-sur-Marne and
L'Epine

Châlons is a proper town with memories of Attila the Hun, Napoléon, and Nazi bombings, whereas l'Epine remains only a spot renowned in the Middle Ages for pilgrimages to its basilica.

In Châlons the **cathedral of St-Etienne** offers windows and artworks of a very high order, and the **church of Notre-Dame-en-Vaux** shows off the meeting of Roman capitals and Gothic arches.

L'Epine's **basilica of Notre-Dame** occupies a site where in the Middle Ages shepherds came upon a statue of the Virgin in a burning thornbush. Resulting pilgrimages attracted such of the eminent faithful as Charles VII, Louis XI, and René of Anjou. Nicolas Froment was moved to create the famous *Buisson Ardent* (burning bush) triptych now in the cathedral of Aix-en-Provence.

Constructed in Flamboyant Gothic style in the 15th century, the basilica is the size of a major cathedral. Its façade presents a fantasy, almost a riot, of architectural details, in particular gargoyles, which in wonderfully varied shapes symbolize the faces of evil and of wicked spirits.

The liveliness of the basilica's exterior is belied by its somber interior, the choir enclosed by a beautiful 16th-century rood screen. If you arrive during services, you will be struck by the spine-tingling sounds from the Renaissance organ bank.

Somewhat surprisingly, this hamlet is home to a pleasantly decorated 40-room hotel, reasonable in price, that prizes quiet and prides itself on its kitchen: **Aux Armes de Champagne**.

Colombey-les-Deux-Eglises

Nothing happens now in this village of fewer than 400 farmers and shopkeepers, and nothing very much ever has, except on the occasions when Charles de Gaulle was at home in his country house, **La Boisserie**, between 1933 and November 9, 1970, when he died there. From his study you can gaze across a rolling green landscape and read the words of the general and president: "This part of Champagne is impregnated with calm, vast, worn, and sad horizons; melancholy woods, pastures, crops, and lands lying fallow; tranquil and rather poor villages of which nothing, for a millennium, has changed the soul.... Silence fills my house. I see night cover the countryside. Then, gazing at stars, I penetrate into the insignificance of things."

Outside town, on a hilly rise grandiosely called "The Mountain," a Cross of Lorraine (the general's double-barred symbol) was erected in 1972. Intimidating in size and impact, it dominates the landscape for miles around.

GETTING AROUND
The fastest route from Paris to Reims is A 4. Those who prefer a slower, more scenic trip can cut off A 4 at about Ferté-sous-Jouarre (and lunch, maybe, at the two-star **Auberge de Condé**), then take Route 3-380 via Château-Thierry.

Railroad buffs will find that trains depart Paris's Gare de l'Est daily for Reims, some trains stopping also at Epernay.

The Champagne Road (brochures are available in English at tourist offices) is divided into three routes designated by colors: blue (the mountain of Reims), red (the Marne valley), and green (the Côte des Blancs). The blue route, about 50 miles long, departs Reims on N 51 in the direction of Soissons and passes through such villages as Jouy, Ecueil, Nogent, Verzy, and Bouzy (visits are possible to Barancourt and Georges Vesselle wineries). The route ends in Ay (visits to Bollinger by appointment only).

The red route, 41 miles along the Marne valley, starts in Ay and winds through Hautvillers to Châtillon-sur-Marne and back to Epernay.

The green route winds for 31 miles along the Côte des Blancs from Epernay on D 51 in the direction of Troyes, then to Menthelon and Chouilly and back to Epernay. Most of the small producers are open only by appointment, which may be arranged through tourist offices in Reims or Epernay.

The **Champagne Air Show** offers ballooning trips of one, two, or three days with accommodations in a château hotel (15 bis, place St-Niçaise, 51100 Reims). At the same address, **Canal Safaris** can custom-tailor canal cruising. A one-day helicopter trip to Champagne is offered to passengers aboard Horizon Cruises' barge trips in Burgundy. A two-day, one-night Spirit of Champagne bus tour for those without time to drive on their own is available from travel agents in Paris.

The trip through Champagne may be combined handily with that to Alsace-Lorraine.

ACCOMMODATIONS REFERENCE

▶ **Aux Armes de Champagne.** 51460 **Courtisols.** Tel: 26-66-96-79.

▶ **Boyer "les Crayères."** 64, boulevard Vasnier, 51100 **Reims.** Tel: 26-82-80-80; Telex: 830959; in U.S., (212) 696-1323.

▶ **La Briqueterie.** 51200 **Vinay.** Tel: 26-54-11-22; Telex: 842007.

▶ **Grand Hôtel.** 4, avenue Maréchal Joffre, 10000 **Troyes.** Tel: 25-79-90-90.

▶ **Moulin du Landion.** 10200 **Dolancourt**, Bar-sur-Aube. Tel: 25-26-12-17.

▶ **Paix.** 9, rue Buirette, 51100 **Reims.** Tel: 26-40-04-08; Telex: 830974.

▶ **Royal Champagne.** 51160 **Champillon.** Tel: 26-52-87-11; Telex: 830111; in U.S., (212) 696-1323.

ALSACE-LORRAINE

By Georgia I. Hesse

The hyphen that forever binds these two distinct provinces is also what divides them: the Vosges range, a granite and sandstone spine that slices the land north to south from Wissembourg and the West German border to Belfort.

West of these mountains lies the plateau of Lorraine, an expanse rich in forests, lakes, and croplands that reaches toward Champagne and the Paris basin. To the east of the Vosges is the narrow plain of Alsace, a region thick with grapevines and half-timbered villages bordered by the river Rhine and facing the homeland of those ancient antagonists the Alemanni, a tribe whose name became synonymous with *Allemagne,* the French for Germany.

The late food writer Waverley Root lumps the two lands together in his so-called Domain of Fat, a happy description for today's traveller, who will find here a wealth not only of hearty cooking but also of history, natural beauty, art and architecture, local traditions and cultures, and important industries (glassmaking in the village of Baccarat in particular).

Both Celtic countries, Lorraine and Alsace have shared a lineage of conquest and liberation almost two thousand years long, from their occupation by Roman legions in 52 and 58 B.C. to the devastating battles of 1914–18 and 1939–45. These frequent struggles have resulted in today's resolute pride in being French, although in both cases that nationality is a surprisingly recent phenomenon. France acquired Alsace in 1648 by the Treaty of Münster (except for Strasbourg, which remained independent until 1681), and annexed Lorraine in 1766 upon the death of Stanislas Leszczyński, the former king of Poland, duke of Lorraine, and, not incidentally, father-in-law of Louis XV.

This intertwining of Germanic and Frankish inheritances gives Lorraine and, especially, Alsace much of their contemporary fascination: the village architecture, imported from beyond the Rhine, of half-timbered houses and wood-sculpted oriels (encorbelled windows) projecting over the street; the substantial Germanic peasant fare of wine-cured sausages and sauerkraut; the Rhenish art created by German masters; the folkloric costumes, songs, and pilgrimages unlike any others in France; even the traditional arts and crafts that are more closely related to those of Germany's Black Forest than to those of the Ile-de-France.

MAJOR INTEREST IN LORRAINE

Nancy
Place Stanislas
The ducal palace (the Musée Historique Lorraine)
Musée des Beaux-Arts

Near Nancy
Bar-le-Duc (15th-century church with macabre tomb sculpture known as "La Squellette"; Sacred Way)
Toul (cathedral of St-Etienne)
St-Nicolas-de-Port (basilica)

Elsewhere in Lorraine
Domrémy-la-Pucelle (birthplace of Joan of Arc)
Verdun (battlefields and monuments)
Avioth (Gothic church)
Metz (cathedral of St-Etienne, notable for the stained-glass windows; museums in former convent-church of the Petits-Carmes)
Vittel area spas
Lunéville ("Little Versailles")
Baccarat (crystal museum, workshops, and sales)

MAJOR INTEREST IN ALSACE

Strasbourg
Cathedral of Notre-Dame (required)

Musée de l'Oeuvre Notre-Dame (pre-Roman, Roman, Medieval, and Renaissance artworks; a must)

La Petite France (ancient quarter of town, featuring half-timbered houses; essential)

Château des Rohan and its museums (not to skip)

Musée Alsacien

Boat rides on the river Ill

La Route du Vin (Wine Road) and its villages

Colmar

Musée d'Unterlinden (required)

Petite Venise ("Little Venice," in the old quarter)

Musée Bartholdi

Walk through the Old Town

Mont-Ste-Odile and the Hohwald region

Château du Haut-Koenigsbourg

Ebersmunster

Munster valley

Murbach

LORRAINE

Lorraine owes its name to the Treaty of Verdun (843), by which Charlemagne's empire—all the Christian lands of Western Europe except the British Isles, southern Italy, and Sicily—was divided among his three grandsons. Charles II (Charles the Bald, or *le Chauve*) took western France, Louis II (Louis the German) the eastern territories, and Lothair I the lands in between, as well as the capitals at Rome and Aix-la-Chapelle and the title of Emperor of the West. Lothair's turf, named Lotharingia after his son and successor, has metamorphosed into modern-day Lorraine.

Lorraine boasts two major cities, Nancy and Metz. In addition to them, their historical, artistic, and culinary attractions, the interest of most North American and British visitors will center on the evidences of World Wars I and II: battlefields, cemeteries, memorials and monuments, the structures of the Maginot Line, etc.

In general, English-speaking travellers are only beginning to savor the delights and benefits of *thermalisme,* or
the spa vacation, an activity enjoyed for the most part by
the French and Germans.

The Parc Naturel Régional de Lorraine, established in
1974, caters to the health-and-fitness prone visitor with
hiking trails, horseback riding, bicycling, picnicking, and
bird-watching. Visitors' centers (Maisons du Parc) have
been arranged to explain some important characteristics
of life in Lorraine: artisan and craft activities, community
arts and rural traditions, and even the production of salt, a
valuable regional product.

Food is another area of interest, and excellent restaurants abound; at least four in the cosmopolitan area of
Nancy alone rate one Michelin rosette. Here you may
sample on their home ground such delicacies as *quiche
Lorraine;* a hearty pork stew named *potée Lorraine* that
immortalizes the great, floppy-eared Celtic breed of hog;
tourte à la Lorraine, a fine marinated meat dish cooked
in a crusty cloak; and *boudin,* or blood pudding, which
the food writer Waverley Root says may be the oldest on
the French menu, since it seems to have been invented in
Tyre by the Assyrians.

Other regional specialties include Gerôme, Lorraine's
most famous cheese, and Marcel Proust's muse, the
madeleine, born in Commercy (buy some at Maison
Grojean on place Charles-de-Gaulle). Bar-le-Duc is renowned for its jams and jellies, particularly those made
of currants.

The *vins gris* native to Lorraine are rosés, and the best
come from Toul, due west of Nancy. They don't compare
with the wines of Alsace but get along well with regional
fare, as do the beers. Lorraine also produces several fruity
eaux-de-vie, the finest of which is probably Mirabelle de
Lorraine, distilled from plums.

Nancy is the center of Lorraine. Most excursions
throughout the area can be staged from there.

NANCY

In style, in appearance, and in essence, Nancy, the seat of
the dukes of Lorraine, lives in the 18th century, the era of
its master-builder, Stanislas Leszczyński. This former king
of Poland was the father of Marie Leszczyńska, who wed
Louis XV and became queen of France. Upon this marriage

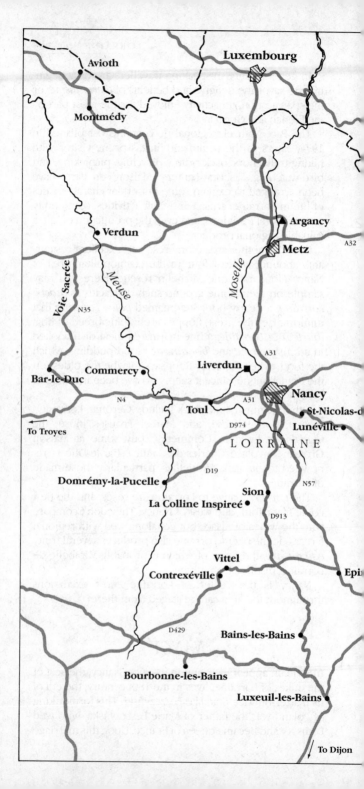

Alsace-Lorraine

0 miles 30
0 kilometers 20

GERMANY

Saarbrücken

E12

Dambach ■   Wissembourg ●

● Haguenau

Saverne ●

N4

Sarrebourg ●   N4

La Wantzenau ●

Marlenheim ●

Rhine

● Baccarat

Strasbourg

Ill

Ottrott ●   Obernai ●
● Ste-Odile

Lorraine-
Vosges

Hohwald

ALSACE

Daumbach-la-Ville ●   ● Ebermunster

St-Dié ●   ● Haut-Koenigsbourg

du Bonhomme   Illhaeusern ■

Lapoutroie ●   Ribeauvillé ●

Orbey ●   Ammerschwihr ●

Hohrodberg ⊠ Thann   Colmar

Gérardmer ●   Wettolsheim △

Munster   Eguisham

● Rouffach

Murbach ⊙   ● Guebwiller

GERMANY

A5

Mulhouse ●

N83

N ↑

To Basel

Louis installed his father-in-law as the duke of Lorraine and Bar, with the understanding that upon Stanislas's death, those lands were to pass to Marie and thus to France. And so it was.

Most of the elegant provincial city Leszczyński created remains. Forming the heart of the town is the aptly named **place Stanislas**, a rectangular breathing space between the Old Town and the commercial area. Originally called place Royale out of loyalty to the crown, it was once the site of a statue of Louis XV that was pulled down during the Revolution. Place Stanislas sits right on the southern edge of the Old Quarter, generally that area between the Arc de Triomphe (18th century, a copy of that of Septimius Severus in Rome) at the southern end of elongated place de la Carrière, and Porte de la Craffe to the north of the church of the Cordeliers. This Old Town was sheltered in the 14th century by a substantial wall, of which only the **Craffe gate** remains. Until after the Revolution, the gate served as a prison; today, it displays Medieval sculptures.

The harmony, the superb detailing, and the majesty of place Stanislas is the work of two talents: the architect Emmanuel Héré, and Jean Lamour, the creator of the gilded wrought-iron grills that distinguish this square from any other in the country. The best and most atmospheric accommodations in town are found in the 18th-century palace right on the square, the **Grand Hôtel de la Reine**, with its **Restaurant Stanislas**.

Of the superb palaces around the place Stanislas, the largest is the **Hôtel de Ville**, or town hall, worth visiting for its grand architectural details, its salons, and the wide-angle view over the square it offers. The whole area is particularly evocative on summer nights, when it is outlined by floodlighting.

Beyond the Arc de Triomphe stretches the **place de la Carrière**, with its 18th-century houses flanked by handsome parades of trees and, in the background, the Palais du Gouvernement. To the right in this remarkable composition is **La Pépinière**, a garden in the style the French call English, offering promenades, a zoo, and a statue by Rodin of the painter Claude Gellée, who was better known as Claude Lorrain.

Neighboring the government palace on the east is the former ducal palace, first constructed in the late 13th century and much reworked (intelligently); it houses the **Musée Historique Lorrain**, a dusty gathering of archaeological and ethnographic items, Medieval sculptures (the most interesting displays), tapestries, furniture, and enough likenesses of the various dukes to make them seem like personal acquaintances.

Across a narrow way from the museum is the **church of the Cordeliers**, in whose crypt lie the remains of the dukes of Lorraine (and a duchess or so) in beautifully worked stone tombs; for this reason it has been likened to St-Denis, the Ile-de-France's repository of crowned heads.

The **Musée des Beaux-Arts**, right on place Stanislas, devotes itself to European paintings from the 14th century to today, showing off such familiars as Manet, Courbet, Delacroix, Dufy, Utrillo, Perugino, Tintoretto, and Rubens. Particularly interesting in this setting is Delacroix's *Death of Charles the Bold at the Battle of Nancy;* ironically, though, native Lorraine artists such as Claude Lorrain and Georges de La Tour are well represented nowhere in town.

Nancy is a pretty, informal town, its people much given to ambling and café-sitting; in conversation they appear to accept—but with some resentment—the greater fame of Strasbourg. Much attention attaches to jazz: Count Basie and Fats Domino play the palace at La Pépinière, as do rock and reggae groups.

Just off place Stanislas, the quite modern **Capucin Gourmand** on rue Gambetta is as popular today for its Lorraine specialties as it was back in the 1950s with the wandering gourmet-writer Samuel Chamberlain.

Between 1871 and 1918, the city welcomed so many refugees as a result of various regional upheavals that a new Nancy grew up to the west, where you find (with some difficulty) the **Musée de l'Ecole de Nancy**, whose collections embody the indigenous style that became a precursor of the so-called modern French style. It houses an exciting collection of late 19th- and early 20th-century furniture, glassware, and faïence and other ceramics by refreshingly unfamiliar artists.

To reach this worthwhile museum, drive south on boulevard de Scarpone until it becomes rue Victor-Hugo, turn west at the church of St-Joseph and the parc Ste-Marie, and continue a short distance to rue Sergent-Blandan. The museum is a jog to the south at 38–46 rue Sergent-Blandan.

South of town proper in the small, resolutely industrial suburb of St-Nicolas-de-Port is—unexpectedly—a superb

basilica in Flamboyant Gothic style, built on the site of an earlier sanctuary that once possessed a most precious ancient relic, a finger bone of Saint Nicholas. Joan of Arc knelt here to ask help on her expedition, as have faithful travellers ever since.

NEAR NANCY

Rewarding excursions of a few hours each can be made to the west and southwest out of Nancy in one long day; the only practical and the most pleasant way to do it is by car.

Toul and Bar-le-Duc

Toul, a little city of about 17,000, is a short drive west of Nancy on A 33. Three centuries were devoted to the construction of its former **cathedral of St-Etienne**, which has not been returned to its former status since being severely damaged during the battles of 1940. Its façade—on the place du Parvis—and its Gothic nave are still admirable. It's just east of the center of town, just inside the old ramparts.

A pleasant walk west of St-Etienne, the **church of St-Gengoult** near the place du Marché is a proud example of the Gothic school of Champagne, raised from the 13th into the 15th centuries. Most appealing is the 16th-century Flamboyant-style cloister.

Just to the east of the church on rue Michâtel, a lovely Renaissance house replete with gargoyles was the home of the 17th-century prelate Jacques Bossuet, while several other treasured Renaissance houses stand on rue de Général-Gengoult, a couple of streets west of the church.

Bar-le-Duc, west of Toul and about 75 km (45 miles) from Nancy, is only slightly larger than Toul but plays a much greater commercial role, as befits its status as a county capital more than a thousand years ago. The town boasts a fairly interesting art and archaeological museum (Musée Barrois) on the west side of town, but almost everybody stops only to visit the **church of St-Etienne**.

For some reason Anne de Lorraine, widow of René de Châlon, prince of Orange, commissioned one Ligier Richier to depict her husband's body in stone as the decomposed corpse it would be three years after his death (he was killed in 1544 during the siege of St-Dizier). The macabre, not to say repellent, *Squellette* may be seen in St-Etienne.

Equally macabre in its way is the Voie Sacrée (Sacred Way), that dangerous stretch of road between Bar-le-Duc and Verdun along which supply convoys rolled night and day during 1916's Battle of Verdun, supplying French defenders in spite of constant threats (and realities) of death and destruction. To pick it up, take N 35 east from Bar-le-Duc across the Marne canal.

Domrémy-La-Pucelle

The pilgrimage to Domrémy is made easily in a one-day excursion southwest from Nancy. (The Colombey just down the road is not de Gaulle's town; Colombey-les-Deux-Eglises is quite a bit farther on.)

With fewer than 300 inhabitants, this village is as sleepy today as it was in 1412 when Isabelle Romée and her husband, Jacques d'Arc, gave birth to Joan (Jeanne in French), the humble peasant girl who was to lead an army, give France a king, and burn at the stake in one of history's most famous martyrdoms. According to the historian Frances Gies, Joan was called Jeanette in the village, and was sometimes given her mother's surname of Romée, as was the country custom. During her military career and for a century afterward, however, she was known as Jeanne *la Pucelle,* or "the Maid."

Although a peasant, Jacques d'Arc was prosperous: His thick-walled house was built of stone in a time when most were of timber. Restored in the 19th century to eliminate side structures that had been added throughout the years, it is simple, solid, unpretentious, and firm—very much like Joan herself.

The village church has been much reworked since Joan's day, but several vestiges the Maid would recognize remain, the basin for holy water and the baptismal font among them.

About a mile away, the **basilica of Bois-Chenu**, consecrated in 1926, rises rather pretentiously above the spot where Joan heard the voices that inspired her mission, those of saints Catherine, Marguerite, and Michael.

Joan's story has touched Frenchmen for half a millennium, not the least of them Charles de Gaulle, who adopted the Cross of Lorraine as the emblem of a Free France besieged.

VERDUN

In 1914 Verdun, about 110 km (67 miles) northwest of Nancy, was, along with Toul, the toughest of French fortresses. Its strategic position had commanded battle lines since the days of the Gauls and then the Romans, under whom it was called Virodunum Castrum.

To visit today the sites where hundreds of thousands of soldiers from both sides died in the epic struggle of World War I is to look back in sadness. That may be why, as years pass and fewer of the dead remain living in memory, fewer foreign visitors make this particular pilgrimage.

The **Citadelle**, in the heart of town near the cathedral of Notre-Dame, is the work of perhaps the most renowned military architect in Europe since the Romans, Sébastien le Prestre de Vauban (1633–1707). In his characteristic star-within-star design (the best example of which is in Lille), the Citadelle sits atop the remains of a tenth-century abbey, houses a **museum of war**, and gives access to the famous tunnels that once sheltered the defensive army.

For anyone who wishes to survey the theater of combat from the air, Verdun's Aero-Club de Rozelier organizes flights over the battlefields; inquire at the *Office de Tourisme* on place Nation.

On the right bank of the Meuse, the "Red Zone" of the battle, drive first to the military cemetery of Faubourg-Pavé (from which the body of one Unknown Soldier was taken to lie beneath the Arc de Triomphe in Paris), then to the monument of the **Maginot Line** and to the Fort de Vaux, on the right bank of the Meuse, a fortification that held out for almost three months against the German onslaughts of 1916. More interesting than Vaux itself are the nearby **museum of the Battle of Verdun** and the sparse ruins of the village of Fleury, which was captured and recaptured 26 times.

Housing the bones of men killed here, the Ossuaire de Douaumont, near the Fort de Douaumont, is the most important French reminder of World War I and is dedicated to the 400,000 French soldiers who died in this one battle. And on the left bank of the Meuse is the **American Cemetery of Romagne-sous-Montfaucon**, which contains more than 14,000 tombs in an eerily peaceful setting of deep lawns, shade trees, and gardens.

Verdun may well be explored in one long day out of

Metz; otherwise, a good hotel choice is **Hostellerie Coq Hardi**, well regarded for decades, with its Michelin one-star restaurant featuring regional specialties.

Avioth

North of Verdun about 40 km (25 miles) via country roads, near the Belgian border, you come upon the hamlet (108 inhabitants) of Avioth. More truthfully, you don't come upon it without some effort, since its name rarely appears except upon large-scale regional maps. From Verdun, follow D 964 north to Stenay, angle east on D 947 to Montmédy, and pick up directional signs to Avioth, five miles to the north of Montmédy.

Those who persist in search of hidden treasures will be rewarded by a magnificent **basilica** founded in the 13th century, some 200 years after the discovery of a miraculous statue of the Virgin Mary at the site. Construction continued for another 200 years or so. Were the stones then as warm and golden in hue as they appear today? Who knows? Gilded in soft late afternoon light, the 70 figures of the Passion seem harmonious and real, as if they had been frozen alive and preserved throughout time, the little angels sounding their trumpets down the centuries.

METZ

Metz, a city of about 118,000 citizens (known as *Messins*), has been important almost forever—or at least since the sixth-century days of the Merovingian ruler Theodoric I, the son of Clovis I and king of Metz. Under Sigibert I and his famous wife, Brunhild, Metz became the capital of Austrasia, one of the two major Merovingian kingdoms, the other being Neustria (with Soissons as its capital).

Today this port on the Moselle river north of Nancy is an industrial town, but a less grim one than most of its northern neighbors. Metz's major attractions are churches, of which it boasts an inordinate number for its size, and museums. In late November it plays home to an international festival of contemporary music that leans toward New Wave.

The treasures of Metz can be appreciated during a one-day round trip from Nancy. If you prefer to spend the night, there are two major hotels in town—**Sofitel** and

Altéa St-Thiébaut—and the very pleasant, 22-room **La Bergerie** in a 16th-century house 12 km (7.5 miles) north in Rugy. Those travellers who prefer to soothe their souls in country settings might settle down in the **Résidence des Vannes** in the village of Liverdun, just 16 km (10 miles) north of Nancy. Poised above the slowly curving Moselle, it's a Michelin one-star restaurant with nine rooms and two apartments.

The nave of Metz's Gothic **cathedral of St-Etienne** soars highest in France after those of St-Pierre in Beauvais and Notre-Dame in Amiens. While the exterior is very richly detailed, it is the interior that makes the church remarkable, with its stunning ensemble of stained glass ranging from the 13th and 14th centuries up to the 20th, including the creations of Marc Chagall. Because of the glass, the cathedral has been nicknamed the Lantern of God. The building's curious design results from the 12th-century linking together of two churches, Notre-Dame-la-Ronde and St-Etienne, across a tiny road. Most of old Metz lies east of a spur of the Moselle river, arranging itself (as is so often the case) around the cathedral.

Four museums are housed in a 17th-century Carmelite convent and its adjoining grain storage shed and several outbuildings. Premier among them, the **Musée d'Art et d'Histoire** is a treasure trove of relics from archaeological digs in the region that have revealed the importance of this Gallo-Roman crossroads town, which became a center of culture under the Carolingians. Exhibitions include evidences of the Romans' skill in engineering baths and sewers.

The three other museums are Beaux-Arts (paintings, engravings, polychrome wood statues); a military collection; and a natural history and zoological collection. The convent is located behind St-Etienne off the rue du Chèvremont.

In good weather, stroll around the **Esplanade**, the adjoining place de la République, and the banks of an offshoot of the Moselle river called **Lac des Cygnes** (Swan Lake), where, on Friday, Saturday, and Sunday evenings a *son-et-lumière* performance is staged.

Near the Esplanade is **St-Pierre-aux-Nonnains**; thought to be the oldest church in France, it was founded by a Benedictine abbey in the seventh century on the site of a fourth-century Roman edifice. Visiting the church usually requires the permission of the *Office de Tourisme,* a couple of blocks away on rue Schuman.

Near the end of August and beginning of September, decorated carts and singers and dancers in folk costumes march in the Fête de Mirabelle to celebrate the little plum from which the fiery liqueur is made.

A very pleasant place for dining in Metz is **La Dinanderie** at 2, rue de Paris, on an island between the Moselle and one of its canals.

VITTEL AND OTHER SPAS

"Taking the waters," or *thermalisme,* in the European sense remains a pastime little known to most North Americans and Australians in their own countries, but is slightly more familiar to the British. The current dieting fad favoring fancy bottled waters has made the name Vittel popular with outsiders who know their waters if not their spas. Wanderers have come here to cure various ills since the days of the Romans; when those bath-happy occupiers departed the springs were forgotten, to be rediscovered only as recently as 1845.

The plains and uplands of the Vosges south of Nancy are rich in healing springs both cold and hot, and the waters emerge both with and without natural carbonation.

Of the spa towns—Vittel, nearby Contrexéville, Bains-les-Bains, Bourbonne-les-Bains, and Luxeuil-les-Bains—the first is the largest (with 6,500 or so permanent residents) and the best known, and offers the possibility of tours and tastings at the bottling factory. The *Foire aux Grenouilles* (Frog Fair) in Vittel takes place the last weekend in April.

The best hotels, however, are in **Contrexéville**, a favorite retreat of Stanislas Leszczyński. Tops are the 29-room **Grand Hôtel Etablissement** next to the baths, with its good **Grill Relais Stanislas**, and the 81-room **Cosmos** near the park. There is something quaint, turn-of-the-century, self-consciously healthful, and studiously manicured about spa villages like Contrexéville. They offer a slightly skewed version of French life that is overlooked by many foreigners.

La Colline Inspirée

About halfway along the Nancy–Vittel route that begins as D 913, a detour of a few miles to the west brings one to Sion and to La Colline Inspirée, or Hill of Inspiration, a lonely place sacred to the gods of war and peace where prayers have been offered up for more than two thousand years.

Celts worshiped here first in what must have been all but total seclusion. Since then the hill has been a pilgrimage site for followers of the Crusades, those liberated from German domination, the faithful freed of the Prussian yoke, the French writer Maurice Barrès (who gave the spot its name), enthusiasts of French unity, and, in 1973's Peace Festival, thousands of former prisoners of Nazi concentration camps.

Epinal

East of Vittel en route to Alsace is Epinal, home to the **Musée Départemental des Vosges et Musée International de l'Imagerie**, which houses local Roman and Gallo-Roman works including a very fine mosaic, Medieval sculptures, and exhibitions of daily private life in the Vosges region. There are also a few outstanding paintings, many drawings, and a display of the history of printmaking from the Middle Ages to today.

On the Wednesday before Easter the children of Epinal draw lighted boats along street gutters flooded for the Fête des Champs-Golots; during June there is an international printmaking festival.

EN ROUTE TO ALSACE

The great Stanislas died in 1766 at **Lunéville** in the château that became known as "Little Versailles," which now presents a *son-et-lumière* show in its chapel and contains a museum of faïence.

Baccarat's crystal factory was established in 1764 and has been making news and quality glassware ever since. A visit to the Musée du Cristal makes the most nonacquisitive traveller acquisitive. Old and new pieces are on display, their production is extremely well documented, and a sales shop lies conveniently at hand.

St-Dié in its little valley at the feet of pine-studded hills grew up around a seventh-century Benedictine monastery and today calls itself, with some pride, the "birthplace of America." U.S. citizens aware of the association

usually make their ways on arrival in town to the Bibliothèque Municipale near the cathedral and its Gothic cloister and ask to be directed to the rare 16th-century book,
Cosmographiae Introductio, a kind of early atlas.

In the *Cosmographiae,* a work of Vosgian academics,
credit is given to Amerigo Vespucci for the discovery of a
new continent and the word "America" is inscribed upon
a map of it for the first time.

From St-Dié, southeast of Baccarat on N 59, the most
direct route to Alsace winds over the Col du Bonhomme
and through the villages of Lapoutroie and Kaysersberg
to Colmar. An alternate route to Colmar via the summer
resort of **Gérardmer** and its lake is more scenic, winding
over the Col de la Schlucht through some of the prettiest Vosges countryside. On the Sunday nearest April 20,
Gérardmer stages its Jonquil Festival, with various musical groups parading through the beflowered town. A
giant fireworks display lights up the night and the lake
in mid-August.

ALSACE

France's most distinctive and, in some eyes, most picturesque province is a green corridor 120 miles long and 32
miles wide wedged between Lorraine on the west, Germany on the north and east, and Switzerland on the
southeast.

A long history of independent kingdoms, duchies, and
other regional entities constitutes one of France's greatest
attractions: her deep and lasting variety. Within that diversity Alsace seems still foreign, a land unto itself with its own
culture, cooking, architecture, tradition, even language.

Even more than Lorraine's, Alsace's history is one of
turmoil and tempest between Germanic and Frankish
peoples. Though Alsatians today are proudly French,
their inheritance is strongly Germanic; witness the Alsatian dialect, which sounds something like Swiss-German
and offends or amuses the ears of almost everyone who
doesn't speak it. The name Alsace itself derives from
Illsass, the dialect word meaning "country of the Ill river."

Alsatian Food and Drink

There is an earthiness, a naturalness, a refreshing absence of vanity in eating and drinking in Alsace. That is not to say there is no *haute cuisine* to be found, however. One of France's 19 Michelin-ranked three-star restaurants, **L'Auberge de l'Ill**, in Illhaeusern, is considered by many epicures the finest in the country, and there are half a dozen places with two-star ratings. Single stars are scattered about like storks' nests.

The province's specialties are soul- as well as stomach-satisfying: the irresistible *choucroute,* wine-cured sauerkraut buried under ham hocks, sausages, smoked bacon, pork slabs, and potatoes; the fatted goose that yields up its liver as foie gras, giving gastronomy *pâté de foie gras en croute;* roasted suckling pig; fried carp and game; *tarte à l'oignon,* an onion tart; *kugelhopf,* a large cake like a Teuton prince's crown; *tuiles,* thin, delicate pastry sheets shaped like roof tiles; *tartes mirabelles,* employing a small, rosy plum; fir-tree honey; and creamy Munster cheese.

Vines have been cultivated in Alsace since 222. Unlike the standard procedure in Bordeaux, Burgundy, and elsewhere, wines here are labeled after the grape: Sylvaner, Pinot (*blanc* and *noir* and even *gris*), Riesling, Muscat, Traminer, Chasselas.

Gewürztraminer means simply a spicy (*gewürz*) Traminer; Tokay d'Alsace is a Pinot Gris; a table wine of blended grapes is called Zwicker, and a Zwicker of blended fine grapes is Edelzwicker. The sparkling Crémant d'Alsace is made by the *méthode champenoise* from the Pinot Blanc or Riesling grape. Rosé d'Alsace is rather well known, but Alsatian reds from Ottrott and Marlenheim are rare.

In 1975 legislation created the *Grand Cru* appellation in Alsace, and it has been awarded to 25 top vineyards. In 1984 late-harvest wines—*Vendanges Tardives*—were recognized. Deep and rich in flavor, they are reminiscent of heavy Sauternes. Even more rare is the sweet *Sélection des Grains Nobles,* produced only in great years from individually selected grapes affected by "noble rot," the fungus mold *Botrytis cinerea,* which enhances flavor. The *eaux-de-vie* (brandylike liqueurs) are forceful but refined. Best known are *framboise* (raspberry), *mirabelle* (plum), *kirsch* (cherry), and *myrtille* (blueberry). Gilbert Miclo Distillery in Lapoutroie, on the route from St-Dié to Colmar, makes the best.

France is much less renowned for its beers than its wines, but Kronenbourg, an Alsatian brew, is widely known and one of the best commercial brands.

Every day of the week except Sunday it's market day somewhere in Alsace. Patricia Wells, the author of *The Food Lover's Guide to France,* reports that the liveliest take place on Tuesdays in Bar-le-Duc; Wednesdays in Gérardmer; Fridays in Haguenau and Strasbourg; and Saturdays in Colmar, Mulhouse, Munster, Strasbourg, and Wissembourg.

In late April to early May the *Foire de Printemps* (Spring Fair) is held in Strasbourg, and in Wissembourg an international folkfest is staged in May. In June Ribeauvillé puts on its *Fête du Kugelhopf,* while Saverne holds its *Festival de la Rose;* Orbey's *Fête de la Tarte au Fromage* (cheese tart) takes place from late June to early July; Sarrebourg's *Fête du Fromage Blanc et des Traditions Rurales* (white cheese and folklore), in July; Ribeauvillé's *Foire aux Vins et Fête Folklorique,* in July; Thann holds a *Fête de la Poitrine Farcie* (stuffed veal breast) in July; Haguenau, the *Fête du Houblon et Semaine Gastronomique* (hops festival and food week) in August; Colmar, the *Foire aux Vins et Représentations Folkloriques* in August; and Obernai, the *Fête des Vendanges* (grape harvest) in October.

The city of Strasbourg is the main departure point for trips through the Alsace area. The *Route du Vin* runs south from near Strasbourg past Obernai, Colmar, then the Munster Valley and on down to Thann, near Mulhouse and the Swiss border.

STRASBOURG

Strataburgum, as its Roman name states, has since its founding been a European crossroads.

The capital of Alsace, seat of the Council of Europe since its foundation in 1949, and one of the three capitals of the European Parliament (the other two are Luxembourg and Brussels), Strasbourg is resolutely international and business-minded in outlook and focus. Yet as Mayor Marcel Rudloff put it, "We *Strasbourgeois* are sometimes accused of being too attached to the past . . . if you pass by our cathedral you will understand why we cannot help feeling attached to such a glorious background."

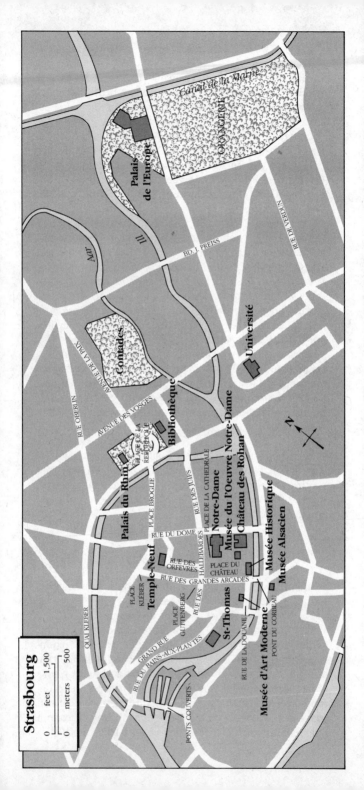

Strasbourg

feet	1,500
0	
meters	500
0	

Canal de la Marne

ORANGERIE

Palais de l'Europe

Aar

Ill

BD. J. PREISS

RUE DE VERDUN

Contades

AVENUE DE LA PAIX

Université

RUE OBERLIN

AVENUE DES VOSGES

Bibliothèque

PLACE DE LA RÉPUBLIQUE

Palais du Rhin

PLACE BROGLIE

RUE DES JUIFS

PLACE DE LA CATHÉDRALE

Notre-Dame

Musée du l'Oeuvre Notre-Dame

Château des Rohan

RUE DU DOME

RUE DES HALLEBARDES

RUE DES ORFEVRES

PLACE DU CHÂTEAU

Musée Historique

Musée Alsacien

Temple-Neuf

RUE DES GRANDES ARCADES

QUAI KLEBER

PLACE KLEBER

PLACE GUTTENBERG

RUE DES

St-Thomas

RUE DE LA DOUANE

Musée d'Art Moderne

PONT DU CORBEAU

GRAND RUE

RUE DU BAINS-AUX-PLANTES

PONTS COUVERTS

N

Doubtless it is evidence of that "glorious background" that the foreign traveller seeks out, but the sense of vitality and contemporary busyness comes as a dividend.

Born in 10 B.C., as Argentoratum, this Roman stronghold that is now Strasbourg was renamed Strataburgum under Clovis, king of the Franks, and developed into a major crossroads of commerce, warfare, and Christianity. In the sixth century Scottish monks set up worship on the site of today's church of St-Thomas, where Albert Schweitzer once served as an organist.

In the 11th century Strasbourg came under the rule of the Hapsburgs, and during the Crusades Frederick Barbarossa had many fortresses and convents built in the region; in 1201 Strasbourg was sanctioned as a free city of the Holy Roman Empire.

From 1336 onward the privilege of staging an annual European fair was granted to Strasbourg, and it is still held here, during the first half of September. The 14th century also saw the city become a center of Rhenish mysticism and then, in the 15th and 16th centuries, a capital of humanism and Protestantism.

Johann Gutenberg perfected the printing press in Strasbourg between 1434 and 1444. A statue of him commands today's **place Gutenberg;** the American Declaration of Independence is for some reason engraved on its pedestal.

In 1681 Louis XIV brought Strasbourg under French rule; in 1871 it was ceded to Germany, but in 1919 it again became French; in 1940 the Germans claimed it, until 1944, when it was once again declared part of France.

Strasbourg is the sixth-largest city in the country and the second-largest port on the Rhine (Rotterdam being first). It's also the seat of several international institutions: the European Court of Human Rights, the European Youth Center, the European Foundation of Science, the International Institute of Human Rights, the Central Committee for Rhine Navigation, and the International Faculty of Comparative Law.

Strasbourg accords great importance to music, staging the **International Music Festival,** Europe's oldest, in June. In addition to enjoying concerts by the Strasbourg Philharmonic and the Percussions of Strasbourg, travellers may be seduced by performances by the Opera of the Rhine, Strasbourg National Theater, Rhine Ballet, Alsatian Theater, and the satirical cabaret Barabli.

A flea market is held Wednesdays through Saturdays on the rue du Vieille-Hôpital.

The heart of old Strasbourg is an egg-shaped near-island within the arms of the River Ill and its canals. At its western end, the quays, canals, and half-timbered houses of La Petite France doze in picturesque memories of the past, while on the east, beyond place Broglie, the opera house, and the Hôtel de Ville, bridges link the old city across the river to the Germanic 19th century.

Beginning in about 1870, the Germans erected grand public buildings in an attempt to create a new city center. Here is the large, beautifully gardened place de la République with its two wings of the Palace of the Rhine on one side and the Théâtre Nationale and Bibliothèque Nationale on the other. The same area includes the place de l'Université and the university buildings, the gardens of the Orangerie, the Palais de Congrès and Palais de l'Europe, and the great port of the Rhine (known as Le Port Autonome; excursions available).

Inside the oval, most major attractions of Strasbourg are within ambling distance of each other: place Kléber, somewhat off-center; the cathedral of Notre-Dame and a cluster of museums to the southeast, right off the river; and several worthwhile churches in the western half of the city.

The Cathedral Quarter

Notre-Dame will stop zealous cathedral visitors right in their tracks. Begun in the Romanesque style in 1015 on the site of a temple to Hercules, it was not declared finished until 1439, by which time it had become mostly—and superbly—Gothic.

Strasbourg's life has been intimately entwined with that of its cathedral. Martin Luther's 95 theses were posted here as well as on the church door in Wittenberg, Germany, and during the ensuing Reformation (about 1520–1689), Strasbourg became a center of the Protestant movement; Protestants and Catholics battled beneath the 14th-century Wise and Foolish Virgins sculpted on the church's right-hand portal. Only in 1681, when the city was seized by Louis XIV, was its cathedral returned to Catholicism.

It was here, in 1725, that Louis XV married Marie Leszczyńska, and here, in 1770, that Marie Antoinette arrived from Vienna en route to her marriage to the future Louis XVI. At the same time, a university student named Johann Wolfgang von Goethe was climbing to the top of the tower and looking woozily into space in attempts to cure his dizzy spells.

In addition to its famous spire and façade, Notre-Dame's treasures include 12th- to 14th-century stained-glass windows (the finest were removed, piece by piece, during World War II, found afterward buried in salt mines in Wurtemberg, and put back in place), the pulpit in Flamboyant Gothic, the 17th-century tapestries, and the **astronomical clock.** The clock runs slow by half an hour and now goes through its daily noon celebrations at 12:30 P.M. Crowds assemble to watch at least half an hour in advance.

A *son-et-lumière* production in the cathedral illustrates Strasbourg's 20-centuries-long history every night except on certain annual holidays; the program is given in German at 8:00 P.M. and in French at 9:00 P.M.

Across the leafy place du Château is the **Musée de l'Oeuvre Notre-Dame**, which is devoted to Alsatian arts from the Middle Ages to the Renaissance, original sculptures from the cathedral (because of weather damage, many of the soft, pink sandstone figures have had to be replaced), Roman and pre-Roman sculptures, and paintings of the Alsatian School.

Also across the place du Château is the Château des Rohan, constructed in 1704 for Cardinal Armand de Rohan-Soubise, bishop of Strasbourg. It now houses the Musée des Beaux-Arts, the Musée Archéologique, and the Musée des Arts Décoratifs.

Renaissance painters and primitives of the Italian school are particularly well represented in the **Beaux-Arts**, with less emphasis on the Spanish (aside from a wonderful El Greco Virgin) and the Dutch-Flemish (but one superb Pieter de Hooch). The collection of still-lifes is highly touted.

The **archaeological museum** devotes itself largely to prehistoric discoveries made in Alsace, but with fine displays of Roman and Merovingian relics. The finest grouping of ceramics in France is on show at **Arts Décoratifs**, including fine faïence from 18th-century Strasbourg, the best of which comes from the famous "blue" period. In addition to the museums, the château houses a stamp and art library.

Good restaurants in varying degrees of informality cluster near the cathedral, of which **Kammerzell** (built between 1467 and 1589) is the best known, largely because of its stunning woodwork. It is a fine place in which to sample regional specialties. Old Alsatian decor and quiet characterize **Zimmer**, a perennial favorite with the *Strasbourgeois* that is located at 8 rue du Temple Neuf.

Winstubs, historic, informal places suited to settling the world's problems over long lunches on traditional fare, abound in the cathedral quarter. The best are **Strissel**, 5, place de la Grande Boucherie; **Tire-Bouchon**, 5, rue des Tailleurs-de-Pierre; **Chez Muller**, 10, place du Marché-aux-Cochons-de-Lait; and **Au Pigeon**, 23, rue des Tonneliers, an amiably rustic spot that has been in business since the Middle Ages.

Three top winstubs that cater more to tourists are the brasserie-like **Le Dauphin**, right across from Notre-Dame; **Aux Armes de Strasbourg**, 9, place Gutenberg, with the best French fries in town; and **L'Ancienne Douane**, 6, rue de la Douane, which has a terrace overlooking the Ill. (Winstubs and brasseries are alike in their informality, simplicity of traditional fare served, and coziness in cold weather. Originally, as their names imply, winstubs were directly in or connected to individual wineries, while brasseries bore the same relationship to breweries. Today, they usually have no physical relationship to a production site, but may serve chiefly one brand of drink.)

The winding streets to the northwest of Notre-Dame are chic shopping country; Strasbourg is one of the smartest of French cities as far as style is concerned. Particularly attractive are the rue des Hallebardes, rue du Dôme, and rue des Orfèvres, this last gaily decorated with banners representing the cities and regions of Alsace. Gastronomic souvenirs, specially packaged—foie gras, sausages, *choucroute,* cheeses, mustards, honey, chocolates, wines, and liqueurs—are found in rich plenty at places such as **Au Bec Fin**, 8, rue des Orfèvres, and **La Toque Blanche**, 36, rue des Hallebardes.

On the north bank of the Ill, the **Musée Historique** (in the 16th-century slaughterhouse) and the **Musée d'Art Moderne** (in the reconstructed customs house) face each other across bustling rue des Grandes Arcades. The former is fascinating to visitors interested in arms, armory, uniforms, and other trappings of war; the latter to enthusiasts of modern French painting, including works by Jean Arp, a *Strasbourgeois,* and stained glass by such makers as Jean Lurçat.

Across the Ill via the Pont du Corbeau, a pleasant bridge from which child murderers and parricides were suspended in iron cages until they drowned, is the **Musée Alsacien**. Occupying three adjoining 16th- and 17th-century houses, it displays to perfection the Alsatian past in costumes, bedchambers, and kitchens—all the essentials of everyday life.

Just off the place de la Cathédrale, the **Hôtel des Rohan** offers 36 stylish rooms furnished in Louis XV fashion or regional rustic decor, but with up-to-date conveniences and even minibars. The clientele is one that appreciates quiet and restrained surroundings and scorns both the prices and the activity of the town's top-rated hotels. Nonetheless, Rohan is surrounded by cathedral and bistro noise and bustle; guests who are bothered by such things should inquire about rooms away from the street.

La Petite France

Once upon a time tanners, fishermen, and millers made this quarter their own. Now, with its narrow streets that wind along the Ill and its canals lined by beautiful 16th- and 17th-century half-timbered houses, La Petite France is the most picturesque part of Strasbourg. The excellent restaurants and small art and gift shops of the district attract a sizable permanent population as well as a touristic one.

The "main" street of this quarter is the rue du Bains-aux-Plantes, but all are worth strolling before taking a little something at **La Maison des Tanneurs**, a restaurant in perhaps the prettiest of the old houses that offers a warm welcome and excellent regional cooking, including *choucroute au Champagne*. **La Würtzmühle**, another possibility, is a triple threat, with a fashionable restaurant accenting fish specialties upstairs, a lively *Bierstub* on the ground floor, and the basement disco, **Le Club des Moulins**, where university students are prone to riot late at night.

Spanning the Ill and forming the ancient ramparts are the **Ponts Couverts**, three bridges topped each with a 14th-century tower. Convenient to this point of architectural and historical interest is a good, informal *Bierstub-winstub* called **L'Ami Schutz**. Of the several other welcoming retreats in the neighborhood, the most attractive because of its curious *orgue de Barbarie* (an antique player-piano), is **Lohkäs**. Students in winter and tourists in summer pack the four-storied restaurant **Au Pont St-Martin** to enjoy the large terrace and panoramic view.

Behind the Ponts-Couverts, a moored barge (*péniche*) serves as a floating disco known as **La Péniche-Le Fantasc**, which draws a steady, more mature group than the Club des Moulins.

Place Kléber

Although it is the commercial heart of the city, place Kléber is nonetheless quite handsome. In the square's center is a statue of a local boy who made good, Général Jean-Baptiste Kléber, born here in 1753 and assassinated in Cairo in 1800. On the statue's base are carved the words with which he replied to an English admiral's suggestion of surrender: "Soldiers, one responds to such insolence only with victories."

A giant parking garage underneath place Kléber is the best place to park while you explore the city. On the north side of the square the enormous, 18th-century **Aubette**, owned by the Kronenbourg brewery, supplies a rotisserie, a brasserie, dancing, snack bars, and a dining room that can seat a thousand hungry people, as well as the largest sidewalk café in eastern France—or maybe anywhere.

An easy amble to east and west are two of the town's top epicurean retreats, **Le Crocodile**, where the renowned chef Emile Jung presides, and **Valentin Sorg**, which offers classic cuisine and a superb view from the 14th floor of a rather off-putting skyscraper.

Just off the place, the **Nouvel Hôtel Maison Rouge** is comfortably old-fashioned in appearance and atmosphere, though guest rooms were renovated not long ago. In the middle of the local price range, it is very handily located for walkers.

Strasbourg's **Hilton Hotel** is just as modern and well outfitted as you might imagine, though rather more than a stroll from the center. It offers all the comforts of international home and some particular amenities for businessmen and small meetings, and its dining room, **La Maison du Boeuf**, ranks highly even in this city full of good restaurants; rates are as up-to-date as the design.

Hôtel Terminus-Gruber, right across the place de la Gare from the railway station, is the choice of travellers who like their inns elegantly turned out in the Old World manner, yet unpretentious and welcoming. The **Cour de Rosemont** dining room is quite good.

Strasbourg University and l'Orangerie

Strasbourg's vitality stems in great part from its university, one of the foremost in France since its founding in the 17th century. Perhaps among its 35,000 students today there is another Goethe, a Napoléon, or a Metternich. A drive around the university and its handsome gardens—and perhaps a stop at its Musée Zoologique—is a pleasant detour en route to the **Palais de l'Europe**.

The Palais is home to both the Council of Europe (21 member states) and the European Parliament (434 members representing more than 270 million people). Guided tours are offered to the public.

Neighboring the Palais is the **Orangerie**, a park laid out by the famous garden architect André Le Nôtre in 1692. A walk through its handsome gardens is preparation for a meal at the beautifully sited **Buerehiesel**. Chef Antoine Westermann serves two-star Michelin cuisine in a rustic, traditional Alsatian house. He ranks among the Maîtres Cuisiniers de France (master chefs), as does his colleague Emile Jung at the aforementioned Crocodile.

LA ROUTE DU VIN

A drive down the 100-mile so-called wine road from **Marlenheim** in the north (due west of Strasbourg) to **Thann** in the south ranks among the most intriguing passages in Europe. People have been known to do it in one day, but they can't have been satisfied with that. Three days should be the minimum.

En route, wine tasting is invited at numerous vineyards. Every twist and turn of the road seems to demand a stop for photographing hill-climbing vineyards, Renaissance town halls and oriels, busy markets, Medieval walls, châteaux in ruins and otherwise, Romanesque clock towers, Gothic churches, streets dressed in brilliant flowers, folk festivals, and shop windows full of good things to eat and drink.

Tradition lives in **Turckheim**, outside Colmar, where at 10:00 on summer evenings the last night watchman extant in Alsace passes through still streets in his greatcoat, carrying halberd, lamp, and trumpet and calling out the hour and "All's well."

Dining throughout the region is universally good; especially recommended are:

- **Hostellerie du Cerf** (Marlenheim)
- **Beau Site** (Ottrott-le-Haut)
- **Clos St-Vincent** (Ribeauvillé)
- **Chambard** (Kaysersberg, hometown of Albert Schweitzer)
- **Aux Armes de France** (Ammerschwir)
- **Auberge du Père Floranc** (Wettolsheim, where winegrowing began in Roman times)
- **Le Caveau** (Eguisheim)
- **Château d' Isenbourg** (Rouffach)
- **Résidence les Violettes** (Guebwiller–Jungholtz)

All but Le Caveau are also inns, cozy for those wanting to sleep off a surfeit of *terrine de foie gras au vieux Gewürztraminer*.

At least nine routes in addition to the Route du Vin have been designed for travellers with special interests: Route des Crêtes (mountaintop road); Route Fleurie (for those interested in gardens, parks, decorated homes); Route de la Plaine et des Forêts (North Vosges regional park, local color and folklore); A l'Assaut des Vieux Châteaux (Assault of Old Castles—for enthusiasts of Medieval ruins); others devoted to open spaces, tobacco, cheese, liqueurs, and even fried carp. (See Getting Around at the end of this chapter.)

There are other places and items of interest in Alsace besides the Route du Vin, of course; we cover them parallel to this route, from Strasbourg, at the northern end of Alsace, running southward through Colmar toward Thann and Mulhouse.

MONT STE-ODILE

Something about the deep green, worn old Vosges inspires brooding, and a good place to indulge in that lonesome mood is this mount, southwest of Strasbourg, dedicated to the patron saint of Alsace.

Away to the south of the convent of Ste-Odile, the so-called **pagan wall** curves through the forests. This wall of immense blocks once must have belted in a camp, a fortification of some sort, in the days before French memory. Was it Gallic? Was it Celtic? Nobody knows, but it makes the Roman road nearby look positively new.

The setting is a fine one for the telling of the tale of

Odile, a blind and weak child born in the seventh century in the village of Obernai just down the hill. She was the daughter of the sullen and loathsome Duke Adalric, a.k.a. Etichon, who, because of her miserable condition and because she was, in any case, a girl, ordered her put to death.

The story twists and turns like today's road up the mountain. Suffice it to say the wicked Etichon lost in the war of life; Odile won and founded a convent in her father's château, Hohenbourg. She also established the abbey of Niedermunster, which served after her death and throughout the Middle Ages as a great pilgrimage site. In the 16th century a fire destroyed most of the antique structures; these were replaced in the 17th century, but an 11th-century chapel survived, and there the ashes of Etichon remain; those of Odile repose nearby in an eighth-century stone sarcophagus.

A day may be spent happily driving south of Mont Ste-Odile in the **Hohwald** glimpsing old châteaux and monasteries in the forests, coming upon neat villages, and slowing down for views that on clear days stretch to Switzerland's Bernese Alps.

When night comes on, you might stay at the attractive **Hôtel du Parc** in Obernai or the small, quiet **Beau Site** in nearby Ottrott-le-Haut, with its one-star Michelin restaurant (wild duck with cassis is a specialty there in autumn). The traditional but not cute pottery, glassware, and wooden goods of Alsace may be purchased at **Dietrich's** on Obernai's place du Marché.

HAUT-KOENIGSBOURG

The reworked feudal castle in Haut-Koenigsbourg (north of Colmar), considered to be the most important in the Vosges, was the seat of Swiss counts before it was burned down by Swedish invaders in 1633 during the Thirty Years' War. It provides some observers with grounds for the argument that ruins can be more satisfying than restorations.

COLMAR

In the days when Charlemagne kept a regal residence on the banks of the river Lauch, a hamlet of workers and farmers grew up around the villa's tower and its dove-cote. The Villa Columbaria, or house of *colombes* (doves), was to give its name to the growing town.

Today Colmar's popularity with some travellers sur-passes even that of Strasbourg's, because it is comfortably smaller (population about 70,000) and less an industrial and business center than a vital repository of art and Alsatian architecture.

In Colmar there is a strong sense of connection with the United States. In 1986 many Americans celebrating the centennial of the Statue of Liberty made pilgrimages here to visit the home of the statue's sculptor, Frédéric Auguste Bartholdi. Since that time Colmariens have been even more conscious of their American ties, as the city's newspapers remind readers that Americans as diverse as Henry Firestone and the film director William Wyler were Alsatian. Colmariens also believe that everybody in the States is familiar with Castroville, a colony formed in Texas in 1844 that is known as "Little Alsace."

Colmar centers on the 13th- to 14th-century **church of St-Martin**, worth seeing particularly for the sculptures on its façade; from the square all the most important sites in town may be investigated in one long day's stroll. The area is also good sidewalk-café country.

Near the church, at 30, rue des Marchands, is the **Musée Bartholdi**, installed in the family home where the sculptor was born. Examples of his sculpture abound in the museum, but even more interesting are his paintings and the porcelain, furniture, family portraits, project mod-els, and other personal effects. All over town the walker will encounter Bartholdi: the statue of Général Rapp in the place of the same name; the Roesselmann fountain, dedicated to local heroes; the winegrowers' fountain; and other monuments. A statue of Bartholdi himself, sculpted in 1907 by the Parisian Louis Noël, stands in a pretty garden near the court of appeals, chisel in hand, his elbow resting on his workstool near a tiny Statue of Liberty.

An extraordinary **Bartholdi grave monument** in the cemetery shows a brave soldier trying, in death, to strug-gle out from under the cracked lid of his tomb. It is unsettling, and worth a detour.

By far the most important site in Colmar is the **Musée d'Unterlinden** at place d'Unterlinden. Installed in the former convent of the Unterlinden Dominicans and in-cluding its chapel and 13th-century cloisters as well as the museum's greatest treasure, the 16th-century **Issenheim Altarpiece** of Mathias Grünewald, Musée d'Unterlinden alone is worth the trip to northeastern France. The museum also houses paintings by local artists, items of historical and folkloric interest, winepresses, stone engravings and sculptures, and some superb stained glass.

Narrow cobbled and beflowered streets flanked by 16th- and 17th-century half-timbered houses curve prettily through **La Petite Venise**, the old town, and the **Krutenau quarter**, once a fortified suburb, near the canals of the Lauch. A good, typical, informal luncheon may be had in the **Caveau St-Pierre**, just off the canal on rue Herse.

Not far away cluster many of the area's handsomest old houses: the old customs house, **Ancienne Douane; Maison Pfister**, ornamented with frescoes and medallions; and **Maison des Têtes**, a Renaissance house occupied by a fine and popular restaurant.

The best hotel in Colmar is the handsome, cozy **Terminus-Bristol**, with its one-star restaurant, **Rendez-vous de Chasse**. Also in town is the elegant **Schillinger** restaurant at 16, rue Stanislas, boasting two stars, and the one-star **Fer Rouge**, at 52, Grand' Rue.

On Saturday the Colmar market is particularly interesting. In early August the Foire aux Vins et Fête Folklorique lures people from all over eastern France, while the first three Saturdays in September, an ideal season for visiting, bring Les Journées de la Choucroute (Sauerkraut Days). During June the Colmar festival features concerts of classical music.

EBERSMUNSTER

Only in the Swiss Vorarlberg will you find Baroque abbeys comparable to Ebersmunster's. This burst of Baroque exuberance was associated with the Counter-Reformation and the desire of Catholic crusaders to move the Church away from the Gothic style, which had begun to seem barbarous. Here is richness that stops short of excess, embodied in a magnificence of gold leaf, stucco ornamentation, a sumptuous high altar, frescoes and paintings in glowing pastels, floral abstractions, garlands and sculptures, and angels as plump as Italian *putti*. The woodwork is remarkable as well, particularly in the choir stalls and in a pulpit supported by Samson, his brow wrinkled with effort. The superb organ is the 18th-century work of André Silbermann; concerts in May show it off.

The history of Ebersmunster, which today has fewer than 500 inhabitants, is as old as that of Christianity in Alsace and edges back into legend. Etichon, the father of Saint Odile, is said to have constructed an abbey here, perhaps to atone for his meanness.

Ebersmunster tends to appear only on large-scale regional maps. To find it (via a highly recommended detour off the Route du Vin), wind due east of Dambach-la-Ville on back roads. More easily, take N 83 for about 20 km (12 miles) northeast of Sélestat.

MUNSTER VALLEY

In the seventh century Irish monks retreated into the rich and quiet valleys west of Colmar, establishing there a monastery, or *munster,* that has been famous from the 15th century onward for its production of the cheese that bears its name. The village of Munster is a modest holiday spot with a handful of small, unpretentious inns, as is Hohrodberg, which is substantially higher in altitude. The best time to visit is in June during the **Albert Schweitzer Music Festival**, when concerts are held in the Romanesque Munster church. The gem of the whole region is the small, circular lake called **Fischboedle**.

MURBACH

"Proud as the dog of Murbach" was a saying understood for the thousand years that the **abbey of Murbach**, bearing upon its coat of arms a silver greyhound, reigned over the region of Guebwiller and enjoyed the protection of Charlemagne and the Holy Roman Empire.

Proud indeed. Founded, according to legend, by Saint Pirmin in 727, it was the repository of the riches of one of the great lords of the day, Count Eberhard of Eguisheim. Murbach's monks were knights; its armies looted and raided and exacted tribute in good feudal tradition, and only ranking nobility could enter its doors. The abbey even minted its own money.

Great imagination is required today to summon up the lost might of Murbach, and imagination is aided only by the serenity of the site, a remote and wooded valley in the foothills of the Vosges. What remains of the abbey are the choir and the transept, with its twin 12th-century towers; the nave has vanished. To find Murbach, take D 430 west up the Vallée de Guebwiller from Guebwiller itself (south of Colmar on the Route du Vin) or, if following the Route des Crêtes, turn east on D 430 from Le Markstein, a winter-sports center.

Mulhouse (moo-LOSE) is of no particular interest to the visitor, who will probably pass through it en route to Burgundy or Switzerland.

GETTING AROUND

Lorraine

The major Autoroute from Paris to Nancy passes through Reims and cuts south through Metz. A more direct route, though probably no faster, follows E 11 and E 12 through Vitry-le-François. For horseback riding and other outdoor touring, see A.R.T.E. Lorraine, Dombrot-le-Sec, Contrexéville 88140.

Alsace

The fastest route from Paris to Strasbourg is Autoroute 4 via Reims. Drivers coming from Nancy and other points in Lorraine may choose from among several routes of varying persuasions; the two major ones are via Sarrebourg to the north and via St-Dié to the south.

Air Inter flies several times daily between Paris (departing from Orly Ouest airport) and Strasbourg, and daily also to Colmar–Houssen. Several trains leave Paris's Gare de l'Est daily for Strasbourg and for Colmar. By early 1989 the French National Railroad plans to have new "Super First Class" service between Paris and Strasbourg on upgraded TEE (Trans-Europ Express) equipment. Welcome lounges at railroad stations similar to airport membership clubs are open to first-class passengers in Paris, Nancy, and Strasbourg.

A car is essential for exploring Alsace. Five rental companies maintain offices in Strasbourg; Avis is right on the railroad square.

Maps of the **Route du Vin** and other itineraries are available from tourism offices in Strasbourg and Colmar.

Barge cruises are available on the rivers and canals of Alsace-Lorraine through various companies. Among the trips is a six-day, seven-night barge cruise from Nancy to

Strasbourg that can be arranged through Horizon Cruises, Ltd., 16000 Ventura Blvd., Suite 200, Encino, CA 91436. Other trips are available from Continental Waterways, Boston, MA; Floating Through Europe, Inc., New York, NY; France Bonjour Travel, Sydney, Australia; Sparks, Slater & Association, Toronto, Ontario, Canada; Continental Waterways, Godalming, Surrey, England. At least one company, Locaboat Plaisance of Joigny in Burgundy, arranges sail-yourself cruises in Alsace-Lorraine.

In Strasbourg, regularly scheduled boat sailings on the Ill and the Rhine depart the Château des Rohan and Promenade Dauphine several times daily, both day and night. Minitrains operate except in midwinter on an hour-long tour that begins near the cathedral, with commentary in English, French, or German.

Sightseeing flights over Strasbourg and the Alsatian plain may be booked at tourist offices.

ACCOMMODATIONS REFERENCE

▶ **Altéa St-Thiébault.** 29, place St-Thiébault, 57000 **Metz.** Tel: 87-37-38-39; Telex: 861815.

▶ **Beau Site.** 67530 **Ottrott.** Tel: 88-95-80-61.

▶ **La Bergerie.** 57640 **Argancy.** Tel: 87-77-82-27.

▶ **Résidence Chambard.** Rue Général-de-Gaulle, 68240 **Kaysersberg.** Tel: 89-47-10-17; Telex: 880272.

▶ **Château d'Isenbourg.** 68250 **Rouffach.** Tel: 89-49-63-53; in U.S., (212) 696-1323 or (201) 235-1990.

▶ **Hostellerie La Cheneaudière.** 67420 **Colroy-La-Roche.** Tel: 88-97-61-64; in U.S., (212) 696-1323. Only 23 rooms in this elegant, gardened retreat in a village of 431 people; two-Michelin-star restaurant.

▶ **Le Clos St-Vincent.** Route de Bergheim, 68150 **Ribeauvillé.** Tel: 89-73-67-65.

▶ **Hostellerie Coq Hardi.** 8, avenue Victoire, 55100 **Verdun.** Tel: 29-86-36-36.

▶ **Cosmos.** Rue Metz, 88140 **Contrexéville.** Tel: 29-08-15-90.

▶ **Aux Ducs de Lorraine.** 16, Route du Vin, 68590 **St-Hippolyte.** Tel: 89-73-00-09. Good headquarters along the Route du Vin.

▶ **Grand Hôtel.** 68410 **Les Trois Epis.** Tel: 89-49-80-65. Beautifully sited 50-room Vosges resort with pool, sauna, solarium, massage, and other amenities.

▶ **Grand Hôtel Etablissement.** 88140 **Contrexéville.** Tel: 29-08-17-30.

▶ **Grand Hôtel de la Reine.** 2, place Stanislas, 54000 **Nancy.** Tel: 83-35-03-01; Telex: 960367.

▶ **Hilton Hotel.** Avenue Herrenschmidt, 67000 **Strasbourg.** Tel: 88-37-10-10; Telex: 890363; in U.S., (212) 697-9370 or (800) 223-1146.

▶ **Nouvel Hôtel Maison Rouge.** 4, rue Francs-Bourgeois, 67000 **Strasbourg.** Tel: 88-32-08-60; Telex: 880130.

▶ **Hôtel au Moulin.** 27, Route de Strasbourg, 67610 **Wantzenau.** Tel: 88-96-27-83. Unpretentious inn in a former mill on the river in a small Strasbourg suburb; two outstanding restaurants and modest prices.

▶ **Hôtel du Parc.** 169, rue Général-Gouraud, 67210 **Obernai.** Tel: 88-95-50-08; Telex: 870615.

▶ **Auberge du Père Floranc.** 9, rue Herzog, 68920 **Wettolsheim.** Tel: 89-80-79-14.

▶ **Résidence des Vannes.** 6, rue de la Porte-Haute, 54460 **Liverdun.** Tel: 83-24-53-87.

▶ **Hôtel des Rohan.** 17–19, rue du Maroquin, 67000 **Strasbourg.** Tel: 88-32-85-11; Telex: 870047; in U.S., (212) 686-9213, (212) 477-1600, (800) 223-1356, or (800) 223-1510.

▶ **Hôtel St-Barnabé.** 68530 **Murbach.** Tel: 89-76-92-15; Telex: 881036. Small, modestly priced valley retreat.

▶ **Sofitel.** Place Paraiges, 57000 **Metz.** Tel: 87-74-57-27; in U.S., (212) 354-3722 or (800) 221-4542.

▶ **Terminus-Bristol.** 7, place de la Gare, 68000 **Colmar.** Tel: 89-23-59-59; Telex: 880248.

▶ **Terminus-Gruber.** 10, place de la Gare, 67000 **Strasbourg.** Tel: 88-32-87-00.

▶ **Résidence les Violettes.** Jungholtz-Thierenbach 68500 **Guebwiller.** Tel: 89-76-91-19.

NORMANDY

By Fred Halliday

Fred Halliday, a frequent contributor to Food and Wine, Connoisseur, *and* Travel & Leisure *magazines, divides his time between his residences in Connecticut and Paris.*

Everyone talks about Normandy's pungent flavor. There is the flavor of its cheeses—Camembert, Livarot, Pont-l'Evêque—strong and unlike anything else in the world. There is the character of its drinks—Calvados and Bénédictine—spirited and flowery. There is the personality of its people, known even among the French for boundless stubbornness. William the Conqueror was Norman; so was Claude Monet.

The Norman landscape, too, has its dichotomy. In the main the division is between the gaming spas of its coast and the terrain of its interior, liberally sprinkled with apple orchards and dairy cows.

History has made a continuous march through Normandy, invading its beaches and passing through crossroads hamlets to its landlocked capital. Tracing those footprints is the visitor's most rewarding objective.

MAJOR INTEREST

Verdant rural landscape, especially in the Pays d'Auge

Calvados and Bénédictine

Camembert and other cheeses

Seacoast, especially the ports of Fécamp and Honfleur, the famous resort of Deauville, and the D-Day landing beaches

Rouen
Cathedral

Antique shops
Museums, especially Musée de la Céramique and
    Musée des Beaux-Arts
Medieval quarter around the rue du Gros Horloge

Bayeux Tapestry

Le Havre
Ferries to the U.K.
Musée des Beaux-Arts André Malraux

Rouen

If there is only one city in France the traveller will pass
through other than Paris, let it be Rouen. It should be seen
well, for it is a crown studded with the gems of France's
history and character. Here is the passion of Joan of Arc,
the very square where she was burned at the stake; here is
the cathedral Monet found so irresistible that he painted it
so many times in so many different ways. Here is a maze of
Medieval streets and architecture to explore on foot—car
traffic is banned. (The railroad station is a good place to
leave your car.) Here are excellent cafés, with the best
Bordeaux lists outside the Médoc; the Norman loves to
dine. Parisian antique dealers come to Rouen to buy; go
into the shops where you see their station wagons—the
ones whose license plate numbers end in 75—illegally
parked outside. And here you can find the best pressed
duck (*canard au sang,* a local specialty) in the world.
When strolling down the rue du Gros-Horloge, remember
that Rouen has wonderful chocolates and caramels, and
any of the sweet shops you find along here will be happy to
send some home. The place du Vieux-Marché itself is a
wide, bustling square; its brasserie is a good place for
lunch. Try hot prawns and Normandy sole, a special treat
for North Americans, who have probably only tasted the
flounder their restaurants *call* sole; it isn't. *Demoiselles à
la crème* (small lobsters in cream sauce) are also interesting. You can wash everything down with the excellent local
cider, but remember, there's a lot of walking to do in the
afternoon, and you'll want to save some room for dinner.

In the center of the city is the old town, which partly
escaped the war and was partly reconstructed from its
damages. Except for a few modern refurbishments, mostly
of glass and Lucite, appearances would make the average
person think that nothing had changed here for 500 years.
Here the visitor enters the Middle Ages down the

quarter-mile amble of old cobblestones that is the rue du Gros Horloge, lined with overhung stucco-and-beam houses (work called *colombage*). Because buildings were originally taxed according to the street space they took up, they were generally constructed with a small ground floor and upper floors—which were not taxed at all—that jutted out over the street. Originally a commercial thoroughfare, the rue du Gros Horloge has retained its hustle-and-bustle character with cafés, the aforementioned sweet shops, and little boutiques that make it worth a trip just for window shopping. Halfway down the street is its namesake, the **Gros Horloge** itself, a big clock spanning the street like a bridge, the pedestrians all walking underneath it and knowing the time.

Catercorner to the clock is a bell tower. If it's open, according to a complex schedule, you can visit a collection of clocks and clockworks inside. From the top of the tower a sparkling view gives out over the whole museumlike village. At your feet there's the quiet Medieval neighborhood of the rue Martinville, lined with half-timbered houses and cloisters. And just ahead looms the **cathedral of Rouen**, whose splendid Gothic logic Monet never tired painting in all its variations.

Among the many other sights, churches, and museums in Rouen is the **Musée de la Céramique**; the city was long an important originator of painted stoneware, and the museum's collection of ceramics from the 18th century is particularly fine, rivaling any ceramic collection in Europe. The **Musée des Beaux Arts** houses works by several name-brand Impressionists as well as art of other periods. The Musée Cornélien and the Musée Flaubert (both writers were natives of Rouen) are worth visiting, but the *grand musée* in Rouen is really its streets. What awaits indoors are primarily the pleasures of the Norman table.

Norman Food and Drink

More than half the dairy output of France—milk, cheese, and butter—is produced in Normandy. It is no wonder, then, that cream forms the basis of Norman cuisine. The velvety white *sauce normande* is used with everything, from eggs to vegetables and chicken, and is particularly fine on seafood, as the world well knows. However, there is another specialty of Rouen the visitor ought to sample.

The **Hôtel de Dieppe**, just across from the railroad

station on Rouen's main square, is a good place to go, not only for its rooms, which are comfortable and tasteful, but for its restaurant, **Le Quatre Saisons**. This is the place to eat the famous *canard au sang,* or pressed duck. As the menu at the Quatre Saisons will explain, their duck is a special variety. The animal is taken from a nearby backwater of the Seine where the local wild breed, the *col vert*—a type that approximates the mallard—crosses quite naturally with the domestic duck and then remains sedentary. The results are happy, as in delicious.

The Quatre Saisons is one of those places that awakens us to the truth: how good the top *centre ville* restaurant can be anywhere in the provinces, especially in the north of France. In an era often submerged by fad and bluff, the table of such an establishment is one of the best reasons for visiting the countryside—no less viable a reason than any art museum or barge tour down a river.

The duck is served at Quatre Saisons with an evident love of theater. You can observe the birds turning in their own juices in a spitarium. At just the right moment the thighs are carved off and taken to the kitchen for extra cooking and special preparation. Then the cart, with its towering duck press, is wheeled beside your table; it is your turn. The carcass is carved, two knives, no hands touching the flesh. Bones, neck, and giblets are pushed, cracked, and pressed in the gleaming machine; the blood is drawn off, the sauce made, poured, flambéed. And *voila!*—served.

Before a three-hour dinner like this, it might be wise to book a room at the hotel.

The bar here, as good a place as any to educate your palate, possesses a splendid array of that heady Norman passion, Calvados. Calva, as its lovers call it, is to the apple what Cognac is to the grape. This distillate of cider is aged in wood and bottled in grades. The least expensive is plain Calvados; then comes Calvados Pays d'Auge Reglémentée. Aging is a factor in grading, and within each grade there are the usual variations of quality according to bottler. One of the finest is Vieux Calvados from the house of Jean-Louis Favennac. To compare it to Cognac would be to belittle it.

You may see people around you quaffing Calvados during the meal; in fact, it is quite correct to do so. This is the *trou normand* (Norman hole) of which you may have heard tell, the idea behind the vivid phrase being that because the Norman meal is very heavy, you have to punch a hole in it—with some Calvados—and then proceed to fill it.

There is likewise a reason to drink Calva at the end of the meal, and a phrase to go along with it. The coffee is *coiffé,* the Normans say, and *recoiffé,* or spiked, with the brandy.

One final note: Many people say they cannot drink brandy because it keeps them awake at night, but report that drinking Calva induces sound sleep—with wild dreams. At any rate, after a Rouen dinner of *canard au sang,* fortified with a *trou normand* and a café *recoiffé,* sound sleep is a safe presumption.

Should the study of spirits prove fascinating, travellers should set their sights on **Fécamp**, a delicious slip of a fishing village cradled in a clef of white chalky cliffs 65 km (40 miles) to the northeast of Rouen. Here, the cathedral where the cordial Bénédictine was discovered in 1510 has been rebuilt as a distillery and the **Musée de la Bénédictine**, entered through massive wrought-iron gates and Gothic arcades. The spacious Salle des Abbés is presided over by stone (or stoned) statues of 16 past abbots. The monk who rediscovered the formula for Bénédictine (it was once lost) is depicted, with a trumpeting angel and a bottle of the elixir, in a stained-glass window.

Fécamp was also the home of Guy de Maupassant, and many of his short stories are dressed in the atmosphere of its streets. Cod fishing is no longer a local industry, but the marina is still interesting and the quai de la Marne receives massive quantities of other fish, as well as cargoes of raw chemicals and timber bound for French sawmills. Along the wharves are canneries, fish-dressing plants, and drydocks for boat repairs. On the place du General Leclerc is the **church of the Trinité**. In its length it rivals the longest in France, being less than ten feet short of Notre-Dame de Paris, and its spire is the quintessence of Norman towers.

Any of the cafés on the place are suitable for a lunch or a snack. Then you can retrace the 70 km (43 miles) back to Rouen, beyond which await the sweet grass smells and running hills of the Pays d'Auge.

The Pays d'Auge

This sun-dappled bocage, a 30-mile-long and 20-mile-wide valley of brooks and hills and farms, with cows

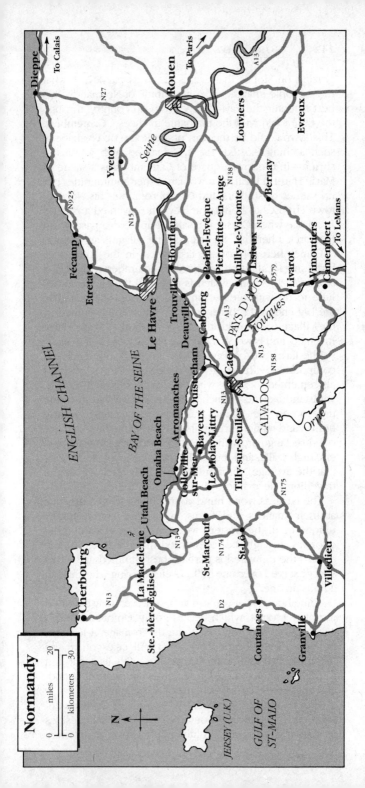

grazing on slopes that are as green as parsley, is what most people imagine when they think of Normandy. It is best to enter the Pays d'Auge from up country, through the little town with the big name in cheese, **Camembert**. This town could be the start of the Route de Fromage, if such a thing existed, for it is marked with a suitable shrine—in the town square of Camembert is a statue to Marie Harel, a local farm woman. Other communities put up statues of soldiers and conquerors, but this Norman town chooses to honor the lady who invented a cheese. In an age when Caesar is a salad, Napoléon a pastry, and Bismarck a herring, who can say the villagers are wrong?

Camembert, of course, tastes best in the land of its birth. In a local bistro or café, the Camembert to ask for is *camembert fermier,* which is made on the farm and has little to do with the perfumed and pasteurized dandies the big cheese factories concoct. The one consumed in the village is rich with the creamy kick that Marie Harel invented, and is worth the trip here.

The farms of the Pays d'Auge are built like enclosed compounds, with silo, granary, coops, and living quarters all cemented together within a continuous wall, as if to withstand a siege—which they might have had to in the time when the Vikings ranged these coasts. Country homes and manors are built along the same lines and are often rectangular, with turrets on the corners, watchtowers, high walls, and moats. This may give you some idea that the average Norman farm is hardly territory for the travelling salesman or, for that matter, the casual tourist.

The farmers won't mind your looking from a distance at their manors and farms, which are architecturally unique in all the Western world. As for approaching the doorway, though, be forewarned that the local attitude toward the uninvited is perhaps best summed up by this sign observed over one bell: "Useless to ring. The château admits no one."

Some homes that you can visit, however, may be found just after **Livarot**, which because of its famous cheese is an obligatory stop on our Route de Fromage. A left turn onto D 47 just beyond the town will take you to the incomparable manor of Coupesarte, with its moat and fortified wall. Just a bit further on is the Château Grand-champ, a 16th-century example of Norman privacy.

About 3 km (2 miles) before Lisieux is **St-Germain-de-Livet**, a château that puts out a real welcome mat. Besides its display of frescoes and lithography, the château offers an approximation of the sort of home atmosphere you might have expected there during the 16th century. Judging by the pitched Norman roofs and massive fireplaces, winters were much more snowy here than they are now.

Lisieux, for centuries a commercial hub (all Pays d'Auge roads lead there), was, with the exception of its cathedral, completely razed by the bombardments of World War II. Although the rebuilt town retains little of its former charm, it nonethelesss remains a busy center of the region's produce and agricultural industry.

The road leaving Lisieux for Pont-l'Evêque (D 579) is particularly picturesque, passing by **Ouilly-le-Vicomte**, where one of the oldest churches in Normandy—parts from the tenth century still survive—can be seen on its lovely islet in the river Touques. Farther downstream is Pierrefitte-en-Auge; the **Auberge des Deux Tonneaux** here is a good place to stop for refreshments or a bed, and the innkeeper can provide you with the key that unlocks the local church. Everything is close together along this route; quaint towns come swiftly one after the other, each with a church that possesses its individual treasures—a rare statuette, a carving, an especially beautiful Virgin.

Pont-l'Evêque, just a few miles beyond, is the last stop on our Route de Fromage. Like Camembert and Livarot, it was severely damaged during World War II and is far from being a garden spot. Yet each of these towns extends its peculiar rewards to the traveller who wants to know the real France. For who can know France without knowing her cheeses? Modern marketing techniques have made this difficult. Nowadays many cheeses are produced at factories, and those earmarked for overseas sale are made to pass various regulations, including (horrors!) taste tests to ensure that they will satisfy differing overseas markets. Particularly hard hit by all this are the fermenting cheeses like Camembert, Livarot, and Pont-l'Evêque, which are tamed for the trip to faraway markets and for "international" tastes. Even the milk for this kind of production is standardized, coming in the main from high-yield, low-butterfat producers—Holstein cows that feed on grain. But in the Pays d'Auge the visitor can taste genuine products made from the milk of the original *race normande* breed, which graze purely on grass, not feedlots. These cheeses will surprise you with their renowned richness, only the barest hint of which exists in the mass-produced products that bear their names.

The D 579 out of Pont-l'Evêque leads to one of the most charming ports on the whole Norman coast: Honfleur.

Honfleur and the Painters of Normandy

There are those who say that Impressionism began in Honfleur. Certainly this claim is supported by the fact that its leading practitioner, Claude Monet, began to paint here, and that his mentor, the outstanding pre-Impressionist painter Eugène Boudin, was a native son. Honfleur has all the basic ingredients for impressionistic painting: water, sky, and flowers. It also has a port that is as pretty as any ever pictured on a postcard, a spot that has long been an attraction to painters. Corot came here; so did Courbet. Honfleur offered yet another important ingredient, a typically Norman one: something the artists called white light, a quality in the sunlight that seemed to let the colors of things stand out in their own essentials. When Monet later set up shop in Giverny, it was this light that would keep him coming back here. Something else about this region that suited French painters was its proximity to Paris, the major art market. And again, something more: the Norman character, affording neighbors who minded their own business.

For these reasons, then, Normandy became a cradle of modern art. And not only French art: in the early 19th century, England's Richard Bonington transferred the blues of Honfleur's beaches to his canvases, and the Dutch Fauvist Kees Van Dongen captured the social elegance of Deauville.

After the darkness of the Barbizon School the palette of modern painting escaped the studio completely and headed for the liberating outdoors, and that outdoors was Normandy. And the movement didn't stop with Impressionism; here Seurat and Signac broke down the white Norman light into seven colors, painting only with these and giving birth to Pointillism. The bold colors of Fauvism followed these Impressionist and Postimpressionist palettes. Contemporary painters continued to live and work in Normandy: Félix Vallotton, Albert Marquet, and Raoul Dufy.

Though there are museums everywhere in Normandy, perhaps even too many for some visitors' taste, the Norman contribution to art is most gratifyingly worked out and illuminated at the **Musée des Beaux-Arts André Malraux** in Le Havre. There is a stunning collection here of works by Raoul Dufy, who was a native of Normandy and depicted its themes: regattas, horse races, outdoor dances, beaches, movement, and explosive color. The André Malraux collection defines Normandy's unique influence on painting with works by Boudin and Monet, Marquet and Van Dongen; ever present in these paintings is the Norman landscape—the sea cliffs of Etretat, the beaches at Deauville and Trouville, and the port of Honfleur. Le Havre itself is a terminal for car ferries making the round trip between France and England and Ireland. The tangle of blocks of postwar construction—Le Havre suffered more damage than any other port in Europe during World War II—has done little to make the town a tourist destination. However, a recommended overnight stop for drivers is the **France et Bourgogne** on the cours République.

At Honfleur there is also the interesting **Musée Eugène-Boudin,** which features works by Boudin himself, his friends, and his artistic offspring. The prophet who helped chart a course for contemporary art is indeed honored in his hometown and throughout his native province.

Honfleur

And Honfleur itself? The little harbor and fishing fleet here remain painterly subjects as compelling now as they were then for Boudin and his friends. For some people this is the essence of Honfleur. To walk around the port, especially when the light is emphasizing a different aspect of some scene—a green door here, a yellow boat there—and to sit over a Belgian beer in a café, contemplating a sunset, are experiences no trip to Normandy should be without.

For an especially bucolic setting in which to enjoy lunch, visit **La Ferme St-Siméon** nearby. The drive up the cliffside to the restaurant gives a seagull's view of Honfleur and arouses the appetite. Swathed in wisteria and rhododendrons, this is *the* picturebook inn of the region. It is also the place that was home away from home for the budding Impressionists, the farm where they came for their meals and, perhaps, to spend a weekend. Now you can, too, though the price is certainly steeper and the service little more professional than when Old Mother Toutain set a table for the starving types Boudin always seemed to be attracting.

The Coast and Casinos

After Honfleur, unless you first cross over to Le Havre and the sea-carved cliffs of Etretat (15 miles east), the Corniche Normande to the west, with its beaches at Trouville and Deauville, will be your next destination.

Trouville has a wide, sandy beach, the north end of which harbors the reasonably priced family hotels, the type the French call "correct," and a casino and a swimming pool—which may tell you something about the temperature of the sea. There is also a commercial fishing fleet docked along the river Touques, giving the spa a nice waterfront animation off-season. The shopping streets are clean and well ordered, the buildings still low enough to allow sunlight to reach the pedestrians. The stroller gets the feeling that Trouville is a town that has kept up to date but has not let progress run rampant.

Deauville, the grande dame of the seacoast, still bespeaks the elegant life. Most typical is the **Normandy**, one of the plushest restaurant-hotels-cum-casinos in the world. The players still dress in black tie and look exactly like Zachary Scott and Jean Harlow. There is a well-protected yacht basin for pleasure craft, two race tracks—steeplechase and the flats—a yearling sale, shows of Norman livestock, and finally, an American film festival that closes the season in September.

But there are also hideous new high-rises that crowd in, cutting off once open spaces and sea perspectives. A heavy population of ex-colonialists from Algeria and elsewhere in North Africa now competes with Parisians for sun space. Although the side streets and main streets of Deauville still host a pleasing variety of boutiques, cute cafés, bizarre clubs (**Club des Canards**, for example), and restaurants, elbow room is at a premium and you feel you are paying a high price for the privilege.

Not far from here is **Cabourg**, a smaller Deauville mostly for families that has remained *toujours élégant,* implacably French, and structured for the longer stay. On the other side of the river Orne from Cabourg is Caen.

Caen and Bayeux

Caen, the capital of lower Normandy and county seat of Calvados, was much fought over, in, and around, with the result that three quarters of it was destroyed in the last war. There are still some interesting places to see here, however. Besides, the people of Caen are stouthearted types who feel a lasting affinity for their Anglo-Saxon brethren-in-arms. Their welcome is especially warm, as is their Calvados, and the *trou normand* is common practice here. The Abbaye aux Hommes, the Romanesque church of St-Etienne and its connected seminary, is well worth seeing, especially as its architectural equivalent can be found no-where else. There is also the singular Château de Caen, begun by William the Conqueror in 1060, and the 16th-century Hôtel d'Escoville. At the city hall you will find a tourism office, a good place for collecting maps and bro-chures on regional points of further interest.

Bayeux, 40 km (25 miles) west of Caen, was the first French town to be liberated during World War II (on June 8, 1944), and so, happily, suffered no damage. Everything remains intact on the old streets of St-Martin and St-Malo; their buildings remain precious treasures of this Medieval crossroads town. The 11th-century **cathedral of Notre-Dame**, with its three-story choir, is another treasure; but housed in the museum across the way is the town's most prized possession, Queen Matilda's **Bayeux Tapestry**, em-broidered with hieroglyphics of Anglo-Norman history.

Almost as long as a football field but not two feet high, the Bayeux Tapestry occupies a building all its own. To read the story of the Norman invasion of England in 1066 from beginning to end, the visitor can follow the tapes-try's length around the four walls of the second-floor viewing room, where the wool-embroidered linen cloth stretches in a continuous band. More than a traditional Gobelins or Aubusson tapestry, it resembles a flowing pictograph, an illuminated comic strip charmingly com-plete with naïve characters in roles that play themselves out across its length, as in a film or a morality play. There is William the Conqueror and Harold of Hastings, plus a cast of hundreds: oarsmen and archers, friars and knights. The English are depicted with mustaches, the Normans with shaved napes. The principals are all labeled and easily recognizable in a sequence of more than 50 subti-tled scenes (Latin and Saxon only, sorry; a pamphlet provides an English translation). The Tapestry is more a storyteller's success than the triumph of an art form. Those coming to view the Bayeux Tapestry with *La Dame à la Licorne* at the Musée Cluny in Paris in mind as an ideal will find that their notions of textile art must be redefined.

In one of those ironies that history seems ever fond to

arrange, it is barely five miles from this depiction of the last Norman invasion of Britain to the site where a more recent invasion occurred on Normandy's own shores.

The Landing Beaches of Normandy

The Allied action that took place on D-Day, the sixth of June, 1944, is well documented and needs no repetition here. The beaches—and the war museums—form a line west from Ouistreham. To visit them, but more specifically, to stand at the headlands above the beaches and just look out, will give an idea of the difficulties encountered that day that no amount of reading or film viewing can offer. The roll call of coast towns rings out with names of invasions: Ste-Mère-Eglise; Omaha Beach (at Colleville); Utah Beach (at La Madeleine); Sword, Juno, and Gold beaches (from Arromanches to Ouistreham). There are markers where the actions took place; here and there broken blockhouses loom. There's a film show at Arromanches and white crosses dotting the green carpets that roll down toward the sea at Omaha Beach.

After the landings the fighting continued. The Battle of Normandy, as it was called, quickly became a desperate struggle. The British, Americans, and Canadians fought so as not to be thrown back into the sea; the Germans fought to keep the Allies from advancing. More than 200,000 homes were destroyed in the onslaught; ports and crossroads like Le Havre, Rouen, Caen, and Lisieux were more than 60 percent flattened. After ten weeks of attack and counterattack, the Battle of Normandy ended on the 21st of August. The Germans had lost 640,000 men, the route to Paris was open, and the world was about to be reordered into the one we know today.

The footprints of history track all over Normandy.

GETTING AROUND

Rouen, in the center of Normandy, is just 139 km (85 miles) from Paris on A 13 (Autoroute de Normandie), which continues for another 125 km (75 miles) past Rouen to Caen. Along the Autoroute from Rouen to Caen are exits for Le Havre, Honfleur, Deauville, and many other points on the Normandy coast. Route N 15 leads north and west from Rouen toward Fécamp and Etretat.

Trains run regularly from the Gare St-Lazare and Gare

Montparnasse in Paris to Rouen, Caen, Le Havre, and all other major cities in Normandy. Travelling by boat from the U.K., the major points of entry in Normandy are: Caen, from Portsmouth; Cherbourg, from Portsmouth and Weymouth; and Dieppe, from Newhaven. There is limited air service from London to Normandy cities on Brit Air, which flies from Gatwick Airport to Cannes and Le Havre, and Air Vendée, which flies from Gatwick to Rouen.

ACCOMMODATIONS REFERENCE

▶ **Château de Montreuil.** 4, chaussée des Capucins, 62170 **Montreuil-sur-Mer.** Tel: 21-81-53-04; Telex: 135205; in U.S., (212) 696-1323. Lovely rooms, superb cuisine, and an attractive garden.

▶ **Auberge des Deux Tonneaux.** Pierrefitte-en-Auge 14130 **Pont-l'Evêque.** Tel: 31-64-09-31.

▶ **Dieppe.** Place Bernard-Tissot, 76000 **Rouen.** Tel: 35-71-96-00; Telex: 180413.

▶ **France et Bourgogne.** 21, cours République, 76600 **Le Havre.** Tel: 35-25-25-40-34.

▶ **Hôtel du Golf.** New-Golf 14800 **Deauville** (3 km/2 miles southeast of Deauville on Route D 278). Tel: 31-88-19-01; Telex: 170488; in U.S., (212) 477-1600 or (800) 223-1510. Quiet, secluded, luxurious hotel with golf course, fine restaurant, and bar.

▶ **Normandy.** 38, rue Jean-Mermoz, 14800 **Deauville.** Tel: 31-88-09-21; Telex: 170617; in U.S., (212) 477-1600 or (800) 223-1510.

▶ **Relais Château d'Audrieu.** 14250 **Tilly-sur-Seuilles** (13 km/9 miles south of Bayeux on Route D 158). Tel: 31-80-21-52; in U.S., (212) 696-1323. A château with 22 unique rooms, each filled with antiques. Restaurant and swimming pool, all set in a gracious park.

▶ **Relais des Gourmets.** 15, rue Geôle, 14300 **Caen.** Tel: 31-86-06-01; Telex: 171657; in U.S., (212) 696-1323. Thirty-two comfortable rooms, no two alike, overlooking a castle of William the Conqueror. Good restaurant.

BRITTANY

By Fred Halliday

Brittany, of the wild, glorious coastline, of oysters, of crêpes and a spirited people, is often described by Frenchmen from Gascony to the Loire valley as "the part of France with the most character. You should go."

But how? Seeing Brittany is not like seeing other parts of France. For one thing it's hard to get to, even from Paris. Air Inter flies there, but space is so limited that reservations must be made far in advance, and then if you don't stick to your schedule, it's quite probable you won't get a seat when you want to return—so it's back to the reservations line.

Also, the roads to Quimper (cam-PEAR) that cover the 522 km (326 miles) from Paris are a mixed bag. There is no direct Autoroute, but it's no bargain for shunpikers either; some of the towns along the way are more obstructions than delights.

For the tourist determined to see Brittany there is one good answer: the train. If you're travelling from Paris, get up early, because the 7:07 A.M. for Quimper, which leaves from the Gare Montparnasse, is the one you want to catch. Why? Because it's the only train that will get you to Quimper before its crêperies close their doors, at 1:00 P.M. sharp.

MAJOR INTEREST

Le Mont-Saint-Michel
Seacoast, especially the dramatic scenery at Pointe
    du Raz and along the beautiful Côte d'Emeraud
Medieval architecture, especially the towns of
    Concarneau, Dinan, and Paimpol

Prehistoric megaliths, especially those at Carnac
   and Locmariaquer
Calvaires, roadside sculptures of saints
Oysters, crêpes, and *galettes*
Tréguier's cathedral

Quimper
Old City
Shops selling local stoneware

St-Malo
Ramparts
Houses from the 15th–17th centuries

To Quimper

If you've got just two weeks in the country that leads the
world in gastronomic pleasure, every meal should be an
important event. Forget the airline food on the world's
fastest trains and save your taste buds for old Quimper.
The 7:07 Paris train pulls into the Quimper station at
12:56 P.M.. This means you've got only four minutes to get
from the station to the crêperies, so you'd better take a
cab from the stand at the entrance to the station. **Crêperie
du Vieux Quimper**, where you tell the cabbie to go, will
not shut the door on any Anglo-Saxons who call ahead
(99-95-31-34) from Paris the day before to say they are
going to be a few minutes late. French trains are always
on time and the Vieux Quimper is only five minutes from
the station, so you should just make it. Dawdle, however,
and you will find out why Bretons are the French with the
most character.

Entering the Crêperie du Vieux Quimper, you will see
that getting up for the 7:07 gets you not only lunch but
into the Breton swing of things right away. The dining
room is full of old beams, antique Quimper dishes (more
about that later) on the walls, and the sizzle of batter
hitting the pan. You just know the crêpes you eat here will
somehow be thinner, hotter, crisper, more delicious than
any to be found in Paris or on most any other table, even
in Brittany. Aside from luncheon and dessert types, there
are two things you should know about crêpes: They are
made with either *froment* (white flour) or *sarrasin* (buckwheat flour). For lunch crêpes take the buckwheat. It will
come sizzling and slightly crunchy. What it is filled with is
your choice. Very good as a base is Gruyère (a Swiss
cheese), to which you can have ham or lettuce added, or

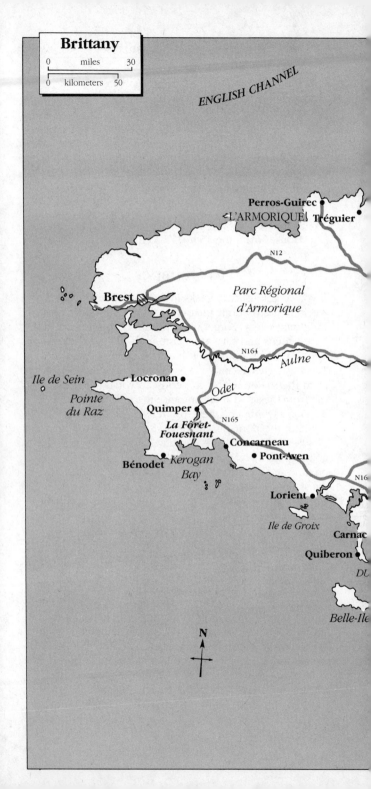

you can have all three. From the more than 20 combinations you might also try mushrooms and seafood. Forget wine, as do the Bretons, and wash your crêpes down with cider. They serve the very best at Vieux Quimper; it's fairly mild, about 6 percent alcohol. If you eat a lot (most diners down two to three crêpes each) and drink a lot (a half to a full bottle is the rule), it would be wise to walk around and see Quimper before taking the wheel of your rental car. Another tip: Before leaving the table, order dessert. Especially recommended is a chocolate crêpe.

Seeing Quimper

Perched way out in Finistère (land's end), where the land smells of the sea, Quimper is one of the larger cities in Brittany where the traditional Breton atmosphere exists in abundance. It can be seen in the many streets closed to cars; in the cathedral, especially its windows, the pride of the town; and in the shops, filled with things Breton. Highly recommended, and on the cathedral square, is **L'Art du Cornouille**, perhaps the best place to buy the city's famous stoneware dishes, which are known throughout the world simply as Quimper. The Henriot factory, just outside the old town and another good place to shop, sells only its own seconds, however, while L'Art du Cornouille sells stoneware (called faïence in France) from many Breton manufacturers at perhaps one-fourth of Western Hemisphere prices—and also has a huge selection you won't find outside Quimper. The shop will dispatch a messenger up the hill to the factory to get what you want if they're out, do all the packing, put everything on a credit card, put on the stamps, add in any duty, and ship to your home. L'Art du Cornouille is also a very good source for grandfather clocks, armoires, and Brittany lace. A nice hotel in Quimper is the **Griffon**.

Quimper is full of architectural surprises. To experience these, follow the pretty Odet and Steir rivers along banks that meander around homes and under buildings.

What is it to be a Breton?

First, the name Quimper is the French spelling of the Breton *Kemper,* meaning "place of the confluence of two rivers." The Breton people and their language are Celtic in origin, their roots extending across the sea to the Cornish coast of England, Ireland, Wales, and Scotland, and to wherever the Celts put a *currah* (bark) in the water. Bretons go so far as to claim that the legend of King Arthur and the Round Table originated in Brittany, not in England, and some "scholars" substantiate the theory.

These Celtic origins are quite apparent in the faces of the people you encounter on the streets. Pick up a walking map at the chamber of commerce (Syndicat d'Initiative, 1, rue du Roc-Gradlon) and join in the flow of blue eyes, fair faces, freckles, and red hair.

For more things Celtic, the annual Festival of Breton Folklore takes place here on the fourth Sunday (and the preceding Friday and Saturday) of July; the Musée Breton, on the quai de l'Odet, has interesting exhibits that highlight the region's heritage.

As the Celts were seafarers, so are the Bretons. You can take a boat down the river Odet to the sea, a trip of 16 kilometers (10 miles). A cruise from Kerogan Bay to the seaside resort of Bénodet, an hour and a half of meandering through forested cliffs and rocky heights, is highly recommended. Consult the Syndicat for details.

As you would expect, a seafaring people take their menu live from the sea. In choosing a Breton dinner, there is only one admonition: Keep it simple. Beware "cuisine." Steer clear of sauces—turbot in béarnaise (nice for Paris but not here), sole meunière—any sauce except *sauce armoricaine* (more about that specialty later). In Brittany the taste is freshness: good staples, simply presented and pure.

Locronan

For the Breton taste you could not do better than at the **Fer à Cheval** in Locronan. Fer à Cheval is a completely captivating inn located in a completely captivating village ten miles from Quimper. Since you must rent a car to see the rest of Brittany properly, Quimper is as good a place as any to do that. From there to Locronan is an easy drive on Route D 39. Arrive while there is still enough light to see Brittany of times past. You will want two hours to walk around the central square and the streets radiating from it.

The village's buildings are entirely of stone, some dating from the 13th century, and are heavily covered with moss because of the proximity to the sea. Unless you have been to western Ireland, you have never seen a village like this. Of course you must also see the musty church right on the square. And sign the book inside; the youngsters in Locronan love to see from how far away their many visitors come. The churchyard is also a must, the markers being so many Celtic crosses. These are similar to the *calvaires,* the sculptures of saints to be seen along Breton roadsides. (A good place to see them is near the church at Bénodet, out of Quimper on Route D 34.)

On the Locronan square itself is possibly the best sweet shop in all of Brittany. Without fail try the *kouign-aman,* the Breton specialty of puff pastry and sugar. Here it's a succulent delicacy, while in places like Paris you will gag on it. This is also a good place to buy tins of Breton *galettes* (butter cookies) for your friends, and *crêpes dentelles* (fluted fruit-filled wafers); raspberry's the best. These are all things to pack as gifts or to open later for a taste of Breton goodness back home; for your night in Locronan, it's *plateau des fruits de mer* at the Fer à Cheval.

The dining room is on the second floor of the hotel overlooking the square. The platter of seafood, known as *cotriade* and which you should not leave Brittany without tasting (somewhere, anywhere, if not here—but is there any other place that does it so well?), comes on a bed of hot French fries, which makes us remember how good the simple potato tastes in this country. On this steaming bed, their briny shells brimming with juices, are assortments of oysters—*belons, fines de claire,* and *cancales*—an overlapping layer of clams and *palourdes* (in succulence, to clams what the capon is to chicken), stray shrimp, crayfish, a spiny *langouste,* a spidery crab, and, best of all, sea snails, periwinkles, and other creatures you'll be delighted to discover. Wash all this down with an icy glass of Muscadet from vineyards near Nantes.

First, of course, make sure there's a room at the inn. Before turning in for the evening, or else in the morning, take a stroll around the square, where you will turn up some artisans' boutiques, including a woolens shop that carries authentic Breton fishermen's sweaters. (People will try to buy yours off your back when you get home.)

To the End of Land's End

This whole part of Brittany, with its gentle green hills rolling down to the sea, ends not far (20 miles) from Locronan at a place called **Pointe du Raz.**

Pointe du Raz is the westernmost point of continental France and one of the world's most dramatic seascapes. It is a 300-foot drop at the end of a long escarpment stuck out like a finger and carved by the furious wind and sea.

The visit down the cliffs can be dangerous, so it is organized. The *tour de la pointe*, which leaves from the parking lot, starts whenever the guide has five people willing to go, and takes an hour and a half. It is wise to wear nonskid shoes and to be in reasonably good shape. Those who stay up at the top will nonetheless enjoy the spectacular panorama of the Atlantic and the Ile de Sein, and can watch from that safe perch the terrible *raz*, the riptide "before which nothing passes without fear or pain" as it races between the island and the point.

Concarneau and the Morbihan Coast

Concarneau is a great attraction, a walled island-city attached to the mainland by two very small bridges. In summer you will encounter within its perfect ramparts happy crowds of the sort that charmed Pinocchio on Stromboli, artistic residents in the midst of their muse, tour-bus passengers looking for restrooms, seafood bistros (try the *friture*), antique shops, pottery sheds, and card and curio shops. Seeing Concarneau in summertime is like visiting a Medieval town during the World Cup or the World Series. In winter, though, the people are gone, many of the shops are closed, and the place seems to lose something.

But a mere hop and a skip farther down the road there are even older sites.

Pont-Aven and Carnac

Eight miles east of Concarneau is Pont-Aven, an artists' colony with a difference: cookies. Pont-Aven was a home to Gauguin and many other painters; see the art museum and galleries here. If you don't have the money to buy art and want something that will fit in your suitcase, you might instead buy a tin of Breton *galettes* in Pont-Aven, since it is home to one of the great cookie companies of the world, Trou Mad. Their tins of delicious butter cookies are relatively cheap and have paintings of Gauguin and various other Breton motifs on the lid. They make wonderful gifts and are available in many card and curio shops on the main route through town.

Carnac preserves the rubble of antiquity and is sort of a mini-Stonehenge along the road. These are Stone Age dolmens, monuments, possibly tombs, dug out of their original sites—which you can also visit. A field of white sabertooth rows of megaliths, a hundred yards wide, half a mile long and numbering 1,099 rocks, runs next to the roadside less than a mile from Carnac along route D 196. No one knows why or how prehistoric man put the stones there; suffice it to say that he did. The largest megalith in the region is at Locmariaquer. This broken giant, measuring some 60 feet in length and weighing nearly 350 tons, is 25 km (15 miles) from Carnac on Route N 165.

Within Carnac, the **Tumulus de St-Michel** provides an intimate look, by candlelight, into a tomb of the prehistoric race that erected these giants in stone then disappeared so completely.

Farther down the coast on a peninsula is Quiberon, a jumping-off point should you wish to visit the bucolic **Belle-Ile**, where there is an extravagant palace, a wild coast lined with grottoes and seabirds, and Sarah Bernhardt's summer retreat. Boats to the isle leave from Quiberon every day, and the ride, always cool and bracing, takes an hour; for information call 97-50-06-90.

Farther east along the coast is La Baule, with its big hotels, casinos, and three-mile-long beach. After that there remains only Nantes—if the nearby Muscadet vineyards interest you.

Rennes

Most visitors would do best to reboard the train at Vannes, just east on the coast from Carnac, or at Quimper, and go back toward Paris as far as Rennes, the key entry point for the **north Breton coast** .

Rennes is the capital of Brittany. Almost any Breton (except a bureaucrat, who probably comes from Paris) will tell you it's "not really Brittany." It certainly is a railhead, though, and Rennes is as close as you can comfortably come (primarily for scheduling reasons) to the great group of North Coast attractions: Le Mont-Saint-Michel (it's actually in Normandy, but makes most sense approached from Rennes), St-Malo (often overlooked, which you shouldn't do), and Brittany's Côte d'Emeraude (Emerald Coast), plus splendid oyster-eating places all along the way.

There's really not much to hold you in Rennes. The rent-a-car agencies are handy to the train station—just follow the signs marked SNCF, the French National Railroad. It's just as well to get an early start toward Mont-Saint-Michel. Though the distance is not great (65 km/40 miles), the turns in the road (N 175) are numerous and you'll probably see some things worth a short stop along the way, so figure a morning or an afternoon to get there comfortably.

Mont-Saint-Michel

According to how the sands at the mouth of the estuary have shifted, this wonder of the Medieval world is either in Normandy or Brittany. Right now it's in Normandy.

Plan your travel time to arrive during daylight. The outline of the island and its spindle-shaped spire visible from far off form one of the most memorable sights in all of France and must not be missed. Watch how it changes as you approach leisurely, the island getting larger, the road descending, the country flattening out into salt marshes, where sheep graze on grass on the fringes of the sea. They are your dinner, the famous *pré-salé*—presalted—sheep of Mont-Saint-Michel. The salt in the marsh grass gives the sheep a delectable taste, and for that reason lamb is the regional specialty.

If you lodge in the Mont-Saint-Michel area it should be at **La Mère Poulard**. Write, phone, telegram ahead. There are not many times this effort is required, but La Mère Poulard is to Mont-Saint-Michel what the Empire State Building is to New York City; it would be madness to leave without experiencing it. Should management claim that a room is not available, try tears. Should they still not yield, you can overnight at St-Malo (35 km/ 20 miles away), where one hotel is as good as another and prices are softer, but remember to reserve for dinner at La Mère Poulard. The pleasure of its table is the great evening joy of Mont-Saint-Michel.

First off, there's the aforementioned *pré-salé,* done to a turn here, where you sit at a long table under wooden beams and the whole room rings with the work of men in leather aprons standing in the fireplace. What are they doing there? Making your dessert.

The sound comes from wire whisks in great copper bowls, the perfect implements for whipping egg whites into mountains of creamy foam to create the frothiest, softest of soufflés that ever emerged from a hearth. Naturally you'll have one.

After dinner, with the whole Mont under lights and (maybe) under stars, is the time to take a stroll—but before dessert, before you lose the lights. La Mère will hold the soufflé for you if you're still at table. Walk outside the walls and down the causeway to take in the entire island lit up, from the sheer ramparts growing out of the gray rock to the spire etched against the night sky.

Both fortress and religious shrine, during the Middle Ages, the Mont was especially rich in pilgrims' gifts. It was protected against sack and invasion by the ferocious tide, which comes roaring in with the speed of a race horse and with enough power to splatter sieging armies against the seawall. This fact of nature, along with—by the grace of the Lord—a hearty band of monks, was the only defense Mont-Saint-Michel ever needed.

One marauding despot devised a subtler ploy and thought to bribe the monks to pull his army up a dumb-waiter to the heights of the Mont, from which the invaders would take the keep from within. All night long, the monks labored, but, at dawn, the drawbridge did not come crashing down—for all night long the monks had drawn the soldiers up the shaft and, one by one, beheaded them.

St-Malo

After Mont-Saint-Michel at night and the sight of the galloping tide that once ran down invading armies as it rushed in, what more can the coast hold? St-Malo, a Renaissance city surrounded by a wall surrounded by the sea.

Here is the Breton port to see, a virtual fort. The Breton corsairs, the men of St-Malo, declared themselves "neither French nor Breton, but Malouïn." If there was ever a Venice of the north of France, a place where seafaring commerce was king with a little piracy thrown in, this is it. The wall was the Malouïns' attempt to protect themselves against their competition and against raids by the English.

The best way to experience this old port is to enter through the ramparts, find a bakery, buy a bag of glazed chestnuts (those of St-Malo are easily the best in France), climb atop the ramparts, and, munching and marching, walk the entire circumference of the wall. Here is an opportunity to take a tour of some of the loveliest Renaissance architecture in France at its second-story level. The height advantage exposes rooflines and other details—extravagant chimney pots, for example—seldom seen in homes of the upper bourgeoisie, as well as a view of the maritime life below. All the while you will be refreshed by the sea, which almost completely rings the city. The spectacle is best when the tide reaches its 30-foot height, for then the sea is at its wildest, but at any time you will get a close-up view of these 15th- to 17th-century buildings, now successfully restored after their almost total destruction during World War II.

A sort of second resurrection of St-Malo is currently visible in the many mansions marked by recent gentrification; wealthy landowners from the surrounding countryside are now flocking to buy vacation homes here, precipitating a flight *to* the city instead of the usual other way around. A couple of good hotels are **La Villefromoy** and the **Valmarin**.

Any great city, especially a port, has a mystique. Along the wall thrust out into the harbor is St-Malo's statue to Jacques Cartier, the first native son to cross the Atlantic, braving the wild seas that begin at the foot of the wall. On his second such voyage Cartier was amazed to find a Breton fishing fleet already in Canadian waters; news of a good fishing spot travelled far even then. The Breton fleet still puts in appearances on the Grand Banks in quest of the singular salmon and cod.

Cancale and Oysters

Along this bay- and inlet-riddled coast, the monstrous tides often leave beaches so naked that it is possible to wade a quarter of a mile out to sea with the water remaining at your ankles. Here in its most productive beds is that most celebrated of Breton produce, the oyster. It couldn't be better met than in one of the famous oyster towns, Cancale. The key to good eating in Brittany, in place after place along the coast and inland, is to order fresh produce, simply prepared.

Cancale oysters are so called because all of those taken from its waters—between Mont-Saint-Michel and St-Malo—have such a strong "personality." An oyster expert, of which there are of course many in France, can taste the difference between a cancale and a belon (a

South Coast oyster) as surely as a wine expert discerns the difference between a Bordeaux and a Burgundy.

So those who stop off on their way from Mont-Saint-Michel to St-Malo or who double back from St-Malo (it's only 11 miles) to the little town sticking out of the mud in the low tide will have themselves a treat.

In keeping an oyster feast simple, all you want is oysters, bread—pumpernickel—and wine (some people also nibble *pommes frites*). The place to go for these is any one of Cancale's bars or cafés facing the port. The wine to order is Muscadet.

A short course on ordering: Oysters in France are sized and priced according to a ubiquitous grading system. The largest size is described on a menu as "000." These are seldom seen. The next are "00"; most menus begin with this size, and these are the costliest. Six will usually do. The next size, the "0," is about a third again as small. Note that the price of the oyster will decline with size, but only within its type; oyster variety is the other price consideration. Cancales and belons—the flat (*plat*) oysters—are usually the most expensive type, followed by *fines de claire* and *papillons*. All are ordered by the dozen in "0" size. A real Breton oyster tasting is one of the musts when you are in Brittany; it is part of the culture, and in no other place in the world can you do it as well.

The French don't wash oysters in fresh water, nor do they soak them in barley water to purge them as it is done in foreign oyster bars and restaurants. The French have a horror of such practices. "Why do you want to wash an oyster?" they ask. Why should you want to purge them? An oyster should taste of the sea! That's the idea. Indeed, it is this sea taste—those of Cancale, for example, are marked with the particularly rich flavor of the plankton in the bay of Mont-Saint-Michel—that makes each oyster a footprint of wherever it comes from. Also, in France oysters are opened by oyster openers. Even in Paris this man is usually Breton. His fingers are as fat and red as his nose and scarred by occasional slips of the knife on the shell. This is all he does in life; as he opens an oyster, in the bat of an eye he knows if it is one to discard or one to put on the pile for your table.

So if this is your first feast on the Breton oyster, watch out. Your tongue is about to be aggressed. No lemon-squirted, watery-eyed candidate for cocktail sauce is this oyster, but something of the sauce primeval—the sea.

Côte d'Emeraud
(The Emerald Coast)

Westward from St-Malo lies the Côte d'Emeraud, a progression of dramatic seascapes, cathedrals, colorful fishing fleets, and quaint villages.

The first stop is St-Servan, with a good sandy bathing beach, a lively spit of forest, and elegant buildings. The town offers lovely views of St-Malo and the Ile du Grand-Bé, with its fortified tower and the tomb of Chateaubriand. Across the Rance estuary and almost facing St-Malo is **Dinard**, the gem of the Côte d'Emeraud. Where St-Malo is walled in and fortified, Dinard is open and social. Where in St-Malo there are history and rocks, in Dinard there is sand. Where in St-Malo there are statues to Jacques Cartier and the mansions of burghers, in Dinard there are casinos, swimming pools, and tennis. The *Grande Plage* is an astonishing beach filled with astonishing bathers. The bikini may be a French invention, but there are plenty of American and English accents here. On the other side of the little peninsula is another beach with a serpentine walk called the *Promenade du Clair de Lune* (Moonlight Promenade).

Save morning daylight for Dinard, too. There are villas niched into its coves and green hills enveloped by the balmy breezes of a mild microclimate. The Gulf Stream ends around here and, having ended, flirts. The climate of Brittany is in general much warmer than you might expect; there is never winter. Finistère exports spring vegetables, shallots, new potatoes, and tomatoes to much of the world year-round. Exuberant bursts of tropical flora—aloe plants, palm trees, mimosa—may surprise you. If you climb the fingerlike green hills that splay out into the Atlantic you will attain the simultaneous pleasures of watching a tempestuous sea and being in a tropical paradise.

An excursion not to be missed is a trip down the Rance. Boats leave from Dinard at the river's mouth and go to where the estuary, gulf size at first, narrows to barge-canal width. This hour-and-a-half journey will show you what the North Breton coast is all about: the river and the sea, and in between, the steep green forest folds that rise to mountainous heights. Back near Dinard, there is a technological wonder to behold at the mouth of the Rance. French engineers have harnessed the dramatic tides that run upriver and convert their fierce power to electricity at the Marémotrice de la France, the world's first tidal-energy station.

Dinan, down where the canal begins and not to be confused with Dinard, is a village filled with so much Medieval charm that, were it indoors, it could pass for a museum. In fact, it *is* almost small enough to qualify, which makes it all the easier to see. The town's crooked old streets (see especially the rue du Jerzual) and antique houses, timbered and overhanging the street, are interspersed with gardens and trees. There are ramparts, a massive château, a great clock tower, and a good crêperie. Dinan is an excellent place to rest and watch the hands of its 15th-century clock turn. The **D'Avaugour** is a good place to stay.

The West Beaches

Farther westward, the beaches of the Côte d'Emeraud open up at every turn. The town of St-Lunaire has two elegant beaches, tennis, a long promenade out to sea, and the Grotte de la Goule-aux-Fées, or Grotto of the Sirens.

Just around the bend is St-Brieuc, cheek by jowl with Lancieux; both are quiet, with less casino action and more family feeling. Then comes St-Cast: seven beaches, two superb lookout points—a popular place with the locals. After several more twists in the road, you'll come to the remarkable, brooding Fort la Latte (one hour away); then the corniche road arrives on what is arguably the most splendid lookout on a whole coast of splendid lookouts: Cap Fréhel. From here, a panorama of sky and sea with plumes of spray shooting off the end of the point, you can look north to England, whence the Bretons came; westward to America, where many went; or back to St-Malo. It is one of the great natural wonders of Brittany, one that gives some understanding of this region's hazards.

After Cap Fréhel the Côte d'Emeraude peters out. There's a charming beach at Le Val-André, a family beach at St-Brieuc that also has a fortified church, but it is at Paimpol where the sun creates a coast of a different color.

The Pink Granite Coast

The landscape now changes to outcroppings of rocks marching seaward, where the surf boils into ribbons of foam. This is not a place to go bathing. Everywhere the rocks are blushed with rose, as if in an eternal sunset. And although they are made of the same stuff, the villages here are more accommodating than the beaches.

Paimpol was celebrated in song and in literature as the most typically Breton town of all. The hero of Pierre Loti's novel *Pêcheur d'Islande* (*An Iceland Fisherman*) comes from here (Breton fishermen make the storm-tossed voyage to Iceland routinely, even in winter); Loti did for Paimpol what Marcel Pagnol did for Marseille. Yet Paimpol is pleasingly sleepy and alone on its rocks. The wild pinks and *bleuets* that bloom there are not trampled under tourists' soles; the stone pier that goes out to sea to welcome the fishing fleet—and a well-sheltered cove it creates, too—does not groan under the crush of humanity. You can find your place in the sun here. Under the pretty parasols that line the beach you can sip a cider, watch the boats, or read a book peacefully.

The town too, like the rocks, is in eternal sunset, or sunrise, being entirely built of pink granite—right down to the quaint church.

But as the song goes, when in Paimpol follow the *la paimpolaise*. And where does she go? Why, to the **Ile de Bréhat**. The island, less than two miles long, is very near—ten minutes from Arcouest—and automobiles are forbidden there. You can spend several hours climbing the slopes and drinking in a surprising variety of wild Breton flora: cedars, fig trees, palm trees. There are great rock crevices down by the sea that in low tide can be used for swimming holes: an ideal way to recharge the spirit for the wear and tear of the road. A little town, Port Clos, and citadel are huddled around its lovely enclosed harbor, where cafés offer light refreshment to those visitors without picnics.

Tréguier

The town of Tréguier is served by a host of attractive beaches, the beach at the nearby resort of **Perros-Guirec** having the most to offer. But it is Tréguier itself that is the most interesting.

If you've come this far, you will have begun to know Brittany and so must see Tréguier, for it contains the major elements of the region's mystique: a saint, the sea, and the products of the sea. All three are centered around the cathedral.

The cathedral of Tréguier is one of the most beautiful in Brittany, both in its scale and its rapport with the town. The **cathedral of St-Tugdual** and its attached cloister rise from the center of the great place du Martray in the middle of the town, where none of the surrounding buildings is close enough to hem them in. The visitor thus gets an upsweeping view of the cathedral and its spire, which soars like a ship's mast above the marketplace.

All towns in Brittany have their churches, but this cathedral is one you should definitely enter—not only for the windows, sculpture, and architecture, or out of devotion, but for the story it tells of the region.

Erected from the 13th to the 15th centuries, the cathedral has three towers that mark three points of the cross, one with a spire, one containing a magnificent rose window. Everywhere the granite is worked with a lightness and finesse that is a lost art. The two Christs, in wood, are particularly fine, but the statue of Saint Yves is especially noteworthy here.

This may be Saint Tugdual's cathedral, but it is Saint Yves who is the more popular here. Indeed, he is the most popular saint in Brittany, where he is known as "Monsieur Saint-Yves." Yves was born in nearby Minichy-Tréguier in the middle of the 13th century. After becoming a priest and finishing his studies in Paris, he returned to Tréguier as the bishop's assistant and did legal work for the poor. Yves argued their cases so well and so purely that he was canonized a hundred years later as the patron saint of lawyers. Along with a page from his prayer book the cathedral possesses Saint Yves's skull, a relic whose closely spaced eye sockets convey the arresting gaze of an expert advocate.

Outside in the square, the sights and sounds of market morning will reanimate you. A good time to catch all French markets at their liveliest is an hour before mealtime, just the time it takes the housewife to go to the market, see what's fresh, and take it home and cook it. Because this is Brittany, the market on Tréguier's place du Martray offers primarily fish. To visitors the produce and its plenty is astonishing.

Everything is raw, cold, and fresh, and heaped in baskets and barrels: sole, mullet, turbot, rays, sea bass, and mackerel; oysters, mussels, clams, lobster, langouste, and more sea creatures. If you have a camper or a boat with a freezer, Tréguier is a good place to fill more than your eyes.

L'Armorique

This is the word that causes so much confusion for writers of menus and cookbooks. After Perros-Guirec it appears on road signs—the *Corniche d'Armorique* begins just a few miles away, then come the *L'Armorique* mountains, then the *Pays Armorique . . . l'Armorique . . . L'Amérique.* A slip of the tongue or pen can cause a jump of 3,000 miles.

Is it correct to call the well-known recipe for lobster in tomato sauce *homard à l'américaine?* Or should it be *homard à l'armoricaine?* There is a story that goes with the untangling tale.

It seems there was a young man from Armorique—the ancient name for Brittany—who went to make his mark in Amérique—to "chercher l'Amérique" as many other Frenchmen had done. This young Breton opened a restaurant there and was astonished at the high quality of the lobsters. "I know what to do with these," he supposedly said, and he prepared them according to an old recipe of his maiden aunt's, an *Armoricaine.* As he worked hard and became famous for the recipe, his restaurant was visited by travelling French chefs (definitely not Breton) who sampled the lobsters and, astonished that so fine a dish could be found in a country with so rude a culinary background, brought it back home to Paris, where it was christened *"homard à l'américaine."* It was quite natural that Parisians might make this mistake, for most of them have never heard of l'Armorique (the name derives from a Breton word meaning "by the sea").

This in fact is the Breton lament: Stuck out on their peninsula, they are the forgotten French. No matter what they do, they hardly ever get recognition, and even when they do someone else gets the credit.

So you will pardon them if they seem a little standoffish. You will not take offense if they speak their Breton tongue when a tourist—Parisian included—is within earshot. It's not that they're rude or suspicious of strangers; it's because they choose not to change the essentials of who they are to suit anyone else. That's why Brittany is "the part of France with the most character." No matter how French it gets it will always be France with a difference.

GETTING AROUND

The gateway to Brittany is Rennes, 350 km (210 miles) from Paris on Autoroute A 11 (Autoroute de l'Oceanne) and three hours from Paris by the Train Grand Vitesse (TGV). There are frequent flights on Air Inter and TAT from all Paris airports to Rennes, Lorient, Quimper, and Brest. (Seats are hard to come by, so reserve far in advance.) Brit Air flies from London's Gatwick Airport to Quimper and Rennes, but most travellers cross the Channel to Brittany on the ferries from Plymouth and Portsmouth to St-Malo.

Buses of the French National Railway Network connect Rennes with the major seaside resorts. The best way to see the countryside, though, is by car. Hertz, Avis, Europcar, and other major car-rental firms have offices in Rennes.

ACCOMMODATIONS REFERENCE

▶ **D'Avaugour.** 1, place du Champ Clos, 22100 **Dinan.** Tel: 96-39-07-49.

▶ **Belle-Etoile.** Le Cabellou-Plage 29110 **Concarneau.** Tel: 98-97-05-73. Twenty-nine comfortable rooms near the beach, surrounded by greenery. Bar and lounge.

▶ **Elizabeth.** 2, rue Cordiers, 35400 **St-Malo.** Tel: 99-56-24-98. Attractive rooms in a 16th-century building.

▶ **Hôtel Au Fer à Cheval.** Route du Bois-de-Nevet, 29 **Locronan.** Tel: 98-91-70-67.

▶ **Griffon et Restaurant Creach Gwenn.** 131, route de Bénodet, 29000 **Quimper.** Tel: 98-90-33-33; Telex: 940063. Standard and moderately priced; the star here is the restaurant.

▶ **Hermitage.** Esplanade François-André, 44500 **La Baule.** Tel: 40-60-37-00; Telex: 710510; in U.S., (212) 477-1600 or (800) 223-1510. A luxurious hotel, with 230 air-conditioned rooms. Wonderful seaside location, with fine restaurants, pool, and tennis courts.

▶ **Manoir de la Rance.** Jouvente 35730 **Pleurtuit** (7 km/ 4 miles south of Dinard on Routes D 114 and D 5). Tel: 99-88-53-76. Eight rooms overlooking the water.

▶ **Manoir du Stang.** 29133 **La Fôret-Fouesnant.** Tel: 98-56-97-37. Charming and elegant, with 26 unique rooms, handsome parks, and refreshing pools.

▶ **La Mère Poulard.** 50116 **Le Mont-Saint-Michel.** Tel: 33-60-14-01; Telex: 170197.

▶ **Reine Hortense.** 19, rue Malouine, 35800 **Dinard.** Tel:

99-46-54-31. Ten luxurious rooms on the beach. No restaurant.

▶ **Valmarin**. 7, rue Jean-XXIII, St-Servan-sur-Mer 35400 **St-Malo**. Tel: 99-81-94-76.

▶ **La Villefromoy**. 7, boulevard Hérbert, Paramé 35400 **St-Malo**. Tel: 99-40-92-20.

THE LOIRE VALLEY

By Georgia I. Hesse

The Loire river, which seems to have few raisons d'être other than enchantment, flows through land that by any name—the garden of France, château country, the domain of butter—is infused with spring and summer richness. The Loire valley suggests idling, an afternoon picnic under leafy trees, back roads and light wines, and perhaps a nap. This is not country to be hurried through, though one-day tours out of Paris exist for that very purpose.

The traveller's Loire includes 15 *départements,* but historical regional names more truly reflect the cultures, habits, and allegiances of the people: Orléanais, Touraine, Anjou (the old capital of which was Angers), Maine, and maybe, by pushing things slightly, Berry.

Following strictly the curving river's course, you could begin in Sancerre (home of the brisk white wine, a lovely rosé, and a lesser-known light red) in the east and wander via Tours and Angers to about Nantes in the west. But driving from Paris you meet the Loire at Orléans; with such a route, Sancerre would be relegated to a Burgundian itinerary.

Starting at Orléans and working west along the river Loire, through Tours to Angers in the west, the tour described here then backtracks to Bourges toward the southeast as a side trip and ends at Sancerre as a jumping-off point for Burgundy.

MAJOR INTEREST

The six most remarkable châteaux: Chambord,
   Blois, Amboise, Chenonceaux, Loches, and Azay-
   le-Rideau
Other important châteaux: Villandry, Langeais,
   Chinon, Chaumont, Cheverny, Ussé
Church of Cunault
Abbey of Fontevraud (Plantagenet tombs)

Tours
Cathedral of St-Gatien
Musée des Beaux-Arts

Angers
The Château (Apocalypse tapestries)
Cathedral of St-Maurice
Musée de Turpin de Crissé

Bourges
Cathedral of St-Etienne
Palais Jacques Coeur
Cistercian abbey of Noirlac

Sancerre

Orléans

A trade and business center since its very beginnings,
Orléans, despite being the largest city on the route from
Paris to the Loire valley, is of little tourist interest today,
possibly because its center was severely damaged by fire
during World War II. Were it not for Joan of Arc, the "Maid
of Orléans," who came to town to relieve it from the
English siege in May of 1429, probably even fewer Loire-
bound travellers would now stop here.

Orléans's one star shines everywhere: on the rue
Jeanne d'Arc, in the Maison de Jeanne d'Arc, the Jeanne
d'Arc school, the statue of Jeanne d'Arc in the place du
Martroi, the chapel and stained-glass windows of Jeanne
d'Arc in the cathedral of Ste-Croix. Then, of course, there
are also the stores that do a brisk business in Joan of Arc
memorabilia (including Joan of Arc key chains) and the
inevitable Café Jeanne d'Arc.

There is an Orléans beyond Jeanne d'Arc, however.
The **Musée des Beaux-Arts**, in the same square as the
cathedral, makes up in modern functionalism for what it
lacks in style. Among the early paintings a Velázquez, a

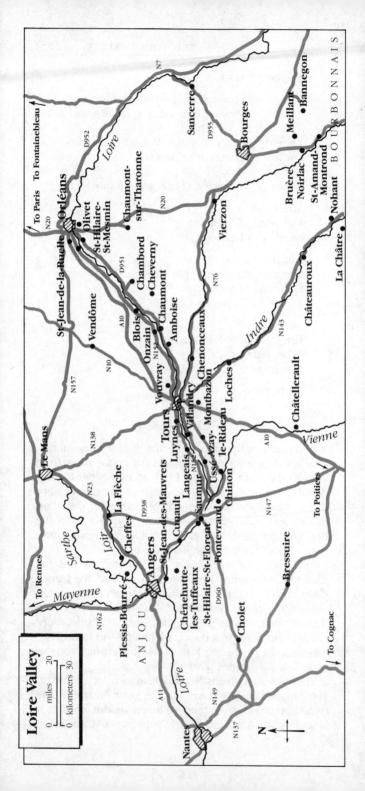

Louis Le Nain, and a Georges de La Tour are standouts, but there are also fine 18th- and 19th-century French paintings, particularly portraits.

The cathedral of Ste-Croix, almost the size of Paris's Notre-Dame, is notable chiefly for the 18th-century woodwork in its chancel.

Orléans's top hotel is the modern, 104-room **Sofitel** right off the river on quai Barentin, in the lower-expensive category. Its dining room, **La Vénerie**, is of a high standard. Otherwise, local hotels are rather ordinary. About 9 km (5 miles) to the southwest in St-Hilaire-St-Mesmin, the small, 19-room **Escale du Port Arthur** enjoys a pretty location and is extremely reasonable in rates. Another reasonable find is **Le Rivage** on rue de la Reine Blanche in Olivet, about 5 km (3 miles) south of Orléans. It offers 21 rooms in an old house on the banks of the Loire; you can expect good meals as well.

The dining scene in Orléans is smarter. Tops in town, at 34, rue Notre-Dame-de-Recouvrance, is **La Crémaillère** (try *ravioli de langoustines*), followed by **Les Antiquaires** (2, rue au Lin) and **La Poutrière**. The last, at 8, rue de la Brèche, is well known for its handsome decor as well as its cuisine.

The Era of the Great Châteaux

In the 15th and 16th centuries everybody who was anybody had to have a château, from Hurault de Cheverny (whose classic castle still belongs to the family) to François I (who needed at least a dozen and employed Cellini as his jeweler, Raphael as his portraitist, and Andrea del Sarto and Leonardo da Vinci as his court painters).

The Italian Renaissance in architecture, which began in Florence around 1420, had by the end of the century been exported to France. The reign of François I (1515–1547) was, in the words of his biographer, Desmond Seward, "the most radiant, the most creative in French history, a reign in which two brilliant cultures came together, those of Gothic France and Renaissance Italy . . . no ruler since Charlemagne has had a more direct influence upon the civilization of France."

The newer châteaux were quite distinct from the *châteaux forts,* or strongholds, of the tenth and 11th centuries, which were dark, dank, dirty, and cold. Over the centuries the *châteaux forts,* some of them veritable fortified towns, metamorphosed from fortresses into palaces. Arrow slits grew into proper windows, naked stone was covered with panels in a fan of colors and complex designs, genuine military-defense structures were translated into architectural caprices, and castles moved from protected heights down onto great greenswards. The châteaux built in the 17th and 18th centuries, on the other hand, are less proper châteaux than country seats (though far more elaborate than country homes or manor houses of today).

Nobody knows exactly how many châteaux exist in the forests and parklands along the Loire. There may be about 300 major ones; the following covers the most significant and attractive.

Château de Chambord

En route from Paris or Sancerre (from the northeast or the east), you come first to Chambord, the valley's biggest and perhaps most incredible château, with 218 rooms, 365 chimneys, a fantasy of turrets, dormers, and gables (Seward likens the roof to "an overcrowded chessboard"). Chambord has a renowned octagonal staircase, a double helix in stone that allows people (or, in its time, horses) ascending to see but never meet those descending.

Some say Leonardo may have been the architect of Chambord, but since he died before serious construction began and since his sketchbooks give no details, odds go to Domenico da Cortona, who may well have shown his model to Leonardo as well as François.

François was passionate about Chambord, continuing to build through good times and bad (at one point the king ordered work to continue even though he hadn't the cash to ransom his son from Spain). Once he even considered diverting the Loire to have it run by the château.

If it is true that Chambord was intended mainly as a hunting lodge, it continues to function as planned, for it commands a giant, 13,000-acre reserve, **le Parc National Cynégétique**, which has been set aside for hunting since 1948.

From April to late September, a 35-minute *spectacle de son et lumière*, "The Combat of Night and Day," is held at the château.

Château de Cheverny

This classic château south of Chambord, constructed in a single, continuous stroke, is more elegant, better dressed,

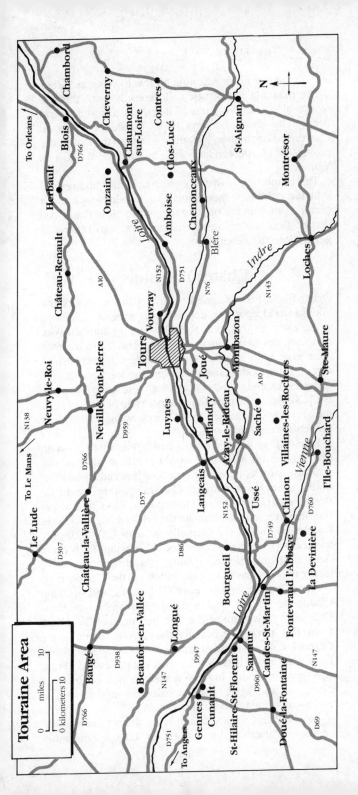

Touraine Area

miles 0   10
kilometers 0   10

and altogether more warming and welcoming as a residence than any of its castle colleagues. For one thing, it retains almost entirely the 17th-century furnishings and decorations from the days of its builder, Hurault de Cheverny. For another, it is still kept within the family, the possession of a descendant of the builder, the Marquis de Vibraye.

The home boasts five Gobelins tapestries and several valuable paintings; the kennels for hunting dogs and a hunting museum are open to the public. More than 2,000 sets of deer antlers testify to the good aim of several generations of Chevernoises.

Château de Blois

Originally, a fort designed to thwart the attacks of the Vikings stood upon this defensive site west of Chambord at the river. Of that, only the 13th-century **Tour du Foix** and **Salle des Etats** remain. To circle the courtyard with your eyes is to see the history of French architecture through the Gothic and early Renaissance periods (the galleries, chapels, and major wing were contributed by Louis XII), past the pure Renaissance style of François I, to the severely classic **Gaston d'Orléans wing**, the work of François Mansart for Louis XIII.

Louis XII took over from Charles VIII in 1498 when Charles, on his way to a tennis match at his castle at Amboise, struck his head upon a door lintel and died a few hours later. Louis married Charles's widow, Anne de Bretagne (Brittany), moved the court to Blois, and began building. His contributions are the brick and stone **Galerie Charles-d'Orléans**, the **Chapelle-St-Calais** (of which only the choir remains), and the **Louis XII wing**. Each has a delightful, airy, informal quality, even though they were too heavily restored—to some tastes—in the 19th century.

François I succeeded Louis XII in 1515, and his wife, Claude de France, Louis's daughter, bought him Blois Château for his amusement. The best parts of Blois date from this period, especially the carved, white stone **Grand Escalier** (Grand Staircase) in an octagonal tower. On a platform at each level, according to Seward, "François' guard paraded in tiers in their striped uniforms of blue, red, and white, holding halberds—and torches at night—to salute him when he rode in."

Blois Château's fairly dull interior, the result of a 19th-century restoration by a pupil of Eugène-Emmanuel

Viollet-le-Duc, pales by comparison with the exciting exterior, save for the fact that so much drama was played out within the walls.

This was the home, after all, of Charles d'Orléans (1391–1465), son of Louis d'Orléans, who was taken prisoner by the English at the Battle of Agincourt and remained a prisoner for 25 years, during which time he polished his great gift of poetry. On his return to France in 1440 Charles married Marie de Clèves; he was 50 years old, she 14. Charles had a part of the old fortress torn down and more livable quarters raised, in which he created a kind of *beaux-arts* court. He was 71 when his son—the future Louis XII—was born.

In 1588 the sniveling Henri III saw to the murder of his rival, the Duc de Guise, on the second floor of the château, and the following year his remarkable mother, Catherine de Médicis (Catherine of the Bad Press, it could be said now), died there. Visitors are dutifully shown the cabinets on the first floor in which Catherine is supposed to have secreted her poisons.

The château includes a *beaux-arts* museum. In June the stunning historical drama "Once Upon a Time, Louis XII" is performed with more than 300 characters in period costume. On various other dates between the end of March and end of September the *son-et-lumière* "Ghosts Like the Night" is shown (in English and French).

Blois the Town

The old quarter around the cathedral of St-Louis is worth exploring for its picturesque houses, the beautiful gardens of the **bishops' palace**, and the statue of the Huguenot Denis Papin, the inventor of the pressure cooker.

The **church of St-Nicolas**, near the château, is the most interesting in Blois; the capitals in the choir should especially be noted. Nearby is the Musée Robert Houdin; the magician Henry Houdini named himself after this master illusionist, who was a native of Blois.

Blois produces shoes and chocolate; almost every chocoholic visitor stops by **Chocolaterie Poulin**, not far from the château on the avenue Gambetta.

Wednesdays and Saturdays are the best market days in Blois. The local restaurant scene has apparently always been bleak: Patricia Wells, in *The Food Lover's Guide to France,* recommends driving 18 km (12 miles) east to Bracieux, where Bernard and Christine Robin prepare regional specialties in an old coaching inn now called **Bernard Robin**. (It was once Le Relais.) At 1, avenue Chambord, it rates two Michelin stars; game dishes are among the best.

The top hostelry in the vicinity (the town proper, of almost 50,000 people, offers little) is the **Domaine des Hauts de Loire**, in its own park just 17 km (11.5 miles) west along the river in Onzain; it also has a fine dining room. Arrangements may be made here for water skiing, fishing, golf, and horseback riding. In the same village, the **Château des Tertres**, in a parklike setting, has only 14 rooms—no restaurant, though—and is pleasant and less expensive.

Château de Chaumont

About 40 km (27 miles) upriver from Tours and just downriver from Blois, this is the fortresslike château Catherine de Médicis gave to Diane de Poitiers when she herself took Chenonceaux. Chaumont isn't undesirable, but Diane was spoiled, and she sulked and betook herself to more gracious Anet, near Paris. Students of symbols and inscriptions will immediately take note of the intertwined *C*s of Charles d'Amboise (one of the 16th-century owners) and of his wife, Catherine; the emblem of *chaud mont* (a volcano or, literally, "hot mountain"); and the intertwined *D*s of Diane de Poitiers that, with the hunting horn here and there, suggest Diane as the classical Diana the Huntress.

Then there are the coat of arms of France, the initials of Louis XII and Anne de Bretagne, the hat of Cardinal d'Amboise, and the coat of arms of Charles d'Amboise. Students of classical carvings have a veritable field day at Chaumont.

Chaumont has an American connection: In the 18th century it was owned by a financier named Le Ray, who supported American independence. Benjamin Franklin, when he was minister to the French court, was frequently entertained at the château. Franklin was able to persuade Le Ray to support freebooter John Paul Jones and thus to become instrumental in the creation of the American Navy.

Château d'Amboise

There is something irresistible about this castle, a bit downriver from Chaumont, toward Tours, although what remains is only a part of the dominant fortress that stood here in the 16th century. Perhaps it's the handsome setting above the town, or the glittering artistic history, or the fact that Leonardo da Vinci worked and died here.

Charles VIII was born to Louis XI and Charlotte of Savoy at Amboise. Only 13 years old when he assumed the throne, Charles began rebuilding and new construction in 1492, eventually creating one of the finest royal residences on the Loire. The masterpiece from this period is the Gothic **Chapelle St-Hubert**, dedicated to the patron saint of the hunt. At one time a portion of the apartments of Queen Anne de Bretagne, the chapel is rich in decoration; the stained-glass windows that were destroyed in 1940 have been suitably replaced by Max Ingrand. From an expedition to Italy (which was undertaken to conquer Naples for the House of Valois), Charles returned with an exuberance of artworks, furniture, fabrics, and people: decorators, gardeners, artists, even a chicken breeder.

When Charles died in 1498 (see the Bourges section), the boy who would become King François I moved to Amboise at the age of six with his mother, Louise of Savoy, and his sister, who would one day become the learned Margaret of Navarre.

As a child, François loved action, shows, tournaments, and display; his enthusiasm for such excesses never left him. In 1518 a particularly diverting mock battle was staged at the château, during which the king and company of 600 men defended a wooden model town against a like force led by the dukes of Bourbon and Vendôme.

"It was the finest mock battle that had ever been seen," Florange wrote, "but it did not please everyone, for some were killed and others terrified."

François enlarged Amboise and made it more magnificent, but his greatest accomplishment was the importation of Leonardo da Vinci, who brought with him his *Mona Lisa* and *Virgin of the Rocks,* both now in the Louvre. This one-man Renaissance spent the last three years of his life in a manor house a cobble's toss from the château, and died there on May 2, 1519.

War, however, has always been insensible to artistic greatness: That August, Leonardo's bones were buried in the cloister of the church of St-Florentin, as he had asked, but during the Wars of Religion his remains and those of hundreds of others were dug up and tossed away. A plaque in the north transept of the Chapelle St-Hubert claims Leonardo's bones are there with others. But nobody knows.

Amboise the Town

After visiting the château, stop first at **Clos-Lucé**, Leonardo's home and now a museum. No originals are displayed, but models from his drawings show the extraordinary talents he had as an engineer. There are also small-scale displays, an armored tank, a helicopter, and a drawbridge among them. Clos-Lucé itself, furnished with 15th- and 16th-century antiques, is worthwhile.

The history of stages and coaching in France draws some wanderers to the **Musée de la Poste** in the 16th-century Hôtel de Joyeuse.

Not far from Clos-Lucé (everything is easily accessible in Amboise), **Le Mail St-Thomas** serves elegant meals in a pretty garden; **Château de Pray**, to the northeast of the village, is a find; quiet, modestly priced, with 16 rooms, it overlooks a park.

A 90-minute *son-et-lumière*, "At the Court of King François," featuring 420 regional citizens in period dress, plays during July and August.

Château de Chenonceaux

At one time, Chenonceaux (south of Amboise), like most other great châteaux along the Loire, came under the sign of the salamander (the symbol of François I). François was not its builder, though; the structure that is admired today is the 16th-century creation of Thomas Bohier, tax collector for Charles VIII, Louis XII, and François I. If you were to explore but a single castle in the Loire, a good choice would be Chenonceaux.

The story of Bohier himself reads somewhat like a Balzac novel, but it is the women who star in the story of the Château of Six Women: Catherine Briçonnet, Bohier's wife; Diane de Poitiers, Henri II's famously beautiful mistress; Catherine de Médicis; Louise of Lorraine, wife and widow of Henri III, who after the king's murder lived out her life in black and white; Madame Dupin, who employed Rousseau as tutor to her son—his *Emile* was written at Chenonceaux; and Madame Pelouze, who restored the whole to its original state.

No castle is more stunning on first approach. Up a superb avenue flanked by plane trees, you approach (no trumpet fanfare, alas) the great keep, the 15th-century *donjon* of the original structure. To the left blooms the **formal garden of Diane**. Diane was the rival of Henri II's wife, Catherine, whose garden to the right is somewhat smaller. Behind the keep, Diane's marvelous **Grande Galerie** (topped off by the image of Catherine, as it happens) spans the river Cher in five bounds.

Unlike some others, this château is extremely well furnished; its rooms and artworks are of great interest. An unfortunate corollary is that Chenonceaux is almost always thronged, so it's best seen out of season.

Catherine took spiteful pleasure, upon Henri's death by jousting, in tossing Diane out of Chenonceaux and into Medieval Chaumont. (Diane never liked Chaumont, and retired to her own, prettier, Anet.)

Chenonceaux's *son-et-lumière,* "In the Times of the Women of Chenonceaux," is presented from June to mid-September.

Medieval Loches

If Chenonceaux seduces with grace, Loches, south of Chenonceaux and southeast of Tours on N 143, strikes right between the eyes with dungeons, turrets, keep, torture chambers, round towers, and ramparts: all the discomforts of home in the Middle Ages.

The town of Loches (about 7,000 people) lies at the foot of what was really a Medieval entrenched camp on the banks of the river Indre.

Loches is a prominent part of the history of the great feudal families of Anjou and Plantagenet. Henri (England's Henry II) created fortifications here; his son, Jean-sans-Terre, had it wrested away from him by King Philippe-Auguste; Jean's brother, Richard the Lion-Hearted, returning from prison in Austria, was so angry he took it back in a three-hour battle; when Richard died, Philippe-Auguste took it back again.

Joan of Arc was here in 1459, but the real *dame du château* is Agnès Sorel, mistress of Charles VII and benefactor of a very good pun: She was known as *la Dame de Beauté* not entirely because of her good looks but more because Charles gave her an estate known as Beauté-sur-Marne. Respects may be paid at the tomb of Agnès Recumbent in the château, where angels support her head, lambs her feet.

Everything in the Medieval enclosure of Loches is

worth seeing; some of its dungeons and cells are open to visitors.

Louis XI liked to put his prisoners into wooden and ironwork cages here and to suspend them from the ceiling of the **Tour Ronde**. One prisoner-cardinal is said to have dangled there for 11 years. Ludovico Sforza, the duke of Milan, spent eight years in the dungeons of **Martelet** (the most oppressive in the complex); Sforza wrote and painted on its walls, and fell dead the moment he observed the sunlight of freedom.

TOURS

In the days of the Pax Romana, under the name of Caesarodunum (Caesar's hill), Tours became a prosperous free city with an administrative center, baths, arenas, and other Roman necessities near the site of the cathedral of St-Gatien.

By the fourth century, Tours (named for a Celtic tribe, the Turones) was the bustling center of Roman Gaul in the west. Five roads, reaching from Spain to Roman settlements in the far north, met in Tours, which allowed for important land commerce in addition to that provided by the river. Saint Martin, today the patron saint of France, was born in what was then called Pannonia (Hungary). Despite his wishes, he was sent off to military duty in northern Gaul, where, near Amiens, he performed the kindness that was to start him down his long religious road.

The story varies in its details. Historian Katherine Scherman, in *The Birth of France,* tells that in a wintry Amiens, Martin came upon a nearly naked beggar at the city gates asking passersby for pity. Martin whipped off his heavy cloak, rent it in two with his sword, and gave half to the beggar. That night he dreamed of Christ, the beggar in the cloak.

In 360 Martin founded a monastery, the first in Gaul, at Ligugé, near Poitiers, and in 372 was named bishop of Tours. He was particularly beloved because of his homely miracles, but he is invoked frequently because of the expression he gave the French language. He died at Candes (about halfway between Tours and Angers) in November 397, and as his body was being transported by boat to Tours trees in the region suddenly leaped into leaf, flowers bloomed, and birds began to sing. The warmth that comes after the first frosts of autumn has ever since been known in France as Saint Martin's Summer.

Candes-St-Martin is important today mainly because of the church that sits atop the place where Martin died. Built in the 12th and 13th centuries, it mixes a quasi-military appearance with lavish decoration on the façade.

As the cult of Saint Martin grew, his constituency prospered. His abbey spread branches to almost all the provinces of France and to other great countries of Europe.

The first French historian, Gregory of Tours, became bishop of the see in 573. In the eighth century the Anglo-Saxon monk Alcuin, brought out of Italy by Charlemagne, created an intellectual and artistic school in Tours that produced such notable illuminated manuscripts as the Bible of Charles le Chauve (the Bald). Tours has experienced bad times (the Norman invasions, the struggles of the Reformation, and the extensive damage done to it during World Wars I and II).

There are about 137,000 Tourangeaux today, working mostly in various medium and heavy industries. An industrial zone between the north bank of the river and the airport has permitted important construction for electronic and metallurgic industries. So far, however, the vital industrial element of the city has been prevented from impinging on the traditional cultural attractions that lure travellers.

As throughout its long history, the university of Tours remains a significant institution, and Touraine continues to boast and believe that the French spoken here is the purest in France.

Music is important to the life of Tours: A summer's schedule will include jazz, rock, and classical concerts, drawing names such as Jango Edwards or Sviatoslav Richter. The Grand Théâtre devotes itself, in the main, to symphonic and choral productions; recitals are held in several churches and in the Salle des Tanneurs; chamber orchestras frequently perform in the Salle des Fêtes of the Hôtel de Ville.

For ticket and other information, inquire at the Comité Départemental de Tourisme, 16, rue Buffon, near the railroad station.

The Old City

Vieux Tours has been tastefully restored. It centers on **place Plumereau**, originally a marketplace for hatters.

Most of the area is off-limits to vehicles, resulting in pleasurably winding streets, lined with a variety of boutiques that offer everything from traditional arts and crafts to today's toys and fashions.

The 15th-century half-timbered houses and gabled façades of the Old City shelter seductive sidewalk cafés and restaurants. Various styles of town houses cluster on **rue Briçonnet** near the **Musée de Gemmail**. (The relatively modern art of *gemmail,* colored glass pieces assembled and artificially lighted from the back or inside to create a contemporary version of stained glass, was invented by the painter John Crotti [1878–1958]. Works of *gemmail* may be original or they may re-create frescoes, mosaics, and the like.)

This tangle of streets also shows off the **Hôtel Gouin**, an ornate Renaissance mansion that somehow survived the battering the area underwent in World War II. Here visitors can view the collections of the Touraine archaeological society, including prehistoric and Gallo-Roman treasures, as well as late Medieval sculptures and other items.

Near the Hôtel Gouin, **La Rôtisserie Tourangelle** is a pleasant, fairly moderate restaurant offering *sandre au sabayon de Vouvray* (a perchlike Loire fish in creamy Vouvray wine sauce) and *aiguillette de canard au fumet de Bourgueil* (sliced duck breast in Bourgueil stock).

Just off the rue des Halles and near the central marketplace are the ruins of the **basilica of St-Martin**, dating from the fifth century, when a sanctuary was built to shelter the remains of Martin. That was destroyed by the Normans but replaced in the 13th century by a magnificent basilica. That in turn was sacked by the Huguenots in 1562 during the Wars of Religion. What's left of *that* are two towers, the Tour Charlemagne and Tour de l'Horloge, both heavily restored. The new basilica of St-Martin, finished in 1924, comprises a corner of the former structure and claims to preserve the tomb of the saint in its crypt, the exact spot where it lay in antiquity.

Elsewhere in the City

From Old Tours it's a pleasant walk east on rue Colbert toward the cathedral of St-Gatien and its quarter. The **Musée du Compagnonnage**, on rue Nationale near the church of St-Julien, is installed in a 16th-century monks' dormitory. It traces the history, techniques, tools, and accomplished works of artisans in the region. (Its name is a happy one: It joins derivatives of the Latin *com-* and *panis,* meaning one with whom bread is shared; the French slang for buddy is *copain,* and the English *companion* clearly shares the same root.)

The 13th-century **church of St-Julien** glows with light shining through the 20th-century stained-glass windows of Max Ingrand; there's a museum of the wines of Touraine in its cloister cellar.

Enthusiasts and collectors of antiquities will not be able to pass by **l'Echiquier** on rue Colbert, probably the best antique shop in town; others are bunched together on the rue de la Scellerie.

Begun in the 13th century and not completed until the 16th, the **cathedral of St-Gatien** shows off the entire, extensive genius of the Gothic style, most of the evolution being visible on the recently restored façade. Romanesque sits in the form of towers upon a Gallo-Roman wall; Flamboyant dances on the façade; Renaissance triumphs in the turret towers.

Inside, the premier attractions are the 13th- to 15th-century stained-glass windows. The top of the south tower is a good position for photography.

In the immediate vicinity of the cathedral, the **Clôitre de la Psalette** (where one sings psalms) has fine 15th- and 16th-century frescoes. The **Musée des Beaux-Arts**, located in a 17th- to 18th-century palace of the archbishops, has attempted to bring alive, in several completely outfitted rooms, the styles of the 18th century: Regency, Louis XV, Louis XVI. This is one of the most comprehensive art museums in the Loire valley, with French paintings from the 15th to 19th century displayed chronologically; the early Italian works are particularly interesting.

Right near the river, off quai d'Orléans, the 12th-century **Tour de Guise** is all that remains of a château of Henry II Plantagenet in which the young Duc de Guise was imprisoned after the murder of his father by Henri III; here Joan of Arc was received by Charles VII. The Musée Historial de Touraine within the château is worth a short stop.

Markets are held daily in Tours, either at the Marché des Halles or place Velpeau, said to be best on weekends. Porcelain, pottery, and wickerwork may be good finds at the flea market on place des Victoires on Wednesdays and Sundays.

A garlic and basil fair puts Tours in good odor near the

end of July; 10 km (6.7 miles) north via A 10, the Touraine music festival is staged in late June at the **Grange de Meslay**, a 13th-century ensemble of farm buildings.

Dining is best and most expensively done in Tours at **Barrier**, on the north bank of the river; near the Tour de Guise, less extravagant local cuisine is offered by **Tuffeaux**, including *blanc de turbot au vin de Layon et melon* (turbot with sweet white wine and melon). Master chef Jean Sabat turns out irresistible pastries here at 76, rue Nationale.

Although Tours itself has several good hotels—the best located for walking is **Univers** on the wide boulevard Heurteloup—travellers in search of serenity (and who don't mind then having to drive into town to sightsee) would prefer the **Domaine de Beauvois** and its fine restaurant, 13 km (8 miles) northwest. The **Domaine des Hauts de Loire** (see the Blois section) and **Château d'Artigny** (see the Azay-le-Rideau section) are also not far away.

Two possibilities in Joué-lès-Tours, cheek-by-jowl with Tours, are **Hôtel des Cèdres** (35 rooms in a country setting; a *gastronomique* restaurant nearby) and **Château de Beaulieu**, a quiet, comfortable, pleasantly priced 19-room discovery.

Villandry

The stunning element of the fortress here, some 20 km (13.5 miles) west of Tours, is not the interior (though that also is worthwhile, especially for 18th-century woodworks), but the gardens. Nothing like them exists elsewhere.

Perfectly manicured, set on three rising terraces, these are ornamental gardens you would want to consider eating. Flowers are plentiful, but there are also geometrical, color-coordinated growths of chard, cabbage, fruit trees—all the good-looking vegetables except the potato, which had yet to arrive in France in the 16th century.

An outstanding restaurant exists in this village of 742 inhabitants: **Cheval Rouge**, in an old house with a pretty garden. Although the cuisine is classic Loire fare, the chef has a flair for creating attractive dishes from fresh seasonal vegetables and fruits.

Azay-le-Rideau

On an autumn afternoon when the air is as golden as the leaves, the pretty promenade to the Château d'Azay, in its setting of woods and water southwest of Tours, seems an invitation to a dream. You will feel you must have lived here in another, more serene life—an elegant escape that was translated from Gothic to Renaissance perfection.

Constructed by financier Gilles Berthelot between 1518 and 1529, Azay is a superb example of Medieval defenses become less useful than graceful, not deadly but decorative.

The château today is a fine Renaissance museum with beautiful furnishings and tapestries. From late May to late September, a *son-et-lumière*, "Since We Have No Other Image of You," features a walk around the château with the disembodied voices of five actors.

The village of Azay (with fewer than 3,000 people) is worth an amble, particularly if it's lunchtime and there's a table on the terrace at **Grande Monarque**, an unpretentious 30-room hotel with a kitchen specializing in local fare, such as green salad in walnut-oil vinaigrette, Loire salmon soufflé, goat cheese (maybe Ste-Maure?), and crunchy *baguettes*.

A morning market is held on Wednesdays, and there's an apple fair in late October.

Only 5 km (3.4 miles) away at Villaines-les-Rochers, the basket weavers of **La Vannerie** turn out beautiful wicker goods and are happy to ship them overseas.

Seven km (4.7 miles) east of Azay-le-Rideau by a back road, at the château in the wide spot of **Saché**, you may pay respects to Honoré de Balzac, who wrote all or part of *Le Père Goriot, La Recherche de l'Absolu,* and other works there. Balzac's bedroom-workroom remains as it was in the mid–19th century; the whole is a small museum.

Philadelphian Alexander Calder (1898–1976) lived and worked on his mobiles and stabiles near Saché from 1953 until his death.

Notable cuisine is served in Saché at **Auberge du XIIᵉ Siècle**, best accompanied by the wine of the area, Azay-le-Rideau.

Among the most regal hostelries in France is **Château d'Artigny**, between Azay-le-Rideau and Tours in the village of **Montbazon** (population of 3,000-plus). It's smart, stylish, and set in its own park, with a heated pool and tennis courts. The kitchen is excellent, and Château d'Artigny's regional wine list is comprehensive. One of Foulques Nera's 20 fortresses was in Montbazon, and its keep remains.

In the same town, **Domaine de la Tortinière** is only slightly less impressive, an old château in its private park overlooking the river Indre and a tenth-century tower ruin on the opposite bank; there are 14 quiet rooms and an outstanding kitchen. Just to the west, occupying a setting by the same river, **Moulin-Fleuri** is small (ten rooms), cozy, and rather more modest in price than la Tortinière.

Langeais

The harmony of this Medieval residence (its appearance from the outside bespeaks more a feudal fortress) results from its having been built in the remarkably short time of five years or so. Fortunately, also, it has never undergone substantial restoration. It lies on the Loire west of Tours and near Azay-le-Rideau. The ruins of a tenth-century keep stand in the gardens.

Within, the *appartements* are unusually well furnished, precisely descriptive of life in the 15th century; Gothic furniture and Flemish tapestries abound. Charles VIII married Anne de Bretagne in the **Grand Salon**.

The comfortable, modestly priced 12-room **Hosten** on rue Gambetta has a Michelin one-star dining room; try the *blanquette de sole et turbot*.

Château d'Ussé

For some reason this massive, fortified, rather grim château, west of Langeais along the Loire, does not play the feature role it should within its company. It always catches photographers with their lenses down, yet it has the very model of a Sleeping Beauty keep. The château bristles like a brush with turrets, clock towers, chimneys, dormers, roof trapdoors (the better for pouring boiling oil), and so forth. In comparison with the fairly fierce exterior, the interior rooms are comfortable, even gracious; the king's bedroom is most interesting.

Château de Chinon

Whereas the château in Chinon is what most travellers come to see—a fortress that played major roles in the nearly endless Anglo-French fights, where Charles VII retreated when the power of Paris really belonged to England's Henry IV, where Joan of Arc came to announce the mission her "voices" had commanded—the Old Town here is at least as provocative.

The château is really three adjoining ruins south of Ussé above the river Vienne: **Fort St-Georges**, of which little remains but memories of the death of Henri II; **Château du Milieu**, entered through the still impressive Tour de l'Horloge and housing the Musée Jeanne-d'Arc; and the **Château de Coudray**, where the Maid resided.

The Middle Ages still can be sensed in the **Old Town**, particularly along rue Voltaire (where the *Office de Tourisme* is) and at the wide area known as **Grand Carroi**, heart of the Medieval action and today the center of ambience.

Just 7 km (4.7 miles) south, across the river, the **Château de Marçay** has 34 guest rooms in a handsome 15th-century fortress, and serves highly rated cuisine.

Rabelais was born at the manor of **La Devinière** near Chinon; it's now a museum of his work.

The Abbey of Fontevraud

Richard the Lion-Hearted is so familiar he seems almost fanciful, the overstated hero, the Superman of antiquity. Paying a pilgrimage to his tomb (or perhaps even more, to that of his parents, Henry II Plantagenet, King of England, and Queen Eleanor of Aquitaine) involves a drive to Fontevraud from Saumur in the west or from Chinon or Ussé in the east. The tiny town of Fontevraud (or Fontevrault, in the old spelling) grew up to support the royal abbey, one of the finest examples of monastic architecture.

In 1099 (when Jerusalem was captured during the First Crusade), a hermit named Robert d'Arbrissel settled in the forested valley of Fontevraud near a formidable spring. Eventually, convents were built at the site: St-Lazarus for lepers and St-Magdalene's for women. An abbess was put in charge and given absolute power. From the 12th century into the 18th century, 36 abbesses, all of princely descent, ruled over Fontevraud.

Today the traveller marches single-mindedly through the Romanesque church, past the high altar (it survived the Revolution and is now enduring archaeological digs at its base), and into the transept room, where, recumbent upon their tombs, lie Richard, Eleanor, Henry, and their daughter-in-law, Isabelle d'Angoulême, third wife of Bad King John Lackland. They are splendid in polychrome limestone (Isabelle is in wood); Eleanor in death, as in life, is reading a book.

> King Henry was I [reads his epitaph]
> Full many a vanquished kingdom I made mine;
> Dukedoms and lordships countless did I hold;
> All nations' sway would not have sated me.
> Today for me eight feet of ground suffice.

Other elements of the abbey—the chapter house, the cloisters, the refectory—are excellent, but the most curious is the old **kitchen**, the only one extant from the Romanesque period in France. It is octagonal, with semicircular attached towers topped by witches' hats in upside-down tiles. Inside, a staff of cooks worked over six wood-fire hearths; smoke soared 89 feet to exit through 20 flues.

Leaving at evening, you may hear church bells in the distance and look back 700 years.

Château de Saumur

To see the château is to feel a sense of déjà vu, its 14th-century silhouette familiar from Christmas cards bearing a likeness of the Limbourg brothers' illumination for *Les Très Riches Heures du Duc de Berry,* now in the Condé museum in Chantilly.

Saumur the town (with about 34,000 inhabitants) has always been renowned for its wines (especially the *mousseux,* or sparkling, ones, such as Crémant de Loire), its cavalry school, and its manufacture of religious medals. It is also Europe's foremost maker of masks for Carnival—and recently has made gains in the electronics industry.

Two fine and distinct museums can be found in the château: the **Musée du Cheval** (Museum of the Horse) and the **Musée des Arts Décoratifs**. In the first, the horse rides through all ages and countries, bareback, saddled, bridled, spurred, and stirruped. The Musée des Arts Décoratifs is notable for its collection of fine ceramics.

Sherman and Patton tanks, the British Conqueror, German Panzers, and landing craft from D-Day are among the items in the **Musée des Blindés** (armored vehicles) near the river and the northern corner of the large place du Chardonnet. The **Musée de Barbet-de-Vaux** shows off historic swords, sabers, uniforms, and other military memorabilia. Guided tours are available in the afternoons; ask for written authority to enter at the office of the cavalry school in the same building (entrance off avenue Foch).

Most unusual is the **Musée du Champignon** (Museum of Mushrooms) in neighboring St-Hilaire-St-Florent, where Louis Bouchard grows the fragrant fungus in the darkness of underground caves.

Sharp-eyed drivers who travel around the riverside cliffs near Saumur will spot dozens of stone-cut homes of present-day troglodytes; some are carpeted and outfitted with electricity, heating, and running water.

Le Prieuré, a restored Renaissance manor in nearby Chênehutte-les-Tuffeaux, offers 35 rooms, two apartments, and fine cuisine in a lovely setting above the river.

Cunault

The Loire's collection of castles, churches, museums, and country inns could not be exhausted in a lifetime. Still, time should be taken for a traipse to the Benedictine monastery's church of Cunault, about 12 km (8.1 miles) northwest of Saumur. The church is thought to embody the finest elements of Romanesque architecture in the Loire Valley. Chiseled figures on the 200 column capitals demand a close look with a long camera lens or binoculars. Some Medieval painted decoration remains.

ANGERS

The old capital of the counts and dukes of Anjou, at the western end of the traditional Loire Valley sightseeing region, occupies a splendid (and easily defensible) site above the banks of the river Maine, about 8 km (5.4 miles) from its confluence with the Loire. During Roman times, it was called Juliomagus; Tacitus mentioned the existence of an ancient people on a local site called Andes or Andecavi; very little is known of this prehistoric culture, however. By Roman times the town served as crossroads for routes from Rennes, Nantes, and Tours. Some second-century baths remain from Gallo-Roman days, as do some portions of the third-century ramparts.

The first House of Anjou (tenth to 12th century) and the second (13th to 15th century) were separated by the dynasties of the Plantagenets and Capets. The first of the Plantagenets was Geoffrey, who plucked a sprig of broom (*plante de genêt*) to put upon his hat, thereby naming a vital line of French and British rulers. Geoffrey's son Henry II (of England) died at Chinon in 1189, as did his son, Richard the Lion-Hearted, ten years later. Anjou became part of the French domain in 1204, though England and France battled over it until the Hundred Years War (1338–1453) had come to an end.

First of the dukes of Anjou was Charles, who received the dukedom as a gift from his brother, Saint Louis (Louis IX), in 1246; he added to it Sicily and the kingdom of Naples by conquest. Good King René (linguist, musician, poet, painter, stage manager of grand entertainments, writer of chivalric sagas) reigned as the last duke before the lands were annexed by King Louis XI in 1474.

During the 1789 revolution, the cathedral became a Temple of Reason.

The small city (about 142,000 Angevins) and its surroundings deserve an exploration of at least three days; Angers is less known but more interesting than either Tours or Orléans. An *entrepôt* for wines, liqueurs (Cointreau), flowers, and agricultural products, Angers hosts an annual wine fair the last two weeks of January and the festival of Anjou at the end of June to early July. For six centuries Angers has been renowned for the production of textiles; today, umbrellas are a specialty.

The **Château d'Angers** bulks high above the Maine—a formidable feudal retreat that looks as if it might even today defeat any conventional-weapons attack. Still standing are the 17 mighty towers, between 130 and 195 feet high, that were once capped by what were called pepperpot roofs (*poivrières*). Formal gardens bloom in the impressive moat.

Inside, magnificent tapestries from the 14th to the 17th century are displayed, including the remarkable **Tenture de l'Apocalypse**, the oldest and largest tapestry known, a 14th-century marvel 551 feet long and more than 16 feet high, woven in seven sections. It is displayed in a room constructed especially for that purpose. The collections also include fine Flemish and other tapestries.

The **cathedral of St-Maurice**, from the 12th and 13th centuries, characterizes Plantagenet-Angevin style; the 12th-century tympanum above the porch is particularly fine. Close observers will note that the Gothic vaulting of the nave—the earliest in Anjou—is rather strange. The stained-glass windows provide a review of the history of the art in France from the 12th to the 18th century. (No stained glass from before the 12th century is known.)

The **Hôpital St-Jean** (12th century) is the oldest hospital in France. It houses ten tapestries of the contemporary artist Jean Lurçat (1892–1966), titled *Song of the World.*

Collections of Greek and Etruscan vases, amphoras, Renaissance art and furnishings, engravings, Chinese and Japanese *objets-d'art,* and enamels are shown in the **Musée de Turpin de Crissé** in the Renaissance mansion known as l'Hôtel Pincé.

In the handsome 15th-century house Logis Barrault, the **Musée des Beaux-Arts** displays the complete works of David d'Angers (1788–1856), some 500 medallions of representatives of the Romantic period (Hugo, Goethe, Chateaubriand, Balzac, and others), items from the Middle Ages such as coffers and sculptures, and works by primitive Flemish, Italian, and Swiss painters.

Angers is a pleasant place to idle away a day by café sitting, ambling, or even indulging in nine holes of golf at nearby **St-Jean-des-Mauvrets**. Markets are held in Angers daily except Mondays. Fish from the Loire are particularly well cooked and served at **Le Toussaint**, at 7, rue Toussaint, and **Le Logis**, at 17, rue du St-Laud. Of local hotels, the best is **Anjou**, with its restaurant **Salamandre**, on the boulevard du Maréchal-Foch, but it might be nicer to try a country retreat such as, 24 km (16.2 miles) away in Cheffes-sur-Sarthe, the **Château de Teildras**: 11 rooms in a 16th-century country house overlooking its own pond and lake.

Angers is also convenient to such sites in the Mayenne valley as the seignorial **Château de Plessis-Bourré**, and the town is admirably suited to promenades along the Loire and drives into the valleys of the Mayenne and Loir.

BOURGES OF BERRY

Bourges and its nearby attractions make a rewarding side trip (out of the Loire valley), roughly south of Orléans or roughly east of Tours. Even today, Bourges, capital of the old region of Grand Berry–Limousin, is a stranger to most foreigners and to many French. The little city of about 80,000 Berruyers sits somewhat off the tourist trails of Burgundy to the east, the Loire to the north, and Brittany-Normandy on the west.

In truth, Bourges is the heart of the matter, only 36 km (24.3 miles) north of the measured center of this measured land, the hamlet of Bruère. That fact did not interest Stendhal at all; he saw Bourges as "surrounded by plains of a bitter ugliness." Only someone born near the up-thrust magnificence of the Alps around Grenoble could feel that way.

Between 80 and 60 B.C., a Celtic people called the Bituriges occupied the site of a future Bourges and called it Avarich (in Latin, Avaricum, "a well-watered place"). Because they believed the town to be an easily defensible site, the Bituriges persuaded their ally, Vercingetorix, not to burn it (as was his custom) in the face of the advancing Roman armies.

Hélas, Vercingetorix gave in, the Romans attacked, and in 52 B.C. massacred some 40,000 citizens of what Caesar had called one of the "most beautiful cities in Gaul."

Bourges prospered under the Romans (though the slaughter remains unforgotten), becoming a major city of Aquitaine, a vital marketplace, and the site of a great amphitheater (at today's place de la Nation). By the third century, Avaricum was hemmed in by a wall crowned with almost 50 towers; remnants of the wall may be seen along rue Bourbonnoux.

Euric, king of the Visigoths, took control of the area in 476. After Pepin the Short (Charlemagne's father) conquered the territory in 762, Bourges became the southern base of the Capetian kingdom.

Lucky cities have their protectors, their enhancers, their patrons; Bourges had all three in the persons of two men: Jean, Duc de Berry, third son of King Jean II the Good and brother of Charles V; and the creative businessman and enthusiast of architecture Jacques Coeur.

In 1360 Berry was still numb from the raids of England's Black Prince (Edward, Prince of Wales) in 1356, and from the general ravages of the Hundred Years War. Jean, returned from captivity in England, was awarded Berry and Auvergne and, through various family inheritances, eventually came also into control of Poitou and Languedoc.

A man of great taste and even greater extravagance, Jean decorated his "empire" with palaces, princely residences, collections of manuscripts, tapestries, rare animals and birds, and jewels. It was he who hired the Flemish artist Pol de Limbourg and his brothers to create

Les Très Riches Heures du Duc de Berry, perhaps the most exquisite of illuminated manuscripts known.

When Jean died at age 76, Charles VII took over. Disinherited from the throne, with half the lands of France in English and Burgundian hands, he endured with fairly good grace the nickname King of Bourges. Luckily, he had as treasurer, minister of finances, whatever, the nimble-minded Jacques Coeur.

Coeur was a canny merchant whose fleet of trading ships, bringing to France the wares of the Levant, the goods of the East, made him the most illustrious financier of his age. Because of Coeur, France began to contend successfully with the great trading republics of Italy, and in 1436 he was summoned by Charles VII to become master of the mint, to reform the coinage and royal expenditure systems. His brilliance resulted in France's increasing supremacy among trading nations in the East, and he went on to represent his country in three embassies.

Jacques, son of a furrier, was born in Bourges in about 1400. Many travellers pay their respects at a handsome half-timbered *pâtisserie* at the corner of rue d'Auron and rue des Armuriers that some guidebooks—and an inscription on the place—cite as his natal home. Michelin, however, characteristically tells the truth: The present building dates from only the early 16th century, and the house it replaced came to Coeur only after his marriage.

Nonetheless, it is intriguing to think of the few yards and many achievements separating this unpretentious corner bakery from the sumptuous Gothic manse, the Palais Jacques Coeur, just up the sloping street.

Bourges the Town

The town will come as a happy surprise to anyone who has planned to see only "the reds of Bourges" in the cathedral and the rich decorations of the Palais Jacques Coeur and then skip away. It is, however, a town not to pass through quickly but to be meandered through and then used as a base for exploration of a countryside as yet unplundered by mass tourism.

In 1963 the first of several Maisons de la Culture was inaugurated in Bourges by André Malraux and Charles de Gaulle, charged with devotion to and promotion of theater, cinema, music, dance, arts and crafts, expositions, and scientific and cultural conferences.

Today the Maison is a home for such happenings as Le Printemps de Bourges, which in late April brings French and foreign singers and songs to the public, putting special emphasis on the discovery of new talent. It houses as well the festival of electro-acoustical music near the end of May and beginning of June.

Other annual goings-on include the Fête de la Vieille Ville (Old Town festival) near the end of May, featuring concerts, plays, and folkloric events; a national fair and exposition during the last half of June; and the Foires Jacques Coeur, with travelling shows and entertainment, held in place Séraucourt, near the Maison de la Culture, from mid-June to mid-July.

In addition, Bourges maintains a national school of music, several experimental music and theater groups, and a national *beaux-arts* academy. In summer, nearby Val d'Auron is the site of water sports.

Cathedral of St-Etienne

"One must see the reds of Bourges and the blues of Chartres," a student of stained glass once said. Well, the blues of Bourges aren't so shabby either.

In fact, the 13th- to 16th-century windows of the cathedral of St-Etienne will cause the stiffest of necks to swivel: This is one of the most astonishing collections in France. Here the impious of the Middle Ages could see moral misbehavior writ large, as in the window depicting the bad rich man, who turns aside from a beggar named Lazarus dying with ulcers, and then dies himself. In agony, he begs Father Abraham for pity, only to be told, "Look, you got yours in life and so did Lazarus. Now your roles are reversed." Or words to that effect.

If the windows are the initial lure of St-Etienne, the Gothic interior—with four side aisles in the place of transepts—is of almost equal interest. Jean de Berry lies entombed in the 12th-century **crypt**.

Circling up the steps of the **north tower** is recommended to enthusiasts of city overviews, photographers who enjoy taking shots of double-winged buttresses through pseudo arrow-slits, and others stout of heart. (This is also called the butter tower, because it was built with funds donated by citizens in return for dispensations allowing them to consume butter and milk during Lent.)

The Old City

Almost the entire heart of the Old City has been preserved or artfully restored. Hosts of half-timbered houses still stand to the north of the cathedral in the vicinity of the **Gallo-Roman wall**. Rue Bourbonnoux (where you can have a pleasant sidewalk luncheon at the **Bar Ramparts**) debouches into place Gordaine with its bustling little park, sidewalk cafés, and the magnificent Renaissance **Hôtel Lallement**, now a museum of decorative arts. The house itself is a major attraction, heightened by collections of 16th- and 17th-century furnishings, tapestries, paintings, and marquetry, in addition to ivories, enamels, and the like.

Smart and trendy shops line the **rue Mirabeau**, veering off place Gordaine, interspersed with fast-food places such as Lucky Burger Luke.

Jacques Coeur's House

One of the handsomest, richest, most elegant, and precisely turned private structures of the Gothic period in France is the Palais Jacques-Coeur, begun in 1443 and completed in fewer than ten years. Seen from its entrance on the place Jacques-Coeur, it seems a fortress that's taken a fanciful turn, with two sculpted false windows on either side of the entrance, from which stony heads spy out—servants, or perhaps Jacques and his wife, Mace. (Place Jacques-Coeur features a small restaurant named, not incidentally, **Jacques Coeur**, called "estimable" by Samuel Chamberlain in the 1960s but now, alas, only pleasant.)

Whatever was beautiful, practical, or inventive was what Coeur wanted and what he got. The Palais Jacques-Coeur contains 43 rooms, of which visitors are permitted in 15 or 16. The most impressive elements are the monumental, ornamental **fireplace** in the banquet room; the storage-loft ceiling in the shape of a wooden, upside-down ship's keel (Coeur's ships brought him the wealth of the Near East and Far East); the several painted ceilings and secret chapels; and—far from least—an engineering system that provided water for hot baths.

One of the mottoes of the man of the house is inscribed on the central tower: "*Dire, Faire, Taire*" (loosely translated, Say it, Do it, Shut up). Having inherited no great coat of arms, the master merchant invented one and had it placed on the palatial façade: a cockleshell for Jacques (reminiscent of the pilgrimages to Santiago—*Jacques*—de Compostela in Spain), a heart (*coeur*), and the words (in translation) "To a valiant heart nothing is impossible."

Just a few steps from the Palais Jacques-Coeur at tiny place Quatre Piliers, the **Hôtel Angleterre** is perhaps the best inn in a city lacking outstanding hotels. Accommodations here are reasonable, clean, and adequate (there are 31 rooms), and the location is the best for taking walks in the town. The Angleterre boasts a pleasant, small dining room.

In the village of Bannegon (297 people) just southeast on D 76, the **Auberge Moulin de Chaméron** is a pleasant, quiet, ten-room retreat handy for exploration of the countryside of Berry.

THE ENVIRONS OF BOURGES

Your plan may well be to see Bourges and then to barge on into Burgundy to the east, but that would mean denying yourself several fine detours in the immediate countryside.

The Cistercian Abbey of Noirlac

About half an hour's drive south of Bourges, Noirlac is the embodiment in pure, white, regional stone of the simple and austere regimens of the Cistercian movement. The stone can also be seen as a reflection of the soul of Saint Bernard, who wished to return his church—which he considered fat and fraught with excesses—to the leanness of earlier Christianity.

The founding Cistercian monks, under their leader, Robert de Clairvaux (a cousin of Saint Bernard's), suffered many privations during their first years (from 1130). The 13th century brought success, but this would be supplanted by the Hundred Years War, the Wars of Religion, and the Revolution. The abbey was eventually sold to a manufacturer of porcelain.

Restoration began in the 1950s and proved enormously

expensive. Today, however, the abbey stands again as one of the best built and most complete of its kind in the country. (Sénanque, near Gordes in Provence, is another top competitor in the rigorous Cistercian race.)

Noirlac is as perfect in its manner as a Gregorian chant.

Château de Meillant

North of Noirlac, across a dense forest, Meillant is an important stop along the route Jacques-Coeur (see the Getting Around section at the end of the chapter) because of its Renaissance western façade, its face of a feudal fortress on the south, its touches of Gothic and Flamboyant.

About a dozen of the 75 rooms in the château, richly decorated and furnished with Cordovan leather hangings, Louis XIV chairs, Bruges tapestries, and Turkish carpets, are open to the public.

Nohant

Fewer than 70 km (47.2 miles) southwest of Bourges, near the small town of La Châtre, young Aurore Dupin—one day to become George Sand—went to live with her grandmother in the château of Nohant when her father died. The author of *Indiana* became George Sand with the publication of that first novel in 1832, and though she lived (passionately) in Paris, having left her husband and two children for several famous liaisons, she returned often to the calm and serenity of Nohant, and died there in 1876.

Despite her stormy romances and her many novels featuring the villages and folk of the Berry region, Sand was known in La Châtre as the Good Lady of Nohant, even serving the villagers from time to time as a local doctor.

The château has become a museum memorializing Sand and her famous guests: Chopin, Liszt, Balzac, Delacroix, Flaubert. The Good Lady (and better novelist) is buried in the family cemetery on the château grounds.

SANCERRE

Outsiders have no image of the tiny town of Sancerre, which lies near the Loire about 37 km (25 miles) northeast of Bourges, other than that of a dry derivative of the *sauvignon blanc* grape. Sancerre is an informal, everyday wine, to be drunk young and inexpensively; while it is predominantly thought of as being white, some reds and rosés also exist, from Pinot grapes.

The little village atop a beehive-shaped hill is a natural hesitation place for drivers eastward-bound from Bourges into Burgundy. They usually park near the Esplanade de la Porte César to inspect the view over the vineyards, and perhaps they have lunch at the modest **Auberge Alphonse Mellot** to try Sancerre on its home ground. The local goat cheeses (try Crottins de Chavignol) and herb cheeses made from cow's milk are delicious.

Annual fairs are held at Sancerre in honor of cheese (the first week in May), wine (around Pentecost and the last Sunday in August), and oysters (the end of October).

GETTING AROUND

The main road from Paris that proceeds through the Loire valley is Autoroute 10, which cuts around Orléans and edges near Blois, heading for Tours. Major route N 20 sweeps south from Paris via Etampes to Orléans, then runs south of Vierzon for Bourges. From Orléans, regional route N 152 leads to Blois and Tours. As always, the best choices if one has time are the yellow local routes, or even the wiggly white ones.

The Loire valley is reached by train from Paris's Gare d'Austerlitz, with about 24 daily trains to Tours, ten or 12 to Bourges, several to Angers. Under construction, the new line of the TGV Atlantique will whisk travellers from Paris to Tours in less than two hours. Rental cars are available at train stations.

Horizon Cruises, Ltd., offers self-drive, château-accommodation programs in the Loire valley and Berry areas as extensions of its Burgundy barge-cruise programs.

Seven-day ballooning adventures are offered in the château country–Loire valley via the Bombard Society of McLean, Virginia, and Arc-en-Ciel in Beaune, France. One-to three-day helicopter cruises with accommodations in châteaux are arranged by Hemphill/Harris Travel Corp. of Encino, California, or Map Travel in Paris. There are short flights out of Blois in July and August by both small plane and helicopter.

In Tours, A.R.T.E. Val-de-Loire-Centre supplies itineraries and makes arrangements for horseback tours, while hiking trips can be arranged along some 750 miles of the Loire by Fédération Française de la Randonnée Pédestre (National Committee for Long-Distance Footpaths) in

Paris. For bicyclists, tours are planned by La Fédération Française de Cyclotourisme in Paris.

A list of captain-it-yourself boats with living accommodations on board will be supplied by Syndicat National des Loueurs de Bateaux de Plaisance, Port de la Bourdonnais, 75007 Paris, or Blakes Holidays, Wroxham, Norwich, Norfolk NR12 8DH, England.

Out of Bourges, the enthusiast of castles and history may wish to drive the tourist route Jacques-Coeur, which shows off more than a dozen châteaux, manors, Noirlac abbey, and so on. A booklet in the *Routes de Beauté* series is available at the Palais Jacques-Coeur in Bourges, where the tourist office can supply a map.

ACCOMMODATIONS REFERENCE

▶ **Angleterre.** 1, place Quatre Piliers, 18000 **Bourges.** Tel: 48-24-68-51.

▶ **Anjou.** 1, boulevard du Maréchal-Foch, 49000 **Angers.** Tel: 41-88-24-82; Telex: 720521.

▶ **Hôtel des Cèdres.** 37300 **Joué-lès-Tours** (10 km/6.7 miles north of town by D 7). Tel: 47-53-00-28.

▶ **Château d'Artigny.** 37520 **Montbazon** (2 km/1.3 miles southwest of town on D 17). Tel: 47-26-24-24; in U.S., (212) 696-1323.

▶ **Château de Beaulieu.** 37300 **Joué-lès-Tours** (5 km/3.4 miles southwest of town by D 86). Tel: 47-53-20-26.

▶ **Château de Marçay.** 37500 **Chinon** (7 km/4.7 miles southeast of town by D 116). Tel: 47-93-03-47; in U.S., (212) 696-1323.

▶ **Château de Pray.** 37400 **Amboise** (2.5 km/1.7 miles northeast of town by D 751). Tel: 47-57-23-67; in U.S., (212) 477-1600 or (800) 223-1510.

▶ **Château de Teildras.** 49125 **Cheffes.** Tel: 41-42-61-08; Telex: 722268; in U.S., (212) 696-1323.

▶ **Château des Tertres.** 41150 **Onzain** (1.5 km/1 mile from town on D 58). Tel: 54-20-83-88.

▶ **Croix Blanche.** 41600 **Chaumont-sur-Tharonne.** Tel: 54-88-55-12.

▶ **Domaine de Beauvois.** 37230 **Luynes** (4 km/2.7 miles northwest of town by D 49). Tel: 47-55-50-11; Telex: 750204; in U.S., (212) 696-1323.

▶ **Domaine des Hauts de Loire.** 41150 **Onzain** (3 km/2 miles northwest of town). Tel: 54-20-72-57.

▶ **Domaine de la Tortinière.** 37250 **Montbazon** (2 km/1.4 miles north of town by N 10 and D 287). Tel: 47-26-00-19; Telex: 752186.

▶ **Escale du Port Arthur.** 45580 St-Hilaire-St-Mesmin. Tel: 38-76-30-36; Telex: 782320.

▶ **Hosten.** 2, rue Gambetta, 37130 **Langeais.** Tel: 47-96-82-12.

▶ **Grande Monarque.** Place de la République, 37190 **Azay-le-Rideau.** Tel: 47-45-40-08.

▶ **Auberge Moulin de Chaméron.** 18210 **Bannegon** (3 km/2 miles southeast of Bourges by D 76). Tel: 48-61-83-80.

▶ **Moulin Fleuri.** 37250 **Montbazon** (5 km/3.4 miles west of town by D 287 and D 87). Tel: 47-26-01-12.

▶ **Le Prieuré.** 49350 **Chênehutte-les-Tuffeaux** (8 km/3.6 miles from Saumur by D 161 and D 751). Tel: 41-67-90-14.

▶ **Le Rivage.** 635, rue de la Reine Blanche, 45160 **Olivet.** Tel: 38-66-02-93.

▶ **Sofitel.** 44, quai Barentin, 45000 **Orléans.** Tel: 38-62-17-39; Telex: 780073.

▶ **Univers.** 5, boulevard Heurteloup, 37000 **Tours.** Tel: 47-05-37-12; in U.S., (212) 477-1600 or (800) 223-1510.

BURGUNDY AND THE RHONE VALLEY

By Georgia I. Hesse

The traveller (as distinct from the geographer) can scarcely tell where Burgundy begins: with a first sight of Vézelay, perhaps, and its hilltop basilica of Ste-Madeleine, where Saint Bernard preached the Second Crusade; it could also be with the first sips of Montrachet slipping seductively down the throat (Alexandre Dumas said that princely elixir should be drunk on your knees with hat off); or even when you first stand before the enormous vessel known as the Treasure of Vix, in Châtillon-sur-Seine, and mentally stumble backward into dim memories of Vercingetorix and first-year Latin.

Burgundy is a bouquet of good things to eat, to drink, to touch and see and feel. It is very sensual country with nothing abstemious about it (except for the considerable world of the Cistercians).

When Charles le Téméraire (the Rash, or, as sometimes rendered, the Bold), last of the Grand Dukes of Burgundy, died in battle in 1477 before the walls of Nancy, his dukedom held sway over Holland, Luxembourg, Flanders, much of today's Belgium, Artois on the English Channel, Picardie, Lorraine, and Franche-Comté. The dukedom was larger than the kingdom of France, which it separated from the Germanic Roman Empire.

Burgundy and the Valley of the Rhône

Burgundy has shrunk to a more comprehensible size: physically speaking, from about Sens in the north to Charlieu and Mâcon in the south, from the Loire in the west to the Saône River in the east, with Dijon as its principal city. After covering Dijon, this section will concentrate on the quadrant northwest of Dijon, then will move south to the Autun-Beaune area.

The Rhône Valley, for its part tied to Burgundy by gastronomy and travellers' traditions, reaches south from Mâcon and the Beaujolais country to Orange (which will be covered in the chapter on Provence), from the Auvergne region in the west to the Jura mountain country, east of Lyon; its center, for the visitor, is the city of Lyon.

MAJOR INTEREST IN BURGUNDY

Food and wine
Romanesque architecture

Dijon
Palais des Ducs
Musée Archéologique

Vézelay
Basilica of Ste-Madeleine

Auxerre
Cathedral of St-Etienne
Abbey of St-Germain
Excursion to village of Chablis
The Châteaux of Tanlay and Ancy-le-Franc

Sens
The Treasury at St-Etienne cathedral

Back roads south of Châtillon-sur-Seine
The Châtillon museum's Treasure of Vix
Abbey of Fontenay
Bussy-Rabutin Château
Semur-en-Auxois

Autun
St-Lazare cathedral's tympanum sculptures
Musée Rolin

Beaune
Center of wine trade
Hôtel-Dieu

Tournus
Former abbey of St-Philibert

Remains of the abbey at Cluny

MAJOR INTEREST IN THE RHÔNE VALLEY

Roman remains
Food

Lyon
Roman theater and Musée de la Civilisation Gallo-
    Romaine
Basilica of Notre-Dame-de-Fourvière
Walking tour of Old Lyon (especially *les traboules*
    passageways)
Museums: Beaux-Arts, Textiles, Decorative Arts

The Walled City of Pérouges

Vienne
Restaurant Pyramide
Temple of Augustus and Livia
St-Romain-en-Gal, Gallo-Roman city
Roman theater
Excursion to Mont Pilat and to Gouffre d'Enfer for
    scenic views

BURGUNDY

Deep in southern Burgundy near the middle-size town of
Mâcon, an enormous limestone escarpment, the Roche
de Solutré, announces the hamlet of Solutré and one of
the most intriguing archaeological sites in Burgundy—or
all of France, for that matter. During the Reindeer Age
(15,000 to 12,000 B.C.) the Solutrean civilization period of
the same name produced precision stone points and
arrowheads, the highest achievement of flint-working in
the ancient Western world.

Digs that began in 1866 revealed the skeletons of at
least 100,000 horses in a bed two and a half acres large
and three feet deep, the earliest evidence of planned
horse consumption in France. (Horsemeat is still eaten in

France, but by law shops selling it must carry a copper-gold horse's head over the door.)

Less dramatically, later excavations have brought to light human remains from the older Aurignacian period and the following Neolithic times, along with tools, pottery, ceramics, and Bronze Age bodies. Some of the finds and their descriptions may be seen on the first floor of the **Musée Municipal des Ursulines** in Mâcon. In the beautiful town of Châtillon-sur-Seine, on the northern borders of Burgundy, the local museum shelters the **Treasure of Vix** and other remarkable relics of prehistoric culture. These artifacts had been buried in a sepulcher with female bones (a warrior princess, perhaps) at nearby Vix in pre-Roman days, and were discovered only in 1953, more than 2,500 years later.

The Celts

Before the Roman Empire, the Celts inhabited vast reaches of Europe stretching from Rumania to Ireland, from the Rhine to the Pyrénées. Theirs was, and is, a fascinating civilization. As described by Oxford historian Barry Cunliffe, in *The Celtic World,* the Celts "were barbarian in the classical sense of the word, energetic, quick-tempered, and 'war-mad'; but their craftsmen created a brilliant art style and by the first century B.C. a truly urban society had begun to develop in many areas. It was against these people that the Roman armies moved in the first centuries B.C. and A.D., leaving only a Celtic fringe in Scotland, Ireland, Wales, and Brittany to survive unconquered."

It was Gaius Julius Caesar who, in the seven years from 58 to 51 B.C., finally conquered the Celts of Gaul and who found a valiant opponent in Vercingetorix, leader of the Arverni tribe. "A man of boundless energy," Caesar wrote of his enemy, "he terrorized waverers with the rigors of an iron discipline."

Vercingetorix and an independent Celtic Gaul found their particular Waterloo on the battlefields of Burgundy in 52 B.C. at Alésia, today's Alise-Ste-Reine.

The House of Burgundy

Burgundy, the name on the land, is derived from the Burgundi, or Burgondiones, a people of Germanic origin who, as a result of wars against the Alemanni tribes, were forced in 411 to take refuge in Gaul under the leadership of Chief Gundicar. The major towns of this first kingdom were Vienne, Lyon, Autun, Mâcon, Besançon, and Geneva. Except for the last two, those towns still come within the territories of Burgundy–Rhône Valley.

The House of Burgundy as one thinks of it today, however, began in 1031 when Robert, son of the king of France, by heredity became the Capetian duke of Burgundy. For the next three centuries, Burgundy stood as a bastion of Christianity under the rules of the abbey of Cluny, followed by the monasteries of Cîteaux, Clairvaux, and some 350 others. The shining light of the whole movement was Saint Bernard (1091–1153), whose eloquence and genius dominated the 12th century. He alone was responsible for the establishment of 160 Cistercian abbeys.

The Romanesque Period

The nature of the feudal, monastic world was sedentary, even static. The barons of feudal times required workers to stay on the land, to produce, to serve as soldiers in the seemingly endless petty wars between neighboring villages. Monasticism made an absolute virtue of not joining the world, of remaining isolated from it.

During the period known as Romanesque (roughly from the 11th to the 12th century), however, dramatic changes led Europeans to move about. Feudal wars slackened, new lands were exploited, new villages built. Reclamation, drainage, and deforestation began in the early 11th century in Burgundy as well as in Normandy and Lombardy. With the advent of two major influences—the cult of relics and the Crusades—great numbers of people began to travel over roads and under conditions that today would be considered impassable and impossible.

All this energy and movement had as one of its manifestations the establishment of churches and abbeys. Architecture became to the Romanesque period what painting was to the Italian Renaissance.

Nowhere can a traveller interested in Romanesque art and architecture enjoy a bigger banquet than in Burgundy, where the regional committee of Burgundian tourism has counted no fewer than 100 *major* Romanesque churches. (Tourism offices in Dijon and other major towns can supply descriptive brochures in English.) The ornamental, often fantastic, sculptural detailing of these churches, especially in column capitals—which enraged the ascetically minded Saint Bernard—delights visitors today.

The historical Burgundy that is best known, however, is that of the proud and powerful Grand Dukes of the West, who ruled from 1364 to 1477: Philippe le Hardi (the Bold), Jean sans Peur (the Fearless), Philippe le Bon (the Good), and Charles le Téméraire (the Rash). Carl Rudolf Friml's musical *The Vagabond King* thus enshrined the worthy dynasty: "And bow down to Burgundy."

Beyond its historical importance Burgundy is, of course, known throughout the world for its food and wine, but because the cooking of the region is synonymous, in many minds, with French cuisine itself, it will not be discussed here. As for wines, there are many excellent publications on the subject (see the Bibliography), and a wine lover could not be properly served by a summary.

DIJON

The good Dijonnais—merchants, city fathers, university professors and students, wine growers and mustard makers—think of their city as a French, even a European *plaque tournante,* or turntable, at the center of great commercial routes from Paris, the Mediterranean, down across the Rhine from West Germany, and over the Alps from Switzerland and Italy.

It is true that motorways from all directions appear to lead to Dijon; that you can whisk here from Paris in an hour and 40 minutes aboard a TGV; that five international airports make access easy to the region (though Dijon proper has only a small civil airport).

It is also true that the Dijon Agglomération boasts properly bustling and traffic-tied industrial and commercial zones to the northeast and to the south of town, where emphasis falls less on Flemish sculpture and half-timbered houses than upon food-processing plants, automobile parts (Peugeot), and pharmaceutical research.

Yet here in the heart of things, at the site of the Roman camp called Divio, a visitor can still summon up the days of the dukes, a period of economic and artistic dominance that for more than a hundred years inspired the envy of states across Europe, especially the kingdom of France.

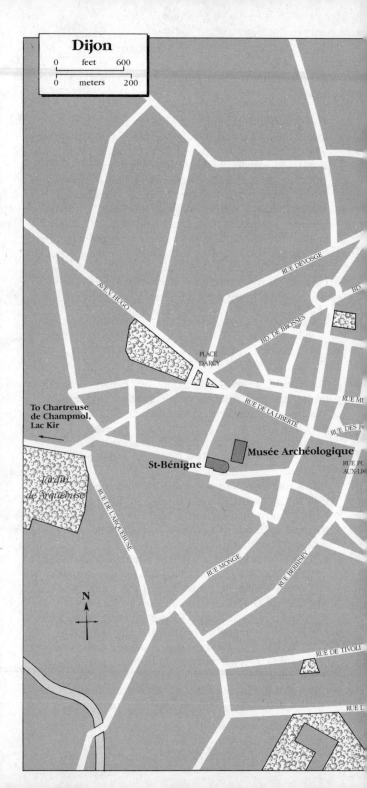

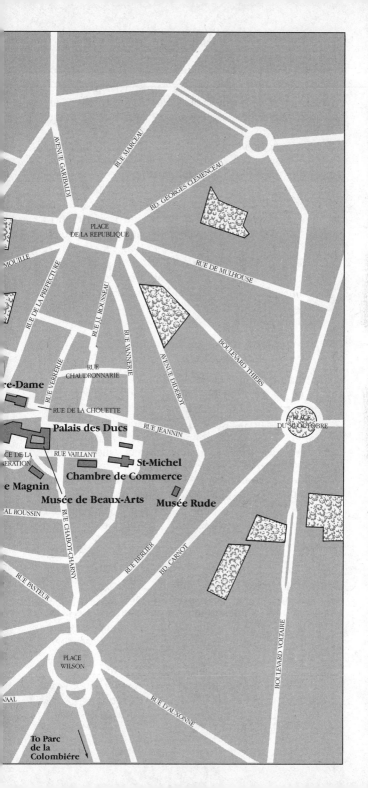

AVENUE GARIBALDI

RUE MARCEAU

BD. GEORGES CLEMENCEAU

PLACE
DE LA REPUBLIQUE

RUE DE MULHOUSE

MOUILLE

RUE DE LA PREFECTURE

RUE J.J. ROUSSEAU

RUE VANNERIE

BOULEVARD THIERS

RUE VERRERIE

RUE
CHAUDRONNARIE

AVENUE DIDEROT

re-Dame

RUE DE LA CHOUETTE

PLACE
DU 30 OCTOBRE

Palais des Ducs

RUE JEANNIN

CE DE LA
ERATION

RUE VAILLANT

St-Michel

Chambre de Commerce

e Magnin

Musée de Beaux-Arts

Musée Rude

AL ROUSSIN

RUE CHABOT-CHARNY

RUE BERLIER

BD. CARNOT

RUE PASTEUR

BOULEVARD VOLTAIRE

PLACE
WILSON

VAAL

RUE D'AUXONNE

To Parc
de la
Colombiére

Dijon is handsome, for one thing, which most metropolises are not. It centers on the hemispheric **place de la Libération** (the former place Royale), a pretty 17th-century layout by Versailles's architect, Jules Hardouin-Mansart.

It is difficult to imagine that after the death of Charles le Téméraire in 1477 the ducal palace had been neglected, ignored, all but abandoned for 300 years. Then, in the 17th century, Louis XIV reinstituted the ducal title for a short time, and Burgundy controlled a government within a government, a *pays d'états* (a kind of parliament of estates, consisting of clergy, nobility, and other citizens).

Dijon's grand days came in the 18th century when, according to the *Encyclopaedia Britannica*, "it became the seat of a bishopric, its streets were improved, its commerce developed, and an academy of science and letters [was] founded; while its literary salons were hardly less celebrated than those of Paris."

Dijon the Town

The **Palais des Ducs et des Etats** bulks just north of the place de la Libération, but only a portion of the palaces—the two towers (Tour de Bar and Tour Philippe-le-Bon), the guardroom (Salle des Gardes), and the kitchens—represents the original complex. These remnants are almost entirely enclosed within the current structures, built in the 17th and 18th centuries.

The west wing of the complex, near the Tour de Bar (named for its most illustrious prisoner, Good King René, Duc de Bar and Lorraine and Comte de Provence), houses the **Musée des Beaux-Arts**, among the richest and most unusual in France.

Taking precedence over the painting and sculpture galleries, the magnificent tombs of Philippe le Hardi and Jean sans Peur (buried along with his wife, Marguerite of Bavaria) in the Salle des Gardes are showstoppers, obsequies in stone, witnesses in great part to the genius of the Flemish sculptor Claus Sluter. There is nothing elsewhere like the alabaster "cloister" of Le Hardi's catafalque, around which parade 41 *pleurants* (mourners)—relatives, friends, soldiers, clergymen—carved from life, heads covered in stony sorrow. Juan de la Huerta reproduced that inspiration for the tomb of Jean and Marguerite.

The tombs so dominate the room that other masterworks might be missed: a scale model of Sluter's *Puits de*

Moïse (*Well of Moses*) from Dijon's Chartreuse (Charterhouse) de Champmol and the painted *Nativity* by Melchior Broederlam, also from Champmol.

Banquets famous throughout the dukedom were prepared in the kitchens, dating from 1435. Six enormous chimneys surround a central, even larger one from which smoky air could soar several stories.

Sculpture is an emphasis in the museum because of Sluter and Dijon native François Rude (responsible for Paris's Arc de Triomphe sculptures). Paintings are displayed according to schools: Italian, German-Swiss, Flemish, 19th-century French.

On rue Vaillant, the **Musée Rude** in the former church of St-Etienne, now the Chambre de Commerce, remembers the local son with moldings of all the sculptor's works that are not in Dijon, including an exact-size replica of the *Marseillaise* bas-relief on the Arc de Triomphe. (Rude and another native born nearby, Saint Bernard, have given their names to squares. On place François-Rude, the shop named **André Grillot** sells gifts and gadgets for oenophiles.)

The gates of the ducal palace and its Cour d'Honneur open on **rue de la Liberté**, a fashionable shopping street where the Dijonnais go to keep themselves *en chic*. No gallivanting gastronome can keep himself from popping in at number 32, where the smart shop **Grey-Poupon** sells and celebrates mustard, a regional resource since the days of the great Gallo-Roman spice route. Considering the hand-painted, museum-quality porcelain containers on display, it's difficult to exit with a mere jar of familiar *moutarde de Dijon*.

On the same street, at number 16, Mulot et Petitjean offers another traditional Dijonnais specialty: *pain d'épice* (spice bread) in several varieties.

Pré aux Clercs et Trois Faisans on place de la Libération serves informal meals including such down-to-earth regional specialties as *coq-au-vin*.

Across rue des Forges (which has fine Renaissance houses), north of the palace, the Gothic **church of Notre-Dame** is best known for its **Jacquemart clock**, to which older Dijonnais remain devoted. Transported all the way from Courtrai (in Belgium) by bullock cart in 1382 on the order of Philippe le Hardi, the Jacquemart figure regularly striking the hours gained great sympathy, and in 1610 was presented with a female companion. Over two centuries, a family was established with the addition of a

Jacquelinet and a Jacquelinette, whose job is sounding the quarter-hours. (University students have been known to attempt outfitting these working worthies with Levi's and sombreros.)

Within Notre-Dame, the chief treasure is an 11th-century Black Virgin, one of the oldest wood sculptures in the country. Two tapestries honor deliverances from war: one from Tournai, Belgium, dedicated after the lifting by the Swiss of a 16th-century siege of Dijon; the other a Gobelins dedicated also to that occupation plus that of the Germans in 1944.

Businessmen in the vicinity of Notre-Dame take their trade to a handy grill, **Le Central**, on place Grangier in the pleasant, unimposing **Central Urbis Hôtel** (a specialty: white turbot in dill cream). Church-architecture enthusiasts will stop by nearby **St-Michel**, with its façade that began in Flamboyant Gothic and ended in Renaissance.

Off the rue des Bons-Enfants, the **Musée Magnin**, occupying a handsome 17th-century town house, is decorated in elegant, mid–19th century fashion and displays the painting collections of Maurice Magnin, given to the nation in 1937. Italian and Flemish canvases hang here as well as French paintings, sketches, and drawings.

West of the palace in the direction of the railway station cluster attractions worth most of a day. The 13th- to 14th-century **cathedral of St-Bénigne** memorializes a missionary priest, apparently martyred in the second century, whose tomb was discovered near Dijon in the sixth century. It is Burgundian Gothic in style.

The crypt, the most interesting feature of St-Bénigne, is the work of an Italian abbot, Guillaume de Volpiano, whose work is also well known in Normandy. This structure is actually the remains of the tenth-century Romanesque basilica that once occupied the site. The transept and choir boast 86 pillars. Some of those in the rotunda still bear their curious capitals; the best have features and forms of monsters.

A visit to the **Musée Archéologique** is a must before making excursions to ancient sites in the Burgundian countryside, because it shows off relics from the early Stone Age and Neolithic epochs, the Bronze Age, Gallo-Roman days, and Merovingian times. Many finds were uncovered at Alise-Ste-Reine and at sanctuaries near the source of the Seine.

The **Jardin de l'Arquebuse** is home to the **Musée d'Histoire Naturelle** in a former barracks of the *arquebusiers* and to a botanical garden. (The *arquebuse* was a gun of matchlock or wheel-lock mechanism much used by the Spanish, Italians, and French in the 15th and 16th centuries. Arquebuse is also the name of a fiery liqueur, which purists prefer to call a vulnerary, since its adherents modestly claim it cures anything. It is very difficult to find; inquire at La Cour aux Vins on rue Jeannin.)

In 1383, Philippe le Hardi founded the charterhouse now known as the **Chartreuse de Champmol** as a quasi-royal necropolis, and filled it with works of the best artists from around his vast lands. Today it is a psychiatric hospital, but visitors are admitted to see the two triumphs that remain: the *Puits de Moïse* (*Well of Moses*) and the chapel door Claus Sluter sculpted between 1395 and 1405.

Enthusiasts of period houses should walk several streets: Porte-aux-Lions, des Forges, de la Chouette, Verrerie, Chaudronnerie, Vannerie, and Amiral-Roussin. Friday is the day when the large, covered central market really hums, and the first two weeks of November bow to cuisine in the Foire Internationale Gastronomique. (Patricia Wells, the food writer, recommends **Simone Porcheret** in this neighborhood for buying cheeses and utensils to go with them.)

Throughout the year, other major happenings in town include L'Hiver Musical (winter musicale), first half of January; L'Eté Musical and L'Estivade (summer musicales with animations in streets and gardens), June through August; and Les Fêtes de la Vigne (wine festival), first half of September.

Dijon's best inns are **Hôtel de la Cloche**, off place Darcy (with superb dining at **Jean-Pierre Billoux**; their specialty is terrine of young pigeon with garlic), and **Le Chapeau Rouge** (also excellent; try the salmon cutlet in Pinot Noir). **La Toison d'Or** joins gastronomy to culture in a 15th- to 16th-century town house with a private museum containing Medieval figures and vineyard tools.

Dining on traditional Burgundian fare is recommended at warm, welcoming **La Chouette** on the street of the same name, which runs between Notre-Dame and the 17th-century Hôtel de Vogüé. (One of Dijon's most important parliamentary mansions, de Vogüé today is occupied by the city's architectural board; it may be visited by anyone interested through application at the Office du Tourisme in place Darcy.)

Du Parc's cuisine and stylish service match its setting near the beautiful Parc de la Colombière, the once-royal domain of the princes of Condé. The park today is a favorite promenading area for the Dijonnais; a small portion of the Via Agrippa that led from Lyon to Trèves is visible.

On a sparkling spring or autumn afternoon, there are few better ways to salute Dijon's famous canon and mayor Kir than to take luncheon at **Le Cygne**, just west of downtown on Lac Kir. While watching canoes, kayaks, and small boats at play, salute the city and its longtime mayor with the drink that he invented: *kir,* classically one-third *crème de cassis* (a black-currant liqueur) and two-thirds white Burgundian Aligoté. (A *kir royale* employs Champagne.)

VEZELAY

Tiny (fewer than 600 inhabitants) hilltop Vézelay, about 90 km (60.7 miles) west of Dijon, is a place of pilgrimage. Its abbey was consecrated by Pope Jean VIII in 878, and it remained significant throughout the glory years of the 12th and 13th centuries.

It is mostly pilgrims of art and history who arrive now, climbing uphill in cars along a skinny one-way street, but their destination is the same: the **basilica of Ste-Madeleine**, among the most impressive of all the Romanesque churches in Burgundy (it has been a basilica since 1920).

In the ninth century, Girart de Roussillon, a Burgundian count, founded a settlement of nuns in the valley below, where St-Père-sous-Vézelay sits today. When that location was repeatedly attacked by the Norman invaders, the decision was taken to reestablish the monastery atop a nearby, more defensible hill.

The relics of Sainte Madeleine (Mary Magdalen) and the miracles accredited to them lured so many pilgrims in the 11th century that the town's population swelled to 10,000 and the church was expanded. Then in 1120 a terrible fire broke out on the eve of July 22, the date of a traditional pilgrimage and the feast day of the saint. It destroyed the entire nave and more than a thousand of the faithful with it.

The story of Mary Magdalen is a fascinating one and had profound effects upon the life and traditions of Medieval France. Early on, her cult became confounded with the story of the Three Marys, which holds that Magdalen, Mary the mother of James, and Mary the wife of Cléophas, driven out of Palestine, arrived miraculously west of Marseille near Arles (at the site now named for them, Stes-Maries-de-la-Mer, in La Camargue). They came in a boat equipped with neither sail nor oars. The company included Lazarus, his sister, Martha, and other people, who proceeded to evangelize Provence. This story still is believed by some Provençals.

Twenty-six years after the great fire, on March 31, 1146, Saint Bernard came to stand on Vézelay's "inspired hill" to preach the Second Crusade to a worshiping crowd that included France's Louis VII. At the time, Bernard, abbot of Clairvaux, was the man of most consequence in Christendom, and Vézelay (along with Autun, Orléans, Le Puy, and Arles) had become an origination point for the most important pilgrimage route, that to Santiago de Compostela, in Spain.

It was from Vézelay that France's Philippe Auguste and England's Richard the Lion-Hearted departed for the Third Crusade in 1190. In the next century, Saint Francis of Assisi founded the first brotherhood of Franciscans, the Frères Mineurs, in France here. In 1248, when the Seventh Crusade began, Saint Louis (Louis IX) made a pilgrimage to Vézelay several times.

In the late 13th century, however, proud Vézelay began a period of decline, with the discovery of more relics of Sainte Madeleine in Provence. Further difficulties were precipitated by the Wars of Religion, the ravages attributed to the Huguenots, and the destruction wrought by the Revolution.

Had Eugène Emmanuel Viollet-le-Duc not been employed in 1840 to restore the whole to its ancient excellence, Vézelay now would attract no more curiosity than a pile of rocks.

Today the basilica of Ste-Madeleine is under the governance of the Franciscans. The feast day, July 22, is celebrated by a great religious manifestation with special music, entertainments, and the like.

The Basilica

In pink-and-ocher stone, Ste-Madeleine dominates a terraced village of brown-roofed houses. The basilica's façade, almost entirely reconstituted in the 19th century, is not universally applauded, but the interior contains artworks acknowledged to be among the finest in the Western world.

The central **Tympanum of Pentecost**, for example, depicts a gigantic Christ in Glory from whose hands the rays of the Holy Ghost reach out to the 12 Apostles. To the right and left of Christ and the Apostles, the people of the world await the Word. These are wonderful, fantastical figures, since the artists of the day knew little of the world and thus imagined most of it: Some appear with the heads of dogs, some with ears like pendants, others more monsters than men.

The column capitals are even more entertaining and as beautifully and imaginatively carved. Here, David defeats a lion; there, Jacob wrestles with an angel. On the right, the bad rich man dies in agony; on the left, Absalom is decapitated.

Some of these capitals are so popular that medallion copies are sold in souvenir shops around the square. Also available near the basilica are handmade textiles and jewelry.

Follow the narrow, crabbed streets of Vézelay to lunch or spend the night at **Poste et Lion d'Or**, a fairly modest but most comfortable hideaway.

In the 1980s, food lovers and aficionados make their pilgrimage to the hamlet of St-Père (some 350 inhabitants) at the foot of Vézelay's hill to dine at celebrated **Espérance** (chef Marc Meneau has earned three Michelin stars for his work) and, perhaps, to stay the night in one of the 21 rooms and apartments. Elegance is the byword here, though nothing is fussy or pompous. Many experienced travellers rank l'Espérance among the two or three top country retreats in France and don't mind paying top price for the quality.

While in St-Père, take a look at **Notre-Dame**, begun in the 13th century and restored in the 19th century by Viollet-le-Duc; the **Musée Archéologique Régional** shelters the finds from digs at nearby Fontaines Salées, a site of Gallo-Roman baths.

AUXERRE

Auxerre (locally pronounced O-sair) is one of the oldest towns in France, known at its beginning as Autricum to the Gauls, Autessiodirum to the Romans. It lies along the great trade routes from Lyon to Boulogne, about halfway between Paris and Dijon, which is some 120 km (81 miles) to its southeast. By the end of the fourth century it was an important center, and even today, despite its population of only slightly more than 40,000, it retains a wealth of art and business activity worthy of a much larger city. And, unlike some rural cities, Auxerre is growing younger; 62 percent of the population is less than 40 years of age.

Auxerre is known throughout France as the birthplace of the great Saint Germain.

Germain was born in 378 to noble parents in the town. He studied and practiced law in Rome and then returned to Gaul, married, and won a high official post. Though later sainted, Germain paid little heed in early life to religion. In 418 he was elected bishop of Auxerre by clergy and the people, much against his will. He changed his life immediately, consecrating himself to prayer and action in defense of the Church. When Saint Germain died at Ravenna, Italy, his body was returned to Auxerre and buried with pomp and circumstance under the abbey church that bears his name.

Saint Germain knew and supported Sainte Geneviève, now the patron saint of Paris. "Exemplified by these two," writes Katherine Scherman in *The Birth of France,* "the cultivation of the Gallo-Roman Christian merged with the tough vitality of the pagan Frank." Saint Germain is memorialized in Paris in the church of St-Germain-l'Auxerrois, behind the Louvre; he is often confused with another Saint Germain, a sixth-century bishop of Paris named Germanus, who lies in St-Germain-des-Prés.

The city's best face is that observed from across the busy river Yonne; from that vantage point the spires of St-Etienne, St-Germain, and St-Pierre-en-Vallée stand skyward as symbols of age and importance.

Marie Noël (1883–1967), a popular poet, gives insight to her fellow citizens:

> The Auxerrois have in their veins both a drop
> of blood and a fantasy.
> It leads them to do good or to do bad,
> To the right or to the left,
> But always a little way off the beaten track.

There does seem to be a very pleasant capriciousness to the daily life of Auxerre, a sturdy and bourgeois business approach joined to a hat-in-the-air, youthful exuberance. Marie Noël herself, a wooden figure topped by a round black hat, neck swathed in gray scarf, contemplates the scene from her perch in front of the Hôtel de Ville.

The present **cathedral of St-Etienne** is the fifth structure built on the site of the original sanctuary founded in 400 by Bishop Saint Amâtre, which had been altered over the years and centuries until it burned down in 1023. Some 500 years of architectural forays followed, and the result can be viewed today. The south tower never has been completed.

Remarkable achievements are the 13th-century stained-glass windows and the 11th-century Romanesque crypt with its superb frescoes, including the unique portrayal of Christ Triumphant astride a white horse surrounded by angels, also on horseback. The treasury holds valuable manuscripts, books of hours, ivories, miniatures, and enamels.

What you first see of the abbey of St-Germain is the Gothic 13th- to 15th-century church. What you remember is the crypt, which essentially constitutes the sixth-century church erected in Saint Germain's honor by Clothilde, Christian wife of the Frankish king Clovis of the Merovingian dynasty. This crypt contains the oldest frescoes yet discovered in France, dating from 858 and depicting the martyrdom of Saint Etienne (Saint Stephen). Still in place, still bearing weight, are beams of oak that are more than 1,100 years old. In this building a rather new museum, photo library, and cultural center make up one of the most valuable historical resources in the country.

In the center of town, the 15th-century Tour de l'Horloge (Clock Tower) is a graceful, storybook structure in Flamboyant style built atop the Gallo-Roman wall and now the heart of the shopping area. One face of the clock features the movements of sun and moon, while the other counts the hours.

Within the grounds of the psychiatric hospital, the six acres of **Clos de la Chaînette** with its few rows of grapes (producing white and rosé wines) are last survivors of the great seventh-century vineyards of Auxerre. At the beginning of the 19th century, Alexandre Dumas regarded the local production as among the greatest of French red wines, mentioning it in the same breath as Château Margaux and Romanée Conti. (One can only wonder, however, what was produced by one famous vineyard known as Migraines.) The phylloxera crisis of the 19th century and increasing urban pressures caused virtually all the other prestigious local vineyards to disappear, but some are being reborn several kilometers away in the environs of **Vaux**.

A revival of the arts of pottery, ceramics, and faïence so celebrated here during the 18th and 19th centuries is under way throughout the region of the Yonne today, and shops selling such crafts have sprung up everywhere, particularly in small towns. In Auxerre, François Brochet is re-creating the tradition of polychrome wood sculpture. New and attractive in form are the works of Pierre Merlier. Shops selling such goods are grouped around the Tour de l'Horloge.

The best restaurants in this area are the **Jardin Gourmand** in Auxerre and **La Petite Auberge** in Vaux, while **Restaurant Maxime** in Auxerre next to (but supposedly not part of) Hôtel Le Maxime is quite good and informal, and puts an emphasis on regional dishes and on fish from nearby rivers. **Hôtel Le Maxime**, a 25-room inn right on the river, is the finest hotel in town and the best located for walking.

SENS

Stop in Sens, at the approximate northern border of Burgundy, about halfway between Fontainebleau and, to the southeast, Auxerre, chiefly to visit the **cathedral of St-Etienne**, dating from 1140. The town itself, counting some 28,000 Sénonais, takes its name from one of the strongest Gallic tribes, the Senones. Its history is proud: The Romans made Sens the capital of one of the provinces of Lyonnaise. It was the seat of an archbishopric when Paris had only a bishop, and when Pope Alexander III was in residence from 1163 to 1164 Sens effectively became the capital of Christianity.

It was at Sens that Abélard was condemned; Saint Louis married Marguerite de Provence in the cathedral. In Sens (and also in the abbey of Pontigny, nearer Auxerre), Saint Thomas à Becket lived six years in exile from England and Henry II.

The good Sénonais are likely to tell the visitor that Sens's cathedral represents the birth of Gothic architecture in France; that opinion is more enthusiastic than accurate. The choir of the cathedral of St-Denis in the Paris suburb of that name is universally acclaimed as the birthplace of Gothic; what *is* certain is that St-Etienne ranks among the first great Gothic edifices in France. Interestingly, the choir of St-Etienne became a model for the rebuilding of the eastern end of England's Canterbury

Cathedral following its disastrous fire in 1174. The work was directed by one Guillaume de Sens (who fell from a scaffold in 1178 and was succeeded by a British William).

Note the early-Gothic Etienne on the central portal (wearing deacon's garb and carrying the Gospel) before entering the nave, where light streams through superb 12th-century to 17th-century stained-glass windows.

The cathedral has always been renowned for the value of its **Treasury**, one of the most highly regarded in Europe, along with those of Ste-Foy, in Conques, and St-Maurice, in Switzerland. Other great collections are housed nearby in the **Palais Synodal** in the Dépôt Lapidaire. Since 1985, many works formerly dispersed throughout the city have been joined together in the **Musées de Sens**, a restoration of part of the cathedral complex.

The collection includes relics, antique textiles, liturgical ornaments, tapestries, mosaics, and silver, ivory, and enamel works; particular attention should, however, be paid to the **vestments of Thomas à Becket**. They appear to have been fitted to a man extremely large and powerful for his time. Among other standouts are a 15th-century Flemish tapestry, *Adoration of the Magi;* a gold and bejeweled fibula (brooch) from Merovingian times; a remarkably carved ivory reliquary, the *Sainte Chasse;* and an eighth-century shroud depicting a gigantic Gilgamesh, the hero of the ancient Babylonian epic.

Joigny

A fine headquarters for exploring all of northwest Burgundy is **A la Côte St-Jacques** in the town of Joigny, about halfway between Sens and Auxerre on the river Yonne. On a grassy terrace above the river, equipped with some private balconies, with an indoor pool and doors opening to the terrace, it is a cultivated oasis. The seven rooms and eight suites bespeak country elegance, and the kitchen, under chef Michel Lorain, is one of the very best in France—three Michelin stars. (The fish called *bar,* lightly smoked with cream of caviar, is not to be passed over.)

The 17th-century Château du Fey in Joigny has been opened as a cooking school (one-week classes) by Anne Willan, whose La Varenne in Paris is one of the best-known such schools in Europe. (For information, write La Varenne in Burgundy, P.O. Box 25574, Washington, DC 20007.)

CHABLIS
AND EAST FROM AUXERRE

"I would give a fortune and all my titles to intoxicate myself on a mixture of Chablis and oysters," Eugène Deschamps once wrote. Or, he might have said, Chablis and turbot or *sole meunière* or escargots or Saint Marcellin cheese.

Chablis, a few miles east of Auxerre, is one of the most famous wine names in the world—and one of the most misused. Outside France, in the United States, in Australia, and in other wine-growing nations it is often employed as an almost generic name for any white, but frequently those of little distinction.

However, as winegrower, writer, and merchant Alexis Lichine points out, "Used correctly, it refers to one of the world's rarest great wines—to the steadily decreasing quantity of magnificent flinty, dry white wines which are made from grapes grown on hilly acres in and around the Burgundian town of Chablis." According to Edward Young, the distinctive taste of the wines results from the pocket of bituminous clay in which they grow, a soil found nowhere else except at Kimmeridge, Dorset, England.

At one time, Chablis boasted some charming old houses and was most picturesque during harvest. As Samuel Chamberlain remembers, "The doors of the wine cellars were open then, and you could hear the creaking of old oak presses and smell the haunting, fruity odor of newly pressed grapes.... Streets were animated with green-stained carts and pretty, full-hipped young grape-pickers."

Unfortunately, on a clear June night in 1940 some far-afield Italian flyers unloaded their bombs on the heart of the unsuspecting and unstrategic town. Fortunately, Chablis's real treasure grew in the chalky hills beyond.

Chablis today is a natural call on a day's excursion out of Auxerre, and it is refreshing, since there's little to do here but sip Chablis (for maximum appreciation, you should request a *grand cru*—Les Bouguerots, Les Blanchots, Les Clos) and lunch or dine at Michel Vignaud's **Hostellerie des Clos**. A conversion of an ancient *clos des hospices,* the *hostellerie* offers 26 quiet, comfortable bedrooms overlooking the gardens to those in search of a real hideaway.

A festival of regional wines is held in Chablis the fourth Sunday in November.

Tonnerre

Tonnerre is little known to foreigners except to passengers aboard the luxury hotel-barges that cruise on the canals of Burgundy. It is worth a stop, however, en route from Auxerre to the châteaux of Tanlay and Ancy-le-Franc, largely because of the beautiful 13th-century hôpital that somehow survived ruinous fires of the 16th century.

Built at the order of Marguerite de Bourgogne, widow of Charles d'Anjou, the hospital is similar in style and purpose to the Hôtel-Dieu in Beaune. The chapel near the high altar contains a very moving *mise au tombeau,* a 15th-century form of Burgundian sculpture that is also called a *saint sépulcre* and, in English, an entombment. Three arresting examples are the one in Tonnerre, one at Notre-Dame in Semur-en-Auxois, another in the hospital in Dijon; the one in Tonnerre features a semi-recumbent Christ being laid upon his tomb by seven mourning figures.

Another reason to hesitate in Tonnerre is the outstanding restaurant and 16-room inn of **Abbaye St-Michel**, which occupies a Benedictine abbey of the 12th century set in its own manicured park. (The unusual and delicious cream of cauliflower soup with shellfish is recommended.)

Two Châteaux

In the 16th century, Burgundian architecture began to change, having come under the influence of Renaissance arts imported from Italy. Unlike the Loire Valley, Burgundy had not seen a burgeoning of château-like country mansions until this period, to which Tanlay and Ancy-le-Franc (both to the east of Tonnerre) as well as Sully, near Autun, belong. **Tanlay** is in essence a comfortable palace, elegant yet unimposing, the kind of noble dwelling most commoners would be happy to call home. It was erected about 1550 on the remains of a feudal fortress.

Several of the handsomely furnished rooms are open to visitors, and the most interesting of them is in the tower where Huguenot conspiracies were hatched during the Wars of Religion. The vault is covered with a most curious fresco from the Fontainebleau school, featuring—together—notable Catholics and Protestants.

Sébastien Serlo, an Italian architect brought to the region (as were so many other artists) by François I, designed **Ancy-le-Franc** for Antoine III de Clermont-Tonnerre in the mid-16th century. It is a harmony of four major structures linked by corner pavilions, the original model of pure Renaissance style in France. Among the 20 beautifully decorated rooms open to the public, the chapel, with its carved woodwork, is most notable.

ALONG THE UPPER SEINE

Châtillon-sur-Seine, farther east of Auxerre, past Tonnerre and Tanlay, straddles the lazily flowing river, its beflowered bridges, pretty houses, winding streets, and coquettish air suggesting that nothing much ever has happened here.

That's not true, sadly. During World War II, the town center was badly mauled; in September 1914, General Joseph Joffre set up headquarters here from which his retreating French troops could counterattack the charging German army; and, just a hundred years before that, Napoléon chose the spot for a congress with the enemies allied against him during the famous Hundred Days.

Today, however, this town of some 8,000 inhabitants is mainly an excursion center, with facilities for horseback riding, tennis, hiking, fishing, and the like. Foreigners and French in search of ancient history come to town, however, to visit one of the most provocative small museums in the country, the **Musée Municipal**.

The handsome 16th-century Renaissance Maison Philandrier houses collections from protohistoric sites in the region: fifth-century ceramics from Mont-Lassois, a bronze alms basin from the chariot tomb at Ste-Colombe, votive sculptures from the sanctuary of Essarois, Gallo-Roman everyday tools and utensils from Vertillum (Vertault).

Sensational, though, are the furnishings from the **tomb of Vix**, discovered in 1953 at the foot of nearby Mont-Lassois. These consisted of the remains of a woman (most likely a Celtic princess) who died in the sixth century B.C. and was buried with goods probably intended to accompany her into the next world (a golden diadem, earrings, bejeweled bracelets), a huge ceremonial chariot, and—one of the most majestic finds of contemporary archaeology—the **Treasure of Vix**. This last is a giant vase five-and-a-half feet high, weighing 460 pounds, and capable of holding 1,162 quarts of liquid (wine, perhaps). A masterpiece in archaic Greek bronze style, it is thought to have been created in about 500 B.C. It is richly decorated with a frieze featuring helmeted warriors and horse-drawn chariots, with Gorgon heads on the handles.

Châtillon offers one of the small, cozy, modestly priced inns that delight travellers who don't wish to make reservations well in advance, as required by more prestigious places. The **Côte d'Or** has ten rooms, a quiet, shady garden, and an agreeable kitchen.

Before departing Châtillon, stop near the **Source de la Douix** at the foot of a rocky hill where waters fountain forth from the limestone earth at a rate of up to 800 gallons a second to mingle, slightly farther along, with those of the Seine. The site is reminiscent of the Fontaine de Vaucluse in Provence, but is much less tourist-ridden.

Fontenay

When Saint Bernard, then abbot of Clairvaux, came to the countryside near Montbard to seek a site for the foundation of a hermitage, he must have felt Nature had designed with him in mind. Set south of Châtillon in a deep valley of intense green, broken in autumn by outbursts of red and golden leaves, the **abbaye de Fontenay** and its grounds are eminently suited to meditation, contemplation, and quiet pursuits.

Originally Fontenay was home to only 12 monks, but that number increased quickly, and the present abbey was constructed and waxed exceedingly prosperous from the 12th through the 15th century. Its buildings consisted of chapel, bakery, dovecote and kennel, church (with dormitories), cloister, infirmary, forge, and hostel.

Decline began in the 16th century, in part due to a system of appointing by royal favor abbots who were uninterested in the traditional roles of abbeys, though largely because of the devastating effects of the Wars of Religion. With the Revolution, Fontenay became a paper mill. It was resold in 1820 to Elie de Montgolfier (of the pioneering family of balloon flights). In 1906 a Montgolfier son-in-law, Edouard Aynard, acquired the abbey, dismantled the factory, and began returning it to its original appearance. The Aynard family currently lives at the abbey and maintains it as a historical monument. In 1981 UNESCO declared Fontenay a Universal Heritage site.

In the history of Cistercian architecture, Fontenay ranks as one of the most successful examples of form joined to monastic ideal (along with Noirlac, in Berry, and Sénanque, in Provence). What was desired, and here achieved, is a reduction of the unnecessary in the creation of admirable proportions—a severe but harmonious simplicity. Fontenay is as spare and elegant as a Gregorian chant.

Even on a summer's day the visitor shivers slightly in the communal dormitory and tries to imagine monks sleeping without warmth on straw mattresses in midwinter; the only heat allowed was in the copying room, where, near a great fireplace, the transcribing of manuscripts was done.

Georges Louis Leclerc, Comte de Buffon, author of the 44-volume classic, *Natural History,* was born in nearby Montbard in 1707. His gardens and study, in what had been a stronghold of the dukes of Burgundy, are open to the public. An association was founded in 1978 to restore Buffon's 18th-century ironworks, and so far has completed the employees' lodgings, the stable, the blast-furnace hall, the refinery, and foundry. It's all quite fitting, since Montbard today is a metallurgical center specializing in steel tubing.

The Montbard Regional Fair is held during the first half of September.

Château Bussy-Rabutin

Marie de Rabutin-Chantal, Marquise de Sévigné, was not the only pithy writer in the family. Her cousin, Roger de Rabutin, Comte de Bussy, had as pointed a pen and as developed a nose for naughty news. Unfortunately, Rabutin could not keep his wit to himself and was exiled by Louis XIV to his château in far-off (from Paris, and therefore from civilization) Burgundy for having ridiculed, in a series of irresistibly amusing couplets, the affair of the king with Marie Mancini.

In exile, Rabutin kept up a lively correspondence with his beautiful and talented cousin (whom he alternately adored and maligned) and wrote a chronicle titled "The Amorous History of the Gauls," satirizing the scandalous goings-on at court. As a result, he was imprisoned in the Bastille for more than a year and then exiled to the country again. Once challenged on his own purity of motives and behavior, Rabutin wrote, "Let me remind you, sir, that I condone only such scandals as I have myself occasioned."

The first castle at Bussy (Bussy is between Fontenay and Alise-Ste-Reine), constructed in the 13th century, had become a powerful fortress under the Rochefort family, and passed into the hands of François de Rabutin in 1602. Roger, his grandson, devoted his years of country confinement to enlarging and beautifying his golden cage.

Of all the public and private rooms, several decorated by Rabutin himself in flights of original fancy, the most interesting may be the master's bedroom, with furniture and woodworks of the day, highlighted by 26 portraits of women, among them Madame de Sévigné.

Bussy-Rabutin's masterpiece, however, may be the **Tour Dorée** (literally "gilded tower," though it comprises only one floor of the structure), which is entirely overwhelmed with paintings that feature mythological subjects as well as contemporary gallants accompanied by cutting, cynical couplets.

Alésia

The heart of the Gallic empire beat its last in 52 B.C. near today's little town (fewer than 800 inhabitants) of Alise-Ste-Reine. A difficult village to find, it is southeast of Montbard/Fontenay near Les Laumes, northwest of Dijon.

Alise was **Alésia**, a hilltop fortress chosen by Vercingetorix for what he planned to make the final rout of the Romans. Tactician though he was, he was no match for Caesar. As Katherine Scherman writes, "Caesar built siege works all around the base of the hill, and in a short time Vercingetorix's big army had exhausted the garrison supplies. In the fierce battle that finally ensued—in which Caesar himself took part, conspicuous to his own men and the enemy alike in the scarlet cloak he always wore in action—the Celtic troops were thoroughly routed and many of them simply ran away and went home."

The great Gaul surrendered himself and his horse to Caesar who, though admitting the enemy's prowess, humiliated him by imprisoning him in Rome and then parading him through the streets. Vercingetorix was finally executed at the foot of the Roman Capitol.

Caesar was a creative conqueror; after all, he wanted a trouble-free Gaul. Celts of rank were awarded Roman citizenship, the Roman monetary system was established, and the Latin language was introduced. "He laid the groundwork for a Roman Europe," says Scherman, "that would fuse the continuing classical Greco-Roman tradition with the fresh Celtic-Teutonic ethos." In a deep sense, classical France was born in these Burgundian fields.

Today, Vercingetorix in bronze bestrides a hill over-looking the village whence the vestiges of Gallo-Roman life come slowly to light: temple, theater, forum, streets, shops, wells, courtyards, even hypocausts, those under-ground furnaces that heated water for the baths. Finds from the embattled earth are displayed at the **Musée Alésia,** and archaeological excavations continue.

On the first or second Sunday of September, Alise celebrates Sainte Reine with a morning parade in appro-priate costumes and an afternoon production of the "Mys-tery of Sainte Reine." Local residents march with torches on the eve of the festival, one of the most attractive of the rural representations in Burgundy.

The Source of the Seine

On the N 71 south of Châtillon and just northwest of Dijon is **St-Seine-l'Abbaye.** Turn north from there in search of *la source de la Seine,* not the easiest spot to find. (Inveterate church inspectors will stop at St-Seine itself, which marks in style the transition from Romanesque to Gothic, and is named not for the river but for a sixth-century Benedic-tine monk, Saint Seigne, who appears in one of the church frescoes in his black monk's robe.)

"Like the Jordan, the Ganges, the Rhine, the Seine is a holy river." So begins Anthony Glyn's *The Seine,* a book that since its publication in 1966 must certainly have inspired hundreds of readers to make their own pilgrim-ages to la Source. (In French *source* means not only source but also spring, fountain, or fountainhead.)

The name Seine derives from that of Sequana, a Roman goddess worshiped in the remote and wooded valley where the river rises. On the site, two temples succeeded the first clay-and-wattle hut, and in the center a spring gushed forth. Slightly downstream, a bathing pool almost 200 feet long lured the faithful from all over France to wash in the holy waters.

As do pilgrims to Lourdes today, the disabled and the merely curious came to cure themselves or to sell nos-trums, votive offerings, and knickknacks. Archaeological digs here have unearthed thousands of various items of tribute, today on show in Dijon's Musée Archéologique and several others in Burgundy.

For 300 years the goddess worked her miracles, but in the third century the temple was smashed and the site desecrated, possibly by invading Burgundians (the Burgondiones). What had been a hive of worshipers reverted to an empty, rather mournful valley.

You approach the source along a narrow road, more like a lane, and see nothing of civilization except the small, rundown Café Sequana and the cranky overseer who claims exhaustion at telling one more traveller precisely where the source is. Through a wet meadow bordered by a fence with signs announcing that the Source is the property of the City of Paris, you eventually find it: an ugly, artificial grotto with a small, bubbling pool in its center and a fat water nymph reclining on a rock. From the pool, a trickle of water runs away through the cow pasture, on its way to Paris and the sea.

SEMUR

Just when you think Burgundy can come up with no more tempting little towns, you round a hill and there stands Semur-en-Auxois, an outsize storybook city of about 5,500 Sémurois on a pink granite outcrop above the valley of the river Armançon west of Dijon, very near Fontenay and Alise-Ste-Reine.

Its profile demands to be painted or at least photographed at once: a bridge that leaps the river toward a parade of picturesque old houses; round towers and ramparts (now a promenade); Medieval gates and the soaring spire of Notre-Dame; and a waterfall of gardens cascading over ancient stones.

In the 14th century, Semur's ramparts supported 18 towers, and as each third of the town was encircled by its own wall, the whole was believed to be impregnable. The treasure was, and is, the **church of Notre-Dame**, founded in the 11th century, restored in the 13th and 14th; eventually it too enjoyed the tender care of Viollet-le-Duc. Within, the second chapel on the left shelters an **entombment** that ranks among the most beautiful created during the late Middle Ages; its monumentality is reminiscent of Dijonnais sculptor Claus Sluter.

The **Musée Municipal et Bibliothèque**, in the former convent of the Jacobins (17th century), exhibits geological and paleontological finds as well as paintings and sculptures from the 13th to the 18th century. The library owns manuscripts and incunabula of great value, including a tenth-century illuminated manuscript, the Missal of

Anne de Bretagne, and an ancient work from the Gutenberg press.

Semur is a lively little place, and stages several happenings during spring and summer: *Course des Chausses et des Desmoiselles* (since 1369), the last half of May; *Fête de la Bauge* (since 1639, oldest horse race in France); *Course à la Timbale d'Argent,* first half of June; and a theater, music, and dance festival during the last 15 days of July and the first week of August.

Lovers of cheese will detour from the route to **Epoisses**, only 12 km (8.1 miles) west of Semur, perhaps not so much because of its château as for a taste of its renowned, buttery Epoisses cheese, produced originally by Cistercian monks. Patricia Wells suggests tasting and buying for picnics at Fromagerie Berthaut; try Epoisses with the fiery liqueur *marc de Bourgogne.*

SAULIEU

There are aspects to Saulieu other than wining, dining, and sleeping, but to many visitors they are mere dividends. The essential attraction in this small, pleasant town (of just more than 3,000 Sédélociens) is the restaurant **Côte d'Or** with its **Résidence** (two rooms, seven apartments, plus 15 simpler rooms in an older, separate building). Owner-chef Bernard Loiseau and his wife, Chantal, have joined contemporary style and comfort to old-fashioned calm, while the kitchen (two Michelin stars) is renowned for lightness and creativity.

Cheese lovers should stop by Laiterie Overney for some of the things good picnics are made of; a newcomer is a five-week cheese washed with local Chablis.

Saulieu's gastronomic reputation was already well established in the 17th century, when it became an important post stop on the route between Paris and Lyon. Rabelais wrote of the good living there (on which, of course, he was an authority), and Madame de Sévigné was made absolutely tipsy by the quality and quantity of food and drink.

In 177 Saint Andoche and two companions, Thyrse and Félix, were martyred at Saulieu, and a church was erected on the spot in 306, to be destroyed before long by the Saracens. The present **basilica of St-Andoche** was begun in the 12th century and has endured several indignities during its long life, including fires that destroyed the choir and transept during the Hundred Years War and the mutilations of the Revolution.

The strong point of St-Andoche is the remarkable set of powerfully carved column capitals somewhat reminiscent of those in Autun, featuring grinning monsters, incredible foliage from an imaginary jungle, and biblical scenes such as the flight to Egypt, the hanging of Judas, the false prophet Balaam and his ass, and more.

Next to St-Andoche, the **Musée Régional** (sometimes called the Musée François-Pompon) exhibits a fine collection of Gallo-Roman steles; Medieval, Renaissance, and Classical sculptures; items of craftwork from the Morvan mountain region; and bronzes, terra-cottas, and the like by Pompon, a native of Saulieu who specialized in animal sculptures. He seemed to like polar bears and tigers in particular.

Today Saulieu supplies much of France with Christmas trees from the forests of the Morvan; they are exported also to the rest of Europe and to North Africa. The woods near the town serve for picnics, hiking, horseback riding, and trout fishing in stocked ponds.

Shops in nearby **Nontron-le-Beau** sell the pleasing handicrafts created by Jean-Louis Pasquet.

AUTUN

Autun and Rome—today nothing of one would stir the slightest inkling of the other. Pleasant, calm (indeed, half-asleep might be a better description) little Autun of about 16,000 citizens snoozes on its slope below the wooded hills of the Morvan (south of Saulieu and west of Beaune).

Autun owes its existence to the demise of Bibracte, a Gallic town at the summit of Mont Beuvray (an easy excursion from Autun), capital of the tribe called Eduens, where Vercingetorix held a council of war in 52 B.C. It was at Bibracte that he took command of the Gallic armies and organized his troops against Julius Caesar. After Vercingetorix was defeated at Alésia, Caesar wiped out Bibracte.

In the days of the Emperor Augustus (27 B.C. to A.D. 14), Autun was established as Augustunum, and it matured into a flourishing city, an important stop on the trade and defensive routes from Lyon to Boulogne. Indeed, contemporary road maps show Autun as the hub of a six-spoked wheel.

During the late Roman Empire (180 to 395) the fame of Autun's schools was widespread, its diocese was one of the oldest in Gaul, and it was the premier suffragan of the mother church in Lyon. Over the centuries an impressive number of abbeys flowered in Autun, including that of St-Martin, founded in the sixth century by the Merovingian Queen Brunhild. It defended its independence even in the face of Cluny.

Brunhild's harsh life (her husband was murdered through the wicked machinations of her sister-in-law, Frédégund) inevitably hardened the queen, who used to retreat from the troubles of her regency to the relative serenity of Autun. Historian Katherine Scherman tells that the quarrels of the two queens and the downfall of her husband King Sigibert I, are the stuff of the Medieval German epic *Niebelungenlied;* Autun is thought to have been the home of the Niebelungs, and Sigibert metamorphosed into Siegfried.

Vestiges of Roman days are: the **Theater**, the largest in Gaul, with seats for 15,000 spectators; the **Porte St-André** on the northeast, one of four gates and 62 towers in the Gallo-Roman wall; **Porte d'Arroux** on the north; and the **Temple de Janus,** of which only two sections remain. Tradition says it was near Porte St-André that Saint Symphorien, one of the most revered martyrs of Roman Gaul, was beheaded as his mother shouted condolences to him from the wall.

After the decline of the Gallo-Roman world, Autun slept for a while, to awake to new prosperity in the Middle Ages, from which dates its major monument, the **cathedral of St-Lazare**, which in its entirety is one of the most important witnesses of Romanesque in Burgundy.

The tall stone spire that marks the cathedral dates from the 15th century, but the church itself is one of the major works of Cluniac art, constructed between 1120 and 1146 and consecrated by Pope Innocent II in 1130. Its artistic marvels are the sculptures (in local gray stone) on the tympanum of the central portal, **The Last Judgment,** and its column capitals in a stippled stone containing mica.

Probably it is best that Autun was in decline during the Renaissance; otherwise "renovations" of these triumphs might have taken place, as happened elsewhere. Following Medieval habit, public works of art are usually anonymous, but the tympanum is signed: "Gislebertus hoc fecit."

The tympanum is a true sermon in stone, designed by the artist to be "read" by illiterates—and paid heed to. An inscription carved in Latin advises, "Let this horror appall those bound by earthly sin." In the center, Christ sits in Byzantine majesty, a figure not yet capable of seeming human. All around him there is wicked and wonderful action: three children bound for Paradise hold on to an angel; a woman headed for Hell is being eaten by serpents; Saint Peter holds the hand of a nude soul; Saint Michael tries to weigh the good and bad honestly, even as Satan pulls the scale down in his direction.

Musée Rolin occupies the 15th-century town house built for Nicolas Rolin, the founder of the Hôtel-Dieu in Beaune. Displayed are Gallo-Roman artifacts, some superb Roman statuary, a Temptation of Eve that is part of a Gislebertus relief, French and Flemish primitive paintings, a 15th-century Nativity by the so-called Master of Moulins; and items of regional archaeological interest.

Also visit the **Hôtel de Ville** for a rich collection of manuscripts; and the **Musée Lapidaire** for Roman and Medieval antiquities.

The unpretentious 50-room Hôtel St-Louis, where Napoléon slept twice, is still in business, but the 30-room **Ursulines** is more comfortable.

The best place in town to eat is the **Hostellerie Vieux Moulin**, near the river; for a better dining experience, drive 43 km (29 miles) east to Chagny and the elegant hotel and three-star restaurant **Lameloise**, which occupies an elegantly reworked antique Burgundian home and provides 25 rooms.

A driving circle of about 70 km (47.2 miles) called Signal d'Uchon will include an exterior view of the lavish **Château de Sully**, northeast of Autun.

BEAUNE

Reverentially, the oenophile approaches Beaune, south of Dijon and east of Autun, admiring the rich slopes of hills and the names of the land: from Dijon, Gevrey-Chambertin, Vougeot, Vosne-Romanée, Aloxe-Corton; from Mâcon in the south, Chassagne-Montrachet, Puligny-Montrachet, Meursault, Volnay, Pommard, and more.

Beaune itself proves to live up to the nobility of its neighboring vineyards. "This is one of the most soul-satisfying of towns," wrote Samuel Chamberlain, "the pure essence of rural France—civilized, bourgeois, unruffled. Its fat chimneys bespeak a well-fed race."

To the traveller, Beaune comes as a respite: It doesn't bustle, it strolls; it need not shout, it chants; it is less chic than comfortable. Beaune, after all, is scarcely an upstart; it's a town of fewer than 22,000 Beaunois that is enjoying a respected old age.

Beaune was a sanctuary for the Gauls, then the Romans (some believe Beaune may have been the "Bibracte" mentioned by Caesar in his *Chronicles*), and, finally, the Great Dukes of Burgundy (before they seized upon Dijon as their capital). Its 14th-century walls and some towers remain, hemming in art and other evidences of the good life.

The **Hôtel-Dieu**, also known as the Hospices de Beaune, was founded in 1443 by Nicolas Rolin, the chancellor of Burgundy under Philippe le Bel, as a charity hospital. Rolin's intentions may not have been quite so splendid as the architecture: Louis XI of France is said to have sniffed, "It is indeed just that having made so many people poor, Rolin should now construct a hospital to shelter them."

Whatever. The hospice catered to the souls as well as the sores of the poor—and in style—for more than 500 years. It was renovated, restored, and altered in 1971, and now serves the aged.

The look has scarcely changed since architect Jehan Wiscrere created its Flamboyant design, the most striking elements of which are visible only after you pass the sober, somewhat formidable façade and step into the courtyard. The multicolored tile roofs, the small towers from which Rapunzel might let down her long hair, the ranks of inviting dormer windows, the eccentric weather vanes—all conspire to put you in the mood of a storybook rather than sickness.

The Grand'Salle served as a ward as well as a church, designed so that patients could share the Mass without leaving their beds. (Beds were scarcely king-size, as the visitor notices, and several of the sick were squeezed into each one, probably with infectious results.) Among several other installations seen, the most interesting are the kitchen and the pharmacy.

The *chef d'oeuvre,* however, is the immense polyptych, **Last Judgment**, by Flemish painter Rogier van der Weyden. On the covers of the panels, Rolin and his wife,

Guigone, appear as they did in life, no warts or wrinkles overlooked. A rather recent display arrangement of van der Weyden's work is quite inventive in its own right.

Chancellor Rolin willed his vineyards to the hospital, and today, the holdings slightly increased, income from the annual wine auction goes to preserve and implement its good works. The mid-November auction is the central event of Les Trois Glorieuses, a three-day festival of feasting watched over by the merry group known as the Confrérie des Chevaliers du Tastevin.

It is fitting that the **Musée du Vin de Bourgogne** is located in Beaune, within a former mansion of the dukes, a handsome wood and stone structure from the 15th and 16th centuries. The history of winemaking is represented by artworks, tools, costumes, and photographs.

The **collegiate church of Notre-Dame**, begun about 1120, is worth visiting particularly because of the collection of tapestries in the choir behind the high altar. Titled "The Life of the Virgin," the collection appears to have one artistic foot in the Middle Ages and one in the Renaissance.

A pleasantly furnished hotel handily located on Maufoux just a couple of curves away from place de la Halle is **Le Cep**, with 46 rooms, the stylish **Bernard Morillon** restaurant, and fairly high prices. Its competition is **La Poste** on boulevard Clemenceau near the city ramparts, with 21 slightly pricey rooms and a one-star dining room; it has a notable wine list with classic labels. Also tops in taste are **Jacques Lainé** (on the north edge of town near promenade des Buttes in a lovely turn-of-the-century home), **Relais de Saulx** (not far from the Hôtel-Dieu; try the *cassolette d'escargots*), **Rôtisserie la Paix** (outside the ramparts to the southeast on rue du Faubourg Madeleine), and **Ermitage de Corton** (about 5 km/3 miles north in Chorey-les-Beaune, with a handful of beautiful rooms and expensive apartments).

Modestly priced with a friendly staff and no restaurant, the **Belle Epoque** sits on faubourg du Bretonnière on the way southwest from town to Autun.

A restaurant lauded by some, swiped at by others, is **Le Petit Truc** in the suburb of Vignoles; in any case, its typical, rustic, warming decor is worth the short detour.

Shopping in Beaune runs less toward fashion than to food and kitchen and table accessories. A worthwhile stop is **Beaune Choses**, where the tableware is almost as irresistible as the pun. **Parfumerie Ambre** is a reliable outlet for those who've exhausted their supply of Azzaro or Hermès or Lanvin. For faïence, porcelain, crystal, and the like, it's **Orfèvrerie Bourguignonne**. Beaune's market bustles on Saturdays right in front of the Hôtel-Dieu.

Only a few kilometers from Beaune, at the rest stop on the A 6 motorway from Auxerre and Paris, the **Archéodrome** displays life-size representations of the important stages of the settlement of Burgundy.

TOURNUS

Traffic tends to bypass Tournus, thundering along A 6. Perhaps that is why the little city (about 7,000 Tournusiens) south of Beaune seems antique and slumbering. It deserves to; it was a settlement of the Eduen tribe long before the Romans came to build a camp. Around 180, Saint Valerien came to Tournus as an evangelist and was martyred on a hill overlooking the river Saône.

History hesitated, it seems, until the ninth century, when monks from Ile de Noirmoutier, off the coast of Brittany, fled the Norman invaders and arrived in this quiet spot to shelter the relics of their founder, Saint Philibert.

Your first stop in town should be the **church of St-Philibert**, reached by taking rue Albert-Thibaudet east off N 6 and passing between two round towers into the place de l'Abbaye. Begun in the late tenth or early 11th century and completed by the end of the 12th, this grand example of early Romanesque style is older than the better-known abbey at Cluny.

The thick-walled crypt and the narthex, with its short, powerful pillars, are the two oldest elements of the abbey, and their solidity, strength, and simplicity are impressive. The nave, with its alternating pink and white stones and unusual arrangement of transverse bays and very tall masonry pillars, soars with a lightness unusual in Romanesque.

The traveller with an interest in prehistory will stop at the **Musée Greuze**, a short walk south of St-Philibert on rue A.-Bessard to inspect the archaeological collections rather than to spend time with the canvases of local painter Jean-Baptiste Greuze, which may seem overly sentimental to today's eyes.

Directly across the narrow street north of the church, the **Musée Perrin-de-Puycousin** occupies the 17th-century treasury building and features reconstitutions of old Burgundian home interiors, complete with wax figures wearing traditional costumes, period furnishings, and a wine cellar.

A couple of good hotels, **De Greuze** and **Le Rempart** (the first with a Michelin two-star restaurant, the second with a one-star), make Tournus a pleasant stop for excursions into the countryside, particularly to **Cluny**.

CLUNY

Cluny nestles among woods and fields in the green valley of the meandering Grosne southwest of Tournus. It is quiet; its Romanesque and Gothic houses breathe deeply; its battles are over. In our times, out of the spotlight, it is a peaceful and small country town of fewer than 5,000 Clusinois.

In the Middle Ages, though, Cluny, as poet Alphonse de Lamartine had it, "as dark as the hood of a monk's cloak," dominated the religious, artistic, intellectual, and political life of Western Europe. Its struggle with the Cistercians and Saint Bernard split Christianity in ways still evidenced today.

Saint Benedict created the order that bears his name at Monte Cassino, in Italy, about 529, but its greatest monastery did not appear for another 400 years—in the wilds of Burgundy.

The abbey at Cluny was founded on September 11, 910, by Guillaume le Pieux (the Pious), duke of Aquitaine. Fewer than a hundred years later it had achieved immense power and prestige: Some 1,500 brotherhoods across France and in England, Germany, Spain, Switzerland, and even Poland depended on Cluny. "Wherever the wind blows," went a saying of the time, "the abbot of Cluny owns."

The immense **abbey** was conceived by one of Cluny's abbots, Saint Hugues de Semur, who laid the first stone in 1088. Major construction was completed in only 20 years, but building went on until 1130. Cluny was the physical as well as spiritual pride of Christendom, remaining the largest church in the world for 500 years until it was exceeded (and then by only ten yards in length) by St. Peter's in Rome.

The Benedictine rule made liturgical prayer the primary occupation of monks, to be complemented by sacred reading, manual labor, practice of the arts, and *opus divinum* (praising God) through the splendor of churches and the beauty of liturgy and hymns.

The rule came to be recognized as the fundamental monastic code of Western Europe. "Its flexibility enabled it to be adapted to the needs of society," writes David Hugh Farmer, "so that monasteries became centers of learning, agriculture, hospitality, and medicine in a way presumably unforeseen by Benedict himself."

Cluniac houses, the first at Barnstaple, the second at Lewes, were introduced to England by William the Conqueror; by the 13th century there were 40 dependencies in England.

"You are the light of the world," Pope Urban II said to Cluny abbot Saint Hugues in 1098. The greatness of Cluny sprang from the genius of its seven great abbots (Pontius is usually excepted) over 250 years. When Peter the Venerable died in about 1157, slow decline set in, perhaps the inevitable result of riches and international power.

The Cistercians

Saint Bernard, a Burgundian from Fontaines, near Dijon, was born to a noble family (his father, a knight, later died on crusade). Educated at Châtillon-sur-Seine, at age 22 he and some 30 companions joined the poverty-stricken monastery of Cîteaux, not far from Nuits-St-Georges and northeast of Beaune. Under Bernard, the Cistercian order was transformed and became the second great Romanesque religious movement.

After only a few years, Bernard was named abbot of the newly formed Clairvaux, some 40 miles southeast of Troyes and east of Sens. Here he found extreme poverty. Largely because of Bernard's intense moral suasion and his brilliant preaching (in Latin), Clairvaux grew steadily, founding houses even in England (the first in North Yorkshire in 1132). At Bernard's death, there were some 350 Cistercian abbeys and 700 monks in residence at Clairvaux.

Food writer Waverley Root sees the Cluny-Clairvaux struggles in terms of eating and drinking. "It is in harmony with the nature of the order," he writes, "that it was the Benedictines who invented, and gave their name to, a rich, sweet, and unctuous liqueur. One would hardly have expected such a development from the Cistercians, whose regulations forbade them to eat meat, fish, eggs, milk dishes, or white bread, and to drink anything other than water.

"When the art of cooking emerged from the monasteries, it had to be Benedictine skills that were passed on to laymen, not Cistercian. The Cistercians had nothing to offer. Even if their ecclesiastical victory had been complete, they could hardly have expected, with their ascetic ideas, to have dominated the gastronomy of a country so fertile and naturally rich in food as Burgundy." (There would be no suspense in wondering which order Root would have joined.)

When Bernard thundered, people listened. He assailed the Benedictine bishops who "can't go four leagues from home without dragging along 60 horses . . . Will the light shine only if it's in a silver or gold candelabra?"

In 1330 the abbey of Cluny bought land in Paris on which to build a residence for abbots attending a college near the Sorbonne; in the late 15th century it was enlarged by Jacques d'Amboise, Bishop of Clermont, with such comforts and ornamentation that even kings and queens slept there as guests. What remains of the luxurious residence constitutes today's **Musée de Cluny** in Paris, which houses the finest examples extant of architectural details, furnishings, and decorative arts of the ecclesiastical style of the period.

Serious decline began for Cluny in the 14th century, the Wars of Religion in the 16th century struck almost a death blow, and the Revolution completed the job. The abbey was closed in 1790, and in 1798 the whole was sold to a merchant from Mâcon, who demolished the nave. By 1823 only the near ruins visible today were left of Cluny's Medieval magnificence.

Cluny Today

What remains of the abbey today are the two Baraban towers at the entrance to the narthex, part of the porch, bits of the south side aisle, a chapel on the south side of the lesser transept, an octagonal belfry known as l'Eau Bénite (Holy Water), and the south end of the larger transept. Even so, this last manages to transmit a sense of the strength, daring, and splendor of the immense abbey.

In the **Farinier**, once the flour or meal barn, remnants of the abbey are displayed, including some capitals from the choir—masterpieces of Romanesque sculpture. There are also various models of the abbey.

An ancient palace, the work of Abbot Jean III de Bourbon, has become the **Musée Ochier**, which houses the collections of the 19th-century Ochier family: some decorations taken from ancient houses, capitals and small columns, a few paintings and portraits, some furniture and *objets d'art,* a collection of ceramics, and some 4,000 books in the museum's library.

A walk around the streets and ramparts of Cluny will reveal several Romanesque houses, and a climb up the 120 steps of the Tour des Fromages is worthwhile for the view.

Across from the abbey's ruins, the modest **Hôtel Bourgogne** has an eminently satisfactory restaurant. However, only 11 km (7.4 miles) east the **Château d'Igé**, a handsome retreat in the tiny village of Igé, offers six rooms and six apartments in a fortified château built by the dukes of Mâcon in the 13th century.

A music festival, Les Grandes Heures, is held in Cluny in August.

THE RHONE VALLEY

Since human history began in Europe, the Rhône, its tributaries, and its valley have constituted a major highway system for invaders, traders, civilizers, and conquerors.

As long ago as 20,000 B.C. Paleolithic man left engravings on the rock walls of caves. Many sites bear witness to the occupations of Neolithic times (around 8000 B.C.), and when the Bronze Age arrived (2000 B.C.) the Rhône had become a watery thoroughfare for the transportation of amber and tin.

In 121 B.C. Roman legions established camps on the left bank of the river at the site of today's Vienne. Lyon was established (as Lugdunum) in 43 B.C. and soon became the capital of the Gauls.

The Burgundian tribes likewise selected Vienne as their capital, in the fifth century, while in the Middle Ages various French kings attempted to seize control of the valley. In 1419 the first fairs held in Lyon were established by the future Charles VII, making the town one of the world's great commercial centers. The fairs lost much of their importance after Medieval times, but the one at Lyon was revived in 1916.

During World War II, Lyon was a headquarters of the Resistance; retreating German armies destroyed many of the river's bridges in 1944.

For the traveller's purposes, the valley of the Rhône stretches from Mâcon in the north to Orange in the south (for Orange, see the Provence chapter), from the regions of Auvergne and Causses on the west to the Alps on the east.

Most visitors to the Rhône valley confine themselves to the cities along the river corridor—Lyon, Vienne, Valence—at the same time complaining about over-industrialization. Yet to the east and particularly to the west of A 7, the rough plateaux, the woods, and the glacier-sliced valleys are almost empty of inhabitants, certainly of travellers. Some fascinating drives may be made through this region, especially in the valley of the Ardèche, north of Orange.

LYON

It is not easy to evade Lyon. Autoroutes from the north (A 6), from the south (A 7), from the east (A 42) and southeast (A 43), and through-routes from all directions are sucked into the maw of the city like so many strands of spaghetti.

The second largest urban area in France, with a population of about half a million and its greater area comprising almost two million, Lyon has to be aggressive to attract the travellers who would otherwise decide to settle down for days in such smaller cities as Strasbourg or Nice.

Yet in some ways Lyon is just an overgrown village. Away from the high-rises and commercial centers that have sprung up during the last two decades or so, along the narrow lanes of Old Lyon, you have something of the sense of a Paris in the 1930s, the one familiar from Gertrude Stein and Alice B. Toklas, of Hemingway and Joyce and Ford Madox Ford.

To orient yourself to Lyon, imagine it as if you are facing north looking down from a helicopter over its peninsula cradled in the arms of the Saône River on the west and the Rhône on the east. Centered over the old railway station near the tip of the peninsula, you would

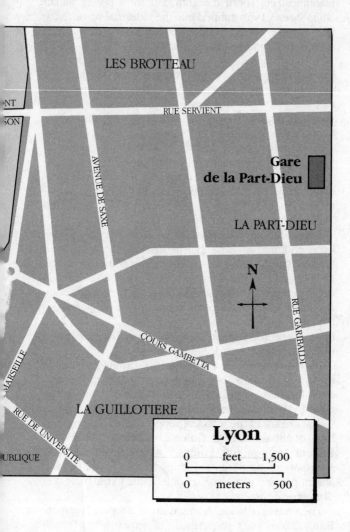

LES BROTTEAU

RUE SERVIENT

NT

SON

AVENUE DE SAXE

Gare
de la Part-Dieu

LA PART-DIEU

N

RUE GARIBALDI

COURS GAMBETTA

MARSEILLE

LA GUILLOTIERE

RUE DE UNIVERSITE

UBLIQUE

Lyon

| 0 | feet | 1,500 |

| 0 | meters | 500 |

murdered, beautiful old houses around place Bellecour were put to the torch, and the very name of the town was changed, to Commune Affranchie (free community).

The 15th century saw the installation of the great fairs that made Lyon a commercial hub, so that when silk manufacturing (until the 16th century a purely Italian craft) spread, Lyon jumped into the industrial world. New fabrics were invented: silks woofed with wool, watered silks, poplins, moirés, and so forth.

In the early 19th century J. M. Jacquard introduced a loom here by which a single workman could do the work of six in creating elaborate fabrics. Homes became factories for piece workers (*canuts*) to whom silk makers supplied fabrics. The center of this activity was today's Croix-Rousse district.

Lyon never has ceased to build upon its industrial inheritance; today's enterprises are grouped in contiguous suburbs. Lyon is also a center for scientific research, engineering, and communications, and has an international airport at Satolas, a fairly new Métro system, and TGV traffic to and from Paris and the south.

The tradition of the literary salon may seem to have been confined to Paris, but it flourished in Lyon from time to time as well, most spectacularly at the end of the 15th century in the days and nights of Louise Labé, la Belle Cordière. (She married Ennemond Perrin, a rope maker, or *cordier*.) Accomplished in several languages, beautiful, a musician and poet, la Belle Cordière held open house for the intelligentsia of her day; she was a precursor of Madame de Sévigné's.

By 1548 there were more than 400 printing studios in town, as well as studios of painters, sculptors, and ceramicists. Rabelais published his *Gargantua* and his *Pantagruel* in Lyon, to be sold during the annual fairs.

The creator of the wooden puppet named Guignol and thus of all the Grand Guignol shows in France was Laurent Mourguet, a Lyonnais weaver born in 1769. André-Marie Ampère, a locally famous physicist and absent-minded professor, gave his name to the basic unit of electrical current.

The Musée Claude Bernard in nearby St-Julien-en-Beaujolais honors the creator of experimental medicine. In 1896 Louis and Auguste Lumière debuted their first films here, and the world witnessed the birth of cinematography.

Fourvière, the Roman Hill

The view from the terrace of the 19th-century **basilica of Notre-Dame-de-Fourvière** is what the Romans saw in the second century—the joining arms of the Saône and the Rhône rivers and, off in the distance, the mountainous horizon that grows up into the Alps. In the foreground, however, those builders saw no metropolis, no industrial suburbs, no towers or hotels or railroad stations testifying to the importance of COURLY (Communauté Urbaine Lyon). Looking at that view, the Romans turned their backs upon the great structures of their own age: the **circus** outside the walls and, within, the theater, the smaller Odéon, and the capitol.

Today's traveller begins an exploration of Lyon atop Fourvière with visits to the handsome stone remains of the **Odéon** (designed for concerts and small conferences) and to the **theater**, the oldest in France and about the size of those in Orange and Arles. (Today the theater serves as venue for an international festival of music and dramatic arts that takes place from mid-June to mid-July.)

If you saw nothing more in Lyon than Fourvière's **Musée de la Civilisation Gallo-Romaine**, adjoining the Roman theater, the trip would have been worthwhile. Opened in 1975, it is an unsurpassed witness to prehistoric, Gallic, and Roman art in France: Paleolithic and Neolithic tools, a chariot from the early Iron Age, a Gallic calendar engraved in bronze, magnificent mosaics, antique glass, pottery, and kitchen utensils.

Perhaps the most valuable find from modern digs in the city was that of the **Claudian Tables**, an inscription on bronze of a speech by Claudius delivered in 48 before the Roman Senate, in which the Lyon-born Emperor urged that the chiefs of Gallic nations might succeed in their attempts to be elected as Roman magistrates.

Vieux (Renaissance) Lyon

The Old Town, comprising the quarters of St-Jean, St-Paul, and St-Georges, stretches along the Saône at the foot of Fourvière, preserving a wealth of at least 300 houses dating from the Renaissance. Along rue Juiverie, rue de la Loge, rue de Gadagne, and around the place du Change march these proud houses shoulder to shoulder, representing the end of the Gothic period, the Italian-inspired Renaissance, the French Renaissance, and pre-Classic days. Normally, the *maisons* Laurençin, Thomassin, Mayet-de-Beauvoir, and Buillioud must be seen from the street and are closed to the public; the Gadagne houses the **Musée Historique**, the **Musée Edouard-Herriot**, and the **Musée de la Marionnette**.

Also of interest in this premier promenade area are the cathedral of St-Jean and the church of St-Paul. Begun in the 11th century, the **cathedral of St-Jean** is a Gothic mass rising upon a Romanesque base; it was the seat of the primate, or first bishop, of Gaul. The façade owes its fine decorations to the 14th century. Inside, the greatest treasure is the 12th-century choir, and some beautiful 13th-century stained glass has survived. On the north side of St-Jean, excavations of a much earlier church are underway. A beautiful lantern-tower and some handsomely sculpted animal figures distinguish the **church of St-Paul**.

In Old Lyon, as in the Croix-Rousse district, the *traboules* form a network of passages tunneling underneath and around the ancient houses, opening into tiny courtyards, leading to otherwise unseen Renaissance galleries, debouching suddenly into minuscule market squares. (*Traboule* derives from the Latin *trans ambulare,* to walk through.)

Bellecour Between the Banks

Place Bellecour and the peninsula of which it is the center, between the Saône on the west and Rhône on the east, is the heart of contemporary Lyon and one of the largest such squares in France, bordered on east and west by handsome, symmetrical Louis XVI houses. It sits atop a large parking garage, a handy central place to leave your car. Place Bellecour is within walking distance from several hotels (in various price ranges), museums, and shopping streets. Smaller than Bellecour but also more animated, **place des Terreaux** was near the confluence of the rivers in Roman times. Today it's the confluence of sidewalk cafés; its fountain is the work of Bartholdi. Walks in the area of Terreaux reveal several curious *traboules,* the Musée des Beaux-Arts, pretty squares, and a collection of renowned restaurants.

Left Bank of the Rhône

The TGV and most other trains deposit travellers at the giant Gare de la Part-Dieu, which has become the center of an entirely new commercial area, with hotels to match. It boasts Le Grand Espace Shopping, with 14 movie houses, 20 restaurants and bars, a bowling alley, a discothèque, and 220 stores. It's also a central departure point for the local Métro. You could get lost in this totally modern complex and never find your way out. (Some trains still arrive from various directions at Gare de Perrache on the peninsula; check your ticket at time of purchase.)

North of Part-Dieu, the 42-acre **Parc de la Tête d'Or** (named Golden Head because of a traditional story that a head of Christ worked in gold once was found buried here) holds Europe's largest rose garden, La Roseraie, with more than five million blossoms in season. It's also a good place to limber up on the huge rowing lake and along jogging paths. There are outstanding zoological and botanical gardens here as well.

The Museums of Lyon

Few French cities outside Paris possess as large and satisfying a collection of museums as Lyon, of which the best known (justifiably) is the **Musée des Beaux-Arts**, off place des Terreaux in the enormous Palais St-Pierre, built in the 17th century as a Benedictine nunnery for gentle ladies. The 90 rooms are devoted to sculptures of various periods and paintings from all the great ages of European art. There are also some Oriental displays. The Musée Gallo-Romaine, described above, is the other museum that should on no account be overlooked.

Of interest chiefly to enthusiasts of fabrics, the **Musée Historique des Tissus** contains the largest collection of textiles in the world, including a recently opened wing of 12 rooms devoted to Oriental rugs, fabrics, and tapestries. The French collections are naturally the most important; overall, fabrics range from the fourth century to today. The museum is about halfway between place Bellecour and the Perrache station and adjoins the **Musée des Arts Décoratifs**. This latter museum is a step back into the 18th century; it is completely outfitted in furniture, *objets d'art,* faïence, tapestries, porcelain, tableware, and so forth. Especially rich is the Italian Renaissance faïence collection.

In Vieux Lyon near the place du Change, the **Musée**

Historique de Lyon shows off a remarkable collection of Romanesque sculptures, furnishings, faïence from Nevers, and descriptions of Lyon throughout the centuries. Part and almost parcel of this museum is the **Musée de la Marionnette**, with an exceptional puppet show of figures from as far away as Kampuchea and Java, but centered, quite naturally, on the Guignols.

If you are strongly inclined toward museum meandering and have leisure time in Lyon, also consider the Musée Guimet d'Histoire Naturelle (all animals represented from mammoths to man, with special emphasis on regional finds); the Musée de l'Imprimerie et de la Banque, which illustrates the importance of banking and printing through the ages; the Musée de la Résistance et de la Déportation, with evidences of the horrors of war and the Nazi death camps; the Musée des Hospices, exhibitions of medical and hospital life from the 17th century on; the Musée Africaine; the brand-new Expositions d'Art Contemporain; and, in the suburbs, the Musée Français de l'Automobile, with cars from 1890 to 1970, including some very prestigious vehicles.

Hotels in Lyon

Lyon's hotels are grouped in nine or ten areas in the city center and its immediate surroundings; most of the best are in Bellecour-Terreaux and Perrache.

Vieux Lyon
La Cour des Loges. Until 1987, no hotel in this great ambling-shopping area could be recommended. Then this strikingly modern, almost futuristic, art-filled inn appeared within a cluster of four 14th-century to 17th-century Medieval and Renaissance houses. The combined effects are stunning, and meld with surprising success. Ancient beamed ceilings have been preserved to look down on bathrooms with two-person tubs.

Rooms are opened by electronically coded keys and offer color TVs and videocassette units; the wine cellar is nobly stocked; and there are thermal baths, a restaurant, and a private garage. All this comes at a price, and it's worth paying.

Bellecour-Terreaux
Sofitel. That this is the best hotel in its area and one of the two tops in Lyon indicates that the city has always lacked

hostelries of an old-fashioned quality to match its size. There is no Crillon here, no Bristol, no Ritz, no Plaza-Athenée. Still, the Sofitel has pretty much everything one needs, a handy location, and a good restaurant, **Les Trois Dômes.**

Grand Hôtel Concorde. Just back from the river, this 14-room hotel is second best in its area, with the pleasant **Le Fiorelle** grill and 12 roomy apartments.

Royal. A fine location on Bellecour adds to the attractiveness of this 90-room member of the Mapotel group; it also has a good grill.

Perrache

Bordeaux et Parc. A suitcase-carrying distance from the railway station, it offers willing service but has no restaurant.

Terminus Perrache. It's right at the corner of the train station and has 140 comfortable rooms but no restaurant.

La Part-Dieu

Frantel. You couldn't call it cozy, but this is the place to witness futuristic France at work in the hotel industry. It's in a good location for those travelling by train, and has two fine restaurants: **L'Arc-en-Ciel,** with a panoramic rooftop view, and **La Ripaille** grill. The hotel proper begins on the 30th floor of a commercial building.

Lyon Airport/Satolas and Bron

Méridien. Very handy for air travellers, with 120 rooms, it has one good restaurant, **La Grande Corbeille,** and a worthwhile *brasserie,* **Auberge le Pichet.**

Novotel Lyon-Nord. Ten km (6.7 miles) out, at the junction of A 6 and N 6, this hotel is intended for motorists who want to stay outside town; it has 107 rooms and an informal restaurant.

Environs

Alain Chapel. This distinguished three-star restaurant in the village of Mionnay, 20 km (13.5 miles) northeast of Lyon, offers 13 rooms in an atmosphere of quiet and rural chic; it is a member of the Relais-et-Châteaux group.

Dining in Lyon

The quality of cooking in Lyon has changed much in past decades—and yet, as the French would always have it, it remains the same.

As recently as 1970, Waverley Root wrote that "the cooking of Lyon fits the character of the city—it is hearty rather than graceful, and is apt to leave you with an overstuffed feeling... my personal experience has been never to have eaten a really good meal in Lyon."

Even so, and whatever it may mean (and in terms of tourism dollars, it means a lot), greater Lyon tots up one three-star, four two-stars, and 11 one-stars (including Mère Brazier). The truth is, not all Lyonnais restaurants are shooting for the stars. As Patricia Wells puts it: "It's a place to roll up your sleeves, put on your walking shoes, turn your thoughts to no-frills eating, and enjoy." In order to enjoy some of the best restaurants in Lyon, you must first make reservations.

The room at the top is that of **Paul Bocuse** in the suburban village of Collonges-au-Mont-d'Or. Bocuse may be the best-known (he is surely the most peripatetic) restaurateur in the world. It may be possible to have a less than memorable meal *chez* Bocuse, but not easily. Like a client for a yacht, if you have to ask the price, forget it. Just settle into the surprisingly unpretentious dining room and order something familiar—leg of lamb, say, or filet of sole, or chicken from Bresse—and realize how unfamiliar really fine, simple cooking can be. Tel: 78-22-01-40.

Virtually all experts agree that a meal should be taken at **Léon de Lyon** (near the Musée des Beaux-Arts) for several reasons, the most persuasive of which is its remarkable presentations of Lyonnais classics. In addition, the decor and ambience are warm, welcoming, and not intimidating; chef Jean-Paul Lacombe is a *maître cuisinier* of France. Tel: 78-28-11-33.

Another *maître cuisinier* is Gérard Nandron of **Nandron**, at 26, quai Jean Moulin. He infuses his traditional cooking with lightness; try the *quenelle de brochet Nantua*. Tel: 78-42-10-26.

Yet another *maître cuisinier,* Jean Vettard, presides over **Vettard** on the place Bellecour. Formal gold and white decor suit the seriousness of the cuisine; the adjoining **Café Neuf** is Vettard at his less complex and expensive. Tel: 78-42-07-59.

Refined, friendly, classic, and yet up-to-date, **Orsi** (Pierre

Orsi at the helm) lures the discerning to 3, place Kléber, in the Left Bank area of Brotteaux, in part, perhaps, to taste his pigeon of Bresse *en cocotte*. Tel: 78-89-57-68.

Philippe Chavent of **La Tour Rose**, in the heart of Vieux Lyon at 16, rue du Boeuf, is being bruited about as the most creative young chef in town; he serves *nouvelle* turns on classic cuisine in a handsome 17th-century town house. Tel: 78-37-25-90. Recently, Chavent opened **Le Comptoir du Boeuf**, just across the street, a wine bar serving excellent wines by the glass to accompany selected cheeses.

Nobody can consume *haute cuisine* at every sitting, and Lyon excels in *bistros, bouchons,* and *cafés*. Right now, try **La Meunière** (in the first *arrondissement* near the Musée des Arts Décoratifs), with a typically brusque boss with a heart of gold, Maurice Debosses, a former Bocuse maître d'; **Le Passage**, in a *traboule* north of the place des Terreaux; **Café des Fédérations** (rue Major-Martin, also in the Terreaux area), with sawdust on the floor, sausages dangling in midair—you get the picture; **Café Gambs**, a hangout for international yuppies in the first block of rue Président-Carnot; **Brasserie Georges**, behind Perrache railway station and about the size of Grand Central Station.

Shopping in Lyon

Fashions, traditional

The street of chic is **rue du Président-Edouard Herriot**, wide and long, connecting place Bellecour to place de Terreaux. Here are the shops of Descamps, Charles Jourdan, Alain Manoukian, and Georges Rech, among other ruiners of budgets. **Rue de la République**, in the same area, also is smart.

Fashions

The one-stop shopping center of **La Part-Dieu** provides a pick of 220 stores, big and small, including Galeries Lafayette, Jelmoli, Darty, and England's imperishable Marks and Spencer. **Rue Saint-Jean**, that crowded pedestrian main street of Vieux Lyon, takes the cake and other items for trendy fashions. Stop on the place du Change and L'Ateyer de Guignol for a gift nobody else has: a traditional Guignol puppet handmade to resemble a friend or yourself (take photographs along).

Antiques

More than 150 galleries offering antiques and high-quality secondhand items are gathered in **Brocante Stalingrad** in the Villeurbanne district. It's the third largest European market for antiques. (*Brocante* is French for secondhand.)

Specialties and silks

In the traditional cloth-making quarter of Croix-Rousse, **La Maison des Canuts** is a cooperative of weavers that operates a museum-cum-retail-outlet. Old cut velvets, damask, and portraits woven in silk are on display, as well as a Jacquard handloom and a demonstration of silk making. Before the Industrial Revolution, some 60,000 looms clattered away in Lyon's family workshops. This cooperative still creates and sells silks at very reasonable prices: ties, scarves, handkerchiefs, foulards, and more.

PEROUGES

Pérouges is one of the most provocative, evocative villages in all Europe, an outcrop of the Middle Ages atop its hill and behind its ramparts only 39 km (26.3 miles) northeast—but centuries removed—from Lyon.

Pérouges owes its name to settlers who arrived from Perugia, Italy, before the Roman occupation. During the Middle Ages, the lords of the Dauphiné and Savoy squabbled over the small but rich (the chief industry was linen weaving) town, leading to the major historical event of local history, the siege of 1468.

On the exterior of the lower of the two city gates (**Porte d'en Bas**), an inscription in somewhat bastardized Latin reads: "Pérouges of the Pérougiens! Impregnable town! Those rogues from Dauphiné wanted to take it, but couldn't. However, they took away the gates, the hinges, and locks, and rolled off with them. The devil take them!"

During the 19th century, Pérouges's prosperity had ebbed, and by 1910 only 90 souls remained to shelter in the shade of the great and gracious linden tree in the heart of the matter, **la place du Tilleul**. Owners of ancient houses began to hack them down, and proud Pérouges seemed about to plunge into the past tense.

Then to the rescue came artists and artisans from Lyon and elsewhere, supported in part by government Beaux-Arts funds. A committee for old Pérouges lured weavers, potters, cabinet makers, and other craftsmen to build shops along the old streets. A few wealthy investors restored handsome merchants' homes with their beamed and sculpted ceilings, huge fireplaces, and immense rooms once covered with frescoes.

Today you will walk narrow, sloping, Medieval streets with rain channels down the center, where once only people of a certain importance could pass under the jutting eaves of houses to keep themselves dry.

It is possible to spend a night in the past here while enjoying the amenities of the present, at **Ostellerie du Vieux Pérouges**, a cozy inn with 25 rooms and an excellent kitchen.

VIENNE

Since the halcyon days between the World Wars, gourmets and gourmands alike have paraded in pilgrimage to a fairly nondescript (except for its Roman ruins) town on the left bank of the Rhône south of Lyon, Vienne. From presidents of the République to wine and food writers, from League of Nations delegates to merchant princes, they have appeared in the pretty little park and at the door of La Pyramide, that "gastronomic temple" once without peer in France or anywhere.

Pyramide (named for a Roman marble that stood in the center of the fourth-century circus) was the inspired creation of Fernand Point, the now legendary super-chef who was considered the foremost restaurateur in the world when he died in 1956 at the age of 57. One of his three Michelin stars faded with him (as is Michelin's practice when a great, presumably irreplaceable, chef dies). Wonder of wonders: Maintained by Point's crew and his admirable wife Marie-Louise ("Mado"), Pyramide quickly regained its third star, under the name Chez Point.

Madame Point died in July 1986, and the three-star rating was again reduced to the two it has today. Last June **Chez Point-Pyramide** was razed, but it has just reopened in a new home on the old site, and with the same chef and staff. Some time in 1989 it will be joined by a 30-room luxury hotel with reasonable rates.

The **cathedral of St-Maurice** (honoring a soldier-saint supposedly martyred nearby in the third century) is notable chiefly for its portal sculptures, long nave, and marvelous capital carvings. Collectors of antiquities will take time also for the **church** and **cloister** of **St-André-le-Bas** and the former **church of St-Pierre**, which today houses a lapidary museum.

Roman Vienne

Half a century before Caesar conquered Gaul, Vienne was established as the capital of the tribal Allobroges; under the Romans, the city preceded Lyon as a metropolis and was the home of such magnificent monuments and residences that the poet Martial dubbed it "Vienne the Beautiful."

Among the relics of Roman Vienne, the **Temple d'Auguste et de Livie** is the grandest, somewhat reminiscent of the Maison Carrée in Nîmes and about its equal in size. Built during the reign of Augustus, it has undergone several permutations, serving as church, Jacobin headquarters during the Revolution, a Temple of Reason, a museum, and a library. It regained its original look in the 19th century.

The **Roman theater**, abandoned as long ago as the fourth century under Emperor Constantine, underwent archaeological work in 1922 and has been returned to an excellent condition. It ranks among the largest theaters of Gaul, and is only slightly smaller in diameter than the Theater of Marcellus in Rome. Productions are still staged here in summer.

Even more interesting to those who enjoy evidences of daily life in past ages, the towns of **St-Romain-en-Gal** and **Ste-Colombe** have been unearthed across the river from Vienne.

St-Romain shows off superb mosaics (in the little museum), a marketplace, warehouses in which dyeing and tanning vessels remain, baths, and sewers. Ste-Colombe was the site of giant baths, palaces, and fine residences.

South of Vienne

From Condrieu, 40 km (27 miles) south of Lyon and south of Vienne, a remarkable route wiggles west along the Crêt de l'Oeillon (splendid views over the mountains and valleys of the Rhône country) to **Mont-Pilat** and **Gouffre d'Enfer** (*enfer* is hell—here an impressive dam site at the end of a rocky, narrow gorge involving a healthful hike) and to the hill hamlet of **Rochetaillée**, with its feudal château ruins.

The end of this particular road comes at St-Etienne, a large industrial town from which you may continue west or cut back to the Rhône route via Annonay and Tournon. Continuing south along the Rhône river from Vienne will bring you to Orange, the Rhône wine country, and Provence, all covered in a later chapter.

In Condrieu, you should plan to stop at **Le Beau Rivage et l'Hermitage du Rhône,** with 26 rooms and four apartments overlooking the river. The lovely terrace restaurant is in fact right on the Rhône, and the kitchen ranks high among those in France.

GETTING AROUND

From Paris, Autoroute A 6 cruises southeast to Beaune, with a cutoff via A 38 to Dijon, and continues via Chalon-sur-Saône and Mâcon to Lyon; A 7 continues to Provence. As usual, the back roads are slower and reveal more of the countryside.

Dijon has no international airport and no regularly scheduled air service; Lyon's Satolas Airport receives flights from Paris and other cities via Air Inter; from Avignon via Air Jet; from Limoges via Air Limousin; from various airports in Southern France, Italy, and Spain via Air Littoral; from Brittany and Normandy via Brit Air; from Clermont-Ferrand and Angoulême via Compagnie Languedoc.

The TGVs (high-speed trains) cover Burgundy, with direct service from Paris to Dijon, Montbard, Beaune, and Chalon-sur-Saône. The train for Lyon also stops at Le Creusot and Mâcon-Loché stations. TGV trains from Besançon and Lausanne, Switzerland, provide service to Dijon, while TGVs from Savoy and Geneva stop at Mâcon-Loché. These swift services are complemented by regular rail services from cities throughout Europe.

In September 1983 the futuristic railway station Lyon Part-Dieu opened to receive new TGV lines that now make the Paris-Lyon run in two hours. Lille-Lyon service, bypassing Paris, runs once daily.

Several companies operate luxury **Burgundy canal cruise-barges,** including Horizon Cruises (which also arranges barge-balloon trips and boat charters; contact Hemphill Harris, 16000 Ventura Blvd., Suite 200, Encino, CA 91436); Abercrombie and Kent (P.O. Box 305, Oak Park, IL 60303 or Sloane Square House, Holbein Place,

London SW1 W8NS); Continental Waterways (11 Beacon St., Boston, MA 02108); Salt & Pepper Tours (310 Madison Ave., Rm. 1821, New York, NY 10017); Floating Through Europe (271 Madison Ave., New York, NY 10016); Quiztour (19, rue d'Athènes, 75009 Paris); Le Duc de Bourgogne (Port de Plaisance, 21000 Dijon); Pro Aqua, Port de Plaisance (quai St-Martin, 89000 Auxerre); and Locaboat Plaisance (quai du Port-au-Bois, 89300 Joigny). Inquire at any regional tourist office for information on short-term boat rentals for four to 12 passengers.

In addition to Horizon Cruises' cruise-ballooning packages, **ballooning in Burgundy** may be arranged through the Bombard Society (6727 Curran St., McLean, VA 22101—Bombard is the operator for Horizon as well); Château Laborde (21200 Meursanges-par-Beaune); and Air Escargot (Remigy, 71150 Chagny).

City tours, wine tours, gastronomic outings, and float and barge trips throughout the area may be booked through regional tourist offices. Several organizations arrange horseback and covered-wagon trips for a day, weekend, or longer, as well as hiking and bicycling trips. A major U.S. operator of bicycling excursions in Burgundy is Progressive Travels, Ltd., P.O. Box 775164, Steamboat Springs, CO 80477.

Automobile tourists interested in vineyards, architecture, and markets may obtain brochures outlining routes at regional tourism offices in major cities.

ACCOMMODATIONS REFERENCE

▶ **Abbaye St-Michel.** Rue St-Michel, 89700 **Tonnerre.** Tel: 86-55-05-99; Telex: 801356; in U.S., (212) 696-1323.

▶ **Alain Chapel.** 01390 **Mionnay-St-André-de-Corcy.** Tel: 78-91-82-02; Telex, 305605; in U.S., (212) 696-1323.

▶ **Le Beau Rivage et l'Hermitage du Rhône.** 2, rue du Beau Rivage, 69420 **Condrieu.** Tel: 74-59-52-24; Telex: 308946; in U.S., (212) 696-1323.

▶ **Belle Epoque.** 15, faubourg Bretonnière, 21200 **Beaune.** Tel: 80-24-66-15.

▶ **Bordeaux et Parc.** 1, rue du Bélier, 69002 **Lyon.** Tel: 78-37-58-73; Telex: 330355.

▶ **Hôtel Bourgogne.** Place de l'Abbaye, 71250 **Cluny.** Tel: 85-59-00-58.

▶ **Central Urbis.** 3, place de la Grangier, 21000 **Dijon.** Tel: 80-30-44-00.

▶ **Le Cep.** 27, rue Maufoux, 21200 **Beaune.** Tel: 80-22-

35-48; Telex: 351256; in U.S., (212) 477-1600 or (800) 223-1510.

▶ **Chapeau Rouge.** 5, rue Michelet, 21000 **Dijon.** Tel: 80-30-28-10; in U.S., (800) 528-1234 or (800) 334-7234; in Canada, (416) 674-3400 or (800) 528-1234; in U.K., (01) 541-0033; in Australia, (02) 438-4733.

▶ **Chapon Fin et Restaurant Paul Blanc.** 01140 **Thoissey.** Tel: 74-04-04-74; in U.S., (212) 696-1323. Madame Paul Blanc and her family oversee this elegant, 25-room inn; one-star cuisine. It's conveniently located for visits to Cluny, Tournus, Mâcon, Bourg-en-Bresse.

▶ **Château d'Igé.** Igé 71960 **Pierreclos.** Tel: 85-33-33-99; in U.S., (212) 696-1323.

▶ **Hôtel de la Cloche.** 14, place Darcy, 21000 **Dijon.** Tel: 80-30-12-32; in U.S., (212) 477-1600 or (800) 223-1510.

▶ **Hostellerie des Clos.** 89800 **Chablis.** Tel: 86-42-10-63.

▶ **Côte d'Or.** Rue Ronot, 21400 **Châtillon-sur-Seine.** Tel: 80-91-13-29.

▶ **Côte d'Or et Résidence.** 2, rue Argentine, 21210 **Saulieu.** Tel: 80-64-07-66.

▶ **A la Côte St-Jacques et la Résidence.** 14, faubourg de Paris, 89300 **Joigny.** Tel: 86-62-09-70; Telex: 801458.

▶ **La Cour des Loges.** 6, rue du Boeuf, 69005 **Lyon.** Tel: 78-42-75-75; Telex: 330831.

▶ **Ermitage de Corton.** Route de Dijon, 21200 **Beaune Nord.** Tel: 80-22-05-28.

▶ **Espérance.** St-Père 89450 **Vézelay** (3 km/2 miles southeast of Vézelay). Tel: 86-33-20-45.

▶ **Frantel.** 129, rue Servient, 69003 **Lyon.** Tel: 78-62-94-12; in U.S., (212) 757-6500/01 or (800) 223-9862; in U.K., (01) 621-1962.

▶ **Grand Hôtel Concorde.** 11, rue Grolée, 69002 **Lyon.** Tel: 78-42-56-21; Telex: 330244; in U.S., (212) 247-7950 or (800) 344-1212; in Australia, (02) 290-3033.

▶ **Hôtel de Greuze.** 5, rue A.-Thibaudet, 71700 **Tournus.** Tel: 85-40-77-77.

▶ **Lameloise.** Place d'Armes, 71150 **Chagny.** Tel: 85-87-08-85; Telex: 801086.

▶ **Hôtel Le Maxime.** 2, quai de la Marine, 89000 **Auxerre.** Tel: 86-52-14-19.

▶ **Méridien.** B.P. 128, 69125 **Lyon-Satolas Aéroport.** Tel: 78-71-91-61; in U.S., (212) 265-4494 or (800) 543-4300; in Canada, (416) 598-3838 or (800) 543-4300; in U.K., (01) 439-1244; in Australia, (02) 235-1174.

▶ **Novotel Lyon-Nord.** Autoroute A 6, Porte-de-Lyon,

69570 **Dardilly**. Tel: 78-35-13-41; in U.S., (800) 221-4542; in Canada, (800) 221-5452; in U.K., (01) 724-1000; in Australia, (02) 246-5955.

▶ **Du Parc**. 49, cours du Parc, 21000 **Dijon**. Tel: 80-65-18-41.

▶ **Hôtel de la Poste**. 1, boulevard Clémenceau, 21200 **Beaune**. Tel: 80-22-08-11; Telex: 350982; in U.S., (212) 477-1600 or (800) 223-1510.

▶ **La Poste et Lion d'Or**. 89450 **Vézelay**. Tel: 86-33-21-23; in U.S., (212) 477-1600 or (800) 223-1510.

▶ **Le Rempart**. 2, avenue Gambetta, 71700 **Tournus**. Tel: 85-51-10-56; Telex: 351019.

▶ **Royal**. 20, place Bellecour, 69002 **Lyon**. Tel: 78-37-57-31; in U.S., (800) 528-1234 or (800) 334-7234; in Canada, (416) 674-3400 or (800) 528-1234; in U.K., (01) 541-0033; in Australia, (02) 438-4733.

▶ **Sofitel**. 20, quai Gailleton, 69002 **Lyon**. Tel: 78-42-72-50; in U.S., (212) 354-3722 or (800) 221-4542; in Canada, (800) 354-3722; in U.K., (01) 724-1000; in Australia, (02) 264-5955.

▶ **Terminus Perrache**. 12, cours de Verdun, 69002 **Lyon**. Tel: 78-37-58-11.

▶ **Hôtel Ursulines**. 14, rue Rivault, 71400 **Autun**. Tel: 85-52-68-00.

▶ **Ostellerie du Vieux Pérouges**. 01800 **Pérouges**. Tel: 74-61-00-88; in U.S., (212) 477-1600 or (800) 223-1510.

THE SAVOY AND THE FRENCH ALPS

By Jonathan Weber

Jonathan Weber is a Senior Editor of World Link *magazine in Geneva. A former correspondent for Fairchild Publications, his articles have also appeared in the* International Herald Tribune, *Paris's* Passion *magazine, and other publications.*

For the sports enthusiast or nature lover, there's no place in France quite like the French Alps. Foreign visitors and Frenchmen alike flock to the Alps to take advantage of an extensive array of outdoor recreational activities or simply to contemplate mountain vistas, rushing streams, and wildflowers. But the region, proud of its independent history yet comfortable in its Frenchness, is more than an outdoor playground. It is a prosperous area rich in historical and cultural diversions and home to the lively small cities of Annecy, Chambéry, and Grenoble.

MAJOR INTEREST

Skiing (December–April)
Hiking (July–August)
Mont Blanc
National and regional natural parks
Cirque du Fer à Cheval
Notre-Dame-de-Toute-Grâce (the church at Plateau d'Assy)

The Abbaye de Hautecombe
The Vauban fortifications at Briançon

Chambéry
The Old City

Annecy
The Old City
Sights relating to Saint François de Sales
Sailing and swimming

Grenoble
The Bastille
Musée Dauphinoise
Musée des Beaux-Arts

Life in the Alps has always had a seasonal quality. In pre-tourist times herds of cows and goats moved up to high Alpine meadows for the summer grazing and re-treated to the valleys before the first autumn snowfalls. Nowadays the ebb and flow of vacationers marks the change of seasons here. Winter brings skiers to the two breeds of ski resorts: the mountain-village-turned-mod-ern-recreational-type (Megève, Chamonix, Morzine, Val-d'Isère), and the integrated vacation complex built from scratch in virgin snowfields (Tignes, Courchevel, La Plagne, Flaine, Avoriaz).

Summertime activities are more varied. The ski towns offer golf, tennis, and swimming, and so do the many lakeside villages and campgrounds. Hikers can take advan-tage of a well-organized network of trails and mountain shelters that allow the well provisioned to stay in the wild for days or even weeks on end. Those who prefer more unusual sports can try rock-climbing, hang gliding, sail-ing, and spelunking. Or, those who think strenuous activi-ties are for the birds can head for Annecy, Chambéry, and Grenoble to shop, visit museums and churches, or just sit in cafés.

The French Alps stretch from north to south along the Italian border, bounded by Lac Léman and Switzerland to the north and the Mediterranean foothills to the south. While the area is mountainous, not all its mountains are created equal. The rugged 10,000- to 14,000-foot-high peaks around Mont Blanc and Ecrins contrast sharply with the gentler mountains near Annecy and Lac Léman and the sunnier slopes south of Grenoble.

Water is everywhere here. The Isère, the Arve, the

Durance, and the Arc rivers cut deep ravines through the mountains, making the region accessible to trains and cars. The lakes of Léman, Annecy, and Bourget are popular with weekend sailors and big enough for steamships. Water cascades down the spectacular falls at Cirque du Fer-à-Cheval and forms icy white glaciers on Mont Blanc; medicinal springs soothe the infirm at Aix-les-Bains and St-Gervais-les-Bains, and mineral water is bottled and sold at Evian-les-Bains.

A great deal of water also sits behind dams waiting to pass through hydro-electric power turbines. This "white oil" fueled a tardy 19th-century industrial revolution in the Alps, as energy-intensive industries such as chemicals and metallurgy sought out cheap sources of electricity. While many of these businesses have since migrated elsewhere or succumbed to deindustrialization, enough remain to create a discouragingly thick smog in some of the major river valleys. This is not plastic vacation paradise. Rather, it is a prosperous and economically diverse area with a growing population. Local industries include the making of wine and cheese in the hills, aluminum and detergent in the valleys, and everything from microchips to church bells in the larger towns. For better or worse, this once-isolated region is now irrevocably integrated into modern France.

Moreover, the mountains look and feel lived-in, and the remote Alpine village, untouched by the modern world, is almost an item of history. All this is to say that those seeking a North American-style wilderness in the Alps are likely to be disappointed. What the Alpine towns lack in quaintness, however, they possess in authenticity.

Historically, the French Alps were divided into two areas: the Savoy to the north and the Dauphiné to the south. The **Savoy**, which occupies the modern administrative departments of the Savoie and the Haute Savoie, was a proud and powerful independent kingdom. It didn't become part of France until 1859, making it the last region to join the nation. The **Dauphiné**, which includes the departments of Isère, Haute Alpes, and Drôme, has been part of France since 1349. While both areas are now firmly French, they retain a subtle kinship not only with one another but with their neighbors across the border; the local cuisine, featuring fondue, dried meats, and a tableside barbecue called *braserade,* seems to be more Swiss than French. And a sense of individualism and self-reliance pervades the culture and traditions of the natives.

Savoy and the French Alps

0   miles   30

0   kilometers   40

To Dijon

Ge

A6

Lyon

Abbe de
Hautecombe

Lac D'A

A41

Lac du
Bourg

Aix-les-Bains

Chambéry

Challes-les-Eaux

D92

Rhone

A7

DAUPHINE

Isère

Grenoble

Gorges
de la Bourne

l'Alpe d'H

Drac

Monêtier-les

Parc Régional
du Vercors

Drôme

Parc Ne
des E

Vallée de la Drôme

N

To Avignon

Gap

N9

Serres-Ponçon

To Nice, Marseilles

THE SAVOY

The early history of the Savoy hardly hints at its later glory. Rome wrested the region from the Celtic Allobroges tribe—who had overrun it in the sixth century B.C.—in 121 B.C. and attached it to the province of Narbonne. It wasn't until the first century A.D. that Rome fully subjugated Savoy. Although settlements sprouted along the Roman road linking Milan and Vienna—notably at Aime and Annecy—no significant ruins from this period remain. In the fifth century, as Christianity became institutionalized, a group of Burgundians migrated here and named the region Savoy from the French *pays des sapins,* or "fir-tree country." The area thus became part of the kingdom of Burgundy, a powerful political entity in France.

The House of Savoy is the oldest sovereign family in Europe. It was founded at the beginning of the 11th century by Count Maurienne Humbert aux Blanches Mains ("white hands"), who received title to the region in exchange for supporting Conrad le Salique, the Holy Roman Emperor. His new kingdom held control of the Alpine passes to Italy and to the Germanic territories to the east and thus had great geopolitical importance. The later Dukes of Savoy fully exploited their position as "porters of the Alps," and many kings were forced to pay humiliating tribute for the right to pass. The kingdom's golden era came in the 14th century when the three Amadeuses—all powerful rulers of the family—extended their domain to Nice, the Jura, Piemonte, and Geneva. At various times Savoy also controlled large chunks of what are now Italy and Switzerland as well as the Mediterranean island of Sardinia. Repeated French invasions—in 1536, in the 17th century (three times), in 1742, and again in 1792—failed to bring Savoy under the control of Paris. But when the Savoy finally joined France, it did so with some relief; an 1860 plebescite showed 130,533 votes in favor of the union and just 235 against.

Chambéry

As the historic capital of the Savoy, Chambéry's fortunes followed those of the House of Savoy. Though it has lost its one-time prominence, the city remains a governmental center. The Château, seat of the Dukes of Savoy, is now occupied by the prefecture and the regional council of Savoie. Today, Chambéry remains a stately but animated town. Nearly all the interesting sites lie in the compact Old City; the tourist office, located on the tree-lined boulevard de la Colonne, is exceptionally helpful in directing visitors to them. There are not many hotels in Chambéry, so it's a good idea to book ahead in summer. The **Grand Hôtel Ducs de Savoie**, across from the railroad station, is a grandly old-fashioned hotel. Its only drawback is the absence of a restaurant. **Les Princes**, on rue de Boigne, is a bit less expensive, and it has a great location and a fine restaurant, which more than compensate for the small rooms.

The **Château** dominates the town. It is actually a collection of buildings on a low, walled hilltop. Many of the original 14th-century structures burned down in the 18th century, and the massive building that now houses the prefecture was erected then. The church, the dungeon, and the treasure tower, however, retain their original Medieval lines. The grounds make for a pleasant walk, but really to see the place the guided tour is a necessity.

Chambéry's **Old City** has numerous small architectural delights in its archways and doorways and well-proportioned squares. On the festive rue Croix-d'Or, the ground floors of beautiful old houses have been converted to shops. The rue de Boigne is a street of grand façades and Italianate porticoes, and it is lined with pastry and candy shops that serve tea. The 15th- to 16th-century cathedral of St-François-de-Sales houses some interesting religious art; the cathedral square is home to fine art galleries. At the intersection of the rue de Boigne and the boulevard de la Colonne lies the slightly bizarre elephant fountain, erected in 1838 in memory of Generale Comte de Boigne's trip to India. It has become, to the chagrin of many residents, one of the most popular monuments in town. At the edge of the Old City is the new cultural center, called L'Espace Malraux, designed by the prominent young Swiss architect Mario Botta and featuring a cinema, a concert hall, and meeting rooms. It is complemented nicely by the Caserne Curial next door, a huge, square army barracks that has been transformed into a tasteful shopping center that should please even the most ardent mall-hater. For a gift of Chambéry origin, try the local chocolate or the famous Opinel knives, available anywhere in town. Another alternative is a bottle of Vermouth. Chambéry has long been a center of Vermouth making, and the distilleries Dolin, on avenue de Grand Ariétaz, and Routin, on rue Emile Romanet, offer guided tours on request (write or call in advance).

For a nice excursion from Chambéry—and a good historical complement to the Château—visit the **Abbaye de Hautecombe**, a beautiful lakeside monastery where the Dukes of Savoy are buried. Take N 201 25 km (15 miles) north to Aix-les-Bains, a Victorian spa town that has lost much of its luster, and then either follow the *tour du lac* around Lac du Bourget or take the boat (summer only) from the main port to the abbey. The recorded tour of the church and tombs is in French, but a free booklet gives a good English translation. There is also a museum with displays on the life and history of the abbey. Hautecombe is still used as a burial place—Umberto II, the last king of Italy, was buried here in 1983—but the Benedictine monks fled the grounds just last year in the face of the tourist invasion.

Aix-les-Bains has been popular with tourists since the Romans began coming here to take the cure in its thermal baths. The **Thermes Nationaux**, just east of the station overlooking the town and the lake, are open all year. The modern facilities were built atop the old Roman baths, the ruins of which are still visible in the cellar. The **Arc de Campanus** and the **Temple de Diane**, both just a stone's throw from the station, are the most significant Roman ruins in the Savoy. Aix also has a beautiful lakefront promenade, several fine parks, and many beautiful Victorian buildings. In fact, the beauty of the place inspired the poet Alphonse de Lamartine both to fall in love and to write some of his finest verse here. The **Musée du Docteur-Faure**, next to the Thermes, houses a fine collection of pre-Impressionist art.

Annecy

If Chambéry is the historic capital of the Savoy, Annecy is its spiritual capital. It was the home of Saint François de Sales, the patron saint of arts and letters, and when Geneva succumbed to the Reformation in the 16th century, Annecy became a regional capital. Magnificently situated on the Lac d'Annecy across from imposing peaks, Annecy today is a prosperous and growing city that has become an extremely popular vacation spot.

Its **Old City** is almost too charming: 17th-century buildings painted in pastel oranges and reds line the trickling rivers and canals, and an excellent flea market takes over the streets and squares on the last Saturday of every month. Annecy bustles with touristy shops and restaurants, and it is necessary to be careful about what you buy and where you eat. Try the **Garcin**, at 11, rue Pâquier, for inexpensive, straightforward French food, or the **Auberge du Lyonnais**, at 9, rue de la République, for a moderately priced meal, or the **Auberge de l'Eridan**, 7, avenue de Chavoires, if you're feeling more upscale.

Annecy's Château, beautifully restored after hundreds of years of abandonment, sits on a small hill above the Old City and provides an excellent view. Along the lakefront are the public gardens and the refreshingly large and informal (for France) Parc du Pâquier. The tourist office is in the Centre Bonlieu, a large modern building across from the park; it won't provide much help with local history, but it's a good place to find out about concerts, boat rentals, and hiking in the nearby mountains.

Saint François de Sales is the undisputed local hero. Born to a prominent Savoyard family in 1567, he studied law in Paris but gave up a promising political career at age 26 to take the vows. Named head of the cathedral of St-Pierre, a large but unremarkable church in the center of the Old City, Saint François led a bitter struggle against Calvinism in the region. His oratory was said to be "soft as honey" and was so persuasive that his fame spread throughout France. In 1606 he joined the renowned lawyer Antoine Favre in founding the Académie Florimontane, one of the earliest literary societies in Europe. It is still headquartered at 18, rue Ste-Clair, its original location.

In 1608, while living in the beautiful Lambert house at 15, rue Jean-Jacques Rousseau, Saint François wrote *Introduction to the Devoted Life,* a spiritual treatise that was the 17th-century equivalent of a best seller. He was also the sponsor of the first convent in the region devoted to the Virgin and was canonized in 1665 (at the church that bears his name just across from the *Mairie*) 43 years after his death. His remains lie at the basilica of the Visitation, an agreeable 20th-century structure just south of the Old City.

Those who like their historical figures a little more profane might want to pay homage to the writer and philosopher Jean-Jacques Rousseau, who fled to Annecy from his native Geneva in 1728. Madame Louise-Eléonore de Warens took the young refugee in, and they began their idyllic liaison. A bust of Rousseau stands on the site of the former de Warens house in the courtyard of the old Episcopal palace.

The **Lac d'Annecy** is unequivocally beautiful; a drive around it makes a good afternoon excursion. The tranquil **St-Germain l'Hermitage**, where Saint François de Sales spent his last days, lies about 16 km (10 miles) around the north end of the lake, off Route D 42. There's a delightful little chapel here and a splendid view of the lake. Just above the church is a nice meadow for picnicking. If you're feeling less rustic, continue up the road to the Col de la Forclaz and have lunch on the terrace of the **La Pricaz** while you watch hang gliders swoop off the ramp next to the restaurant. The drive back down toward the lower lake and Albertville is harrowing but pretty.

On the lake road, D 909A, just south of the turnoff for Route D 42, lies the charming port town of Talloires, where there are two excellent inns. The **Auberge du Père Bise** has 25 rooms, lovely grounds, and one of the most prestigious restaurants in France; it is essential to make reservations far in advance. The **Abbaye** occupies a 17th-century abbey. Its antique- and tapestry-filled rooms are equaled only by the stunning lakeside location and excellent dining room.

The Countryside

Evian-les-Bains, a dignified old spa town on Lac Léman, is most appealing to gamblers, connoisseurs of fine hotels, and those who intend to take the (cold) waters. But for anyone coming from Switzerland (by lake steamer, for example), it's also a good starting point for a summertime driving tour of the Haute Savoie. Begin on D 902 toward Morzine, which passes through the spectacular **Gorges du Pont du Diable** (Devil's Bridge); you can descend for a close look in summers.

From Morzine, Route D 354 meanders over the mountains toward Samoëns, past the ski trails of Les Gets, providing superb vistas and many good opportunities for walking. **Samoëns** is a perfectly tended village of fewer than 2,000 inhabitants. It is well worth a stop, if only for the **Jaysinia**, a remarkable botanic garden devoted to Alpine plants from around the globe. It was the gift of Marie-Louise Juy, a local shepherdess who married a peddler named Ernest Cognacq. Together they made good and founded the Parisian department store La Samaritaine.

From Samoëns, it's just a 20-minute drive up to **Cirque du Fer à Cheval**. The Cirque is a flat valley floor surrounded by a near-perfect semicircle of towering cliff walls and angular peaks, the highest of which sit directly on the border with Switzerland. In spring and early summer, an incredible array of some 30 waterfalls spills down the mountains. Hiking opportunities range from a quick jaunt up to one of the waterfalls to a 12-hour trek over the mountains to Chamonix. Bicycles are for rent next to the welcome center.

South of the road leading into the Cirque is the Maison de la Reserve at **Sixt-Fer-à-Cheval**. It's open at least a few hours a day all year round and is a friendly place that offers good information on the flora and fauna of the nearby nature reserve. Sixt itself is a pleasant, low-key town and a good base for serious exploration of the area. Unfortunately, the only direct route from Sixt to Chamonix is on foot. By car, it's necessary to backtrack through Samoëns to Cluses and take the Autoroute.

In the spa town of Plateau d'Assy, on the way to Chamonix about 20 minutes off the Autoroute north of Fayet, is **Notre-Dame-de-Toute-Grâce**, a controversial and fascinating church. Begun in 1937 and consecrated in 1950, the church features the work of a remarkable array of prominent 20th-century artists. The huge mosaic on the front of the building is by Fernand Léger, the painting of Saint François de Sales is by Pierre Bonnard and that of Saint Dominique is by Henri Matisse, the spectacular tapestry over the altar is by Jean Lurçat, and the ceramic just to the right of the entrance (now being restored) is by Marc Chagall. There are sculptures by Jacques Lipchitz and Germaine Richier, and wood carvings by the Savoyard artist Demaison. The overall effect is sacrilegious for some—in part because it is dedicated to the Virgin and her powers of comforting the afflicted (this is a spa town, remember)—but wonderful for lovers of modern art. Be sure to see the crypt also (entrance in the back).

The Chamonix-Mont Blanc area is a hiker's paradise, a fact not lost on Europe's hoards of hikers. The resulting overcrowding would almost make it a destination worth skipping were not **Mont Blanc** such a truly grand and powerful sight. You'll need a guide to climb the glacier-covered peak itself, but many easier walks yield great views of the massive mountain. If you want to save your strength, take a ski lift up one of the mountains and then walk from there. The tourist office, located near the church and the *Mairie* in the old town square at Chamonix, has hiking information.

The town of **Chamonix** today may make you wish you'd been there 30 years ago; its charms are somewhat swamped by new development and tourists. The town claims to be the world capital of mountaineering, and its guide school is renowned and exclusive; only recently has the school admitted members not born in Chamonix. The small mountaineering museum, with its display of primitive early equipment, shows just how brave the early climbers were.

Chamonix has no shortage of restaurants; the best is **Albert Ier**, at 119, impasse du Montenvers. It is especially pleasant in the summer, when dinner is served in the garden. The address is also home to a friendly family hotel with moderately priced rooms; ask for one with a view of the mountains. A more expensive choice is the **Auberge du Bois Prin**, just outside of the center of town in les Moussoux.

From Chamonix take N 212 south through the resorts of St-Gervais-les-Bains and Megève and the pleasant Gorges de l'Arly. A turn to the west at Ugine will take you back toward Annecy, while continuing south on N 212 will bring you to Albertville. This ugly industrial town has nothing to recommend it except its convenient location at a train and road intersection; this position is what led organizers to choose Albertville as host of the 1992 Winter Olympic Games, although the town itself is not a sports center. Most of the Olympic events will be scattered throughout the numerous ski resorts within easy reach. Those looking for lodging in Albertville might try the **Million**, the nicest hotel in town, or the **Berjann**. The restaurant at the Million is one of the region's finest.

From Albertville, a detour up D 925 to the northeast leads through the charming **Beaufort** region, famous for an excellent cheese made there. The cheese factory at Beaufort offers tours. Beaufort is also a good spot to buy local handicrafts, such as wooden household items, and pewter mugs and plates. The vacation boom has sideswiped this region (although the hydroelectric boom hit it full force), so it's a bit calmer than some of the neighboring areas.

The Isère valley south of Albertville, served by road and rail, is the access route to some of Europe's best ski stations, including Courchevel, Méribel, Val Thorens, La Plagne, Les Arcs, Tignes, and Val-d'Isère. The town of

Aime has a first-rate 11th-century Romanesque church and an excellent roadside restaurant, complete with ancient vaulted ceiling, called **L'Atre**. At Bourg-St-Maurice, where the rail line terminates, you can head by car toward Italy over Col du Petit St-Bernard (where Hannibal is supposed to have made his fateful crossing of the Alps), or toward Val-d'Isère, the 8,900-foot-high Col d'Isèran, and the **Parc National de la Vanoise**. The park, in the remotest part of the Savoy, has some 300 miles of hiking paths. You can enter the park from almost any of the towns along D 902 out of Val-d'Isère or from N 6 south of the park. The tourist offices at Modane, Val-d'Isère, and Bourg-St-Maurice are helpful, as is the Maison du Parc in Chambéry.

Skiing

Skiing in the French Alps is a serious business: The resorts are huge and well equipped, and though they tend to lack charm, they provide an endless variety of slopes. Unlike American ski centers, they are usually not organized around a single base lodge. Instead, the newer stations have multiple clusters of apartments, shops, hotels, and concessions, and ski lifts and restaurants are strewn far and wide across the massive, treeless expanses of snow. The modern stations were developed primarily as real-estate projects and have acres of cheap, small apartments owned by middle-class families. Most visitors rent these apartments when they come to the resorts for stays of more than a weekend; prices start at about $300 for a studio during a non-holiday week. Bookings for both apartments and hotels can be made easily through the tourist offices at the individual resorts.

Typical of the newer resorts are Courchevel, Méribel, and Val-Thorens, which are linked by ski lifts and together make up an area called **Les Trois Vallées**. Courchevel is for the ultra-chic (it boasts many luxury hotels, the fanciest being the new **Byblos des Neiges**), while Méribel caters to families and attracts many British visitors; both have skiing to suit every taste. Val-Thorens has extensive off-trail skiing possibilities and exceptional high-altitude runs, which allow for summer skiing.

La Plagne is another large, modern resort, especially good for beginning and intermediate skiers. Experts might be frustrated by the abundance of broad, gentle trails; only the spectacular runs from the Bellecôte glacier offer a real challenge. La Plagne also has limited summer skiing. Neighboring **Les Arcs**, accessible by cable car from Bourg-St-Maurice, has 73 ski lifts and attracts many international visitors.

Farther up the Isère valley, Val-d'Isère and Tignes are the best destinations for accomplished skiers. The hometown of Olympic skiing champion Jean-Claude Killy, **Val-d'Isère** is a real village that existed long before the skiing boom, and its facilities are second to none. The mountains above Val-d'Isère are very high and offer many harrowing expert trails and superb off-trail skiing. **Tignes**, which shares much of the same skiing domain, is a new resort complex several miles away. Both are popular with a young, fast crowd, drawn in part by the hopping nightlife in Val-d'Isère.

Chamonix, a family resort in the summer, becomes younger and more hip during the ski season. The ski installations are spread across the valley and are not linked with one another, so it's necessary to choose your destination carefully according to your aptitude; Chamonix, therefore, is not ideal for a group including both expert and novice skiers. **Les Grands Montets** at Argentière, up the valley from Chamonix, has some of the best ski slopes in the Alps.

For a slightly different flavor, try the domain called **Les Portes du Soleil**, on the Swiss border in the northeast corner of the Haute Savoie. It centers on **Avoriaz**, a modern resort done with more taste than some others, and includes a string of nine small ski centers, some in France and some in Switzerland. Except at Avoriaz itself, the lift installations are less comprehensive than elsewhere. Connections between the different ski areas are not always easy, but the smaller villages are pleasantly low-key. As its name indicates, the region is very sunny, but it is not especially high and is best for intermediate skiers.

In the southern Alps, the biggest ski centers are L'Alpe d'Huez and Les Deux-Alpes. **L'Alpe d'Huez** boasts a fine array of long, uncrowded, high-altitude expert trails, as well as a good beginners' area. **Les Deux-Alpes**, also quite high, has summer skiing.

The ski season extends from December to April, but good snow is not assured outside of January, February, and March; at the beginning and end of the season, try to head for the higher altitudes. If at all possible, avoid the Christmas holidays and mid-February, when French schools take their winter break. Weekend ski traffic can be horrendous, especially along the Isère valley. The only way to avoid it is to travel late at night.

THE DAUPHINE

Despite the extensive reach of the Savoyard empire, it never succeeded in absorbing the Dauphiné to the immediate south. The Dauphiné was an independent feudal kingdom from the early 11th century until 1349, when the mercurial King Humbert II, bankrupt after the Crusades, sold his domain to Philippe VI of France. This is not to say that the Dauphiné was a peaceful place. Fierce wars with the Italian kingdoms from 1494–1515 brought Pierre Terrail Bayard, the *chevalier sans peur et sans reproche* ("the knight without fear and without faults"), to prominence as lieutenant-general of the Dauphiné. Religious wars racked the region in the second half of the 16th century, when the indomitable general and politician François de Lesdiguières ruled as a virtual viceroy. Later the Dauphiné was in the vanguard of the French Revolution; some say the revolution started with the "day of tiles" in 1788, when the Grenoble citizenry erected barricades and fought off royal troops with roof tiles in reaction to edicts from Louis XVI that threatened local sovereignty.

Grenoble

The history of the Dauphiné is inseparable from the history of Grenoble, a bustling and picturesque city at the junction of the Drac and Isère rivers. The Romans built an important fortified settlement here called Gratianopolis in honor of the emperor Gratian; from that came the name Grenoble. Today, Grenoble is a major regional capital with an important university, budding high-tech industry, and a solid but unimposing tourist infrastructure. It is also a good example of intelligent urban planning, with a sparkling downtown shopping district served by a new tram line, and a controlled urban sprawl.

While significantly larger than Annecy or Chambéry, Grenoble is still small enough to be easily navigated. A tranquil and elegant hotel is the **Park**, on the Parc Paul-Mistral near the Hôtel de Ville. Grenoble is an excellent place to get a reasonably priced top-flight meal. At **L'Escalier**, 6, place de Lavellette, old stone walls combine with ultra-contemporary furniture and fixtures to stunning effect; the atmosphere is informal, the clientele slightly yuppie, and the food excellent. Try tiny and friendly **A Ma Table**, at 92, cour Jacques-Jaurès, for fish specialties.

If you like to begin your sightseeing with a proper panorama, take the cable car from the riverbank north of the Old Town up to the **Bastille**, a set of early 19th-century fortifications perched on the big hill overlooking the city. On the Bastille, you can scramble around the chaotic collection of archways, stairways, and tunnels that once defended Grenoble against invasion from the north, then stroll back down to the city (cable-car tickets are one-way or round trip). On the way down, stop at the **Musée Dauphinoise**, located in an old cloister. The museum has a fascinating multimedia exhibit on the evolution of village life in the region, but no English translations are available. However, non-French speakers can still enjoy the paintings that evoke the mystical spirits of the mountains.

At the bottom of the hill is a pizzeria-lined quay, and just across the photogenic bridge is the **Old Town**. The Flamboyant Gothic building near the river is the late 15th-century Palais de Justice, home of the original Dauphinoise parliament. Across the place St-André to the right is the home of Lesdiguières, complete with a tower dating from the 14th century. The building now houses the Musée Stendhal, honoring the novelist (born Marie-Henri Beyle), who is one of the city's most famous sons.

A piece of the old Roman wall is visible near the garish Maison de Tourism. The 14th-century Tour d'Ile on the quai Jongkind is another interesting site, part of Grenoble's early fortifications. The **Musée des Beaux-Arts**, or Musée de la Peinture et de la Sculpture, facing the botanical gardens near place de Verdun, has one of France's better collections of contemporary art, and its classical collections are among the best to be found at a provincial museum.

Outside Grenoble, mountains spread out in every direction. To the southwest lies the regional park of **Vercors**, which, unlike the national parks, is relatively crowded and not very wild. The park offers courses on the natural features of the area and instruction in rock-climbing, spelunking, and cross-country skiing. The landscape here is gentler and lusher than in the High Alps; the **Gorges de la Bourne** is among the more dramatic gorges in the region.

East of Grenoble is high-mountain country, with several major ski stations (L'Alpe d'Huez, Les Deux-Alpes) and the national park of Ecrins, another high-mountain wilderness park with abundant hiking opportunities. Due south of Grenoble, Route N 85 leads toward Gap, following the route Napoléon took when he made his famous return from Elba. However, the highly touted Route Napoléon is actually just a road with an occasional incongruous statue of the general sitting in a field. It's a pretty ride, though, and a good route south to the Mediterranean coast (and therefore crowded in summer).

From Gap, if you're not heading for the sea, take N 94 or the train northeast to Briançon, which, at an elevation of 4,300 feet, is the highest town in France. You'll pass the Lac de Serre-Ponçon, which has an exceptionally pretty lakeside campground and a number of good picnic spots. **Briançon** is a spectacular, unsung little town set in a high mountain pass almost on the Italian border. Its strategic position explains the remarkable **fortifications**, a masterpiece of protection built by Louis XIV's famous engineer Vauban. The Old Town is surrounded by layered, jutting walls, and a string of nine forts lines ridges around the city. The defenses were put to their most serious test in 1815, when an Austro-Savoyard army, which had already seized most of the Dauphiné, laid seige to the town. Briançon held out against an attacking army 20 times as strong for four months, until the treaty of Paris was signed. Since then, it's been known as *"petit ville, grand renom"* ("little city, big reputation").

Founded as the Gallo-Roman settlement of Brigantium, Briançon has the feel of a place apart, and indeed its political history is unusual; it was long an autonomous semi-republic, called an *escarton,* which had purchased its right to self-government. Its pure air gave it a minor reputation as a spa; now Briançon is trying to build its tourist appeal with a new ski lift linking it to nearby ski resorts. If you're spending the night here, the **Vauban,** with its very friendly proprietor, is a good choice of hotel.

GETTING AROUND

Annecy, Chambéry, Grenoble, and Geneva are the gateways to the Alps. Frequent TGV service puts all four cities within three and a half hours of Paris by rail, and the highway connections are also good, if somewhat slower. It's not worth flying from Paris, but if you're starting from outside the country, Geneva, with its international airport, might be the best gateway. From Italy, the tunnels of Mont Blanc and Fréjus, as well as several seasonal mountain roads, provide auto access.

Despite occasional heavy traffic, the Alps are indisputably car country. Trains serve the major river valleys to Chamonix, Bourg-St-Maurice, and Briançon, and there are buses to the big resort towns, but unless you're headed for a single destination you'll be much better off driving yourself. The A 41 Autoroute provides the basic north-south link west of the mountains, and from there the well-engineered *Routes Nationales*—along with the A 40 Autoroute to Chamonix—bring you into the high country along the river valleys. Secondary roads follow all manner of improbable routes through the mountains, where the going tends to be slow but scenic. Outside of July and August, check with the tourist office before planning an elaborate touring itinerary; any route that doesn't involve extensive backtracking will cross mountain passes that are not open all year round. Tire chains are a good idea in winter even if you're sticking to the main roads, and they're equally advisable in spring and fall if you're planning any high-altitude routes. A word of warning: Something about the mountain air makes people drive like fools on the narrow, winding roads; about all you can do is remain calm.

The summer tourist season is short—essentially limited to July and August—and crowded. Hikers can get detailed information on trails and refuges from the Maison de la Randonée in Grenoble and from the various tourist offices mentioned above. Travel in the spring and fall is a mixed bag; there aren't many tourists, but many places are closed and the weather is fickle.

ACCOMMODATIONS REFERENCE

▶ **Abbaye.** Route du Port, 74290 **Talloires**. Tel: 50-60-77-33; Telex: 385307; in U.S., (212) 696-1323.

▶ **Albert Ier.** 119, impasse du Montenvers, 74400 **Chamonix**. Tel: 50-53-05-09; Telex: 380779; in U.S., (212) 477-1600 or (800) 223-1510.

▶ **La Berjann.** 33, route de Tours, 73200 **Albertville**. Tel: 79-32-47-88.

▶ **Auberge du Bois Prin.** Les Moussoux 74400 **Chamonix**. Tel: 50-53-33-51; in U.S., (212) 696-1323.

▶ **Byblos des Neiges.** Jardin Alpin, 73120 **Courchevel**. Tel: 79-08-12-12; Telex: 980580; in U.S., (212) 477-1600 or (800) 223-1510.

▶ **Château de Challes**. 73190 **Challes-les-Eaux**. Tel: 79-72-86-71; in U.S., (800) 528-1234 or (800) 334-7234. Just 6 km (4 miles) south of Chambéry, this 71-room hostelry is set apart by its manicured garden and private park; quiet, civilized.

▶ **Château de Trivier**. 73190 **Challes-les-Eaux**. Tel: 79-85-07-27. This very model of a castle sits in greenery surrounded by peaks. The Clanet family oversees the château of the *seigneurs* of Trivier. Excellent cooking; thermal treatments available.

▶ **Auberge du Choucas**. 17, rue de la Fruitière, 05220 **Monêtier-les-Bains**. Tel: 92-24-42-73. In a high-altitude village between Grenoble and Briançon, this 18th-century farmhouse has been turned into a cozy, rustic retreat with 13 rooms right in the heart of Alpine adventure country. Good headquarters for family outdoor activities.

▶ **Grand Hôtel Ducs de Savoie**. 6, place de la Gare, 73000 **Chambéry**. Tel: 79-69-54-54; Telex: 320910.

▶ **Grand Paradis**. 73150 **Val-d'Isère**. Tel: 79-06-11-73; in U.S., (212) 477-1600 or (800) 223-1500. With large rooms and spacious balconies overlooking the mountains, this fine hotel also has a nightclub and a panoramic restaurant (where in season hotel guests are obliged to eat).

▶ **Million**. 8, place de la Liberté, 73200 **Albertville**. Tel: 79-32-25-15; in U.S., (212) 696-1323.

▶ **Ombremont**. Route du Tunnel, 73370 **Le Bourget-du-Lac**. Tel: 79-25-00-23; Telex: 980832; in U.S., (212) 696-1323. North of Chambéry and across the lake from Aix-les-Bains, this 20-room, two-apartment inn boasts an outstanding kitchen and a smashing garden setting. It's a very good value in the luxury class.

▶ **Park Hôtel**. 10, place Paul-Mistral, 38000 **Grenoble**. Tel: 76-87-29-11; Telex: 32076; in U.S., (212) 477-1600 or (800) 223-1510.

▶ **Auberge du Père Bise**. Route du Port, 74290 **Talloires**. Tel: 50-60-72-01; in U.S., (212) 696-1323.

▶ **Les Princes**. 4, rue de Boigne, 73000 **Chambéry**. Tel: 79-33-45-36.

▶ **Royal**. 745000 **Evian-les-Bains**. Tel: 50-75-14-00; Telex: 385759; in U.S., (212) 838-3110 or (800) 223-6800. The most prestigious (and rather stuffy) address in town offers a superb view from its hilltop park; 158 rooms, 32 apartments, swimming, golf, and tennis.

▶ **Vauban**. 13, avenue Générale-de-Gaulle, 05100 **Briançon**. Tel: 92-21-12-11.

▶ Association des Maries des Stations Français de

Sports Hiver, 61, boulevard Haussmann, 75008 Paris. Tel: (01) 47-23-61-72. This association can provide information on the facilities, lodging, and transportation at all the French ski resorts, although it does not book accommodations; not all representatives speak English.

PROVENCE AND THE COTE D'AZUR

By Bruce Alderman
With Georgia I. Hesse

Bruce Alderman lived in southern France for many years, working as a correspondent for Reuters, Time, *and* Newsweek. *Now Paris bureau chief for* Variety, *he is also working toward a doctorate in French history.*

For many people, Provence and the Riviera fuse into one glamorous, sun-splashed image—the south of France. The legendary Fitzgeralds, the casinos, and the topless bathers cast an aura so strong that it is easy to forget that the Riviera, or Côte d'Azur, is only a small part of Provence.

La Provence and the Côte d'Azur share the same history. Yet while the Côte d'Azur is primarily Provençal, the reverse is not the case. Many Provençaux, with their deep-rooted sense of tradition, would be aghast at the thought of being identified with the Riviera. For its part, the Côte d'Azur, throughout years of intense development and constant political change, has been trying to carve out its own regional character.

Another reason why it is inappropriate to lump Provence and the Côte d'Azur together is because they can be two completely different travel destinations. You could easily fly into Nice, spend two weeks on the coast, and never venture into the "real" Provence. Or you could take a train to Avignon and explore centuries-old towns and villages, never setting foot on the Riviera.

However, thinking of the two entities as completely separate would be misleading as well. Step just north of Cannes and you can discover a village as Provençal as anything the playwright Marcel Pagnol ever imagined.

The best approach is therefore first to look at the intertwining realities of Provence and the Côte d'Azur and later divide the two for the sake of practical travel planning. After all, the geographical range of La Provence–Côte d'Azur is vast, extending from the Italian border to Avignon, and from the Mediterranean to Vaison-la-Romaine. It is a rich and diversified territory that includes the swamps and bird sanctuaries of La Camargue in the west near Arles; the towering mountains and thick, fire-prone forests in the east by the Côte d'Azur; the sparkling beaches and steep cliffs in the south; and the rolling hills and riverbeds of the Rhône and Durance valleys in the north.

La Provence itself extends from the Rhône River to Toulon; the Côte d'Azur from Hyères to Monaco and the Italian border.

MAJOR INTEREST

Provence
Art
Roman and Greek ruins
Early Christian antiquities
Vineyards
Beaches
Natural parks and forests

Côte d'Azur
Seaside resorts
Gambling
Modern-art museums
Roman ruins

The similarities between Provence and the Côte d'Azur run deep. Even in the glitziest parts of the Riviera there are traces of Provence—a Latin flavor both in food and temperament, a Roman cultural heritage, and a certain laid-back lifestyle that typifies the Mediterranean. When you enter Provence–Côte d'Azur you know you have arrived in the Mediterranean region: The intense sunlight, blue skies, dry climate, olive trees, chalky hills, and red-tiled roofs are unmistakable.

But Provence is more than just a Mediterranean land. Provençal is a style, a language, and a history—starting with the Roman Republic and Empire, developing into a kingdom ruled independently of France until the 15th century, and then becoming a special-statute state of the ancien régime—until the French Revolution created Provence as an administrative region.

While the significance of Provence spans millennia, the Côte d'Azur has become well known only during the past hundred years—mostly since World War II—as a result of the rise of mass vacations and retirement opportunities. Over those years, the Côte d'Azur came into its own, thanks to its beaches, hotels, condominiums, and the distinctiveness of Nice, the area's center. Not only does Nice neighbor Italy, but for several centuries the city stood apart politically from the rest of Provence, allying itself instead with the Savoies to the east. In fact, Nice didn't definitively become French until 1860.

But traditions die hard here. There are still fishermen in St-Tropez who speak Provençal, just as there are in Marseille. You can eat the stewy *daube* or garlicky *aioli* of Provence nearly everywhere. And the architecture—even the new buildings—has an overriding regional unity.

The Côte d'Azur hasn't been alone in attracting newcomers: All of Provence has become France's sun belt. Millions of Parisians and other northerners have migrated south to escape gray skies and city pressures. Some have been retirees, but a large part are among the most educated and highest-paid workers in France: doctors, lawyers, engineers, and administrators. Even these new Provençaux feel a kinship with those who have been here for generations—united by climate, the proximity of the sea, and the easygoing lifestyle.

In 1962, another wave of immigrants hit the region: *pieds-noirs,* French colonists returning to the mainland after Algeria achieved independence. The *pieds-noirs* brought a new, large segment of political and social influence: Conservative politically, they share a common North African culture.

The *pieds-noirs* were followed by waves of ethnic Algerian, Moroccan, and Tunisian immigrant workers. Economic stagnation in France in the late 1970s and 1980s

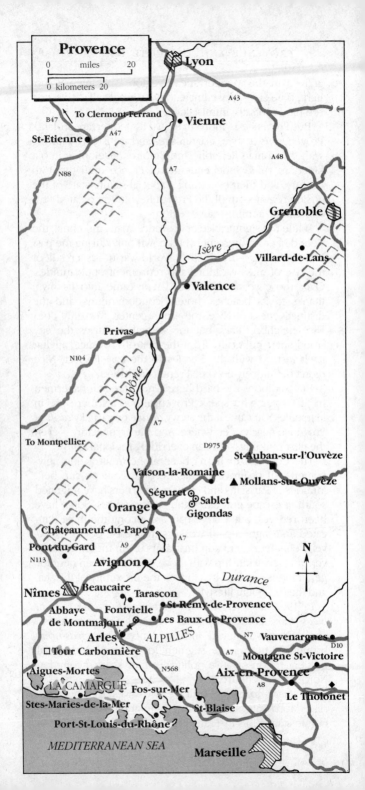

Provence

| 0 | miles | 20 |
| 0 | kilometers | 20 |

To Clermont-Ferrand

B47

St-Etienne

A47

N88

Vienne

A43

A7

Grenoble

A48

Isère

Villard-de-Lans

Valence

Privas

Rhône

N104

To Montpellier

D975

St-Auban-sur-l'Ouvèze

Vaison-la-Romaine

Mollans-sur-Ouvèze

Séguret

Sablet

Orange

Gigondas

Châteauneuf-du-Pape

A9

A7

Pont-du-Gard

N113

Avignon

Durance

N

Nîmes

Beaucaire

Tarascon

St-Rémy-de-Provence

Fontvielle

Abbaye
de Montmajour

Les Baux-de-Provence

ALPILLES

Vauvenargues

N7

D10

Arles

Montagne St-Victoire

Tour Carbonnière

Aix-en-Provence

A7

Aigues-Mortes

LA CAMARGUE

Fos-sur-Mer

N568

A8

Le Tholonet

Stes-Maries-de-la-Mer

Port-St-Louis-du-Rhône

St-Blaise

MEDITERRANEAN SEA

Marseille

Lyon

and a slowness to assimilate foreigners have caused a backlash of prejudice against these non-French immigrants. As a result Provence and the Côte d'Azur have both shifted to the far right. (Until recently, Marseille, Avignon, and Arles had a left-leaning political tradition, while the wealthier Nice, Cannes, and Antibes were conservative strongholds.) Shifting political values aside, Provence and the Côte d'Azur officially form one of 23 regional governments in France. On a practical level, this means a strong regional network for tourism and cultural affairs.

The real binding factor of Provence is the language, Provençal being a regional variation of the old Occitan. Today the dialect itself is quickly disappearing, but its lasting effects can be heard here even in the accents of the young. Strong local differences within Provence can be heard as well. Because Provençal was never a written language, a great ancient oral tradition of tales, legends, and proverbs has been and continues to be passed down.

LA PROVENCE

Flying into Marseille-Marignan airport to visit Provence is somehow to miss the whole point. Provence should unfold itself gradually, slowly, deliberately. Provence is as much a state of mind as it is a geographic entity.

In nearly every corner of Provence, small, wondrous discoveries await those willing to find them. Even the most unlikely and unheard-of village can offer an archaeological treasure, a 12th-century church, a beautiful view, or a culinary delight.

So forget the plane. Instead, take the train from Paris or Lyon; Provence is best discovered from the north southward. Rent a car at Avignon or Marseille and cherish the countryside, with its lavender fields and back roads, where the smells of thyme and rosemary permeate the air beneath a brilliant sun.

As close as it may come, however, Provence is not paradise. There are blots on the landscape. But in Provence every cloud has its silver lining. For example, one of the most frightening industrial structures on the Mediterranean, the Fos chemical and oil-refining complex, sits next to one of the oldest and most important archaeological sites in France: St-Blaise, its foundation dating from the sixth century B.C. Above all, Provence provides a window into Western history: Marseille and Fos were founded by the Phoenicians. Provence itself was settled later by the Romans; their traces are still in Arles, Vaison-la-Romaine, Orange, and St-Rémy, to name just a few.

Perhaps the most lasting Roman influence is on the name Provence itself. The word comes from Provincia Romana, or Roman Province. To simplify things: At one time, Provincia stretched all the way to the Spanish border and served as the strategic link between Rome and the Iberian Peninsula. It was called Provincia Narbonnaise and was soon divided into two administrative regions: Narbonnaise I (now Languedoc and Aquitaine) and Narbonnaise II (Provence).

When the Germanic invaders swept through Gaul in the fifth century, Narbonnaise I fell quickly. Narbonnaise II resisted longer, and even after the empire's fall the Germanic tribes continued to refer to Narbonnaise II as the Provincia Romana. The name stuck.

The Roman impact on Gaul was at its greatest in Provence because of the region's nearness to Italy. In fact, Provence's indigenous Celtic and Ligurian populations quickly adopted a hybrid Gallo-Roman culture that survived both the empire's fall and the tribal invasions from the north; the victorious Alemanni were few in number in Provence, and their lasting influence was therefore relatively small.

At the same time, Catholicism was on the rise. Churches were built on top of Roman temples. (Few of the early churches stand today, and often only remnants survive—such as the fifth-century foundation of the cathedral of St-Sauveur in Aix.)

As the empire crumbled, bishops and deacons became the new moral and political leaders. Most of these church officials came from the prominent Gallo-Roman families—relatives of Roman senators, officials, or large landowners. The Catholic Church replaced the empire; its authority here lasted more than 12 centuries. The Church played a very large role in the daily lives of the Provençaux, who were less spiritually religious than they were piously attached to Catholicism's material customs and traditions.

Creation of the Spirit of Provence

In 972, Count Guillaume and his armies took control of the region from invading Moors and formed the Comté de Provence, which during the next five hundred years existed as a separate state—sometimes allied with the Aragons and sometimes with Naples, but always independent of France and attached more often than not to the Holy Roman Empire.

The court (at Aix) became a center for art and poetry. The Provençal language flourished, thanks to travelling troubadours and their epic songs of courtly love. The golden age of the troubadours came in the 12th century, at a time when castle life was brutish and violent. The troubadours softened the mores of these harsh times by introducing a glorification of idealized love between man and woman.

Meanwhile, the French kings had embarked on territorial expansion, and Provence was one of their major targets. For several hundred years Provence was the scene of bloody feudal rivalries among different ruling powers and ambitious leaders. By the 15th century, members of the Anjou branch of the French monarchy had become rulers of Provence. The Comté de Provence eventually became French peacefully—in 1481—as the result of an inheritance.

Now part of France, the region slowly transformed. During the next four hundred years, Provençal gradually disappeared as the common spoken language. In the 19th century, dramatic economic and social changes—railroads, industry, and tourism—further eroded what was once Provence's dreamy isolation from the bustle of Paris.

In reaction to the changes, a group led by the poet Frédéric Mistral founded a movement—called le Félibrige—advocating a return to the old traditions. The organization tried to revive a Provence of legend: a peaceful, rural community of peasant farmers, bourgeois, and fishermen held together by the Provençal language—and a great faith in the Roman Catholic Church.

Reality was elsewhere, however. Since the last decades of the 19th century, Provence has developed into a modern and technologically oriented region whose past is nevertheless still stamped on nearly every corner of every town.

Throughout its history Provence was also clearly divided into rural villages and main cities. Each major city—Arles, Marseille, Aix, Avignon—followed its own particular historical growth.

The rural villages, until recently comprising by far the majority of the population, were always tight-knit communities. A sense of community is in fact a very strong Provençal tradition; each village and town has a main square or boulevard that is the center of local social life.

MAJOR INTEREST IN PROVENCE

Avignon
Palais des Papes
Pont d'Avignon
Rhône wine country to the north

Orange
Roman theater and ruins

Les Baux
The fortress

Arles
Van Gogh colors and landscapes
Roman amphitheater and theater
Early Christian sites

The Camargue

Aix-en-Provence
The city's natural light
Cours Mirabeau
Cézanne interest

Marseille
Vieux Port views
Bouillabaisse
Château d'If

AVIGNON

Avignon benefits from a strategic geographic location: on a major north-south water route—the Rhône River— halfway between Spain and Italy. This was partly what led the popes to Avignon in the 14th century. Unfortunately, the city's position also has a climatic disadvantage: In the winter the powerful, icy mistral wind sweeps down the

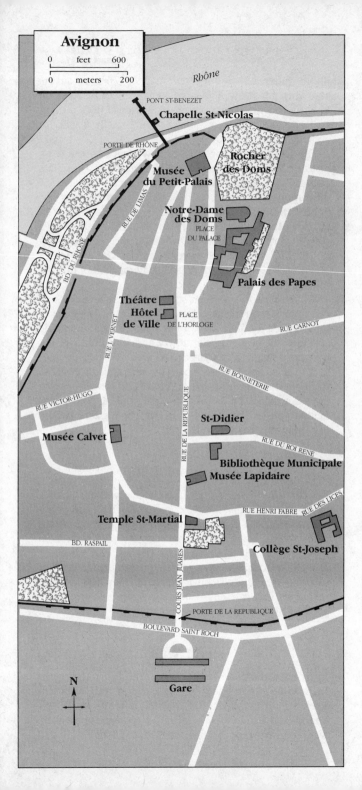

Rhône valley, blowing through Avignon's narrow streets and whipping around its large squares. Because Avignon is at the northwestern corner of Provence, it is a good place to start a visit to the region, especially if you are arriving from the north.

The first-time visitor is always awestruck by the city's massive Medieval monuments—the imposing Palais des Papes (Popes' Palace), the wall that encircles the city, and the famous bridge where "*on y danse.*" Considering Avignon proper's relatively small size and population (91,000), the weight of history can seem heavy. Lawrence Durrell noted: "The past embalmed it, the present could not alter it." A Provençal proverb cautions: "He who leaves Avignon, loses his good sense." Avignon leaves no one indifferent.

While Avignon's somber, sometimes disarrayed Gothic center may support such observations, the city is not just a museum of the past. It vibrates with various economic activities, including small industry, agriculture, and freight transport. Avignon's incorporated area (175,000 people) spans the socioeconomic spectrum and adds diversity to the walled center. Though Avignon is no longer a major university town—it lost its university during the French Revolution—it does have a small but growing annex of the university in Marseille.

The Papal State

For centuries, Avignon has been a state within a state, a city of tolerance that has welcomed foreigners and political and religious refugees from around Europe in times when freedom and travel have been at a premium. Even today, Avignon is among a group of "free" French cities: French law forbids certain released prisoners to live in or near the area of their convicted crime; they must take up residence in a free city—such as Avignon. Political refugees are also sent to live in one of these *villes libres*.

The Wall

In front of the train station you come face-to-face with twin stone towers and the outside of the wall that stretches for two-and-a-half miles around the city. Don't be fooled: Despite their Medieval appearance, the towers were constructed in 1863, and most of the wall and

ramparts were heavily reconstructed at about the same
time and again 30 years later.

The original wall went up between 1359 and 1370
under the direction of Pope Innocent VI. Twelve gates
were built into guard towers. Military invasions and bandits weren't the only worries; the wall also protected
Avignon from Rhône river floods.

Immediately inside the gates the city offers its puzzling
contrasts: the main boulevard, for example, cours Jean-
Jaurès–rue de la République, a busy street overflowing
with overpriced cafés, restaurants, and shops. Every few
yards, a monument or alluring building stands out. One
example: the **Temple St-Martial**, a Benedictine monastery
founded in 1378. Major sections of the monastery and its
church were destroyed or rebuilt in the 19th century
when the boulevard was constructed to join the train
station with the Palais des Papes. Avignon's Office de Tourisme now occupies a corner of one of the old buildings.

Farther down the street is the **Musée Lapidaire**, built as
a chapel for a Jesuit college in 1620. The building is
hailed as one of the most beautiful examples of French
Baroque architecture and houses a magnificent collection
of antiquities.

Just past the museum and behind the rue de la République is the **church of St-Didier**. This fine example of
Provençal Gothic style, constructed during the papal period in 1356, has not been significantly retouched. Next to
the church is the **Restaurant St-Didier**. In a town that
offers little between standard French fast food and ridicu-
lously·overpriced and pretentious restaurants, Le Didier
is a fine choice. Its owner and chef, Christian Etienne, is a
young, energetic Avignon native who learned his trade at
the Ritz in Paris. He often comes to the tables to take
orders and talk with customers. The St-Didier's fare is
light and imaginative with a Provençal flavor at high but
relatively reasonable prices.

Nearby on the rue Joseph Vernet, off the rue de la
République, is the **Musée Calvet**, which occupies an elegant 18th-century mansion and houses an impressive collection of paintings and archaeological treasures. The rue
de la République ends at the large **place de l'Horloge**
(bell tower), a pedestrian mall and the center of near
round-the-clock activity during most of the tourist season
and especially during the Festival d'Avignon theater extravaganza in August. The several unexceptional outdoor
café-restaurants that line one side of the square are con-

stantly packed, providing a captive audience for street performers.

The square's two monumental buildings—the Hôtel de Ville and the Théâtre—were both heavily reconstructed in the last century. In August, during the Festival d'Avignon (unlike the proper ambience at Aix's music festival), a month-long carnival atmosphere animates this onetime Catholic capital: The town is invaded by thousands of theatergoers, actors, performers of all types, vagabonds, thieves, drug dealers, and just plain tourists. The festival has two faces: the official, highly acclaimed Classic Performances at the Théâtre—Shakespeare, Molière, etc., all in French—and the "Festival Off," in which dozens of offbeat and less-established troupes put on performances ranging from one-man shows to traditional plays to experimental theater in various locations around town.

The Palais des Papes

The main show in Avignon is nonetheless the Palais des Papes, just north of the place de l'Horloge. The heavily fortified palace is a reminder that Avignon was—for 73 years, from 1305 to 1378—the capital of Christianity. Contested antipopes stayed until 1417, when the schism between Rome and Avignon ended.

Chance played a part in bringing popes to the city. For years, the popes in Rome were consolidating their power over temporal leaders. The new papal position was clear: The pope was not just the vicar of Saint Peter but of Jesus Christ himself. The pope was heir to the spiritual kingdom, directly under God, and therefore was above individual monarchs and territorial rulers. The French kings did not agree and maintained that they were sovereign in matters concerning the Church in France. In 1303, King Philippe le Bel arrested the pope for interfering in the affairs of the French Church. This blow severely weakened the Roman Church.

Two years later Clement V, the former archbishop of Bordeaux, was elected pope. In 1309, he came to Avignon to prepare for a Church council to be held in Vienne, just up the Rhône. Grave security problems in Italy—war and rebellion against the papal state—made his return to Rome unwise.

The next elected pope, in 1316, was Jean XXII, the bishop of Avignon. He, too, decided to stay in his city, and was installed as pope in the bishop's palace. His successor, Benoît XII, another Frenchman, also chose Avignon as his residence. He ordered the demolition of the bishop's palace and, in its place, the construction in 1336 of a *demeure* worthy of a pope.

Benoît XII was succeeded by Frenchman Clement VI, who not only more than doubled the palace's size, but in 1348 purchased Avignon itself from Queen Jeanne of Naples, who was also the countess of Provence. From that moment until the French Revolution, Avignon was a papal state. Several other important buildings date from the early papal period: The **Petit Palais**, at the northern part of the square in front of the palace, was the residence for archbishops and bishops; during the past few years it became home to a superb museum of Medieval painting and sculpture, featuring some 400 Italian canvases of the 13th to 16th centuries and regional Avignon paintings from the 14th and 15th centuries. The Italian paintings are special treasures. The **Livrée Ceccano** (now a municipal library), just south of St-Didier church, was built by Cardinal Ceccano, the archbishop of Naples, in 1330. Some of the original painted ceilings remain intact.

Avignon at Apogee

During the popes' residence, Avignon became one of the most important cities of the Western world. Nearly the entire papal administration, including the College of Cardinals, lived here. The city developed significant economic and cultural activities, partly because the Avignon popes were immensely rich due to taxes collected from states and from church *domaines*. However, Avignon's prestige long outlasted the Avignon popes—the last of them, Grégoire XI, abandoned the city in 1376.

The return of the popes to Rome didn't end the story, it only made it more interesting. After Grégoire's death an Italian pope was elected. Months later, the French protested the election, claiming it was held under the menace of the Roman population. The French cardinals then elected a second pope (a so-called antipope), who took his seat at Avignon. The Church was now divided in two: England, the German Empire, Poland, Hungary, Bohemia, Flanders, and most of Italy were in favor of the Roman pope; Spain, France, Savoie, Scotland, Sicily, and Portugal were on Avignon's side.

The schism ended in 1417 with the election of a pope seated at Rome who united not only the two Western churches but also Constantinople and the Eastern Church, which had had its own pope. Afterward, Avignon was governed by Rome until it became French during the Revolution in 1793—a fact the Church didn't accept until 1814.

The Pont d'Avignon

Standing next to the palace is the 12th-century cathedral of Notre-Dame des Doms. Past the cathedral, steps rise to the **Rocher des Doms**, a rocky hill that offers a panoramic view of the valley, the neighboring town of Villeneuve-lès-Avignon, and especially the Pont St-Bénézet, a.k.a. the Pont d'Avignon. To visit the bridge, of which only a partial span and four of the original 22 arches remain, walk westward through the Porte du Rhône, just past the Petit Palais.

Legend has it that an angel appeared before a simple shepherd, Bénézet (later sainted), and ordered him to build a bridge over the Rhône. Between 1177 and 1185 he built a wooden bridge, which was destroyed in 1226 but reconstructed in stone. In spanning the river the bridge crossed the small Ile de la Barthelasse. Most of the dancing noted in the song "Sur le Pont d'Avignon" probably took place in taverns located on this island under the bridge's arches.

The bridge was also once a place for prayer. The chapel of St-Nicolas still stands on the second pillar and is open daily to paid visits. Built in the 13th century on Romanesque lines, the chapel was enlarged in 1513. Over the centuries the ravaging Rhône eroded St-Bénézet's arches, and repeated attempts to rebuild the fallen supports eventually failed. In 1715 the chapel was closed for purposes of worship.

RHONE WINE COUNTRY

"The Rhône is a river of wine," writes Alexis Lichine, and he puts the geography nicely. "It drains vineyards on its broad delta plain, along the steep cliffs above Avignon, in the Cévennes and Jura mountains, and around the Lake of Geneva. Yet the only wines to bear the name are those which come from the central section—the Côtes du Rhône."

These Côtes extend from Lyon in the north to Avignon in the south, a strip about 140 miles long.

In the company of the greatest Bordeaux and Burgundy wines, whose names are shouted aloud, those of the Rhône are whispered: Condrieu, Côte Rôtie, Château Grillet, Gigondas, Hermitage, Saint-Péray, Tavel, and Châteauneuf-du-Pape.

Yet the Rhônes have much to recommend them. They are eminently drinkable, for one thing; for another, usually they are reasonable in price.

The most famous of these is Châteauneuf-du-Pape, and the *pape* (pope) referred to is generally considered to be Pope John XXII, who from 1316 to 1333 built a new castle (*château neuf*) in the sloping hills about 17 km (11 miles) north of Avignon. (The château was mostly ruined in 1552 during the Wars of Religion, and its remaining keep was wiped out during bombings on August 20, 1944. Only one provocative façade remains to hint at the majesty of the original.)

Even among the worldly, extravagant Avignon popes, John XXII was notorious for high living and debauchery. He slept on an ermine-trimmed pillow shared, it was said, by a nearly endless parade of pretty *desmoiselles*. Soon his reputation began to enhance that of his wines. As Frederick Wildman, Jr., reminds us in *A Wine Tour of France,* "He let it be known that his Châteauneuf-du-Pape was not only a glory to taste, but—and he stood as living proof—also a rejuvenator and aphrodisiac of remarkable potency. The fortunes of Châteauneuf-du-Pape were made."

Today, Châteauneuf, off D 192 halfway between Orange and Avignon and home to about 2,000 inhabitants, most of them wine enthusiasts, is the most interesting village in the valley for the traveller who has time for only one stop.

A few sites in town are worth hesitation—notably the **Château des Papes** for its splendid views over the valley—but the main attraction is wine: drinking it, fine dining to accompany it, visiting vineyards, spending a night in seductive surroundings.

The largest estate of Châteauneuf today is **Mont-Redon**, to the north of town on Route d'Orange. Born as Mourredon in the 14th century, it has been a property of the Plantin family for three generations and is now the largest producer of little-known white Châteauneuf as well as the familiar reds and less highly bred bottles called simply Côtes-du-Rhône. Cellar visits are conducted on weekdays; the tasting and sales room is open daily.

A lighter, more "modern" Châteauneuf is produced by the **Château des Fines Roches** domaine, which also, handily, maintains a fine inn and outstanding restaurant in the highly picturesque 19th-century château. Just south of the village via D 17 and a marked private road winding through vineyards, Fines Roches is renowned for lamb dishes perfectly suited to its wines. The seven rooms are only moderately expensive; the winery itself is open for visitors daily between March and December.

A wine fair is held in autumn in Châteauneuf; the date depends on the harvest (usually mid- to late September). The restaurant **La Mule du Pape,** touted by discerning gourmets such as Samuel Chamberlain, serves elegant meals in the center of town on the place de la Fontaine, though time has slightly dimmed its luster.

Travellers who have time to familiarize themselves with other towns and other bottlings might consider (from north to south) Tain-l'Hermitage (17 km/11 miles north of Valence, across the Rhône from Tournon), Gigondas (17 km/11 miles east of Orange, only 650 inhabitants but two estates to visit), or Tavel (15 km/9 miles northwest of Avignon; there are four estates in its immediate vicinity).

Two small, modestly priced inns in attractive settings are near Gigondas: **Les Florets** (15 rooms) and **Montmirail,** in the nearby hamlet of that name (46 rooms). Tavel is known for the **Auberge de Tavel,** a one-star Michelin restaurant with 11 modestly priced rooms and a swimming pool.

—Georgia I. Hesse

ORANGE

Orange, just 31 km (19 miles) north of Avignon by Routes A 7 or N 7, shares with Nîmes and Arles important souvenirs of Roman Gaul: a theater, a gymnasium, and a commemorative arch that lived on as evidence of the importance of Roman Arausio long after that city of some 85,000 was trampled by Alemannic and Visigothic invaders. Later, the battered monuments were used as rock quarries for the construction of homes and fortifications.

Orange is one of the most momentous sites in the history of Christianity: In 529 the Council of Orange, convened here, declared for Augustinian predeterminism and against all forms of Pelagian doctrines of free will.

By the 13th century the original Celtic market town upon which the Romans built had become a holding of the German duchy of Nassau, later joined to the Dutch house of Orange. In the 17th century it fell to Louis XIV and the French.

From Celtic days to our own, Orange sat right on France's main north-south route, the commercial Roman road that became Route Nationale 7. Today, however, the town of some 27,000 people has been bypassed by A 7, the Autoroute du Soleil, and it is possible—though not recommended—to hurry by without hesitation.

The plane trees, the sleepy, shady squares, the sidewalk cafés where strollers sit, musing and unmoving, mark Orange as a southern, Provençal town. The works of long-gone Rome remain the major lure.

Orange's **theater** usually is considered the best-looking and best-preserved in existence, having been constructed during the last decade of the first century B.C. under Emperor Augustus. It follows the Greek plan of a semicircle of tiers facing the orchestra and stage and was about the same size as that in Arles, with a marble and mosaic backdrop of niches, columns, statues, and other decorations. From the square behind the theater, the backdrop and its supporting wings were known to Louis XIV as the "finest wall in the kingdom."

Long ago, the stage lost all its accoutrements, but the acoustics remain unsullied, and classical plays are still performed on a regular basis, watched by the theater's imperial statue (all Roman theaters had one; only the one in Orange remains), a 10-foot-2-inch-tall Augustus, discovered, somewhat the worse for fall and burial, in the orchestra pit.

Near the theater, excavations proceed on an early **temple** and **gymnasium**—the latter is one of only three known in France. Off a courtyard, the gym boasted baths (of course), open and enclosed running tracks, and a dais for the awarding of prizes. Orange's **Arc de Triomphe** in the triple-arched style was completed about A.D. 26 and is the third largest, as well as the best-preserved, in France.

In 1939, French art collector Count William de Belleroche (whose family had lived for two centuries in Britain) presented to the city some 400 works by one Sir Frank Brangwyn: prints, drawings, watercolors, engravings, all showing town and country activities in France and England and now on display in the **Musée Municipal**.

Orange is the source of some fragrant, long-lasting

milled soaps in the French tradition, fine and useful gifts with scents of lavender, orange, and herbs.

The smartest place to stay in the immediate area of Orange is **Château de Rochegude**, about 15 km (9 miles) north via D 976 and D 111. The base of the castle-like structure and its keep have been overlooking the valley for eight centuries. The 25 rooms range from expensive to very expensive; the four apartments are in the latter category. The dining room has earned one Michelin star.

In town, on the way to Caderousse and Nîmes, the **Altéa** offers 99 rooms for moderately high prices; it has a good restaurant and pleasant dining terrace.

A one-Michelin-star restaurant, **Le Pigraillet** (on the road that enters the Parc de la Colline St-Eutrope on the south), specializes in duck and local wines. **Le Forum** is an unpretentious but satisfying restaurant at 3, rue Mazeau, very near the Théâtre Antique.

Travellers who seek historical passages may make an excursion of about 100 km (62 miles) to the northeast, departing Orange on D 975. It links the Rhône valley and the high Alps via a 4,210-foot-high pass, the Col de Perty, and is probably the route used by Hannibaı and his elephant train (and army of 60,000 men) in 218 B.C. Many attractive old villages lie along the way, Mollans-sur-Ouvèze and St-Auban-sur-l'Ouvèze among them.

—*Georgia I. Hesse*

LES BAUX-DE-PROVENCE

A towering rock plateau—a natural fortress—formed of twisted limestone weathered into haunting forms. Below, on either side, two valleys: On one side, a pastoral scene from the tales of Daudet, is the Vallée d'Entreconque; on the other, a tormented landscape, the Val d'Enfer (Valley of Hell) in the cracks of the Alpilles mountains. Atop the rock plateau are ruins of a feudal fortress, carved out of stone, and long since destroyed by successive wars waged against the castle's powerful and ambitious rulers: This is Les Baux.

Isolated in the countryside northeast of Arles, Les Baux still stimulates the imagination as it did seven hundred years ago when it gave birth to the phenomenon of the troubadours and the ideal of courtly love. At night, when spotlights illuminate the towering ruins, Les Baux is an eerie reminder of time's conquest of man. Today it is a lively touristic and artistic center of fewer than 500 permanent inhabitants. It is also a meeting point for a segment of France's extreme right, the royalist parties, who hold an annual rally near the village.

Because the village of Les Baux sits on such a small rock plateau—only 2,600 feet long and 650 feet wide—no cars are allowed on its streets. The village is split into two: the early-Medieval ghost town—*ville morte* (dead town)—and the latter-day Provençal village, with its arts-and-crafts shops, restaurants, museums, and exceptional Renaissance mansions.

The village has a few moderately priced hotels and restaurants; in the summer hotel reservations are a must. While you can get a snack or a decent meal with a spectacular view or charming ambience almost anywhere in Les Baux, it would be a shame to come here and not try—budget willing—the **Oustaù de Baumanière**, one of France's outstanding restaurants, and one of only 18 in the country that merit three Michelin stars. The food here runs to heavy dishes with rich sauces; the house specialty is local lamb cooked in a crust. Baumanière also has 25 elegantly rustic and comfortable rooms and a swimming pool and tennis courts, in a restored Provençal farmhouse. Down the road is the less expensive, but charmingly rustic, **La Cabro d'Or**, with 22 rooms and a good restaurant.

Bauxite

While historians debate the exact origins of the name Les Baux—some say it means "high place" in Ligurian, others contend it's Provençal for cave, and still others believe it's a derivative of Balthazar, one of the three Wise Men—there is no question that Les Baux gave us the word *bauxite,* for the mineral mined in the nearby Alpilles chain.

Feudal Les Baux

The story of Les Baux is one of a regional feudal power engaged in nearly incessant (and typically losing) wars and rebellions lasting several hundred years. The princes of Les Baux were often cruel and ambitious warmongers. Nevertheless, their court was considered highly refined and brilliant, especially during the 12th and 13th centuries, when it was frequented by troubadours.

When Provence became French in 1481, Les Baux revolted against Louis XI and the castle was destroyed (not for the first or last time). The Renaissance brought better times for Les Baux; the castle was rebuilt and splendid mansions were constructed, including the Hôtel de Manville and the Hôtel de Brion—the latter now housing a museum of printing, with artifacts from the beginnings of printing in the West.

The Renaissance of Les Baux didn't last long. The lords of Les Baux supported the wrong causes all too often: the Protestants; the Duke of Orléans against King Louis XIII; and Aixois insurgents rebelling against Cardinal Richelieu. As a result, the king ordered a military occupation of Les Baux, and the castle and city ramparts were torn down for the last time. Les Baux became a ghost town as its three thousand inhabitants moved away to greener pastures.

Les Baux Redux

The writings of Mistral (of the Félibrige movement; see also Arles) and Daudet helped Les Baux regain some of its past glory by rediscovering its historic importance and above all its touristic potential. Daudet's tales tell of a peaceful, pastoral village coping with economic hardships and displaying a fervent attachment to the Church and its traditions.

One of his stories describes a centuries-old Christmas ritual still performed today: the midnight mass procession—the *fête des bergers* (shepherds' festival)—in the now significantly modified 12th-century church of St-Vincent.

Church authorities often forbade the fête because of suspicions that it was rooted in paganism. The procession provides a good show for the several hundred people, mostly visitors, who cram into the small church on Christmas Eve. Provençal music—flute and tambourine—replaces traditional Christmas carols.

Excursions from Les Baux

Along the route from Arles to Les Baux is the **Abbaye de Montmajour**, a fascinating Romanesque fortress monastery often captured on van Gogh's canvases. A visit lasts two hours. Views of the landscape from Montmajour suggest the scenes van Gogh painted a hundred years ago. Also along the same route is the Medieval village of Fontvieille, where Daudet's windmill—le Moulin de Daudet—is a good vantage point from which to see the Alpilles, a small Daudet museum, and (in the summer) large crowds. Out of Les Baux to the northeast is **St-Rémy-de-Provence**, a charming little town of 8,000 where van Gogh spent his last days in the Monastère St-Paul-de-Mausole, on the outskirts near Glanum. The remains of a Greco-Roman city in Glanum are the best-preserved in Europe. To the northwest are the twin fortress castles of **Tarascon** and **Beaucaire**—each on its own side of the Rhône river.

ARLES

Perhaps no other city has been so dramatically immortalized on canvas as Arles, thanks to Vincent van Gogh. He spent only one year here (1888–1889), during which he was ridiculed, persecuted, and interned. Nevertheless, he painted some two hundred canvases in a feverish outburst of creativity that was inspired by Arles: its people, their customs, and the countryside.

Today very little of van Gogh's Arles remains, except the hospital cell in which he was held in solitary confinement for a fit of madness. Recently the hospital—the Hôtel-Dieu—was converted into a van Gogh center and shopping mall (!) to commemorate the one hundredth anniversary of the painter's arrival in the Provençal city.

If most of the buildings van Gogh painted have disappeared, the light and colors of the city and its rural surroundings have not, nor have most of Arles's main attractions. Arles was both the capital of Roman Gaul and the center of Provençal folklore, and many reminders of its prestigious past still exist: the amphitheater, the Roman theater, the Alyscamps burial ground, early Christian art (in museums), and Medieval ramparts and churches. Important archaeological digs are uncovering a Roman circus next to the Alyscamps, and several largely intact villas in Arles's right-bank twin, Trinquetaille. The city offers a day pass for all of its museums and monuments.

Arles is on the left bank of the Rhône River, about 35 km (22 miles) south of Avignon on Route N 570 and on the train line from Paris to Marseille and the Côte d'Azur. Arles makes a good base for visiting Les Baux, the Abbaye de Montmajour, St-Rémy-de-Provence, and the Camargue; most of these places were painted by van Gogh. You can easily spend three days in this area and still feel rushed.

Coming in by the southbound train from Avignon, you will pass a *paysage* described one hundred years ago by van Gogh: "Before arriving at Tarascon [just north of Arles] I noticed a magnificent landscape of immense yellowish crags strangely entangled with the most imposing forms. The valleys were lined with small, round trees covered with olive-colored or gray-colored leaves." In Arles, van Gogh wrote: "I saw magnificent reddish land planted with vineyards, and at the foot of nearby mountains, the finest lilies."

Van Gogh arrived at the Arles train station and went through the same Medieval ramparts at the Porte de la Cavalerie that you will on your way into the center of the city. Van Gogh eventually rented a room in the "Maison Jaune" (Yellow House), where he spent most of his time at Arles. World War II bombings completely destroyed the building, which stood in front of the city's gates at 2, place Lamartine. His "Café du Nuit" is now a Monoprix supermarket.

Van Gogh was not interested in Arles's rich Roman vestiges. He did often paint the Roman amphitheater, but only during bullfights (which are still fought today). He also cherished the black and red colors of local Arlesian dress.

Roman Arles

The amphitheater and the neighboring Roman theater are witnesses to Arles's prestigious place in the Roman world. The name Arles was derived from Arelate, "city of swamps." Arles was then surrounded by swamps and marshes that have since been drained. The Camargue is the last remaining one. Despite the inhospitable environment, the Romans developed Arles as an important port and economic center.

The rise of the city dates from 49 B.C., after Julius Caesar overcame the city of Marseille during the civil war between his supporters and those of rival Pompey; Marseille had sided with Pompey, the loser. As punishment, the winners shifted Rome's trading activity from Marseille to Arles. A canal was built to join Arles with the Mediterranean Sea. Arles also inherited the major portion of Marseille's territory, which extended along the coast to Nice.

During Arles's golden period (first through fourth centuries A.D.) the emperors endowed it with monuments worthy of a major Roman city: a circus, a triumphal arch, a 12,000-seat theater, lavish baths, an aqueduct, temples, and the amphitheater, les Arènes.

Les Arènes, carved out of rock, is relatively well preserved today. During the Middle Ages it was used as a military camp and it later became a city within a city, with some two hundred houses and two chapels built inside and outside its walls. The city cleared out the houses and their residents in 1825, and shortly afterward the amphitheater was restored to its original state.

Next to les Arènes are the ruins of the **Roman theater**, which was constructed several years before the amphitheater, in about A.D. 30, during the first years of the reign of Augustus. Today the theater is mostly in ruin. Several artifacts found here, including a statue of Augustus, are at the **Musée Lapidaire Païen**, nearby in the place de la République. The museum occupies a 17th-century Gothic church; plans are under way to transfer it to a large building just outside the city. The museum also houses statues, sarcophagi, and Roman columns found throughout the Arlesian region.

Augustus and Caesar weren't the only prominent Roman rulers who supported Arles. Constantine (288–337) adopted Arles as one of his two capitals (Constantinople was the other). He brought his family, friends, dignitaries, and his treasury here but stayed only for short periods.

Constantine ordered new construction at Arles, embellishing the ramparts ordered by Caesar and Augustus and enlarging the city to include the right bank of the Rhône, Trinquetaille. Arles therefore earned the title of Duplex Arelas (double city).

Arles became the sole capital of the Western Empire in 395, during the Germanic invasions, when Emperor Theodosius transferred the seat of government here from Trèves.

Arles's importance in the Christian Roman Empire explains why the city has several early Christian churches. An important Paleo-Christian museum, the **Musée Lapidaire Chrétien**, located behind the place de la République, is considered to have the richest collection of sarcophagi after the Vatican Museum. Most of these, dating from the fourth century, were transferred in excellent condition from the late empire burial grounds at Alyscamps.

The **Alyscamps** was the only archaeological site that interested van Gogh, although that was only thanks to Gauguin, who set out to study and paint the sacred burial ground when he came down to Arles to join his friend.

Outside the old city's ramparts to the southeast and crammed in between factories and houses, the Alyscamps is a tomb- and tree-lined walkway—all that remains of the Roman necropolis—that now leads to the 12th-century church of St-Honorat (now being restored).

Arles after the Romans

After the Germanic tribes overran the Roman Empire, Arles fell into the hands of the Visigoths, then, in succession, the Burgunds, the Franks, the Saracens, and finally the Carolingian Franks—who were later to establish the Holy Roman Empire under Charlemagne. Charlemagne's descendants further divided the new empire with each succession. Arles was first integrated into the kingdom of Provence, then became the capital of the kingdom of Burgundy-Provence (from 934 to 1032). Such was the enduring importance of Arles that Emperor Frederick Barbarossa of the Holy Roman Empire (then in effect German) was crowned king of Arles at the **church of St-Trophime** in 1178.

St-Trophime, in the place de la République, just west of the Roman theater, is the most interesting of Arles's early-Christian buildings. It was a major stopping point along the Medieval Christian pilgrimage route to Santiago de Compostela in Spain. Built from the ruins of a fifth-century church, St-Trophime is an example of early Provençal Romanesque architecture, strongly influenced by Roman and Greek style.

The church's cloisters (12th to 14th centuries) contain intricately sculptured cornices that recount the resurrection of Christ and the glorification of Arles's patron saints.

Saint Trophime the man was a significant figure in the early history of the Catholic Church. Recognized as having evangelized Arles near the end of the second century, he was one of the city's first bishops, therefore making him one of the first Christian dignitaries.

Provençal Arles

Arles's historical glory ended in the 13th century, when the city was fully integrated with the Comté de Provence.

Of all Provence's major cities, none embodies the Provençal tradition more than Arles. Frédéric Mistral's Félibrige movement and the writings of Alphonse Daudet helped create this image. In 1896, Mistral founded the Musée Arlaten, on the rue Balze next to the Musée Lapidaire Chrétien (but the entrance to the latter is on the rue de la République). Inside, the history of Arles is traced from prehistoric times to the 20th century with an amazing collection of furniture, local dress, documents, and works of art.

Like every typical Provençal town, Arles has its main café-lined avenue, the boulevard des Lices. Here is the city's only four-star hotel, the reasonably priced **Jules César**, in a rebuilt 17th-century convent. The hotel's restaurant, **Lou Marquès**, which specializes in Arlesian cooking, provides a relaxed yet somehow fussy atmosphere.

Arles is not just a trip to the past. The annual Rencontres Internationales de la Photographie has built a solid reputation for its summer photo exhibitions. While the shows take place in different sites in the city, the **Musée Réattu** houses a permanent collection. Located on the banks of the Rhône next to the ruins of Constantine's baths, the museum also has 57 drawings by Picasso and one of his paintings.

Just out of town is an outrageous yet worthwhile recreation of van Gogh's Pont de Langlois. The bridge itself is an authentic period piece, brought in from Fos-sur-Mer. Even the Rhône has changed since van Gogh painted Arlesians washing clothes in it; a canal has diverted it almost half a mile from its original site.

NIMES

The main reason to visit Nîmes, a mere 25 km or so (about 15 miles) southwest of Avignon and northwest of Arles, is to see its grand Roman ruins: The Arènes (amphitheater), the Temple de Diane, and the Maison Carrée are among the best-preserved Roman monuments in Europe. In addition, a 30-mile-long Roman aqueduct comes down from Uzès in the north and along the route crosses the famous Pont-du-Gard, a three-tier bridge that is one of the engineering and architectural wonders of the Roman Empire, standing miraculously intact.

Because of the close geographical grouping of its monuments (all within walking distance from the train station), Nîmes is easily visited in a short day trip from any of several bases. From Montpellier, Arles, or Avignon, for example, the trip takes 30 minutes by train. From Avignon by car, the trip should include a slight detour north for a visit to the Pont-du-Gard. There is a good hotel right in Nîmes, however, the **Impérator**, with a lovely garden and excellent dining outdoors in season.

Religious differences have been particularly disastrous for the city. Nîmes was a victim of the Albigensian Crusades in the 13th century. In the 16th century, it was one of the most important Calvinist centers in France, and the site of a major massacre of Catholics. The Catholic Louis XIII brought the city under submission in 1629. Despite an official tolerance for Huguenots, religious hatred and tension continued until the 18th century. The Revolution was bloody in Nîmes, fiercely fought between royalist Catholics and Protestant republicans.

Nîmes once had a strong textile industry based on wool and silk. Its serge became world famous, thanks to Levi-Strauss, who produced blue jeans from *material de Nîmes*—denim.

Today Nîmes is a sprawling city of 130,000, the center of strong agricultural and food-processing industries, and is in the heart of France's main (by quantity) wine-producing region. Recently the area has been hard hit by Common Market measures to reduce European wine surpluses. Many farmers have been forced out of the wine-producing business, and others have converted their fields to higher-quality vines or have introduced different crops altogether.

Roman Nîmes

Nîmes was occupied long before the Romans founded it in 121 B.C. In fact, Nîmes was the capital of the Volques Arecomices, an indiginous tribe. The city grouped several villages around a hill dominated by a freshwater spring. A fountain—later during the Roman era considered among the most famous in the world—was built and named after a local god, Nemausus, from whom the name Nîmes derived.

Nîmes owes most of its glorious Roman monuments to Agrippa, friend and counselor to Augustus. The **Maison Carrée** (Square House) was a monument, built in 1 B.C., to Agrippa's two sons born from a marriage with Augustus's daughter Julia. Modeled after a Greek temple, the

Maison Carrée overlooked the long-since-disappeared forum. The house is not actually square, but rather rectangular; the Romans considered a building square if its angles were symmetrical.

The **amphitheater** is nearly identical to the one in Arles. Its façade is better preserved, however. Historians believe that the Nîmes amphitheater was constructed around A.D. 70. Today, matadors rather than gladiators awe spectators in the ancient arena, which holds 21,000 people. It is frequently used for bullfights (usually in the Provençal style: no killing of the bull). Over the centuries, the amphitheater was used as a Visigoth fort, a stronghold for an association of Medieval knights, and, finally, a village of 2,000, complete with a chapel. It was restored to its original state in the 19th century.

LA CAMARGUE

The Camargue—a triangle between two branches of the Rhône River and Mediterranean Sea—is the closest thing France has to open wilderness. Vast and varied, the Camargue includes a beachside resort—Stes-Maries-de-la-Mer—an immense bird sanctuary, a zoological park, rice paddies, and sea-salt mines.

A car is a must to see the Camargue, although buses run from Arles to Stes-Maries. Numerous small ranches near Stes-Maries offer horseback tours of the Camargue's most inaccessible spots. (Tour promoters also take visitors out on safaris by Jeep.) For the horseback route try Port-Dromar (Tel: 90-97-91-92), where owners Claude and Kiki go out once or twice daily. The Camargue horse, now a recognized breed in France, is small, barrel-bellied, with tiny ears and heavy feet. Its primary function, over the centuries, was to roam the swamps with the *gardian,* the Camargue cowboy, to manage herds of bulls.

If cowboy dress is your thing, reasonably priced, classic Camargue clothing can be bought at the **Botte Gardiane** in Stes-Maries, next to the Musée Baroncelli. The clothes—slick leather boots, large-brimmed black hats, and traditional shirts—are made in Nîmes and Arles.

Nature lovers can also enjoy the Camargue in the off-season, although by late November most of the pink flamingos and other birds have headed south. In winter, the Camargue is a deserted, magical land that, because of its isolation, should be visited with caution, especially the small back roads and paths. Stes-Maries almost shuts down completely in winter, but it's during this time that it's at its most charming.

Stes-Maries-de-la-Mer

Neither a St-Tropez nor a Miami Beach, Stes-Maries-de-la-Mer has its own appeal that you can appreciate if you don't expect too much. In the height of the summer season—July and August—this village of 2,000 inhabitants is overrun with French and northern European tourists in search of a seaside vacation quieter and more modest than they would find on the Côte d'Azur.

The town does offer a Medieval fortified church—which still dominates the skyline as it did when van Gogh painted it—a bullfighting ring, and wide white-sand beaches.

Avoid going at the end of May, when the gypsy pilgrimage turns the area into the "Mecca of the Golfe du Lion," as Frédéric Mistral described it one hundred years ago. The gypsy pilgrims arrive for the procession celebrating the legend of the two Saint Marys.

Its roots based on the New Testament, the legend first appeared in local church documents in the 13th century and goes as follows: Shortly after the death of Christ, several disciples, including Marie-Salomé and Marie-Jacobe, were cast out from Jerusalem on a small sailless boat and told "You will perish . . . without sail . . . without food. Go forward to your sad shipwreck."

But by miracle the boat arrived safely on the shores near Stes-Maries-de-la-Mer. From here the disciples dispersed to the north and east in Gaul to spread the gospel. The legend thus places Stes-Maries as the first holy spot in France. The gypsy pilgrimage and procession—which includes what is claimed to be the boat itself—takes place May 25, the day Saint Marie-Jacobe is supposed to have died.

Stes-Maries's restaurants are mostly pizzerias or purveyors of modest tourist fare, although an unpretentious waterfront snack-bar/hotel, **Les Vagues**, facing the new marina, serves one specialty of the area: *tellines,* a small shellfish cooked in a garlic sauce.

For the best meal in town, try the **Brûleur de Loups**, on the avenue Gilbert-Leroy. The prices are reasonable, the cuisine is regional, and the restaurant is decorated in elegant 1930s style.

While Stes-Maries-de-la-Mer has several hotels, the best

bet is to stay in one of the numerous cabana-type lodgings outside of town, such as the nearby **Auberge Cavalière**. Slightly farther out of town is the pricey (meals included though) but spectacularly located **Mas de la Fouque**. Set off in the Camargue about 4 km (2.5 miles) from Stes-Maries, the Fouque has a swimming pool and spacious grounds, and its rooms have outdoor (but secluded) sunken tubs.

AIGUES-MORTES

In *Impressions of a Voyage,* Alexandre Dumas remarked, "We noticed Aigues-Mortes or rather we noticed its walls, because not one house or building is higher than its ramparts. This Gothic city appears like a jewel carefully wrapped in a case of stone."

Dumas's description still holds nearly a hundred years later. Aigues-Mortes, which is just 45 km (28 miles) south of both Arles and Nîmes, is one of the few cities in France—along with Carcassonne—whose walls are intact. The small town, with a population of only 4,000, makes a good base from which to visit the surrounding Camargue. It has two excellent hotels and several top restaurants; best to avoid it during the busy July to August season, however.

Aigues-Mortes was created by the French king Louis IX—Saint Louis—out of a sandy desert bordered by estuaries and swamps—hence the name, which means "dead water." Aigues-Mortes's history and fame thus belong to Medieval royal France. In fact, for nearly a hundred years Aigues-Mortes enjoyed the status of being the kingdom's only Mediterranean port. Saint Louis encouraged neighboring inhabitants to move to his newly created but highly inhospitable town by offering them generous tax breaks. Thousands moved in, and the port was used by traders from throughout the northern Mediterranean coast: Catalonia, Genoa, and Provence. At its height, its population was 15,000.

After Saint Louis chose Aigues-Mortes as his Mediterranean port, he used it twice to embark on crusades to the "Orient," once in 1248 to Egypt and the second time, in 1270, to Tunis. The king died on that last trip, and historians believe the cause of death was malaria he contracted in the swampy and mosquito-infested area surrounding Aigues-Mortes.

Most of the ramparts and walls were built by Saint Louis's sons and successors, Philippe III and Philippe Auguste. Although Aigues-Mortes was heavily fortified, its greatest defensive asset was the swamps, which rendered the city unapproachable by all but one road. To guard that road, the king built the **Tour Carbonnière**. The fortress tower still stands today, virtually untouched, just out of town on Route N 579.

A visit to **the ramparts** begins at the castle and the massive **Tour de Constance**. The tower—originally isolated by a ditch—was the centerpiece of Aigues-Mortes's defense and contained the city's arsenal.

Next to the tower, in the place d'Armes through the main entrance into the city, is the **Hostellerie des Remparts**, a cozy three-star hotel in a converted 18th-century two-story guardhouse with a view of the tower.

The main square of this small town is named after its founder—Saint Louis. Several restaurants, café terraces, and the *Office de Tourisme* are on the square. Unusual for such a small place, Aigues-Mortes has two fine restaurants, one of which—**Minos**—is here on the place St-Louis. The Minos has a vine-covered terrace overlooking a statue of the king. The service is friendly; the specialty is fish and a local Camargue meat dish in sauce, *gardiane*.

Just off the square on the rue Amiral-Courbet is another rustic hotel, the **St-Louis**. Its enclosed private terrace can be a welcome retreat during the crowded season.

Aigues-Mortes's second major restaurant is of national renown, **La Camargue**. Many come to the town just to eat in this converted, centuries-old, rustic Camarguais house and listen to gypsy and flamenco music. Reservations are necessary for dining on the terrace in July and August, and the restaurant is closed in January and February. Plaques mark the booths where dignitaries, former President Georges Pompidou among them, have eaten. The specialties are regional—*tellines,* shellfish, *boeuf gardiane* in a black-olive sauce. The restaurant is pricey, but worth it.

AIX-EN-PROVENCE

It doesn't take an art scholar to understand why Cézanne was captivated by Aix (pronounced "X"). All it takes is experiencing an afternoon sun casting a reddish hue on the massive Montagne St-Victoire and reflecting off the city's rose-colored tile roofs and well-groomed orange Baroque buildings.

The biggest asset of Aix is an intrinsic and unified Baroque architectural beauty that forms an enchanting whole. Sitting on a café terrace and doing absolutely nothing is one of the great attractions of this posh student town. Throughout most of its history, Aix has cultivated a noble air and an elitist front. Its reputation for the good life, especially among upper-middle-class Parisians, has been responsible for making it one of France's fastest-growing cities. Aix has mushroomed from 30,000 people before World War II to nearly 140,000 today. The growth, however, has taken place outside of what is referred to as Old Aix, which has remained virtually unchanged during the past two hundred years.

Aix has been known for its waters since Roman times. Today the town boasts dozens of fountains, but only one—in the middle of cours Sextius—gives forth mineral water.

In the second and third centuries B.C., Aix was the capital of an important Celtic-Ligurian community. Its ruins can still be visited, at Entremont, just outside the city. In 123 B.C. the Greeks in Marseille called on their Roman allies for military help against the Celtic Ligurians. The Roman armies led by the proconsul Caius Sextius Calvinus defeated the Celts and founded a military out-post on land that contained underground springs. The camp was named Aquae Sextiae, which was eventually shortened to just Aix. Today the Hôtel des Thermes—with its thermal-water cure—stands next to the site of the old Roman baths. (A few years ago a scandal struck when it was discovered that the pure water of Aix was not so pure after all.)

Under the Roman Empire, Aix became an important city and was lavishly rewarded with temples and amphitheaters. However, successive calamities, including the Moorish invasions of the ninth century, caused the destruction of Aix's fabulous Roman buildings.

Another landmark—the court palace of Provence—fell victim to architectural snobbishness. When Provence became French in 1481, the old palace was used as the parliament building—a sort of courthouse—for the Provence region. By the early 18th century the practical need for more modern facilities and a mania for architectural symmetry led to the demolition of the palace.

Cours Mirabeau

The best example of this fashion for symmetry is the cours Mirabeau—a short tree-lined boulevard created in the late 17th century as a promenade based on a triple architectural harmony: the uniform height of the buildings, and the length (1,452 feet) and width (145 feet) of the street.

Along one side of the cours stand a half-dozen majestic *hôtels particuliers* (city mansions) constructed during the 17th and early 18th centuries. Today the buildings house several street-level *pâtisseries* where you can buy Aix's gourmet specialty, *calissons* (a soft, almond paste candy, still handmade in the city's several *calisson* factories).

On the cours's other side are less impressive Baroque buildings, notable only for the numerous large sidewalk cafés that front them. In the summertime trees on both sides of the cours form a green roof that shields the cafés from the Provençal sun. During most of the year the café terraces are filled with sippers who spend hours watching the parade of hundreds of passersby. Buskers, clowns, and other sidewalk performers add spice. The cours remains the center of life in Aix, as it was three hundred years ago.

Recently the Aixois committed another architectural faux pas when they tore down the exquisite four-star Hôtel Roi-René to make room for a modern replacement. The loss of Roi-René has made the **Augustins** even more appealing. On a side street off the cours—the rue de la Masse—this former convent is intimate, and each room has a charming Medieval air. Make sure to ask for one with a balcony (there are only two); they cost about 100 francs more but are worth it, looking out over a small, quiet courtyard with a view of a 15th-century bell tower and a panorama of tiled rooftops.

At the bottom of the cours, in front of a statue of Good King René—the last great ruler of Provence—stands Aix's most famous café: **Les Deux Garçons**. During the First Empire the café was the meeting place of the "Golden Youth," and after that, under the Restoration, the "Romantic Youth." Later it became the favorite café of Cézanne, Emile Zola, and others. Now it is protected as a national landmark.

In recent years the cours has lost some of its spark. Just as one example, during Aix's music festival, which lasts nearly two months, from late June to early August, heavily armed police patrol the street to stop any music played after 10:00 P.M.—which, not surprisingly, has soured the formerly festive atmosphere more than a bit.

Even so, Aix's music festival is still a big event. It is really two different festivals: **Aix en Musique**, daily free classical and folk concerts in various locations around the city; and the **Festival d'Aix**—the opera festival—which features highly acclaimed performances under the stars in a newly renovated theater at the 17th-century archbishop's palace (on rue Gaston de Saporta, next to the cathedral). Tickets must be reserved months in advance, and cost an average of 400 francs. Aix's festival has become a major stepping-stone for up-and-coming opera stars. The theater runs three different operas per festival and specializes in Mozart. For information and reservations call 42-23-37-81.

Festival time or not, for a break from the more touristy and higher-priced cours take a two-minute walk to the majestic place de L'Hôtel de Ville in the center of the Old City, Vieil Aix. An almost enclosed courtyard, the place is dominated by the 17th-century city hall and the former Halles aux Grains, now a post office. Just behind it is the small daily produce market—one of the most outstanding in Provence. At the small market you can find a vast selection of Provençal specialties, including braids of garlic cloves, fresh and dried herbs, fresh goat cheese, and melons.

Parallel to the cours, on the rue Espariat, is the 17th-century Hôtel Boyer d'Equilles, a natural history museum. The paleontological collection includes dinosaur eggs and ancient seashells.

Despite the fresh food available, Aix is not especially known for its restaurants. The city is filled with eating places, though, and while very few offer gastronomical treats, nearly all of them—except for some chain restaurants—are small, intimate, and charming, or else well situated with comfortable outside terraces. These places are scattered throughout the center of the Old City, and you can't go wrong by just wandering around checking out menus and decor until the fancy hits. Try the relaxed and rustic **Comté d'Aix**, on the rue de Couronne.

The Aix Cathedral

Passing through the place de L'Hôtel de Ville en route to the cathedral, you must go under the ancient bell tower. The large white stones on the tower's bottom date from

Roman times; the rest was built in the 11th century and rebuilt in the 16th.

The tower marks what most historians now believe to be the boundary of ancient Roman Aix. It was perhaps the guard tower of the military outpost, Aquae Sextiae. Beyond the tower and away from the cours begins what was once the main Roman street, now called the rue Gaston de Saporta. This is the hub of a part of Aix's student life: The political science building and the foreign student institute sit side by side facing the hybrid and architecturally interesting **cathedral of St-Sauveur**.

The cathedral's mélange of styles clashes with the studied symmetry of the other structures of Aix. While many *hautain* Aixois took swipes at its lack of continuity ("Ugly and irregular," noted one university president in 1739), archaeologists find it a gold mine of information.

Its styles span two thousand years of Western history, with traces of Roman, early Christian, Romanesque, Gothic, and Renaissance architecture. Recent digs proved that the cathedral was built on the site of a former Roman building, and Roman stones were used to build one wall of the 12th-century Romanesque section. Inside, there is a remarkable triptych of the Burning Bush by Nicolas Froment, King René's court painter. The painting remains shuttered most of the year and you must ask the keeper or guide to open it. The baptistery dates from the fourth and fifth centuries, and the bell tower from the early 15th century. Next to the cathedral, and accessible through the courtyard of the adjoining archbishop's palace, is a small Medieval cloister, well worth visiting for its sculptured cornices. In the place de l'Archevêché (Archbishop) is the **Snack Bar Charlie et Maggie**; open during the summer until midnight or later, this is a great place to eat a quick and not too expensive meal outside.

Paul Cézanne in Aix

Paul Cézanne may be Aix's best-known native, but it's only recently that he has become the city's favorite son. While he lived here the eccentric Cézanne was at odds with the staid Aixois. Children mocked him and his fellow citizens shunned him. Until 1985 no Cézanne painting hung in the city. Today, the **Musée Granet**, to the south of the cours Mirabeau off the rue d'Italie, houses several major Cézannes.

Cézanne preferred working away from the city, mostly

in the foothills of the imposing Montagne St-Victoire, which he painted more than 60 times. He also had a workshop just outside Old Aix, past the cathedral, at what is now 9, avenue Paul Cézanne. American admirers have restored the workshop to the same state it was in at the time of Cézanne's death in 1906.

Excursions from Aix

The chalky white massif of **Montagne St-Victoire** dominates Aix and the surrounding countryside. At sunset it turns a brilliant red. St-Victoire can be easily climbed and is well marked. The summit provides a 17th-century chapel and a panoramic view of the valley. The massif received its name in the 16th century as a reminder of the Roman victory over the Teutons in 102 B.C.

Route D 17 east from Aix borders the southern side of St-Victoire; along the route are several lovely villages, including Le Tholonet (with its 19th-century Château Noir), St-Antonin, and Pourrières.

Along the route on the northern side of the mountain, D 10, is the village of Vauvenargues, where Picasso lived until 1961. The castle of Vauvenargues, unfortunately, is not open to the public.

MARSEILLE

Marseille, a mere 30 km (18 miles) south of elegant, well-heeled Aix, strikes terror in the hearts of some travellers because of its reputation as a nest of gangsters. That's too bad, because this port town is so endowed with charm and beauty that limiting a visit here to changing trains at the Gare St-Charles would be a shame.

If nothing else, a quick morning boat ride from the Vieux Port to the Château d'If to see the castle made famous by Alexandre Dumas's *Count of Monte Cristo* is well worth the approximately two-hour detour. The trip across the harbor lets you view Marseille the right way, from the water, so you can feel a closer identification with the Marseillais, whose town has been linked to the sea for 26 centuries. The château was built by François I from 1524 to 1528 as a fort, after Marseille had been held under siege by the armies of Spanish ruler Charles V. It was converted into a prison in 1634 and shut down in 1872 when the third Republic was established.

Marseille has several prominent museums and monuments, including the **Musée des Beaux-Arts**, which contains one of France's richest painting collections, and the
Vieille Charité—a 17th- to 18th-century hospital that has
been converted into a vast cultural center housing a new
archaeological museum. The city's most famous monument is no doubt the **cathedral of Notre-Dame de la
Garde**, high on a hill above the city.

Marseille's tarnished reputation is, in fact, part of its
attraction. Maverick, mysterious, violent, passionate, and
Byzantine, Marseille is a teeming, sprawling, hilly port
town of one million inhabitants, most of whom were—or
are descended from—immigrants: Italians, Arabs, North
African Jews, and Spaniards.

For centuries Marseille was focused more toward the
Orient and Africa than toward Europe, because it was a
major trading and commercial center, especially during
the Renaissance. Today sections of the city—Porte d'Aix,
for example—are much like the souk in Algiers.

Throughout its long history Marseille has been independent and often rebellious. Neither royalist nor conservative, Marseille has been fiercely democratic ever since
it was founded as a Hellenistic republic in 600 B.C.

The story of France's national anthem, *La Marseillaise,* is
an example. During the Revolution fervent Marseillais revolutionaries marched to Paris, singing a military chant written in Strasbourg all along the route as a battle cry. The song
thereafter became synonymous with the Revolution—
much to the chagrin of its composer, who was a royalist.

Ancient Marseille

The Marseillais have a well-founded reputation of being
great tellers of tall tales, and they've got a whopper for the
founding of their city by the Phoenicians in 600 B.C. The
Marseillais themselves are not the source of the legend; it
comes from the third-century Latin historian Justin. As he
described it, a Greek leader, Protis, went in search of
Celtic-Ligurian king Segobia Nannus to ask permission to
found a city on the coast of his territory. The day Protis
arrived, King Nannus was preparing a wedding-day festival for his daughter. Custom was to choose the groom at
the festival. The Greeks were invited. The king told his
daughter to offer water to the man of her choice. She
chose Protis. As a gift, the king granted Protis the land to
found his port, which became known as Massalia.

For the Greeks, Marseille was the perfect site. French geographer Vidal de la Blanche noted: "With its small islands, acropolis, detached hills and cliffs, small river and deep port, Massalia is the classic type of a Greek city."

Developed as an independent but distinctly Hellenistic republic, Marseille quickly emerged as a powerful mercantile and political center. Its control spread throughout the region, including Nice to the east and Agde to the west.

The city's fortunes changed in 49 B.C., when Julius Caesar's army crushed it for siding with Pompey during Rome's civil war. Marseille paid dearly for the blunder, losing its navy, port, and territories—all except Nice. The city then slipped into the shadows for centuries. You can witness much of this history in the Jardin des Vestiges (see below) and in the nearby Musée d'Histoire de Marseille, with a collection that includes a well-preserved third-century Roman ship.

The Vieux Port

The Vieux Port (Old Port) is a protected basin that cuts right into the center of Marseille. The new port, La Joliette, lies at the Marseille end of a 45-mile-long seaside complex that stretches west to the Port-St-Louis-du-Rhône. Now used by pleasure boaters, tour guides, and fishermen, the Vieux Port is lined with restaurants—most of which are unscrupulous tourist traps that serve bogus bouillabaisse at seemingly reasonable prices. The few honest establishments have banded together and created a bouillabaisse certificate that guarantees authentic traditional quality.

Real bouillabaisse is a Marseillais specialty, and shouldn't be missed. **Michel**, 6, rue des Catalans, serves the best. The fish is bought fresh every morning from the Vieux Port market, and only the proper high-quality Mediterranean fish—such as *Saint-Pierre* and *rascasse*—is used. A real bouillabaisse is made with at least four different types of fish.

The **Miramar** restaurant, at 12, quai Port, is less expensive and nearly as good. It has the advantage of being easy to find and affords a lovely view of the Vieux Port.

Just behind the Vieux Port is La Bourse de Commerce, a modern shopping complex that nevertheless is near two points of interest—the best hotel in Marseille, the Altéa, and the **Jardin des Vestiges**, an archaeological site with Greek, Roman, and early Christian ruins. (The walls of Marseille's original port have been uncovered here.)

What the **Altéa** lacks in intimacy it makes up for in convenience, comfort, and view. A seven-story modern hotel, its prices go up with the floors. Be sure to ask for a room with a view of the Vieux Port.

If you want a quieter hideaway in Marseille, a good choice would be **Le Petit Nice**, with its **Restaurant Passedat**, along the corniche John F. Kennedy, south of town along the coast. Less expensive but nevertheless charming is the **Concorde-Palm Beach**, with its seaside fish restaurant, **La Réserve**. Palm Beach is farther south on the corniche route. Also on the attractive corniche route is **Parc Borély** and its 18th-century château, which houses the **Musée d'Archéologie Méditerranéenne**— France's second-largest collection of Egyptian antiquities (after the Louvre).

COTE D'AZUR

The contemporary impression of the French Riviera as a place for beautiful people dies hard. Despite packed beaches and some tacky condos, the Côte d'Azur is still in fact dazzling. Each succeeding generation has had its own images of the chic and rich who have made the Riviera their partying ground. Today we dream of the dolce vita days of Bardot and swinging, topless St-Tropez, while 30 years ago people reminisced about F. Scott Fitzgerald's Antibes crowd. Fitzgerald himself wrote in *Tender Is the Night* about Rosemary Hoyt being driven along the Riviera: "The resplendent names—Cannes, Nice, Monte Carlo— began to glow through their torpid camouflage, whispering of old kings come here to dine or die, of rajahs tossing Buddha's eyes to English ballerinas, of Russian princes turning the weeks into Baltic twilights in the lost caviar days."

Today Arab sheikhs may have replaced Russian and English royalty, and the entire coast is crawling with thrill- and sun-seekers of all types and classes, but the jet and moneyed set still come here.

The Côte d'Azur is two distinctly different worlds: the coast and the *arrière-pays,* or backcountry. The latter includes the French Alps, less than an hour's drive north from Nice. The *arrière-pays* presents startlingly beautiful countryside (the rocky Vallée des Merveilles, the Gorges Rouges, and the Trois Corniches) and interesting villages—the tiny, Medieval Colmars-les-Alpes, for example. These must be approached by car, and seeing them requires several days. Unless you have a lot of time to spend, it's best to concentrate on the coast and those areas closest to it.

MAJOR INTEREST ON THE COTE D'AZUR

Art and archaeology museums

Iles d'Hyères
Nature and relative tranquillity

St-Tropez
Fishing-port charm with glitz

Cannes
Film Festival
Beach lunching

Antibes/Juan-les-Pins/Cap d'Antibes
Swinging summer beach resort at Juan-les-Pins
More exclusive resorts at Cap d'Antibes

St-Paul-de-Vence
Art interest and atmosphere
Fondation Maeght
Colombe d'Or restaurant

Nice
Promenade des Anglais
Old Nice
Musée Chagall
Cimiez
Musée Matisse

Perched villages

Monaco
Monte-Carlo Casino

Menton
Genteel Belle Epoque beauty

The Late Rise of the Côte d'Azur

The name Côte d'Azur was coined in 1887 by Stephen Liegeard, politician and writer, who published a book on the Riviera entitled *La Côte d'Azur*. The new name was adopted almost immediately by the region and the rest of the French.

Liegeard described the area as a "coast of light, of warm breezes, and mysterious and balmy forests . . . from Genoa to Hyères, the route is short but delicious."

Perhaps the first visitor to discover the French Riviera was Hercules, who, according to legend, created the port of Villefranche-sur-Mer with his own hands. The first real tourist, in the modern sense, came in the 18th century: an Englishman, Tobias Smollett. What he saw wasn't exactly what's printed in today's vacation brochures. In his *Letters from Nice* he explained how he narrowly escaped from bandits in the Maures hills and almost drowned while crossing the then bridgeless river Var. He found the streets of Nice "full of excrement," the servants "repulsively dirty," and that "day and night, flies and fleas" swarm. The overall picture Smollett painted was a rosy one, however—he also told of the Riviera's natural beauty and lovely climate—and it attracted a great many English travellers to the city. Later, Russians and French followed.

The second half of the 19th century was the Riviera's Belle Epoque. "Princes and princes, everywhere princes!" remarked Guy de Maupassant in 1888. The railroad made it possible to travel from Vienna to Cannes in 31 hours in a luxurious Pullman sleeping car. By the end of the century a weekly St. Petersburg-Vienna-Cannes line carried the privileged to the azure coast. Casinos, splendid villas, and grand hotels were built along the beaches; Champagne, caviar, and money flowed.

The Era of the Summer Season

Yet it wasn't until the 1920s that the Riviera became a summer, sea-bathing resort. Until then people came to the coast to escape northern winters By summertime most of the Riviera set had either gone home or migrated to Normandy and Brittany. A worldly Russian, Marie Bashkirtseff, described the Riviera in summer as a desolate place: "It's deserted. I'm ready to cry, I'm suffering so." Stepping into the sea for a dip was only for those with a medical prescription, not yet a general fashion.

Summer tourism slowly came to the coast after World War I, thanks to American soldiers. Antibes was the first hot spot. John Dos Passos remarked that "rich British and French would rather be dead than be seen here in the

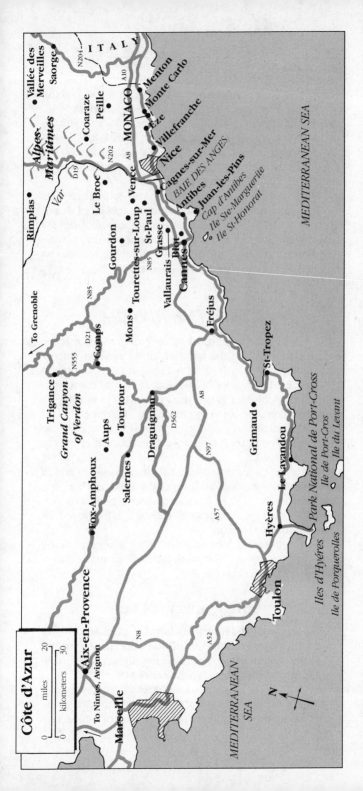

summer. The place is too hot for them. But for us Americans, the temperatures seem perfect and the bathing delicious. The sun cult is just beginning." Gertrude Stein, Rudolph Valentino, Picasso, the Fitzgeralds, and Rex Ingram were among the first summer tourists coming to Antibes in the early 1920s. World War I also affected the visitors from Europe: The October Revolution brought an end to the Russian monarchy.

The major change in the Côte d'Azur took place after 1936, when the Socialist government, the Front Populaire, granted French workers the right to paid vacations in July and August. For the first time a vacation on the Riviera was possible for the masses. And the masses did indeed come, and indeed they still do.

ART ON THE RIVIERA

The beauty of light and nature in Provence came to be appreciated only in the late 19th century, when Vincent van Gogh moved to Arles from Paris (in 1886), hoping to "... establish 'a school of the Midi' similar to contemporary artists' colonies in Brittany." Following in van Gogh's brushstrokes, the Fauves centered in St-Tropez, Picasso settled in Antibes, Matisse moved to Nice, Chagall chose Vence, and countless other artists have found their way to this sunny land.

Today, art of the past (especially Impressionist) and of the present is as integral a part of the Riviera as sun, sea, garlic, and wine. More than 30 museums of various persuasions stud the coast and hills along a 116-mile stretch from Toulon to Menton.

Nice is a natural starting place for an adventure in the Riviera's sea of art, followed here by other locations, listed in alphabetical order.

Museums in Nice

Travellers intrigued by archaeology as well as art discover a double-barreled attraction in the **Villa des Arènes** on the site of Roman Cemenelum, now **Cimiez**, a sophisticated residential area. When Henri Matisse died in a nearby house in 1954, his widow donated a great number of works to Nice, specifying the 17th-century villa as the spot where they should be displayed. The rich collection includes paintings, drawings, sketches, models, bronze sculptures, and the artist's personal effects.

The fascinating archaeological museum on the villa's ground floor contains exhibits from excavations in the neighborhood; nearby Roman baths and an arena are open to the public.

In 1971 the **Musée National Message Biblique Marc Chagall** opened, also in Cimiez, to house the artist's gifts to France: 17 canvases of biblical inspiration, 300 graphic works, five sculptures, a tapestry, three stained-glass windows, and a huge mosaic. The lively, glowing, amusing fantasies are well served by the light and airy museum.

Most museums don't inspire laughter, but the **Musée International d'Art Naïf** on the avenue du Val Marie in far western Nice does just that. The Anatole Jakovsky bequest of some 600 canvases (about half on display at any one time) features amateur art from many countries, prominently including that of Jakovsky and other Yugoslavs. Childish, primitive, and illusory, the works are simultaneously well crafted, harmonious, and ingenious.

On avenue des Baumettes in western Nice, not far off the promenade des Anglais, the **Musée des Beaux-Arts Jules Chéret** devotes itself to 17th- and 18th-century European paintings, a collection of sculptures by Jean-Baptiste Carpeaux, 19th- and 20th-century landscapists, many posters and studies of founder Chéret, and several Impressionist works.

On rue de France in a little park just off the promenade des Anglais, the **Musée Masséna** (named for a local boy made Napoleonic general) illustrates the history, folklore, town planning, home decoration, and paintings of Nice and its region, and houses some paintings from Italian, Spanish, and Flemish schools.

Nice museums devoted to subjects other than art include the **Musée d'Histoire Naturelle**, near place Garibaldi in Old Nice; the **Musée Maritime**, on the grounds of the Nice Château; the **Musée Terra Amata**, a fascinating and unique exhibition of a prehistoric habitat on the very site of its discovery, on boulevard Carnot east of the port; and **Musée Vieux-Logis**, a priory outfitted with artworks and items from daily life of the 14th to 17th centuries, in St-Barthélemy on the northern edge of town.

Museums Elsewhere on the Côte d'Azur

Antibes. The **Musée Picasso**, in the Grimaldi castle, is among the most popular museums in the region. It shows off paintings, drawings, tapestries, sculptures, ceramics, and lithographs of the prolific artist. He produced a surprising number of them during his six-month stint as curator of an antiquities museum, during which time he also used the rooms as a studio.

The antiquities Picasso oversaw are now in the **Musée d'Archéologie**, in the St-André Bastion, part of the city's old fortifications: 300,000 items illustrate four thousand years of regional history.

Biot. This pretty village of flower markets, ceramic shops, and glassworks is known chiefly for the stark, light, altogether admirable **Musée National Fernand Léger**, created by the Cubist's widow in his honor in 1957, two years after his death. Madame Nadia Léger made it a gift to France in 1964. The 348 works on display include ceramics, stained glass, paintings, mosaics, and even tapestries. The museum is located southeast of the village, off Route D 4.

Cagnes-sur-Mer. In 1902, Jean Renoir bought a property in Cagnes named Les Collettes, built a house there, and lived in it with his wife for the last 12 years of his life. Now the **Musée Renoir**, the house remains as it was, containing a few artworks, furniture, and, in the studio, the artist's wheelchair (he suffered from rheumatoid arthritis in his final years and painted with brushes strapped to his hand); the delightful garden will be familiar to you from many paintings.

Haut-de-Cagnes, the now-fashionable older part of Cagnes, clusters around the reworked, 14th-century Grimaldi castle, today the **Château-Musée**. Like the castle's current appearance, the collections are nothing if not eclectic, the two most interesting constituting a museum of the olive tree and a museum of modern Mediterranean art.

Grasse. An elegant if small country house in a garden on the southwest edge of the hill town has become the **Villa Fragonard**. Fittingly enough, it's on the boulevard Jean-Honoré Fragonard, named for the 18th-century painter born in the village. Copies of panels painted for the Countess du Barry (originals are in New York City's Frick Collection) are displayed, as are original drawings, paintings, sketches, and etchings. (**Maison Fragonard** is among the most-visited *parfumeries* in this city of perfume-makers.)

An exceptionally interesting portrayal of the art and history of eastern Provence is shown in Grasse's **Musée d'Art et d'Histoire de Provence**, in a handsome 18th-century mansion just an amble from the Villa Fragonard off place du Cours. Collections extend from prehistoric and Gallo-Roman remains to fine Moustiers china, rural tools, Louis XIV furniture, and paintings by local artists.

Menton. The **Musée des Beaux-Arts**, also called Musée Palais Carnolès, occupies the former summer residence of Monaco's Grimaldi Prince Anthony I on avenue de la Madonne. It was later a casino, then the home of American Dr. Edward P. Aldiss. A museum since 1977, it displays various French and Italian old masters as well as contemporary works—one by England's Graham Sutherland.

Right on the quai Napoléon in Menton's 17th-century bastion, the **Musée Jean Cocteau** features the writer's fantasies in art: ceramics, paintings, gray-white tesserae (pebble paintings). A ticket to this museum also allows entrance to the **Salle des Mariages** in the old Hôtel de Ville, a room decorated by Cocteau in pseudo Greek-temple style.

Menton's **Musée Municipal** is a repository of ancient arts and archaeology.

St-Jean-Cap-Ferrat. The setting alone of the **Villa Ephrussi de Rothschild**, the only one on this beautiful wooded peninsula that is open to the public, would satisfy an artistic temperament. The baroness's art collections and those of her wealthy father and husband (together often called the Musée d'Ile de France) are only heightened in quality by the villa and its furnishings: Savonnerie carpets, Beauvais and Aubusson tapestries, Chinese vases, and the like. The gardens and their ornamentation also are magnificent.

St-Paul-de-Vence. One of the best modern art collections in France as well as one of the region's top tourist attractions, the **Fondation Maeght** was raised in the midst of a tangled pine forest in the early 1960s by Paris gallery owners and publishers Aimé and Marguerite Maeght. Even the architect was an artist, the Spaniard José Luis Sert. In such an environment, the works of Calder, Arp, Zadkine, Miró, Braque, Bonnard, Chagall, Léger, Kandinsky, Giacometti, and others seem peculiarly happy and at home. The foundation also has living quarters for artists and a vast art library. (St-Paul is reached from Cagnes-sur-

Mer via Routes D 6 and D 7.) On its main square, the 15-room inn and restaurant **La Colombe d'Or** keeps a stunning collection of paintings that artists—Modigliani, Bonnard, Dufy, Picasso, and Utrillo among them—presented to owner Paul Roux in their leaner days in return for his hospitality. An overnight stay or a fine meal in such surroundings is a small price to pay for such an atmosphere; rooms are expensive, but the wall painting might be by Rouault.

St-Tropez. Works of universally high quality have been hung in the **Musée de l'Annonciade**, which occupies a former chapel right off the port. Signac, Derain, Maillol, Seurat, Vuillard, Vlaminck, Utrillo, Dufy, and the rest of that crowd are represented here.

Toulon. The **Musée d'Art et d'Archéologie** and the **Musée d'Histoire Naturelle** are both located in a large, modernized building on boulevard Maréchal Leclerc in the heart of the new town. The antiquities are well arranged and include Oriental as well as Western finds; paintings extend from the 13th century to today. Toulon also boasts an outstanding **Musée Maritime**.

Vallauris. In this bustling little town just to the north of Cannes, where Picasso came to create ceramics for several years after World War II, the centrally located château contains the **Musée Municipal**, with its exhibitions of ceramics from Etruscan times to our own, as well as the **Musée National la Guerre et la Paix** (War and Peace), a priory chapel decorated with an immense composition Picasso executed in 1952.

Vence. The old market town is now a car-crowded resort in all seasons. Serenity now reigns here only in the **Chapelle du Rosaire**, which Matisse designed and decorated—down to the candles and vestments—between 1947 and 1951. Of it (and perhaps of his astonishing versatility), the artist wrote: "Despite its imperfections I think it is my masterpiece . . . the result of a lifetime devoted to the search for truth." (The chapel is open only on Tuesday and Thursday mornings and afternoons.)

Villefranche. Another chapel well worth a detour is **Chapelle St-Pierre**, right by the little port, once a fisherman's sanctuary, entirely painted from top to bottom, inside and out, by Cocteau in 1957.

Personalized art trips to museums and—equally enjoyable—to the homes and/or studios of the Nice-Riviera school of contemporary artists are arranged by P.A.T., the creation of Canadian Pat Hyduk, at 2, allée des Ormes, Les Hauts de Vaugrenier, 06270 Villeneuve-Loubet (9 km/5 miles west of Cagnes); Tel: 93-20-37-60.

In addition, P.A.T. operates Riviera on Request, which arranges for personalized antique-hunting and shopping excursions, gastronomic events, wine tours, and yacht charters. Contact: Unitravel Riviera, 119 bis, boulevard Carnot, 06110 Le Cannet (next to Cannes); Tel: 93-68-25-50.

An affiliate in the United States is Langcom International, 250 S. Beverly Dr., Beverly Hills, CA 90212; Tel: (213) 273-7833.

—*Georgia I. Hesse*

ILES D'HYERES

The four islands of Hyères form an oasis of unspoiled beauty just off the highly developed Côte d'Azur, thanks to strict environmental-protection controls. Of the four islands, only two are completely open to visitors: Ile de Port-Cros and Ile de Porquerolles. A major portion of the third, Ile de Levant, is reserved for the French navy, and part of it harbors a large nudist colony. The fourth, Ile de Bagaud, is an off-limits national park reserve. Boats for the Ile de Port-Cros and the Ile de Porquerolles leave from Lavendou and Hyères. Lavendou is a bit off the beaten track, between Toulon and St-Tropez, but from there the crossing takes only 35 minutes. From Hyères, the boats leave less frequently and the trip takes one and a half hours.

Ile de Port-Cros

For a quiet holiday amid some of the Mediterranean's most striking natural scenery, Port-Cros should top anyone's list. Motor vehicles are forbidden in the national park, and smoking, camping, and hunting are outlawed.

The island has one tiny village of 30 inhabitants, and few restaurants. Nevertheless, it does have a hotel, the **Manoir**, which has only 26 rooms, so reservations must be made long in advance. (The hotel is closed from October 15 to Easter.) Several footpaths provide for a tranquil hike through the island's forests and hills. The path through the Vallée de la Solitude takes two and a half hours and leads to the southern coast. Along the way are some of the small forts rebuilt by Napoléon Bonaparte after the English and Spanish occupied the islands in 1793.

The most interesting of the forts is Estissac (open June through September). Built in the 17th century, the fort is on the path to the bay of Port-Man, a three-hour round-trip walk that leads to the northeast part of the island. Less hilly and well shaded than the Vallée de la Solitude path, this one ends in a magnificent horseshoe-shaped bay ringed by woods.

Tourism aside, the main activity of the island is the preservation of endangered Mediterranean marine species, including fish. Recently, monk seals from throughout the western Mediterranean were captured and brought to the island to protect them from extinction.

Ile de Porquerolles

More developed than Port-Cros, Porquerolles nevertheless is car-free and has only a few hotels, including the secluded and moderately priced **Mas du Langoustier** and the more modest **Ste-Anne**. The island has wide white-sand beaches and countless nature walks.

ST-TROPEZ

St-Trop—as the hip call it—is indeed *trop*. Situated off the main highway, it requires a detour. This is both a blessing and a curse. These days it's more of a curse because it seems everybody wants to go to St-Tropez, and as a result the traffic snarls are intolerable on the small roads that lead in and out of this glitzy resort.

Those in the know, however, still go there, preferring the hidden St-Trop. They're the ones who have villas tucked away just outside the town. They have their own swimming pools so they avoid the crowded beaches. Or they know the right secluded beaches—located mostly south of the city.

These people include top writers—Françoise Sagan; movie directors—Claude Zidi; photographers—David Hamilton; actors and singers—Charles Aznavour and, of course, Brigitte Bardot.

In spite of the congestion, St-Trop's old town center has kept much of its Provençal fishing-port charm. Some of the old-timers remain, and a few of them even still make a living fishing.

CANNES

For two weeks in May, Cannes becomes the world's cinema capital, and stargazers can catch the likes of Roman Polanski or Tony Curtis walking down the Croisette. Cannes is a city of other conventions, too, with year-round events from parapsychology meetings to television-program trade fairs.

Cannes's natural beauty, grand hotels, and mild climate are the keys to its success. A city of 72,000 residents, it seems to have an equal number of luxury shops, snack bars, and restaurants.

Cannes is not quaint and quiet. It does not attract the real jet set—except during the film festival. The city has no cultural attractions or major historical monuments. It does have two islands, 40 minutes off its coast, that do: the Iles de Lérins.

It is impossible to find a hotel in Cannes during the film festival; most are booked many months in advance. Nevertheless, the city is an exciting place at festival time. The festival was once a small, relaxed, but glamorous event held at the old Palais Croisette (scheduled to be demolished to make way for a Hilton hotel) and attended by Hollywood film greats. Grace Kelly met her future husband, the prince of Monaco, here during the festival of 1955.

In 1982 the festival was moved from the old Palais to a new venue, the Palais des Festivals, unaffectionately dubbed "the bunker" because of its heavy and unimaginative architecture—almost a symbol of how the festival has lost most of its human dimensions. Security is tight and entry to the screenings is strictly by invitation only. Thirty thousand professionals, journalists, and film lovers cram the huge bunker, and the numbers grow annually.

Still, it's worth breathing the charged atmosphere of the largest gathering of the world's cinematic industry while Cannes is awash in film billboards and starlets pose for the paparazzi, sometimes in very provocative postures. Meanwhile, thousands of people will be basking on Cannes's wide white-sand beaches.

The Croisette

During the festival, the major players—actors, directors, and producers—stay on the Croisette, a long, seaside avenue that begins at the Palais des Festivals and ends at the Palm Beach casino. The Croisette has three palace hotels: the **Majestic**, **Carlton**, and **Martinez**. From five in the afternoon until two in the morning, the Majestic bar and poolside terrace are packed with festivalgoers, journalists, and gawkers.

The festival's underbelly is at **Le Petit Carlton** (no relation to the Carlton), a small snack bar on the rue d'Antibes, where the European film crowd—overflowing onto the street—swigs endless beers until 4:00 A.M.

After the festival, the hotels empty out and Cannes quiets down. This is a good time to come. Although the three sumptuous Croisette hotels brim with romance and history, they are also very expensive. Seaside rooms are nearly double the rates of the others. In many ways the three hotels are interchangeable, although the Martinez has been modernized. It also has the best restaurant: **l'Orangerie**.

Less splendid than its Croisette sisters is the **Splendid**, one of the best hotel buys in Cannes. Just off the port, the Splendid is almost as comfortable as the other three but more homey and less fussy. It, too, has rooms facing the sea. To get away from the bustling center try the **Montfleury**, located on a hill overlooking the sea.

Beach Lunching

One of the pleasures of Cannes is lunching on the beach. A dozen beachside restaurants offer similar fare that is several steps up from—and many francs more than—typical snack food. Expect to pay 120 to 250 francs for any seaside meal. The Martinez serves an especially elaborate and impressive buffet.

In the evening **La Mère Besson**, behind the Croisette at 13, rue des Frères-Pardignac, serves traditional Provençal food. During the season, and especially during conventions or festivals, reservations here are imperative.

THE ILES DE LERINS

To get away from the crowds in Cannes, try hopping a boat at the Gare Maritime (next to the Palais) for the Iles de Lérins. From April to September boats leave regularly, taking 15 minutes to get to Ile Ste-Marguerite and 30 minutes to the smaller and quieter Ile St-Honorat. Both islands have conserved their natural beauty, and motor vehicles are banned.

Ile St-Honorat

In 410, Honorat, the son of a Roman consul, founded a monastery on the island—one of the first in the Christian world. The island was chosen because of the Lérins's isolation and barren solitude. The monastery's reputation spread quickly. Among its inhabitants were Saint Cassian, the founder of St-Victor in Marseille, and Saint Patrick of Ireland.

The original monastery was destroyed by the Moors in the eighth century but was rebuilt and fortified two hundred years later. The tenth-century tower still stands and is open to visitors.

After centuries of decline, the monastery was finally shut, and the island sold, during the French Revolution. Monks returned in 1869, however, after the bishop of Fréjus purchased the island. A new monastery was built on the ruins of the old one and a sect of Cistercian monks moved in. Cistercians still live here today.

Although the island receives about 150,000 visitors a year, you can still find quiet spots for a picnic and swim, especially in early June.

Ile Ste-Marguerite

Ile Ste-Marguerite is larger and more touristic than Honorat, although its development has been tightly controlled by the government. The island has numerous nature trails through its 400 acres of forests, as well as the 17th-century Fort Royal, built with remains of Gallo-Roman monuments and construction materials. Originally a private castle, the fort has been converted into a sinister-looking prison.

ANTIBES, JUAN-LES-PINS, CAP D'ANTIBES

Antibes and its neighbors, Juan-les-Pins and Cap d'Antibes, contrast and complement each other. Antibes is one of the oldest ports on the Mediterranean; Juan-les-Pins was built in the late 19th century. While today these two towns are full of summer tourists, the Cap—the peninsula separating the two—remains one of the exclusive locations on the Riviera.

About 30 km (18 miles) east of Nice, and only a stone's throw from Cannes, the area is easily accessible by train, bus, or car. Also in the vicinity is **Biot** (several km/a couple of miles northwest), featuring Medieval architecture and the **Musée National Fernand Léger** (on the St-Andre road; see Art on the Riviera, above).

Summertime, especially in July, during the top-notch jazz festival Juan-les-Pins swings, its nightclubs, cafés, and streets jammed with people late into the night. During the day the fine sand beaches are packed.

Juan-les-Pins's older cousin, Antibes, was founded in the fifth century B.C. by Greeks as Antipolis, or the city that faces. What it faced has always puzzled historians. Over the centuries, Antibes was a military stronghold and ancient fortifications remain.

One of the city's most interesting attractions is the **Musée Picasso**, located in a castle reconstructed in the 16th century (see Art on the Riviera). Not far from the museum, on the rue Clemenceau, is a typical Provençal market bordered by streets that contain several Medieval houses. The place Nationale is a bustling square with outdoor cafés and two comfortable, small, moderately priced hotels, **Caméo** and the **Auberge Provençale**.

Of course, the most famous restaurant on the Riviera is **La Bonne Auberge**, located just outside of Antibes. While its classic Provençal cuisine remains highly rated (two Michelin stars), the restaurant is suffering from its international reputation and has lost its romantic touch.

To get away from the crowds, head to Cap d'Antibes. For deep pockets, there's the **Hôtel du Cap d'Antibes**, with its superb view of the Mediterranean and its famous restaurant, **Pavillon Eden Roc**. Most of the top Hollywood stars stay at the hotel during the Cannes Film Festival. With a car, cruise the Cap in search of an off-the-beaten-track beach. They still exist, but don't expect a deserted oasis. More likely the beach will be an extension of a seaside restaurant.

Jazz came to Antibes–Juan-les-Pins with the first Americans, Frank Jay Gould and F. Scott Fitzgerald. Over the years all the greats have passed through: Louis Armstrong, Count Basie, Dizzy Gillespie, and Ray Charles. Most of the shows are played outdoors on a stage that borders the sea.

ST-PAUL-DE-VENCE

At one time St-Paul was the center for Europe's most vibrant artistic minds: Marc Chagall, Jacques Prévert, Georges Braque, Pablo Picasso, Yves Montand, Simone Signoret, André Malraux, and James Baldwin are but a few of those who have made this village perched on a hillside their home or meeting place in the fairly recent past. Time has taken its toll, and few of that generation are left. Nevertheless, the tradition continues, thanks in part to the Fondation Maeght, a modern-art museum and artists' community (see Art on the Riviera).

St-Paul, with its 2,600 inhabitants, is invaded by tourists on spring holidays and during the peak summer season. Yet even at its busiest time, St-Paul is quieter than the beach resorts. March and late September are excellent times to visit here. The village itself has a Medieval fortress wall, a rebuilt Romanesque church, and narrow, hilly, winding alleys full of art galleries and craft shops.

Surrounding St-Paul are forested parks where several hotels are located, among them the **Mas d'Artigny**. This outstanding Relais et Châteaux property, on a 16-acre park, has some reasonably priced rooms in off-season; most of them include large private balconies with views of the woods. Waking up to birds singing in the morning in this calm, pastoral setting is a far cry from the hubbub of the coast. For big spenders, 25 rooms have their own swimming pools—an extravagance that can be very appealing for a honeymoon or other special occasion.

La Colombe d'Or

Many people just pass through St-Paul to have a meal at La Colombe d'Or—an inexpensive but rather exclusive restaurant-hotel that has welcomed heads of state, artists, and actors.

Catherine Deneuve says that if she wants to be seen she goes to Maxim's in Paris; if she wants a quiet meal away from the crowds, she eats at the Colombe d'Or. During most of the year meals are served in its main dining room, which houses an impressive collection of modern art from many of the artists who have actually eaten or stayed here—Chagall, Picasso, Braque, Matisse, and Miró (see Art on the Riviera). In warm weather seating is available on the terrace, offering an unobstructed view of the valley below.

It's always best to reserve a table here no matter what the time of year. The fare is traditional, and unexceptional, Provençal; the service is friendly and informal; the prices are moderate. The Colombe d'Or's hotel, with only 24 rooms, is usually booked solid at peak season. The hotel also has a heated swimming pool.

Vence

Vence, with 13,400 inhabitants, is much larger than St-Paul. You must pass through Vence to get to St-Paul, and it's well worth your time to stop, if only to see the Medieval walls and interesting cathedral. Rebuilt throughout the centuries, the cathedral is constructed in part with stones from the Carolingian period and has a late-19th-century Rococo façade.

Just outside of Vence on Route D 2210 is Matisse's **Chapelle du Rosaire**, built by the artist for Dominican monks in 1948.

NICE

Although Nice is awash in year-round sunshine, the hint of problems is never very far away. The glorious and grandiose days of the 19th and early 20th centuries are gone forever. Their spirit hangs over the city, though, never letting it forget that it was once the splendid playground of Europe's aristocracy.

Today the city is a volatile mixture of rich retirees, working-class Arab and enterprising *pied-noir* immigrants, a large dose of winter and summer tourists, and dashes of underworld-controlled nightclubs and bars. Prostitutes roam the streets.

The center of the Riviera and by far its largest city (population 340,000), Nice is the capital of the Côte d'Azur. Like most of the cities on the coast, it is an ancient town, founded by the Marseillais in 350 B.C. It was first Roman, and then part of Provence until 1388, when it was taken over by the Savoies of northern Italy and Switzerland. Nice didn't become French until 1861.

Protected by the Baie des Anges to the south and the Alps in the north, the city has milder weather than its Riviera neighbors. It also has wide, numerous beaches and several major museums—including the Chagall and the Matisse—a major jazz festival, a Mardi Gras, a spectacular flower pageant, and several ancient monuments.

The Promenade des Anglais

The promenade, a long and bustling avenue that borders the bay, is lined with dozens of large hotels, posh apartment buildings, and museums. For a pleasant and affordable lunch with a clear view of the bay, go up to the seventh-story poolside restaurant in the modern and high-priced **Beach Regency Hotel**. If you stay there, the higher the room the better—it's quieter. Seaside rooms are usually more costly, but the scenery is worth it. This large, unpretentious hotel is a favorite among American businessmen, but its location at the far west end of the promenade makes it inconvenient for visiting the city.

The promenade begins at the other end of Nice, in the east by the Jardin Albert I, and runs westward for what seems to be forever. At number 1 is the modern, comfortable **Méridien**. The promenade's older and grander hotels were built at the turn of the century, the grandest of all, with its Empire and Napoléon III decor, being the **Négresco**. Constructed in 1912 by a Hungarian immigrant, Henri Négresco, the hotel is now a national monument.

Before starting the hotel, Négresco was director of the city casino's restaurant—one of the *hauts lieux* frequented by the richest people in the world, including the Rockefellers and the Singers. Négresco built his hotel to attract this upper-crust clientele. Unfortunately World War I was declared a year later, and the hotel was turned into a hospital. Négresco died a ruined man shortly after the war. The hotel survived, however, and flourished with the coming of Americans and the surprising discovery that summer on the Riviera can be even more fun than winter. Today you never know who you might bump into at the Négresco, from Elton John and Richard Chamberlain to heads of state.

The hotel's restaurant, the formal and expensive **Chantecler**, is considered among France's finest. The inspired cuisine of chef Jacques Maximin is Niçoise. Many food critics consider the desserts to be the best in France; chocolate is the specialty. The prices are often as awe-inspiring as the cuisine.

The Négresco aside, Nice's grand hotels have a musty feel. The entire city is not above this description, perhaps because the retirement community represents about 40 percent of the population. This has also had an impact on Nice's city government, which is highly conservative. Its long-standing mayor, Jacques Médecin, is aligned with the extreme right. Municipal police have been given increased powers even though French law forbids it.

Old Nice

East of the promenade and away from the beach is the old center of town. Old Nice is full of animation—smacking of Italian influence—and has many small, inexpensive restaurants and pizzerias. For a view of the bay and the city from here, climb the Colline du Château.

The oldest part of Nice is actually **Cimiez**, to the north. Cimiez sits on a hill where the Romans settled a camp in the first century B.C. At its height, in the third century A.D., Cimiez had 20,000 residents and was the capital of a small eastern Gaul province called Alpes Maritimae—today's Alpes-Maritimes *département.*

During the third century the Romans built thermal baths and arenas in Cimiez. The Roman amphitheater still stands today but is in bad shape. Nice's jazz festival, which takes place in July in and around the amphitheater, is a relaxed affair, one ticket providing entry to concerts throughout the day. The event coincides with the older and more renowned Antibes festival. A temporary restaurant in the park surrounding the amphitheater serves New Orleans food.

Another special event in Nice is Carnaval, a colorful, explosive bacchanal with burlesque floats and fireworks that is held ten days before Mardi Gras.

THE PERCHED VILLAGES

Like aeries, like tree houses, like nature's mysterious "hanging" rocks, the more than 60 "perched" villages of the Côte d'Azur sit on hilltops above the Riviera or cling precariously to the flanks of mountains, digging their toes into the rock.

Villages perchés, the French call them, haunts and hideaways, peasant dwelling places from the past that range from the now-chic Eze overhanging Monte-Carlo, to Saorge clinging catlike to a spur of the Alpes-Maritimes to Gourdon, crouching around its 13th-century fortress and battling the ghosts of Saracens.

Most of the villages cluster in the high reaches north of Nice, this way or that, in a range roughly from the Grand Canyon of the Verdon in the west to very near the Italian border in the east—east or west of roads marked N 204, D 19, or N 202. Others may be reached by driving north from Cannes or Fréjus or Toulon, east from Manosque or south from Digne: What's essential is a large-scale map of the region.

For centuries, the country people built their rampart-sheltered retreats in this way, hiding out from Alemannic and other invaders, from Muslim pirates and other mercenaries of the Middle Ages, from lawless raiders of the Renaissance. Some of the towns, nearly deserted, seem to grow out of the hillside stones, their arcaded streets as tangled and intriguing as fairy tales.

They tend to have wonderful names, too: Rimplas and Le Broc and Fox-Amphoux and Tourtour.

Tourtour

As of this writing, 384 people live here, ambling through its small square in the shade of two 17th-century elms. An occasional visitor may be cited for parking irregularities by the policeman, who wants someone to chat with.

The main occupation in Tourtour would seem to be eating, since the comely little hamlet boasts not one but two remarkable restaurants: **Chênes Verts**, slightly west of town on route Villecroze, and the dining room of **La Bastide**, route Draguignan, a 25-room inn of imposing size and shape that looks down upon its swimming pool and out to an uninterrupted horizon. (Most of its rooms are expensive, but then such privileged isolation is these days.)

It is also possible to spend a night or so in comfort for substantially less cost in Tourtour at the **Auberge St-Pierre** (just east of town on D 51, 15 rooms, its own park, quiet) or **Petite Auberge** (just south on D 77, 15 rooms, cozy, beautiful view). Both are just outside the town and are inexpensive. Tourtour is 10 km (6 miles) from Aups and 11 km (7 miles) from Salernes; it is better just to drive west of Grasse to Draguignan on N 562, about 55 km (35 miles), continue on a wiggle named 557, then arc north on 77.

From the metropolis of Tourtour it's a hop and a

skipped stone to **Trigance**, which almost isn't there at all (122 inhabitants), at the entrance to the wild Gorges du Verdon. (The most direct route is via N 85 from Cannes through Grasse to le Logis du Pin, then a left hook to Comps on D 21 and a short swivel north on N 555.) What you do here is hide out at the eight-room **Château de Trigance**, pretending to be a Medieval person of privilege and paying a very reasonable rate for that experience. (The round-trip drive through the **Grand Canyon of the Verdon** is one of the most exciting in France and can be accomplished in one long day out of Trigance.)

The Central Area

Driving from west to east, the collector of perched villages may be content just to see them as relics, as rural phenomena in a countryscape stuffed with cities. On the other hand, a few sport sites of interest beyond their own sinuous streets: In **Grimaud**, 10 km (6 miles) from St-Tropez, the 11th-century Romanesque basilica and the one-Michelin-star restaurant, **Les Santons**; in **Mons**, 40 km (25 miles) west of Grasse, the church with five 17th-century altarpieces, and the fountain-centered squares; in **Tourette-sur-Loup**, just west of Vence, the church's artistic treasures and the many craft shops; in **Peille**, 25 km (16 miles) north of Nice, the church and gorgeous old, covered passageways; in **Coaraze**, not far from Peille, the cemetery, the artisan shops, and the chapel of Our Lady of Sorrow.

East of Nice

Saorge, northeast of Nice on N 204, a road that climbs up gorges through the Roya valley, ranks among the most photogenic of the perched towns, its houses backed against the steep slopes as if afraid of falling forward into the river. The streets are stairways, the views sensational.

Most stylish, most celebrated, easiest to reach of the perched villages (but worth the while despite all that) is **Eze**, looking down upon Nice, Monte-Carlo, and the blue Mediterranean. To walk in the steps of Frederick Nietzsche, take the mule path named after him down toward the lower corniche; he dreamed up *Thus Spake Zarathustra* while walking this same path.

More than two thousand lucky cliff-hangers live atop this rocky spike and somehow, in cars, negotiate its skinny streets. Visitors put themselves up at the **Château Eza** (six very expensive rooms, three apartments) or at the older, more traditional **Château de la Chèvre d'Or** (five rooms, three apartments, just as expensive), both with smashing settings and superb dining rooms. These are definitely places for leading the oysters-Champagne-wild strawberries life.

—*Georgia I. Hesse*

MONACO

Monaco, situated on a 450-acre rock extending into the sea, is crammed with towering highrises, one-armed bandits, armed policemen, and a pampered population that pays no taxes and serves no one but their illustrious prince, Rainier III, the 26th head of the Grimaldi family, Monaco's founders. Popular legend has it that in 1297 François Grimaldi and his men, disguised as monks, took the rock by force. The Grimaldi family has been its lords ever since.

Make no mistake, the Monégasques revere their sovereign prince, who runs this postage-stamp principality like a father. His rebellious daughter her royal highness Princess Stephanie aside, Rainier III has been successful in keeping his kingdom in check. Monaco is the closest thing to a crimeless, clean, fiscally sound paradise on earth. Before rushing out to apply for citizenship, though, remember that of Monaco's 27,000 inhabitants, only 4,500 are full-fledged citizens. The rest, alas, are mere mortals—rich, maybe, but taxpaying.

Not everyone is welcomed in this quasi-police state. It's not unheard of for officers to stop questionable-appearing travellers and inform them not to linger in Monaco. Rainier is after image, and shabby people have no role to play in his film script. Except, of course, for the thousands of immigrant workers who stay out of sight in Monaco's small food-processing factories.

Monaco's high elevation by the sea creates a micro-climate that results in extremely mild winter temperatures. The tiny principality consists of Monaco (the old town), La Condamine (its bustling port), Monte-Carlo (casinos and shops), and Fontvielle (small industry). The city of Monaco houses the royal family, the administration, and the famed Musée Océanographique.

The prince's palace offers 35-minute guided tours from

June to October but is closed to the public the rest of the year. Every day come rain or even snow, the colorful changing of the palace guard takes place at 11:55 A.M. The oldest part of the palace was built in the 13th century as a fortress and rebuilt in Italian Renaissance style in the 15th and 16th centuries.

Musée Océanographique

Prince Albert I, a sea explorer and inventor of underwater photographic techniques, created the Musée Océano-graphique in 1899. It took ten years to build the monumental white-stone building on a promontory that hangs over the sea. Nearby are the Jardin St-Martin and Monaco's cathedral.

Included in the museum's collection are 10,000 species of shellfish, a zoological exhibition of rare marine animals, and an immense aquarium stocked with Mediterranean and tropical fish. The aquarium is one of the largest and oldest in the world.

Monte-Carlo Casino

Monte-Carlo is the shining crown in the amazing success story of this fairyland. Today its name is so well known around the world, and its image so strong, that no one can mistake Monte-Carlo for anything other than what it is—a high-rolling, high-class gambling mecca that tries hard to be platinum to Las Vegas's tinsel.

This wasn't always the case. More than a hundred years ago Monaco was a poor, isolated rock run by a comic-opera prince, Floristan I. This artistic prince painted while his principality headed for bankruptcy. He had already lost his major source of income—agricultural products from the fields of Menton and Roquebrune, two areas annexed to France in 1848. Floristan I preferred painting his aquarelles to running Monaco, so he abdicated the throne, which went to his son, Charles III.

Almost out of desperation the new prince approved construction of a gambling house in the small village of Monte-Carlo, to be run by two Frenchmen—Aubert and Langlois—who had had their gambling license pulled by Napoléon III and had chosen Monaco because it wasn't under Napoléon's jurisdiction. The two men told Charles III that casinos would attract rich tourists from the Côte d'Azur.

The first Monte-Carlo gambling house was a disaster. Not only was the casino uncomfortably small and horribly decorated, but getting to Monaco from Nice was virtually impossible. Finally François Blanc, a banker, tried his hand. Blanc had already succeeded in Hamburg, but in 1862 Bismarck had come to power and outlawed gambling. Blanc packed his bags and headed for Monaco.

He explained to the now-weary Prince Charles III that "Monte-Carlo's vocation is written in its history... the Phoenicians founded Monaco, and it's incontestable that Greeks are the greatest gamblers in the world." Blanc spared no expense in putting up his casino. To do the job he called in architect Charles Garnier, who later expanded his fame by building the Paris Opéra. Garnier's casino was pompous and grandiose.

To overcome the transportation problem, Blanc arranged for an extension of the main railroad to Monaco. The train cut travelling time from Nice to Monaco from four hours to 15 minutes, and Monte-Carlo was finally on the map.

To welcome the new gamblers, Blanc built the **Hôtel de Paris**, one of the world's most glamorous hostelries. Today it has a rooftop restaurant with a fabulous view of the coast, a discotheque, and a cabaret.

To finance the Monte-Carlo Casino, the hotel, and the restaurant, Blanc and Charles III formed the new Société des Bains de Mer. Within a few years, the casino and Monaco were awash in European royalty and, subsequently, in millions of francs. So great was the casino's income that Charles III decided to exonerate the Monégasques from paying taxes.

Decline and Rebirth

Monte-Carlo's reputation suffered greatly over the years. By the time Rainier III took power, 95 percent of Monaco's economy was reliant on the sagging and aging gambling industry. Rainier decided to transform the rock into a fiscal paradise with a broader economic base, including business and light industry. The turning point in Monaco's modern-day fortunes was Rainier's marriage in 1956 to American actress Grace Kelly, who created a powerful public-relations machine for the principality. Much to the sadness of Monaco and the rest of the world, the princess died in a car accident in 1982.

Rainier also threw open Monaco's doors to real-estate

speculators, who some observers contend have turned this country-club country into a high-rise horror. He introduced American-style gambling, and brought in the sprawling 636-room **Loews Hotel**—the antithesis of the Paris—or Monaco's other splendid Belle Epoque hotel, the **Hermitage**. Loews, the most "American" and modern of the major hotels, has its own casino and cabaret. The seven-story hotel is built over the water, and its seaside rooms are the only reason to book into this otherwise characterless and suffocating place. In fact, these seaside rooms are among the best accommodations on the Riviera, as they give the impression that you are on an ocean cruise.

MENTON

"Cannes is for living, Monte-Carlo for playing, and Menton for dying," goes the old wheeze. Indeed, it's true that Menton always has appealed to the elderly, largely because the steep mountains behind it wall out the miserable mistral and create milder winters than elsewhere along the Riviera.

Menton is the last stop along the Côte d'Azur before Italy, France's last Riviera hurrah. Once Geoffrey Bocca (in *Bikini Beach*) wrote of it, "At various times ... Menton has belonged to France, Italy, and Monaco, and it has been a separate republic. But none of this has ever succeeded in making it interesting."

Today, Menton *is* interesting, possibly because more than any city on this tourist-trammeled coast, it retains a gentility, an understated and upper-crust classiness, a Belle Epoque beauty.

Menton, in its quieter corners, still speaks of the late 19th and early 20th centuries, when Katherine Mansfield joined Blasco Ibáñez on local celebrity lists. European aristocracy mingled with *les artistes* (successful ones, that is) on the broad terraces of the promenade du Soleil, still the chosen spot for strolling.

Today, the visitor comes to town to see the Jean Cocteau, the Palais Carnolès, and the municipal museums (see Art on the Riviera section), to attend the chamber music festival on the Italianate parvis St-Michel in August, to admire the fine Baroque church of St-Michel, to celebrate the lemon festival on Shrove Tuesday (Menton's lemons are for lemon connoisseurs), and to photograph and quietly enjoy the Jardin Biovès in the heart of town, the tropical gardens near the Villa Val Rahmeh, and the Jardin des Colombières edging the smart Garavan residential area.

Menton is outfitted with hotels in all categories except, for some reason, the grandest. Because of its location right on the promenade du Soleil, the nod frequently goes to **Princess et Richmond**; although it has no restaurant, it has 43 rooms and reasonable prices by Riviera standards. **Chambord**, which enjoys a somewhat quieter location near the Jardin Biovès, also has no dining room and ranks in the same price category.

For dining, the choice is clear: **Chez Mireille-l'Ermitage** on the promenade du Soleil near the casino, where in clement weather meals are served on a sunny terrace.

—*Georgia I. Hesse*

GETTING AROUND

The gateway to the south of France is Nice. It is about seven hours from Paris by the Trains à Grande Vitesse (TGV) and its international airport services flights from Paris as well as from New York, London, and other major cities around the world. From Nice you can make easy train and bus connections to Cannes, Monaco, Avignon, Aix-en-Provence, Marseille, and all other major towns and cities in the region. Larger towns, among them Marseille, Arles, Avignon, and Nîmes, are directly serviced by train from Paris. (If you are beginning a tour of Provence and the Côte d'Azur from the north, you can take the TGV directly from Paris to Avignon.) Even the smaller villages—such as Les Baux and St-Paul-de-Vence—are usually connected to larger towns by frequent bus service.

Autoroute A 8 and other major roads connect towns throughout the south. The most scenic road, though, is the old, winding corniche that follows the Riviera all the way from Menton to St-Tropez.

ACCOMMODATIONS REFERENCE

▶ **Altéa**. Rue Neuve St-Martin, 13001 **Marseille**. Tel: 91-91-91-29; Telex: 401886; in U.S., (212) 757-6500 or (800) 223-9862.

▶ **Altéa**. Route de Caderousse, 84100 **Orange**. Tel: 90-34-24-10.

▶ **D'Arlatan**. 26, rue du Sauvage, 13200 **Arles**. Tel: 90-93-56-66; Telex: 441203; in U.S., (212) 477-1600 or (800) 223-1510. Former mansion of the counts of Arlatan; old Provençal furniture and setting.

▶ **Augustins.** 3, rue Masse, 13100 **Aix-en-Provence.** Tel: 42-27-28-59; Telex: 441052.

▶ **La Bastide de Tourtour.** Route Draguignan, 83690 **Tourtour.** Tel: 94-70-57-30; in U.S., (212) 696-1323.

▶ **Beach Regency.** 233, promenade des Anglais, 06000 **Nice.** Tel: 94-83-91-51; in U.S., (212) 714-2323 or (800) 522-5568.

▶ **Cabro d'Or.** 13520 **Les Baux-de-Provence.** Tel: 90-54-33-21; Telex: 40180; in U.S., (212) 696-1323.

▶ **Le Caméo.** Place Nationale, 06600 **Antibes.** Tel: 93-34-24-17.

▶ **Hôtel du Cap d'Antibes.** Boulevard Kennedy, 06600 **Antibes.** Tel: 93-61-39-01.

▶ **Carlton Intercontinental.** 58, boulevard de la Croisette, 06400 **Cannes.** Tel: 93-68-91-68; in U.S., (402) 498-4300 or (800) 44-UTELL.

▶ **Auberge Cavalière.** 13460 **Stes-Maries-de-la-Mer.** Tel: 90-97-84-62.

▶ **Chambord.** 6, avenue Boyer, 06500 **Menton.** Tel: 93-35-94-19.

▶ **Château de la Chèvre d'Or.** 06360 **Eze-Village.** Tel: 93-41-12-12; in U.S., (212) 696-1323.

▶ **Château Eza.** 06360 **Eze-Village.** Tel: 93-41-12-24; in U.S., (212) 477-1600 or (800) 223-1510.

▶ **Château des Fines Roches.** 84230 **Châteauneuf-du-Pape.** Tel: 90-83-70-23.

▶ **Château de Rochegude.** 84100 **Rochegude.** Tel: 75-04-81-88.

▶ **Château de Trigance.** 83840 **Trigance.** Tel: 94-76-91-18.

▶ **La Colombe d'Or.** Place de Gaulle, 06570 **St-Paul-de-Vence.** Tel: 93-32-80-02; Telex: 970607; in U.S., (212) 477-1600 or (800) 223-1510.

▶ **Concorde-Palm Beach.** 2, promenade de la Plage, 13008 **Marseille.** Tel: 91-76-20-00; in U.S., (800) THE-OMNI.

▶ **Europe.** 12, place Crillon, 84000 **Avignon.** Tel: 90-82-66-92; Telex: 431965. Napoléon stayed in this grandiose (and expensive) hotel.

▶ **Les Florets.** Gigondas 84190 Beaumes-de-Venise. Tel: 90-65-85-01.

▶ **Hermitage.** Square Beaumarchais, **Monte-Carlo** 98000 Monaco. Tel: 93-50-67-31; Telex: 479432.

▶ **Impérator.** Place A.-Briand, 30000 **Nîmes.** Tel: 66-21-90-30; Telex: 490635; in U.S., (212) 686-9213 or (800) 223-1356.

▶ **Jules César.** Boulevard des Lices, 13200 **Arles.** Tel: 90-93-43-20; in U.S., (212) 696-1323.

▶ **Loews Hotel.** Avenue Spélugues, **Monte-Carlo** 98000 Monaco. Tel: 93-50-65-00.

▶ **Majestic.** 6, boulevard de la Croisette, 06400 **Cannes.** Tel: 93-68-91-00; Telex: 470787; in U.S., (212) 593-2988 or (800) 223-5652.

▶ **Le Manoir.** 83145 **Ile de Port-Cros.** Tel: 94-05-90-52.

▶ **Martinez.** 73, boulevard de la Croisette, 06400 **Cannes.** Tel: 93-68-91-91; in U.S., (212) 838-3100 or (800) 213-6800.

▶ **Mas d'Artigny.** Chemin des Salettes, 06570 **St-Paul-de-Vence.** Tel: 93-32-84-54; Telex: 470601; in U.S., (212) 696-1323.

▶ **Mas de la Fouque.** 13460 **Stes-Maries-de-la-Mer.** Tel: 90-47-81-02; Telex: 403155.

▶ **Mas du Langoustier.** 83400 **Ile de Porquerolles.** Tel: 94-58-30-09.

▶ **Méridien.** 1, promenade des Anglais, 06000 **Nice.** Tel: 93-82-25-25; in U.S., (201) 235-1990.

▶ **Montfleury.** 25, avenue Beauséjour, 06400 **Cannes.** Tel: 93-68-91-50; in U.S., (212) 354-3722 or (800) 221-4542.

▶ **Montmirail. Montmirail** 84190 Beaumes-de-Venise. Tel: 90-65-84-01.

▶ **Négresco.** 37, promenade des Anglais, 06000 **Nice.** Tel: 94-88-39-51; in U.S., (212) 593-2988 or (800) 223-5652.

▶ **Oustaù de Baumanière.** 13520 **Les-Baux-de-Provence.** Tel: 90-97-33-87; in U.S., (212) 696-1323.

▶ **Paris.** Place du Casino, **Monte-Carlo** 98000 Monaco. Tel: 93-50-80-80; Telex: 469925. The Grand Dame. Its two restaurants—La Grille and the newly opened and astronomically priced Louis XVI—are among the best in Monte-Carlo.

▶ **Petite Auberge.** 83690 **Tourtour.** Tel: 94-70-57-16.

▶ **Le Petit Nice.** Anse de Maldormé, 13007 **Marseille.** Tel: 91-52-14-39; in U.S., (212) 696-1323.

▶ **Princess et Richmond.** 617, promenade du Soleil, 06500 **Menton.** Tel: 93-35-80-20.

▶ **Auberge Provençale.** Place Nationale, 06600 **Antibes.** Tel: 93-34-13-24.

▶ **Pullman Le Pigonnet.** 5, avenue Pigonnet, 13090 **Aix-en-Provence.** Tel: 42-59-02-90; Telex: 410692. This four-star hotel occupies an old Provençal house surrounded by trees.

▶ **Hostellerie des Remparts**. 6, place Anatole-France, 30220 **Aigues-Mortes**. Tel: 66-53-82-77.

▶ **Ste-Anne**. 83400 **Ile de Porquerolles**. Tel: 94-58-30-04.

▶ **St-Louis**. Rue Amiral-Courbet, 30220 **Aigues-Mortes**. Tel: 66-53-72-68; Telex: 485465.

▶ **Auberge St-Pierre**. 83690 **Tourtour**. Tel: 94-70-57-17.

▶ **Splendid**. 4, rue Felix-Faure, 06400 **Cannes**. Tel: 93-99-53-11.

▶ **Auberge de Tavel**. 30126 **Tavel**. Tel: 66-50-03-41.

TOULOUSE AND THE SOUTH

By Fred Halliday

As elsewhere, the population of France is shifting sunward. More and more people want to live where there is less and less winter. It is not yet clear which of the country's regions will be reanimated most in this southern shift, but what seems certain, as we head toward the 21st century, is that a prime center of French development will be the city of Toulouse and its environs.

MAJOR INTEREST

Cathar heritage

Toulouse
Basilica of St-Sernin
Les Jacobins
Tomb of Saint Thomas Aquinas
Hôtel Bernuy
Musée des Augustins

Gascony

Albi
Cathedral of St-Cecil
Musée Toulouse-Lautrec

Gaillac
Cordes
Castelnaudary

Canal du Midi
Carcassonne

The Old South

At the turn of the first millennium the south of France was a land distinctly apart from the north. It rallied around Toulouse, and when its counts sought leadership they did not look to Paris, but to the king of Aragon, in Spain. At that time a line between the north and south of France cut a political and cultural division that was deeper than the Mason-Dixon line ever established in the United States. To the north were the kings of the fleur-de-lis, the green realm of Tours and the Loire; to the south, the dry Midi (the word for midday, an apt name for this land where the sun shines as if it were always noon): hot towns on orange escarpments, the scent of wild lavender, olive trees. The region's culture and influences belonged to a meridional swath stretching from Aragon to Toulouse and on to the Italian frontier. It remains today almost what it was then.

The Latin south had its own Gallo-Roman language, the *langue d'oc,* a tongue more akin to Spanish than to French. The Midi observed its own traditions: The wife ruled in the family; the husband, its invited guest, was permitted unlimited travel to make war and fortunes. It had, and has, its own cuisine, based on oil instead of the cream of the north. This vast southern land, part of which was called Languedoc, stretched to Bordeaux on the Atlantic, bulged north to gobble up Cognac, cut across the Massif Central to Vichy, and from there to Valence across the Rhône and on to the Italian Alps. It was very rich, and separate from France in most every temporal detail. Then it tried to have its own religion, too.

The Cathar Revolt

This is perhaps the most important native development in the history of France, for had it not occurred, it is difficult to say what the map of France, or of Europe, for that matter, would look like today. Up to the 10th and 11th centuries, Toulouse and the land under its control, the Toulousain Midi, had proceeded tranquilly in its own style within the Catholic world. But when it turned from Rome and developed its own spiritual doctrine, the pope noticed and directed the attention of France's kings to the

Languedoc. What they saw, as they gazed on this vast territory, was their chance.

The official Church term for the religion called Catharism was the Albigensian heresy, named for Albi, a rich city 50 km (30 miles) northeast of Toulouse, where the new philosophy quickly put down roots in a soil most ready to receive it.

What was Catharism? The agonizing question confronting the thoughtful 11th-century Albigensian was: If God is all good, how could He create a world that is so bad? Answer: He didn't; the devil did, or at least the material part, including the flesh from which all sin springs. The spiritual part, to which comes all grace and salvation, was credited to God. Man was thus divided between good and evil, between flesh and spirit, a conflict in need of a resolution that would take more than one lifetime. The Cathars believed it could be accomplished through re-incarnation. Each new life would lead to a greater purging, or catharsis (the Greek word for purifying, which gave the religion its name), until the individual was perfected and ready for heaven. Cathar priests, closest to this goal, were called *parfaits*. Because in its metamorphosis the spirit could pass through even base animals (but not fish, curiously), a good Cathar did not kill or eat animals for fear he might kill a brother. Good Cathars also observed absolute chastity, and could not swear oaths.

According to Catharism, Christ never was made man, since all flesh was evil, but existed as a spirit, an illusion who created the desired effect among his followers. There fore a temporal ruler such as the pope was frowned upon, as was paying the taxes to him that Rome demanded; when the Cathar *parfaits* encouraged people not to pay, they gained converts and made the pope frown.

Rome sent a fact-finding team to look into charges that Church corruption in the Toulousain Midi had made an alternative church attractive. This embassy, however, was butchered as they crossed into the region. The pope then sent the Spanish-born Domingo de Guzmán, the man who would become Saint Dominic, founder of the Dominican order of friars. At the same time he interested the kings of France in one of his favorite words: crusade. Saint Dominic tried using his powers of persuasion. The crusade carried the whip and the sword. Both armies and priests crossed into the Midi. They coerced, they contended. Then they laid siege.

The Cathars fought valiantly, but one by one their citadels fell. It is not entirely accurate, however, to say they only fell, for they also crackled; funeral pyres to a civilization, they were burned with their inhabitants inside. In this way the Catholic Church saved itself. There are no blacker pages in all of Medieval history.

In 1271 Toulouse and all Languedoc came under the scepter of France. The victory was total. The crown had won its vast and rich territory, a large opening onto the Mediterranean Sea, and a Latin population to leaven what had been up until then a mostly Germanic culture. The Church got what it wanted: all those souls back under Rome's aegis. In 1321 the last *parfait* was found and burned.

At the moment, Catharism is enjoying something of a revival in France, not just as a religion but as a mode of thought. In reply to the "What are you?" religious question, certain French people find it smart to say, "I'm Cathar." It's as fashionable as Dior.

Now, 700 years later, the south is rising again in several ways.

TOULOUSE

Some say that this magnificent sun capital on the Garonne River southeast of Bordeaux is called the Pink City because of the pinkish Medieval bricks its buildings are made of. Others say that the brick is pink because of Toulouse's revolutionary soul, that it thus shows its true colors as the perennial ally of rebellion. In any case, the framework of this city's past lives in its splendid buildings.

The **basilica of St-Sernin** tells the story of pre-Cathar Toulouse. Emerging from the Roman Empire very much a rebel in favor of Christianity, the city consecrated its first cathedral on a site along the path where, in the middle of the third century A.D., Saturninus (Sernin), the bishop of Toulouse, had been lashed to a mad bull and dragged through the streets to his martyrdom. Today's rue du Taur (Bull Street) is said to be the route the bull took. The basilica rising at the end of this street is the largest Romanesque edifice in the world, designed so that pilgrims could arrive en masse and have space to parade around the display of relics.

No brief description can give significant detail or communicate, even in part, the emotional impact made by

St-Sernin. As viewed from the east, the tower and criss-crossing transept and choir alone form an architectural ensemble of such harmony as is seldom seen in structures as massive or built in so diverse an array of materials as this one.

The interior is immense, the nave just over 100 yards long. Crossing the nave at right angles is a transept nearly 70 yards wide. Everything soars on colonnades that reach up to a ceiling 65 feet high. This enormous cavity is filled with reliefs, statues, altars, paintings, crypts, chapels, reliquaries, frescoes, and sculpted capitals—all of which total what may be the world's supreme Romanesque statement, handed down to us from that period's artistic pinnacle.

Les Jacobins

With the defeat of the Cathars, Toulouse was called upon to give symbolic assurance that its loyalty to Rome was renewed. So commanded, the city expressed its fealty in the architecture of **Les Jacobins**, a monastery and church built to house the Dominican order. (Dominicans were known as Jacobins because their first house in Paris was on the rue St-Jacques.) These followers of Saint Dominic were responsible for the Inquisition that continued to crush the Cathars. Les Jacobins would be the rampart from which they could defend the faith—and rampart it is.

As the Dominicans were preachers (*frères prêcheurs*) or arguers, their church was not a place where the saying of Mass was central, but was primarily a preaching hall, which is evident in its physical plan. Outside, the building looks like a fort, a place to withstand a siege; inside, it is not the altar that greets the eye, but the lectern. And something seems to be missing: decoration. In all this immense space there is barely a nod toward pleasing the physical senses. This is not the basilica of St-Sernin, whose encrusted decor and priceless art objects make obvious its devotion to beauty. The church of the Dominicans was a platform, a stronghold from which to put forth arguments. It is ironic that all this lack of decoration only serves to point up the one vain element permitted: the red and gold fan vaulting rising up to the roof at the east end of the church. Typically Toulousain, it is the finest in the world, and an admitted inspiration to the Surrealist painter Salvador Dalí. The **Tomb of Saint Thomas Aquinas** is here, too, a gilded casket.

After pondering the esthetics of the hall, you have only

to go through the small door beside the pamphlet counter to see from whence its arguments emanated: Outside is an immense Dominican cloister, with the monastery beside it. A walk down the cloister's length will open up your view to the sky and the octagonal tower overhead.

The Renaissance Mansions

Among the chief beneficiaries of the Cathar revolt were businessmen. Before Cathar dominance, the growth of the commercial class had been sorely hampered by the Catholic Church's interdiction against drawing interest from lending capital. The Cathars changed all that, permitting interest on loans; businessmen embraced the new philosophy and came to be counted among its earliest and staunchest supporters. When the Church re-established its authority, it reasoned that it could not so easily repress this profitable practice, which had endured in some places for as long as two centuries. So the merchant class continued to rise unimpeded, and its prosperity provided a whole new impetus for building.

The Renaissance businessman was rich, but he still could not build palaces as imposing as those of the nobles, or monuments as impressive as the Church's, like Les Jacobins. What the merchants left in prosperous Toulouse came in the shape of town houses, each one based on commerce, flaunting the spreading wealth, and dedicated to the man who built it. This was new; it was a phenomenon that helped shape the face of Toulouse, which harbors as fine a string of city mansions as will be found anywhere in France.

In the 16th century Toulouse achieved worldwide renown for the quality of its dyes. Fortunes were made in their trade, and mansions of the merchants who made good in the business stand as testimony. The rue Gambetta boasts the **Hôtel Bernuy**, one of the finest dwellings in Toulouse. Because it is now a high school, access to the courtyard is easy, and unobtrusive visitors are free to poke around, especially if they look like students or teachers who might belong there. The dye merchant de Bernuy was rich enough to ransom François I when that French monarch was imprisoned, and the lavish sculpting in out-of-the-way places, on balcony undersides, for example, shows that nothing was too good for him. Even more ostentatious is the nearby **Hôtel d'Assézat**, named after its proud owner, another dye merchant.

There are many more places worth visiting in the Pink City. With the few mentioned so far, the door has barely been opened. Certainly to be included on any list is the **Musée des Augustins**, the largest museum in Toulouse. Its exceptional stone sculptures from the Romanesque, Gothic, and Renaissance periods have brought the museum national recognition, but equally remarkable is a singular collection of the works of Toulouse painters, starting with examples from the 17th century (Chalette) and marching picturesquely through to Toulouse-Lautrec himself.

The cloister of this former monastery, itself faultlessly restored, presents a rare opportunity to amble within the meticulous balances of Medieval times; even the soil underfoot is original. The massive organ within the chapel sets the very air against the face ashiver. A visit to this museum opens a window to the cultural soul of Toulouse.

Impressive, too, are the place du Capitole and the **Capitole** building, or city hall. Its name refers to the post-Carolingian *capitouls,* or consuls, who administered the city under the courts of Toulouse. The Tourist Office, housed in the only remnant of the ancient structure, provides good maps and brochures. Also look for the remarkable frescoes in the Capitole's *Salle des Illustres.*

To find the spirit of Toulouse, walk the rue du Taur—where the martyr was dragged—on a warm evening at sunset. Massive brick bell towers, triumphant and glowing and rosy in the twilight, abound; the street is crowded with Toulousains hurrying to galleries or shops along the rue St-Rome. Go down the rue des Gestes, paved with the restaurants you came to France to find: cheap, cute, and good. There's the **Lechefrites**, which means "lick a French fry." (You won't find anyone doing anything so fulsome within its interior, decorated with checked tablecloths.) Lechefrites boasts a complete dinner menu for 90 francs, which naturally comes with French fries, and naturally they're good enough to lick.

For something fancier, try **La Belle Epoque**, 3, rue Pargaminières. The food is a little bit of regional, a little bit of *nouvelle;* as for the atmosphere, it's downright festive. Take the tasting menu, and your glasses will be kept full of Sauterne. The name of this wine means literally "to jump," and the wine keeps La Belle Epoque jumping late into the night. In any case, the Belle Epoque is the kind of place where guests are made to feel very welcome.

On the other hand, **Vanel**, at 22, rue Maurice-Fontvieille, is a restaurant where only the serious eater need venture. This, one of the great temples of gastronomy of France, is as quiet as a church during collection time. Regulars are received by Lucien Vanel himself. This owner chef has a wonderful way with game birds. Just as important, Vanel's Burgundies are, as they say, to die for; but at prices that are not.

A nice place to stay near the fringe of town is the **Hôtel de Brienne** on boulevard Maréchal. From there you can take a taxi to the center of town, and on the other side the open road is near.

OUTSIDE TOULOUSE

The country around Toulouse is intensely interesting. It can be divided into two parts: the **Fallen Cities** section, a ring of Cathar fortresses perched on precarious over-looks, with the holy city of Albi as its axis; and **Gascony**, land of d'Artagnan and Armagnac, one of the great gastro-nomic regions of France.

The north-flowing river Gers lies west of Toulouse and lends its name to the picturesque province that is part of Gascony. The whole region is bursting with subtropical plants growing on undulating hills that roll up and down from the river as it winds along its shallow banks. There are fields of sunflowers, golden wheat, and vineyards—grapes for Armagnac, the wild, distilled essence of Gascony, best appreciated when held under the nose in a large glass.

Gascony

"We must keep the flame," says a bottler of Armagnac. What he means is that the distillers of this regional nectar should not succumb to the pressure afoot to tame its spirit to please an international taste, to make Armagnac less fiery. Doing so means distilling the spirit twice, the way Cognac is, to make it "smooth" (i.e., drinkable by everyone). But from time immemorial Gascony has dis-tilled its spirit just once, opting for fire rather than silki-ness in the throat. If you want smoothness, argues the Gascon, there's always Cognac up north, while there's no fire like real Armagnac's anywhere. None indeed.

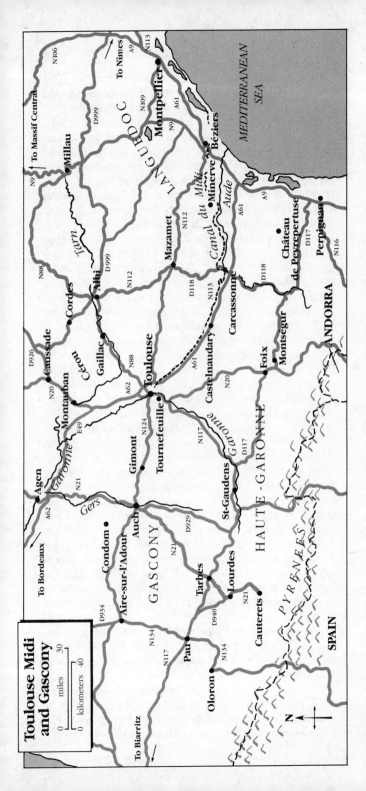

Toulouse Midi and Gascony

miles 0 30
kilometers 0 40

N

To Massif Central
To Nîmes
MEDITERRANEAN SEA
Millau
Montpellier
Béziers
LANGUEDOC
Minerve
Canal du Midi
Aude
Château de Peyrepertuse
Perpignan
Mazamet
Cordes
Albi
Gaillac
Caussade
Montauban
Toulouse
Carcassonne
Castelnaudary
Foix
Montségur
ANDORRA
Agen
Gimont
Tournefeuille
St-Gaudens
Garonne
Gers
Condom
Auch
GASCONY
Aire-sur-l'Adour
Tarbes
Lourdes
HAUTE-GARONNE
Cauterets
Pau
Oloron
PYRENEES
SPAIN
To Bordeaux
To Biarritz
Tarn
Céou

N106
N113
A9
D999
N109
N9
A61
N88
D999
N112
D999
N112
D118
N113
A61
D118
N116
D926
N20
A62
N88
A62
N21
N124
N117
D117
N20
E49
D929
N21
N21
D934
N134
D940
N117
N134

From Toulouse and into the Gers toward Auch is a good place to find real Armagnac. For fine, single-distilled brands, look for the labels Montesquiou and Sempé.

Gascony is also a good place to find rather special accommodations. At Gimont, try the **Château de Larroque** for something grand and classic. But for full-bore Gascon gastronomy, as well as the region's hospitality, the only name you need to know is André Daguin, at the **Hôtel de France** in **Auch**. Owner/chef Daguin, holding forth in his inimitable style over the years, has become firmly entrenched as a star in the French gastronomic galaxy. Everybody making a pilgrimage to France has heard of Daguin since, it seems, forever. But Auch is a little bit away from things, so Daguin isn't visited as much as the other great chefs, making him possibly the most widely discussed and untasted chef in the world. From Toulouse, Auch is an easy drive (less than an hour on the N 124), though it is recommended that those who eat in the restaurant stay at the hotel. After such a meal as you'll get there—why fool around with lunch—sleep, not the highway, will be wanted. There are great big beds and down pillows in which to sink softly to the wildest of Armagnac dreams. The restaurant downstairs is the place where the Gascon will be bearded in his den. So think big; there is nothing small, "international," or in any way "light" about Daguin's cuisine. It is rich, round, and tasty, if insolently perfumed. On a platter of fresh foie gras, for example, each slice will be flavored differently, one tasting of tarragon, another of rosemary, one of raspberry, another of rosehip. Daguin is thoroughly Gascon. He comes out of the kitchen. He hovers. He asks, "Is the lamb perfect?" Without waiting for a reply, he may snatch the fork from your hand and taste what's on it. Do all he advises on food, but when it comes to wine, if you have a mind of your own, stick to it; Daguin has a partiality for local reds, especially Madiran, which seems to some who dine in his restaurant like a truck-horse teamed with a Ferrari.

While in Auch go to the **cathedral of Ste-Marie** to see the remarkable 16th-century choir stalls. The 113 of them took 50 years to carve; made of oak, many are heavily sculpted with figures from the Bible, history, mythology, and legend. Such works can be seen elsewhere in Europe, but none as exquisite as these. The town itself is charming, and a good place to load up on Armagnacs and plum brandy, another regional specialty (plum trees are everywhere). The countryside around Auch is one of farms and rivers. Condom, north of Auch and a bit farther on toward the Atlantic Coast, is also a good place for buying local products.

Albi

Albi is a city of Cathars and painting, a home to heretics and to native son Henri de Toulouse-Lautrec (1864–1901), who is honored here with a museum. Albi was a holy city, but one in opposition to Rome and its Church Triumphant. Albi offered sanctuary to heretics, to those inspired losers who came to be called Albigensians and were eventually crushed by the Church in a bloody crusade.

The residue of the Catholic-Cathar struggle is all around, but looms largest in the eloquent **cathedral of Ste-Cécile**. Some people think this edifice looks more like a fortress than a house of worship; in truth, it is both.

Built by the Church after the success of its campaign against the Cathars, the cathedral at Albi was intended as a symbol of Roman Catholicism's return to rule. The bold, ochre-colored cathedral is an original synthesis of Catholic and military architecture that towers over a city where the first element could not have existed without the second. Inside are the remnants of a consummate decorative statement that could have left no doubt about the Church's return to power: statues of no fewer than 97 saints, which once perched overhead on the rood screen. (The Cathars didn't believe in saints.) Most were lost to the French Revolution; the only figures that remain are the Virgin, Christ on the cross, Saint John, and Adam and Eve; the rest have never been returned.

While Toulouse is called the Pink City, Albi is called "The Red"; today's Albigeois revel in their bright red brick buildings and the sunny outdoors. They love to stroll the streets and narrow alleyways that wind through the vest-pocket metropolis, all of which seem to end in the great squares, either by the cathedral or the **Palais de la Berbie**, the archbishop's palace. The main topic of conversation in the cafés seems to be rugby, the national sport of the Midi. The playing of the game is the region's biggest celebration of a Sunday.

Not to be ignored in this corrida-like atmosphere, however, is Albi's great museum to one of the world's great modern masters. The life of Henri de Toulouse-Lautrec is well known today. Enter the **Musée Toulouse-Lautrec** within the walls of the Palais de la Berbie, and enter his world. Here is a collection of the artist's work that can only be described as massive. Here are all the artist's friends: Aristide Bruant, Jane Avril, and La Goulue from the music hall; blond Miss Dolly from Le Havre, by way of England, and Missa Godebski, the exquisite wife of the producer; acrobats; circus performers; and many others, all companions on Lautrec's random nighttime walks through life and Paris. (Also of interest in the same building is an architectural gallery and the 13th-century Chapelle de Notre-Dame.)

Even after all this—cathedral, Cathars, cafés, and Lautrec—the mute, mystical feeling of Albi is not exhausted. There is the Vieux Pont (Old Bridge) across the river Tarn, which gives a view onto the city from the heights of the shore opposite. Too, there is Lautrec's birthplace on a picturesque old street with the famous salon, and the staircase down which this eager local boy tumbled and broke both legs, stunting the physical but not artistic growth of a man who went on to become one of the most famous painters of his time.

The River Tarn

The lovely Tarn is easily the most underrated river in France. Few outside the country sing its praises. Following it from Albi to Gaillac will present to the curious visitor many secret curves and high banks. At **Gaillac**, a town for lounging, there are crossroads, turns in the Tarn, and usually soft skies overhead. Along the Tarn's right bank are the white wine-producing hills of Gaillac, with Sauvignon, Sémillon, and Muscat grapes; along the opposite shore are the red-wine vineyards of Gamay and Syrah grapes, among others. The cafés of Gaillac are agreeable places to sample the yield.

The Fallen Cities

Around Albi, describing a wide circle from north to south, are the cities of siege, the sites where the heretics holed up and were burned. Their citadels are still standing, to be walked and picked over; the isolation that once protected them now yields the poetry of their time. Tours are now organized from the Bureau de Tourisme in Toulouse, opening the door to these fabulous sites, the lost Midi of the Cathars.

To the northwest is Cordes, to the southeast (northeast of Carcassonne) Minerve—two water wells with far different stories.

Cordes

Here is a plunge straight into the heart of France, but an upward one. Carved into a prominent rocky outcropping high in the hills over the Cérou valley, Cordes, meaning ropes, in its very name expresses the hope of the heretics who climbed its rocky pathway to the sky.

Originally conceived and built by the count of Toulouse, Raymond VII, the fortified city was designed to withstand the siege of German and French crusaders from the north and serve as refuge for the many Cathars roaming the Languedoc in search of a home. But Simon de Montfort, leader of the Albigensian Crusade, was as persistent as he was terrible. As the Cathar citadels fell one by one, Cordes-sur-Ciel remained intact. When in 1234 three of the pope's inquisitors were finally allowed inside, presumably signaling that the Catholic repression was about to begin, a curious thing happened: Almost the next day these emissaries were found dead at the bottom of a 300-foot-deep well.

The well still exists. So do the ancient cobblestone streets, with their Medieval workplaces—a smith here, a weaver there, an engraver, a sculptor, a picturemaker, a woodcarver. All these crafts are now afforded work spaces in this city of sanctuary so that their industry might keep up the old buildings, and keep the ancient noble professions alive.

Because of its fortified site (two moats surround it) and its powerful economic position, Cordes survived the crusade and entered the post-Cathar period in good shape. Most cities and citadels, despite their moats, fell to far worse fates.

Minerve

The fires of French history once smoked with an unholy incense in this village at the foot of the Montagne Noir (Black Mountain). Still, in walking these streets today, you feel an austerity that simmers in the heat, and even now here live a people who don't give up easily. That was the way it was in the first quarter of the 13th century. The

story of the well in Minerve, however, has a different
ending than the story of the well in Cordes.

Led by Simon de Montfort, the northerners besieged
Minerve for six weeks; onslaught after onslaught was
turned back in the head-spinning heat of June and July.
Then the tenacious conqueror, recognizing the importance of the town's water source, positioned a large cata-
pult on the heights overlooking the well and buried the
well with rocks. The sun did not rest: Resistance faded.

As elsewhere, the Cathars had two choices in the face
of this defeat—reconversion to the Catholic faith or death
by flames. In keeping with those who had striven and lost
before them, they opted for the second fate. For two days
sticks were laid down in the square and tarred. Then the
Cathars, 190 of them, some singing and some sobbing,
took seats on this kindling, which was then ignited.

Farther south, in Montségur, the last Cathar citadel fell,
200 more Cathars burning as a group. The great heresy
was thought to be no more. But as this part of France
reawakens, interest in its early history revives. And that
interest encompasses the Cathars and the religion Roman
Catholicism tried so hard to eradicate 700 years ago.

Castelnaudary

Here is a citadel of the sun. Those who take the trouble to
come down here—it's no trouble really, just 55 km (34
miles) down Route N 113 from Toulouse on the way to
Carcassonne—will take in a pre-Medieval town whose
well-ordered ranks of stone buildings spiral ever upward
toward a cathedral, while all around the town flows the
Canal du Midi, with its refreshing swimming holes in
greenswards flanked by shade trees. But what is really
savory about Castelnaudary is the dish that everyone who
goes to France (or inside a French restaurant) hears
about, half as many try, but only few get to taste in its
authentic form: cassoulet. It was born in Castelnaudary
(or Carcassonne some say, or Toulouse say others, but
probably it really did originate in Castelnaudary). Cassoulet is made in a *cassolo,* a locally produced squat clay pot
with a hollow handle, of lingot beans, shank joints and
ribs of pork, lean, local sausages, and confit (preserves)
of goose; it is what some people call "rich."

Fortunately, Castelnaudary is also a great town for a
walk. It's big enough for a stay of a day and a night, and if
the sun is shining, a few days more. The rabbit-warren

streets are not closed in and dark as they are in northern Medieval cities. Here the sun streams in, igniting the rose flecks in the granite walls and making the stones shine. Rues Soumet and Contresty are typically narrow, over-hung by wrought-iron balconies. Shops offer Castel-naudary pottery (including authentic *cassolos* for your kitchen), ceramics, glassware, locally made furniture, and wrought iron, also a specialty of the area.

There are major buildings in Castelnaudary, too. The **church of St-Michel** is beautifully severe under its 14th-century tower. Those who love the grandiose could spend an afternoon admiring the nave, its choir, its transept, its bizarre communion table in wrought iron, and its two chapels. The **Présidial** sits on the city's oldest inhabited spot, a fortress carved in rock, from which Castelnaudary got its name, coming from a corruption of Roman words meaning "New Castle." Dismantled in part by Richelieu and next a prison, the Présidial currently houses some government agencies and an interesting apothecary museum.

Good regional cooking is everywhere in Castelnau-dary: especially at the **Auberge Monnereau**, 22, cours de la République; at **Le Fourcade** (try the leg of lamb roasted as it twists on a string) on the route de Carcassonne, a mere 50 yards from the Canal du Midi—they pack boat lunches; and at **La Belle Epoque** (they do a cassoulet in a fireplace), 55, rue Général Dejean.

Among the best places to stop for a night or two are **Chez Pinelou**, **Mapotel les Palmes**, and **Hostellerie Etienne** (Etienne wears a toque blanche).

Especially worth a look, if not a gambol on its waters, is the **Canal du Midi**. Watered by springs and sources from high up the neighboring Montagne Noire, the canal flows all the way to Sète on the Mediterranean. Its banks are lined with fragrant roses, cypress, palms, bougainvillea, and rose-tiled Mediterranean villages.

CARCASSONNE

At first sight, the colossal fortress city of Carcassonne, its Medieval double walls and towers surrounding it for more than a mile, will make you feel as though you had just jumped back 600 years. The spell is even stronger if you come to Carcassonne at night or in the off-season, when a desolate calm descends upon the Cité.

Carcassonne, 37 km (23 miles) west of Castelnaudary and 92 km (57 miles) west of Toulouse on Route N 113, is actually two cities separated by the river Aude. The newer city, around the train station, is of little interest. Instead, head by cab, bus, or on foot (it is a 30-minute walk) to the Cité, Carcassonne's Medieval wonderland. There are several rustic and first-class hotels in the Cité, shops and banks that service visitors as well as the Cité's thousand or so residents, and many restaurants. The four-star hotel **Cité** is full of Medieval charm—but at a high price. The **Donjon** is smaller and less expensive; recently renovated and modernized, it has nevertheless kept some of its Medieval feel. Service is friendly, and the hotel staff helps organize tours of the village.

The Cité's Walls

Although the Cité's towers have been tinkered with, the architect who did the dirty deed in the 19th century, Viollet-le-Duc, had a solid foundation to build upon. A good many of Carcassonne's 50 towers and concentric interior and exterior walls have not been altered. The original fortress was built by the Romans during the third and fourth centuries, although the first Roman garrison had been established here several hundred years earlier. Geographic considerations—the river Aude, the hilltop view, the site's location between Toulouse and the Mediterranean—made Carcassonne an important military garrison. Sections of the original Roman wall may still be seen to the left of Pont Levis (the Roman portion comprises the sections in which the stores are packed more tightly than they are in the others), and several Gallo-Roman relics are on display at the **Musée Lapidaire** in the Château.

The Visigoths swept into the region in the fifth century and dealt a death blow to Roman control. Carcassonne then became a Visigoth stronghold, and it wasn't until the Arab invasions in the eighth century that the Visigoths lost their control. It took nearly a hundred years, and all the soldiers of Charlemagne, to dislodge the Moors from Carcassonne and the rest of the Narbonne region.

Legend has it that Carcassonne owes its name to a Moorish woman, Dame Carcas. In the ninth century the Moors invaded and occupied the fortress. Responding to the invasion, Charlemagne laid siege to the city and captured the Moorish king Balaak. When the Moor refused to convert to Christianity, the French killed him.

Balaak's wife, Dame Carcas, resolutely continued to hold the fortress and kept the Christians outside the walls. The siege lasted five years, and nearly all of the Dame's soldiers died of hunger and thirst. Even so, Carcas showered her last five gallons of water over the wall, tricking Charlemagne into believing that she had provisions to burn. Just to make sure her point was made, Carcas gathered the last of the remaining wheat and fed it to the last sow, which she heaved over the walls. The poor beast burst open upon hitting the ground, revealing all of the wheat. Convinced he was defeated, Charlemagne about-faced his army and began a retreat. Wanting an audience with the emperor, Carcas began to sound the bells of the fortress. "Carcas is ringing," the soldiers shouted, or in French, *"Carcas sonne,"* which is how the town got its name.

Carcas met with the emperor and was converted to Christianity. Charlemagne was so taken by the woman's courage, it is said, that he asked her to stay and be the master of the city. He wed her to one of his noblemen, Trencavel, which was then the custom when a great lord wanted to keep a woman for himself without marrying her. Together, Carcas and Trencavel founded the dynasty of the viscounts of Carcassonne.

Charlemagne's death marked the beginning of the decline of his empire and the gradual disappearance of centralized power. Carcassonne became the feudal territory of the Trencavels. During their reign the city enjoyed a long period of economic prosperity, thanks to weaving, metal forging (for the cavalry), carpentry, masonry, and agriculture.

The Cathar Crusades

By 1209 Carcassonne was a well-protected, prosperous city, visited by troubadours and livened by tournaments, hunts, and festivals. Most of the festive activities took place in the space between the two encircling walls—the *lices.*

Then began the crusade against the Cathars. Although Raymond-Roger de Trencavel, Carcassonne's lord, was a Catholic, he was a strong believer in protecting the right to freedom of worship—an opinion that was not shared by many of his fellow lords. Called to Montpellier to an assembly of knights who asked him to chase all heretics from his city, Trencavel replied: "I offer a city, a roof, a shelter, a loaf of bread, and my sword to all those banned who will soon wander throughout Provence, without a city, or a roof, or asylum, or bread." Trencavel's speech led to his downfall. Carcassonne was attacked by 20,000 men; Trencavel was captured and imprisoned. He soon died in one of the towers of his own fortress.

The crusade against the Cathars ended, and the Inquisition, carried out by Dominican monks, followed. The room of the Inquisition, **Tour de l'Inquisition**, can be visited as part of a 45-minute guided tour of the **Château Comtal** (the Count's Castle) and the walls and ramparts. The entrance to the Château is on rue Viollet-Le-Duc. For a regional meal, try the informal **Sénéchal** on the same street; it serves traditional food and overlooks a courtyard garden. Probably the best restaurant is **Pont Levis**, just outside the Cité and near the bridge of the same name. The waiters won't turn up their noses if you order a cassoulet, and the desserts are *nouvelle* and divine.

Major sections of the interior wall were built from 1209 to 1240, during the period between the two major sieges of the city and coinciding with the reign of the very Catholic King of France, Louis IX, a.k.a. Saint Louis. Carcassonne attacked the Royal Army in 1240 and Saint Louis punished the rebellious inhabitants by burning the village that stood outside the wall of the Cité. He had a new town built on the left bank of the river Aude: today's modern Carcassonne, or Ville Basse (lower city). The Ville Basse is now a bustling city of 41,000, but it is of very little touristic or cultural interest. Nevertheless, it is a major regional agricultural center and has light textile-manufacturing activities, and it is surrounded by a military base and barracks.

Saint Louis also ordered the building of the Cité's outer wall to bolster the fortress's defensive invulnerability. His son, Philippe III, put the finishing touches on the fortress. Carcassonne became an impregnable stone wonder and a military model for the rest of Europe. It earned the title "Maiden of Languedoc." It is no coincidence that no one ever attacked the Cité again.

Looking at the towers, you can see how the defense of the Cité was carried out. Archers were situated on four floors of the major towers behind narrow-slitted openings just big enough to shoot an arrow through but not large enough for enemy arrows to penetrate. Wooden platforms atop the towers were equipped with ramps from which heavy iron balls were rolled and dropped on the luckless invaders below. During the fort's renovation in the 19th century, Viollet-Le-Duc reconstructed several of these *hourds-montes*. Thanks to his efforts, Carcassonne is the perfect place to study Medieval assault and defense tactics.

A comparison of Medieval and Renaissance stained-glass windows may be made at the **basilica of St-Nazaire**, whose original stones were blessed by Pope Urbain in 1096. The Medieval windows are darker, more saturated, more intense in color. The art of making stained glass had become a lost art as long ago as the 16th century. The church was reconstructed in the 13th century; its western façade was later modified, horribly, by Viollet-Le-Duc.

The architect had political connections and is responsible for so many restorations across the face of France that a phrase has actually passed into the French language to forever sit in judgment of his efforts: *"Violé par Viollet"* ("Raped by Viollet").

In front of the church's main entrance is the somewhat expensive **La Crémade** restaurant (1, rue Plô). Along with the formal and pricey **Jardin de la Tour** (rue Porte d'Aude), the two are considered Carcassonne's most pricey.

Regional Food and Drink

Carcassonne and the surrounding area is home to excellent foie gras and cassoulet. Accompany a cassoulet with a regional wine—Corbières or the lighter Minervois. For dessert try a bottle of Blanquette de Limoux, the Champagne of Languedoc. The Cité has several regional gourmet shops that sell local wines and other specialties, such as *confits*.

Bastille Day in Carcassonne

Carcassonne's busy summer tourist season quiets down in September, but if the crowds don't bother you, July is a good time to visit. For all hotels in and near the Cité, reserve well in advance, especially for the Bastille Day (July 14th) celebration. The Bastille Day fireworks at the Cité rival the Parisian event. In addition, the recently enlarged outdoor amphitheater on the southern rampart is the scene of various concerts and plays throughout the month-long Festival de la Cité in July.

Excursions from Carcassonne

Carcassonne's region is rich in Medieval forts and castles as well as vineyards. The most spectacular castle is the **Château de Peyrepertuse**, sitting on a mountain crest about 55 km (35 miles) south of Carcassonne, in the middle of the Corbières wine region. Access is difficult; inquire locally.

—Bruce Alderman with Fred Halliday

GETTING AROUND

From Paris, Toulouse is well serviced by train—just five hours by the rapid TGV—and by air. Connections by bus and train from Toulouse to other cities and even smaller towns are excellent, and the region is crisscrossed by excellent roads. Several major rental-car firms have outlets in Toulouse. In Castelnaudary, you can board barges for a cruise on the Canal du Midi. Blue Line Boats, whose logo is "Green France in a blue boat," is a good way to go. Contact: Blue Line, 11400 Castelnaudary; Tel: 68-23-17-51.

ACCOMMODATIONS REFERENCE

▶ **Hôtel de Brienne.** 20, boulevard Maréchal, 31000 **Toulouse.** Tel: 61-23-60-60.

▶ **Les Chanterelles.** Route D 63, 31170 **Tournefeuille.** Tel: 61-86-21-86. Ten rooms set in a lovely garden.

▶ **Château de Larrogue.** Route Toulouse, 32200 **Gimont.** Tel: 62-67-77-44; Telex: 531135.

▶ **Chez Pinelou.** La Bastide d'Anjou 11400 **Castelnaudary.** Tel: 62-60-11-63.

▶ **Cité.** Place Eglise, 11000 **Carcassonne.** Tel: 68-25-03-34; Telex: 500829.

▶ **Donjon.** 2, rue Comte-Roger, 11000 **Carcassonne.** Tel: 68-71-08-80; Telex: 505012.

▶ **Grand Ecuyer.** Rue Voltaire, 81170 **Cordes.** Tel: 63-56-01-03. Beautiful rooms and an excellent restaurant in a Gothic building.

▶ **Hostellerie Etienne.** La Bastide d'Anjou 11400 **Castelnaudary.** Tel: 68-60-10-18.

▶ **Hôtel de France.** Place Libération, 32000 **Auch.** Tel: 62-05-00-44; Telex: 520474.

▶ **Mapotel les Palmes.** 10, rue Maréchal-Foch, 11400 **Castelnaudary.** Tel: 68-23-03-10; in U.S., (800) 528-1234.

▶ **La Réserve**. Route Cordes, 81000 **Albi**. Tel: 63-60-79-79; in U.S., (212) 696-1323. An elegant, 20-room member of the Château et Relais group, set in a large garden.

▶ **Hostellerie St-Antoine**. 17, rue St-Antoine, 81000 **Albi**. Tel: 63-54-04-04; Telex: 520850. All 56 rooms are furnished with antiques.

▶ **Hostellerie du Vieux Cordes**. Rue de la République, 81170 **Cordes**. Tel: 63-56-00-12. A 13th-century château with 20 rooms.

BORDELAIS, COGNAC, AND THE DORDOGNE

By Georgia I. Hesse

A vineyard-rich slice of limestone plain called the Bordelais edges the wide Gironde River, which flows into the Atlantic, its waters joined by those of the tributaries Garonne and Dordogne.

The Bordelais, the heart of the old province of Guyenne (sometimes Guienne), covers almost all the modern department of the Gironde. It is also the linchpin of ancient Aquitaine.

The Cognac region in the Charente lies north of Bordeaux and the rivers.

The Dordogne, one of France's longest rivers, rises in the plateau known as the Massif Central; for most of its life capricious and tumultuous, it has recently been tamed by dams, artificial lakes, and hydroelectric stations. Still, it remains a capricious river in places (especially along the 38-mile run from Sarlat to St-Cyprien), slicing through the history and prehistory of mankind.

For some reason, the regions of Bordeaux, the Bordelais, Cognac, and the valley of the Dordogne remain among the lesser-roamed major regions of France, despite being home to some of the world's greatest wines, most fascinating human antiquities, and most magical landscapes. The best times to visit these areas—as for many parts of France—are May and June or September and October.

MAJOR INTEREST

Bordeaux
Grand-Théâtre
Musée des Beaux-Arts
Musée d'Aquitaine
Cathedral of St-André
Musée des Arts Décoratifs
Walk from esplanade des Quinconces along
    Garonne River to place de la Bourse
The Vinothèque

Throughout the Bordelais
Wine châteaux and tastings
St-Emilion

Cognac
Saintes, Roman and Medieval sites
Royan, traditional seaside resort and casinos

Along the Dordogne
Prehistoric sights, especially caves
Drive along the Cingle de Trémolat
Les Eyzies-de-Tayac area of prehistoric sites
Sarlat-la-Canéda, old town for strolling
Domme, La Roque-Gageac, and Beynac-et-Cazenac,
    scenic villages
Monpazier
Rocamadour scenic Medieval religious site
Pech-Merle prehistoric cave site

In the 12th century, Eleanor of Aquitaine was the most powerful person here. Her lands, inherited in 1137 upon the death of her father the duke, stretched north from the Pyrénées to the Loire and east from the Atlantic to central Auvergne, constituting a region at least as large as the kingdom of France itself.

Realizing that, Louis VI (called Louis the Fat), who was rather ill, seized the prize for his son, Louis the Young. The Capetian prince married Eleanor in 1137, the year he became Louis VII, gaining not only a wife but also a dowry comprising Guyenne, Périgord, Limousin, Poitou, Angoumois, Saintonge, Gascony, Auvergne, and Toulouse.

After 15 years of misunderstandings, manipulations, and machinations, Louis VII arranged the pronounce-

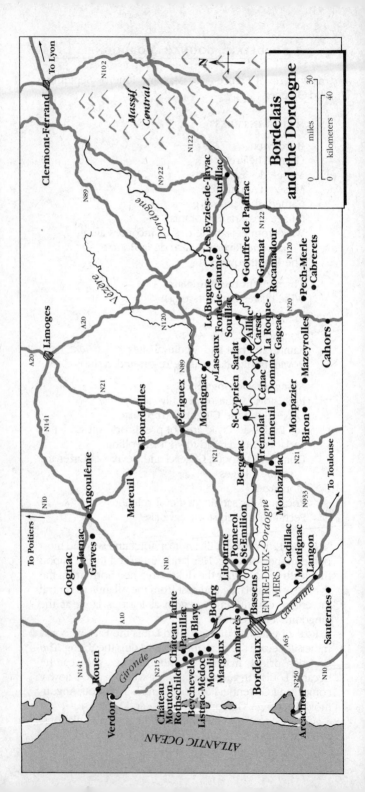

Bordelais and the Dordogne

ment of divorce from his wife by the Council of Beaugency. Two months later, Eleanor (with her lands) married Henri Plantagenêt, who himself held Anjou, Maine, Touraine, and Normandy.

The marriage of Eleanor and Henri was disastrous for France and the house of Capet, and the situation only worsened when, two years later, Henri was crowned Henry II of England (as a descendant of William the Conqueror). The French-English struggles that ensued were to last almost precisely 300 years, culminating in the Hundred Years War. Everywhere in the Bordelais and the valley of the Dordogne, evidences of this epic antagonism are at hand.

As Desmond Seward writes in *The Hundred Years War:* "The protagonists are among the most colorful in English and French history: Edward III, the Black Prince, and the even more formidable Henry V; the splendid but inept John II who died a prisoner in London; the sickly, limping intellectual Charles V, who very nearly overcame the English; and the enigmatic Charles VII (Joan of Arc's *dauphin*), who at last drove them out. The supporting English cast included such men as Sir John Chandos, John of Gaunt, the Duke of Bedford and Old Talbot, as well as Sir John Fastolf—the original of Shakespeare's Falstaff. On the French side were figures like the Constable du Guesclin, the Bastard of Orléans, and the "witch-saint from Domremy."

THE BORDELAIS

BORDEAUX

Henry James wrote, "Bordeaux is . . . dedicated to the worship of Bacchus in the most discreet form."

Patricia Wells mentions no gods: "I find Bordeaux a rather stuffy, characterless town—too snooty *bourgeois* for those of us who are not part of the clan. . . ."

"Take Versailles," Victor Hugo opined, "add Antwerp to it, and you have Bordeaux."

Bordeaux means business and has since the days of the

Romans, who introduced the vine into the region. During the 14th century and the Hundred Years War the wine trade never slowed, and in the 18th century the keys to Bordeaux's port were the heaviest in the kingdom. Only the Revolution of 1789, followed by the Napoleonic wars and some miserable harvests, succeeded in defoliating the success of the vineyards. Not until after World War II did the sun of success and sales shine fully on Bordeaux again.

Today, despite its distance of 60 miles from the sea, Bordeaux, including Verdon, Bassans, Ambès, Blaye, and Pauillac on the Gironde estuary, is France's major industrial port.

Whether you arrive by train, plane, ship, or car, it is the business of business that you notice here first: the warehouses and cargo sheds that march along both banks of the Garonne, the new university city on the outskirts, several industrial zones, the still-burgeoning fair-sports-convention-hotel-exposition conglomeration known as Le Lac (the lake), and Mériadeck, a new commercial quarter. (Much of the current economic expansion of Bordeaux results from the efforts of Jacques Chaban-Delmas in his positions as mayor, president of the regional council, and occasional candidate for the French presidency.)

Every day in summer boat tours on the river show off Bordeaux's bustling port and industrial areas, but most travellers head first for the old city center.

Classic Bordeaux

The center of things civilized is **place de la Comédie**, site of the Roman forum and a Gallo-Roman temple torn down by Louis XIV and replaced by today's magnificent Grand-Théâtre. Wide avenues and tree-lined esplanades radiate out from here: cours de l'Intendance, the best street for smart, idle strolling; cours Georges Clemenceau, a flagstone-paved shopping street that links place Gambetta to place Tourny; and the allées de Tourny, along which chic boutiques edge fashionable sidewalk cafés. Keep your eyes open for the **Brasserie de Noailles** along Tourny; it speaks of the 1930s and is a super place to relax with a seafood snack and a few glasses of dry, snappy Entre-deux-Mers.

Any amble here should be the cure for the delusion

that Bordeaux is aloof and indifferent. It is simply itself, with a refreshing absence of the usual rivalry with Paris.

First things first: settling in. Although some bigger and more modern hotels have been built in the new developments, the most satisfactory choice for travellers who like to sleep near the heart of the matter is **Grand Hôtel et Café de Bordeaux**, right on place de la Comédie. It's a very comfortable inn, neither brisk nor brusque, which also affords you the luxury of dining in a Michelin-starred restaurant.

Before you start exploring, make three stops on cours du 30-Juillet, which runs the short distance from place de la Comédie to the esplanade des Quinconces. Here are the *Office de Tourisme* (with maps, details of special events, etc.), the Maison du Vin de Bordeaux (for tastings, vineyard touring information, and reservations, etc.), and **La Vinothèque** (a wine store the size of a warehouse).

Right across from the hotel, the **Grand-Théâtre** is one of the handsomest in France, inside and out, an echo of Greece in 18th-century stone. Performances the year round (and especially during the prestigious music festival in May) play under its magnificent Bohemian crystal chandelier. Guided tours of the theater are given Tuesday through Friday from mid-July to the end of September, and on Saturday the rest of the year.

Many of the major attractions cluster around the Hôtel de Ville, near place Pey-Berland, which occupies the 18th-century **Palais des Rohan**, built for the archbishop and prince of the noted and sometimes notorious Rohan family. People who have time to see everything in town may want to tour the building on weekday mid-afternoons, but others will admire the gardens behind and then visit the museums installed in the two galleries: **Musée des Beaux-Arts** and **Musée d'Aquitaine**.

The Beaux-Arts' collections of paintings and sculptures extend from the 15th century to the 20th, and are arranged by national schools. The museum is particularly rich in Dutch art. It also includes works by three men born in Bordeaux: Odilon Redon, André Lhote, and Albert Marquet.

The Aquitaine displays a treasury of prehistoric and ancient relics, tools, and artworks, ranging from the Paleolithic period to the Renaissance. Among the most famous (and, today, humorous) items is the fat little *Venus de Laussel,* sculpted some 20,000 years before Christ.

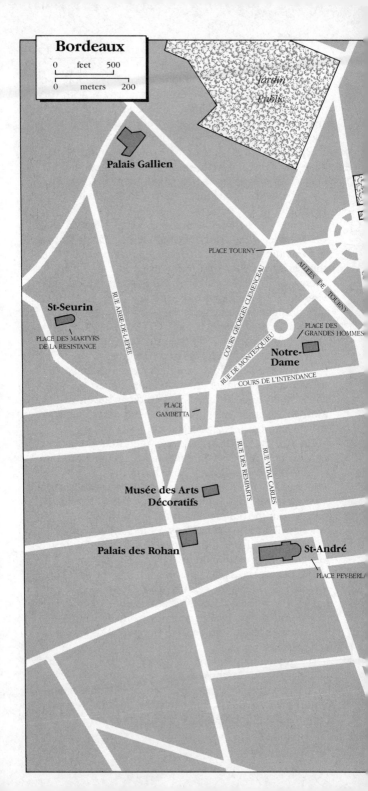

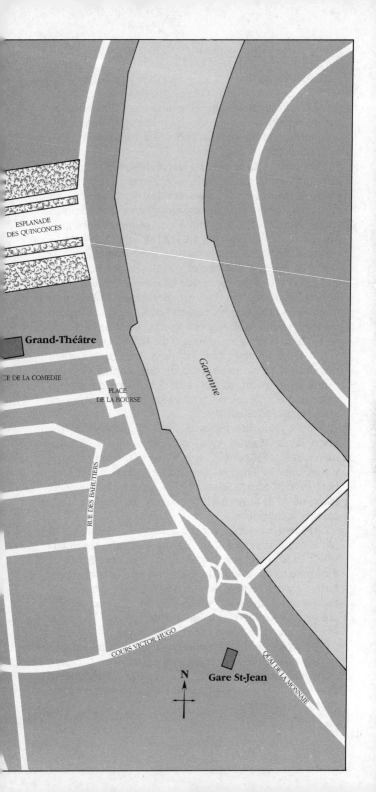

Almost facing the Rohan Palace, the **cathedral of St-André** was built in the 11th century and has endured several reincarnations. Its most important elements are the Porte Royale, with its extraordinary 13th-century sculptures, and the curious belfry, the Tour Pey-Berland, isolated on the grounds.

The nearby **Musée des Arts Décoratifs** owns handsome furniture groupings as well as glassware, enamels, silverwork, and ceramics from around the Continent. Of particular interest are the *pots-Jaqueline,* rustic, traditional pieces from Lille that are reminiscent of English Toby jugs. Also on place Pey-Berland, the Jean Moulin Centre documents World War II and the Resistance movement.

Within walking distance of the Musée des Beaux-Arts and just north of the esplanade Charles de Gaulle on rue Robert-Lateulade, the **Pullman-Mériadeck** is the most modern and most highly ranked hotel in town, a step up from the Grand in all respects except old-fashioned coziness. There is also good dining at the Pullman.

Not far from the public gardens, the **Palais Gallien** remembers Rome in its third-century amphitheater remains. At **St-Seurin,** off the place des Martyrs de la Résistance, there is a paleo-Christian site with a necropolis, sarcophagi, and amphorae.

A walk from the esplanade des Quinconces to the place de la Bourse, past classical façades and wine-merchants' town houses, reveals one of the most elegant waterfronts in Europe. The gentle curve of the river here gave Bordeaux its old nickname, Port of the Moon. Place de la Bourse itself shows off harmonious 18th-century architecture.

Travellers who enjoy the tranquillity of a country inn by night while sightseeing in the city bustle by day might select **La Réserve,** just southwest of town near Pessac on the route to Arcachon. The 20 rooms and one apartment have a garden setting, there is an excellent restaurant on the premises, the good vines of Médoc grow all around, and the atmosphere is calm and welcoming. The cellar stores bottles that cost more than the rooms.

The *Office de Tourisme* keeps a list of rural celebrations in the Bordeaux region—a fatted oxen parade, a pony fair, an oyster festival, a flower show among them. Foreign guests will be wined and dined to within a centimeter of collapse.

Dining in Bordeaux

Surprisingly, in the recent past Bordeaux suffered a dearth of fine restaurants. Today the situation is sunnier. Among the tops for cuisine and atmosphere, or both, are: **Le Chapon Fin**, still in its original style and location on Montesquieu and serving the traditional stews, soups, and roasts; **Christian Clément-Dubern**, on the elegant allées de Tourny; it is named for the new, young chef who took over Dubern and installed creative cuisine. There is lighter and less expensive cuisine upstairs at Le Petit Dubern; **La Chamade** has elegant service and cuisine in an 18th-century cellar; Francis Garcia, formerly of the Chapon-Fin, now works at **Le Bistrot du Clavel (Gare)**, near the St-Jean railway station, where regulars include members of the local soccer team. Some say **Chez Philippe**, on place du Parlement, serves the best seafood in town.

Also: **Jean Ramet**, contemporary, fresh decor, just off Tourny; **Le Rouzic**, chef Michel Gautier's masterworks, near Grand-Théâtre; **Bolchoï**, for folkloric food and drinks on the first floor; **Tupina**, behind the quai de la Monnaie. (Chef J. P. Xiradakis—a Gascon despite his Greek-sounding name—is president of the association for the preservation of Southwestern culinary traditions; this is a casual and colorful bistro.)

The highest ranking in the region usually goes to **Saint-James**, southeast of town in suburban Bouliac, where chef Jean-Marie Amat superbly cooks whatever's fine from the market; the shady terrace and views of Bordeaux add to the enjoyment of the whole.

Shopping in Bordeaux

As far as couture in Bordeaux is concerned, you could be shopping in Paris. This is especially true along the cours de l'Intendance and rue Ste-Catherine (they meet at place de la Comédie). For shopping with a difference, consider custom-engraved glassware from **Mazauque** on rue des Bahutiers; everything for your favorite wine enthusiast from **Humbert** on the cours Victor-Hugo; cheeses from Jean d'Alos on rue de Montesquieu off l'Intendance; wines and wine-associated eccentricities plus a museum and tastings at **Hôtel des Vins** on rue Abbé-de-l-Epée; books, many from Great Britain, on everything at **Librairie Mollat**, on rue Vital-Carles.

Sip while shopping at the **Salon de Thé/Pour La Maison,** not far from the Palais Rohan on rue des Remparts: Antiques, gifts, tableware, embroideries, and decorative light fixtures are to be considered while consuming a *café filtre.*

Antiques are best found in the area of Notre-Dame, the St-Michel quarter, and around place Gambetta; flea markets change locations daily—ask at the *Office de Tourisme;* the best of a handful of covered markets is at **place des Grands-Hommes** (here, take a little something at the Belle Epoque **Bar des Grands-Hommes**).

Le Golf in the Area

When thinking of Bordeaux, Pomerol not putters, and châteaux not clubs readily come to mind. Nonetheless, the region of the Aquitaine is rapidly expanding its golf courses. Three outstanding public courses in the Gironde are Golf d'Arcachon, about 65 km (40 miles) from Bordeaux; Bordeaux-Lac, in the Bordeaux's new sporting-exhibition area; and Golf Country Club de l'Ardilouse, at Lacanau-Océan, 60 km (37 miles) west of Bordeaux. All are open year-round. In addition, as elsewhere in France, private clubs may allow members of top American clubs to play their courses and use club facilities. Inquire at the *Office de Tourisme.* At Bordeaux-Lac, sportive types may also swim, ice skate, shoot clay pigeons, boat, and play squash.

WINES AND VINES

To many oenophiles worldwide, the Bordeaux region is unchallenged as the greatest winescape on the globe. Here, after all, vines, first imported from Greece, have grown happily since the beginning of the Christian era. North of Bordeaux blush the noble "red princes" of **Médoc** (the big four are Château Lafite, Château Latour, Château Margaux, and Mouton-Rothschild; others are St-Estèphe, Pauillac, and St-Julien). These are wines that age with grace: "All the angles grow round in the bottle," say the Médociens.

Here, also, mature great whites: the sumptuous **Sauternes,** south of Bordeaux, the dry and nifty **Graves** between Sauternes and the city. Across the Garonne and the

Dordogne to the east, the rewarding reds of **St-Emilion**, **Pomerol**, and **Fronsac** are at home, with Château Pétrus shining the most brilliantly among the Pomerols.

Then there are the crisp whites of **Entre-deux-Mers**, in the triangle where the two rivers meet to become the Gironde, and the **Côtes de Blaye** on the east bank of the Gironde. These are the delicious everyday wines the French term great "ordinaires." Other *appellations* are prestigious on their own: **Côte de Bourg**, just south of Blaye, and **Pecharmant**, to name but two.

The prettiest time to wander these winelands is in autumn: It is also the hectic picking time, when visitors are not greeted with glee and frequently are not greeted at all. Except when picking and crushing are in progress, though, it is possible to visit most of the properties; plan an itinerary with the assistance of wine authorities in Bordeaux.

In general, great Bordeaux châteaux are more chary of welcoming outsiders than are those in other regions of France.

A few châteaux, such as **Beychevelle** and **Lafite**, operate guided tours on a regular basis. (Beychevelle owes its name to *baisse-voile*, or "lowered sail," a salute demanded by the 17th-century owner, the Duc d'Eperon, who demanded respect and a toll.) To visit others, write or call ahead for an appointment (it's easiest to deal with the agencies in Bordeaux). Not to be missed (reservations required) is the museum of **Château Mouton-Rothschild** in its caves: Artworks from various historical periods that have to do with wine and grapes, magnificent tapestries and glassware, and so forth are here.

In general it's easiest to visit estates and wineries that display the signs *Vente au détail* (approximately "individual sales") or *Dégustation* (tastings). In some villages and at some estates, the reception center even sells light meals to be accompanied by wine purchased on the spot: **Listrac-Médoc** near Moulis is an example.

As in the case of St-Emilion (see the next section), a few wine villages are worth visiting in themselves: **Blaye**, with a citadel constructed by Louis XIV's great military architect, Sébastien le Prestre de Vauban (a good hotel-restaurant there is **La Citadelle**); **Cadillac**, where part of the ramparts remain—while there you should visit the Château Fayau, and, in autumn, attend the *vin nouveau* festival.

An uncommonly good headquarters for tours of the

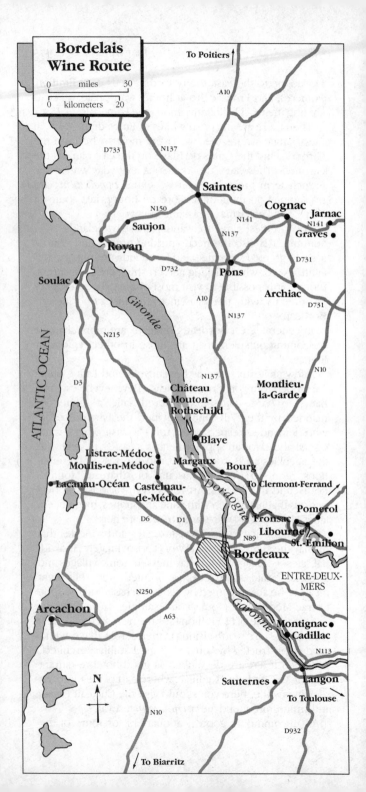

Bordelais
Wine Route

miles 0 — 30
kilometers 0 — 20

To Poitiers ↑

A10

D733

N137

Saintes

Cognac

Jarnac

N141

Saujon

N150

N141

Graves

N137

Royan

D732

Pons

D731

Soulac

A10

Archiac

Gironde

D731

N137

ATLANTIC OCEAN

N215

N137

Montlieu-la-Garde

N10

D3

Château Mouton-Rothschild

Blaye

Listrac-Médoc
Moulis-en-Médoc

Margaux

Bourg

To Clermont-Ferrand

Lacanau-Océan

Castelnau-de-Médoc

Dordogne

Pomerol

D6

D1

Fronsac

Libourne

N89

St.-Emilion

Bordeaux

ENTRE-DEUX-MERS

Arcachon

N250

Garonne

A63

Montignac

Cadillac

N113

N

Sauternes

Langon

N10

To Toulouse

D932

↓ To Biarritz

Médoc is the **Relais de Margaux** in the village of Margaux, about 25 km (14 miles) northwest of Bordeaux, where 18 splendid rooms and three apartments and a pampering staff are joined by a most able chef. Château visits can be arranged. The luxurious Relais has a splendid wine cellar and is expensive—but worth it.

St-Emilion

Of all the wine towns in the Bordeaux region, St-Emilion (about 65 km/40 miles east of Bordeaux near Libourne) is the most provocative and enticing. Sitting atop its little limestone hill overlooking the Dordogne, it seduces even non-oenophiles. The very best time to visit is during the annual Jurade, a ritual dating from Medieval times in which several councilmen dressed in ermine-edged scarlet robes parade through town to a hilltop ruin known as **La Tour du Roi** (the King's Tower). From there, they pronounce in stentorian chant the result of the year's harvest, echoed by the townsfolk in the square below who cheer "Hallelujah!" in increasingly excited tones. The Jurade is held in late September or early October, depending upon the harvest. ("And what would you say if one year the wine was no good?" a *jurat* was asked. "We should pronounce it 'insufficiently fine,'" he answered solemnly.)

Two figures step out of history in St-Emilion: the fourth-century Gallo-Roman poet and proconsul Ausonius and the eighth-century Breton monk Emilion. The first is remembered in the classic wines produced by the nearby Château Ausone (they may have been served to the Roman emperor), while the latter gave his name to the town. Today, the peace of the golden-stoned village of 3,000 inhabitants belies its bloody history of battles between English and French during the Hundred Years War; between Catholics and Huguenots during the Wars of Religion; and between the radical Jacobins and the moderate Girondists near the end of the French Revolution in 1792. (The Girondists were so-named because their most persuasive members came from Bordeaux—in the Gironde.)

St-Emilion sits on two levels. About the only place for drivers to park is on the upper, near the **Eglise Collégiale**, from which the whole village may easily be explored on foot. The church is rather disappointing in the interior, but its cloister is worth a short stop. From the church a cobbled street winds through the porte de la Cadène and down to the lower level, the center of town. The **place du Marché**, lively during Sunday markets, is somnolent most of the time, with the buying and selling (of wines, mostly) proceeding slowly, if at all. (The best wine shop in town is **Le Cellier des Gourmets** on le Castellot.)

St-Emilion's major treasure, the **Eglise Monolithe**, is entered from the square; a sign on the door tells which shop is keeping the key. The rare subterranean church, the largest and most important of its kind in France, was hewn from the rock walls of several adjoining caves by Benedictine monks at the beginning of the 12th century. Stripped during the revolution of decorations, treasures, and even the bones of the buried monks, it is today a massive, cold, forbidding, almost mystical space. (The hack marks still show in its bays, vaults, and on its pillars.) The tower of this marvel reaches aboveground clear to the upper level of the town (on the place du Clocher, where cars are parked) like "a finger of God (rising) from a sea of vines," as wine writer Ernst Hornickel put it.

At the end of the market square, the 13th-century **chapel of the Trinity** stands on top of a grotto known as **L'Hermitage St-Emilion**, which was supposedly the cave in which the hermit lived, sleeping on a bed cut out of the rock and drinking from a spring that still bubbles, as if the saint were to return by evening. Next to the chapel, the **catacombs** are another poignant underground curiosity.

The **Hostellerie de Plaisance** on place du Clocher is a pleasant, informal, 12-room inn with a kitchen that serves regional fare and boasts an impressive list of St-Emilion wines. For rural, family-style dining, **Logis de la Cadène** is the best in town, although **Chez Germaine**, across the street from the inn, also is recommended. On the main street, rue Guadet, the **Galerie Jean Guyot** boasts excellent buys in regional pottery.

Between St-Emilion and Pomerol, the Château Cheval Blanc produces what experts consider the most highly bred of the St-Emilion wines. It is open only by appointment on weekdays, as is the equally renowned Château Figeac.

COGNAC

"The Charente is a rolling patch of French countryside just north of Bordeaux where the actinic quality of the sunlight is extraordinary, and where the majority of rural postmen have liver trouble." So Samuel Chamberlain approaches his study of the world-famous brandy from Cognac, a small city-port on the Charente River about 65 km (40 miles) north of Bordeaux where the great château builder François I was born in 1494.

Cognac the Brandy

Wines have been grown in the Charente region since the Romans planted vines there in A.D. 300; with salt, the Roman wines were a major export to England, the Netherlands, and Scandinavia. However, the white table wines have never been very good, and even today they tend toward tartness, meanness, and cloudiness, so that the postman who stops to take an occasional glass on his rounds will not only make the mails tardy but will give himself a *crise de foi.*

More than three centuries ago, however, it was discovered that the same spirits, when distilled, metamorphose into an elixir permitting no competition for excellence from anything except Armagnac. Besides, the government had begun to exact a heavy tax on wine exports that did not extend to distilled, or "concentrated," wines.

It was the English and the Dutch who in the 17th century began to import this *vin brûlé,* or "burnt wine" (from the distillation process), which in Dutch is *brande-wijn* and was long ago Anglicized as *brandy*.

The production of Cognac is complicated; travellers who wish to make a short study of it will find more than enough information in the *Office de Tourisme* in the town of Cognac. Suffice it to say here that the name Cognac may be put on the label only if the grapes have been grown in an area comprising about 150,000 acres outside the town. Aging is all-important, as is the use of Limousin oak for the casks.

The seven grades of Cognac come from territories spreading out from the towns of Cognac and Jarnac as from a bull's-eye: Closest in is *Grande* or *Fine Grande*

Champagne (nothing to do with the region of the bubbly), followed by *Petite Champagne,* by *Borderies,* by the rings of *Fins Bois, Bons Bois,* and *Bois Ordinaires.* Finally, on the coast and islands of Oléron and Ré, there is *Bois à Terroir.*

According to wine connoisseur Alexis Lichine, the star device on labels began about a hundred years ago when the first three-star Cognac was designated for the Australian market. (Today, 90 percent of Cognacs sold are three stars.) Younger and less worthwhile spirits have no stars and, as Lichine puts it, "are best drunk with soda." The third type is designated V.S.O.P. (for Very Superior Old Pale). For export, some firms add such names as Réserve, Extra, X.O., and Cordon Bleu to the label.

Because Cognacs don't age after bottling, a Cognac made in 1814 but bottled in 1815 would now be only a year old, or younger than one produced in 1983 and bottled today. While V.S.O.P.s are at least five years old and sometimes ten, increasingly high costs of production for older ones means that one day they will be priced out of the market. A sweet liqueur made in the Cognac region, Pineau des Charentes, may be drunk as an apéritif.

Cognac the Town

It is possible to make an excursion (or a pilgrimage) to Cognac from Bordeaux in one long day, but a more satisfactory solution is to combine the visit there with ones to Saintes and Royan.

Your first stop in Cognac should be at the *Office de Tourisme* right near the heart of things—on place François-Ier—in order to discover which *chais* (wine sheds or storage places) are open to the public on what days: **Otard** (in the former château where François was born), **Polignac, Martell, Hennessy,** and others. The office can also arrange visits to the respected glass factory of **St-Gobain** and provide information about *son-et-lumière* performances in the firm's château.

On place Jean-Monnet, near the tourist office, a **Cognathèque** provides information about Cognacs and also sells an enormous selection of them at reasonable prices. Also available for purchase are the deep-blue glasses used by professional tasters. The **Musée du Cognac,** in the Dupuy d'Angeac town house (set in the kind of unmanicured park the French term *accidenté*), joins archaeology to art to the *eau-de-vie* industry in a fascinating manner. Fossils, ceramics, tools for viticulture, paintings—all meet in this entirely engaging museum.

The making of Cognac leaves its mark everywhere in the town (about 21,000 Cognaçais), even on many buildings near distilleries, which have assumed a curious brown shade created by a fungus that lives on the mere vapors of the distillation process. Aside from visits to the *chais* and museum, your primary pastime in Cognac will be walking along Grand-Rue, with its pretty 15th-century half-timbered houses, and the more aristocratic rue Saulnier, where town houses of the 16th and 17th centuries stand proudly. Right at the edge of the old quarter, the **church of St-Léger** boasts a beautiful rose window in Flamboyant style.

The best answer for both dining and staying the night in Cognac's neighborhood is **Moulin de Cierzac**, about 15 km (8 miles) south near St-Fort-sur-le-Né. The Moulin is a peaceful 17th-century country house that offers 10 rooms, a one-star Michelin dining room (oyster *cassolette à la Fine Champagne,* October to April), and a marvelous collection of Cognacs. There is an informal atmosphere here—and the Moulin is a good value per franc.

Local fairs are staged in Cognac in May and November; here, as is so often the case elsewhere, the liveliest market days are Saturday and Sunday.

SAINTES

Hurtling by on A 10 from Tours and Poitiers to Bordeaux, you will have no sense at all of Saintes, an ancient and attractive town of about 28,000 Saintais, or Santons, that today is sliced in two by the Charente. In Roman days the town occupied mainly the left bank as a major trading city called Mediolanum Santonum.

In Medieval times, under Plantagenêt domination, the town watched year in and year out as thousands of pilgrims passed through the Arc de Germanicus and crossed the bridge, bound for the shrine of Santiago de Compostela in Spain. Today a regional center of industry, agricultural markets, and crafts, Saintes well deserves at least one day of exploration.

Arriving from the east and Cognac or the coast and Royan, you will slow down along the animated main street, a meeting of avenue Gambetta and cours National et Lemercier, perhaps in search of a seat at one of the sidewalk cafés shadowed by plane trees (the **Brasserie Louis** on Gambetta, for example). From this perspective, Saintes seems pleasant enough—animated, well-supplied with shops, but of little individuality.

In its Old Town, however, and in what were once suburbs on the right bank, Saintes boasts witnesses of every age since that of the Romans and Saint Eutropius.

As usual, traipsing begins best in the Old Town, which surrounds the cathedral of St-Pierre and place du Marché. The cathedral, built atop a Roman structure, owes today's appearance mainly to the 15th century and is only of passing interest. Up rue St-Michel and a jog to the left on rue Victor Hugo, the **Musée des Beaux-Arts** is housed in the classic, 17th-century Hôtel Présdial in the center of an attractive pedestrian district. Beautifully restored in the modern manner (i.e., the exhibitions can be seen clearly), the Présdial's seven rooms house Saintonge ceramics from the 11th century up to today as well as paintings from the 17th, 18th, and 19th centuries. (The best restaurant in this part of town is that in the hotel **Commerce Mancini**, nearby on rue des Messageries.)

An amble past the flowery place de Nivelle, the center of municipal goings-on, leads to the **Musée Dupuy-Mestreau**, an example of the regional collections in which France excels. The *hôtel* itself is handsome in woodworks, fireplaces, and ceilings, and the displays include items of maritime importance, stamps, peasant headdresses and costumes, weapons, and reconstituted rooms in regional style. From here, it's a pleasant walk back along the quai de Verdun, lined with handsome old 17th- and 18th-century mansions with gardens and wrought-iron balconies.

Farther out, on what was once the western rim of the city, the **church of St-Eutrope** ranks among the most important in western France. Its prize remains the lower, half-buried church that Pope Urban II consecrated in 1096. The body of the saint rests here in its sarcophagus, secure in a scene of sturdy, fat Roman pillars, some of their capitals decorated with unlikely looking vegetables.

Beyond, an amphitheater almost the size of that in Nîmes once held 20,000 spectators; today grass grows over the tiers. Built in the first century, it is among the oldest remaining from the Roman world, and it is a moving setting for the musical performances staged here on many summer nights.

The **Arc de Germanicus** has been standing on the right

bank of the river, the Gambetta side, since 1842, when the Roman bridge on which it originally stood had to be demolished. (Prosper Mérimée, author of the *Carmen* on which Bizet's opera was based and an inspector of historical monuments, insisted it be saved.) The wonder of this arch, built of local limestone in the year A.D. 19, is that its inscriptions, by one Caius Julius Rufius, may still be read in dedication to Germanicus, Emperor Tiberius, and his son Drusus.

Nearby, the **archaeological museum** and its park show off remains of walls, churches, and houses from Roman days; archaeologically inclined visitors may sometimes arrange to see the digs still going on in the immediate region. In the center of town on the right bank is the Benedictine **abbaye aux Dames**, which dates from 1047. Not far from the railway station, a stud farm (*haras*) houses about 60 handsome horses of varying breeds. It is open to visitors on many late afternoons throughout the year.

As in Cognac, there is a scarcity of outstanding inns in central Saintes. The best here is out past the amphitheater on the way to Royan: **Relais du Bois St-Georges** stands in a large park where quiet and good living are bywords, families and dogs are welcome, and no pretensions are required.

ROYAN

Travellers from places other than France will thoroughly enjoy or completely deplore Royan, west of Cognac and Saintes, depending upon their views of what is or is not typically French.

Almost nothing remains of the old port of Royan on the northern lip of the mouth of the Gironde. During the liberating battles of autumn 1944 German troops holed up here and in other nearby pockets, but their retreats were bombed by Allied forces in April 1945, less than a month before the armistice of May 8.

Today, Royan is nicknamed "Queen of the *Côte de Beauté*," and it is the largest and most modern sea resort between La Baule up north in Brittany and Biarritz south on the Spanish border. There are those who wax nostalgic about old Royan, the Royan of elegant cliffside chalets, of breezy Victorian hostelries with wide corridors and intimidating façades and concierges, of palatial casinos in Renaissance or Baroque dress. It is said that some sense of the olden days may be glimpsed in the smart suburb of Pontaillac, although most visitors stop there not because of nostalgia but to play at the Sporting-Casino.

Today, expressions such as *resto en vogue* (trendy restaurant) are more suggestive of Royan than *aristocratique* or *traditionel*. Indeed, the top tourist attraction in town is a triumph of reinforced concrete dating from 1958, the **church of Notre-Dame**. Seen from the front, the soaring belfry (almost 215 feet high) suggests the giant prow of a ship sailing into town from the Atlantic.

The heart of the modern town curves around the Grande Conche, a large bay flanked on the north by a fine sandy beach and a seafront promenade backed by shops, banks, and apartment houses. Across the bay, the port swells with resting trawlers, sardine-fishing boats, and pleasure craft, right at the foot of the **Grand Casino**. (In European fashion, the visitor to the casinos is expected to be properly dressed, quiet, serious, and to respect an atmosphere utterly unlike those in Reno, Las Vegas, or Atlantic City.)

The resort setting may best be admired by driving northwest of town on the coastal road in the direction of the **Forêt de la Courbe**. Rounding the various *conches* (bays, coves), on cliffs above or down by sandy dunes where sea pines blow, you will begin to appreciate the natural beauty that brings inland souls to this place. The best day along **la Grande Côte** between Royan and the lighthouse in the Forêt de la Courbe is a cold, windy one when waves batter in and spray drenches the windshield.

Looking right out at the beach, the **Family Golf Hotel** is the best one in town, though it's quite modest and has no restaurant. Better is the **Résidence de Rohan**, just a couple of miles north along the coast. It is a 22-room inn occupying a handsomely furnished 19th-century home, and it is comfortable but far from ostentatious (no dining room).

For dining, **Le Squale** and **Le Chalet** stand out. They are both solid, middle-ground restaurants offering such dishes as salmon in a parsley cream sauce, grilled sole, and oysters.

THE DORDOGNE

The green, serene valley of the Dordogne is inexplicably spooky. One tends to drive carefully, as if expecting the mysterious, prehistoric Cro-Magnon man, who 40,000 years ago called this valley home, to materialize in the rear-view mirror.

Perhaps it is the autumnal, light-and-shadow haze that hangs above the countryside almost all year long—a drapery as delicate as a Japanese screen. Maybe it's the flickering forms of willows and poplars that reflect themselves in the clear waters of the Dordogne and its tributary, the Vézère.

The Dordogne ranks among the longest rivers in France, taking both its source and its name from the meeting place of the Dore with the Dogne near the town of Clermont-Ferrand and the Puy de Sancy, at 6,184 feet the highest peak in the Massif Central. From its birthplace, the river used to skip swiftly over its volcanic bed and slice through narrow ravines, but it has been slowed down today by dams and artificial lakes created to supply energy for mighty power stations. Those who wish to follow the river along (and about and around) its length will start upstream at Bort-les-Orges and continue down to Libourne, about 500 km (300 miles) west.

On the other hand, the Dordogne of lore, legend, and archaeological interest can best be explored by beginning at Bergerac, east of Bordeaux and St-Emilion, and proceeding with measured pace east toward Souillac and the Gouffre de Padirac, making detours north and south en route. The river roams through the regions of Périgord and Quercy, rich in underground caverns.

It is not nature, however, but the mark of mankind that dominates in so many places along the Dordogne and throughout this region. No other place on earth is so rich in evidences of early man, who left his art and his tools behind in Paleolithic times. The most intriguing and most advanced of these early peoples were the **Cro-Magnons**, a tall (about 5 feet, 11 inches in average height) and erect race that recorded elements of its existence on the cave walls of the Dordogne-Vézère.

It is the shades of these prehistoric civilizations, the enticing Medieval villages, and the evidences of the strug-

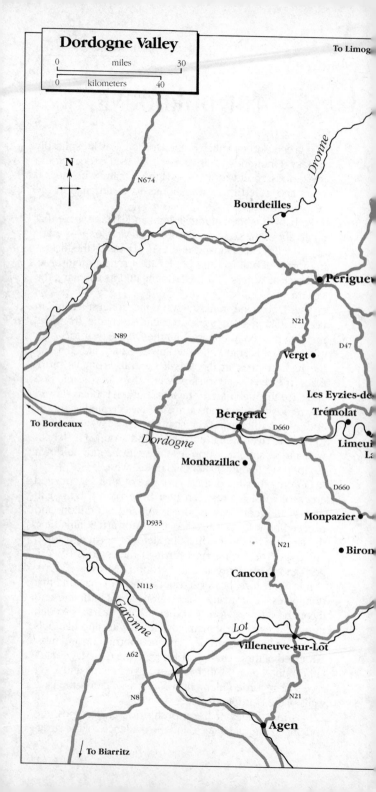

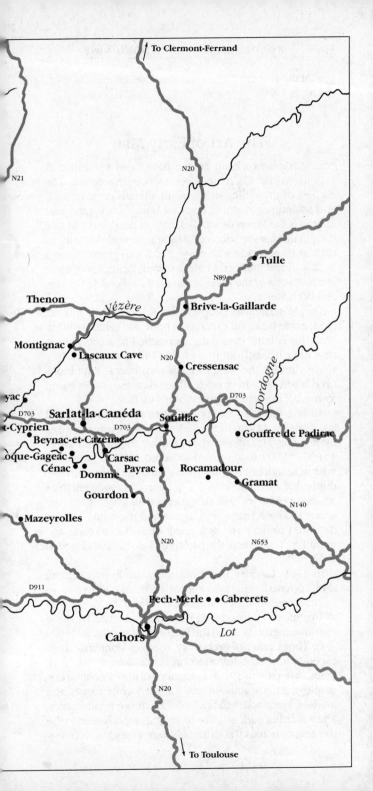

gles of the Hundred Years War that lure the traveller here today.

The Art of Early Man

Prehistoric artworks in France have been unearthed at sites from the Charente River to northern Spain. The earliest of these, line drawings of animals on cave walls and sculptures in stone, horn, or bone (among the best known is the **Venus de Laussel**, now in Bordeaux's Musée d'Aquitaine), were succeeded by simple wall decorations such as those made with outspread hands placed upon a rock wall and outlined in black or red. Examples of these are best seen in the caves at Bara-Bahau, Font-de-Gaume, and Pech-Merle.

The Magdalenian people, who flourished in this region, made beautiful carvings in bone and reindeer horn. With this culture, cave painting reached its acme: Horses rear their heads from bodies shot full of arrows; a deer slumps under the weight of his own horns; a multicolored bison steps from one to three dimensions, his hump formed of the natural curve of the rock face.

Among the most exceptional cave paintings yet found are those in **Lascaux cave**, a few miles northeast of Les Eyzies near Montignac. These works, dating from about 14,000–13,500 B.C., were discovered in 1940 by young boys in search of a dog that had fallen into a hole. The cave, dubbed "the Sistine Chapel of Périgord," was opened to an amazed public in 1948. Alas, despite all precautions, the green sickness (moss and algae) and the white (calcite deposits) proliferated as a result of carbon dioxide and humidity. To preserve the paintings, Lascaux was closed in 1963.

In 1983, **Lascaux II**, a brilliant facsimile in a cement shell, opened near the original cave after ten years of labor. Here are archaeological finds from the site as well as ingeniously reproduced paintings, achieved by using the same methods as did the Paleolithic peoples.

Le Thot Center of Prehistory, south of Montignac, is an excellent one-stop introduction to the animals, environment, cave painting, and civilizations of the Paleolithic era, employing films, audiovisuals, still photographs, casts, and models. Here you will find a list of recommended sites. The adjoining park is home to animals represented in the paintings, such as the extremely rare Przewalski's horse.

Many of the prehistoric sites mentioned here are covered in more detail in the following sections.

BERGERAC TO LES EYZIES

There is no compelling reason for the traveller to visit Bergerac, although from an economic standpoint it is the most important town along the Dordogne. If you arrive at noon, however, there *is* an excellent excuse for stopping: the restaurant known as **Le Cyrano**, in honor of the local 17th-century duelist and writer who won fame only posthumously in the writing of Edmond Rostand. Le Cyrano offers the regional wines of Bergerac (fruity red, dry, or sweet white) to accompany fine local dishes. Restaurants in the Dordogne are committed to serving well the finest dishes of the Périgord and Quercy cuisines: truffles, fois gras of geese and ducks in various persuasions, *confits* (preserved goose, duck, and pork dishes), truffle or cepe omelettes, garlic soup, sautéed potatoes from Sarlat, Limousin beef with *sauce Périgeaux, Chabichou,* and Pouligny-St-Pierre cheeses.

After lunch you might visit the **Musée du Tabac**, unique in France, dedicated to the history, influence on society, and growth of the "American weed."

Wine enthusiasts will certainly want to make a detour south (about 30 km/18 miles round-trip) to **Monbazillac**, from the vineyards of which comes the heavy, sweet dessert wine that has made the term "noble rot" a synonym for perfection throughout centuries. The vineyard's elegant 16th-century château is open as a museum of Calvinism, but photographing its exterior may be satisfaction enough for non-Calvinists. The wine may be tasted; buying is also encouraged at the shop near the castle gate.

From Bergerac, D 660 (which becomes D 703) runs east toward **Lanquais château**, an architectural mishmash rising from the ruins of a fortress battered by the English during the Hundred Years War. Students of Louis XIII furniture will admire the interiors.

Near the pleasant village of **Trémolat**, the road climbs a coil of white cliffs from which there's a splendid view of the *Cingle de Trémolat* (*cingle* means "meander" in French). Below, the Dordogne bends in remarkable S-curves through fields that look like green or golden chessboards. If twilight is approaching, wait for the sun to set over the ordered landscape. A fine overnight retreat,

Le Vieux Logis, awaits in Trémolat. The accent at Logis, a handsome old country mansion set in pleasant gardens, is on dignified quiet and comfort; only well-behaved dogs are allowed, for example.

Past Limeuil, where the Dordogne meets the Vézère, drivers bound for Les Eyzies will cruise through the town of Le Bugue and into prehistory. (If you're in Le Bugue at lunchtime, try the river terrace of l'**Albuca** in the unassuming, always-busy Hôtel Royal-Vézère.)

LES EYZIES

High, ocher cliffs rise from the narrow green valley that shelters the village (about 800 people) of Les Eyzies-de-Tayac, east of Trémolat on the Vézère. Prehistoric man lived here during the Ice Ages, occupying caves for tens of thousands of years and leaving behind a legacy of tools, weapons, pottery, and—particularly provocative—the marvelous works of art that are their cave paintings. (In ancient times, the bed of the Vézère lay some 90 feet above today's level, and the caves were more accessible than they are today.) Les Eyzies makes a natural head-quarters for investigations of the prehistory evident in the surrounding area. (Another suggestion is Sarlat-la-Canéda, of which more later.) Although it is a small town, Les Eyzies sports two outstanding inns: **Le Centen-aire**, with 26 rooms, and **Cro-Magnon**, with 24. Both kitchens are acclaimed, but the Cro-Magnon's gardened grounds and large outdoor pool give it an edge (and it's slightly less costly). Besides, local tradition has it that Cro-Magnon remains were found at what is today the latter's men's room. Both are popular and centers of the town's activity, with English-speaking visitors gathering at dinnertime to tell tales of what they've seen. From Easter through September, a lively Monday market fills Les Eyzies' main street.

Les Eyzies' **Musée National de Préhistoire** occupies the castle of the barons of Beynac, and from modest beginnings it has grown to rank among the best of its kind in France. Discoveries in the region are described and out-lined, while many original objects and reproductions of paintings are displayed. A visit to this museum is required as an introduction to the sites themselves. Nearby, an amusing statue of Cro-Magnon man, as envisioned by sculptor Paul Dardé in 1930, stares out from beneath an overhanging rock.

Around Les Eyzies

Just outside the village, where the mouth of the St-Cyprien valley opens, the grotto of **Font-de-Gaume** (just east of town off D 47) makes believers of those who would doubt the creative talents of Paleolithic man. The frescoes at the grotto form a veritable catalog of creatures of the hunt: bison, mammoths, horses, reindeer, and more. A well-fed horse outlined in black relief thrusts its front legs against a bend in the wall, while another wall helps form the hump of a multicolored buffalo.

Stalactites, stalagmites, and more eccentric formations fill the cave of **Grand Roc** (to the north on D 47), many of them younger than the paintings within. At the grotto of **Rouffignac** (just north of Les Eyzies on a spur off D 6) an electric railway passes through two and a half miles of underground galleries, their walls alive with engravings, drawings, and paintings.

The prehistory museum in Les Eyzies provides a list of recommended sites in the immediate neighborhood. It includes **La Mouthe** (just a croissant's toss south of town; the first cave to be discovered), **Grotte des Combarelles** (a short detour east of town on D 47; portrayals of nearly 300 animals), and **Bara-Bahau**, a short spurt west of Le Bugue (very early flintwork engravings).

SARLAT

It is easy not to stop in Sarlat-la-Canéda, east of Les Eyzies, if you careen past on the "modern" rue de la République (1837). The "traverse," as it is called by the locals, cuts unheedingly right through the old quarter and is lined by rather nondescript houses. Off to each side, however, the old stone buildings with their slate roofs still march around circuitous streets that are now safeguarded as historic monuments.

Sarlat's most famous son is Etienne de la Boétie, magistrate of the Bordeaux parliament in the 16th century but better-known internationally as a prolific political writer and close friend of Montaigne. His house, with its handsome gables, mullioned windows, and medallions—an exuberance in Renaissance style—still stands right across from the cathedral. From this *place* (the cathedral may be skipped) runs a tangle of arches and alleyways recently and tastefully restored to their original beauty.

The marketplace in front of the **Hôtel de Ville** bustles and bubbles during the Wednesday and, particularly, Saturday markets. Sarlat is sought out for products of the Dordogne and Périgord: unbeatable walnut oils, foie gras, black truffles, *chabichou* cheese, canned *confits d'oie,* dried mushrooms, a walnut-flavored liqueur named Eau de Noix, and a wonderful chocolate treat called *éphémères,* from Confolens. Patricia Wells suggests that picnickers pick up a loaf of rye bread or sourdough *pain de seigle* from the B. Pauliac bakery.

In summer, the classics of Molière, Shakespeare, and their like go on stage during the Sarlat theater festival. At any time, Sarlat is for strolling; you might stay overnight at **La Couleuvrine**, an old house wedged into the city wall (unpretentious and popular with younger travellers who like to be in the heart of things), or **Hostellerie Meysset**, on a hill above town in a wooded setting (calmer, ideal for slower-moving travellers).

THE DORDOGNE NEAR SARLAT

South of Sarlat the Dordogne meanders at the foot of golden rock walls crowned by beetling castles and perilously perched villages. There are several attractions clustered in this area.

The **Château de Montfort**, just beyond the village of Carsac, sits on its rock outcrop above a wide bend in the Dordogne, its towers and turrets threatening at any moment to teeter over into the view. Today privately owned, the château has lived a history of sieges, battles, and reconstructions, having been burned to the ground in 1214 by Simon de Montfort in one of his anti-Albigensian crusades. To call its style a mélange is to understate.

Domme

From near Cénac, the road climbs up a crag to Domme, a village of fewer than a thousand people whose ancestors were embroiled in the struggles of the Reformation. At a mere suggestion, any one of them will tell the tale of Huguenot Captain Geoffroi de Vivans, who with daring (say Protestants) or trickery (say Catholics) took the town in the middle of the night in 1588.

From Domme's Belvédère de la Barre you can look over the rich, crop-checkered valley where the Dordogne eases slowly between its poplar-lined banks. The **Château de Beynac** and the great cliff of La Roque-Gageac thrust their silhouettes against the sky. The caves (the entrance is near the covered market) that sheltered the townspeople during the Hundred Years War and the Wars of Religion are rich in stalactites, stalagmites, and bones of Ice Age bison and rhinoceri; the trek through the caves leads to the pretty Promenade des Falaises (cliff walk) and then to the Promenade des Remparts.

Those who can't bear to leave Domme quite yet may lunch at the very fine **Esplanade** and even, if departure still seems premature, stay over in one of the inn's modest but clean and adequate rooms.

La Roque-Gageac

It seems unlikely that La Roque-Gageac should exist at all: Perhaps it and its fewer than 500 Gageacs are figments of an inspired imagination. Flat faces of old stone houses reflect themselves in the river, while behind them narrow alleyways scale the cliff face and lead to the humble 12th-century church. The castle at the west end of the village is a 19th-century imitation of a 15th-century style; still, it appears very authentic in this setting.

La Roque is best seen and photographed from the west: If you arrive from the east, make sure to see the western approach before leaving.

Beynac

Beynac-et-Cazenac, and especially the views from its formidable château, stay in the traveller's mind long after leaving. Somehow, a fierce past lies lightly on this pastel, impressionistic countryside.

The Capets and Plantagenêts were rivals here, and Richard the Lion-Hearted employed the thuggish Mercadier to pillage the countryside on his royal behalf. He seized Beynac in 1189, but the indefatigable Montfort wiped it out in 1214. A great part of today's château dates from the 13th century; the well-restored hall of state is notable, and there's the smashing view from the battlements. It's all a setting for a Cecil B. De Mille epic.

There is not much to do here except gaze into the distance and imagine the forces of Richard the Lion-Hearted attacking. That done, it's time to eat a little something on the terrace of the small inn called **Bonnet**.

In the Middle Ages Beynac was one of four grand baronies of Périgord, with Biron (castle also worth seeing), Bourdeilles (outstanding furnishings in its castle), and Mareuil (castle less interesting, rebuilt since 1965).

MONPAZIER

Not all of the Hundred Years War was devoted to destruction. Constant struggles between the French and English forces necessitated the construction of fortified towns, mostly along disputed frontiers. These *bastides* (*bastide* derives from the old-French verb *bastir,* to build) are among the most interesting examples of military architecture in France.

Sitting a straight shot south of Les Eyzies to Mazeyrolles and then a dash to the west, Monpazier is among the two or three best-preserved *bastides* still functioning as towns 700 years after being built.

French and English *bastides* once faced each other wall to wall near the rivers Garonne, Lot, and Dordogne. They were all new towns, and whether French or English they adhered to an identical plan. Unlike old villages with their narrow and crooked streets, the new towns conformed to a checkerboard or rectangular design of straight streets that cut across alleys, and small spaces that acted as drains, firebreaks, or latrines. At the center of each town, a *cornière* (plazalike square) was surrounded by roofed arcades. Nearby stood a church, commonly fortified.

Life in the new towns was fairly good for the defending citizenry: Houses could be bought and sold, offspring were free to marry at will, and town affairs were conducted by locally elected consuls, though under the watchful eye of the king's bailiff.

Monpazier was an English *bastide,* founded on January 7, 1284, by Edward I, and later joined by Beaumont, Molières, and Roquepine. Attackers and defenders often changed roles in those confusing days, and Monpazier was assaulted by both sides with some regularity, depending upon which forces were in power at the time. In 1594 and 1637, Monpazier also served as a center for some of the fiercest peasant revolts in the region.

Remarkably, Monpazier retains its grid pattern, its fortified church (restored in the 16th century), and its roomy
square flanked by covered galleries. The sturdy old
houses still stand, and the measuring standards for judging weights hang in place in the covered market.

Shops selling souvenirs, fruits and vegetables, and arts
and crafts snuggle into the arcades today, shading themselves from the summer sun, and it seems as though the
whole place has been hibernating since the 13th century.

ROCAMADOUR

Narrow roads from Les Eyzies, Sarlat, Beynac, or any
number of other little towns skitter eastward to Rocamadour, east of N 20 and south of the Dordogne, a gathering
place for pilgrims in the past and a required stop for
tourists today.

Although the site is one of the most stunning in all
Europe, Rocamadour is sometimes skipped over by travellers who scorn it as over-commercialized. Yet in a sense
the town has always been the same, with streets full of
buyers and sellers, often dealing in religious trinkets.

It's important to approach from the road from l'Hospi-
talet and to look down and out from the small terrace of
the hamlet. Below, the river Alzou wanders through the
wide gorge, while houses and shops climb its banks,
nearly standing on each other's shoulders as they cling to
the steep cliff face, rising to the château on the summit.

Nobody knows who Saint Amadour was, though it is
generally acknowledged that he was a pious hermit. The
current theory is that he was Zaccheus, who came here
with his wife, Saint Veronica (she who wiped the face of
Christ on the route to Calvary), and after her death lived
on, alone, on the cliff. He first was called *roc amator*
("one who knows and loves the rock"), hence the name
Rocamadour. It is said that miracles began to occur as
soon as the saint's bones were buried near the altar in the
tiny **chapel of the Virgin**.

The resultant pilgrimages attracted thousands of the
faithful, some of whom made this a stop en route to
Santiago de Compostela. French kings, Saint Louis among
them, came here, as did England's Henry II, Saint Bernard, Blanche of Castille, and thousands upon thousands
of unremembered believers. Repentant sinners were a
major source of revenue, paying severe penances in coin

and then climbing the 216 steps (the *Via Sancta*) on bleeding knees to chapels atop the summit, known as the Ecclesiastical City.

Life was rarely peaceful in Rocamadour: In 1183, Henri Court-Mantel, rebelling against his father, Henri Plantagenêt, sacked the oratory in search of riches, only to die soon after in Martel, claiming to regret his actions. Legend has it that during the Wars of Religion, pillaging Protestants dug up the body of Saint Amadour and tossed it into a fire, in which it refused to burn. The abbey finally fell to the Revolution of 1789. Today the wealth and the splendor have vanished, but Rocamadour lives on, a fascinating witness to history and religious hysteria.

The entrance to the town is through the 13th-century Figuier Gate, where you will find yourself in a swirl of souvenir shops lining rue Roland le Preux. It's off-putting but must be braved. The street passes through Porte Salmon and becomes rue de la Couronnerie, growing somewhat less cute and more intriguing along the way.

The point of Rocamadour, however, is the **Ecclesiastical City**, reached either by lift or by the self-same 216 steps, past shops and hotels on terraces along the way. The cluster of buildings at the top (most of them were restored during the 19th century) includes the fort, the seven churches on place St-Amadour, the Basilique St-Sauveur, the Chapelle Miraculeuse, and the Chapelle St-Michel.

Major treasures are the **Black Virgin and Child**, a wood sculpture above the altar in the Chapelle Miraculeuse; the chapel bell that rings on its own when a miracle is about to occur; and the **iron sword** on the wall of Chapelle Notre-Dame that tradition holds to be Durandal, the weapon of Roland.

On the open space in front of the church, a small but rewarding museum is open to guided tours. The main street offers two museums: Roland-le-Preux (waxworks) and the Historial.

The delicious regional goat cheese, *chabichou,* should be available at cafés in town, perhaps at **Jehan de Valon**. The best is produced by the Ferme Jean Lacoste between Rocamadour and Gramat.

Rocamadour is another good center for exploration of the local countryside. In town, **Beau Site et Notre Dame** is the choice inn, a 55-room hostelry of agreeable nature and decoration that's always full. Several km (a couple of miles) away, on the road leading southeast to Gramat, the unassuming **Auberge de la Garenne** is one of those warm, welcoming inns in which the French countryside excels, a calm retreat after a day's exploration.

Near Gramat, the **Château de Roumégouse** offers 14 rooms and two apartments to travellers looking for elegance in their home away from the madding crowd. Also near Gramat, the rather new **Parc de Vision** (Safari Park), 94 acres of regional plants and trees, is home to various wild European animals, including some beasts such as wild oxen and bison descended from prehistoric species.

While in Rocamadour and vicinity, sample the fine plum brandy from the Ségala distillery: *eau-de-vie du Vieux Pigeonnier.*

Gouffre de Padirac

If there is time to view only one *gouffre* (chasm) on a trip to France, that one should be the Gouffre de Padirac, only a few minutes' drive northeast of Rocamadour. Elevators make the descent into a vast and mysterious—and definitely touristy—underground world of galleries and rivers created by rainwater percolating through fine limestone. After a visit to Padirac, on foot and flat-bottomed boat, the legend ascribing it to a face-off between Satan and Saint Martin will seem more probable to you.

Pech-Merle

About 25 km (15 miles) south of Rocamadour, off to the east of N 20 and near the wide spot of Cabrerets, the cave of Pech-Merle is one of the most exciting of the painted caverns, since Lascaux can no longer be seen. It's entered through a chamber used by prehistoric man 20,000 years ago. Bison and mammoth parade in a frieze, human footprints of 200 centuries past are perfect in petrification, and two horses suffer the stenciled hands of would-be attackers.

The **Musée Amédée-Lemozi** at the site illustrates the prehistory of Pech-Merle and other nearby sites.

Two remarkable hostelries may keep the wanderer near Pech-Merle and its region: **La Pescalerie** in Cabrerets, a gracious 17th-century country house where fine regional meals are served family-style; and the more lordly and extremely fashionable but no less inviting **Château de Mercuès**, a 12th-century castle of the bishops of Cahors.

CAHORS

The perfumed air of the Midi breathes ever so slightly in the sleepy streets of Cahors and stirs the plane trees along boulevard Gambetta, which is lined by sidewalk cafés and seductive shops. (Among regional items, the most interesting are the ceramics in brilliant and beautiful shades of gold, green, and a wine red.)

The boulevard, the main artery of Cahors, celebrates the favorite local son, Léon-Michel Gambetta, the 19th-century barrister and activist who floated over the German lines in a balloon, became war minister and prime minister, and gave his name to squares and streets all over France.

Cahors sits above a loop in the river Lot and serves as an excursion center for the valleys of the Lot and Célé, with their pretty perched villages (see the Provence chapter), fortress churches, troglodyte caves, and châteaux. In town, look for the **Pont Valentré**, still a commanding example of Medieval military-bridge design, and the admirable tympanum and cloisters of the **cathédrale St-Etienne**.

Saturday is the best market day in Cahors, as elsewhere, though there is action on Wednesdays also. The Cahors wines, rich, powerful, and little-known outside France, may best be tasted at **La Taverne**, which has the best selection of them in the country. The wines nobly support the café's renowned dishes, which feature precious truffles.

GETTING AROUND

Bordeaux usually serves as the starting point for travellers to the region who arrive by air (13 daily one-hour flights from Paris Orly-Ouest or Roissy) or rail (at least ten trains arrive daily from Paris's Austerlitz station).

Driving a car is recommended here, as it is everywhere in France when you want to seek out remote valleys, small hotels, and little-known villages. Either pick up a rental car in Bordeaux or drive from Paris via the Loire valley and Poitiers.

Pleasure boats may be rented in many ports, including Arcachon, Pauillac, Royan, Verdon, and Bordeaux.

In Bordeaux, a guided boat tour shows off the Old City; departures are from quai Louis-XVIII, near the Quinconques.

Bus tours of from four to eight days may be booked through the *Office de Tourisme* in Bordeaux.

ACCOMMODATIONS REFERENCE

▶ **Beau Site et Notre-Dame**. 46500 **Rocamadour**. Tel: 65-33-63-08; Telex: 520421; in U.S., (800) 334-7234; in Canada, (416) 674-3400 or (800) 528-1234; in U.K., (01) 541-0050-9766.

▶ **Le Centenaire**. 24620 **Les Eyzies-de-Tayac**. Tel: 53-06-97-18; Telex: 541921; in U.S., (212) 696-1323; in Australia, (02) 957-4511.

▶ **Château de Mercuès**. 46090 **Cahors**. Tel: 65-20-00-01.

▶ **Château de Roumégouse**. 46500 **Gramat**. Tel: 65-33-63-81; in U.S., (212) 696-1323.

▶ **La Couleuvrine**. 24200 **Sarlat-la-Canéda**. Tel: 53-59-27-80.

▶ **Cro-Magnon**. 24620 **Les Eyzies-de-Tayac**. Tel: 53-06-97-06; Telex: 570637.

▶ **Esplanade**. Domme 24250. Tel: 53-28-31-41.

▶ **Family Golf Hôtel**. 28, boulevard F. Garnier, 17200 **Royan**. Tel: 46-05-14-66.

▶ **Auberge de la Garenne**. 46500 **Rocamadour**. Tel: 65-33-65-88.

▶ **Grand Hôtel**. 2, place de la Comédie, 33000 **Bordeaux**. Tel: 56-90-33-44; Telex: 541658; in U.S., (212) 477-1600 or (800) 223-1510.

▶ **Hostellerie Meysset**. 24200 **Sarlat-la-Canéda**. Tel: 53-59-08-29.

▶ **Moulin de Cierzac**. **Cierzac** 17520 Cognac. Tel: 45-83-01-32.

▶ **La Pescalerie**. 46330 **Cabrerets**. Tel: 65-31-22-55.

▶ **Hostellerie de Plaisance**. Place du Clocher, 33330 **St-Emilion**. Tel: 57-24-72-32.

▶ **Pullman Mériadeck**. 5, rue Robert-Lateulade, 33000 **Bordeaux**. Tel: 56-90-92-37; Telex: 540565.

▶ **Relais du Bois St-Georges**. Rue Royan, 17100 **Saintes**. Tel: 46-93-50-99; Telex: 790488.

▶ **Relais de Margaux**. 33460 **Margaux**. Tel: 56-88-38-30; in U.S., (212) 696-1323.

▶ **La Réserve**. Avenue Bourgailh, 33600 **l'Alouette**. Tel: 56-07-13-28; in U.S., (212) 696-1323.

▶ **Résidence de Rohan**. 17640 **Conche de Nauzan** (2.5 km/1.5 miles northwest of Royan). Tel: 46-39-00-75.

▶ **Sofitel Aquitania**. 33300 **Bordeaux le Lac**. Tel: 56-50-83-80; Telex: 691320; in U.S., (212) 354-3722 or (800) 221-4542; in Canada, (800) 221-4542; in U.K., (01) 724-1000; in

Australia, (02) 264-5955. Among the new resort-conference types, 212 rooms, good dining room, and semicoffee shop.

▶ **Vieux Logis. Trémolat** 24510 Ste-Alvère. Tel: 53-22-80-06; Telex: 541025.

BIARRITZ
AND THE
PYRENEES

By Fred Halliday

Biarritz, that old Hemingway haven of *The Sun Also Rises,* sits pleased as punch on the Gascony sea—pleased with her wide sandy beaches and green rolling breakers, her promenades and wedding-cake spas, her ballrooms, swimming pools, casinos, crowds of high rollers in Rolls-Royces, and her matchless Café de Paris, *the* Café de Paris apart from which there is no other.

Biarritz is all the more impressive considering that not too long ago—up to the mid-19th century—it was only a sleepy fishing village where there was nothing more exciting to do than watch the Basques mending their nets or going down to the sea in their eel boats.

Then Biarritz was discovered by nobility on the lam. A Spanish countess who was on the outs with the Spanish royalty, and who couldn't be seen in San Sebastián in Spain—then the "in" resort—wanted to be as close to the action as possible. *Voilà,* she, with her daughter, settled on Biarritz, a mere 40 km (25 miles) up the coast. Napoléon III later married the daughter, who became the Empress Eugénie. Napoléon built a palace for his bride so she wouldn't be lonely, and her royal friends came running. Could the bourgeoisie of Europe do any less? The stampede was on. Biarritz was on its way to becoming a major international resort. The Basque country was beaten back a little bit, the eel boats moved farther south.

But Biarritz is still Basque France and her original heritage is still around.

At the doorstep of Biarritz to the east is Bayonne (of the ham). South, along the coast, is the appealing little resort of St-Jean-de-Luz, and still farther along, of course, is pretty San Sebastián, its harbor defined by mountains sticking up from the sea, like a small-scale Rio de Janeiro. Eastward, from the coast, mountains and the music of Bizet beckon: Biarritz is the gateway to the Golden Hills, the Pyrénées.

MAJOR INTEREST

Biarritz
Café de Paris
Victorian casino
Café François: outstanding foie gras

Musée Basque, in Bayonne

The Pyrénées
Waters of Pau and Lourdes
Pont d'Espagne
Cirque de Gavarnie
Aspé and Aure valleys
St-Bertrand-de-Comminges
Foix
Grotte de Niaux Grotto
Cathar citadel of Montségur
Abbey of St-Martin-de-Canigou

Biarritz, the old Basque port that nobility remodeled as a resort more than a century ago, does in fact unfold itself in a regal way. The **Hôtel Palais**, the villa that Napoléon built for Eugénie de Montijo, is at one end of the seaside promenade. That is one of the things you do in Biarritz, you promenade, or you watch other people promenading. The Hôtel du Palais offers accommodations that are as palatial as you'll find at any hotel in France, and if you are looking for that sort of thing (and Biarritz is the appropriate place to find it) you are sure to be charmed. From the hotel's end of the promenade you can set out on a walk of 15 to 20 minutes— past the most interesting spots in town with glimpses of the sea in between—to the **Plage de la Côte des Basques**.

Midway down the promenade, a statue of the Virgin sits

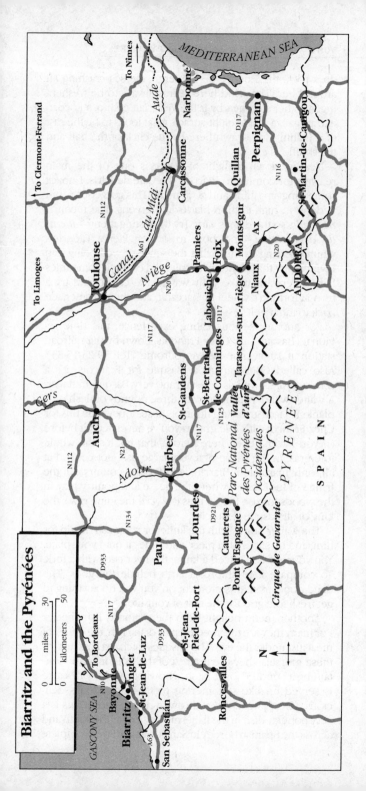

Biarritz and the Pyrénées

MEDITERRANEAN SEA

To Nîmes

To Clermont-Ferrand

To Limoges

To Bordeaux

GASCONY SEA

Narbonne

Carcassonne

Quillan

Perpignan

St-Martin-de-Canigou

Toulouse

Pamiers

Foix

Montségur

Ax

ANDORRA

Niaux

Tarascon-sur-Ariège

Labouiche

St-Bertrand-de-Comminges

St-Gaudens

Auch

Tarbes

Lourdes

Cauterets

Pont d'Espagne

Parc National des Pyrénées Occidentales

Vallée d'Aire

Cirque de Gavarnie

PYRÉNÉES

SPAIN

Pau

St-Jean-Pied-de-Port

Roncesvalles

Bayonne

Anglet

Biarritz

St-Jean-de-Luz

San Sebastián

Aude

Canal du Midi

Ariège

Gers

Adour

N112

A61

N20

N117

N125

N134

N21

D933

N117

D933

N10

A63

D921

D117

D117

N116

N20

N112

miles

0   30

kilometers

0   50

N

on a rock, the **Rocher de la Vierge**, the sea crashing all around her. The wind here seems always to be freshening. Another stop nearby is the Victorian **casino**, a Rococo extravaganza that at night attracts what looks to be the cast of a Fellini film, drawn here by the click of the ball and the shuffle of cards.

Nearby, down a flight of stairs, is one of the main reasons for coming to Biarritz: the **Café de Paris**. Unpack something smashing and go at night. This gorgeous room is done in high-fashion blacks and greens. The menu is *nouvelle,* so the dishes vary. Try the tasting menu—*menu de dégustation*—and bow to owner Pierre Laporte's whim. Bearing in mind that the sense of well-being and invincibility that comes with splendid eating is sometimes false, afterward make your way to the casino and try a turn at fortune's wheel or baccarat, and then promenade back to the hotel.

For another serious eating experience, this time regional (Basque), try **Chez François**, down by the railroad station at 10, avenue de l'Aerodrome (Tel: 59-23-15-83). Also called Chez Pantchoa, Basque for François, it's a *charcuterie* as well as a restaurant, very Basque in flavor. A waiter wanders around with three pounds of flesh on a plank: It's foie gras. And none of those dopey little tins for Chez François. It's foie gras as you've never seen it before (if you haven't been here before, that is). It's the whole foie gras, in the shape of a very large fish, not cooked at all, only marinated. Biarritz is in Basque country, on the fringe of les Landes, where the geese and poultry play in the woods for use in foie gras *cru* (*cru* meaning raw), the king of all Basque delicacies.

The waiter points with the knife, or you push the tip for him, and he slices off a piece and slides it onto your plate. You yourself don't need a knife; the liver cuts with a fork. To compare it to ambrosia is to belittle the gods. The deed done, from this moment on you will do anything to get fresh foie gras for the rest of your life.

Another menu delight from the region is fish cheeks. For many they are the sweetest part of the fish, the oyster of meat just under the eye. The Basques catch sea bass just for these morsels; they use the rest of the fish for soup. Containing a hundred jowls or so, a bowl of cheeks with sauce is served up like shimmering pasta—and it looks delicious. (Don't worry, they throw away the eyes.) This is a very popular dish in the fishermen's cafés to the south and across the Spanish border in San Sebastian. For a complete range of Basque tastes, try **Bahea** (Basque for peace and quiet) in Biriatou, 28 km (17 miles) south of Biarritz on the Spanish frontier (Tel: 59-20-76-36).

Like Biarritz, **St-Jean-de-Luz** to the south is a Basque fishing village with a royal past and a Spanish association. No less a person than Louis XIV was married here, to the Infanta of Spain. For regional seafood specialties try the **Tavern Basque** at 5, rue de la République. If your taste runs to *royale,* however, there is the restaurant at the Grand Hôtel.

As for **Bayonne**, so close to Biarritz: If you are curious about the origins of the Basques (an enigma, and all enigmas are fascinating) and their culture, you'll want to visit the **Musée Basque.** Aside from being the official capital of the Basque country (on the French side of the border, anyway), Bayonne also has the aforementioned ham, famous throughout the world, and is the unofficial capital of espadrilles—the canvas shoes that have made their rope-soled mark on half the beaches of the world. If you want to see *jai alai,* this is its French capital, too.

Then turn from the sea and set your sights on the most underrated mountains of Europe.

Southeast of Bayonne, near the Spanish border, is St-Jean-Pied-de-Port, from which a road goes over the mountains through a pass to the Spanish town of Roncevalles (Roncevaux in French). It was here that Roland blew his horn to summon Charlemagne—and, as the 12th-century *Chanson de Roland* has it, save France.

THE PYRENEES

It is impossible to do the entire Pyrénées in one trip. Start instead with a taste of its special essentials. Among the separate ingredients: staggering mountain vistas, gently rolling hills, smart spas, underground rivers, ruins of ancient civilizations, and miracle cures—all shrouded in the sweet country air of a gentle climate.

Pau

Pau, about 75 km (45 miles) southeast of Biarritz, is a town populated by the smart set. With enlarged livers and all the other impacted ills of advanced civilization, visitors come for the waters, seeking to cure their cirrhosis, obesity, high blood pressure, nervous conditions, respiratory problems, rheumatism, and spasms. And why not? The waters, south of Pau, bubble forth in some of the most exquisite locations in France: Beaucens, Eaux-Chaudes, Eaux-Bonnes. Visitors leave feeling purified and relaxed.

On the other hand, **Lourdes** (only 50 km/30 miles southeast of Pau) is a town for the poor, who come by tour bus from Spain and Italy as well as France. They also have their *maladies:* a club foot, blindness, a tumor. That the rich and the poor should each enjoy their own kind of waters is of no consequence. Pilgrims to Lourdes mount imposing steps to a tabernacle and come away with a prayer for a cure. The miraculous power of Lourdes—officially recognized by the Catholic Church—began with the appearance of the Blessed Virgin at a local grotto. Now the city of Lourdes has more hotel rooms than any other city in France except Paris.

The High Pyrénées

After Pau (a good base for exploration) and Lourdes, the road (D 921) leads to the high Pyrénées. At **Pont d'Espagne** and its glacier lake are the snowcapped vistas and waterfalls that tumble into verdant glades. Then go on to the **Cirque de Gavarnie**—a natural amphitheater set in a circle (*cirque*) of mountains and plunging waterfalls around a breathtaking plateau. Sixty miles of national park stretch along the Aspe and Aure valleys and offer a good chance to see wildlife, such as bears, badgers, foxes, mountain birds, and eagles.

All the green glades might instill in the traveller a yearning for a village retreat, maybe one with a monastery and, even better, a good restaurant. There is just such a place nearby, to the east of N 117, with lodgings.

St-Bertrand-de-Comminges

St-Bertrand-de-Comminges is the perfect little town away from it all. Off the beaten track but comfortable, it is also adorable—and inexpensive, too. It has everything to recommend it for a mid-Pyrénées stay. It's on a hill. It has a 12th-century church with attached cloister whose carvings are in surprisingly good condition. The church's carved wooden choir is intact, superbly crafted and meticulously maintained. Down the hill on the plain is another charming church, plus Roman ruins, antique grottoes with prehistoric cave paintings (rudimentary animals), and even prehistoric handprints (blown-ash technique). Whenever a group large enough gathers, a university student will lead a tour of the caves. Should you miss this, however, a youngster from the concession—which seems to be family-run—will be perfectly willing to take you on a more leisurely tour of his own.

As for hotels in St-Bertrand, you will like the **Comminges**, not fancy, but cute. The little family restaurant just off the main square, **Chez Simone**, open daily for dinner, sometimes takes guests, sometimes makes lunch. It welcomes customers on a drop-in basis.

From St-Bertrand-de-Comminges, the route east to Foix on N 117 runs through St-Gaudens. There, the **Villa Nymphus et Serena** has what are probably the most beautiful baths in this region full of spas.

The serendipitous bather should know that throughout this whole region of baths, there are special rates available for a single day or even an afternoon. In this way, you could bathe your way across France.

Foix

From Medieval times on, Foix has been a special place; its complete name is Foix-le-Château. The bustling town grew up at the foot of the château, which is perched on a rock and belonged to a lofty count of Foix. As he dominated the eastern Pyrénées, so does the city today; its spokes radiate out into the countryside, with the château at the hub.

There is a farmers' market down in the town, near the river Ariège. On the river's banks are most of the small hotels, among them the **Barbacane**, with moderate prices, and **Hôtel du Lac**, inexpensive, both with restaurants. Either would be a good choice for a base to explore Foix and its environs, which are rich in both history and natural wonders. The local cuisine relies heavily on grilled meat, much of it lamb, prepared with fresh herbs.

It's worth it to walk up to the fairy-tale hill site of the château. The tops of its three towers provide stunning views. Inside are exhibitions from the prehistoric and Medieval periods; the area is particularly well endowed with artifacts from these times. All around this lovely town are traces of history. An enchanting season to visit Foix is early fall, when the château is floodlit at night, and folklore festivals with lots of dancing take place down in the streets.

In case it rains, head a few miles away to **Labouiche**, where you can take a boat ride on an underground river. An hour's ride transports you past illuminated limestone stalagmites and stalactites.

The Cave People of Niaux

If you have a taste for caves and prehistoric cave paintings, the moving **Grotte de Niaux** is not to be missed. Herds of 20,000-year-old horses, deer, and bison leap across a long strip of cave. They are magnificently painted, remarkably well-preserved, and give a fine representation of the fare of our hunting ancestors. Niaux, 16 km (10 miles) down the Ariège from Foix and just south of Tarascon, is now, with the closing of the Lascaux caves, one of the finest displays of prehistoric art in France open to the public. It is anyone's guess, however, how long it will be before the French scholastics who run it will also look askance at the daily procession before the treasure of Niaux. Those with an interest in our priceless human patrimony should therefore see Niaux now, before it is closed.

Montségur

Not far from Foix is Montségur, the relic of another bygone age, but one much closer to our own—the 13th century, the time of the great religious war for the south of France. (For more information on the Cathar revolt in the making of France, see the Toulouse and the South chapter.) At Montségur, a fortress town high on a rock outcropping about 35 km (20 miles) west of Foix, the Cathars made their last stand against the pope's crusading hosts, led by Hughes des Archis, the battering ram of the Inquisition. The siege lasted six months, and in the end, by bribe, it succeeded. As at other Cathar citadels in the Midi, the survivors were given a choice: Renounce their faith and embrace Catholicism or burn. Two hundred and ten men, women, and children chose the fire over the pope.

The village that then rested at the foot of Montségur remains, and is in some ways functioning as it did then. Its *gîtes* serve up exceptional meals of local game at long wooden tables. The locals are friendly; they will tell you about the horrible fire in the ruined fortress on top of the rock. On certain nights the villagers say, they can still see the glow. Legend also has it that three Cathar priests escaped the siege, bearing with them the storied treasure of Montségur, with its most priceless object: the Holy Grail.

There are several ways out of these locations seemingly lost in time: either up through Toulouse, with its bright lights and shopping streets, or through Perpignan, with its Catalan charm. If Perpignan is your way, passage there through the **abbey of St-Martin-du-Canigou** is strongly recommended. The 11th-century Cluniac abbey is spectacularly perched atop a mountain at the edge of a cliff; within view of the monastery is a glacier field. A few hours' reflection under snowcapped peaks will do you a world of good before you reenter the world of traffic and baggage.

GETTING AROUND
The Pyrénées is well serviced by flights from Paris to airports in Biarritz, Lourdes, Pau, Perpignan, and Toulouse (see the chapter on Toulouse and the South). Rail and bus service to almost all towns is excellent. However, the best way to explore the region is by car (you will find outlets of major rental agencies in Toulouse). Route N 117 cuts across the region from Bayonne to Toulouse, providing access to the roads that crisscross the Pyrénées. Hiking trails in the region are superb; for information, contact Fédération Française de la Randonnée Pédestre, 8, avenue Marceau, 75008 Paris.

ACCOMMODATIONS REFERENCE
▶ **Barbacane.** 1, avenue Lérida, 09000 **Foix.** Tel: 61-65-50-44.

▶ **Chez Simone.** 31510 **St-Bertrand-de-Comminges.** Tel: 61-88-30-70.

▶ **Comminges.** 31510 **St-Bertrand-de-Comminges.** Tel: 61-88-31-43.

▶ **Hôtel du Lac.** 09000 **Foix.** Tel: 61-65-12-50.

▶ **Hôtel Palais.** 1, avenue Impératrice, 64200 **Biarritz.** Tel: 59-24-09-40; Telex: 570000; in U.S., (201) 235-1990.

CHRONOLOGY OF THE HISTORY OF FRANCE

Prehistory

France is one of the most rewarding countries in Europe for travellers in search of prehistoric art and architecture *in situ*. Naturally, delicate and portable pieces such as the plump, lumpy Venus figures repose comfortably in museums. Still, astonishing wall paintings and engravings remain in caves once occupied by Paleolithic hunters, chiefly in the Dordogne valley and the central Pyrénées. The Carnac and Locmariaquer districts of Brittany show off dozens of archaeological sites: standing stone alignments, megalithic tombs, passage graves, tumuli.

Prehistoric cultures in France are impressively old by any standards. English archaeologist Jacquetta Hawkes reports (in the *Atlas of Ancient Archeology*): "Le Vallonet cave, near Menton, is the oldest inhabited site in Europe, perhaps a million years old, and the other sea caves on this coast (the Côte d'Azur), the Grimaldi caves and the Observatory, near Monaco, and Lazaret, in the suburbs of Nice, contain early occupations representative of Neanderthal man and his predecessors."

Following these ancient, Acheulean, cultures, the main ones evidenced in France are the Mousterian (60,000–39,000 B.C.), Châtelperron (33,000 B.C.), Aurignacian (30,000 B.C.), Gravettian (24,000 B.C.), Solutréan (17,000 B.C.), and Magdalenian (15,000 B.C.).

- **15,000–10,000 B.C.:** Cave art in sites around Les Eyzies in the Dordogne: Lascaux, Font de Gaume, Cap Blanc, La Mouthe, Les Combarelles, and many cave shelters (*abri*).
- **3,800–2,000 B.C.:** Tombs and stone alignments (avenues of upright stones, *menhirs,* some 14–20 feet high), tumuli (earth-covered mound tombs), megaliths. The Menac alignment, near to and

northeast of Brittany's Carnac on D 196, boasts more than a thousand standing stones.

- **3,500 B.C.:** Megalithic tombs in southern France, particularly the Grotte des Fées near Arles.
- **600–50 B.C.:** The *oppidum,* or hilltop fort, of Vix, in Burgundy near Châtillon-sur-Seine.

Other prehistoric cultures are represented in pottery (Impressed Ware, about 5,000 B.C.), Chassey pottery (3,500 B.C., southern France), and open-air huts and farming settlements in the north of France.

The Celtic Period

The Celts, an Indo-European race, arrived in waves from the east, beginning about 1,000 B.C., bringing decorative La Tène art (the Basse-Yutz flagon, the Janus head from Roquepertuse); hilltop strongholds (*oppida*); a warrior aristocracy; and many divinities as well as the Druids. Eventually they were driven out by the Romans, though keeping a toehold in Brittany.

The Coming of the Greeks

- **About 600 B.C.:** Founding of the trading colony of Marseille (Massilia) by the Phocéans.

The Romans and Gallo-Romans

- **121 B.C.:** Romans establish Gallia Narbonensis (Provence).
- **58–51 B.C.:** Caesar conquers Gaul.
- **53 B.C.:** Vercingétorix battles Caesar, loses.
- **A.D.162:** Arrival of the first Alemannic hordes.
- **c. 250:** Christianity comes to the Gallo-Romans.
- **c. 355:** Invasions of Gaul by Franks, Alemanni, Saxons.
- **373–397:** Saint Martin is bishop of Tours.
- **418–507:** The Visigoths rule the south, out of Toulouse.
- **443:** The Burgundians establish themselves in the Rhône valley.
- **451:** Attila and his Huns are defeated by the Romans and their allies in the Battle of the Catalaunian Fields near Troyes.
- **481:** Merovingian Clovis I crowned king of the Franks.

- **c. 496**: Clovis is crowned at Reims and the Franks become Christian.
- **c. 511**: All Gaul is divided into three parts: Austrasia, Neustria, Burgundy.
- **c. 630**: The first Benedictine monasteries are built.
- **732**: Charles Martel (the Hammer), son of Pepin of Herstal, defeats the Moors at the Battle of Poitiers.
- **741**: Pepin the Short (*le Brèf*), father of Charlemagne, is proclaimed king.
- **788**: Death of Roland, in the Pyrénées, when Charlemagne's army, returning from Spain, is ambushed. He is immortalized in the Medieval epic, the *Chanson de Roland*.
- **800**: Charlemagne is crowned emperor in Rome.
- **843**: The Frankish empire is partitioned by the Treaty of Verdun.

The Romanesque Era

- **910**: Foundation of the abbey of Cluny.
- **From c. 950**: Expansion is the theme, with clearing of lands, growth of population, broadening of trade with fairs, movement of peoples on pilgrimages, building of new towns. Romanesque art is exemplified in Vézelay, Autun, Conques, and Sénanque, among other towns. Old French moves away from Latin in this time; monks at Jumièges add vocalizations to traditional Gregorian chants.
- **987**: Hugues Capet ("little cloak") is crowned king of the Franks, creating the Capetian dynasty (direct line to 1328, collateral until 1848).
- **1066**: William the Conqueror (*Guillaume le Conquérant*), duke of Normandy, conquers England.
- **1090 (?)–1153**: Days of Saint Bernard of Clairvaux.
- **1095–1099**: First Crusade, led by Raymond IV, count of Toulouse, and Godfrey of Bouillon (now Belgium). The Crusades continue periodically until 1250.
- **1115**: Saint Bernard founds Cistercian abbey of Clairvaux.
- **1122**: Birth of Eleanor of Aquitaine, queen consort of Louis VII of France, then of Henry II of England, mother of many children, including English Kings Richard the Lion-Hearted and (Bad King) John. She lived until 1204.
- **c. 1132**: Cathedrals begun at Vézelay and Autun.

- **1137**: Start of construction of cathedral of St-Denis, first monumental Gothic structure.
- **1137–1180**: Major conflicts with England between Louis VII and Henry II.
- **c. 1140**: Development of Catharism, one of the Albigensian heresies.
- **1147–1149**: Disastrous Second Crusade, preached by Saint Bernard at Vézelay.
- **1150–1167**: Universities founded at Paris and Oxford.
- **1163**: Cornerstone of Notre-Dame de Paris laid.
- **1189–1192**: Third Crusade, led by France's Philippe Auguste, England's Richard I (the Lion-Hearted), and Holy Roman Emperor Frederick I.

In Gothic Times

- **c. 1200–1300**: Medieval France lives and creates at full flower; trade and population expansion continue. Gothic art gives birth to cathedrals at Amiens, Beauvais, Chartres, Reims; stained glass brings light to those at Bourges, Laon, Notre-Dame, etc. Polyphonic music is heard at Notre-Dame.
- **1208**: Beginning of the Albigensian Crusade.
- **1202–1204**: Fourth Crusade, Constantinople seized.
- **1210–1294**: Construction of Reims' cathedral of Notre-Dame.
- **1226**: Accession of Louis IX, king, crusader; reigned 44 years; canonized as Saint Louis, 1297.
- **1233**: Start of the Papal Inquisition.
- **1246–1248**: Construction of Sainte-Chapelle, one of finest examples of Gothic, in Palais de Justice on Ile de la Cité, Paris.
- **1253**: Foundation of the Sorbonne, to become nucleus of the University of Paris, by Robert de Sorbon.
- **1270**: Gothic cathedrals begun in Toulouse, Narbonne.

Late Gothic

- **1300–1400+**: Decoration and ornamentation come to architecture in Radiant Gothic (cathedrals of Strasbourg, Metz) and Flamboyant Gothic (flowing, flame-like forms), mostly in Normandy and Picardie.

- **1309–1378:** The "Babylonian captivity" of the popes in Avignon.
- **1328:** Accession of Philippe VI, first of the House of Valois.
- **1333:** Edward III of England claims the French crown.
- **1337–1453:** The Hundred Years War; it begins with dynastic squabbles between France and England.
- **1348–1351:** The Black Death kills as many as half the inhabitants of Europe.
- **1349:** The heir to the throne inherits the Dauphiné region; each kingly heir is afterward known as the Dauphin.
- **1356:** Edward, the Black Prince, son of England's Edward III, captures King John II (the Good) in the Battle of Poitiers.
- **c. 1360:** The portrait of Burgundian Duke Jean le Bon (now in the Louvre) marks the debut of French portraiture.
- **1378–1417:** The Great Schism; rival popes in Rome and Avignon.
- **1407:** War breaks out between the Burgundians and the Armagnacs.
- **1415:** The Battle of Azincourt (Agincourt in English) in northern France, won by Henry V of England (and of Shakespeare).
- **1429:** Joan of Arc raises the English siege of Orléans and accompanies Charles VII to Reims and his coronation.
- **1431:** Joan of Arc is burned at the stake in Rouen on May 30; she is canonized in 1920.

The Renaissance

- **c. 1450:** Somewhere about here the Renaissance begins, moving out of the so-called Dark Ages with burgeoning trade, improving economy, renewed interest in building and the arts. The influence of Italy is a dramatic force in architecture (François I imports Italian artists in all fields), and Italian Mannerism influences painting and music, while the 16th century is a triumph for French sculpture.
- **1451:** Financier and minister Jacques Coeur is arrested, accused of having poisoned Agnès Sorel, Charles VII's mistress; he will die fighting the Turks in 1456.

- **1453**: The Hundred Years War comes to a shaky end as England loses all its possessions in France except Calais.
- **1455–1485**: Wars of the Roses in England between Houses of Lancaster and York, involving Henry IV's queen, Margaret of Anjou, daughter of René-le-Bon.
- **1469–1470**: Foundation of France's first printing house.
- **1477**: Charles le Téméraire, duke of Burgundy, dies; Burgundy and Picardie pass to the crown, other lands to Emperor Maximilian I, and the France-Hapsburg quarrels begin.
- **1484**: Meeting of the Estates-General in Tours; town representatives join clergy and nobility as the Third Estate.
- **1492**: Discovery of America by Christopher Columbus.
- **1515**: Accession of François I of Angoulême, who reigns for 32 years, fights four major wars, becomes the greatest masterbuilder and art patron of French history with the help of Cellini, da Vinci, et al.
- **1517**: Martin Luther posts his 95 theses on the door of the castle church in Wittenberg.
- **1524**: Italian Giovanni da Verrazano, sailing under the French flag, explores the New England coast, and becomes the first European to enter New York Bay.
- **1534–1542**: Jacques Cartier departs St-Malo and ventures up the St. Lawrence in Canada, giving France claims to the region.
- **1547**: Henri II, husband of Catherine de Médicis, lover of Diane de Poitiers, ascends to the throne.
- **1547–1559**: Henri II persecutes the Huguenots.
- **1561**: Persecution of Huguenots stopped, briefly, by Edict of Orléans.
- **1562–1598**: Wars of Religion—Catholics led by the Guise family, Protestants by the Bourbons.
- **1572**: St. Bartholomew's Day Massacre, August 24, on orders of Catherine de Médicis.
- **1589**: Henri of Navarre becomes Henri IV, first of the House of Bourbon; becomes a Catholic in 1593 and claims "Paris is worth a Mass."
- **1598**: The Edict of Nantes grants freedom (conditional) to Huguenots.
- **1609**: Samuel de Champlain establishes French colony in Quebec.

Louis XIII

- **1610**: Henri IV is assassinated, succeeded by Louis XIII with his great ministers, Cardinals Richelieu and Mazarin.
- **1620**: Pilgrims arrive at Plymouth Rock after a three-month voyage.
- **c. 1630–1700**: Art styles in France reflect serenity, i.e., Poussin; classical values in literature are expressed by Racine's tragedies; Montaigne creates the essay (from 1571).
- **1635**: The *Académie Française* is founded to promote education and the arts. France involves itself in the Thirty Years War on the side of Denmark and Sweden against Germany.

Louis XIV and the Classic Century

- **1643**: Louis XIV becomes king, to reign for 72 years.
- **1648–1653**: The *Fronde* is a series of outbreaks caused by the efforts of *Parlement* to limit royal authority; eventually, Parlement will be joined by the nobility and the people of Paris.
- **1661–1715**: Louis XIV's Sun King period sees a flowering of Baroque art and architecture (Versailles, with Le Vau, Le Nôtre, Le Brun, others); painting (Georges de la Tour, Claude Le Lorrain, others); literature (Cornéille, Racine, La Fontaine, Molière, La Rochefoucauld, others); music (Lully, Couperin); and philosophy, science, and mathematics (Pascal and many others).
- **1685**: Revocation of the Edict of Nantes; half a million Huguenots leave France.
- **1700–1800**: The science and reason century starts off with Descartes's truths; the French Enlightenment is born in works of Montesquieu, Voltaire, Rousseau, Diderot. In art, Rococo emerges with Watteau, Neoclassicism with David.
- **1701–1714**: War of the Spanish Succession; the duke of Anjou and grandson of Louis XIV becomes Spanish King Felipe V over other claimants from around Europe.

Louis XV and the Enlightenment

- **c. 1715**: The economy booms, inspiring the sophistication of salons, receptions, construction of more châteaux, and a passion for knowledge.

- **1715**: Death of Louis XIV, succeeded by Louis XV, who loses Canada to the English and enjoys such favorites as Madame de Pompadour and Madame Du Barry.
- **1751**: First volume of Denis Diderot's *Encyclopédie* is published.
- **1768**: France buys Corsica from Genoa.
- **1769**: Napoléon Bonaparte (Buonaparte) is born in Ajaccio, Corsica.
- **1774**: Louis XVI and Marie-Antoinette come to power.
- **1777**: Marie-Joseph-Paul-Yves-Roch-Gilbert du Motier, marquis de Lafayette, arrives in America, is made a major general by the Continental Congress, serves in many battles. (In 1789, Lafayette creates the modern French flag.)
- **1783**: First manned free-balloon flight accomplished by brothers Joseph Michel and Jacques Etienne Montgolfier, over Paris.

The Revolution

- **1789**: Outbreak of the French Revolution; Louis and Marie-Antoinette beheaded in 1793. This is followed by the Continent-wide French Revolutionary Wars until 1802. Names and concepts that now enter the world's languages are: Girondists, Jacobins, Cordeliers, the Convention, the Revolutionary Tribunal, the Directory, the Terror.
- **1792**: France is declared a republic, but the wars, uprisings, and massacres go on.
- **1794**: Maximilien Marie Isidore Robespierre, chief architect of the Terror, dies on the guillotine.
- **1796–1804**: Napoléon's successes against the Austrians, Milan, Genoa, Mamelukes of Egypt, etc.

The 19th Century

- **1800–40**: Romanticism replaces Neoclassicism and Rococo; Rousseau a leader. Hugo expresses in novels the new desire for freedom; Delacroix in paint the appeal of exotic locales.
- **1803–1815**: Napoleonic Wars against European powers.
- **1804**: Napoléon is crowned Emperor of the French and civil law is codified in the *Code Napoléon*.
- **1805**: Napoléon crowns himself King of Italy; Vis-

count Horatio Nelson defeats combined French and Spanish forces at Battle of Trafalgar; Napoléon triumphs over Russians and Austrians at Austerlitz.

- **1812**: Napoléon's disastrous Russian campaign.
- **1814**: Continent-wide Wars of Liberation against Napoléon.
- **1814**: Napoléon abdicates, receives the island of Elba as a principality; the Bourbon dynasty is restored with Louis XVIII as king.
- **1815**: The 100 Days: During the Congress of Vienna, Napoléon lands at Cannes and marches to Paris. Louix XVIII flees and Napoléon rules until beaten by the British and Prussians in the Battle of Waterloo; exiled to the British island of St. Helena, where he dies in 1821.
- **1815–1816**: The White Terror—Royalist uprisings, persecutions of Jacobins and Bonapartists.
- **1824**: Charles X, brother of Louis XVIII, gains the throne.
- **1825**: Louis Braille invents script for the blind.
- **1830**: The July Revolution forces abdication of Charles X; he is succeeded by Louis-Philippe and the House of Orléans.
- **1840–1880**: The official Beaux-Arts school of Paris sets an international style for public buildings and sculpture with such examples as the Paris Opéra and Bartholdi's Statue of Liberty. Realist painting is influenced by Daguerre and photography. Balzac provides a realistic look at social classes.
- **1848**: The February Revolution brings about the abdication of Louis-Philippe and installation of Louis Napoléon Bonaparte (nephew of Napoléon I) as president of the Second Republic.
- **1852**: The president becomes Napoléon III, Emperor of the French, to begin the Second Empire.
- **1854–1870**: France takes part in the Crimean War, takes Nice and Savoy from Austria, extends her possessions in Southeast Asia, aids in the construction of Suez Canal, and sees the collapse of the Mexican Empire established for Maximilian of Hapsburg.
- **1870–1871**: Franco-Prussian War—Napoléon III is defeated at Sedan, taken prisoner; the Third Republic is proclaimed, with Louis-Adolphe Thiers as president.
- **1874**: First exhibition of the Impressionists opens

April 15; canvases by Cézanne, Degas, Monet, Berthe Morisot, Pissarro, Renoir, Sisley, 21 others; the school is named for Monet's *Impression, Sunrise*.

- **1879–1896**: France expands into parts of Central Africa, Tunis, Indochina, and Madagascar.
- **1889**: Paris International Exhibition stars the Eiffel Tower.
- **1880–1900**: *Fin-de-Siècle* period in art and literature—Flaubert, Zola, Verlaine, Rimbaud; Cézanne, Gauguin.
- **1890**: Birth of Charles de Gaulle.
- **1895**: The brothers Louis Jean and August Lumière patent first device for making and projecting films.
- **1894–1906**: The Dreyfus Affair, a case revolving around supposed treason, brings the left wing to power, raises issues of anti-Semitism, and helps split church and state (Alfred Dreyfus exonerated in 1906).

The 20th Century

- **1900–1909**: France is the center of experimentation in the arts; Fauvism (Matisse a leader, 1905), Cubism (Picasso et al.); Diaghilev in Paris alters classical ballet; new sounds of music (Debussy, Satie, Stravinsky).
- **1909**: Louis Blériot is the first man to fly an airplane across the Channel.
- **1914**: World War I is occasioned by the murder of Archduke Francis Ferdinand, heir to the Austro-Hungarian throne, at Sarajevo, Yugoslavia, June 28.
- **1916**: Beginning of Dada movement in arts (Arp, Tzara).
- **1918**: Allied counter-offensive begins; Franco-German armistice at Compiègne, November.
- **1919**: Treaty of Versailles returns Alsace and Lorraine to France, gives her mandates over other lands; France becomes a founding member of the League of Nations.
- **1925**: Exhibition of Surrealists, now in their heyday: Breton, De Chirico, Dalí, Tanguy, Ernst, Magritte; in literature, Eluard, Cocteau, heirs of Baudelaire, Rimbaud and, eventually, Freud.
- **1929**: Beginning of worldwide Great Depression.
- **1936**: Germany occupies the demilitarized Rhineland; no action from France or England.

- **1939**: World War II; after a series of unanswered German takeovers, culminating in an attack on Poland, France declares war on Germany, September 3.
- **1940**: German army occupies Paris, June 14; Vichy government headed by Henri Philippe Pétain; Third Republic ends; Charles de Gaulle forms a government in exile in England; Résistance is formed.
- **1942–1943**: Existentialism in literature and philosophy; publication of Albert Camus's *The Stranger* and Jean-Paul Sartre's *Being and Nothingness*.
- **1944**: Allies land in Normandy, June 6, and in the south of France, August 15, to liberate France; Charles de Gaulle forms a provisional government.
- **1945**: Germany capitulates.
- **1946**: De Gaulle resigns, succeeded by Félix Gouin and Georges Bidault.
- **1948**: The United States's Marshall Plan for the recovery of Europe begins.
- **1954–1956**: France loses Equatorial Africa, Indochina, Morocco, Tunisia, and West Africa because of independence movements and wars.
- **1957**: European Common Market comes into being with France as a founding member.
- **1959**: Having dealt with the Algerian question as prime minister under René Coty, de Gaulle becomes president of the Fifth Republic until 1969.
- **1962**: Algeria is granted independence.
- **1969**: De Gaulle retires from the presidency, succeeded by Georges Pompidou.
- **1970**: De Gaulle dies and is buried near his home at Colombey-les-Deux-Eglises.
- **1974**: Valéry Giscard d'Estaing is elected third president of the Fifth Republic.
- **1981**: François Mitterrand is elected president of France; reelected for a second seven-year term in 1988.

INDEX